Tor Books by Steven Erikson

THE MALAZAN BOOK OF THE FALLEN
Gardens of the Moon
Deadhouse Gates
Memories of Ice
House of Chains
Midnight Tides
The Bonehunters
Reaper's Gale
Toll the Hounds
Dust of Dreams
The Crippled God

THE KHARKANAS TRILOGY
Forge of Darkness
Fall of Light

MALAZAN NOVELLAS
Bauchelain and Korbal Broach
Crack'd Pot Trail
The Wurms of Blearmouth
The Fiends of Nightmaria

WITNESS
The God Is Not Willing

The Devil Delivered and Other Tales
This River Awakens
Willful Child
Willful Child: Wrath of Betty
Willful Child: The Search for Spark

HOUSE OF CHAINS

STEVEN ERIKSON

Tor Publishing Group
New York

HOUSE OF CHAINS

Copyright © 2002 by Steven Erikson

First published in Great Britain in 2002 by Bantam.

Excerpt from *Midnight Tides* © copyright 2004 by Steven Erikson

All rights reserved.

Map by Neil Gower

A Tor Book
Published by Tom Doherty Associates/Tor Publishing Group
120 Broadway
New York, NY 10271

www.tor-forge.com

Tor® is a registered trademark of Macmillan Publishing Group, LLC.

ISBN 978-0-7653-4881-4

Our books may be purchased in bulk for promotional, educational, or business use. Please contact your local bookseller or the Macmillan Corporate and Premium Sales Department at 1-800-221-7945, ext. 5442, or by email at MacmillanSpecialMarkets@macmillan.com.

First Edition: August 2006
First Mass Market Edition: March 2007

Printed in the United States of America

23 22 21 20 19 18 17 16 15 14

For Mark Paxton MacRae, for the KO
punch. This one's all yours, my friend.

ACKNOWLEDGEMENTS

The author wishes to thank his cadre of readers, Chris Porozny, Richard Jones, David Keck and Mark Paxton MacRae. Clare and Bowen as always. Simon Taylor and the crew at Transworld. And the terrific (and patient) staff at Tony's Bar Italia: Erica, Steve, Jesse, Dan, Ron, Orville, Rhimpy, Rhea, Cam, James, Konrad, Darren, Rusty, Phil, Todd, Marnie, Chris, Leah, Ada, Kevin, Jake, Jamie, Graeme and the two Doms. Thanks also to Darren Nash (for the yeast always rises) and Peter Crowther.

Contents

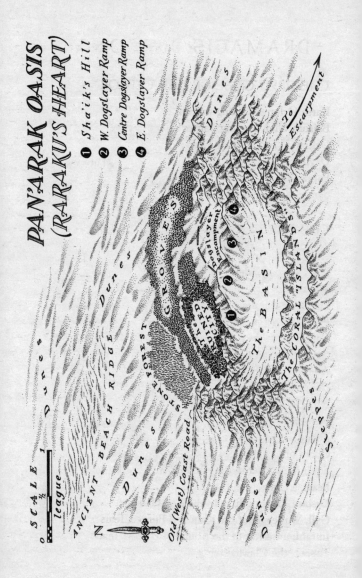

PAN'ARAK OASIS
(RARAKU'S HEART)

1. Sha'ik's Hill
2. W. Dogslayer Ramp
3. Centre Dogslayer Ramp
4. E. Dogslayer Ramp

SCALE
0   ½   1   league

N

Dunes

ANCIENT BEACH RIDGE   Dunes

Dunes

STONEFOREST

GROVES

THE RUINED CITY

Dogslayer Encampment

The Basin

The Coral "Islands"

Dunes

Steppes

To Escarpment

Old (West) Coast Road

DRAMATIS PERSONAE

THE URYD TRIBE OF THE TEBLOR

Karsa Orlong, a young warrior
Bairoth Gild, a young warrior
Delum Thord, a young warrior
Dayliss, a young woman
Pahlk, Karsa's grandfather
Synyg, Karsa's father

THE ADJUNCT'S ARMY

Adjunct Tavore
Fist Gamet/Gimlet
T'amber
Fist Tene Baralta
Fist Blistig
Captain Keneb
Grub, his adopted son
Admiral Nok
Commander Alardis
Nil, a Wickan warlock
Nether, a Wickan witch
Temul, a Wickan of the Crow Clan (survivor of the Chain of Dogs)
Squint, a soldier in the Aren Guard
Pearl, a Claw
Lostara Yil, an officer in the Red Blades
Gall, Warleader of the Khundryl Burned Tears
Imrahl, a warrior of the Khundryl Burned Tears
Topper, the Clawmaster

MARINES OF THE 9th COMPANY, 8th LEGION

Lieutenant Ranal
Sergeant Strings
Sergeant Gesler
Sergeant Borduke
Corporal Tarr
Corporal Stormy
Corporal Hubb
Bottle, a squad mage
Smiles
Koryk, a half-Seti soldier
Cuttle, a sapper
Truth
Pella
Tavos Pond
Sands
Balgrid
Ibb
Maybe
Lutes

SELECTED HEAVY INFANTRY OF THE 9th COMPANY, 8th LEGION

Sergeant Mosel
Sergeant Sobelone
Sergeant Tugg
Flashwit
Uru Hela
Bowl
Shortnose

SELECTED MEDIUM INFANTRY OF THE 9th COMPANY, 8th LEGION

Sergeant Balm
Sergeant Moak
Sergeant Thom Tissy
Corporal Deadsmell
Corporal Burnt
Corporal Tulip
Throatslitter
Widdershins
Galt
Lobe
Stacker
Ramp
Able

OTHER SOLDIERS OF THE MALAZAN EMPIRE

Sergeant Cord, 2nd Company, Ashok Regiment
Ebron, 5th squad, mage
Limp, 5th squad
Bell, 5th squad
Corporal Shard, 5th squad
Captain Kindly, 2nd Company
Lieutenant Pores, 2nd Company
Jibb, Ehrlitan Guard
Gullstream, Ehrlitan Guard
Scrawl, Ehrlitan Guard
Master Sergeant Braven Tooth, Malaz City Garrison
Captain Irriz, renegade
Sinn, refugee
Gentur

Mudslinger
Hawl

NATHII

Slavemaster Silgar
Damisk
Balantis
Astabb
Borrug

OTHERS ON GENABACKIS

Torvald Nom
Calm
Ganal

SHA'IK'S ARMY OF THE APOCALYPSE

Sha'ik, The Chosen One of the Whirlwind Goddess
(once Felisin of House Paran)
Felisin Younger, her adopted daughter
Toblakai
Leoman of the Flails
High Mage L'oric
High Mage Bidithal
High Mage Febryl
Heboric Ghost Hands
Kamist Reloe, Korbolo Dom's mage
Henaras, a sorceress
Fayelle, a sorceress
Mathok, Warleader of the Desert Tribes
T'morol, his bodyguard
Corabb Bhilan Thenu'alas, an officer in Leoman's
company

Scillara, a camp follower
Duryl, a messenger
Ethume, a corporal
Korbolo Dom, a renegade Napan
Kasanal, his hired assassin

OTHERS

Kalam Mekhar, an assassin
Trull Sengar, a Tiste Edur
Onrack, a T'lan Imass
Cutter, an assassin (also known as **Crokus**)
Apsalar, an assassin
Rellock, Apsalar's father
Cotillion, Patron of Assassins
Traveller
Rood, a Hound of Shadow
Blind, a Hound of Shadow
Darist, a Tiste Andii
Ba'ienrok (Keeper), a hermit
Ibra Gholan, a T'lan Imass Clan Leader
Monok Ochem, a Bonecaster of the Logros T'lan Imass
Haran Epal, a T'lan Imass
Olar Shayn, a T'lan Imass
Greyfrog, a demon familiar
Apt, a matron demon (Aptorian) of Shadow
Azalan, a demon of Shadow
Panek, a child of Shadow
Mebra, a spy in Ehrlitan
Iskaral Pust, a priest of Shadow
Mogora, his D'ivers wife
Cynnigig, a Jaghut
Phyrlis, a Jaghut
Aramala, a Jaghut

Icarium, a Jhag
Mappo Runt, a Trell
Jorrude, a Tiste Liosan Seneschal
Malachar, a Tiste Liosan
Enias, a Tiste Liosan
Orenas, a Tiste Liosan

HOUSE OF CHAINS

PROLOGUE

Verge of the Nascent, the 943rd Day of the Search
1159 Burn's Sleep

Grey, bloated and pocked, the bodies lined the silt-laden shoreline for as far as the eye could see. Heaped like driftwood by the rising water, bobbing and rolling on the edges, the putrefying flesh seethed with black-shelled, ten-legged crabs. The coin-sized creatures had scarcely begun to make inroads on the bounteous feast the warren's sundering had laid before them.

The sea mirrored the low sky's hue. Dull, patched pewter above and below, broken only by the deeper grey of silts and, thirty strokes of the oar distant, the smeared ochre tones of the barely visible upper levels of a city's inundated buildings. The storms had passed, the waters were calm amidst the wreckage of a drowned world.

Short, squat had been the inhabitants. Flat-featured, the pale hair left long and loose. Their world had been a cold one, given the thick-padded clothing they had worn. But with the sundering that had changed, cataclysmically. The air was sultry, damp and now foul with the reek of decay.

The sea had been born of a river on another realm. A massive, wide and probably continent-spanning artery of fresh water, heavy with a plain's silts, the murky depths home to huge catfish and wagon-wheel-sized spiders, its shallows crowded with the crabs and carnivorous, rootless plants. The river had poured its torrential volume onto this vast, level landscape. Days, then weeks, then months.

Storms, conjured by the volatile clash of tropical airstreams with the resident temperate climate, had driven the flood on beneath shrieking winds, and before the inexorably rising waters came deadly plagues to take those who had not drowned.

Somehow, the rent had closed sometime in the night just past. The river from another realm had been returned to its original path.

The shoreline ahead probably did not deserve the word, but nothing else came to Trull Sengar's mind as he was dragged along its verge. The beach was nothing more than silt, heaped against a huge wall that seemed to stretch from horizon to horizon. The wall had withstood the flood, though water now streamed down it on the opposite side.

Bodies on his left, a sheer drop of seven, maybe eight man-heights to his right, the top of the wall itself slightly less than thirty paces across; that it held back an entire sea whispered of sorcery. The broad, flat stones underfoot were smeared with mud, but already drying in the heat, duncoloured insects dancing on its surface, leaping from the path of Trull Sengar and his captors.

Trull still experienced difficulty comprehending that notion. *Captors.* A word he struggled with. They were his brothers, after all. Kin. Faces he had known all his life, faces he had seen smile, and laugh, and faces – at times – filled with a grief that had mirrored his own. He had stood at their sides through all that had happened, the glorious triumphs, the soul-wrenching losses.

Captors.

There were no smiles, now. No laughter. The expressions of those who held him were fixed and cold.

What we have come to.

24

The march ended. Hands pushed Trull Sengar down, heedless of his bruises, the cuts and the gouges that still leaked blood. Massive iron rings had been set, for some unknown purpose, by this world's now-dead inhabitants, along the top of the wall, anchored in the heart of the huge stone blocks. The rings were evenly spaced down the wall's length, at intervals of fifteen or so paces, for as far as Trull could see.

Now, those rings had found a new function.

Chains were wrapped around Trull Sengar, shackles hammered into place on his wrists and ankles. A studded girdle was cinched painfully tight about his midriff, the chains drawn through iron loops and pulled taut to pin him down beside the iron ring. A hinged metal press was affixed to his jaw, his mouth forced open and the plate pushed in and locked in place over his tongue.

The Shorning followed. A dagger inscribed a circle on his forehead, followed by a jagged slash to break that circle, the point pushed deep enough to gouge the bone. Ash was rubbed into the wounds. His long single braid was removed with rough hacks that made a bloody mess of his nape. A thick, cloying unguent was then smeared through his remaining hair, massaged down to the pate. Within a few hours, the rest of his hair would fall away, leaving him permanently bald.

The Shorning was an absolute thing, an irreversible act of severance. He was now outcast. To his brothers, he had ceased to exist. He would not be mourned. His deeds would vanish from memory along with his name. His mother and father would have birthed one less child. This was, for his people, the most dire punishment – worse than execution by far.

Yet, Trull Sengar had committed no crime.

And this is what we have come to.

They stood above him, perhaps only now comprehending what they had done.

A familiar voice broke the silence. 'We will speak of him

now, and once we have left this place, he will cease to be our brother.'

'We will speak of him now,' the others intoned, then one added, 'He betrayed you.'

The first voice was cool, revealing nothing of the gloat that Trull Sengar knew would be there. 'You say he betrayed me.'

'He did, brother.'

'What proof do you have?'

'By his own tongue.'

'Is it just you who claims to have heard such betrayal spoken?'

'No, I too heard it, brother.'

'And I.'

'And what did our brother say to you all?'

'He said that you had severed your blood from ours.'

'That you now served a hidden master.'

'That your ambition would lead us all to our deaths—'

'Our entire people.'

'He spoke against me, then.'

'He did.'

'By his own tongue, he accused me of betraying our people.'

'He did.'

'And have I? Let us consider this charge. The southlands are aflame. The enemy's armies have fled. The enemy now kneels before us, and begs to be our slaves. From nothing, was forged an empire. And still our strength grows. Yet. To grow stronger, what must you, my brothers, do?'

'We must search.'

'Aye. And when you find what must be sought?'

'We must deliver. To you, brother.'

'Do you see the need for this?'

'We do.'

'Do you understand the sacrifice I make, for you, for our people, for our future?'

'We do.'

'Yet, even as you searched, this man, our once-brother, spoke against me.'

'He did.'

'Worse, he spoke to defend the new enemies we had found.'

'He did. He called them the Pure Kin, and said we should not kill them.'

'And, had they been in truth Pure Kin, then . . .'

'They would not have died so easily.'

'Thus.'

'He betrayed you, brother.'

'He betrayed us all.'

There was silence. *Ah, now you would share out this crime of yours. And they hesitate.*

'He betrayed us all, did he not, brothers?'

'Yes.' The word arrived rough, beneath the breath, mumbled – a chorus of dubious uncertainty.

No-one spoke for a long moment, then, savage with barely bridled anger: 'Thus, *brothers*. And should we not heed this danger? This threat of betrayal, this poison, this plague that seeks to tear our family apart? Will it spread? Will we come here yet again? We must be vigilant, brothers. Within ourselves. With each other. Now, we have spoken of him. And now, he is gone.'

'He is gone.'

'He never existed.'

'He never existed.'

'Let us leave this place, then.'

'Yes, let us leave.'

Trull Sengar listened until he could no more hear their boots on the stones, nor feel the tremble of their dwindling steps. He was alone, unable to move, seeing only the mud-smeared stone at the base of the iron ring.

The sea rustled the corpses along the shoreline. Crabs scuttled. Water continued to seep through the mortar, insinuate the Cyclopean wall with the voice of muttering ghosts, and flow down on the other side.

Among his people, it was a long-known truth, perhaps the only truth, that Nature fought but one eternal war. One foe. That, further, to understand this was to understand the world. Every world.

Nature has but one enemy.

And that is imbalance.

The wall held the sea.

And there are two meanings to this. My brothers, can you not see the truth of that? Two meanings. The wall holds the sea.

For now.

This was a flood that would not be denied. The deluge had but just begun – something his brothers could not understand, would, perhaps, never understand.

Drowning was common among his people. Drowning was not feared. And so, Trull Sengar would drown. Soon.

And before long, he suspected, his entire people would join him.

His brother had shattered the balance.

And Nature shall not abide.

BOOK ONE

FACES IN THE ROCK

The slower the river, the redder it runs.

Nathii saying

CHAPTER ONE

Children from a dark house
choose shadowed paths.

Nathii folk saying

The dog had savaged a woman, an old man and a child before the warriors drove it into an abandoned kiln at the edge of the village. The beast had never before displayed an uncertain loyalty. It had guarded the Uryd lands with fierce zeal, one with its kin in its harsh, but just, duties. There were no wounds on its body that might have festered and so allowed the spirit of madness into its veins. Nor was the dog possessed by the foaming sickness. Its position in the village pack had not been challenged. Indeed, there was nothing, nothing at all, to give cause to the sudden turn.

The warriors pinned the animal to the rounded back wall of the clay kiln with spears, stabbing at the snapping, shrieking beast until it was dead. When they withdrew their spears they saw the shafts chewed and slick with spit and blood; they saw iron dented and scored.

Madness, they knew, could remain hidden, buried far beneath the surface, a subtle flavour turning blood into something bitter. The shamans examined the three victims; two had already died of their wounds, but the child still clung to life.

In solemn procession he was carried by his father to the Faces in the Rock, laid down in the glade before the

31

Seven Gods of the Teblor, and left there.

He died a short while later. Alone in his pain before the hard visages carved into the cliff-face.

This was not an unexpected fate. The child, after all, had been too young to pray.

All of this, of course, happened centuries past.

Long before the Seven Gods opened their eyes.

Urugal the Woven's Year
1159 Burn's Sleep

They were glorious tales. Farms in flames, children dragged behind horses for leagues. The trophies of that day, so long ago, cluttered the low walls of his grandfather's longhouse. Scarred skull-pates, frail-looking mandibles. Odd fragments of clothing made of some unknown material, now smoke-blackened and tattered. Small ears nailed to every wooden post that reached up to the thatched roof.

Evidence that Silver Lake was real, that it existed in truth, beyond the forest-clad mountains, down through hidden passes, a week – perhaps two – distant from the lands of the Uryd clan. The way itself was fraught, passing through territories held by the Sunyd and Rathyd clans, a journey that was itself a tale of legendary proportions. Moving silent and unseen through enemy camps, shifting the hearthstones to deliver deepest insult, eluding the hunters and trackers day and night until the borderlands were reached, then crossed – the vista ahead unknown, its riches not even yet dreamed of.

Karsa Orlong lived and breathed his grandfather's tales. They stood like a legion, defiant and fierce, before the pallid, empty legacy of Synyg – Pahlk's son and Karsa's father. Synyg, who had done nothing in his life, who tended his horses in his valley and had not once ventured into hostile lands. Synyg, who was both his father's and his son's greatest shame.

True, Synyg had more than once defended his herd of horses from raiders from other clans, and defended well, with honourable ferocity and admirable skill. But this was only to be expected from those of Uryd blood. Urugal the Woven was the clan's Face in the Rock, and Urugal was counted among the fiercest of the seven gods. The other clans had reason to fear the Uryd.

Nor had Synyg proved less than masterful in training his only son in the Fighting Dances. Karsa's skill with the bloodwood blade far surpassed his years. He was counted among the finest warriors of the clan. While the Uryd disdained use of the bow, they excelled with spear and atlatl, with the toothed-disc and the black-rope, and Synyg had taught his son an impressive efficiency with these weapons as well.

None the less, such training was to be expected from any father in the Uryd clan. Karsa could find no reason for pride in such things. The Fighting Dances were but preparation, after all. Glory was found in all that followed, in the contests, the raids, in the vicious perpetuation of feuds.

Karsa would not do as his father had done. He would not do . . . *nothing*. No, he would walk his grandfather's path. More closely than anyone might imagine. Too much of the clan's reputation lived only in the past. The Uryd had grown complacent in their position of pre-eminence among the Teblor. Pahlk had muttered that truth more than once, the nights when his bones ached from old wounds and the shame that was his son burned deepest.

A return to the old ways. And I, Karsa Orlong, shall lead. Delum Thord is with me. As is Bairoth Gild. All in our first year of scarring. We have counted coup. We have slain enemies. Stolen horses. Shifted the hearthstones of the Kellyd and the Buryd.

And now, with the new moon and in the year of your naming, Urugal, we shall weave our way to Silver Lake. To slay the children who dwell there.

He remained on his knees in the glade, head bowed

beneath the Faces in the Rock, knowing that Urugal's visage, high on the cliff-face, mirrored his own savage desire; and that those of the other gods, all with their own clans barring 'Siballe, who was the Unfound, glared down upon Karsa with envy and hate. None of their children knelt before them, after all, to voice such bold vows.

Complacency plagued all the clans of the Teblor, Karsa suspected. The world beyond the mountains dared not encroach, had not attempted to do so in decades. No visitors ventured into Teblor lands. Nor had the Teblor themselves gazed out beyond the borderlands with dark hunger, as they had often done generations past. The last man to have led a raid into foreign territory had been his grandfather. To the shores of Silver Lake, where farms squatted like rotted mushrooms and children scurried like mice. Back then, there had been two farms, a half-dozen outbuildings. Now, Karsa believed, there would be more. Three, even four farms. Even Pahlk's day of slaughter would pale to that delivered by Karsa, Delum and Bairoth.

So I vow, beloved Urugal. And I shall deliver unto you a feast of trophies such as never before blackened the soil of this glade. Enough, perhaps, to free you from the stone itself, so that once more you will stride in our midst, a deliverer of death upon all our enemies.

I, Karsa Orlong, grandson of Pahlk Orlong, so swear. And, should you doubt, Urugal, know that we leave this very night. The journey begins with the descent of this very sun. And, as each day's sun births the sun of the next day, so shall it look down upon three warriors of the Uryd clan, leading their destriers through the passes, down into the unknown lands. And Silver Lake shall, after more than four centuries, once again tremble to the coming of the Teblor.

Karsa slowly lifted his head, eyes travelling up the battered cliff-face, to find the harsh, bestial face of Urugal, there, among its kin. The pitted gaze seemed fixed upon him and Karsa thought he saw avid pleasure in those dark pools. Indeed, he was certain of it, and would describe it as

34

truth to Delum and Bairoth, and to Dayliss, so that she might voice her blessing, for he so wished her blessing, her cold words . . . *I, Dayliss, yet to find a family's name, bless you, Karsa Orlong, on your dire raid. May you slay a legion of children. May their cries feed your dreams. May their blood give you thirst for more. May flames haunt the path of your life. May you return to me, a thousand deaths upon your soul, and take me as your wife.*

She might indeed so bless him. A first yet undeniable expression of her interest in him. Not Bairoth – she but toyed with Bairoth as any young unwedded woman might, for amusement. Her Knife of Night remained sheathed, of course, for Bairoth lacked cold ambition – a flaw he might deny, yet the truth was plain that he did not lead, only follow, and Dayliss would not settle for that.

No, she would be his, Karsa's, upon his return, the culmination of his triumph that was the raid on Silver Lake. For him, and him alone, Dayliss would unsheathe her Knife of Night.

May you slay a legion of children. May flames haunt the path of your life.

Karsa straightened. No wind rustled the leaves of the birch trees encircling the glade. The air was heavy, a lowland air that had climbed its way into the mountains in the wake of the marching sun, and now, with light fading, it was trapped in the glade before the Faces in the Rock. Like a breath of the gods, soon to seep into the rotting soil.

There was no doubt in Karsa's mind that Urugal was present, as close behind the stone skin of his face as he had ever been. Drawn by the power of Karsa's vow, by the promise of a return to glory. So too hovered the other gods. Beroke Soft Voice, Kahlb the Silent Hunter, Thenik the Shattered, Halad Rack Bearer, Imroth the Cruel and 'Siballe the Unfound, all awakened once more and eager for blood.

And I have but just begun on this path. Newly arrived to my eightieth year of life, finally a warrior in truth. I have heard the oldest words, the whispers, of the One, who will unite the Teblor, who will bind the clans one and all and lead them into the lowlands and so begin the War of the People. These whispers, they are the voice of promise, and that voice is mine.

Hidden birds announced the coming of dusk. It was time to leave. Delum and Bairoth awaited him in the village. And Dayliss, silent yet holding to the words she would speak to him.

Bairoth will be furious.

The pocket of warm air in the glade lingered long after Karsa Orlong's departure. The soft, boggy soil was slow to yield the imprint of his knees, his moccasined feet, and the sun's deepening glare continued to paint the harsh features of the gods even as shadows filled the glade itself.

Seven figures rose from the ground, skin wrinkled and stained dark brown over withered muscles and heavy bones, hair red as ochre and dripping stagnant, black water. Some were missing limbs, others stood on splintered, shattered or mangled legs. One lacked a lower jaw while another's left cheekbone and brow were crushed flat, obliterating the eye-socket. Each of the seven, broken in some way. Imperfect. Flawed.

Somewhere behind the wall of rock was a sealed cavern that had been their tomb for a span of centuries, a short-lived imprisonment as it turned out. None had expected their resurrection. Too shattered to remain with their kin, they had been left behind, as was the custom of their kind. Failure's sentence was abandonment, an eternity of immobility. When failure was honourable, their sentient remnants would be placed open to the sky, to vistas, to the outside world, so that they might find peace in watching the passing of eons. But, for these seven, failure had not been honourable. Thus, the darkness of a tomb had been their sentence. They had felt no bitterness at that.

That dark gift came later, from outside their unlit prison, and with it, opportunity.

All that was required was the breaking of a vow, and the swearing of fealty to another. The reward: rebirth, and freedom.

Their kin had marked this place of internment, with carved faces each a likeness, mocking the vista with blank, blind eyes. They had spoken their names to close the ritual of binding, names that lingered in this place with a power sufficient to twist the minds of the shamans of the people who had found refuge in these mountains, and on the plateau with the ancient name of Laederon.

The seven were silent and motionless in the glade as the dusk deepened. Six were waiting for one to speak, yet that one was in no hurry. Freedom was raw exultation and, even limited as it was to this glade, the emotion persisted still. It would not be long, now, until that freedom would break free of its last chains – the truncated range of vision from the eye-sockets carved into the rock. Service to the new master promised travel, an entire world to rediscover and countless deaths to deliver.

Urual, whose name meant Mossy Bone and who was known to the Teblor as Urugal, finally spoke. 'He will suffice.'

Sin'b'alle – Lichen For Moss – who was 'Siballe the Unfound, did not hide the scepticism in her voice. 'You place too much faith in these fallen Teblor. *Teblor.* They know naught, even their true name.'

'Be glad that they do not,' said Ber'ok, his voice a rough rasp through a crushed throat. Neck twisted and head leaning to one side, he was forced to turn his entire body to stare at the rock-face. 'In any case, you have your own children, Sin'b'alle, who are the bearers of the truth. For the others, lost history is best left lost, for our purposes. Their ignorance is our greatest weapon.'

'Dead Ash Tree speaks the truth,' Urual said. 'We could not have so twisted their faith were they cognizant of their legacy.'

Sin'b'alle shrugged disdainfully. 'The one named Pahlk

also . . . *sufficed*. In your opinion, Urual. A worthy prospect to lead my children, it seemed. Yet he failed.'

'Our fault, not his,' Haran'alle growled. 'We were impatient, too confident of our efficacy. Sundering the Vow stole much of our power—'

'Yet what has our new master given of his, Antler From Summer?' Thek Ist demanded. 'Naught but a trickle.'

'And what do you expect?' Urual enquired in a quiet tone. 'He recovers from his ordeals as we do from ours.'

Emroth spoke, her voice like silk. 'So you believe, Mossy Bone, that this grandson of Pahlk will carve for us our path to freedom.'

'I do.'

'And if we are disappointed yet again?'

'Then we begin anew. Bairoth's child in Dayliss's womb.'

Emroth hissed. 'Another century of waiting! Damn these long-lived Teblor!'

'A century is as nothing—'

'As nothing, yet as everything, Mossy Bone! And you know precisely what I mean.'

Urual studied the woman, who was aptly named Fanged Skeleton, recalling her Soletaken proclivities, and its hunger that had so clearly led to their failure so long ago. 'The year of my name has returned,' he said. 'Among us all, who has led a clan of the Teblor as far along our path as I have? You, Fanged Skeleton? Lichen For Moss? Spear Leg?'

No-one spoke.

Then finally Dead Ash Tree made a sound that might have been a soft laugh. 'We are as Red Moss, silent. The way *will* be opened. So our new master has promised. He finds his power. Urual's chosen warrior already possesses a score of souls in his slayer's train. *Teblor* souls at that. Recall, also, that Pahlk journeyed alone. Yet Karsa shall have two formidable warriors flanking him. Should he die, there is always Bairoth, or Delum.'

'Bairoth is too clever,' Emroth snarled. 'He takes after Pahlk's son, his uncle. Worse, his ambition is only for himself. He feigns to follow Karsa, yet has his hand on Karsa's back.'

'And mine on his,' Urual murmured. 'Night is almost upon us. We must return to our tomb.' The ancient warrior turned. 'Fanged Skeleton, remain close to the child in Dayliss's womb.'

'She feeds from my breast even now,' Emroth asserted.

'A girl-child?'

'In flesh only. What I make within is neither a girl, nor a child.'

'Good.'

The seven figures returned to the earth as the first stars of night blinked awake in the sky overhead. Blinked awake, and looked down upon a glade where no gods dwelt. Where no gods had ever dwelt.

The village was situated on the stony bank of Laderii River, a mountain-fed, torrential flow of bitter-cold water that cut a valley through the conifer forest on its way down to some distant sea. The houses were built with boulder foundations and rough-hewn cedar walls, the roofs thick-matted, humped and overgrown with moss. Along the bank rose latticed frames thick with strips of drying fish. Beyond a fringe of woods, clearings had been cut to provide pasture for horses.

Mist-dimmed firelight flickered through the trees as Karsa reached his father's house, passing the dozen horses standing silent and motionless in the glade. Their only threat came from raiders, for these beasts were bred killers and the mountain wolves had long since learned to avoid the huge animals. Occasionally a rust-collared bear would venture down from its mountain haunt, but this usually coincided with salmon runs and the creatures showed little interest in challenging the horses, the village's dogs, or its fearless warriors.

Synyg was in the training kraal, grooming Havok, his prized destrier. Karsa could feel the animal's heat as he approached, though it was little more than a black mass in the darkness. 'Red Eye still wanders loose,' Karsa growled. 'You will do nothing for your son?'

His father continued grooming Havok. 'Red Eye is too young for such a journey, as I have said before—'

'Yet he is mine, and so I shall ride him.'

'No. He lacks independence, and has not yet ridden with the mounts of Bairoth and Delum. You will lodge a thorn in his nerves.'

'So I am to walk?'

'I give you Havok, my son. He has been softly run this night and still wears the bridle. Go collect your gear, before he cools too much.'

Karsa said nothing. He was in truth astonished. He swung about and made his way to the house. His father had slung his pack from a ridgepole near the doorway to keep it dry. His bloodwood sword hung in its harness beside it, newly oiled, the Uryd warcrest freshly painted on the broad blade. Karsa drew the weapon down and strapped the harness in place, the sword's leather-wrapped two-handed grip jutting over his left shoulder. The pack would ride Havok's shoulders, affixed to the stirrup-rig, though Karsa's knees would take most of the weight.

Teblor horse-trappings did not include a rider's seat; a warrior rode against flesh, stirrups high, the bulk of his weight directly behind the mount's shoulders. Lowlander trophies included saddles, which revealed, when positioned on the smaller lowlander horses, a clear shifting of weight to the back. But a true destrier needed its hindquarters free of extra weight, to ensure the swiftness of its kicks. More, a warrior must needs protect his mount's neck and head, with sword and, if necessary, vambraced forearms.

Karsa returned to where his father and Havok waited.

'Bairoth and Delum await you at the ford,' Synyg said.

'Dayliss?'

Karsa could see nothing of his father's expression as he replied tonelessly, 'Dayliss voiced her blessing

40

to Bairoth after you'd set out for the Faces in the Rock.'

'She blessed Bairoth?'

'She did.'

'It seems I misjudged her,' Karsa said, struggling against an unfamiliar stricture that tightened his voice.

'Easy to do, for she is a woman.'

'And you, Father? Will you give me your blessing?'

Synyg handed Karsa the lone rein and turned away. 'Pahlk has already done so. Be satisfied with that.'

'Pahlk is not my father!'

Synyg paused in the darkness, seemed to consider, then said, 'No, he is not.'

'Then will you bless me?'

'What would you have me bless, son? The Seven Gods who are a lie? The glory that is empty? Will I be pleased in your slaying of children? In the trophies you will tie to your belt? My father, Pahlk, would polish bright his own youth, for he is of that age. What were his words of blessing, Karsa? That you surpass his achievements? I imagine not. Consider his words carefully, and I expect you will find that they served him more than you.'

' "Pahlk, Finder of the Path that you shall follow, blesses your journey." Such were his words.'

Synyg was silent for a moment, and when he spoke his son could hear the grim smile though he could not see it. 'As I said.'

'Mother would have blessed me,' Karsa snapped.

'As a mother must. But her heart would have been heavy. Go, then, son. Your companions await you.'

With a snarl, Karsa swung himself onto the destrier's broad back. Havok swung his head about at the unfamiliar seating, then snorted.

Synyg spoke from the gloom. 'He dislikes carrying anger. Calm yourself, son.'

'A warhorse afraid of anger is next to useless. Havok shall have to learn who rides him now.' At that, Karsa drew a leg back and with a flick of the single rein swung the

41

destrier smartly round. A gesture with his rein hand sent the horse forward onto the trail.

Four blood-posts, each marking one of Karsa's sacrificed siblings, lined the path leading to the village. Unlike others, Synyg had left the carved posts unadorned; he had only gone so far as to cut the glyphs naming his three sons and one daughter given to the Faces in the Rock, followed by a splash of kin blood which had not lasted much beyond the first rain. Instead of braids winding up the man-high posts to a feathered and gut-knotted headdress at the peak, only vines entwined the weathered wood, and the blunted top was smeared with bird droppings.

Karsa knew the memory of his siblings deserved more, and he resolved to carry their names close to his lips at the moment of attack, that he might slay with their cries sharp in the air. His voice would be their voice, when that time arrived. They had suffered their father's neglect for far too long.

The trail widened, flanked by old stumps and low-spreading juniper. Ahead, the lurid glare of hearths amidst dark, squat, conical houses glimmered through the woodsmoke haze. Near one of those firepits waited two mounted figures. A third shape, on foot, stood wrapped in furs to one side. *Dayliss. She blessed Bairoth Gild, and now comes to see him off.*

Karsa rode up to them, holding Havok back to a lazy lope. He was the leader, and he would make the truth of that plain. Bairoth and Delum awaited him, after all, and which of the three had gone to the Faces in the Rock? Dayliss had blessed a follower. Had Karsa held himself too aloof? Yet such was the burden of those who commanded. She must have understood that. It made no sense.

He halted his horse before them, was silent.

Bairoth was a heavier man, though not as tall as Karsa or, indeed, Delum. He possessed a bear-like quality that he had long since recognized and had come to self-consciously affect. He rolled his shoulders now, as if loosening them for the journey, and grinned. 'A bold beginning, brother,' he rumbled, 'the theft of your father's horse.'

'I did not steal him, Bairoth. Synyg gave me both Havok and his blessing.'

'A night of miracles, it seems. And did Urugal stride out from the rock to kiss your brow as well, Karsa Orlong?'

Dayliss snorted at that.

If he had indeed stridden onto mortal ground, he would have found but one of us three standing before him. To Bairoth's jibe Karsa said nothing. He slowly swung his gaze to Dayliss. 'You have blessed Bairoth?'

Her shrug was dismissive.

'I grieve,' Karsa said, 'your loss of courage.'

Her eyes snapped to his with sudden fury.

Smiling, Karsa turned back to Bairoth and Delum. '"The stars wheel. Let us ride."'

But Bairoth ignored the words and instead of voicing the ritual reply he growled, 'Ill chosen, to unleash your wounded pride on her. Dayliss is to be my wife upon our return. To strike at her is to strike at me.'

Karsa went motionless. 'But Bairoth,' he said, low and smooth, 'I strike where I will. A failing of courage can spread like a disease – has her blessing settled upon you as a curse? I am warleader. I invite you to challenge me, now, before we quit our home.'

Bairoth hunched his shoulders, slowly leaned forward. 'It is no failing of courage,' he grated, 'that stays my hand, Karsa Orlong—'

'I am pleased to hear it. "The stars wheel. Let us ride."'

Scowling at the interruption, Bairoth made to say something more, then stopped. He smiled, relaxing once again. He glanced over at Dayliss and nodded, as if silently reaffirming a secret, then intoned, '"The stars wheel. Lead us, Warleader, into glory."'

Delum, who had watched all in silence, his face empty of expression, now spoke in turn. '"Lead us, Warleader, into glory."'

Karsa in front, the three warriors rode the length of the village. The tribe's elders had spoken against the journey, so no-one came out to watch them depart. Yet Karsa knew that none could escape hearing them pass, and he knew that, one day, they would come to regret that they had been witness to nothing more than the heavy, muffled thump of hoofs. None the less, he wished dearly for a witness other than Dayliss. Not even Pahlk had appeared.

Yet I feel as if we are indeed being watched. By the Seven perhaps. Urugal, risen to the height of the stars, riding the current of the wheel, gazing down upon us now. Hear me, Urugal! I, Karsa Orlong, shall slay for you a thousand children! A thousand souls to lay at your feet!

Nearby, a dog moaned in restless sleep, but did not awaken.

On the north valley side overlooking the village, at the very edge of the tree line, stood twenty-three silent witnesses to the departure of Karsa Orlong, Bairoth Gild and Delum Thord. Ghostly in the darkness between the broadleafed trees, they waited, motionless, until long after the three warriors had passed out of sight down the eastern track.

Uryd born. Uryd sacrificed, they were blood-kin to Karsa, Bairoth and Delum. In their fourth month of life they had each been given to the Faces in the Rock, laid down by their mothers in the glade at sunset. Offered to the Seven's embrace, vanishing before the sun's rise. Given, one and all, to a new mother.

'Siballe's children, then and now. 'Siballe, the Unfound, the lone goddess among the Seven without a tribe of her own. And so, she had created one, a secret tribe drawn from the six others, had taught them of their individual blood ties – in order to link them with their unsacrificed kin. Taught them, as well, of their own special purpose, the destiny that would belong to them and them alone.

She called them her Found, and this was the name by

which they knew themselves, the name of their own hidden tribe. Dwelling unseen in the midst of their kin, their very existence unimagined by anyone in any of the six tribes. There were some, they knew, who might suspect, but suspicion was all they possessed. Men such as Synyg, Karsa's father, who treated the memorial blood-posts with indifference, if not contempt. Such men usually posed no real threat, although on occasion more extreme measures proved necessary when true risk was perceived. Such as with Karsa's mother.

The twenty-three Found who stood witness to the beginning of the warriors' journey, hidden among the trees of the valley side, were by blood the brothers and sisters of Karsa, Bairoth and Delum, yet they were strangers as well, though at that moment that detail seemed to matter little.

'One shall make it.' This from Bairoth's eldest brother.

Delum's twin sister shrugged in reply and said, 'We shall be here, then, upon that one's return.'

'So we shall.'

Another trait was shared by all of the Found. 'Siballe had marked her children with a savage scar, a stripping away of flesh and muscle on the left side – from temple down to jawline – of each face, and with that destruction the capacity for expression had been severely diminished. Features on the left were fixed in a downturned grimace, as if in permanent dismay. In some strange manner, the physical scarring had also stripped inflection from their voices – or perhaps 'Siballe's own toneless voice had proved an overwhelming influence.

Thus bereft of intonation, words of hope had a way of ringing false to their own ears, sufficient to silence those who had spoken.

One would make it.

Perhaps.

Synyg continued stirring the stew at the cookfire when the door opened behind him. A soft wheeze, a dragged foot, the clatter of a walking stick against the doorframe. Then a harsh accusatory question.

'Did you bless your son?'

'I gave him Havok, Father.'

Somehow Pahlk filled a single word with contempt, disgust and suspicion all at once: 'Why?'

Synyg still did not turn as he listened to his father make a tortured journey to the chair closest to the hearth. 'Havok deserved a final battle, one I knew I would not give him. So.'

'So, as I thought.' Pahlk settled into the chair with a pained grunt. 'For your horse, but not for your son.'

'Are you hungry?' Synyg asked.

'I will not deny you the gesture.'

Synyg allowed himself a small, bitter smile, then reached over to collect a second bowl and set it down beside his own.

'He would batter down a mountain,' Pahlk growled, 'to see you stir from your straw.'

'What he does is not for me, Father, it is for you.'

'He perceives only the fiercest glory possible will achieve what is necessary – the inundation of the shame that is you, Synyg. You are the straggly bush between two towering trees, child of one and sire to the other. This is why he reached out to me, reached out – do you fret and chafe there in the shadows between Karsa and me? Too bad, the choice was always yours.'

Synyg filled both bowls and straightened to hand one to his father. 'The scar around an old wound feels nothing,' he said.

'To feel nothing is not a virtue.'

Smiling, Synyg sat in the other chair. 'Tell me a tale, Father, as you once did. Those days following your triumph. Tell me again of the children you killed. Of the women you cut down. Tell me of the burning homesteads, the screams of the cattle and sheep trapped in the flames. I would see those fires once more, rekindled in your eyes. Stir the ashes, Father.'

'When you speak these days, son, all I hear is that damned woman.'

'Eat, Father, lest you insult me and my home.'

'I shall.'

'You were ever a mindful guest.'

'True.'

No more words were exchanged until both men had finished their meals. Then Synyg set down his bowl. He rose and collected Pahlk's bowl as well, then, turning, he threw it into the fire.

His father's eyes widened.

Synyg stared down at him. 'Neither of us shall live to see Karsa's return. The bridge between you and me is now swept away. Come to my door again, Father, and I shall kill you.' He reached down with both hands and pulled Pahlk upright, dragged the sputtering old man to the door and without ceremony threw him outside. The walking stick followed.

They travelled the old trail that paralleled the spine of the mountains. Old rockslides obscured the path here and there, dragging firs and cedars down towards the valley below, and in these places bushes and broadleafed trees had found a foothold, making passage difficult. Two days and three nights ahead lay Rathyd lands, and of all the other Teblor tribes it was the Rathyd with whom the Uryd feuded the most. Raids and vicious murders entangled the two tribes together in a skein of hatred that stretched back centuries.

Passing unseen through Rathyd territories was not what Karsa had in mind. He intended to carve a bloody path through real and imagined insults with a vengeful blade, gathering a score or more Teblor souls to his name in the process. The two warriors riding behind him, he well knew, believed that the journey ahead would be one of stealth and subterfuge. They were, after all, but three.

But Urugal is with us, in this, his season. And we shall

announce ourselves in his name, and in blood. We shall shock awake the hornets in their nest, and the Rathyd shall come to know, and fear, the name of Karsa Orlong. As will the Sunyd, in their turn.

The warhorses moved cautiously across the loose scree of a recent slide. There had been a lot of snow the past winter, more than Karsa could recall in his lifetime. Long before the Faces in the Rock awoke to proclaim to the elders, within dreams and trances, that they had defeated the old Teblor spirits and now demanded obeisance; long before the taking of enemy souls had become foremost among Teblor aspirations, the spirits that had ruled the land and its people were the bones of rock, the flesh of earth, the hair and fur of forest and glen, and their breath was the wind of each season. Winter arrived and departed with violent storms high in the mountains, the savage exertions of the spirits in their eternal, mutual war. Summer and winter were as one: motionless and dry, but the former revealed exhaustion while the latter evinced an icy, fragile peace. Accordingly, the Teblor viewed summers with sympathy for the battle-weary spirits, while they detested winters for the weakness of the ascendant combatants, for there was no value in the illusion of peace.

Less than a score days remained in this, the season of spring. The high storms were diminishing, both in frequency and fury. Though the Faces in the Rock had long ago destroyed the old spirits and were, it seemed, indifferent to the passage of seasons, Karsa secretly envisioned himself and his two companion warriors as harbingers of one last storm. Their bloodwood swords would echo ancient rages among the unsuspecting Rathyd and Sunyd.

They cleared the recent slide. The path ahead wound down into a shallow valley with a highland meadow open to the bright afternoon sunlight.

Bairoth spoke behind Karsa. 'We should camp on the other side of this valley, Warleader. The horses need rest.'

'Perhaps your horse needs rest, Bairoth,' Karsa replied. 'You've too many feast nights on your bones. This journey shall make a warrior of you once again, I trust. Your back has known too much straw of late.' *With Dayliss riding you.*

Bairoth laughed, but made no other reply.

Delum called, 'My horse needs rest as well, Warleader. The glade ahead should make a good camp. There are rabbit runs here and I would set my snare.'

Karsa shrugged. 'Two weighted chains about me, then. The warcries of your stomachs leave me deafened. So be it. We shall camp.'

There would be no fire, so they ate the rabbits Delum had caught raw. Once, such fare would have been risky, for rabbits often carried diseases that could only be killed by cooking, most of them fatal to the Teblor. But since the coming of the Faces in the Rock, illnesses had vanished among the tribes. Madness, it was true, still plagued them, but this had nothing to do with what was eaten or drunk. At times, the elders had explained, the burdens laid upon a man by the Seven proved too powerful. A mind must be strong, and strength was found in faith. For the weak man, for the man who knew doubt, rules and rites could become a cage, and imprisonment led to madness.

They sat around a small pit Delum had dug for the rabbit bones, saying little through the course of the meal. Overhead, the sky slowly lost its colour, and the stars had begun their wheel. In the gathering gloom Karsa listened to Bairoth sucking at a rabbit skull. He was ever last to finish, for he left nothing and would even gnaw, on the next day, the thin layer of fat from the underside of the skin. Finally, Bairoth tossed the empty skull into the pit and sat back, licking his fingers.

'I have given,' Delum said, 'some thought as to the journey ahead. Through Rathyd and Sunyd lands. We should not take trails that set us against skyline or even bare rock. Therefore, we must take lower paths. Yet these

49

are ones that will lead us closest to camps. We must, I think, shift our travelling to night.'

'Better, then,' Bairoth nodded, 'to count coup. To turn the hearthstones and steal feathers. Perhaps a few lone sleeping warriors can give us their souls.'

Karsa spoke. 'Hiding by day, we see little smoke to tell us where the camps are. At night, the wind swirls, so it will not help us find the hearths. The Rathyd and Sunyd are not fools. They will not build fires beneath overhangs or against rock-faces – we shall find no welcoming wash of light on stone. Also, our horses see better during the day, and are more sure-footed. We shall ride by day,' he finished.

Neither Bairoth nor Delum said anything for a moment.

Then Bairoth cleared his throat. 'We shall find ourselves in a war, Karsa.'

'We shall be as an arrow of the Lanyd in its flight through a forest, changing direction with each twig, branch and bole. We shall gather souls, Bairoth, in a roaring storm. War? Yes. Do you fear war, Bairoth Gild?'

Delum said, 'We are three, Warleader.'

'Aye, we are Karsa Orlong, Bairoth Gild and Delum Thord. I have faced twenty-four warriors and have slain them all. I dance without equal – would you deny it? Even the elders have spoken in awe. And you, Delum, I see eighteen tongues looped on the thong at your hip. You can read a ghost's trail, and hear a pebble roll over from twenty paces. And Bairoth, in the days when all he carried was muscle – you, Bairoth, did you not break a Buryd's spine with your bare hands? Did you not drag a warhorse down? That ferocity but sleeps within you and this journey shall awaken it once more. Any other three . . . aye, glide the dark winding ways and turn hearthstones and pluck feathers and crush a few windpipes among sleeping foes. A worthy enough glory for any other three warriors. For us? No. Your warleader has spoken.'

Bairoth grinned over at Delum. 'Let us gaze upward and

witness the wheel, Delum Thord, for scant few such sights remain to us.'

Karsa slowly rose. 'You follow your warleader, Bairoth Gild. You do not question him. Your faltering courage threatens to poison us all. Believe in victory, warrior, or turn back now.'

Bairoth shrugged and leaned back, stretching out his hide-wrapped legs. 'You are a great warleader, Karsa Orlong, but sadly blind to humour. I have faith that you shall indeed find the glory you seek, and that Delum and I shall shine as lesser moons, yet shine none the less. For us, it is enough. You may cease questioning that, Warleader. We are here, with you—'

'Challenging my wisdom!'

'Wisdom is not a subject we have as yet discussed,' Bairoth replied. 'We are warriors as you said, Karsa. And we are young. Wisdom belongs to old men.'

'Yes, the elders,' Karsa snapped. 'Who would not bless our journey!'

Bairoth laughed. 'That is our truth and we must carry it with us, unchanged and bitter in our hearts. But upon our return, Warleader, we shall find that that truth has changed in our absence. The blessing will have been given after all. Wait and see.'

Karsa's eyes widened. 'The elders will *lie*?'

'Of course they will lie. And they will expect us to accept their new truths, and we shall – no, we must, Karsa Orlong. The glory of our success must serve to bind the people together – to hold it close is not only selfish, it is potentially deadly. Think on this, Warleader. We will be returning to the village with our own claims. Aye, no doubt a few trophies with us to add proof to our tale, but if we do not share out that glory then the elders will see to it that our claims shall know the poison of disbelief.'

'Disbelief?'

'Aye. They will believe but only if they can partake of our glory. They will believe us, but only if we in turn believe them – their reshaping of the past, the blessing that was not given, now given, all the villagers lining our ride out. They were all there, or so they will tell you, and, eventually, they will themselves come to believe it, and will have the scenes carved into their minds. Does this still confuse you, Karsa? If so, then we'd best not speak of wisdom.'

'The Teblor do not play games of deceit,' Karsa growled.

Bairoth studied him for a moment, then he nodded. 'True, they do not.'

Delum pushed soil and stones into the pit. 'It is time to sleep,' he said, rising to check one last time on the hobbled horses.

Karsa eyed Bairoth. *His mind is as a Lanyd arrow in the forest, but will that aid him when our bloodwood blades are out and battlecries sound on all sides? This is what comes when muscle turns to fat and straw clings to your back. Duelling with words will win you nothing, Bairoth Gild, except perhaps that your tongue will not dry out as quickly on a Rathyd warrior's belt.*

'At least eight,' Delum murmured. 'With perhaps one youth. There are indeed two hearths. They have hunted the grey bear that dwells in caves, and carry a trophy with them.'

'Meaning they are full of themselves.' Bairoth nodded. 'That's good.'

Karsa frowned at Bairoth. 'Why?'

'The cast of the enemy's mind, Warleader. They will be feeling invincible, and this will make them careless. Do they have horses, Delum?'

'No. Grey bears know the sound of hoofs too well. If they brought dogs on the hunt, none survived for the return journey.'

'Better still.'

They had dismounted, and now crouched near the edge of the tree line. Delum had slipped ahead to scout the

Rathyd encampment. His passage through the tall grasses, knee-high stumps and brush of the slope beyond the trees had not stirred a single blade or leaf.

The sun was high overhead, the air dry, hot and motionless.

'Eight,' Bairoth said. He grinned at Karsa. 'And a youth. He should be taken first.'

To make the survivors know shame. He expects us to lose. 'Leave him to me,' Karsa said. 'My charge will be fierce, and will take me to the other side of the camp. The warriors still standing will turn to face me one and all. That is when you two will charge.'

Delum blinked. 'You would have us strike from behind?'

'To even the numbers, yes. Then we shall each settle to our duels.'

'Will you dodge and duck in your pass?' Bairoth asked, his eyes glittering.

'No, I will strike.'

'They will bind you, then, Warleader, and you shall fail in reaching the far side.'

'I will not be bound, Bairoth Gild.'

'There are nine of them.'

'Then watch me dance.'

Delum asked, 'Why do we not use our horses, Warleader?'

'I am tired of talking. Follow, but at a slower pace.'

Bairoth and Delum shared an unreadable look, then Bairoth shrugged. 'We will be your witnesses, then.'

Karsa unslung his bloodwood sword, closing both hands around the leather-wrapped grip. The blade's wood was deep red, almost black, the glassy polish making the painted warcrest seem to float a finger's width above the surface. The weapon's edge was almost translucent, where the blood-oil rubbed into the grain had hardened, coming to replace the wood. There were no nicks or notches along the edge, only a slight rippling of the line where damage had repaired itself, for blood-oil clung to its memory and would little tolerate denting or scarring. Karsa held the weapon out before him, then slipped forward through the high grasses, quickening into the dance as he went.

Reaching the boar trail leading into the forest that Delum had pointed out, he hunched lower and slipped onto its hard-packed, flattened track without breaking stride. The broad, tapered sword-point seemed to lead him forward as if cutting its own silent, unerring path through the shadows and shafts of light. He picked up greater speed.

In the centre of the Rathyd camp, three of the eight adult warriors were crouched around a slab of bear meat that they had just unwrapped from a fold of deer hide. Two others sat nearby with their weapons across their thighs, rubbing the thick blood-oil into the blades. The remaining three stood speaking to one another less than three paces from the mouth of the boar trail. The youth was at the far end.

Karsa's sprint was at its peak when he reached the glade. At distances of seventy paces or less, a Teblor could run alongside a galloping warhorse. His arrival was explosive. One moment, eight warriors and one youth at rest in a clearing, the next, the tops of the heads of two of the standing warriors were cut off in a single horizontal blow. Scalp and bone flew, blood and brain sprayed and spat across the face of the third Rathyd. This man reeled back, and pivoted to his left to see the return swing of Karsa's sword, as it swept under his chin, then was gone from sight. Eyes, still held wide, watched the scene tilt wildly before darkness burgeoned.

Still moving, Karsa leapt high to avoid the warrior's head as it thudded and rolled across the ground.

The Rathyd who had been oiling their swords had already straightened and readied their weapons. They split away from each other and darted forward to take Karsa from either side.

He laughed, twisting around to plunge among the three

54

warriors whose bloodied hands held but butchering knives. Snapping his sword into a close-quarter guard, he ducked low. Three small blades each found their mark, slicing through leathers, skin and into muscle. Momentum propelled Karsa through the press, and he took those knives with him, spinning to rip his sword through a pair of arms, then up into an armpit, tearing the shoulder away, the scapula coming with it – a curved plate of purple bone latticed in veins attached by a skein of ligaments to a twitching arm that swung in its flight to reach skyward.

A body dived with a snarl to wrap burly arms around Karsa's legs. Still laughing, the Uryd warleader punched down with his sword, the pommel crunching through the top of the warrior's skull. The arms spasmed and fell away.

A sword hissed towards his neck from the right. Still in close-quarter guard, Karsa spun to take the blade with his own, the impact ringing both weapons with a pealing, sonorous sound.

He heard the closing step of the Rathyd behind him, felt the air cleave to the blade swinging in towards his left shoulder, and he pitched instantly down and to his right. Wheeling his own sword around, arms extending as he fell. The edge swept above and past the warrior's savage downstroke, cut through a pair of thick wrists, then tore through abdomen, from belly-button and across, between ribcage and point of hip, then bursting clear.

Still spinning as he toppled, he renewed the swing that had been staggered by bone and flesh, twisting his shoulders to follow the blade as it passed beneath him, then around to the other side. The slash cleared the ground at a level that took the last Rathyd's left leg at the ankle. Then the ground hammered into Karsa's right shoulder. Rolling away, his sword trailing crossways across his own body, deflecting but not quite defeating a downward blow – fire tearing into his right hip – then he was beyond the warrior's reach – and the man was shrieking and stumbling an awkward retreat.

Karsa's roll brought him upright once more, into a crouch that spurted blood down his right leg, that sent stinging stabs into his left side, his back beneath his right shoulder blade, and his left thigh where the knives were still buried.

He found himself facing the youth.

No more than forty, not yet at his full height, lean of limb as the Unready often were. Eyes filled with horror.

Karsa winked, then wheeled around to close on the one-footed warrior.

His shrieks had grown frenzied, and Karsa saw that Bairoth and Delum had reached him and had joined in the game, their blades taking the other foot and both hands. The Rathyd was on the ground between them, limbs jerking and spurting blood across the trampled grass.

Karsa glanced back to see the youth fleeing towards the woods. The warleader smiled.

Bairoth and Delum began chasing the floundering Rathyd warrior about, chopping pieces from his flailing limbs.

They were angry, Karsa knew. He had left them nothing.

Ignoring his two companions and their brutal torture, he plucked the butchering knife from his thigh. Blood welled but did not spurt, telling him that no major artery or vein had been touched. The knife in his left side had skittered along ribs and lay embedded flat beneath skin and a few layers of muscle. He drew the weapon out and tossed it aside. The last knife, sunk deep into his back, was harder to reach and it took a few attempts before he managed to find a sure clasp of its smeared handle and then pull it out. A longer blade would have reached his heart. As it was, it would probably be the most irritating of the three minor wounds. The sword-cut into his hip and through part of a buttock was slightly more serious. It would have to be carefully sewn, and would make both riding and walking painful for a while.

Loss of blood ·or a fatal blow had silenced the

dismembered Rathyd, and Karsa heard Bairoth's heavy steps approach. Another scream announced Delum's examination of the other fallen.

'Warleader.' Anger made the voice taut.

Karsa slowly turned. 'Bairoth Gild.'

The heavy warrior's face was dark. 'You let the youth escape. We must hunt him, now, and it will not be easy for these are his lands, not ours.'

'He is meant to escape,' Karsa replied.

Bairoth scowled.

'You're the clever one,' Karsa pointed out, 'why should this baffle you so?'

'He reaches his village.'

'Aye.'

'And tells of the attack. Three Uryd warriors. There is rage and frenzied preparations.' Bairoth allowed himself a small nod as he continued. 'A hunt sets out, seeking three Uryd warriors. Who are on foot. The youth is certain on this. Had the Uryd had horses, they would have used them, of course. Three against eight, to do otherwise is madness. So the hunt confines itself, in what it seeks, in its frame of thought, in all things. Three Uryd warriors, on foot.'

Delum had joined them, and now eyed Karsa without expression.

Karsa said, 'Delum Thord would speak.'

'I would, Warleader. The youth, you have placed an image in his mind. It will harden there, its colours will not fade, but sharpen. The echo of screams will become louder in his skull. Familiar faces, frozen eternal in expressions of pain. This youth, Karsa Orlong, will become an adult. And he will not be content to follow, he will lead. He *must* lead; and none shall challenge his fierceness, the gleaming wood of his will, the oil of his desire. Karsa Orlong, you have made an enemy for the Uryd, an enemy to pale all we have known in the past.'

'One day,' Karsa said, 'that Rathyd warleader shall kneel before me. This, I vow, here, on the blood of his kin, I so vow.'

The air was suddenly chill. Silence hung in the glade except for the muted buzz of flies.

Delum's eyes were wide, his expression one of fear.

Bairoth turned away. 'That vow shall destroy you, Karsa Orlong. No Rathyd kneels before an Uryd. Unless you prop his lifeless corpse against a tree stump. You now seek the impossible, and that is a path to madness.'

'One vow among many I have made,' Karsa said. 'And each shall be kept. Witness, if you dare.'

Bairoth paused from studying the grey bear's fur and defleshed skull – the Rathyd trophies – and glanced back at Karsa. 'Do we have a choice?'

'If you still breathe, then the answer is no, Bairoth Gild.'

'Remind me to tell you one day, Karsa Orlong.'

'Tell me of what?'

'What life is like, for those of us in your shadow.'

Delum stepped close to Karsa. 'You have wounds that need mending, Warleader.'

'Aye, but for now, only the sword-cut. We must return to our horses and ride.'

'Like a Lanyd arrow.'

'Aye, just so, Delum Thord.'

Bairoth called out, 'Karsa Orlong, I shall collect for you your trophies.'

'Thank you, Bairoth Gild. We shall take that fur and skull, as well. You and Delum may keep those.'

Delum turned to face Bairoth. 'Take them, brother. The grey bear better suits you than me.'

Bairoth nodded his thanks, then waved towards the dismembered warrior. 'His ears and tongue are yours, Delum Thord.'

'It is so, then.'

Among the Teblor, the Rathyd bred the fewest horses; despite this, there were plenty of wide runs from glade to glade down which Karsa and his companions could ride. In one of the clearings they had come upon an adult and two youths tending to six destriers. They had ridden them down, blades flashing, pausing only to collect trophies and gather up the horses, each taking two on a lead. An hour before darkness fell, they came to a forking of the trail, rode down the lower of the two for thirty paces, then released the leads and drove the Rathyd horses on. The three Uryd warriors then slipped a single, short rope around the necks of their own mounts, just above the collar bones, and with gentle, alternating tugs walked them backwards until they reached the fork, whereupon they proceeded onto the higher trail. Fifty paces ahead, Delum dismounted and backtracked to obscure their trail.

With the wheel taking shape overhead, they cut away from the rocky path and found a small clearing in which they made camp. Bairoth cut slices from the bear meat and they ate. Delum then rose to attend to the horses, using wet moss to wipe them down. The beasts were tired and left unhobbled to allow them to walk the clearing and stretch their necks.

Examining his wounds, Karsa noted that they had already begun to knit. So it was among the Teblor. Satisfied, he found his flask of blood-oil and set to repairing his weapon. Delum rejoined them and he and Bairoth followed suit.

'Tomorrow,' Karsa said, 'we leave this trail.'

'Down to the wider, easier ones in the valley?' Bairoth asked.

'If we are quick,' Delum said, 'we can pass through Rathyd land in a single day.'

'No, we lead our horses higher, onto the goat and sheep trails,' Karsa replied. 'And we reverse our path for the length of the morning. Then we ride down into the valley once more. Bairoth Gild, with the hunt out, who will remain in the village?'

The heavy man drew out his new bear cloak and wrapped it about himself before answering. 'Youths. Women. The old and the crippled.'

'Dogs?'

'No, the hunt will have taken those. So, Warleader, we attack the village.'

'Yes. Then we find the hunt's trail.'

Delum drew a deep breath and was slow in its release. 'Karsa Orlong, the village of our victims thus far is not the only village. In the first valley alone there are at least three more. Word will go out. Every warrior will ready his sword. Every dog will be unleashed and sent out into the forest. The warriors may not find us, but the dogs will.'

'And then,' Bairoth growled, 'there are three more valleys to cross.'

'Small ones,' Karsa pointed out. 'And we cross them at the south ends, a day or more hard riding from the north mouths and the heart of the Rathyd lands.'

Delum said, 'There will be such a foment of anger pursuing us, Warleader, that they will follow us into the valleys of the Sunyd.'

Karsa flipped the blade on his thighs to begin work on the other side. 'So I hope, Delum Thord. Answer me this, when last have the Sunyd seen an Uryd?'

'Your grandfather,' Bairoth said.

Karsa nodded. 'And we well know the Rathyd warcry, do we not?'

'You would start a war between the Rathyd and Sunyd?'

'Aye, Bairoth.'

The warrior slowly shook his head. 'We are not yet done with the Rathyd, Karsa Orlong. You plan too far in advance, Warleader.'

'Witness what comes, Bairoth Gild.'

Bairoth picked up the bear skull. The lower jaw still hung from it by a single strip of gristle. He snapped it off and tossed it to one side. Then he drew out a spare bundle of leather straps. He began tightly wrapping the cheek bones, leaving long lengths dangling beneath.

Karsa watched these efforts curiously. The skull was too heavy even for Bairoth to wear as a helm. Moreover, he would need to break the bone away on the underside, where it was thickest around the hole that the spinal cord made.

Delum rose. 'I shall sleep now,' he announced, moving off.

'Karsa Orlong,' Bairoth said, 'do you have spare straps?'

'You are welcome to them,' Karsa replied, also rising. 'Be sure to sleep this night, Bairoth Gild.'

'I will.'

For the first hour of light they heard dogs in the forested valley floor below. These faded as they backtracked along a high cliffside path. When the sun was directly overhead, Delum found a downward wending trail and they began the descent.

Midway through the afternoon, they came upon stump-crowded clearings and could smell the smoke of the village. Delum dismounted and slipped ahead.

He returned a short while later. 'As you surmised, Warleader. I saw eleven elders, thrice as many women, and thirteen youths – all very young, I imagine the older ones are with the hunt. No horses. No dogs.' He climbed back onto his horse.

The three Uryd warriors readied their swords. They then each drew out their flasks of blood-oil and sprinkled a few drops around the nostrils of their destriers. Heads snapped back, muscles tensed.

'I have the right flank,' Bairoth said.

'And I the centre,' Karsa announced.

'And so I the left,' Delum said, then frowned. 'They will scatter from you, Warleader.'

'I am feeling generous today, Delum Thord. This village shall be to the glory of you and Bairoth. Be sure that no-one escapes on the other side.'

'None shall.'

'And if any woman seeks to fire a house to turn the hunt, slay her.'

'They would not be so foolish,' Bairoth said. 'If they

61

do not resist they shall have our seed, but they shall live.'

The three removed the reins from their horses and looped them around their waists. They edged further onto their mounts' shoulders and drew their knees up.

Karsa slipped his wrist through the sword's thong and whirled the weapon once through the air to tighten it. The others did the same. Beneath him, Havok trembled.

'Lead us, Warleader,' Delum said.

A slight pressure launched Havok forward, three strides into a canter, slow and almost loping as they crossed the stump-filled glade. A slight shifting to the left led them towards the main path. Reaching it, Karsa lifted his sword into the destrier's range of vision. The beast surged into a gallop.

Seven lengthening strides brought them to the village. Karsa's companions had already split away to either side to come up behind the houses, leaving him the main artery. He saw figures there, directly ahead, heads turning. A scream rang through the air. Children scattered.

Sword lashed out, chopped down easily through young bone. Karsa glanced to his right and Havok shifted direction, hoofs kicking out to gather in and trample an elder. They plunged onward, pursuing, butchering. On the far sides of the houses, beyond the refuse trenches, more screams sounded.

Karsa reached the far end. He saw a single youth racing for the trees and drove after him. The lad carried a practice sword. Hearing the heavy thump of Havok's charge closing fast – and with the safety of the forest still too far in front of him – he wheeled.

Karsa's swing cut through practice sword then neck. A head thrust from Havok sent the youth's decapitated body sprawling.

I lost a cousin in such a manner. Ridden down by a Rathyd. Ears and tongue taken. Body strung by one foot from a branch. The head propped beneath, smeared in excrement. The deed is answered. Answered.

62

Havok slowed, then wheeled.

Karsa looked back upon the village. Bairoth and Delum had done their slaughter and were now herding the women into the clearing surrounding the village hearth.

At a trot, Havok carried him back into the village.

'The chief's own belong to me,' Karsa announced.

Bairoth and Delum nodded, and he could see their heightened spirits, from the ease with which they surrendered the privilege. Bairoth faced the women and gestured with his sword. A middle-aged, handsome woman stepped forward, followed by a younger version – a lass perhaps the same age as Dayliss. Both studied Karsa as carefully as he did them.

'Bairoth Gild and Delum Thord, take your first among the others. I will guard.'

The two warriors grinned, dismounted and plunged among the women to select one each. They vanished into separate houses, leading their prizes by the hand.

Karsa watched with raised brows.

The chief's wife snorted. 'Your warriors were not blind to the eagerness of those two,' she said.

'Their warriors, be they father or mate, will not be pleased with such eagerness,' Karsa commented. *Uryd women would not—*

'They will never know, Warleader,' the chief's wife replied, 'unless you tell them, and what is the likelihood of that? They will spare you no time for taunts before killing you. Ah, but I see now,' she added, stepping closer to stare up at his face. 'You thought to believe that Uryd women are different, and now you realize the lie of that. All men are fools, but now you are perhaps a little less so, as truth steals into your heart. What is your name, Warleader?'

'You talk too much,' Karsa growled, then he drew himself straight. 'I am Karsa Orlong, grandson of Pahlk—'

'Pahlk?'

'Aye.' Karsa grinned. 'I see you recall him.'

'I was a child, but yes, he is well known among us.'

'He lives still, and sleeps calm despite the curses you have laid upon his name.'

She laughed. 'Curses? There are none. Pahlk bowed his head to beg passage through our lands—'

'You lie!'

She studied him, then shrugged. 'As you say.'

One of the women cried out from one of the houses, a cry more pleasure than pain.

The chief's wife turned her head. 'How many of us will take your seed, Warleader?'

Karsa settled back. 'All of you. Eleven each.'

'And how many days will that take? You want us to cook for you as well?'

'Days? You think as an old woman. We are young. And, if need be, we have blood-oil.'

The woman's eyes widened. The others behind her began murmuring and whispering. The chief's wife spun and silenced them with a look, then she faced Karsa once more. 'You have never used blood-oil in this fashion before, have you? It is true, you will know fire in your loins. You will know stiffness for days to come. But, Warleader, you do not know what it will do to each of us women. I do, for I too was young and foolish once. Even my husband's strength could not keep my teeth from his throat, and he carries the scars still. There is more. What for you will last less than a week, haunts us for months.'

'And so,' Karsa replied, 'if we do not kill your husbands, you will upon their return. I am pleased.'

'You three will not survive the night.'

'It will be interesting, do you not think,' Karsa smiled, 'who among Bairoth, Delum and me will find need for it first.' He addressed all the women. 'I suggest to each of you to be eager, so you are not the first to fail us.'

Bairoth appeared, nodded at Karsa.

The chief's wife sighed and waved her daughter forward. 'No,' Karsa said.

The woman stopped, suddenly confused. 'But . . . will

you not want a child from this? Your first will carry the most seed—'

'Aye, it will. Are you past bearing age?'

After a long moment, she shook her head. 'Karsa Orlong,' she whispered, 'you invite my husband to set upon you a curse – he will burn blood on the stone lips of Imroth herself.'

'Yes, that is likely.' Karsa dismounted and approached her. 'Now, lead me to your house.'

She drew back. 'The house of my husband? Warleader – no, please, let us choose another one—'

'Your husband's house,' Karsa growled. 'I am done talking and so are you.'

An hour before dusk, and Karsa led the last of his prizes towards the house – the chief's daughter. He and Bairoth and Delum had not needed the blood-oil, a testament, Bairoth claimed, to Uryd prowess, though Karsa suspected the true honour belonged to the zeal and desperate creativity of the women of the Rathyd, and even then, the last few for each of the warriors had been peremptory.

As he drew the young woman into the gloomy house with its dying hearth, Karsa swung shut the door and dropped the latch. She turned to face him, a curious tilt to her chin.

'Mother said you were surprisingly gentle.'

He eyed her. *She is as Dayliss, yet not. There is no dark streak within this one. That is . . . a difference.* 'Remove your clothes.'

She quickly climbed out of the one-piece hide tunic. 'Had I been first, Karsa Orlong, I would have made home for your seed. Such is this day in my wheel of time.'

'You would have been proud?'

She paused to give him a startled look, then shook her head. 'You have slain all the children, all the elders. It will be centuries before our village recovers, and indeed it may not, for the anger of the warriors may turn them on each other, and on us women – should you escape.'

65

'Escape? Lie down, there, where your mother did. Karsa Orlong is not interested in escape.' He moved forward to stand over her. 'Your warriors will not be returning. The life of this village is ended, and within many of you there shall be the seed of the Uryd. Go there, all of you, to live among my people. And you and your mother, go to the village where I was born. Await me. Raise your children, my children, as Uryd.'

'You make bold claims, Karsa Orlong.'

He began removing his leathers.

'More than claims, I see,' she observed. 'No need, then, for blood-oil.'

'We will save the blood-oil, you and I, for my return.'

Her eyes widened and she leaned back as he moved down over her. In a small voice, she asked, 'Do you not wish to know my name?'

'No,' he growled. 'I will call you Dayliss.'

And he saw nothing of the shame that filled her young, beautiful face. Nor did he sense the darkness his words clawed into her soul.

Within her, as within her mother, Karsa Orlong's seed found a home.

A late storm had descended from the mountains, devouring the stars. Treetops thrashed to a wind that made no effort to reach lower, creating a roar of sound overhead and a strange calm among the boles. Lightning flickered, but the thunder's voice was long in coming.

They rode through an hour of darkness, then found an old campsite near the trail the hunt had left. The Rathyd warriors had been careless in their fury, leaving far too many signs of their passage. Delum judged that there were twelve adults and four youths on horseback in this particular party, perhaps a third of the village's entire strength. The dogs had already been set loose to range in packs on their own, and none accompanied the group the Uryd now pursued.

Karsa was well pleased. The hornets were out of the nest, yet flying blind.

They ate once more of the ageing bear meat, then Bairoth once again unwrapped the bear skull and resumed winding straps, this time around the snout, pulling them taut between the teeth. The ends left dangling were long, an arm and a half in length. Karsa now understood what Bairoth was fashioning. Often, two or three wolf skulls were employed for this particular weapon – only a man of Bairoth's strength and weight could manage the same with the skull of a grey bear. 'Bairoth Gild, what you create shall make a bright thread in the legend we are weaving.'

The man grunted. 'I care nothing for legends, Warleader. But soon, we shall be facing Rathyd on destriers.'

Karsa smiled in the darkness, said nothing.

A soft wind flowed down from upslope.

Delum lifted his head suddenly and rose in silence. 'I smell wet fur,' he said.

There had been no rain as yet.

Karsa removed his sword harness and laid the weapon down. 'Bairoth,' he whispered, 'remain here. Delum, take with you your brace of knives – leave your sword.' He rose and gestured. 'Lead.'

'Warleader,' Delum murmured. 'It is a pack, driven down from the high ground by the storm. They have no scent of us, yet their ears are sharp.'

'Do you not think,' Karsa asked, 'that they would have set to howling if they had heard us?'

Bairoth snorted. 'Delum, beneath this roar they have heard nothing.'

But Delum shook his head. 'There are high sounds and there are low sounds, Bairoth Gild, and they each travel their own stream.' He swung to Karsa. 'To your question, Warleader, this answer: possibly not, if they are unsure whether we are Uryd or Rathyd.'

Karsa grinned. 'Even better. Take me to them, Delum Thord. I have thought long on this matter of Rathyd dogs, the loosed packs. Take me to them, and keep your throwing knives close to hand.'

Havok and the other two destriers had quietly flanked the warriors during the conversation, and now all faced upslope, ears pricked forward.

After a moment's hesitation, Delum shrugged and, crouching, set off into the woods. Karsa followed.

The slope grew steeper after a score of paces. There was no path, and fallen tree trunks made traverse difficult and slow, though thick swaths of damp moss made the passage of the two Teblor warriors virtually noiseless. They reached a flatter shelf perhaps fifteen paces wide and ten deep, a high crack-riven cliff opposite. A few trees leaned against the rock, grey with death. Delum scanned the cliffside, then made to move towards a narrow, dirt-filled crevasse near the left end of the cliff that served as a game trail, but Karsa restrained him with a hand.

He leaned close. 'How far ahead?'

'Fifty heartbeats. We've still time to make this climb—'

'No. We position ourselves here. Take that ledge to the right and have your knives ready.'

With baffled expression, Delum did as he was told. The ledge was halfway up the cliffside. Within moments he was in place.

Karsa moved towards the game trail. A dead pine had fallen from above, taking the same path in its descent, coming to rest half a pace to the trail's left. Karsa reached it and gave the trunk a nudge. The wood was still sound. He quickly climbed it, then, feet resting on branches, he twisted round until he faced the flat expanse of shelf, the game trail now almost within arm's reach to his left, the bole and cliff at his back.

Then he waited. He could not see Delum from his position unless he leaned forward, which might well pull the tree away from the cliffside, taking him with it in a loud, probably damaging fall. He would have to trust, therefore, that Delum would grasp what he intended, and act accordingly when the time came.

A skitter of stones down the trail.

The dogs had begun the descent.

Karsa drew a slow, deep breath and held it.

The pack's leader would not be the first. Most likely the second, a safe beat or two behind the scout.

The first dog scrambled past Karsa's position in a scatter of stones, twigs and dirt, its momentum taking it a half-dozen paces out onto the flat shelf, where it paused, nose lifting to test the air. Hackles rising, it moved cautiously towards the shelf's edge.

Another dog came down the trail, a larger beast, this one kicking up more detritus than the first. As its scarred head and shoulders came into view, Karsa knew that he had found the pack's leader.

The animal reached the flat.

Just as the scout began swinging his head around.

Karsa leapt.

His hands shot out to take the leader on the neck, driving the beast down, spinning it onto its back, his left hand closing on the throat, his right gripping both flailing, kicking front legs just above the paws.

The dog flew into a frenzy beneath him, but Karsa held firm.

More dogs tumbled in a rush down the trail, then fanned out in sudden alarm and confusion.

The leader's snarls had turned to yelps.

Savage teeth had ripped into Karsa's wrist, until he managed to push his chokehold higher under the dog's jaw. The animal writhed, but it had already lost and they both knew it.

As did the rest of the pack.

Karsa finally glanced up to study the dogs surrounding him. At his lifting of head they all backed away – all but one. A young, burly male, who ducked low as it crept forward.

Two of Delum's knives thudded into the animal, one in

the throat and the other behind its right shoulder. The dog pitched to the ground with a strangled grunt, then lay still. The others of the pack retreated still further.

The leader had gone motionless beneath Karsa. Baring his teeth, the warrior slowly lowered himself until his cheek lay alongside the dog's jawline. Then he whispered into the animal's ear. 'You heard the deathcry, friend? That was your challenger. This should please you, yes? Now, you and your pack belong to me.' As he spoke, his tone soft and reassuring, he slowly loosened his grip on the dog's throat. A moment later, he leaned back, shifted his weight to one side, withdrawing his arm entirely, then releasing the dog's forelimbs.

The beast scrambled to its feet.

Karsa straightened, stepped close to the dog, smiling to see its tail droop.

Delum climbed down from the ledge. 'Warleader,' he said as he approached, 'I am witness to this.' He retrieved his knives.

'Delum Thord, you are both witness and participant, for I saw your knives and they were well timed.'

'The leader's rival saw his moment.'

'And you understood that.'

'We now have a pack that will fight for us.'

'Aye, Delum Thord.'

'I will go ahead of you back to Bairoth, then. The horses will need calming.'

'We shall give you a few moments.'

At the shelf's edge, Delum paused and glanced back at Karsa. 'I no longer fear the Rathyd, Karsa Orlong. Nor the Sunyd. I now believe that Urugal indeed walks with you on this journey.'

'Then know this, Delum Thord. I am not content to be champion among the Uryd. One day, all the Teblor shall kneel to me. This, our journey to the outlands, is but a scouting of the enemy we shall one day face. Our people have slept for far too long.'

70

'Karsa Orlong, I do not doubt you.'

Karsa's answering grin was cold. 'Yet you once did.'

To that, Delum simply shrugged, then he swung about and set off down the slope.

Karsa examined his chewed wrist, then looked down at the dog and laughed. 'You've the taste of my blood in your mouth, beast. Urugal now races to clasp your heart, and so, you and I, we are joined. Come, walk at my side. I name you Gnaw.'

There were eleven adult dogs in the pack and three not quite full-grown. They fell in step behind Karsa and Gnaw, leaving their lone fallen kin unchallenged ruler of the shelf beneath the cliff. Until the flies came.

Towards midday, the three Uryd warriors and their pack descended into the middle of the three small valleys on their southeasterly course across Rathyd lands. The hunt they tracked had clearly been driven to desperation, to have travelled so far in their search. It was also evident that the warriors ahead had avoided contact with other villages in the area. Their lengthening failure had become a shame that haunted them.

Karsa was mildly disappointed in that, but he consoled himself that the tale of their deeds would travel none the less, sufficient to make their return journey across Rathyd territory a deadlier and more interesting task.

Delum judged that the hunt was barely a third of a day ahead. They had slowed their pace, sending outriders to either side in search of a trail that did not yet exist. Karsa would not permit himself a gloat concerning that, however; there were, after all, two other parties from the Rathyd village, these ones probably on foot and moving cautiously, leaving few signs of their stealthy passage. At any time, they might cross the Uryd trail.

The pack of dogs remained close on the upwind side, loping effortlessly alongside the trotting horses. Bairoth had simply shaken his head at hearing Delum's recount of

Karsa's exploits, though of Karsa's ambitions, Delum curiously said nothing.

They reached the valley floor, a place of tumbled stone amidst birch, black spruce, aspen and alder. The remnants of a river seeped through the moss and rotting stumps, forming black pools that hinted nothing of their depth. Many of these sinkholes were hidden among boulders and treefalls. Their pace slowed as they cautiously worked their way deeper into the forest.

A short while later they came to the first of the mud-packed, wooden walkways the Rathyd of this valley had built long ago and still maintained, if only indifferently. Lush grasses filling the joins attested to this particular one's disuse, but its direction suited the Uryd warriors, and so they dismounted and led their horses up onto the raised track.

It creaked and swayed beneath the combined weight of horses, Teblor and dogs.

'We'd best spread out and stay on foot,' Bairoth said.

Karsa crouched and studied the roughly dressed logs. 'The wood is still sound,' he observed.

'But the stilts are seated in mud, Warleader.'

'Not mud, Bairoth Gild. Peat.'

'Karsa Orlong is right,' Delum said, swinging himself back onto his destrier. 'The way may pitch but the cross-struts underneath will keep it from twisting. We ride down the centre, in single file.'

'There is little point,' Karsa said to Bairoth, 'in taking this path if we then creep along it like snails.'

'The risk, Warleader, is that we become far more visible.'

'Best we move along it quickly, then.'

Bairoth grimaced. 'As you say, Karsa Orlong.'

Delum in the lead, they rode at a slow canter down the centre of the walkway. The pack followed. To either side, the only trees that reached to the eye level of the mounted warriors were dead birch, their leafless, black branches wrapped in the web of caterpillar nests. The living trees –

72

aspen and alder and elm – reached no higher than chest height with their fluttering canopy of dusty-green leaves. Taller black spruce was visible in the distance. Most of these looked to be dead or dying.

'The old river is returning,' Delum commented. 'This forest slowly drowns.'

Karsa grunted, then said, 'This valley runs into others that all lead northward, all the way to the Buryd Fissure. Pahlk was among the Teblor elders who gathered there sixty years ago. The river of ice filling the Fissure had died, suddenly, and had begun to melt.'

Behind Karsa, Bairoth spoke. 'We never learned what the elders of all the tribes discovered up there, nor if they had found whatever it was they were seeking.'

'I did not know they were seeking anything in particular,' Delum muttered. 'The death of the ice river was heard in a hundred valleys, including our own. Did they not travel to the Fissure simply to discover what had happened?'

Karsa shrugged. 'Pahlk told me of countless beasts that had been frozen within the ice for numberless centuries, becoming visible amidst the shattered blocks. Fur and flesh thawing, the ground and sky alive with crows and mountain vultures. There was ivory, but most of it was too badly crushed to be of any worth. The river had a black heart, or so its death revealed, but whatever lay within that heart was either gone or destroyed. Even so, there were signs of an ancient battle in that place. The bones of children. Weapons of stone, all broken.'

'This is more than I have ever—' Bairoth began, then stopped.

The walkway, which had been reverberating to their passage, had suddenly acquired a deeper, syncopating thunder. The walkway ahead made a bend, forty paces distant, to the left, disappearing behind trees.

The pack of dogs began snapping their jaws in voiceless warning. Karsa twisted round, and saw, two hundred paces behind them on the walkway, a dozen

73

Rathyd warriors on foot. Weapons were lifted in silent promise.

Yet the sound of hoofs – Karsa swung forward again, to see six riders pitch around the bend. Warcries rang in the air.

'Clear a space!' Bairoth bellowed, driving his horse past Karsa, and then Delum. The bear skull sprang into the air, snapping as it reached the length of the straps, and Bairoth began whirling the massive, bound skull over his and his horse's head, using both hands, his knees high on his destrier's shoulders. The whirling skull made a deep, droning sound. His horse loped forward.

The Rathyd riders were at full charge. They rode two abreast, the edge of the walkway less than half an arm's length away on either side.

They had closed to within twenty paces of Bairoth when he released the bear skull.

When two or three wolf skulls were used in this fashion, it was to bind or break legs. But Bairoth's target was higher. The skull struck the destrier on the left with a force that shattered the horse's chest. Blood sprayed from the animal's nose and mouth. Crashing down, it fouled the beast beside it – no more than the crack of a single hoof against its shoulder, but sufficient to make it veer wildly, and plunge down off the walkway. Legs snapped. The Rathyd warrior flew over his horse's head.

The rider of the first horse landed with bone-breaking impact on the walkway, at the very hoofs of Bairoth's destrier. Those hoofs punched down on the man's head in quick succession, leaving a shattered mess.

The charge floundered. Another horse went down, stumbling with a scream over the wildly kicking beast that now blocked the walkway.

Loosing the Uryd warcry, Bairoth drove his mount forward. A surging leap carried them over the first downed destrier. The Rathyd warrior from the other fallen horse was just clambering clear and had time to look up

74

to see Bairoth's sword-blade reach the bridge of his nose.

Delum was suddenly behind his comrade. Two knives darted through the air, passing Bairoth on his right. There was a sharp report as a Rathyd's heavy sword-blade slashed across to block one of the knives, then a wet gasp as the second knife found the man's throat.

Two of the enemy remained, one each for Delum and Bairoth, and so the duels could begin.

Karsa, after watching the effect of Bairoth's initial attack, had wheeled his mount round. Sword in his hands, blade flashing into Havok's vision, and they were charging back down the walkway towards the pursuing band.

The dog pack split to either side to avoid the thundering hoofs, then raced after rider and horse.

Ahead, eight adults and four youths.

A barked order sent the youths to either side of the walkway, then down. The adults wanted room, and, seeing their obvious confidence as they formed an inverted V spanning the walkway, weapons ready, Karsa laughed.

They wanted him to ride down into the centre of that inverted V – a tactic that, while it maintained Havok's fierce speed, also exposed horse and rider to flanking attacks. Speed counted for much in the engagement to come. The Rathyd's expectations fit neatly into the attacker's intent – had that attacker been someone other than Karsa Orlong. 'Urugal!' he bellowed, lifting himself high on Havok's shoulders. 'Witness!' He held his sword, point forward, over his destrier's head, and fixed his gaze on the Rathyd warrior on the V's extreme left.

Havok sensed the shift in attention and angled his charge just moments before contact, hoofs pounding along the very edge of the walkway.

The Rathyd directly before them managed a single backward step, swinging a two-handed overhead chop at Havok's snout as he went.

Karsa took that blade on his own, even as he twisted and threw his right leg forward, his left back. Havok turned beneath him, surged in towards the centre of the walkway.

The V had collapsed, and every Rathyd warrior was on Karsa's left.

Havok carried him diagonally across the walkway. Keening his delight, Karsa slashed and chopped repeatedly, his blade finding flesh and bone as often as weapon. Havok pitched around before reaching the opposite edge, and lashed out his hind legs. At least one connected, flinging a shattered body from the bridge.

The pack then arrived. Snarling bodies hurling onto the Rathyd warriors – most of whom had turned when engaging Karsa, and so presented exposed backs to the frenzied dogs. Shrieks filled the air.

Karsa spun Havok round. They plunged back into the savage press. Two Rathyd had managed to fight clear of the dogs, blood spraying from their blades as they backed up the walkway.

Bellowing a challenge, Karsa drove towards them.

And was shocked to see them both leap from the walkway.

'Bloodless cowards! I witness! Your youths witness! These damned dogs witness!'

He saw them reappear, weapons gone, scrambling and stumbling across the bog.

Delum and Bairoth arrived, dismounting to add their swords to the maniacal frenzy of the surviving dogs as they tore unceasing at fallen Rathyd.

Karsa drew Havok to one side, eyes still on the fleeing warriors, who had been joined now by the four youths. 'I witness! Urugal witnesses!'

Gnaw, black and grey hide barely visible beneath splashes of gore, panted up to stand beside Havok, his muscles twitching but no wounds showing. Karsa glanced back and saw that four more dogs remained, whilst a fifth had lost a foreleg and limped a red circle off to one side.

'Delum, bind that one's leg – we will sear it anon.'

'What use a three-legged hunting dog, Warleader?' Bairoth asked, breathing heavy.

'Even a three-legged dog has ears and a nose, Bairoth Gild. One day, she will lie grey-nosed and fat before my hearth, this I swear. Now, is either of you wounded?'

'Scratches.' Bairoth shrugged, turning away.

'I have lost a finger,' Delum said as he drew out a leather strap and approached the wounded dog, 'but not an important one.'

Karsa looked once more at the retreating Rathyd. They had almost reached a stand of black spruce. The warleader sent them a final sneer, then laid a hand on Havok's brow. 'My father spoke true, Havok. I have never ridden such a horse as you.'

An ear had cocked at his words. Karsa leaned forward and set his lips to the beast's brow. 'We become, you and I,' he whispered, 'legend. Legend, Havok.' Straightening, he studied the sprawl of corpses on the walkway, and smiled. 'It is time for trophies, my brothers. Bairoth, did your bear skull survive?'

'I believe so, Warleader.'

'Your deed was our victory, Bairoth Gild.'

The heavy man turned, studied Karsa through slitted eyes. 'You ever surprise me, Karsa Orlong.'

'As your strength does me, Bairoth Gild.'

The man hesitated, then nodded. 'I am content to follow you, Warleader.'

You ever were, Bairoth Gild, and that is the difference between us.

CHAPTER TWO

There are hints, if one scans the ground with a clear and
sharp eye, that this ancient Jaghut war, which for the Kron
T'lan Imass was either their seventeenth or eighteenth, went
terribly awry. The Adept who accompanied our expedition
evinced no doubt whatsoever that a Jaghut remained alive
within the Laederon glacier. Terribly wounded, yet
possessing formidable sorcery still. Well beyond the
ice river's reach (a reach which has been diminishing
over time), there are shattered remains of T'lan Imass,
the bones strangely malformed, and on them the flavour of
fierce and deadly Omtose Phellack lingering to this day.

Of the ensorcelled stone weapons of the Kron, only
those that were broken in the conflict remained, leading
one to assume that either looters have been this way,
or the T'lan Imass survivors (assuming there were any)
took them with them . . .

The Nathii Expedition of 1012
Kenemass Trybanos, Chronicler

'I believe,' Delum said as they led their horses down
from the walkway, 'that the last group of the hunt
has turned back.'

'The plague of cowardice ever spreads,' Karsa growled.

'They surmised at the very first,' Bairoth rumbled,
'that we were crossing their lands. That our first attack
was not simply a raid. So, they will await our return,

and will likely call upon the warriors of other villages.'

'That does not concern me, Bairoth Gild.'

'I know that, Karsa Orlong, for what part of this journey have you not already anticipated? Even so, two more Rathyd valleys lie before us. I would know. There will be villages – do we ride around them or do we collect still more trophies?'

'We shall be burdened with too many trophies when we reach the lands of the lowlanders at Silver Lake,' Delum commented.

Karsa laughed, then considered. 'Bairoth Gild, we shall slip through these valleys like snakes in the night, until the very last village. I would still draw hunters after us, into the lands of the Sunyd.'

Delum had found a trail leading up the valley side.

Karsa checked on the dog limping in their wake. Gnaw walked alongside it, and it occurred to Karsa that the three-legged beast might well be its mate. He was pleased with his decision to not slay the wounded creature.

There was a chill in the air that confirmed their gradual climb to higher elevations. The Sunyd territory was higher still, leading to the eastern edge of the escarpment. Pahlk had told Karsa that but a single pass cut through the escarpment, marked by a torrential waterfall that fed into Silver Lake. The climb down was treacherous. Pahlk had named it Bone Pass.

The trail began to wind sinuously among winter-cracked boulders and treefalls. They could now see the summit, six hundred steep paces upward.

The warriors dismounted. Karsa strode back and lifted the three-legged dog into his arms. He set it down across Havok's broad back and strapped it in place. The animal voiced no protest. Gnaw moved up to flank the destrier.

They resumed their journey.

The sun was bathing the slope in brilliant gold light by the time they had closed to within a hundred paces of the summit, reaching a broad ledge that seemed – through a sparse forest of straggly, wind-twisted oaks – to run the length of the valley side. Scanning the terrace's sweep to his right, Delum voiced a grunt, then said, 'I see a cave. There,' he pointed, 'behind those fallen trees, where the shelf bulges.'

Bairoth nodded and said, 'It looks big enough to hold our horses. Karsa Orlong, if we are to begin riding at night . . .'

'Agreed,' Karsa said.

Delum led the way along the terrace. Gnaw scrambled past him, slowing upon nearing the cave mouth, then crouching down and edging forward.

The Uryd warriors paused, waiting to see if the dog's hackles rose, thus signalling the presence of a grey bear or some other denizen. After a long moment, with Gnaw motionless and lying almost flat before the cave entrance, the beast finally rose and glanced back at the party, then trotted into the cave.

The fallen trees had provided a natural screen, hiding the cave from the valley below. There had been an over-hang, but it had collapsed, perhaps beneath the weight of the trees, leaving a rough pile of rubble partially block-ing the entrance.

Bairoth began clearing a path to lead the horses through. Delum and Karsa took Gnaw's route into the cave.

Beyond the mound of tumbled stones and sand, the floor levelled out beneath a scatter of dried leaves. The setting sun's light painted the back wall in patches of yellow, revealing an almost solid mass of carved glyphs. A small cairn of piled stones sat in the domed chamber's centre.

Gnaw was nowhere to be seen, but the dog's tracks crossed the floor and vanished into an area of gloom near the back.

Delum stepped forward, his eyes on a single, oversized glyph directly opposite the entrance. 'That Bloodsign is neither Rathyd nor Sunyd,' he said.

'But the words beneath it are Teblor,' Karsa asserted.

'The style is very . . .' Delum frowned, 'ornate.'

Karsa began reading aloud, ' *"I led the families that survived. Down from the high lands. Through the broken veins that bled beneath the sun . . ."* Broken veins?'

'Ice,' Delum said.

'Bleeding beneath the sun, aye. *"We were so few. Our blood was cloudy and would grow cloudier still. I saw the need to shatter what remained. For the T'lan Imass were still close and much agitated and inclined to continue their indiscriminate slaughter."* ' Karsa scowled. 'T'lan Imass? I do not know those two words.'

'Nor I,' Delum replied. 'A rival tribe, perhaps. Read on, Karsa Orlong. Your eye is quicker than mine.'

' *"And so I sundered husband from wife. Child from parent. Brother from sister. I fashioned new families and then sent them away. Each to a different place. I proclaimed the Laws of Isolation, as given us by Icarium whom we had once sheltered and whose heart grew vast with grief upon seeing what had become of us. The Laws of Isolation would be our salvation, clearing the blood and strengthening our children. To all who follow and to all who shall read these words, this is my justification—"* '

'These words trouble me, Karsa Orlong.'

Karsa glanced back at Delum. 'Why? They signify nothing of us. They are an elder's ravings. Too many words – to have carved all these letters would have taken years, and only a madman would do such a thing. A madman, who was buried here, alone, driven out by his people—'

Delum's gaze sharpened on Karsa. 'Driven out? Yes, I believe you are correct, Warleader. Read more – let us hear his justification, and so judge for ourselves.'

Shrugging, Karsa returned his attention to the stone wall. ' *"To survive, we must forget. So Icarium told us. Those things that we had come to, those things that softened us. We must abandon them. We must dismantle our . . ."* I know not that word, *"and shatter each and every stone, leaving no*

81

evidence of what we had been. We must burn our . . ."
another word I do not know, "and leave naught but ash. We
must forget our history and seek only our most ancient of
legends. Legends that told of a time when we lived simply. In the
forests. Hunting, culling fish from the rivers, raising horses.
When our laws were those of the raider, the slayer, when all was
measured by the sweep of a sword. Legends that spoke of feuds,
of murders and rapes. We must return to those terrible times. To
isolate our streams of blood, to weave new, smaller nets of
kinship. New threads must be born of rape, for only with
violence would they remain rare occurrences, and random. To
cleanse our blood, we must forget all that we were, yet find what
we had once been—"'

'Down here,' Delum said, squatting. 'Lower down. I
recognize words. Read here, Karsa Orlong.'

'It's dark, Delum Thord, but I shall try. Ah, yes. These
are . . . names. "I have given these new tribes names, the names
given by my father for his sons." And then a list. "Baryd,
Sanyd, Phalyd, Urad, Gelad, Manyd, Rathyd and Lanyd.
These, then, shall be the new tribes . . ." It grows too dark to
read on, Delum Thord, nor,' he added, fighting a sudden
chill, 'do I desire to. These thoughts are spider-bitten.
Fever-twisted into lies.'

'Phalyd and Lanyd are—'

Karsa straightened. 'No more, Delum Thord.'

'The name of Icarium has lived on in our—'

'Enough!' Karsa growled. 'There is nothing of meaning
here in these words!'

'As you say, Karsa Orlong.'

Gnaw emerged from the gloom, where a darker fissure
was now evident to the two Teblor warriors.

Delum nodded towards it. 'The carver's body lies within.'

'Where he no doubt crawled to die,' Karsa sneered. 'Let
us return to Bairoth. The horses can be sheltered here. We
shall sleep outside.'

Both warriors turned and strode back to the cave mouth.
Behind them, Gnaw stood beside the cairn a moment

longer. The sun had left the wall, filling the cave with shadows. In the darkness, the dog's eyes flickered.

Two nights later, they sat on their horses and looked down into the valley of the Sunyd. The plan to draw Rathyd pursuers after them had failed, for the last two villages they had come across had been long abandoned. The surrounding trails had been overgrown and rains had taken the charcoal from the firepits, leaving only red-rimmed black stains in the earth.

And now, across the entire breadth and length of the Sunyd valley, they could see no fires.

'They have fled,' Bairoth muttered.

'But not from us,' Delum replied, 'if the Sunyd villages prove to be the same as those Rathyd ones. This is a flight long past.'

Bairoth grunted. 'Where, then, have they gone?'

Shrugging, Karsa said, 'There are Sunyd valleys north of this one. A dozen or more. And some to the south as well. Perhaps there has been a schism. It matters little to us, except that we shall gather no more trophies until we reach Silver Lake.'

Bairoth rolled his shoulders. 'Warleader, when we reach Silver Lake, will our raid be beneath the wheel or the sun? With the valley before us empty, we could camp at night. These trails are unfamiliar, forcing us to go slowly in the dark.'

'You speak the truth, Bairoth Gild. Our raid will be in daylight. Let us make our way down to the valley floor, then, and find us a place to camp.'

The wheel of stars had travelled a fourth of its journey by the time the Uryd warriors reached level ground and found a suitable campsite. Delum had, with the aid of the dogs, killed a half-dozen rock hares during the descent, which he now skinned and spit while Bairoth built a small fire.

Karsa saw to the horses, then joined his two companions

at the hearth. They sat, waiting in silence for the meat to cook, the sweet smell and sizzle strangely unfamiliar after so many meals of raw food. Karsa felt a lassitude settle into his muscles, and only now realized how weary he had become.

The hares were ready. The three warriors ate in silence.

'Delum has spoken,' Bairoth said when they were done, 'of the words written in the cave.'

Karsa shot Delum a glare. 'Delum Thord spoke when he should not have. Within the cave, a madman's ravings, nothing more.'

'I have considered them,' Bairoth persisted, 'and I believe there is truth hidden within those ravings, Karsa Orlong.'

'Pointless belief, Bairoth Gild.'

'I think not, Warleader. The names of the tribes – I agree with Delum when he says there are, among them, the names of our tribes. "Urad" is far too close to Uryd to be accidental, especially when three of the other names are unchanged. Granted, one of those tribes has since vanished, but even our own legends whisper of a time when there were more tribes than there are now. And those two words that you did not know, Karsa Orlong. "Great villages" and "yellow bark"—'

'Those were not the words!'

'True enough, but that is the closest Delum could come to. Karsa Orlong, the hand that inscribed those words was from a place and time of sophistication, a place and a time where the Teblor language was, if anything, more complex than it is now.'

Karsa spat into the fire. 'Bairoth Gild, if these be truths as you and Delum say, I still must ask: what value do they hold for us now? Are we a fallen people? That is not a revelation. Our legends all speak of an age of glory, long past, when a hundred heroes strode among the Teblor, heroes that would make even my own grandfather, Pahlk, seem but a child among men—'

Delum's face in the firelight was deeply frowning as he cut in, 'And this is what troubles me, Karsa Orlong. Those legends and their tales of glory – they describe an age little different from our own. Aye, more heroes, greater deeds, but essentially the same, in the manner of how we lived. Indeed, it often seems that the very point of those tales is one of instruction, a code of behaviour, the proper way of being a Teblor.'

Bairoth nodded. 'And there, in those carved words in the cave, we are offered the explanation.'

'A description of how we would be,' Delum added. 'No, of how we *are*.'

'None of it matters,' Karsa growled.

'We were a defeated people,' Delum continued, as if he hadn't heard. 'Reduced to a broken handful.' He looked up, met Karsa's eyes across the fire. 'How many of our brothers and sisters who are given to the Faces in the Rock – how many of them were born flawed in some way? Too many fingers and toes, mouths with no palates, faces with no eyes. We've seen the same among our dogs and horses, Warleader. Defects come of inbreeding. That is a truth. The elder in the cave, he knew what threatened our people, so he fashioned a means of separating us, of slowly clearing our cloudy blood – and he was cast out as a betrayer of the Teblor. We were witness, in that cave, to an ancient crime—'

'We are fallen,' Bairoth said, then laughed.

Delum's gaze snapped to him. 'And what is it that you find so funny, Bairoth Gild?'

'If I must needs explain, Delum Thord, then there is no point.'

Bairoth's laughter had chilled Karsa. 'You have both failed to grasp the true meaning of all this—'

Bairoth grunted, 'The meaning you said did not exist, Karsa Orlong?'

'The fallen know but one challenge,' Karsa resumed. 'And that is to rise once more. The Teblor were once few, once defeated. So be it. We are no longer few. Nor have we known defeat since that time. Who from the lowlands dares venture into our territories? The time has come, I now say, to face that challenge. The Teblor must rise once more.'

Bairoth sneered, 'And who will lead us? Who will unite the tribes? I wonder.'

'Hold,' Delum rumbled, eyes glittering. 'Bairoth Gild, from you I now hear unseemly envy. With what we three have done, with what our warleader has already achieved – tell me, Bairoth Gild, do the shadows of the ancient heroes still devour us whole? I say they do not. Karsa Orlong now walks among those heroes, and we walk with him.'

Bairoth slowly leaned back, stretching his legs out beside the hearth. 'As you say, Delum Thord.' The flickering light revealed a broad smile that seemed directed into the flames. '"Who from the lowlands dares venture into our territories?" Karsa Orlong, we travel an empty valley. Empty of Teblor, aye. But what has driven them away? It may be that defeat stalks the formidable Teblor once more.'

There was a long moment when none of the three spoke, then Delum added another stick to the fire. 'It may be,' he said in a low voice, 'that there are no heroes among the Sunyd.'

Bairoth laughed. 'True. Among all the Teblor, there are but three heroes. Will that be enough, do you think?'

'Three is better than two,' Karsa snapped, 'but if need be, two will suffice.'

'I pray to the Seven, Karsa Orlong, that your mind ever remain free of doubt.'

Karsa realized that his hands had closed on the grip of his sword. 'Ah, that's your thought, then. The son of the father. Am I being accused of Synyg's weakness?'

Bairoth studied Karsa, then slowly shook his head. 'Your father is not weak, Karsa Orlong. If there are doubts to speak of here and now, they concern Pahlk and his heroic raid to Silver Lake.'

Karsa was on his feet, the bloodwood sword in his hands.

Bairoth made no move. 'You do not see what I see,' he said quietly. 'There is the potential within you, Karsa Orlong, to be your father's son. I lied earlier when I said I prayed that you would remain free of doubt. I pray for the very opposite, Warleader. I pray that doubt comes to you, that it tempers you with its wisdom. Those heroes in our legends, Karsa Orlong, they were terrible, they were monsters, for they were strangers to uncertainty.'

'Stand before me, Bairoth Gild, for I will not kill you whilst your sword remains at your side.'

'I will not, Karsa Orlong. The straw is on my back, and you are not my enemy.'

Delum moved forward with his hands full of earth, which he dropped onto the fire between the two other men. 'It is late,' he muttered, 'and it may be as Bairoth suggests, that we are not as alone in this valley as we believe ourselves to be. At the very least, there may be watchers on the other side. Warleader, there have been only words this night. Let us leave the spilling of blood for our true enemies.'

Karsa remained standing, glaring down at Bairoth Gild. 'Words,' he growled. 'Yes, and for the words he has spoken, Bairoth Gild must apologize.'

'I, Bairoth Gild, beg forgiveness for my words. Now, Karsa Orlong, will you put away your sword?'

'You are warned,' Karsa said, 'I will not be so easily appeased next time.'

'I am warned.'

Grasses and saplings had reclaimed the Sunyd village. The trails leading to and from it had almost vanished beneath brambles, but here and there, among the stone foundations of the circular houses, the signs of fire and violence could be seen.

Delum dismounted and began poking about the ruins. It was only a few moments before he found the first bones.

Bairoth grunted. 'A raiding party. One that left no survivors.'

Delum straightened with a splintered arrow shaft in his hands. 'Lowlanders. The Sunyd keep few dogs, else they would not have been so unprepared.'

'We now take upon ourselves,' Karsa said, 'not a raid, but a war. We journey to Silver Lake not as Uryd, but as Teblor. And we shall deliver vengeance.' He dismounted and removed from the saddle pack four hard leather sheaths, which he began strapping onto Havok's legs to protect the horse from the brambles. The other two warriors followed suit.

'Lead us, Warleader,' Delum said when he was done, swinging himself onto his destrier's back.

Karsa collected the three-legged dog and laid it down once more behind Havok's withers. He regained his seat and looked to Bairoth.

The burly warrior also remounted. His eyes were hooded as he met Karsa's gaze. 'Lead us, Warleader.'

'We shall ride as fast as the land allows,' Karsa said, drawing the three-legged dog onto his thighs. 'Once beyond this valley, we head northward, then east once more. By tomorrow night we shall be close to Bone Pass, the southward wend that will take us to Silver Lake.'

'And if we come across lowlanders on the way?'

'Then, Bairoth Gild, we shall begin gathering trophies. But none must be allowed to escape, for our attack on the farm must come as a complete surprise, lest the children flee.'

They skirted the village until they came to a trail that led them into the forest. Beneath the trees there was less undergrowth, allowing them to ride at a slow canter. Before long, the trail began climbing the valley side. By dusk, they reached the summit. Horses steaming beneath them, the three warriors reined in.

They had come to the edge of the escarpment. To the north and east and still bathed in golden sunlight, the horizon was a jagged line of mountains, their peaks capped in snow with rivers of white stretching down their flanks. Directly before them, after a sheer drop of three hundred or more paces, lay a vast, forested basin.

'I see no fires,' Delum said, scanning the shadow-draped valley.

'We must now skirt this edge, northward,' Karsa said. 'There are no trails breaking the cliffside here.'

'The horses need rest,' Delum said. 'But we are highly visible here, Warleader.'

'We shall walk them on, then,' Karsa said, dismounting. When he set the three-legged dog onto the ground, Gnaw moved up alongside her. Karsa collected Havok's single rein. A game trail followed the ridgeline along the top for another thirty paces before dropping slightly, sufficient to remove the silhouette they made against the sky.

They continued on until the wheel of stars had completed a fifth of its passage, whereupon they found a high-walled cul de sac just off the trail in which to make camp. Delum began preparing the meal while Bairoth rubbed down the horses.

Taking Gnaw and his mate with him, Karsa scouted the path ahead. Thus far, the only tracks they had seen were those from mountain goats and wild sheep. The ridge had begun a slow, broken descent, and he knew that, somewhere ahead, there would be a river carrying the run-off from the north range of mountains, and a waterfall cutting a notch into the escarpment's cliffside.

Both dogs shied suddenly in the gloom, bumping into Karsa's legs as they backed away from another dead-end to the left. Laying a hand down to calm Gnaw, he found the beast trembling. Karsa drew his sword. He sniffed the air, but could smell nothing awry, nor was there any sound from the dark-shrouded dead-end and Karsa was close enough to hear breathing had there been anyone hiding in it.

He edged forward.

A massive flat slab dominated the stone floor, leaving only a forearm's space on the three sides where rose the rock walls. The surface of the slab was unadorned, but a faint grey light seemed to emanate from the stone itself. Karsa moved closer, then slowly crouched down before the lone, motionless hand jutting from the slab's nearmost edge. It was gaunt, yet whole, the skin a milky blue-green, the nails chipped and ragged, the fingers patched in white dust.

Every space within reach of that hand was etched in grooves, cut deep into the stone floor – as deep as the fingers could reach – in a chaotic, cross-hatched pattern.

The hand, Karsa could see, was neither Teblor nor low-lander, but in size somewhere in between, the bones prominent, the fingers narrow and overlong and seeming to bear far too many joints.

Something of Karsa's presence – his breath perhaps as he leaned close in his study – was sensed, for the hand spasmed suddenly, jerking down to lie flat, fingers spread, on the rock. And Karsa now saw the unmistakable signs that animals had attacked that hand in the past – mountain wolves and creatures yet fiercer. It had been chewed, clawed and gnawed at, though, it seemed, never broken. Motionless once more, it lay pressed against the ground.

Hearing footsteps behind him, Karsa rose and turned. Delum and Bairoth, weapons out, made their way up the trail. Karsa strode to meet them.

Bairoth rumbled, 'Your two dogs came skulking back to us.'

'What have you found, Warleader?' Delum asked in a whisper.

'A demon,' he replied. 'Pinned for eternity beneath that stone. It lives, still.'

'The Forkassal.'

'Even so. There is much truth in our legends, it seems.'

Bairoth moved past and approached the slab. He crouched down before the hand and studied it long in the gloom, then he straightened and strode back. 'The Forkassal. The demon of the mountains, the One Who Sought Peace.'

'In the time of the Spirit Wars, when our old gods were young,' Delum said. 'What, Karsa Orlong, do you recall of that tale? It was so brief, nothing more than torn pieces. The elders themselves admitted that most of it had been lost long ago, before the Seven awoke.'

'Pieces,' Karsa agreed. 'The Spirit Wars were two, perhaps three invasions, and had little to do with the Teblor. Foreign gods and demons. Their battles shook the mountains, and then but one force remained—'

'In those tales,' Delum interjected, 'are the only mention of Icarium. Karsa Orlong, it may be that the T'lan Imass – spoken of in that elder's cave – belonged to the Spirit Wars, and that they were the victors, who then left never to return. It may be that it was the Spirit Wars that shattered our people.'

Bairoth's gaze remained on the slab. Now he spoke. 'The demon must be freed.'

Both Karsa and Delum turned to him, struck silent by the pronouncement.

'Say nothing,' Bairoth continued, 'until I have finished. The Forkassal was said to have come to the place of the Spirit Wars, seeking to make peace between the contestants. That is one of the torn pieces of the tale. For the demon's effort it was destroyed. That is another piece. Icarium too sought to end the war, but he arrived too late, and the victors knew they could not defeat him so they did not even try. A third piece. Delum Thord, the words in the cave also spoke of Icarium, yes?'

'They did, Bairoth Gild. Icarium gave the Teblor the Laws that ensured our survival.'

'Yet, were they able, the T'lan Imass would have laid a stone on him as well.' After these words, Bairoth fell silent.

Karsa swung about and walked to the slab. Its luminescence was fitful in places, hinting of the sorcery's antiquity, a slow dissolution of the power invested in it. Teblor elders worked magic, but only rarely. Since the awakening of the Faces in the Rock, sorcery arrived as a visitation, locked within the confines of sleep or trance. The old legends spoke of vicious displays of overt magic, of dread weapons tempered with curses, but Karsa suspected these were but elaborate inventions to weave bold colours into the tales. He scowled. 'I have no understanding of this magic,' he said.

Bairoth and Delum joined him.

The hand still lay flat, motionless.

'I wonder if the demon can hear our words,' Delum said.

Bairoth grunted. 'Even if it could, why would it understand them? The lowlanders speak a different tongue. Demons must also have their own.'

'Yet he came to make peace—'

'He cannot hear us,' Karsa asserted. 'He can do no more than sense the presence of someone . . . of something.'

Shrugging, Bairoth crouched down beside the slab. He reached out, hesitated, then settled his palm against the stone. 'It is neither hot nor cold. Its magic is not for us.'

'It is not meant to ward, then, only hold,' Delum suggested.

'The three of us should be able to lift it.'

Karsa studied Bairoth. 'What do you wish to awaken here, Bairoth Gild?'

The huge warrior looked up, eyes narrowing. Then his brows rose and he smiled. 'A bringer of peace?'

'There is no value in peace.'

'There must be peace among the Teblor, or they shall never be united.'

Karsa cocked his head, considering Bairoth's words.

'This demon may have gone mad,' Delum muttered. 'How long, trapped beneath this rock?'

'There are three of us,' Bairoth said.

'Yet this demon is from a time when we had been defeated, and if it was these T'lan Imass who imprisoned this demon, they did so because they could not kill him. Bairoth Gild, we three would be as nothing to this creature.'

'We will have earned its gratitude.'

'The fever of madness knows no friends.'

Both warriors looked to Karsa. 'We cannot know the mind of a demon,' he said. 'But we can see one thing, and that is how it still seeks to protect itself. This lone hand has fended off all sorts of beasts. In that, I see a holding on to purpose.'

'The patience of an immortal.' Bairoth nodded. 'I see the same as you, Karsa Orlong.'

Karsa faced Delum. 'Delum Thord, do you still possess doubts?'

'I do, Warleader, yet I will give your effort my strength, for I see the decision in your eyes. So be it.'

Without another word the three Uryd positioned themselves along one side of the stone slab. They squatted, hands reaching down to grip the edge.

'With the fourth breath,' Karsa instructed.

The stone lifted with a grinding, grating sound, a sifting of dust. A concerted heave sent it over, to crack against the rock wall.

The figure had been pinned on its side. The immense weight of the slab must have dislocated bones and crushed muscle, but it had not been enough to defeat the demon, for it had, over millennia, gouged out a rough, uneven pit for half the length of its narrow, strangely elongated body. The hand trapped beneath that body had clawed out a space for itself first, then had slowly worked grooves for hip and shoulder. Both feet, which were bare, had managed something similar. Spider webs and the dust of ground stone covered the figure like a dull grey shroud, and the stale air that rose from the space visibly swirled in its languid escape, heavy with a peculiar, insect-like stench.

The three warriors stood looking down on the demon.

It had yet to move, but they could see its strangeness even so. Elongated limbs, extra-jointed, the skin stretched taut and pallid as moonlight. A mass of blue-black hair spread out from the face-down head, like fine roots,

93

forming a latticework across the stone floor. The demon was naked, and female.

The limbs spasmed.

Bairoth edged closer and spoke in a low, soothing tone. 'You are freed, Demon. We are Teblor, of the Uryd tribe. If you will, we would help you. Tell us what you require.'

The limbs had ceased their spasming, and now but trembled. Slowly, the demon lifted her head. The hand that had known an eternity of darkness slipped free from under her body, probed out over the flat stone floor. The fingertips cut across strands of hair and those strands fell to dust. The hand settled in a way that matched its opposite. Muscles tautened along the arms, neck and shoulders, and the demon rose, in jagged, shaking increments. She shed hair in black sheets of dust until her pate was revealed, smooth and white.

Bairoth moved to take her weight but Karsa snapped a hand out to restrain him. 'No, Bairoth Gild, she has known enough pressure that was not her own. I do not think she would be touched, not for a long time, perhaps never again.'

Bairoth's hooded gaze fixed on Karsa for a long moment, then he sighed and said, 'Karsa Orlong, I hear wisdom in your words. Again and again, you surprise me – no, I did not mean to insult. I am dragged towards admiration – leave me my edged words.'

Karsa shrugged, eyes returning once more to the demon. 'We can only wait, now. Does a demon know thirst? Hunger? Hers is a throat that has not known water for generations, a stomach that has forgotten its purpose, lungs that have not drawn a full breath since the slab first settled. Fortunate it is night, too, for the sun might be as fire to her eyes—' He stopped then, for the demon, on hands and knees, had raised her head and they could see her face for the first time.

Skin like polished marble, devoid of flaws, a broad brow over enormous midnight eyes that seemed dry and flat, like onyx beneath a layer of dust. High, flaring cheekbones, a wide mouth withered and crusted with fine crystals.

'There is no water within her,' Delum said. 'None.' He backed away, then set off for their camp.

The woman slowly sat back onto her haunches, then struggled to stand.

It was difficult to just watch, but both warriors held back, tensed to catch her should she fall.

It seemed she noticed that, and one side of her mouth curled upward a fraction.

That one twitch transformed her face, and, in response, Karsa felt a hammerblow in his chest. *She mocks her own sorry condition. This, her first emotion upon being freed. Embarrassment, yet finding the humour within it. Hear me, Urugal the Woven, I will make the ones who imprisoned her regret their deed, should they or their descendants still live. These T'lan Imass – they have made of me an enemy. I, Karsa Orlong, so vow.*

Delum returned with a waterskin, his steps slowing upon seeing her standing upright.

She was gaunt, her body a collection of planes and angles. Her breasts were high and far apart, her sternum prominent between them. She seemed to possess far too many ribs. In height, she was as a Teblor child.

She saw the waterskin in Delum's hands, but made no gesture towards it. Instead, she turned to settle her gaze on the place where she had lain.

Karsa could see the rise and fall of her breath, but she was otherwise motionless.

Bairoth spoke. 'Are you the Forkassal?'

She looked over at him and half-smiled once more.

'We are Teblor,' Bairoth continued, at which her smile broadened slightly in what was to Karsa clear recognition, though strangely flavoured with amusement.

'She understands you,' Karsa observed.

Delum approached with the waterskin. She glanced at him and shook her head. He stopped.

Karsa now saw that some of the dustiness was gone from her eyes, and that her lips were now slightly fuller. 'She recovers,' he said.

'Freedom was all she needed,' Bairoth said.

'In the manner that sun-hardened lichen softens in the night,' Karsa said. 'Her thirst is quenched by the air itself—'

She faced him suddenly, her body stiffening.

'If I have given cause for offence—'

Before Karsa drew another breath she was upon him. Five concussive blows to his body and he found himself lying on his back, the hard stone floor stinging as if he was lying on a nest of fire-ants. There was no air in his lungs. Agony thundered through him. He could not move.

He heard Delum's warcry – cut off with a strangled grunt – then the sound of another body striking the ground.

Bairoth cried out from one side, 'Forkassal! Hold! Leave him—'

Karsa blinked up through tear-filled eyes as her face hovered above his. It moved closer, the eyes gleaming now like black pools, the lips full and almost purple in the starlight.

In a rasping voice she whispered to him in the language of the Teblor, 'They will not leave you, will they? These once enemies of mine. It seems shattering their bones was not enough.' Something in her eyes softened slightly. 'Your kind deserve better.' The face slowly withdrew. 'I believe I must needs wait. Wait and see what comes of you, before I decide whether I shall deliver unto you, Warrior, my eternal peace.'

Bairoth's voice from a dozen paces away: 'Forkassal!'

She straightened and turned with extraordinary fluidity. 'You have fallen far, to so twist the name of my kind, not to mention your own. I am Forkrul Assail, young warrior – not a demon. I am named Calm, a Bringer of Peace, and I warn you, the desire to deliver it is very strong in me at the moment, so remove your hand from that weapon.'

'But we have freed you!' Bairoth cried. 'Yet you have struck Karsa and Delum down!'

She laughed. 'And Icarium and those damned T'lan Imass will not be pleased that you undid their work. Then again, it is likely Icarium has no memory of having done so, and the T'lan Imass are far away. Well, I shall not give them a second chance. But I do know gratitude, Warrior, and so I give you this. The one named Karsa has been chosen. If I was to tell you even the little that I sense of his ultimate purpose, you would seek to kill him. But I tell you there would be no value in that, for the ones using him will simply select another. No. Watch this friend of yours. Guard him. There will come a time when he stands poised to change the world. And when that time comes, I shall be there. For I bring peace. When that moment arrives, cease guarding him. Step back, as you have done now.'

Karsa dragged a sobbing breath into his racked lungs. At a wave of nausea he twisted onto his side and vomited onto the gritty stone floor. Between his gasping and coughing, he heard the Forkrul Assail – the woman named Calm – stride away.

A moment later Bairoth knelt beside Karsa. 'Delum is badly hurt, Warleader,' he said. 'There is liquid leaking from a crack in his head. Karsa Orlong, I regret freeing this . . . this creature. Delum had doubts. Yet he—'

Karsa coughed and spat, then, fighting waves of pain from his battered chest, he climbed to his feet. 'You could not know, Bairoth Gild,' he muttered, wiping the tears from his eyes.

'Warleader, I did not draw my weapon. I did not seek to protect you as did Delum Thord—'

'Which leaves one of us healthy,' Karsa growled, staggering over to where Delum lay across the trail. He had been thrown some distance, by what looked to be a single blow. Slanting crossways across his forehead were four deep impressions, the skin split, yellow liquid oozing from the punched-through bone underneath. *Her fingertips*. Delum's eyes were wide, yet cloudy with confusion. Whole sections of his face had gone slack, as if no underlying thought could hold them to an expression.

Bairoth joined him. 'See, the fluid is clear. It is thought-blood. Delum Thord will not come all the way back with such an injury.'

'No,' Karsa murmured, 'he will not. None who lose thought-blood ever do.'

'It is my fault.'

'No, Delum made a mistake, Bairoth Gild. Am I killed? The Forkassal chose not to slay me. Delum should have done as you did – nothing.'

Bairoth winced. 'She spoke to you, Karsa Orlong. I heard her whispering. What did she say?'

'Little I could understand, except that the peace she brings is death.'

'Our legends have twisted with time.'

'They have, Bairoth Gild. Come, we must wrap Delum's wounds. The thought-blood will gather in the bandages and dry, and so clot the holes. Perhaps it will not leak so much then and he will come some of the way back to us.'

The two warriors set off for their camp. When they arrived they found the dogs huddled together, racked with shivering. Through the centre of the clearing ran the tracks of Calm's feet. Heading south.

A crisp, chill wind howled along the edge of the escarpment. Karsa Orlong sat with his back against the rock wall, watching Delum Thord move about on his hands and knees among the dogs. Reaching out and gathering the beasts close, to stroke and nuzzle. Soft, crooning sounds issued from Delum Thord, the smile never leaving the half of his face that still worked.

The dogs were hunters. They suffered the manhandling with miserable expressions that occasionally became fierce, low growls punctuated with warning snaps of their jaws – to which Delum Thord seemed indifferent.

Gnaw, lying at Karsa's feet, tracked with sleepy eyes Delum's random crawling about through the pack.

It had taken most of a day for Delum Thord to return to them, a journey that had left much of the warrior behind. Another day had passed whilst Karsa and Bairoth waited to see if more would come, enough to send light into his eyes, enough to gift Delum Thord with the ability to once more look upon his companions. But there had been no change. He did not see them at all. Only the dogs.

Bairoth had left earlier to hunt, but Karsa sensed, as the day stretched on, that Bairoth Gild had chosen to avoid the camp for other reasons. Freeing the demon had taken Delum from them, and it had been Bairoth's words that had yielded a most bitter reward. Karsa had little understanding of such feelings, this need to self-inflict some sort of punishment. The error had belonged to Delum, drawing his blade against the demon. Karsa's sore ribs attested to the Forkrul Assail's martial prowess – she had attacked with impressive speed, faster than anything Karsa had seen before, much less faced. The three Teblor were as children before her. Delum should have seen that, instantly, should have stayed his hand as Bairoth had done.

Instead, the warrior had been foolish, and now he crawled among the dogs. The Faces in the Rock held no pity for foolish warriors, so why should Karsa Orlong? Bairoth Gild was indulging himself, making regret and pity and castigation into sweet nectars, leaving him to wander like a tortured drunk.

Karsa was fast running out of patience. The journey must be resumed. If anything could return Delum Thord to himself, then it would be battle, the blood's fierce rage searing the soul awake.

Footsteps from uptrail. Gnaw's head turned, but the distraction was only momentary.

Bairoth Gild strode into view, the carcass of a wild goat draped over one shoulder. He paused to study Delum

Thord, then let the goat drop in a crunch and clatter of hoofs. He drew his butchering knife and knelt down beside it.

'We have lost another day,' Karsa said.

'Game is scarce,' Bairoth replied, slicing open the goat's belly.

The dogs moved into an expectant half-circle, Delum following to take his place among them. Bairoth cut through connecting tissues and began flinging blood-soaked organs to the beasts. None made a move.

Karsa tapped Gnaw on the flank and the beast rose and moved forward, trailed by its three-legged mate. Gnaw sniffed at the offerings, each in turn, and settled on the goat's liver, while its mate chose the heart. They each trotted away with their prizes. The remaining dogs then closed in on what remained, snapping and bickering. Delum pounced forward to wrest a lung from the jaws of one of the dogs, baring his own teeth in challenge. He scrambled off to one side, hunching down over his prize.

Karsa watched as Gnaw rose and trotted towards Delum Thord, watched as Delum, whimpering, dropped the lung then crouched flat, head down, while Gnaw licked the pooling blood around the organ for a few moments, then padded back to its own meal.

Grunting, Karsa said, 'Gnaw's pack has grown by one.' There was no reply and he glanced over to see Bairoth staring at Delum in horror. 'See his smile, Bairoth Gild? Delum Thord has found happiness, and this tells us that he will come back no further, for why would he?'

Bairoth stared down at his bloodied hands, at the butchering knife gleaming red in the dying light. 'Know you no grief, Warleader?' he asked in a whisper.

'No. He is not dead.'

'Better he were!' Bairoth snapped.

'Then kill him.'

Raw hatred flared in Bairoth's eyes. 'Karsa Orlong, what did she say to you?'

Karsa frowned at the unexpected question, then shrugged. 'She damned me for my ignorance. Words that could not wound me, for I was indifferent to all that she uttered.'

Bairoth's eyes narrowed. 'You make of what has happened a jest? Warleader, you no longer lead me. I shall not guard your flank in this cursed war of yours. We have lost too much—'

'There is weakness in you, Bairoth Gild. I have known that all along. For years, I have known that. You are no different from what Delum has become, and it is this truth that now haunts you so. Did you truly believe we would all return from this journey without scars? Did you think us immune to our enemies?'

'So *you* think—'

Karsa's laugh was harsh. 'You are a fool, Bairoth Gild. How did we come this far? Through Rathyd and Sunyd lands? Through the battles we have fought? Our victory was no gift of the Seven. Success was carved by our skill with swords, and by my leadership. Yet all you saw in me was bravado, as would come from a youth fresh to the ways of the warrior. You deluded yourself, and it gave you comfort. You are not my superior, Bairoth Gild, not in anything.'

Bairoth Gild stared, his eyes wide, his crimson hands trembling.

'And now,' Karsa growled, 'if you would survive. Survive this journey. Survive *me*, then I suggest you teach yourself anew the value of following. Your life is in your leader's hands. Follow me to victory, Bairoth Gild, or fall to the wayside. Either way, I will tell the tale with true words. Thus, how would you have it?'

Emotions flitted like wildfire across Bairoth's broad, suddenly pale face. He drew a half-dozen tortured breaths.

'I lead this pack,' Karsa said quietly, 'and none other. Do you challenge me?'

Bairoth slowly settled back on his haunches, shifting the grip on the butchering knife, his gaze settling, level now on

101

Karsa's own. 'We have been lovers a long time, Dayliss and I. You knew nothing, even as we laughed at your clumsy efforts to court her. Every day you would strut between us, filled with bold words, always challenging me, always seeking to belittle me in her eyes. But we laughed inside, Dayliss and I, and spent the nights in each other's arms. Karsa Orlong, it may be that you are the only one who will return to our village – indeed, I believe that you will make certain of it, so my life is as good as ended already, but I do not fear that. And when you return to the village, Warleader, you will make Dayliss your wife. But one truth shall remain with you until the end of your days, and that is: with Dayliss, it was not I who followed, but you. And there is nothing you can do to change that.'

Karsa slowly bared his teeth. 'Dayliss? My wife? I think not. No, instead I shall denounce her to the tribe. To have lain with a man not her husband. She shall be shorn, and then I shall claim her – as my slave—'

Bairoth launched himself at Karsa, knife flashing through the gloom. His back to the stone wall, Karsa could only manage a sideways roll that gave him no time to find his feet before Bairoth was upon him, one arm wrapping about his neck, arching him back, the hard knife-blade scoring up his chest, point driving for his throat.

Then the dogs were upon them both, thundering, bone-jarring impacts, snarls, the clash of canines, teeth punching through leather.

Bairoth screamed, pulled away, arm releasing Karsa.

Rolling onto his back, Karsa saw the other warrior stumbling, dogs hanging by their jaws from both arms, Gnaw with his teeth sunk into Bairoth's hip, other beasts flinging themselves forward, seeking yet more holds. Stumbling, then crashing to the ground.

'Away!' Karsa bellowed.

The dogs flinched, tore themselves free and backed off, still snarling. Off to one side, Karsa saw as he scrambled upright, crouched Delum, his face twisted into a wild smile, his eyes glittering, hands hanging low to the ground and spasmodically snatching at nothing. Then, his gaze travelling past Delum, Karsa stiffened. He hissed and the dogs fell perfectly silent.

Bairoth rolled onto his hands and knees, head lifting.

Karsa gestured, then pointed.

There was the flicker of torchlight on the trail ahead. Still a hundred or more paces distant, slowly nearing. With the way sound was trapped within the dead-end, it was unlikely the fighting had been heard.

Ignoring Bairoth, Karsa drew his sword and set off towards it. If Sunyd, then the ones who approached were displaying a carelessness that he intended to make fatal. More likely, they were lowlanders. He could see now, as he edged from shadow to shadow on the trail, that there were at least a half-dozen torches – a sizeable party, then. He could now hear voices, the foul tongue of the lowlanders.

Bairoth moved up alongside him. He had drawn his own sword. Blood dripped from puncture wounds on his arms, streamed down his hip. Karsa scowled at him, waved him back.

Grimacing, Bairoth withdrew.

The lowlanders had come to the cul de sac where the demon had been imprisoned. The play of torchlight danced on the high stone walls. The voices rose louder, edged with alarm.

Karsa slipped forward in silence until he was just beyond the pool of light. He saw nine lowlanders, gathered to examine the now-empty pit in the centre of the clearing. Two were well armoured and helmed, cradling heavy crossbows, longswords belted at their hips, positioned at the entrance to the cul de sac and watching the trail. Off to one side were four males dressed in earth-toned robes, their hair braided, pulled forward and knotted over their breastbones; none of these carried weapons.

The remaining three had the look of scouts, wearing tight-fitting leathers, armed with short bows and hunting

103

knives. Clan tattoos spanned their brows. It was one of these who seemed to be in charge, for he spoke in hard tones, as if giving commands. The other two scouts were crouched down beside the pit, eyes studying the stone floor.

Both guards stood within the torchlight, leaving them effectively blind to the darkness beyond. Neither appeared particularly vigilant.

Karsa adjusted his grip on the bloodsword, his gaze fixed on the guard nearest him.

Then he charged.

Head flew from shoulders, blood fountaining. Karsa's headlong rush carried him to where the other guard had been standing, to find the lowlander no longer there. Cursing, the Teblor pivoted, closed on the three scouts.

Who had already scattered, black-iron blades hissing from their sheaths.

Karsa laughed. There was little room beyond his reach in the high-walled cul de sac, and the only chance of escape would have to be through him.

One of the scouts shouted something then darted forward.

Karsa's wooden sword chopped down, splitting tendon, then bone. The lowlander shrieked. Stepping past the crumpling figure, Karsa dragged his weapon free.

The remaining two scouts had moved away from each other and now attacked from the sides. Ignoring one – and feeling the broad-bladed hunting knife rip through his leather armour to score along his ribs – Karsa batted aside the other's attack and, still laughing, crushed the lowlander's skull with his sword. A back slash connected with the other scout, sent him flying to strike the stone wall.

The four robed figures awaited Karsa, evincing little fear, joined in a low chant.

The air sparkled strangely before them, then coruscating fire suddenly unfolded, swept forward to engulf Karsa.

It raged against him, a thousand clawed hands, tearing,

raking, battering his body, his face and his eyes.

Karsa, shoulders hunching, walked through it.

The fire burst apart, flames fleeing into the night air. Shrugging the effects off with a soft growl, Karsa approached the four lowlanders.

Their expressions, calm and serene and confident a moment ago, now revealed disbelief that swiftly shifted to horror as Karsa's sword ripped into them.

They died as easily as had the others, and moments later the Teblor stood amidst twitching bodies, blood gleaming dark on his sword's blade. Torches lay on the stone floor here and there, fitfully throwing smoky light to dance against the cul de sac's walls.

Bairoth Gild strode into view. 'The second guard escaped up the trail, Warleader,' he said. 'The dogs now hunt.'

Karsa grunted.

'Karsa Orlong, you have slain the first group of children. The trophies are yours.'

Reaching down, Karsa closed the fingers of one hand in the robes of one of the bodies at his feet. He straightened, lifting the corpse into the air, and studied its puny limbs, its small head with its peculiar braids. A face lined, as would be a Teblor's after centuries upon centuries of life, yet the visage he stared down upon was scaled to that of a Teblor newborn.

'They squealed like babes,' Bairoth Gild said. 'The tales are true, then. These lowlanders are like children indeed.'

'Yet not,' Karsa said, studying the aged face now slack in death.

'They died easily.'

'Aye, they did.' Karsa flung the body away. 'Bairoth Gild, these are our enemies. Do you follow your warleader?'

'For this war, I shall,' Bairoth replied. 'Karsa Orlong, we shall speak no more of our . . . village. What lies between us must await our eventual return.'

'Agreed.'

* * *

105

Two of the pack's dogs did not return, and there was nothing of strutting victory in the gaits of Gnaw and the others as they padded back into the camp at dawn. Surprisingly, the lone guard had somehow escaped. Delum Thord, his arms wrapped about Gnaw's mate – as they had been throughout the night – whimpered upon the pack's return.

Bairoth shifted the supplies from his and Karsa's destriers to Delum's warhorse, for it was clear that Delum had lost all knowledge of riding. He would run with the dogs.

As they readied to depart, Bairoth said, 'It may be that the guard came from Silver Lake. That he will bring to them warning words of our approach.'

'We shall find him,' Karsa growled from where he crouched, threading the last of his trophies onto the leather cord. 'He could only have eluded the dogs by climbing, so there will be no swiftness to his flight. We shall seek sign of him. If he has continued on through the night, he will be tired. If not, he will be close.' Straightening, Karsa held the string of severed ears and tongues out before him, studied the small, mangled objects for a moment longer, then looped his collection of trophies round his neck.

He swung himself onto Havok's back, collected the lone rein.

Gnaw's pack moved ahead to scout the trail, Delum among them, the three-legged dog cradled in his arms.

They set off.

Shortly before midday, they came upon signs of the last lowlander, thirty paces beyond the corpses of the two missing dogs – a crossbow quarrel buried in each one. A scattering of iron armour, straps and fittings. The guard had shed weight.

'This child is a clever one,' Bairoth Gild observed. 'He will hear us before we see him, and will prepare an ambush.' The warrior's hooded gaze flicked to Delum. 'More dogs will be slain.'

Karsa shook his head at Bairoth's words. 'He will not

ambush us, for that will see him killed, and he knows it. Should we catch up with him, he will seek to hide. Evasion is his only hope, up the cliffside, and then we will have passed him, and so he will not succeed in reaching Silver Lake before us.'

'We do not hunt him down?' Bairoth asked in surprise.

'No. We ride for Bone Pass.'

'Then he shall trail us. Warleader, an enemy loose at our backs—'

'A child. Those quarrels might well kill a dog, but they are as twigs to us Teblor. Our armour alone will take much of those small barbs—'

'He has a sharp eye, Karsa Orlong, to slay two dogs in the dark. He will aim for where our armour does not cover us.'

Karsa shrugged. 'Then we must outpace him beyond the pass.'

They continued on. The trail widened as it climbed, the entire escarpment pushing upward in its northward reach. Riding at a fast trot, they covered league after league until, by late afternoon, they found themselves entering clouds of mist, a deep roaring sound directly ahead.

The path dropped away suddenly.

Reining in amidst the milling dogs, Karsa dismounted.

The edge was sheer. Beyond it and on his left, a river had cut a notch a thousand paces or more deep into the cliffside, down to what must have been a ledge of some sort, over which it then plunged another thousand paces to a mist-shrouded valley floor. A dozen or more thread-thin waterfalls drifted out from both sides of the notch, issuing from fissures in the bedrock. The scene, Karsa realized after a moment, was all wrong. They had reached the highest part of the escarpment's ridge. A river, cutting a natural route through to the lowlands, did not belong in this place. Stranger still, the flanking waterfalls poured out from riven cracks, not one level with another, as if the mountains on both sides were filled with water.

'Karsa Orlong,' Bairoth had to shout to be heard over the

roar rising from far below, 'someone – an ancient god, perhaps – has broken a mountain in half. That notch, it was not carved by water. No, it has the look of having been cut by a giant axe. And the wound . . . bleeds.'

Not replying to Bairoth's words, Karsa turned about. Directly on his right, a winding, rocky path descended on their side of the cliff, a steep path of shale and scree, gleaming wet.

'This is our way down?' Bairoth stepped past Karsa, then swung an incredulous look upon the warleader. 'We cannot! It will vanish beneath our feet! Beneath the hoofs of the horses! We shall descend indeed, like stones down a cliffside!'

Karsa crouched and pried a rock loose from the ground. He tossed it down the trail. Where it first struck, the shale shifted, trembled, then slid in a growing wave that quickly followed the bouncing rock, vanishing into the mists.

Revealing rough, broad steps.

Made entirely of bones.

'It is as Pahlk said,' Karsa murmured, before turning to Bairoth. 'Come, our path awaits.'

Bairoth's eyes were hooded. 'It does indeed, Karsa Orlong. Beneath our feet there shall be a truth.'

Karsa scowled. 'This is our trail down from the mountains. Nothing more, Bairoth Gild.'

The warrior shrugged. 'As you say, Warleader.'

Karsa in the lead, they began the descent.

The bones were lowlander in scale, yet heavier and thicker, hardened into stone. Here and there, antlers and tusks were visible, as well as artfully carved bone helms from larger beasts. An army had been slain, their bones then laid out, intricately fashioned into these grim steps. The mists had quickly laid down a layer of water, but each step was solid, broad and slightly angled back, the pitch reducing the risk of slipping. The Teblor's pace was slowed only by the cautious descent of the destriers.

It seemed that the rockslide Karsa had triggered had

cleared the way as far down as the massive shelf of stone where the river gathered before plunging over to the valley below. With the roaring tumble of water growing ever closer on their left and jagged, raw rock on their right, the warriors descended more than a thousand paces, and with each step the gloom deepened around them.

Pale, ghostly light broken by shreds of darker, opaque mists commanded the ledge that spread out on this side of the waterfall. The bones formed a level floor of sorts, abutting the rock wall to the right and appearing to continue on beneath the river that now roared, massive and monstrous, less than twenty paces away on their left.

The horses needed to rest. Karsa watched Bairoth make his way towards the river, then glanced over at Delum, who huddled now among Gnaw's pack, wet and shivering. The faint glow emanating from the bones seemed to carry a breath unnaturally cold. On all sides, the scene was colourless, strangely dead. Even the river's immense power felt lifeless.

Bairoth approached. 'Warleader, these bones beneath us, they continue under the river to the other side. They are deep, almost my height where I could see. Tens of thousands have died to make this. Tens of tens. This entire shelf—'

'Bairoth Gild, we have rested long enough. There are stones coming down from above – either the guard descends, or there will be another slide to bury what we have revealed. There must be many such slides, for the lowlanders used this on the way up, and that could not have been more than a few days ago. Yet we arrived to find it buried once more.'

Sudden unease flickered through Bairoth's expression, and he glanced over to where small stones of shale pattered down from the trail above. There were more now than there had been a moment ago.

They gathered the horses once more and approached the shelf's edge. The descent before them was too steep to hold a slide, the steps switchbacking for as far down as the Teblor could see. The horses balked before it.

'Karsa Orlong, we shall be very vulnerable on that path.'

'We have been so all along, Bairoth Gild. That lowlander behind us has already missed his greatest opportunity. That is why I believe we have outdistanced him, and that the stones we see falling from above portend another slide and nothing more.' With that Karsa coaxed Havok forward onto the first step.

Thirty paces down they heard a faint roar from above, a sound deeper in timbre than the river. A hail of stones swept over them, but at some distance out from the cliff wall. Muddy rain followed for a short time thereafter.

They continued on, until weariness settled into their limbs. The mists might have lightened for a time, but perhaps it was nothing more than their eyes growing accustomed to the gloom. The wheels of sun and stars passed unseen and unseeing over them. The only means of measuring time was through hunger and exhaustion. There would be no stopping until the descent was complete. Karsa had lost count of the switchbacks; what he had imagined to be a thousand paces was proving to be far more. Beside them, the river continued its fall, nothing but mists now, a hissing deluge bitter cold, spreading out to blind them to the valley below and the skies above. Their world had narrowed to the endless bones under their moccasins and the sheer wall of the cliff.

They reached another shelf and the bones were gone, buried beneath squelching, sodden mud and snarled bundles of vivid green grasses. Fallen tree branches cloaked in mosses littered the area. Mists hid all else.

The horses tossed their heads as they were led, finally, onto level ground. Delum and the dogs settled down into a clump of wet fur and skin. Bairoth stumbled close to Karsa. 'Warleader, I am distraught.'

Karsa frowned. His legs were trembling beneath him, and he could not keep the shivering from his muscles.

'Why, Bairoth Gild? We are done. We have descended Bone Pass.'

'Aye.' Bairoth coughed, then said, 'And before long we will come to this place again – to climb.'

Karsa slowly nodded. 'I have thought on this, Bairoth Gild. The lowlands sweep around our plateau. There are other passes, directly south of our own Uryd lands – there must be, else lowlanders would never have appeared among us. Our return journey will take us along the edge, westward, and we shall find those hidden passes.'

'Through lowlander territories the entire way! We are but two, Karsa Orlong! A raid upon the farm at Silver Lake is one thing, but to wage war against an entire tribe is madness! We will be hunted and pursued the entire way – it cannot be done!'

'Hunted and pursued?' Karsa laughed. 'What is new in that? Come, Bairoth Gild, we must find somewhere dry, away from this river. I see treetops, there, to the left. We shall make ourselves a fire, we shall rediscover what it is like to be warm, our bellies full.'

The ledge's slope led gently down a scree mostly buried beneath mosses, lichens and rich, dark soil, beyond which waited a forest of ancient redwoods and cedars. The sky overhead revealed a patch of blue, and shafts of sunlight were visible here and there. Once within the wood, the mists thinned to a musty dampness, smelling of rotting treefalls. The warriors continued on another fifty paces, until they found a sunlit stretch where a diseased cedar had collapsed some time past. Butterflies danced in the golden air and the soft crunch of pine-borers was a steady cadence on all sides. The huge, upright root-mat of the cedar had left a bare patch of bedrock where the tree had once stood. The rock was dry and in full sunlight.

Karsa began unstrapping supplies while Bairoth set off to collect deadwood from the fallen cedar. Delum found a mossy patch warmed by the sun and curled up to sleep. Karsa considered removing the man's sodden clothes, then, seeing the rest of the pack gather around Delum, he simply shrugged and resumed unburdening the horses.

A short while later, their clothes hanging from roots close to the fire, the two warriors sat naked on the bedrock, the chill slowly yielding from muscle and bone.

'At the far end of this valley,' Karsa said, 'the river widens, forming a flat before reaching the lake. The side we are now on becomes the south side of the river. There will be a spar of rock near the mouth, blocking our view to the right. Immediately beyond it, on the lake's southwest shore, stands the lowlander farm. We are very nearly there, Bairoth Gild.'

The warrior on the other side of the hearth rolled his shoulders. 'Tell me we shall attack in daylight, Warleader. I have found a deep hatred for darkness. Bone Pass has shrivelled my heart.'

'Daylight it shall be, Bairoth Gild,' Karsa replied, choosing to ignore Bairoth's last confession, for its words had trembled something within him, leaving a sour taste in his mouth. 'The children will be working in the fields, unable to reach the stronghold of the farmhouse in time. They will see us charging down upon them, and know terror and despair.'

'This pleases me, Warleader.'

The redwood and cedar forest cloaked the entire valley, showing no evidence of clearing or logging. There was little game to be found beneath the thick canopy, and days passed in a diffuse gloom relieved only by the occasional treefall. The Teblor's supply of food quickly dwindled, the horses growing leaner on a diet of blueleaf, cullan moss and bitter vine, the dogs taking to eating rotten wood, berries and beetles.

Midway through the fourth day, the valley narrowed, forcing them ever closer to the river. Travelling through the deep forest, away from the lone trail running alongside the river, the Teblor had ensured that they would remain undiscovered, but now, finally, they were nearing Silver Lake.

They arrived at the river mouth at dusk, the wheel of stars awakening in the sky above them. The trail flanking the river's boulder-strewn bank had seen recent passage, leading northwestward, but no sign of anyone's returning. The air was crisp above the river's rushing water. A broad fan of sand and gravel formed a driftwood-cluttered island where the river opened out into the lake. Mists hung over the water, making the lake's far north and east shores hazy. The mountains reached down on those distant shores, kneeling in the breeze-rippled waves.

Karsa and Bairoth dismounted and began preparing their camp, though on this night there would be no cookfire.

'Those tracks,' Bairoth said after a time, 'they belong to the lowlanders you killed. I wonder what they'd intended on doing in the place where the demon was imprisoned.'

Karsa's shrug was dismissive. 'Perhaps they'd planned on freeing her.'

'I think not, Karsa Orlong. The sorcery they used to assail you was god-aspected. I believe they came to worship, or perhaps the demon's soul could be drawn out from the flesh, in the manner of the Faces in the Rock. Perhaps, for the lowlanders, it was the site of an oracle, or even the home of their god.'

Karsa studied his companion for a long moment, then said, 'Bairoth Gild, there is poison in your words. That demon was not a god. It was a prisoner of the stone. The Faces in the Rock are true gods. There is no comparison to be made.'

Bairoth's heavy brows rose. 'Karsa Orlong, I make no comparison. The lowlanders are foolish creatures, whilst the Teblor are not. The lowlanders are children and are susceptible to self-deception. Why would they not worship that demon? Tell me, did you sense a living presence in that sorcery when it struck you?'

Karsa considered. 'There was . . . something. Scratching

113

and hissing and spitting. I flung it away and it then fled. So, it was not the demon's own power.'

'No, it wasn't, for she was gone. Perhaps they worshipped the stone that had pinned her down – there was magic in that as well.'

'But not living, Bairoth Gild. I do not understand the track of your thoughts, and I grow tired of these pointless words.'

'I believe,' Bairoth persisted, 'that the bones of Bone Pass belong to the people who imprisoned the demon. And this is what troubles me, Karsa Orlong, for those bones are much like the lowlanders' – thicker, yes, but still childlike. Indeed, it may be that the lowlanders are kin to that ancient people.'

'What of it?' Karsa rose. 'I will hear no more of this. Our only task now is to rest, then rise with the dawn and prepare our weapons. Tomorrow, we slay children.' He strode to where the horses stood beneath the trees. Delum sat nearby amidst the dogs, Gnaw's three-legged mate cradled in his arms. One hand stroked the beast's head in mindless repetition. Karsa stared at Delum for a moment longer, then turned away to prepare his bedding.

The river's passage was the only sound as the wheel of stars slowly crossed the sky. At some point in the night the breeze shifted, carrying with it the smell of woodsmoke and livestock and, once, the faint bark of a dog. Lying awake on his bed of moss, Karsa prayed to Urugal that the wind would not turn with the sun's rise. There were always dogs on lowlander farms, kept for the same reason as Teblor kept dogs. Sharp ears and sensitive noses, quick to announce strangers. But these would be lowlander breeds – smaller than those of the Teblor. Gnaw and his pack would make short work of them. And there would be no warning . . . so long as the wind did not shift.

He heard Bairoth rise and make his way over to where the pack slept.

Karsa glanced over to see Bairoth crouched down beside

Delum. Dogs had lifted their heads questioningly and were now watching as Bairoth stroked Delum's upturned face.

It was a moment before Karsa realized what he was witnessing. Bairoth was painting Delum's face in the battle-mask, black, grey and white, the shades of the Uryd. The battle-mask was reserved for warriors who knowingly rode to their deaths; it was an announcement that the sword would never again be sheathed. But it was a ritual that belonged, traditionally, to ageing warriors who had elected to set forth on a final raid, and thus avoid dying with straw on their backs. Karsa rose.

If Bairoth heard his approach, he gave no sign. There were tears running down the huge warrior's broad, blunt face, whilst Delum, lying perfectly still, stared up at him with wide, unblinking eyes.

'He does not comprehend,' Karsa growled, 'but I do. Bairoth Gild, you dishonour every Uryd warrior who has worn the battle-mask.'

'Do I, Karsa Orlong? Those warriors grown old, setting out for a final fight – there is nothing of glory in their deed, nothing of glory in their battle-mask. You are blind if you think otherwise. The paint hides nothing – the desperation remains undisguised in their eyes. They come to the ends of their lives, and have found that those lives were without meaning. It is that knowledge that drives them from the village, drives them out to seek a quick death.' Bairoth finished with the black paint and now moved on to the white, spreading it with three fingers across Delum's wide brow. 'Look into our friend's eyes, Karsa Orlong. Look closely.'

'I see nothing,' Karsa muttered, shaken by Bairoth's words.

'Delum sees the same, Warleader. He stares at . . . nothing. Unlike you, however, he does not turn away from it. Instead, he sees with complete comprehension. Sees, and is terrified.'

'You speak nonsense, Bairoth Gild.'

'I do not. You and I, we are Teblor. We are warriors. We can offer Delum no comfort, and so he holds on to that dog, the beast with misery in its eyes. For comfort is what he seeks, now. It is, indeed, all he seeks. Why do I gift him the battle-mask? He will die this day, Karsa Orlong, and perhaps that will be comfort enough for Delum Thord. I pray to Urugal that it be so.'

Karsa glanced skyward. 'The wheel is nearly done. We must ready ourselves.'

'I am almost finished, Warleader.'

The horses stirred as Karsa rubbed blood-oil into his sword's wooden blade. The dogs were on their feet now, pacing restlessly. Bairoth completed his painting of Delum's face and headed off to attend to his own weapons. The three-legged dog struggled in Delum's arms, but he simply held the beast all the tighter, until a soft growl from Gnaw made the whimpering warrior release it.

Karsa strapped the boiled leather armour onto Havok's chest, neck and legs. When he was done, he turned to see Bairoth already astride his own horse. Delum's destrier had also been armoured, but it stood without a rein. The animals were trembling.

'Warleader, your grandfather's descriptions have been unerring thus far. Tell me of the farmstead's layout.'

'A log house the size of two Uryd houses, with an upper floor beneath a steep roof. Heavy shutters with arrow-slits, a thick, quickly barred door at the front and at the back. There are three outbuildings; the one nearest the house and sharing one wall holds the livestock. Another is a forge, whilst the last one is of sod and likely was the first home before the log house was built. There is a landing on the lakeshore as well, and mooring poles. There will be a corral for the small lowlander horses.'

Bairoth was frowning. 'Warleader, how many lowlander generations have passed since Pahlk's raid?'

Karsa swung himself onto Havok's back. He shrugged in answer to Bairoth's question. 'Enough. Are you ready, Bairoth Gild?'

'Lead me, Warleader.'

Karsa guided Havok onto the trail beside the river. The mouth was on his left. To the right rose a high, raw mass of rock, treed on top, leaning out towards the lakeshore. A wide strand of round-stoned beach wound between the pinnacle and the lake.

The wind had not changed. The air smelled of smoke and manure. The farm's dogs were silent.

Karsa drew his sword, angled the glistening blade near Havok's nostrils. The destrier's head lifted. Trot to canter, onto the pebbled beach, lake on the left, rock wall sliding past to the right. Behind him, he heard Bairoth's horse, hoofs crashing down into the stones, and, further back, the dogs, Delum and his horse, the latter lagging to stay alongside its once-master.

Once clear of the pinnacle, they would shift hard right, and in moments be upon the unsuspecting children of the farm.

Canter to gallop.

Rock wall vanishing, flat, planted fields.

Gallop into charge.

The farm – smoke-blackened ruins barely visible through tall corn plants – and, just beyond it, sprawled all along the lake's shore and back, all the way to the foot of a mountain, a town.

Tall, stone buildings, stone piers and wood-planked docks and boats crowding the lake's edge. A wall of stones enclosing most of the structures inland, perhaps the height of a full-grown lowlander. A main road, a gate flanked by squat, flat-topped towers. Woodsmoke drifting in a layer above the slate rooftops.

Figures on those towers.

More lowlanders – more than could be counted – all scurrying about now, as a bell started clanging. Running towards the gate from the cornfields, farming implements tossed aside.

Bairoth was bellowing something behind Karsa. Not a warcry. A voice pitched with alarm. Karsa ignored it, already closing in on the first of the farmers. He would take a few in passing, but not slacken his pace. Leave these children to the pack. He wanted the ones in the town, cowering behind the now-closing gate, behind the puny walls.

Sword flashed, taking off the back of a farmer's head. Havok ran down another, trampling the shrieking woman under his hoofs.

The gate boomed as it shut.

Karsa angled Havok to the left of it, eyes on the wall as he leaned forward. A crossbow quarrel flitted past, striking the furrowed ground ten paces to his right. Another whistled over his head.

No lowlander horse could clear this wall, but Havok stood at twenty-six hands – almost twice the height and mass of the lowlander breeds – and, muscles bunching, legs gathering, the huge destrier leapt, sailing over the wall effortlessly.

To crash, front hoofs first, onto the sloped roof of a shack. Slate tiles exploded, wood beams snapped. The small structure collapsed beneath them, chickens scattering, as Havok stumbled, legs clawing for purchase, then surged forward onto the muddy cart ruts of the street beyond.

Another building, this one stone-walled, reared up before them. Havok slewed to the right. A figure suddenly appeared at the building's entrance, a round face, eyes wide. Karsa's crossover chop split the lowlander's skull where he stood just beyond the threshold, spinning him in place before his legs folded beneath him.

Hoofs pounding, Havok swept Karsa down the street towards the gate. He could hear slaughter in the fields and the road beyond – most of the workers had been trapped outside the town, it seemed. A dozen guards had succeeded in dropping a bar and had begun fanning out to take defensive positions when the warleader burst upon them.

Iron helm crunched, was torn from the dying child's head as if biting at the blade as it was dragged free. A backhanded slash separated another child's arm and shoulder from his body. Trampling a third guard, Havok pivoted, flinging his hindquarters around to strike a fourth child, sending him flying to crash up against the gate, sword spinning away.

A longsword – its blade as puny as a long knife's to Karsa's eyes – struck his leather-armoured thigh, cutting through two, perhaps three of the hardened layers, before bouncing away. Karsa drove his sword's pommel into the lowlander's face, felt bone crack. A kick sent the child reeling. Figures were scattering in panic from his path. Laughing, Karsa drove Havok forward.

He cut down another guard, whilst the others raced down the street.

Something punched the Teblor's back, then a brief, stinging blossom of pain. Reaching over, Karsa dragged the quarrel free and flung it away. He dropped down from the horse, eyes on the barred gate. Metal latches had been locked over the bar, holding the thick plank in place.

Taking three strides back, Karsa lowered one shoulder, then charged it.

The iron pins holding the hinges between blocks of mortared stone burst free with the impact, sending the entire gate toppling outward. The tower on Karsa's right groaned and sagged suddenly. Voices cried out inside it. The stone wall began to fold.

Cursing, the Teblor scrambled back towards the street as the entire tower collapsed in an explosion of dust.

Through the swirling white cloud, Bairoth rode, threads of blood and gore whipping from his bloodsword, his mount leaping to clear the rubble. The dogs followed, and with them Delum and his horse. Blood smeared Delum Thord's mouth, and Karsa realized, with a faint ripple of shock, that the warrior had torn out a farmer's throat with his own teeth, as would a dog.

Hoofs spraying mud, Bairoth reined in.

Karsa swung himself back onto Havok, twisted the destrier round to face down the street.

A square of pikemen approached at a trot, their long-poled weapons wavering, iron blades glinting in the morning light. They were still thirty paces distant.

A quarrel glanced off the rump of Bairoth's horse, coming from a nearby upper floor window.

From somewhere outside the wall came the sound of galloping horses.

Bairoth grunted. 'Our withdrawal shall be contested, Warleader.'

'Withdrawal?' Karsa laughed. He jutted his chin towards the advancing pikemen. 'There can be no more than thirty, and children with long spears are still children, Bairoth Gild. Come, let us scatter them!'

With a curse, Bairoth unlimbered his bear skull bolas. 'Precede me, then, Karsa Orlong, to hide my preparation.'

Baring his teeth in fierce pleasure, Karsa urged Havok forward. The dogs fanned out to either side, Delum positioning himself on the warleader's far right.

Ahead, the pikes slowly lowered, hovering at chest height as the square halted to plant their weapons.

Upper floor windows on the street opened then, and faces appeared, looking down to witness what would come.

'Urugal!' Karsa bellowed as he drove Havok into a charge. 'Witness!' Behind him he heard Bairoth riding just as hard, and within that clash of sounds rose the whirring flow of the grey bear skull, round and round, and round again.

Ten paces from the readied pikes, and Bairoth roared. Karsa ducked low, pitching Havok to the left even as he slowed the beast's savage charge.

Something massive and hissing whipped past him, and

120

Karsa twisted to see the huge bolas strike the square of soldiers.

Deadly chaos. Three of the five rows on the ground. Piercing screams.

Then the dogs were among them, followed by Delum's horse.

Wheeling his destrier once again, Karsa closed on the shattered square, arriving in time to be alongside Bairoth as the two Teblor rode into the press. Batting aside the occasional, floundering pike, they slaughtered the children the dogs had not already taken down, in the passage of twenty heartbeats.

'Warleader!'

Dragging his bloodsword from the last victim, Karsa turned at Bairoth's bellow.

Another square of soldiers, this time flanked by cross-bowmen. Fifty, perhaps sixty in all, at the street's far end.

Scowling, Karsa glanced back towards the gate. Twenty mounted children, heavily armoured in plate and chain, were slowly emerging through the dust; more on foot, some armed with short bows, others with double-bladed axes, swords or javelins.

'Lead me, Warleader!'

Karsa glared at Bairoth. 'And so I shall, Bairoth Gild!' He swung Havok about. 'This side passage, down to the shoreline – we shall ride around our pursuers. Tell me, Bairoth Gild, have we slain enough children for you?'

'Aye, Karsa Orlong.'

'Then follow!'

The side passage was a street almost as wide as the main one, and it led straight down to the lake. Dwellings, trader stores and warehouses lined it. Shadowy figures were visible in windows, in doorways and at alley mouths as the Teblor raiders thundered past. The street ended twenty paces before the shoreline. The intervening space, through which a wide, wood-planked loadway ran down to the docks and piers, was filled with heaps of detritus, dominant among them a huge pile of bleached bones, from which poles rose, skulls affixed to their tops.

Teblor skulls.

Amidst this stretch of rubbish, squalid huts and tents filled every clear patch, and scores of children had emerged from them, bristling with weapons, their rough clothing bedecked with Teblor charms and scalps, their hard eyes watching the warriors approach as they began readying long-handled axes, two-handed swords, thick-shafted halberds, whilst yet others strung robust, recurved bows and nocked over-long, barbed arrows – which they began to draw, taking swift aim.

Bairoth's roar was half horror, half rage as he sent his destrier charging towards these silent, deadly children.

Arrows flashed.

Bairoth's horse screamed, stumbled, then crashed to the ground. Bairoth tumbled, his sword spinning away through the air as he struck, then broke through, a sapling-walled hut.

More arrows flew.

Karsa shifted Havok sharply, watched an arrow hiss past his thigh, then he was among the first of the lowlanders. Bloodsword clashed against an axe's bronze-sheathed shaft, the impact tearing the weapon from the man's hands. Karsa's left hand shot out to intercept another axe as it swung towards Havok's head. He plucked it from the man, sent it flying, then lunged forward the same hand to take the lowlander by the neck, lifting him clear as they continued on. A single, bone-crunching squeeze left the head lolling, the body twitching and spilling piss. Karsa flung the corpse away.

Havok's onward plunge was brought to a sudden halt. The destrier shrieked, slewed to one side, blood gushing from its mouth and nostrils, dragging with it a heavy pike, its iron head buried deep in the horse's chest.

The beast stumbled, then, with a drunken weave, it began toppling.

Karsa, screaming his fury, launched himself from the dying destrier's back. A sword point rose to meet him, but Karsa batted it aside. He landed atop at least three tumbling bodies, hearing bones snap beneath him as he rolled his way clear.

Then he was on his feet, bloodsword slashing across the face of a lowlander, ripping black-bearded jaw from skull. An edged weapon scored deep across his back. Spinning, Karsa swung his blade under the attacker's outstretched arms, chopped deep between ribs, jamming at the breastbone.

He tugged fiercely, tearing his sword free, the dying lowlander's body cartwheeling past him.

Heavy weapons, many of them bearing knotted Teblor fetishes, surrounded him, each striving to drink Uryd blood. They fouled each other as often as not, yet Karsa was hard-pressed blocking the others as he fought his way clear. He killed two of his attackers in the process.

Now he heard another fight, nearby, from where Bairoth had crashed into the hut, and, here and there, the snap and snarl of the dogs.

His attackers had been silent until a moment ago. Now, all were screaming in their gibbering tongue, their faces filled with alarm, as Karsa wheeled once more and, seeing more than a dozen before him, attacked. They scattered, revealing a half-crescent line of lowlanders with bows and crossbows.

Strings thrummed.

Searing pain along Karsa's neck, twin punches to his chest, another against his right thigh. Ignoring them all, the warleader charged the half-crescent.

More shouts, sudden pursuit from the ones who had scattered, but it was too late for that. Karsa's sword was a blur as he cut into the archers. Figures turning to run. Dying, spinning away in floods of blood. Skulls shattering. Karsa carved his way down the line, and left a trail of eight figures, some writhing and others still, behind him, by the time the first set of attackers reached him. He pivoted to meet them, laughing at the alarm in their tiny, wizened, dirt-smeared faces, then he lunged into their midst once more.

They broke. Flinging weapons away, stumbling and scrambling in their panic. Karsa killed one after another, until there were no more within reach of his bloodsword. He straightened, then.

Where Bairoth had been fighting, seven lowlander bodies lay in a rough circle, but of the Teblor warrior there was no sign. The screams of a dog continued from further up the street, and Karsa ran towards the sound.

He passed the quarrel-studded corpses of the rest of the pack, though he did not see Gnaw among them. They had killed a number of lowlanders before they had finally fallen. Looking up, he saw, thirty paces down the street, Delum Thord, near him his fallen horse, and, another fifteen paces beyond, a knot of villagers.

Delum was shrieking. He had taken a dozen or more quarrels and arrows, and a javelin had been thrust right through his torso, just above the left hip. He had left a winding trail of blood behind him, yet still he crawled forward – to where the villagers surrounded the three-legged dog, beating it to death with walking sticks, hoes and shovels.

Wailing, Delum dragged himself on, the javelin scraping alongside him, blood streaming down the shaft.

Even as Karsa began to run forward, a figure raced out from an alley mouth, coming up slightly behind Delum, a long-handled shovel in its hands. Lifting high.

Karsa screamed a warning.

Delum did not so much as turn, his eyes fixed on the now-dead three-legged dog, as the shovel struck the back of his head.

There was a loud crunch. The shovel pulled away, revealing a flat patch of shattered bone and twisted hair.

Delum toppled forward, and did not move.

His slayer spun at Karsa's charge. An old man, his tooth-less mouth opening wide in sudden terror.

Karsa's downward chop cut the man in half down to the hips.

Tearing his bloodsword free, the warleader plunged on, towards the dozen or so villagers still gathered around the pulped corpse of the three-legged dog. They saw him and scattered.

Ten paces beyond lay Gnaw, leaving his own blood-trail as, back legs dragging, he continued towards the body of his mate. He raised his head upon seeing Karsa. Pleading eyes fixed on the warleader's.

Bellowing, Karsa ran down two of the villagers and left their twitching corpses sprawled in the muddy street. He saw another, armed with a rust-pitted mattock, dart between two houses. The Teblor hesitated, then with a curse he swung about and moments later was crouched beside Gnaw.

A shattered hip.

Karsa glanced up the street to see the pike-wielding soldiers closing at a jog. Three mounted men rode in their wake, shouting out commands. A quick look towards the lakeside revealed more horsemen gathering, heads turned in his direction.

The warleader lifted Gnaw from the ground, tucking the beast under his left arm.

Then he set off in pursuit of the mattock-wielding villager.

Rotting vegetables crowded the narrow aisle between the two houses which, at the far end, opened out into a pair of corralled runs. As he emerged into the track between the two fence lines, he saw the man, still running, twenty paces ahead. Beyond the corrals was a shallow ditch, carrying sewage down to the lake. The child had crossed it and was plunging into a tangle of young alders – there were more buildings beyond it, either barns or warehouses.

Karsa raced after him, leaping across the ditch, the

hunting dog still under his arm. The jostling was giving it great pain, the Teblor knew. He contemplated slitting its throat.

The child entered a barn, still carrying his mattock.

Following, Karsa ducked low as he plunged through the side doorway. Sudden gloom. There were no beasts in the stalls; the straw, still piled high, looked old and damp. A large fishing boat commanded the wide centre aisle, flipped over and resting on wooden horses. Double sliding doors to the left, one of them slightly pushed back, the ropes from the handle gently swinging back and forth.

Karsa found the last, darkest stall, where he set Gnaw down on the straw. 'I shall return to you, my friend,' he whispered. 'Failing that, find a way to heal, then journey home. Home, among the Uryd.' The Teblor cut a thong of leather from his armour strappings. He tore from his belt-bag a handful of bronze sigils bearing the tribal signs, then strung the thong through them. None hung loose, and so would make no sound. He tied the makeshift collar round Gnaw's thick, muscled neck. Then he laid one hand lightly upon the dog's shattered hip and closed his eyes. 'I gift this beast the soul of the Teblor, the heart of the Uryd. Urugal, hear me. Heal this great fighter. Then send him home. For now, bold Urugal, hide him.'

He withdrew his hand and opened his eyes. The beast looked up at him calmly. 'Make fierce your long life, Gnaw. We will meet again, this I vow upon the blood of all the children I have slain this day.'

Shifting grip on his bloodsword, Karsa turned away and departed the stall without another backward glance.

He padded towards the sliding door, looked out.

A warehouse stood opposite, high-ceilinged with a loading loft beneath its slate-tiled roof. From within the building came the sounds of bolts and bars dropping into place. Smiling, Karsa darted across to where the loading chains dangled from pulleys, his eyes on the doorless loft platform high overhead.

As he prepared to sling his sword back over a shoulder, he saw, with a start, that he was festooned with arrows and quarrels, and realized, for the first time, that much of the blood sheathing his body was his own. Scowling, he pulled the darts out. There was more blood, particularly from his right thigh and the two wounds in his chest. A long arrow in his back had buried its barbed head deep into muscle. He attempted to drag the arrow free, but the pain that resulted came close to making him faint. He settled for snapping the shaft just behind the iron head, and this effort alone left him chilled and sweating.

Distant shouts alerted him to a slowly closing cordon of soldiers and townsfolk, all hunting him. Karsa closed his hands around the chains, then began climbing. Every time he lifted his left arm, his back flashed with agony. But it had been the flat of a mattock's blade that had felled Gnaw, a two-handed blow from behind – the attack of a coward. And nothing else mattered.

He swung himself onto the platform's dusty floorboards, padded silently away from the opening as he drew his sword once more.

He could hear breathing, harsh and ragged, below. Low whimpering between gasps, a voice praying to whatever gods the child worshipped.

Karsa made his way towards the gaping hole in the centre of the platform, careful to keep his moccasins from dragging, lest sawdust drift down from between the floorboards. He came to the edge and looked down.

The fool was directly beneath him, crouched down, trembling, the mattock held ready as he faced the barred doors. He had soiled himself in his terror.

Karsa carefully reversed grip on his sword, held it out point downward, then dropped from the ledge.

The sword's tip entered atop the man's pate, the blade driving down through bone and brain. As Karsa's full weight impacted the warehouse floor, there was a massive, splintering sound, and Teblor and victim both plunged through, down into a cellar. Shattered floorboards crashed down around them. The cellar was deep, almost Karsa's height, stinking of salted fish yet empty.

Stunned by the fall, Karsa feebly groped for his sword, but he could not find it. He managed to raise his head slightly, and saw that something was sticking out of his chest, a red shard of splintered wood. He was, he bemusedly realized, impaled. His hand continued searching for his sword, though he could not otherwise move, but found only wood and fish-scales, the latter greasy with salt and sticking to his fingertips.

He heard the sound of boots from above. Blinking, Karsa stared up as a ring of helmed faces slowly swam into view. Then another child's face appeared, unhelmed, his brow marked in a tribal tattoo, the expression beneath it strangely sympathetic. There was a lot of conversation, hot with anger, then the tattooed child gestured and everyone fell silent. In the Sunyd dialect of the Teblor, the man said, 'Should you die down there, warrior, at least you'll keep for a time.'

Karsa sought to rise once more, but the shaft of wood held him fast. He bared his teeth in a grimace.

'What is your name, Teblor?' the child asked.

'I am Karsa Orlong, grandson of Pahlk—'

'Pahlk? The Uryd who visited centuries ago?'

'To slay scores of children—'

The man's nod was serious as he interjected, 'Children, yes, it makes sense for your kind to call us that. But Pahlk killed no-one, not at first. He came down from the pass, half starved and fevered. The first farmers who'd settled here took him in, nourished him back to health. It was only then that he murdered them all and fled. Well, not all. A girl escaped, made her way back along the lake's south shore to Orbs, and told the detachment there – well, told them everything they needed to know about the Teblor. Since that time, of course, the Sunyd slaves have told us even more. You are Uryd. We've not reached your tribe –

128

you've had no bounty hunters as yet, but you will. Within a century, I'd hazard, there will be no more Teblor in the fastnesses of Laederon Plateau. The only Teblor will be the ones branded and in chains. Plying the nets on the fishing boats, as the Sunyd now do. Tell me, Karsa, do you recognize me?'

'You are the one who escaped us above the pass. Who came too late to warn his fellow children. Who, I know now, is full of lies. Your tiny voice insults the Teblor tongue. It hurts my ears.'

The man smiled. 'Too bad. You should reconsider, in any case, warrior. For I am all that stands between your living or dying. Assuming you don't die of your wounds first. Of course, you Teblor are uncommonly tough, as my companions have just been reminded, to their dismay. I see no blood frothing your lips, which is a good sign, and rather astonishing, since you've four lungs, while we have two.'

Another figure had appeared and now spoke to the tattooed man in stentorian tones, to which he simply shrugged. 'Karsa Orlong of the Uryd,' he called down, 'soldiers are about to descend, to tie ropes to your limbs so you can be lifted out. It seems you're lying on what's left of the town's factor, which has somewhat abated the anger up here, since he was not a well-liked man. I would suggest, if you wish to live, that you not resist the, uh, warleader's nervous volunteers.'

Karsa watched as four soldiers were slowly lowered down on ropes. He made no effort to resist as they roughly bound his wrists, ankles and upper arms, for the truth was, he was incapable of doing so.

The soldiers were quickly dragged back up, then the ropes were drawn taut, and Karsa was steadily lifted. He watched the shaft of splintered wood slowly withdrawing from his chest. It had entered high, just above his right shoulder blade, through muscles, reappearing just to the right of his clavicle on that side. As he was pulled free, pain overwhelmed him.

A hand was then slapping him awake. Karsa opened his eyes. He was lying on the warehouse floor, faces crowding him on all sides. Everyone seemed to be speaking to him at once in their thin, weedy tongue, and though he could not understand the words raw hatred rode the tone, and Karsa knew he was being cursed, in the name of scores of lowlander gods, spirits and mouldering ancestors. The thought pleased him, and he smiled.

The soldiers flinched back as one.

The tattooed lowlander, whose hand had awakened him, was crouched down at Karsa's side. 'Hood's breath,' he muttered. 'Are all Uryd like you? Or are you the one the priests spoke of? The one who stalked their dreams like Hood's own Knight? Ah well, it doesn't matter, I suppose, for it seems their fears were unfounded. Look at you. Half dead, with a whole town eager to see you and your companion flayed alive – there's not a family to be found not in mourning, thanks to you. Grasp the world by the throat? Not likely; you'll need Oponn's luck to live out the hour.'

The broken arrow shaft had been driven deeper into Karsa's back with the fall, gouging into the bone of his shoulder blade. Blood was spreading out on the floorboards beneath him.

There was a commotion as a new lowlander arrived, this one tall for his kind, thin with a severe, weather-lined face. He was dressed in shimmering clothes, deep blue and trimmed with gold thread sewn into intricate patterns. The guard spoke to him at length, though the man himself said nothing, nor did his expression change. When the guard was finished, the newcomer nodded, then gestured with one hand and turned away.

The guard looked down at Karsa once more. 'That was Master Silgar, the man I work for, most of the time. He believes you will survive your wounds, Karsa Orlong, and so has prepared for you a ... a lesson, of sorts.' The man straightened and said something to the soldiers. There followed a brief argument, which concluded with an indifferent shrug from one of the soldiers.

Karsa's limbs were lifted once more, two lowlanders to each, the men straining to hold him as they carried him to the warehouse doors.

The blood dripping down from his wounds was slowing, pain retreating behind a dull lassitude in the Teblor's mind. He stared up at blue sky as the soldiers carried him to the centre of the street, the sounds of a crowd on all sides. They set him down propped up against a cart wheel, and Karsa saw before him Bairoth Gild.

He had been tied to a much larger spoked wheel, which itself rested against support poles. The huge warrior was a mass of wounds. A spear had been driven into his mouth, exiting just below his left ear, leaving the lower jaw shattered, bone gleaming red amidst torn flesh. The stubs of deep-driven quarrels crowded his torso.

But his eyes were sharp as they met Karsa's own.

Villagers filled the street, held back by a cordon of soldiers. Angry shouts and curses filled the air, punctuated every now and then by wails of grief.

The guard positioned himself between Karsa and Bairoth, his expression mockingly thoughtful. Then he turned to Karsa. 'Your comrade here will tell us nothing of the Uryd. We would know the number of warriors, the number and location of villages. We would know more of the Phalyd as well, who are said to be your match in ferocity. But he says nothing.'

Karsa bared his teeth. 'I, Karsa Orlong, invite you to send a thousand of your warriors to wage war among the Uryd. None shall return, but the trophies will remain with us. Send two thousand. It matters not.'

The guard smiled. 'You will answer our questions, then, Karsa Orlong?'

'I will, for such words will avail you naught—'

'Excellent.' The guard gestured with one hand. A lowlander stepped up to Bairoth Gild, drawing his sword.

Bairoth sneered at Karsa. He snarled, the sound a mangled roar that Karsa nevertheless understood, 'Lead me, Warleader!'

The sword slashed. Through Bairoth Gild's neck. Blood sprayed, the huge warrior's head flopping back, then rolling from a shoulder to land with a heavy thump on the ground.

A savage, gleeful roar erupted from the villagers.

The guard approached Karsa. 'Delighted to hear that you will co-operate. Doing so buys you your life. Master Silgar will add you to his herd of slaves once you've told us all you know. I don't think you will be joining the Sunyd out on the lake, however. No hauling of nets for you, Karsa Orlong, I'm afraid.' He turned as a heavily armoured soldier appeared. 'Ah, here is the Malazan captain. Ill luck, Karsa Orlong, that you should have timed your attack to coincide with the arrival of a Malazan company on its way to Bettrys. Now then, assuming the captain has no objections, shall we begin the questioning?'

The twin trenches of the slave-pits lay beneath the floor of a large warehouse near the lake, accessed through a trap-door and a mould-smeared staircase. One side held, for the moment, only a half-dozen lowlanders chained to the tree trunk running the length of the trench, but more shackles awaited the return of the Sunyd net-haulers. The other trench was home to the sick and dying. Emaciated low-lander shapes huddled in their own filth, some moaning, others silent and motionless.

After he had done describing the Uryd and their lands, Karsa was dragged to the warehouse and chained in the second trench. Its sides were sloped, packed with damp clay. The centre log ran along the narrow, flat bottom, half-submerged in blood-streaked sewage. Karsa was taken to the far end, out of the reach of any of the other slaves, and shackles were fixed to both wrists and both ankles – whereas, he saw, among everyone else a single shackle sufficed.

132

They left him alone then.

Flies swarmed him, alighting on his chilled skin. He lay on his side against one of the sloping sides. The wound within which the arrow-head remained was threatening to close, and this he could not allow. He shut his eyes and began to concentrate until he could feel each muscle, cut and torn and seeping, holding fast around the iron point. Then he began working them, the slightest of contractions to test the position of the arrow-head – fighting the pulses of pain that radiated out with each flex. After a few moments, he ceased, let his body relax, taking deep breaths until he was recovered from his efforts. The flanged iron blade lay almost flat against his shoulder blade. Its tip had scoured a groove along the bone. There were barbs as well, bent and twisted.

To leave such an object within his flesh would make his left arm useless. He needed to drive it out.

He began to concentrate once more. Ravaged muscles and tissue, a path inward of chopped and sliced flesh.

A layer of sweat sheathed him as he continued to focus his mind, preparing, his breaths slowing, steadying.

He contracted his muscles. A ragged scream forced its way out. Another welter of blood, amidst relentless pain. The muscles spasmed in a rippling wave. Something struck the clay slope and slid down into the sewage.

Gasping, trembling, Karsa lay motionless for a long while. The blood streaming down from his back slowed, then ceased.

'Lead me, Warleader!'

Bairoth Gild had made those words a curse, in a manner and from a place of thought that Karsa did not understand. And then, Bairoth Gild had died senselessly. Nothing the lowlanders could do threatened the Uryd, for the Uryd were not as the Sunyd. Bairoth had surrendered his chance for vengeance, a gesture so baffling to Karsa that he was left stunned.

A brutal, knowing glare in Bairoth's eyes, fixed solely on

Karsa, even as the sword flashed towards his neck. He would tell the lowlanders nothing, yet it was a defiance without meaning – but no, there *was* meaning . . . *for Bairoth chose to abandon me.*

A sudden shiver took him. *Urugal, have my brothers betrayed me? Delum Thord's flight, Bairoth Gild's death – am I to know abandonment again and again? What of the Uryd awaiting my return? Will they not follow when I proclaim war against the lowlanders?*

Perhaps not at first. No, he realized, there would be arguments, and opinions, and, seated around the camp hearths, the elders would poke smouldering sticks into the fire and shake their heads.

Until word came that the lowlander armies were coming.

And then they will have no choice. Would we flee into the laps of the Phalyd? No. There will be no choice but to fight, and I, Karsa Orlong, will be looked upon then, to lead the Uryd.

The thought calmed him.

He slowly rolled over, blinking in the gloom, flies scattering all around his face.

It took a few moments of groping in the sludge to find the arrow-head and its stubby, splintered fragment of shaft. He then crouched down beside the centre log to examine the fittings holding the chains.

There were two sets of chains, one for his arms and one for his legs, each fixed to a long iron rod that had been driven through the trunk, the opposite end flattened out. The links were large and solid, forged with Teblor strength in mind. But the wood on the underside had begun to rot.

Using the arrow-head, he began gouging and digging into the sewage-softened wood around the flange.

Bairoth had betrayed him, betrayed the Uryd. There had been nothing of courage in his last act of defiance. Indeed, the very opposite. They had discovered enemies to the Teblor. Hunters, who collected Teblor trophies. These were truths that the warriors of all the tribes needed to hear, and delivering those truths was now Karsa's sole task.

He was not Sunyd, as the lowlanders were about to discover.

The rot had been drawn up the hole. Karsa dug out the soaked, pulpy mass as far as the arrow-head could reach. He then moved on to the second fitting. The iron bar holding his leg chains would be tested first.

There was no way to tell if it was day or night outside. Heavy boots occasionally crossed the plank floor above him, too random to indicate a set passage of time. Karsa worked unceasingly, listening to the coughs and moans of the lowlanders chained further down the trunk. He could not imagine what those sad children had done, to warrant such punishment from their kin. Banishment was the harshest sentence the Teblor inflicted on those among the tribe whose actions had, with deliberate intent, endangered the survival of the village, actions that ranged from carelessness to kin-murder. Banishment led, usually, to death, but that came of starvation of the spirit within the one punished. Torture was not a Teblor way, nor was prolonged imprisonment.

Of course, he reconsidered, it may be that these lowlanders were sick because their spirits were dying. Among the legends, there were fragments whispering that the Teblor had once owned slaves – the word, the concept, was known to him. Possession of another's life, to do with as one wished. A slave's spirit could do naught but starve.

Karsa had no intention of starving. Urugal's shadow protected his spirit.

He tucked the arrow-head into his belt. Setting his back against the slope, he planted his feet against the log, one to either side of the fitting, then slowly extended his legs. The chain tautened. On the underside of the trunk, the flange was pulled into the wood with a steady splintering, grinding sound.

The shackles dug into his hide-wrapped ankles.

He began to push harder. There was a solid crunch, then the flange would go no further. Karsa slowly relaxed. A kick sent the bar thumping free on the other end. He rested for a few moments, then resumed the process once more.

After a dozen tries he had managed to pull the bar up the span of three fingers from where it had been at the beginning. The flange's edges were bent now, battered by their assault on the wood. His leggings had been cut through and blood gleamed on the shackles.

He leaned his head back on the damp clay of the slope, his legs trembling.

More boots thumped overhead, then the trapdoor was lifted. The glow of lantern light descended the steps, and within it Karsa saw the nameless guard.

'Uryd,' he called out. 'Do you still breathe?'

'Come closer,' Karsa challenged in a low voice, 'and I will show you the extent of my recovery.'

The lowlander laughed. 'Master Silgar saw true, it seems. It will take some effort to break your spirit, I suspect.' The guard remained standing halfway down the steps. 'Your Sunyd kin will be returning in a day or two.'

'I have no kin who accept the life of slavery.'

'That's odd, since you clearly have, else you would have contrived to kill yourself by now.'

'You think I am a slave because I am in chains? Come closer, then, child.'

'"Child," yes. Your strange affectation persists, even while we *children* have you at our mercy. Well, never mind. The chains are but the beginning, Karsa Orlong. You will indeed be broken, and had you been captured by the bounty hunters high on the plateau, by the time they'd delivered you to this town you'd have had nothing left of Teblor pride, much less defiance. The Sunyd will worship you, Karsa Orlong, for killing an entire camp of bounty hunters.'

'What is your name?' Karsa asked.

'Why?'

The Uryd warrior smiled in the gloom. 'For all your words, you still fear me.'

136

'Hardly.'

But Karsa heard the strain in the guard's tone and his smile broadened. 'Then tell me your name.'

'Damisk. My name is Damisk. I was once a tracker in the Greydog army during the Malazan conquest.'

'Conquest. You lost, then. Which of our spirits has broken, Damisk Greydog? When I attacked your party on the ridge, you fled. Left the ones who had hired you to their fates. You fled, as would a coward, a broken man. And this is why you are here, now. For I am chained and you are beyond my reach. You come, not to tell me things, but because you cannot help yourself. You seek the pleasure of gloating, yet you devour yourself inside, and so feel no true satisfaction. Yet we both know, you will come again. And again.'

'I shall advise,' Damisk said, his voice ragged, 'my master to give you to the surviving bounty hunters, to do with you as they will. And I will watch—'

'Of course you will, Damisk Greydog.'

The man backed up the stairs, the lantern's light swinging wildly.

Karsa laughed.

A moment later the trapdoor slammed down once more, and there was darkness.

The Teblor warrior fell silent, then planted his feet on the log yet again.

A weak voice from the far end of the trench stopped him. 'Giant.'

The tongue was Sunyd, the voice a child's. 'I have no words for you, lowlander,' Karsa growled.

'I do not ask for words. I can feel you working on this Hood-damned tree. Will you succeed at whatever it is you are doing?'

'I am doing nothing.'

'All right, then. Must be my imagination. We're dying here, the rest of us. In a most terrible, undignified manner.'

'You must have done great wrong—'

The answering laugh was a rasping cough. 'Oh indeed, giant. Indeed. We're the ones who would not accept Malazan rule, so we held on to our weapons and hid in the hills and forests. Raiding, ambushing, making nuisances of ourselves. It was great fun. Until the bastards caught us.'

'Careless.'

'Three of you and a handful of your damned dogs, raiding an entire *town*? And you call me careless? Well, I suppose we both were, since we're here.'

Karsa grimaced at the truth of that. 'What is it you want, lowlander?'

'Your strength, giant. There are four of us over here who are still alive, though I alone am still conscious . . . and very nearly sane. Sane enough, that is, to comprehend the fullest ignobility of my fate.'

'You talk too much.'

'For not much longer, I assure you. Can you lift this log, giant? Or spin it over a few times?'

Karsa was silent for a long moment. 'What would that achieve?'

'It would shorten the chains.'

'I have no wish to shorten the chains.'

'Temporarily.'

'Why?'

'Spin the damned thing, giant. So our chains wrap around it again and again. So, with one last turn, you drag us poor fools at this end under. So we drown.'

'You would have me kill you?'

'I applaud your swift comprehension, giant. More souls to crowd your shadow, Teblor – that's how your kind see it, yes? Kill me, and I will walk with honour in your shadow.'

'I am not interested in mercy, lowlander.'

'How about trophies?'

'I cannot reach you to take trophies.'

'How well can you see in this gloom? I've heard that Teblor—'

'I can see. Well enough to know that your right hand is closed in a fist. What lies within it?'

'A tooth. Just fallen out. The third one since I've been chained down here.'

'Throw it to me.'

'I will try. I am afraid I'm somewhat . . . worse for wear. Are you ready?'

'Throw.'

The man's arm wavered as he lifted it.

The tooth flew high and wide, but Karsa's arm shot out, chain snapping behind it, and he snatched the tooth from the air. He brought it down for a closer look, then grunted. 'It's rotted.'

'Probably why it fell out. Well? Consider this, too. You will succeed in getting water right through the shaft, which should soften things up even more. Not that you've been up to anything down there.'

Karsa slowly nodded. 'I like you, lowlander.'

'Good. Now drown me.'

'I will.'

Karsa slipped down to stand knee-deep in the foul muck, the fresh wounds around his ankles stinging at the contact.

'I saw them bring you down, giant,' the man said. 'None of the Sunyd are as big as you.'

'The Sunyd are the smallest among the Teblor.'

'Must be some lowlander blood from way back, I'd imagine.'

'They have fallen far indeed.' Karsa lowered both arms, chains dragging, until his hands rested beneath the log.

'My thanks to you, Teblor.'

Karsa lifted, twisted the log, then set it down once more, gasping. 'This will not be quick, lowlander, and for that I am sorry.'

'I understand. Take your time. Biltar slid right under in any case, and Alrute looks about to the next time. You're doing well.'

He lifted the log once more, rolled it another half-twist.

Splashes and gurgling sounds came from the other end.

Then a gasp. 'Almost there, Teblor. I'm the last. One more – I'll roll myself under it, so it pins me down.'

'Then you are crushed, not drowned.'

'In this muck? No worries there, Teblor. I'll feel the weight, true, but it won't cause me much pain.'

'You lie.'

'So what? It's not the means, it's the end that matters.'

'All things matter,' Karsa said, preparing once more. 'I shall twist it all the way round this time, lowlander. It will be easier now that my own chains are shorter. Are you ready?'

'A moment, please,' the man sputtered.

Karsa lifted the log, grunting with the immense weight pulling down on his arms.

'I've had a change of heart—'

'I haven't.' Karsa spun the log. Then dropped it.

Wild thrashing from the other end, chains sawing the air, then frantic coughing.

Surprised, Karsa looked up. A brown-smeared figure flailed about, sputtering, kicking.

Karsa slowly sat back, waiting for the man to recover. For a while, there was naught but heavy gasping from the other end of the log. 'You managed to roll back over, then under and out. I am impressed, lowlander. It seems you are not a coward after all. I did not believe there were such as you among the children.'

'Sheer courage,' the man rasped. 'That's me.'

'Whose tooth was it?'

'Alrute's. Now, no more spinning, if you please.'

'I am sorry, lowlander, but I must now spin it the opposite way, until the log is as it was before I started.'

'I curse your grim logic, Teblor.'

'What is your name?'

'Torvald Nom, though to my Malazan enemies, I'm known as Knuckles.'

'And how came you to learn the Sunyd tongue?'

140

'It's the old trader language, actually. Before there were bounty hunters, there were Nathii traders. A mutually profitable trade between them and the Sunyd. The truth is, your language is close kin to Nathii.'

'The soldiers spoke gibberish.'

'Naturally; they're soldiers.' He paused. 'All right, that sort of humour's lost on you. So be it. Likely, those soldiers were Malazan.'

'I have decided that the Malazans are my enemy.'

'Something we share, then, Teblor.'

'We share naught but this tree trunk, lowlander.'

'If you prefer. Though I feel obliged to correct you on one thing. Hateworthy as the Malazans are, the Nathii these days are no better. You've no allies among the lowlanders, Teblor, be sure of that.'

'Are you a Nathii?'

'No. I'm Daru. From a city far to the south. The House of Nom is vast and certain families among it are almost wealthy. We've a Nom in the Council, in fact, in Darujhistan. Never met him. Alas, my own family's holdings are more, uh, modest. Hence my extended travels and nefarious professions—'

'You talk too much, Torvald Nom. I am ready to turn this log once more.'

'Damn, I was hoping you'd forgotten about that.'

The iron bar's end was more than halfway through the trunk, the flange a blunt, shapeless piece of metal. Karsa could not keep the aching and trembling from his legs, even as the rest periods between efforts grew ever longer. The larger wounds in his chest and back, created by the splinter of wood, had reopened, leaking steadily to mix with the sweat soaking his clothes. The skin and flesh of his ankles were shredded.

Torvald had succumbed to his own exhaustion, shortly after the log had been returned to its original position, groaning in his sleep whilst Karsa laboured on.

For the moment, as the Uryd warrior rested against the clay slope, the only sounds were his own ragged gasps, underscored by softer, shallow breaths from the far end of the trunk.

Then the sound of boots crossed overhead, first in one direction, then back again, and gone.

Karsa pushed himself upright once more, his head spinning.

'Rest longer, Teblor.'

'There is no time for that, Torvald Nom—'

'Oh, but there is. That slavemaster who now owns you will be waiting here for a while, so that he and his train can travel in the company of the Malazan soldiers. For as far as Malybridge, at least. There's been plenty of bandit activity from Fool's Forest and Yellow Mark, for which I acknowledge some proprietary pride, since it was me who united that motley collection of highwaymen and throat-slitters in the first place. They'd have already come to rescue me, too, if not for the Malazans.'

'I will kill that slavemaster,' Karsa said.

'Careful with that one, giant. Silgar's not a pleasant man, and he's used to dealing with warriors like you—'

'I am Uryd, not Sunyd.'

'So you keep saying, and I've no doubt you're meaner – you're certainly bigger. All I was saying is, be wary of Silgar.'

Karsa positioned himself over the log.

'You have time to spare, Teblor. There's no point in freeing yourself if you're then unable to walk. This isn't the first time I've been in chains, and I speak from experience: bide your time, an opportunity will arise, if you don't wither and die first.'

'Or drown.'

'Point taken, and yes, I understood your meaning when you spoke of courage. I admit to a moment of despair.'

'Do you know how long you have been chained here?'

'Well, there was snow on the ground and the lake's ice had just broken.'

Karsa slowly glanced over at the barely visible, scrawny figure at the far end. 'Torvald Nom, even a lowlander should not be made to suffer such a fate.'

The man's laugh was a rattle. 'And you call *us* children. You Teblor cut people down as if you were executioners, but among my kind, execution is an act of mercy. For your average condemned bastard, prolonged torture is far more likely. The Nathii have made the infliction of suffering an art – must be the cold winters or something. In any case, if not for Silgar claiming you – and the Malazan soldiers in town – the locals would be peeling the skin from your flesh right now, a sliver at a time. Then they'd lock you inside a box to let you heal. They know that your kind are immune to infections, which means they can make you suffer for a long, long time. There's a lot of frustrated townsfolk out there right now, I'd imagine.'

Karsa began pulling on the bar once more.

He was interrupted by voices overhead, then heavy thumping, as of a dozen or more barefooted arrivals, the sound joined now by chains slithering across the warehouse floor.

Karsa settled back against the opposite trench slope.

The trapdoor opened. A child in the lead, lantern in hand, and then Sunyd – naked but for rough-woven short skirts – making a slow descent, their left ankles shackled with a chain linking them all together. The lowlander with the lantern walked down the walkway between the two trenches. The Sunyd, eleven in all, six men and five women, followed.

Their heads were lowered; none would meet Karsa's steady, cold regard.

At a gesture from the child, who had halted four long paces from Karsa's position, the Sunyd turned and slid down the slope of their trench. Three more lowlanders had appeared, and followed them down to apply the fixed shackles to the Teblor's other ankles. There was no resistance from the Sunyd.

143

Moments later, the lowlanders were back on the walk-way, then heading up the steps. The trapdoor squealed on its hinges, closing with a reverberating thump that sent dust drifting down through the gloom.

'It is true, then. An Uryd.' The voice was a whisper.

Karsa sneered. 'Was that the voice of a Teblor? No, it could not have been. Teblor do not become slaves. Teblor would rather die than kneel before a lowlander.'

'An Uryd . . . *in chains*. Like the rest of us—'

'Like the Sunyd? Who let these foul children come close and fix shackles to their legs? No. I am a prisoner, but no bindings shall hold me for long. The Sunyd must be reminded what it is to be a Teblor.'

A new voice spoke from among the Sunyd, a woman's. 'We saw the dead, lined up on the ground before the hunters' camp. We saw wagons, filled with dead Malazans. Townsfolk were wailing. Yet, it is said there were but three of you—'

'Two, not three. Our companion, Delum Thord, was wounded in the head, his mind had fallen away. He ran with the dogs. Had his mind been whole, his bloodsword in his hands—'

There was sudden murmuring from the Sunyd, the word *bloodsword* spoken in tones of awe.

Karsa scowled. 'What is this madness? Have the Sunyd lost *all* the old ways of the Teblor?'

The woman sighed. 'Lost? Yes, long ago. Our own children slipping away in the night to wander south into the lowlands, eager for the cursed lowlander coins – the bits of metal around which life itself seems to revolve. Sorely used, were our children – some even returned to our valleys, as scouts for the hunters. The secret groves of bloodwood were burned down, our horses slain. To be betrayed by our own children, Uryd, this is what broke the Sunyd.'

'Your children should have been hunted down,' Karsa said. 'The hearts of your warriors were too soft. Blood-kin is cut when betrayal is done. Those children ceased being Sunyd. I will kill them for you.'

'You would have trouble finding them, Uryd. They are scattered, many fallen, many now sold into servitude to repay their debts. And some have travelled great distances, to the great cities of Nathilog and Genabaris. Our tribe is no more.'

The first Sunyd who had spoken added, 'Besides, Uryd, you are in chains. Now the property of Master Silgar, from whom no slave has ever escaped. You will be killing no-one, ever again. And like us, you will be made to kneel. Your words are empty.'

Karsa straddled the log once more. He grasped hold of the chains this time, wrapping them about his wrists as many times as he could.

Then he threw himself back. Muscles bunching, legs pushing down on the log, back straightening. Grinding, splintering, a sudden loud crack.

Karsa was thrown backward onto the clay slope, chains snapping around him. Blinking the sweat from his eyes, he stared down at the log.

The trunk had split, down its entire length.

There was a low hiss from the other end, the rustle of freed chains. 'Hood take me, Karsa Orlong,' Torvald whispered, 'you don't take insults well, do you?'

Though no longer attached to the log, Karsa's wrists and ankles were still chained to the iron bars. The warrior unravelled the chains from his battered, bleeding forearms, then collected one of the bars. Laying the ankle chain against the log, he drove the bar's unflanged end into a single link, then began twisting it with both hands.

'What has happened?' a Sunyd asked. 'What was that sound?'

'The Uryd's spine has snapped,' the first speaker replied in a drawl.

Torvald's laugh was a cold chuckle. 'The Lord's push for you, Ganal, I'm afraid.'

'What do you mean, Nom?'

The link popped, sending a piece whipping across the trench to thud against the earthen wall.

Karsa dragged the chain from his ankle shackles. Then he set to splitting the one holding his wrists.

Another popping sound. He freed his arms.

'What is happening?'

A third crack, as he snapped the chain from the iron bar he had been using – which was the undamaged one, its flange intact, sharp-edged and jagged. Karsa clambered from the trench.

'Where is this Ganal?' he growled.

All but one of the Sunyd lying in the opposite trench shrank back at his words.

'I am Ganal,' said the lone warrior who had not moved. 'Not a broken spine after all. Well then, warrior, kill me for my sceptical words.'

'I shall.' Karsa strode down the walkway, lifting the iron bar.

'If you do that,' Torvald said hastily, 'the others will likely raise a cry.'

Karsa hesitated.

Ganal smiled up at him. 'If you spare me, there will be no alarm sounded, Uryd. It is night, still a bell or more before dawn. You will make good your escape—'

'And by your silence, you will all be punished,' Karsa said.

'No. We were all sleeping.'

The woman spoke. 'Bring the Uryd, in all your numbers. When you have slain everyone in this town, then you can settle judgement upon us Sunyd, as will be your right.'

Karsa hesitated, then he nodded. 'Ganal, I give you more of your miserable life. But I shall come once more, and I shall remember you.'

'I have no doubt, Uryd,' Ganal replied. 'Not any more.'

'Karsa,' Torvald said. 'I may be a lowlander and all—'

'I shall free you, child,' the Uryd replied, turning from

146

the Sunyd trench. 'You have shown courage.' He slid down to the man's side. 'You are too thin to walk,' he observed. 'Unable to run. Do you still wish for me to release you?'

'Thin? I haven't lost more than half a stone, Karsa Orlong. I can run.'

'You sounded poorly earlier on—'

'Sympathy.'

'You sought sympathy from an Uryd?'

The man's bony shoulders lifted in a sheepish shrug. 'It was worth a try.'

Karsa pried the chain apart.

Torvald pulled his arms free. 'Beru's blessing on you, lad.'

'Keep your lowlander gods to yourself.'

'Of course. Apologies. Anything you say.'

Torvald scrambled up the slope. On the walkway, he paused. 'What of the trapdoor, Karsa Orlong?'

'What of it?' the warrior growled, climbing up and moving past the lowlander.

Torvald bowed as Karsa went past, a scrawny arm sweeping out in a graceful gesture. 'Lead me, by all means.'

Karsa halted on the first step and glanced back at the child. 'I am warleader,' he rumbled. 'You would have me lead you, lowlander?'

Ganal said from the other trench, 'Careful how you answer, Daru. There are no empty words among the Teblor.'

'Well, uh, it was naught but an invitation. To precede me up the steps—'

Karsa resumed his climb.

Directly beneath the trapdoor, he examined its edges. He recalled that there was an iron latch that was lowered when locked, making it flush with the surrounding boards. Karsa jammed the chain-fixing end of the iron bar into the join beneath the latch. He drove it in as far as he could, then began levering, settling his full weight in gradual increments.

A splintering snap, the trapdoor jumping up slightly. Karsa set his shoulders against it and lifted.

The hinges creaked.

The warrior froze, waited, then resumed, slower this time.

As his head cleared the hatchway, he could see faint lantern-glow from the far end of the warehouse, and saw, seated around a small round table, three lowlanders. They were not soldiers – Karsa had seen them earlier in the company of the slavemaster, Silgar. There was the muted clatter of bones on the tabletop.

That they had not heard the trapdoor's hinges was, to Karsa's mind, remarkable. Then his ears caught a new sound – a chorus of creaks and groans, and, outside, the howl of a wind. A storm had come in from the lake, and rain had begun spraying against the north wall of the warehouse.

'Urugal,' Karsa said under his breath, 'I thank you. And now, witness . . .'

One hand holding the trapdoor over him, the warrior slowly slid onto the floor. He moved far enough to permit Torvald's equally silent arrival, then he slowly lowered the hatch until it settled. A gesture told Torvald to remain where he was, understanding indicated by the man's fervent nod. Karsa carefully shifted the bar from his left hand to his right, then made his way forward.

Only one of the three guards might have seen him, from the corner of his eye, but his attention was intent on the bones skidding over the tabletop before him. The other two had their backs to the room.

Karsa remained low on the floor until he was less than three paces away, then he silently rose into a crouch.

He launched himself forward, the bar whipping horizontally, connecting with first one unhelmed head, then on to the second. The third guard stared open-mouthed. Karsa's swing finished with his left hand grasping the red-smeared end of the bar, which he then drove crossways into the lowlander's throat. The man was thrown back over his chair, striking the warehouse doors and falling in a heap.

Karsa set the bar down on the tabletop, then crouched down beside one of the victims and began removing his sword-belt.

Torvald approached. 'Hood's own nightmare,' he muttered, 'that's what you are, Uryd.'

'Take yourself a weapon,' Karsa directed, moving on to the next corpse.

'I will. Now, which way shall we run, Karsa? They'll be expecting northwest, back the way you came. They'll ride hard for the foot of the pass. I have friends—'

'I have no intention of running,' the warleader growled, looping both sword-belts over a shoulder, the scabbarded longswords looking minuscule where they rested against his back. He collected the flanged bar once more. He turned to find Torvald staring at him. 'Run to your friends, lowlander. I will, this night, deliver sufficient diversion to make good your escape. Tonight, Bairoth Gild and Delum Thord shall be avenged.'

'Don't expect me to avenge *your* death, Karsa. It's madness – you've already done the impossible. I'd advise you to thank the Lady's pull and get away while you can. In case you've forgotten, this town's full of soldiers.'

'Be on your way, child.'

Torvald hesitated, then he threw up his hands. 'So be it. For my life, Karsa Orlong, I thank you. The family of Nom will speak your name in its prayers.'

'I will wait fifty heartbeats.'

Without another word Torvald headed to the warehouse's sliding doors. The main bar had not been lowered into its slots; a smaller latch loosely held the door to the frame. He flipped it back, pushed the door to one side, sufficient only to pop his head out for a quick look. Then he shoved it open slightly more, and slipped outside.

Karsa listened to his footfalls, the splash of bare feet in mud, hurrying away to the left. He decided he would not wait fifty heartbeats. Even with the storm holding fast the darkness, dawn was not far away.

The Teblor slid the door back further and stepped outside. A track narrower than the main street, the wooden buildings opposite indistinct behind a slanting curtain of hard rain. To the right and twenty paces distant, light showed from a single murky window on the upper floor of a house standing next to a side street.

He wanted his bloodsword, but had no idea where it might be. Failing that, any Teblor weapon would suffice. And he knew where he might find some.

Karsa slid the door shut behind him. He swung right and, skirting the edge of the street, made his way towards the lakefront.

The wind whipped rain against his face, loosening the crusted blood and dirt. The shredded leathers of his shirt flapped heavily as he jogged towards the clearing, where waited the camp of the bounty hunters.

There had been survivors. A careless oversight on Karsa's part; one he would now correct. And, in the huts of those cold-eyed children, there would be Teblor trophies. Weapons. Armour.

The huts and shacks of the fallen had already been stripped, the doors hanging open, rubbish strewn about. Karsa's gaze settled on a nearby reed-walled shack clearly still occupied. He padded towards it.

Ignoring the small door, the warrior threw his shoulder against a wall. The reed panel fell inward, Karsa plunging through. There was a grunt from a cot to his left, a vague shape bolting into a sitting position. Iron bar swung down. Blood and bits of bone sprayed the walls. The figure sank back down.

The small, lone room of the shack was cluttered with Sunyd objects, most of them useless: charms, belts and trinkets. He did find, however, a pair of Sunyd hunting knives, sheathed in beaded buckskin over wood. A low altar caught Karsa's attention. Some lowlander god, signified by a small clay statue – a boar, standing on its hind legs.

The Teblor knocked it to the earthen floor, then shattered it with a single stomp of his heel.

Returning outside, he approached the next inhabited shack.

The wind howled off the lake, white-maned waves crashing up the pebbled beach. The sky overhead was still black with clouds, the rain unceasing.

There were seven shacks in all, and in the sixth one – after killing the two men entwined together in the cot beneath the skin of a grey bear – he found an old Sunyd bloodsword, and an almost complete set of armour that, although of a style Karsa had never seen before, was clearly Teblor in origin, given its size and the sigils burned into the wooden plates. It was only when he began strapping it on that he realized that the grey, weathered wood was blood-wood – bleached by centuries of neglect.

In the seventh hut he found a small jar of blood-oil, and took the time to remove the armour and rub the pungent salve into its starved wood. He used the last of it to ease the sword's own thirst.

He then kissed the gleaming blade, tasting the bitter oil.

The effect was instantaneous. His heart began pounding, fire ripping through his muscles, lust and rage filling his mind.

He found himself back outside, staring at the town before him through a red haze. The air was foul with the stench of lowlanders. He moved forward, though he could no longer feel his legs, his gaze fixing on the bronze-banded door of a large, timbered house.

Then it was flying inward, and Karsa was entering the low-ceilinged hallway beyond the threshold. Someone was shouting upstairs.

He found himself on the landing, face to face with a broad-shouldered, bald child. Behind him cowered a woman with grey-streaked hair, and behind her – now fleeing – a half-dozen servants.

The bald child had just taken down from the wall a

151

longsword still in its jewel-studded scabbard. His eyes glittered with terror, his expression of disbelief remaining frozen on his features even as his head leapt from his shoulders.

And then Karsa found himself in the last room upstairs, ducking to keep his head beneath the ceiling as he stepped over the last of the servants, the house silent behind him. Before him, hiding behind a poster bed, a young female lowlander.

The Teblor dropped his sword. A moment later he held her before him, her feet kicking at his knees. He cupped the back of her head in his right hand, pushed her face against his armour's oil-smeared breastplate.

She struggled, then her head snapped back, eyes suddenly wild.

Karsa laughed, throwing her down on the bed.

Animal sounds came from her mouth, her long-fingered hands snatching up at him as he moved over her.

The female clawed at him, her back arching in desperate need.

She was unconscious before he was done, and when he drew away there was blood between them. She would live, he knew. Blood-oil was impatient with broken flesh.

He was outside in the rain once more, sword in his hands. The clouds were lightening to the east.

Karsa moved on to the next house.

Awareness drifted away then, for a time, and when it returned he found himself in an attic with a window at the far end through which streamed bright sunlight. He was on his hands and knees, sheathed in blood, and to one side lay a child's body, fat and in slashed robes, eyes staring sightlessly.

Waves of shivering racked him, his breath harsh gasps that echoed dully in the close, dusty attic. He heard shouts from somewhere outside and crawled over to the round, thick-glassed window at the far end.

Below was the main street, and he realized that he was

near the west gate. Glass-distorted figures on restless horses were gathering – Malazan soldiers. As he watched, and to his astonishment, they suddenly set forth for the gate. The thundering of horse hoofs quickly diminished as the party rode westward.

The warrior slowly sat back. There was no sound from directly beneath him, and he knew that no-one remained alive in the house. He knew, also, that he had passed through at least a dozen such houses, sometimes through the front door, but more often through recessed side and rear doors. And that those places were now as silent as the one in which he now found himself.

The escape has been discovered. But what of the bounty hunters? What of the townsfolk who have yet to emerge onto the street, though the day is already half done? How many did I truly kill?

Soft footfalls below, five, six sets, spreading out through the room under him. Karsa, his senses still heightened beyond normal by the blood-oil, sniffed the air, but their scent had yet to reach him. Yet he knew – these were hunters, not soldiers. He drew a deep breath and held it for a moment, then nodded to himself. *Yes, the slavemaster's warriors. Deeming themselves cleverer than the Malazans, still wanting me for their master.*

Karsa made no move – any shift of weight would be heard, he well knew. Twisting his head slowly, he glanced back at the attic's hatch. It was closed – he'd no recollection of doing so, so probably it was the trapdoor's own weight that had dropped it back into place. But how long ago? His gaze flicked to the child's corpse. The blood dripping from his gaping wounds was thick and slow. Some time had passed, then.

He heard someone speak, and it was a moment before he realized that he could understand the language. 'A bell, sir, maybe more.'

'So where,' another asked, 'is Merchant Balantis? Here's his wife, their two children . . . four servants – did he own more?'

There was more movement.

'Check the lofts—'

'Where the servants slept? I doubt fat old Balantis could have climbed that ladder.'

'Here!' another voice cried from further in. 'The attic stairs are down!'

'All right, so the merchant's terror gave him wings. Go up and confirm the grim details, Astabb, and be quick. We need to check the next house.'

'Hood's breath, Borrug, I nearly lost my breakfast in the last place. It's all quiet up there, can't we just leave it at that? Who knows, the bastard might be chopping up the next family right now.'

There was silence, then: 'All right, let's go. This time, I think Silgar's plain wrong. That Uryd's path of slaughter is straight for the west gate, and I'd lay a year's column he's heading for T'lan Pass right now.'

'Then the Malazans will run him down.'

'Aye, they will. Come on.'

Karsa listened as the hunters converged on the front door then headed back outside. The Teblor remained motionless for another dozen heartbeats. Silgar's men would find no further scenes of slaughter westward along the street. This fact alone would bring them back. He padded across to the trapdoor, lifted it clear, and made his way down the blood-spattered wooden steps. There were corpses strewn along the length of the hallway, the air foul with the reek of death.

He quickly moved to the back door. The yard outside was churned mud and puddles, a heap of pavestones off to one side awaiting the arrival of labourers. Beyond it was a newly built low stone wall, an arched gate in its centre. The sky overhead was broken with clouds carried on a swift wind. Shadows and patches of sunlight crawled steadily over the scene. There was no-one in sight.

Karsa crossed the yard at a sprint. He crouched down at the arched gate. Opposite him ran a rutted, narrow track, parallel to the main street, and beyond it a row of irregular heaps of cut brush amidst tall yellow grasses. The back walls of houses reared behind the heaps.

He was on the western side of the town, and here there were hunters. It followed, then, that he would be safer on the eastern side. At the same time, the Malazan soldiers appeared to be quartered there . . . though he'd watched at least thirty of them ride out through the west gate. Leaving how many?

Karsa had proclaimed the Malazans his enemy.

The warrior slipped out onto the track and headed east. Hunched low, he ran hard, his eyes scanning the way ahead, seeking cover, expecting at any moment the shout that would announce his discovery.

He moved into the shadows of a large house that leaned slightly over the alley. In another five strides he would come to the wide street that led down to the lakeshore. Crossing it undetected was likely to prove a challenge. Silgar's hunters remained in the town, as did an unknown number of Malazans. Enough to cause him trouble? There was no telling.

Five cautious strides, and he was at the edge of the street. There was a small crowd at the far end, lakeside. Wrapped bodies were being carried out of a house, whilst two men struggled with a young, naked, blood-splashed woman. She was hissing and trying to claw at their eyes. It was a moment before Karsa recollected her. The blood-oil still burned within her, and the crowd had drawn back in obvious alarm, their attention one and all fixed on her writhing form.

A glance to the right. No-one.

Karsa bolted across the street. He was but a single stride from the alley opposite when he heard a hoarse shout, then a chorus of cries. Skidding through sluicing mud, the warrior raised his sword and snapped his gaze towards the distant crowd.

To see only their backs, as they fled like panicked deer,

155

leaving the wrapped corpses strewn in their wake. The young woman, suddenly released, fell to the mud shrieking, one hand snapping out to clamp on the ankle of one of her captors. She was dragged through the mud for a body length before she managed to foul the man's stride and send him sprawling. She clambered atop him with a snarl.

Karsa padded into the alley.

A bell started a wild clanging.

He continued on, eastward, parallel to the main street. The far end, thirty or more paces distant, seemed to face onto a long, stone-walled, single level building, the windows visible bearing heavy shutters. As he raced towards it, he saw three Malazan soldiers dart across his field of vision – all were helmed, visors lowered, and none turned their heads.

Karsa slowed his pace as he neared the alley's end. He could see more of the building ahead now. It looked somehow different from all the others in the town, its style more severe, pragmatic – a style the Teblor could admire.

He halted at the alley mouth. A glance to his right revealed that the building before him fronted onto the main street, beyond which was a clearing to match that of the west gate, the edge of the town wall visible just beyond. To his left, and closer to hand, the building came to an end, with a wooden corral flanked by stables and outbuildings. Karsa returned his attention to his right and leaned out slightly further.

The three Malazan soldiers were nowhere to be seen.

The bell was still pealing somewhere behind him, yet the town seemed strangely deserted.

Karsa jogged towards the corral. He arrived with no alarms raised, stepped over the railing, and made his way along the building's wall towards the doorway.

It had been left open. The antechamber within held hooks, racks and shelves for weapons, but all such weapons had been removed. The close dusty air held the memory of

156

fear. Karsa slowly entered. Another door stood opposite, this one shut.

A single kick sent it crashing inward.

Beyond, a large room with a row of cots on either side. Empty.

The echoes of the shattered door fading, Karsa ducked through the doorway and straightened, looking around, sniffing the air. The chamber reeked of tension. He felt something like a presence, still there, yet somehow managing to remain unseen. The warrior cautiously stepped forward. He listened for breathing, heard nothing, took another step.

The noose dropped down from above, over his head and down onto his shoulders. Then a wild shout, and it snapped tight around his neck.

As Karsa raised his sword to slice through the hemp rope, four figures descended behind him, and the rope gave a savage yank, lifting the Teblor off his feet.

There was a sudden splintering from above, followed by a desultory curse, then the crossbeam snapped, the rope slackening though the noose remained taut around Karsa's throat. Unable to draw breath, he spun, sword cleaving in a horizontal slash – that passed through empty air. The Malazan soldiers, he saw, had already dropped to the floor and rolled away.

Karsa dragged the rope free of his neck, then advanced on the nearest scrambling soldier.

Sorcery hammered him from behind, a frenzied wave that engulfed the Teblor. He staggered, then, with a roar, shook it off.

He swung his sword. The Malazan before him leapt backward, but the blade's tip connected with his right knee, shattering the bone. The man shrieked as he toppled.

A net of fire descended on Karsa, an impossibly heavy web of pain that drove him to his knees. He sought to slash at it, but his weapon was fouled by the flickering strands. It began constricting as if it possessed a life of its own.

The warrior struggled within the ever-tightening net, and in moments was rendered helpless.

The wounded soldier's screams continued, until a hard voice rumbled a command and eerie light flashed in the room. The shrieks abruptly stopped.

Figures closed in around Karsa, one crouching down near his head. A dark-skinned, scarred face beneath a bald, tattoo-stitched pate. The man's smile was a row of gleaming gold. 'You understand Nathii, I take it. That's nice. You've just made Limp's bad leg a whole lot worse, and he won't be happy about that. Even so, you stumbling into our laps will more than make up for the house arrest we're presently under—'

'Let's kill him, Sergeant—'

'Enough of that, Shard. Bell, go find the slavemaster. Tell him we got his prize. We'll hand him over, but not for nothing. Oh, and do it quietly – I don't want the whole town outside with torches and pitchforks.' The sergeant looked up as another soldier arrived. 'Nice work, Ebron.'

'I damned near wet my pants, Cord,' the man named Ebron replied, 'when he just threw off the nastiest I had.'

'Just shows, don't it?' Shard muttered.

'Shows what?' Ebron demanded.

'Well, only that clever beats nasty every time, that's all.'

Sergeant Cord grunted, then said, 'Ebron, see what you can do for Limp, before he comes round and starts screaming again.'

'I'll do that. For a runt, he's got some lungs, don't he just.'

Cord reached down and carefully slid his hand between the burning strands to tap a finger against the bloodsword. 'So here's one of the famed wooden swords. So hard it breaks Aren steel.'

'Look at the edge,' Shard said. 'It's that resin they use that makes that edge—'

'And hardens the wood itself, aye. Ebron, this web of yours, is it causing him pain?'

The sorcerer's reply came from beyond Karsa's line of

sight. 'If it was you in that, Cord, you'd be howling to shame the Hounds. For a moment or two, then you'd be dead and sizzling like fat on a hearthstone.'

Cord frowned down at Karsa, then slowly shook his head. 'He ain't even trembling. Hood knows what we could do with five thousand of these bastards in our ranks.'

'Might even manage to clean out Mott Wood, eh, Sergeant?'

'Might at that.' Cord rose and stepped away. 'So what's keeping Bell?'

'Probably can't find no-one,' Shard replied. 'Never seen a whole town take to the boats like that before.'

Boots sounded in the antechamber, and Karsa listened to the arrival of at least a half-dozen newcomers.

A soft voice said, 'Thank you, Sergeant, for recovering my property—'

'Ain't your property any more,' Cord replied. 'He's a prisoner of the Malazan Empire, now. He killed Malazan soldiers, not to mention damaging imperial property by kicking in that door there.'

'You cannot be serious—'

'I'm always serious, Silgar,' Cord quietly drawled. 'I can guess what you got in mind for this giant. Castration, a cut-out tongue, hobbling. You'll put him on a leash and travel the towns south of here, drumming up replacements for your bounty hunters. But the Fist's position on your slaving activities is well enough known. This is occupied territory – this is part of the Malazan Empire now, like it or not, and we ain't at war with these so-called Teblor. Oh, I'll grant you, we don't appreciate renegades coming down and raiding, killing imperial subjects and all that. Which is why this bastard is now under arrest, and he'll likely be sentenced to the usual punishment: the otataral mines of my dear old homeland.' Cord moved to settle down beside Karsa once more. 'Meaning we'll be seeing a lot of each other, since our detachment's heading home. Rumours of rebellion and such, though I doubt it'll come to much.'

Behind him, the slavemaster spoke. 'Sergeant, the Malazan hold upon its conquests on this continent is more than precarious at the moment, now that your principal army is bogged down outside the walls of Pale. Do you truly wish for an incident here? To so flout our local customs—'

'Customs?' Still gazing down at Karsa, Cord bared his teeth. 'The Nathii custom has been to run and hide when the Teblor raid. Your studious, deliberate corruption of the Sunyd is unique, Silgar. Your destruction of that tribe was a business venture on your part. Damned successful it was, too. The only flouting going on here is yours, with Malazan law.' He looked up, his smile broadening. 'What in Hood's name do you think our company's doing here, you perfumed piece of scum?'

All at once tension filled the air as hands settled on sword-grips.

'Rest easy, I'd advise,' Ebron said from one side. 'I know you're a Mael priest, Silgar, and you're right on the edge of your warren right now, but I'll turn you into a lumpy puddle if you make so much as a twitch for it.'

'Order your thugs back,' Cord said, 'or this Teblor will have company on his way to the mines.'

'You would not dare—'

'Wouldn't I?'

'Your captain would—'

'No, he wouldn't.'

'I see. Very well. Damisk, take the men outside for a moment.'

Karsa heard receding footsteps.

'Now then, Sergeant,' Silgar continued after a moment, 'how much?'

'Well, I admit I was considering some kind of exchange. But then the town's bells stopped. Which tells me we're out of time. Alas. Captain's back – there, the sound of the horses, coming fast. All of this means we're all official, now, Silgar. Of course, maybe I was stringing you along all the time, until you finally went and offered me a bribe. Which, as you know, is a crime.'

The Malazan troop had arrived at the corral, Karsa could hear. A few shouts, the stamping of hoofs, a brief exchange of words with Damisk and the other guards standing outside, then heavy boots on the floorboards.

Cord turned. 'Captain—'

A rumbling voice cut him off. 'I thought I'd left you under house guard. Ebron, I don't recall granting you permission to rearm these drunken louts...' Then the captain's words trailed away.

Karsa sensed the smile on Cord's face as he said, 'The Teblor attempted an assault on our position, sir—'

'Which no doubt sobered you up quick.'

'That it did, sir. Accordingly, our clever sorcerer here decided to give us back our weapons, so that we could effect the capture of this overgrown savage. Alas, Captain, matters have since become somewhat more complicated.'

Silgar spoke. 'Captain Kindly, I came here to request the return of my slave and was met with overt hostility and threats from this squad here. I trust their poor example is not indicative of the depths to which the entire Malazan army has fallen—'

'That they're definitely not, Slavemaster,' Captain Kindly replied.

'Excellent. Now, if we could—'

'He tried to bribe me, sir,' Cord said in a troubled, distressed tone.

There was silence, then the captain said, 'Ebron? Is this true?'

'Afraid it is, Captain.'

There was cool satisfaction in Kindly's voice as he said, 'How unfortunate. Bribery is a crime, after all . . .'

'I was just saying the same thing, sir,' Cord noted.

'I was invited to make an offer!' Silgar hissed.

'No you wasn't,' Ebron replied.

Captain Kindly spoke. 'Lieutenant Pores, place the

slavemaster and his hunters under arrest. Detach two squads to oversee their incarceration in the town gaol. Put them in a separate cell from that bandit leader we captured on the way back – the infamous Knuckles is likely to have few friends locally. Barring those we strung up beside the road east of here, that is. Oh, and send in a healer for Limp – Ebron seems to have made something of a mess in his efforts on the unfortunate man.'

'Well,' Ebron snapped, 'I ain't Denul, you know.'

'Watch your tone, Mage,' the captain calmly warned.

'Sorry, sir.'

'I admit to some curiosity, Ebron,' Kindly continued. 'What is the nature of this spell you have inflicted on this warrior?'

'Uh, a shaping of Ruse—'

'Yes, I know your warren, Ebron.'

'Yes, sir. Well, it's used to snare and stun dhenrabi in the seas—'

'*Dhenrabi*? Those giant sea-worms?'

'Yes, sir.'

'Well, why in Hood's name isn't this Teblor dead?'

'Good question, Captain. He's a tough one, he is, ain't he just.'

'Beru fend us all.'

'Aye, sir.'

'Sergeant Cord.'

'Sir?'

'I have decided to drop the charges of drunkenness against you and your squad. Grief for lost ones. An understandable reaction, all things considered. This time. The next abandoned tavern you stumble into, however, is not to be construed as an invitation to licentiousness. Am I understood?'

'Perfectly, sir.'

'Good. Ebron, inform the squads that we are departing this picturesque town. As soon as possible. Sergeant Cord, your squad will see to the loading of supplies. That will be all, soldiers.'

'What of this warrior?' Ebron asked.

'How long will this sorcerous net last?'

'As long as you like, sir. But the pain—'

'He seems to be bearing up. Leave him as he is, and in the meantime think of a way to load him onto the bed of a wagon.'

'Yes, sir. We'll need long poles—'

'Whatever,' Captain Kindly muttered, striding away.

Karsa sensed the sorcerer staring down on him. The pain had long since faded, no matter what Ebron's claims, and indeed, the steady, slow tensing and easing of the Teblor's muscles had begun to weaken it.

Not long, now . . .

CHAPTER THREE

Among the founding families of
Darujhistan, there is Nom.

The Noble Houses of Darujhistan
Misdry

'I missed you, Karsa Orlong.'

Torvald Nom's face was mottled blue and black,
his right eye swollen shut. He had been chained to
the wagon's forward wall and was slouched down amidst
rotting straw, watching as the Malazan soldiers levered the
Teblor onto the bed using stripped-down saplings that had
been inserted beneath the limbs of the huge, net-wrapped
warrior. The wagon shifted and groaned as Karsa's weight
settled on it.

'Pity the damned oxen,' Shard said, dragging one of the
saplings free, his breath harsh and his face red with
exertion.

A second wagon stood nearby, just within the field of
Karsa's vision as he lay motionless on the weathered boards.
In its back sat Silgar, Damisk, and three other Nathii lowlanders. The slavemaster's face was white and patchy, the
blue and gold trim of his expensive clothes stained and
wrinkled. Seeing him, Karsa laughed.

Silgar's head snapped around, dark eyes fixing like knives
on the Uryd warrior.

'Taker of slaves!' Karsa sneered.

The Malazan soldier, Shard, climbed onto the wagon's wall and leaned over to study Karsa for a moment, then he shook his head. 'Ebron!' he called out. 'Come look. That web ain't what it was.'

The sorcerer clambered up beside him. His eyes narrowed. 'Hood take him,' he muttered. 'Get us some chains, Shard. Heavy ones, and lots of them. Tell the captain, too, and hurry.'

The soldier dropped out of sight.

Ebron scowled down at Karsa. 'You got otataral in your veins? Nerruse knows, that spell should have killed you long ago. What's it been, three days now. Failing that, the pain should have driven you mad. But you're no madder than you were a week ago, are you?' His scowl deepened. 'There's something about you . . . something . . .'

Soldiers were suddenly clambering up on all sides, some dragging chains whilst others held back slightly with crossbows cocked.

'Can we touch this?' one asked, hesitating over Karsa.

'You can now,' Ebron replied, then spat.

Karsa tested the magical constraints in a single, concerted surge that forced a bellow from his throat. Strands snapped.

Answering shouts. Wild panic.

As the Uryd began dragging himself free, his sword still in his right hand, something hard cracked into the side of his head.

Blackness swept over him.

He awoke lying on his back, spread-eagled on the bed of the wagon as it rocked and jolted beneath him. His limbs were wrapped in heavy chains that had been spiked to the boards. Others crisscrossed his chest and stomach. Dried blood crusted the left side of his face, sealing the lid of that eye. He could smell dust, wafting up from between the boards, as well as his own bile.

Torvald spoke from somewhere beyond Karsa's head. 'So

you're alive after all. Despite what the soldiers were saying, you looked pretty much dead to me. You certainly smell that way. Well, almost. In case you're wondering, friend, it's been six days. That gold-toothed sergeant hit you hard. Broke the shovel's shaft.'

A sharp, throbbing pain bloomed in Karsa's head as soon as he tried to lift it clear of the foul-smelling boards. He grimaced, settling once more. 'Too many words, lowlander. Be quiet.'

'Quiet's not in my nature, alas. Of course, you don't have to listen. Now, you might think otherwise, but we should be celebrating our good fortune. Prisoners of the Malazans is an improvement over being Silgar's slaves. Granted, I might end up getting executed as a common criminal – which is, of course, precisely what I am – but more likely we're both off to work in the imperial mines in Seven Cities. Never been there, but even so, it's a long trip, land and sea. There might be pirates. Storms. Who knows? Might even be the mines aren't so bad as people say. What's a little digging? I can't wait for the day they put a pickaxe in your hands – oh my, won't you have some fun? Lots to look forward to, don't you think?'

'Including cutting out your tongue.'

'Humour? Hood take me, I didn't think you had it in you, Karsa Orlong. Anything else you want to say? Feel free.'

'I'm hungry.'

'We'll reach Culvern Crossing by tonight – the pace has been torturously slow, thanks to you, since it appears you weigh more than you should, more even than Silgar and his four thugs. Ebron says you don't have normal flesh – same for the Sunyd, of course – but with you it's even more so. Purer blood, I suppose. Meaner blood, that's for sure. I remember, once, in Darujhistan, I was just a lad, a troop arrived with a grey bear, all chained up. Had it in a huge tent just outside Worrytown, charged a sliver to see it. First day, I was there. The crowd was huge. Everyone'd thought grey bears had died out centuries ago—'

'Then you are all fools,' Karsa growled.

'So we were, because there it was. Collared, chained down, with red in its eyes. The crowd rushed in, me in it, and that damned thing went wild. Broke loose like those chains were braids of grass. You wouldn't believe the panic. I got trampled on, but managed to crawl out from under the tent with my scrawny but lovely body mostly intact. That bear – bodies were flying from its path. It charged straight for the Gadrobi Hills and was never seen again. Sure, there's rumours to this day that the bastard's still there, eating the occasional herder ... and herd. Anyway, you remind me of that grey bear, Uryd. The same look in your eyes. A look that says: *Chains will not hold me.* And that's what has me so eager to see what will happen next.'

'I shall not hide in the hills, Torvald Nom.'

'Didn't think you would. Do you know how you will be loaded onto the prison ship? Shard told me. They'll take the wheels off this wagon. That's it. You'll be riding this damned bed all the way to Seven Cities.'

The wagon's wheels slid down into deep, stony ruts, the jarring motion sending waves of pain through Karsa's head.

'You still here?' Torvald asked after a moment.

Karsa remained silent.

'Oh well,' the Daru sighed.

Lead me, Warleader.

Lead me.

This was not the world he had expected. The lowlanders were both weak and strong, in ways he found difficult to comprehend. He had seen huts built one atop another; he had seen watercraft the size of entire Teblor houses.

Expecting a farmstead, they had found a town. Anticipating the slaughter of fleeing cowards, they had instead been met with fierce opponents who stood their ground.

And Sunyd slaves. The most horrifying discovery of all. Teblor, their spirits broken. He had not thought such a thing was possible.

I shall snap those chains on the Sunyd. This, I vow before the Seven. I shall give the Sunyd lowlander slaves in turn – no. To do such would be as wrong as what the lowlanders have done to the Sunyd, have done, indeed, to their own kin. No, his sword's gathering of souls was a far cleaner, a far purer deliverance.

He wondered about these Malazans. They were, it was clear, a tribe that was fundamentally different from the Nathii. Conquerors, it seemed, from a distant land. Holders to strict laws. Their captives not slaves, but prisoners, though it had begun to appear that the distinction lay in name only. He would be set to work.

Yet he had no desire to work. Thus, it was punishment, intended to bow his warrior spirit, to – in time – break it. In this, a fate to match that of the Sunyd.

But that shall not happen, for I am Uryd, not Sunyd. They shall have to kill me, once they realize that they cannot control me. And so, the truth is before me. Should I hasten that realization, I shall never see release from this wagon.

Torvald Nom spoke of patience – the prisoner's code. Urugal, forgive me, for I must now avow to that code. I must seem to relent.

Even as he thought it, he knew it would not work. These Malazans were too clever. They would be fools to trust a sudden, inexplicable passivity. No, he needed to fashion a different kind of illusion.

Delum Thord. You shall now be my guide. Your loss is now my gift. You walked the path before me, showing me the steps. I shall awaken yet again, but it shall not be with a broken spirit, but with a broken mind.

Indeed, the Malazan sergeant had struck him hard. The muscles of his neck had seized, clenched tight around his spine. Even breathing triggered lancing stabs of pain. He sought to slow it, shifting his thoughts away from the low roar of his nerves.

The Teblor had lived in blindness for centuries, oblivious of the growing numbers – and growing threat – of the lowlanders. Borders, once defended with vicious determination, had for some reason been abandoned, left open to the poisoning influences from the south. It was important, Karsa realized, to discover the cause of this moral failing. The Sunyd had never been among the strongest of the tribes, yet they were Teblor none the less, and what befell them could, in time, befall all the others. This was a difficult truth, but to close one's eyes to it would be to walk the same path yet again.

There were failings that must be faced. Pahlk, his own grandfather, had been something far less than the warrior of glorious deeds that he pretended to be. Had Pahlk returned to the tribe with truthful tales, then the warnings within them would have been heard. A slow but inexorable invasion was under way, one step at a time. A war on the Teblor that assailed their spirit as much as it did their lands. Perhaps such warnings would have proved sufficient to unite the tribes.

He considered this, and darkness settled upon his thoughts. No. Pahlk's failing had been a deeper one; it was not his lies that were the greatest crime, it was his lack of courage, for he had shown himself unable to wrest free of the strictures binding the Teblor. His people's rules of conduct, the narrowly crafted confines of expectations – its innate conservatism that crushed dissent with the threat of deadly isolation – these were what had defeated his grandfather's courage.

Yet not, perhaps, my father's.

The wagon jolted once more beneath him.

I saw your mistrust as weakness. Your unwillingness to participate in our tribe's endless, deadly games of pride and retribution – I saw this as cowardice. Even so, what have you done to challenge our ways? Nothing. Your only answer was to hide yourself away – and to belittle all that I did, to mock my zeal . . .

Preparing me for this moment.

Very well, Father, I can see the gleam of satisfaction in your eyes, now. But I tell you this, you delivered naught but wounds upon your son. And I have had enough of wounds.

Urugal was with him. All the Seven were with him. Their power would make him impervious to all that besieged his Teblor spirit. He would, one day, return to his people, and he would shatter their rules. He would unite the Teblor, and they would march behind him . . . down into the lowlands.

Until that moment, all that came before – all that afflicted him now – was but preparation. He would be the weapon of retribution, and it was the enemy itself that now honed him.

Blindness curses both sides, it seems. Thus, the truth of my words shall be shown.

Such were his last thoughts before consciousness once more faded away.

Excited voices awoke him. It was dusk and the air was filled with the smell of horses, dust and spiced foods. The wagon was motionless under him, and he could now hear, mingled with the voices, the sounds of many people and a multitude of activities, underscored by the rush of a river.

'Ah, awake once more,' Torvald Nom said.

Karsa opened his eyes but did not otherwise move.

'This is Culvern Crossing,' the Daru went on, 'and it's a storm swirling with the latest news from the south. All right, a small storm, given the size of this latrine pit of a town. The scum of the Nathii, which is saying a lot. The Malazan company's pretty excited, though. Pale's just fallen, you see. A big battle, lots of sorcery, and Moon's Spawn retreated – likely headed to Darujhistan, in fact. Beru take me, I wish I was there right now, watching it crossing the lake, what a sight that'd be. The company, of course, are wishing they'd been there for the battle. Idiots, but that's soldiers for you—'

'And why not?' Shard's voice snapped as the wagon rocked slightly and the man appeared. 'The Ashok Regiment deserves better than to be stuck up here hunting bandits and slavers.'

170

'The Ashok Regiment is you, I presume,' Torvald said.

'Aye. Damned veterans, too, one and all.'

'So why *aren't* you down south, Corporal?'

Shard made a face, then turned away with narrowed eyes. 'She don't trust us, that's why,' he murmured. 'We're Seven Cities, and the bitch don't trust us.'

'Excuse me,' Torvald said, 'but if she – and by that I take you to mean your Empress – doesn't trust you, then why is she sending you home? Isn't Seven Cities supposedly on the edge of rebellion? If there's a chance of you turning renegade, wouldn't she rather have you here on Genabackis?'

Shard stared down at Torvald Nom. 'Why am I talking to you, thief? You might damn well be one of her spies. A Claw, for all I know.'

'If I am, Corporal, you haven't been treating me very well. A detail I'd be sure to put in my report – this secret one, the one I'm secretly writing, that is. *Shard*, wasn't it? As in a piece of broken glass, yes? And you called the Empress "bitch"—'

'Shut up,' the Malazan snarled.

'Just making a rather obvious point, Corporal.'

'That's what you think,' Shard sneered as he dropped back down from the side of the wagon and was lost from sight.

Torvald Nom said nothing for a long moment, then, 'Karsa Orlong, do you have any idea what that man meant by that last statement?'

Karsa spoke in a low voice, 'Torvald Nom, listen well. A warrior who followed me, Delum Thord, was struck on the head. His skull cracked and leaked thought-blood. His mind could not walk back up the path. He was left helpless, harmless. I, too, have been struck on the head. My skull is cracked and I have leaked thought-blood—'

'Actually, it was drool—'

'Be quiet. Listen. And answer, when you will, in a whisper. I have awakened now, twice, and you have observed—'

Torvald interjected in a soft murmur. 'That your mind's lost on the trail or something. Is that what I have observed? You babble meaningless words, sing childhood songs and the like. All right, fine. I'll play along, on one condition.'

'What condition?'

'That whenever you manage to escape, you free me as well. A small thing, you might think, but I assure you—'

'Very well. I, Karsa Orlong of the Uryd, give my word.'

'Good. I like the formality of that vow. Sounds like it's real.'

'It is. Do not mock me, else I kill you once I have freed you.'

'Ah, now I see the hidden caveat. I must twist another vow from you, alas—'

The Teblor growled with impatience, then relented and said, 'I, Karsa Orlong, shall not kill you once I have freed you, unless given cause.'

'Explain the nature of those causes—'

'Are all Daru like you?'

'It needn't be an exhaustive list. "Cause" being, say, attempted murder, betrayal, and mockery of course. Can you think of any others?'

'Talking too much.'

'Well, with that one we're getting into very grey, very murky shades, don't you think? It's a matter of cultural distinctions—'

'I believe Darujhistan shall be the first city I conquer—'

'I've a feeling the Malazans will get there first, I'm afraid. Mind you, my beloved city has never been conquered, despite its being too cheap to hire a standing army. The gods not only look down on Darujhistan with a protective eye, they probably drink in its taverns. In any case – oh, shhh, someone's coming.'

Bootsteps neared, then, as Karsa watched through slitted eyes, Sergeant Cord clambered up into view and glared for a long moment at Torvald Nom. 'You sure don't look like a Claw . . .' he finally said. 'But maybe that's the whole point.'

'Perhaps it is.'

Cord's head began turning towards Karsa and the Teblor closed his eyes completely. 'He come around yet?'

'Twice. Doing nothing but drooling and making animal sounds. I think you went and damaged his brain, assuming he has one.'

Cord grunted. 'Might prove a good thing, so long as he doesn't die on us. Now, where was I?'

'Torvald Nom, the Claw.'

'Right. OK. Even so, we're still treating you as a bandit – until you prove to us you're something otherwise – and so you're off to the otataral mines with everyone else. Meaning, if you *are* a Claw, you'd better announce it before we leave Genabaris.'

'Assuming, of course,' Torvald smiled, 'my assignment does not require me to assume the disguise of a prisoner in the otataral mines.'

Cord frowned, then, hissing a curse, he dropped down from the side of the wagon.

They heard him shout, 'Get this damned wagon on that ferry! Now!'

The wheels creaked into sudden motion, the oxen lowing.

Torvald Nom sighed, leaning his head against the wall and closing his eyes.

'You play a deadly game,' Karsa muttered.

The Daru propped one eye open. 'A game, Teblor? Indeed, but maybe not the game you think.'

Karsa grunted his disgust.

'Be not so quick to dismiss—'

'I am,' the warrior replied, as the oxen dragged the wagon onto a ramp of wooden boards. 'My causes shall be "attempted murder, betrayal, mockery, and being one of these Claws".'

'And talking too much?'

'It seems I shall have to suffer that curse.'

Torvald slowly cocked his head, then he grinned. 'Agreed.'

173

* * *

In a strange way, the discipline of maintaining the illusion of mindlessness proved Karsa's greatest ally in remaining sane. Days, then weeks lying supine, spread-eagled and chained down to the bed of a wagon was a torture unlike anything the Teblor could have imagined possible. Vermin crawled all over his body, covering him in bites that itched incessantly. He knew of large animals of the deep forest being driven mad by blackflies and midges, and now he understood how such an event could occur.

He was washed down with buckets of icy water at the end of each day, and was fed by the drover guiding the wagon, an ancient foul-smelling Nathii who would crouch down beside his head with a smoke-blackened iron pot filled with some kind of thick, seed-filled stew. He used a large wooden spoon to pour the scalding, malty cereal and stringy meat into Karsa's mouth – the Teblor's lips, tongue and the insides of his cheeks were terribly blistered, the feedings coming too often to allow for healing.

Meals became an ordeal, which was alleviated only when Torvald Nom talked the drover into permitting the Daru to take over the task, ensuring that the stew had cooled sufficiently before it was poured into Karsa's mouth. The blisters were gone within a few days.

The Teblor endeavoured to keep his muscles fit through sessions, late at night, of flexing and unflexing, but all his joints ached from immobility, and for this he could do nothing.

At times, his discipline wavered, his thoughts travelling back to the demon he and his comrades had freed. That woman, the Forkassal, had spent an unimaginable length of time pinned beneath that massive stone. She had managed to achieve some movement, had no doubt clung to some protracted sense of progress as she clawed and scratched against the stone. Even so, Karsa could not comprehend her ability to withstand madness and the eventual death that was its conclusion.

Thoughts of her left him humbled, his spirit weakened by his own growing frailty in these chains, in the wagon bed's rough-hewn planks that had rubbed his skin raw, in the shame of his soiled clothes, and the simple, unbearable torment of the lice and fleas.

Torvald took to talking to him as he would a child, or a pet. Calming words, soothing tones, and the curse of talking too much was transformed into something Karsa could hold on to, his desperate grip ever tightening.

The words fed him, kept his spirit from starving. They measured the cycle of days and nights that passed, they taught him the language of the Malazans, they gave him an account of the places they travelled through. After Culvern Crossing, there had been a larger town, Ninsano Moat, where crowds of children had clambered onto the wagon, poking and prodding him until Shard arrived to drive them away. Another river had been crossed there. Onward to Malybridge, a town of similar proportions to Ninsano Moat, then, seventeen days later, Karsa stared up at the arched stone gateway of a city – Tanys – passing over him, and on either side, as the wagon made its rocking way down a cobbled street, huge buildings of three, even four levels. And all around, the sounds of people, more lowlanders than Karsa had thought possible.

Tanys was a port, resting on tiered ridges rising from the east shore of the Malyn Sea, where the water was brackish with salt – such as was found in a number of springs near the Rathyd borderlands. Yet the Malyn Sea was no turgid, tiny pool; it was vast, for the journey across it to the city called Malyntaeas consumed four days and three nights.

It was the transferring onto the ship that resulted in Karsa's being lifted upright – unwheeled wagon bed included – for the first time, creating a new kind of torture as the chains took his full weight. His joints screamed within him and gave voice as Karsa's shrieks filled the air, continuing without surcease until someone poured a fiery, burning liquid down his throat, enough to fill his stomach, after which his mind sank away.

When he awoke he found that the platform that held him remained upright, strapped to what Torvald called the main mast. The Daru had been chained nearby, having assumed the responsibility for Karsa's care.

The ship's healer had rubbed salves into Karsa's swollen joints, deadening the pain. But a new agony had arrived, raging behind his eyes.

'Hurting?' Torvald Nom murmured. 'That's called a hangover, friend. A whole bladder of rum was poured into you, lucky bastard that you are. You heaved half of it back up, of course, but it had sufficiently worsened in the interval to enable me to refrain from licking the deck, leaving my dignity intact. Now, we both need some shade or we'll end up fevered and raving – and believe me, you've done enough raving for both of us already. Fortunately in your Teblor tongue, which few if any aboard understand. Aye, we've parted ways with Captain Kindly and his soldiers, for the moment. They're crossing on another ship. By the way, who is Dayliss? No, don't tell me. You've made quite a list of rather horrible things you've got planned for this Dayliss, whoever he or she is. Anyway, you should have your sea-legs by the time we dock in Malyntaeas, which should prepare you somewhat for the horrors of Meningalle Ocean. I hope.

'Hungry?'

The crew, mostly Malazans, gave Karsa's position wide berth. The other prisoners had been locked below, but the wagon bed had proved too large for the cargo hatch, and Captain Kindly had been firm on his instructions not to release Karsa, in any circumstances, despite his apparent feeble-mindedness. Not a sign of scepticism, Torvald had explained in a whisper, just the captain's legendary sense of caution, which was reputedly extreme even for a soldier. The illusion seemed to have, in fact, succeeded – Karsa had been bludgeoned into a harmless ox, devoid of any glimmer of intelligence in his dull eyes, his endless, ghastly smile evincing permanent incomprehension. A giant, once warrior, now less than a child, comforted only by the shackled bandit, Torvald Nom, and his incessant chatter.

'Eventually, they'll have to unchain you from that wagon bed,' the Daru once muttered in the darkness as the ship rolled on towards Malyntaeas. 'But maybe not until we arrive at the mines. You'll just have to hold on, Karsa Orlong – assuming you're still pretending you've lost your mind, and these days I admit you've got even me convinced. You *are* still sane, aren't you?'

Karsa voiced a soft grunt, though at times he himself was unsure. Some days had been lost entirely, simply blank patches in his memory – more frightening than anything else he'd yet to experience. Hold on? He did not know if he could.

The city of Malyntaeas had the appearance of having been three separate cities at one time. It was midday when the ship drew into the harbour, and from his position against the main mast Karsa's view was mostly unobstructed. Three enormous stone fortifications commanded three distinct rises in the land, the centre one set back further from the shoreline than the other two. Each possessed its own peculiar style of architecture. The keep to the left was squat, robust and unimaginative, built of a golden, almost orange limestone that looked marred and stained in the sunlight. The centre fortification, hazy through the woodsmoke rising from the maze of streets and houses filling the lower tiers between the hills, appeared older, more decrepit, and had been painted – walls, domes and towers – in a faded red wash. The fortification on the right was built on the very edge of the coastal cliff, the sea below roiling amidst tumbled rocks and boulders, the cliff itself rotted, pock-marked and battle-scarred. Ship-launched projectiles had battered the keep's sloped walls at some time in the past; deep cracks radiated from the wounds, and one of the square towers had slumped and shifted and now leaned precariously outward.

Yet a row of pennants fluttered beyond the wall.

Around each keep, down the slopes and in the flat, lowest stretches, buildings crowded every available space, mimicking its particular style. Borders were marked by wide streets, winding inland, where one style faced the other down their crooked lengths.

Three tribes had settled here, Karsa concluded as the ship eased its way through the crowds of fisherboats and traders in the bay.

Torvald Nom rose to his feet in a rustle of chains, scratching vigorously at his snarled beard. His eyes glittered as he gazed at the city. 'Malyntaeas,' he sighed. 'Nathii, Genabarii and Korhivi, side by side by side. And what keeps them from each other's throats? Naught but the Malazan overlord and three companies from the Ashok Regiment. See that half-ruined keep over there, Karsa? That's from the war between the Nathii and the Korhivi. The whole Nathii fleet filled this bay, flinging stones at the walls, and they were so busy with trying to kill each other that they didn't even notice when the Malazan forces arrived. Dujek Onearm, three legions from the 2nd, the Bridgeburners, and two High Mages. That's all Dujek had, and by day's end the Nathii fleet was on the bay's muddy bottom, the Genabarii royal line holed up in their blood-red castle were all dead, and the Korhivi keep had capitulated.'

The ship was approaching a berth alongside a broad, stone pier, sailors scampering about on all sides.

Torvald was smiling. 'All well and good, you might be thinking. The forceful imposition of peace and all that. Only, the city's Fist is about to lose two of his three companies. Granted, replacements are supposedly on the way. But when? From where? How many? See what happens, my dear Teblor, when your tribe gets too big? Suddenly, the simplest things become ungainly, unmanageable. Confusion seeps in like fog, and everyone gropes blind and dumb.'

A voice cackled from slightly behind and to Karsa's left. A bandy-legged, bald officer stepped into view, his eyes on the berth closing ahead, a sour grin twisting his mouth. In Nathii, he said, 'The bandit chief pontificates on politics, speaking from experience no doubt, what with having to manage a dozen unruly highwaymen. And why are you telling this brainless fool, anyway? Ah, of course, a captive and uncomplaining audience.'

'Well, there is that,' Torvald conceded. 'You are the First Mate? I was wondering, sir, about how long we'd be staying here in Malyntaeas—'

'You were wondering, were you? Fine, allow me to explain the course of events for the next day or two. One. No prisoners leave this ship. Two. We pick up six squads of the 2nd Company. Three, we sail on to Genabaris. You're then shipped off and I'm done with you.'

'I sense a certain unease in you, sir,' Torvald said. 'Have you security concerns regarding fair Malyntaeas?'

The man's head slowly turned. He regarded the Daru for a moment, then grunted. 'You're the one might be a Claw. Well, if you are, add this to your damned report. There's Crimson Guard in Malyntaeas, stirring up the Korhivi. The shadows ain't safe, and it's getting so bad that the patrols don't go anywhere unless there's two squads at the minimum. And now two-thirds of them are being sent home. The situation in Malyntaeas is about to get very unsettled.'

'The Empress would certainly be remiss to discount the opinions of her officers,' Torvald replied.

The First Mate's eyes narrowed. 'She would at that.'

He then strode ahead, bellowing at a small group of sailors who'd run out of things to do.

Torvald tugged at his beard, glanced over at Karsa and winked. 'Crimson Guard. That's troubling indeed. For the Malazans, that is.'

Days vanished. Karsa became aware once again as the wagon bed pitched wildly under him. His joints were afire, as his weight was shifted, chains snapping taut to jolt his limbs. He was being wheeled through the air, suspended from a pulley beneath a creaking framework of beams. Ropes whipped about, voices shouting from below. Overhead, seagulls glided above masts and rigging. Figures clung to that rigging, staring down at the Teblor.

The pulley squealed, and Karsa watched the sailors get smaller. Hands gripped the bed's edges on all sides, steadying it. The end nearest his feet dropped further, drawing him slowly upright.

He saw before him the mid- and foredecks of a huge ship, over which swarmed haulers and stevedores, sailors and soldiers. Supplies were piled everywhere, the bundles being shifted below decks through gaping hatches.

The bed's bottom end scraped the deck. Shouts, a flurry of activity, and the Teblor felt the bed lifted slightly, swinging free once more, then it was lowered again, and this time Karsa could both hear and feel the top edge thump against the main mast. Ropes were drawn through chains to bind the platform in place. Workers stepped away, then, staring up at Karsa.

Who smiled.

Torvald's voice came from one side, 'Aye, it's a ghastly smile, but he's harmless, I assure you all. No need for concern, unless of course you happen to be a superstitious lot—'

There was a solid crack and Torvald Nom's body sprawled down in front of Karsa. Blood poured from his shattered nose. The Daru blinked stupidly, but made no move to rise. A large figure strode to stand over Torvald. Not tall, but wide, and his skin was dusky blue. He glared down at the bandit chief, then studied the ring of silent sailors facing him.

'It's called sticking the knife in and twisting,' he growled in Malazan. 'And he got every damned one of you.' He turned and studied Torvald Nom once more. 'Another stab like that one, prisoner, and I'll see your tongue cut out and

180

nailed to the mast. And if there's any other kind of trouble from you or this giant here, I'll chain you up there beside him then toss the whole damned thing overboard. Nod if you understand me.'

Wiping the blood from his face, Torvald Nom jerked his head in assent.

The blue-skinned man swung his hard gaze up to Karsa. 'Wipe that smile off your face or a knife will kiss it,' he said. 'You don't need lips to eat and the other miners won't care either way.'

Karsa's empty smile remained fixed.

The man's face darkened. 'You heard me . . .'

Torvald raised a hesitant hand, 'Captain, sir, if you will. He does not understand you – his brain is addled.'

'Bosun!'

'Sir!'

'Gag the bastard.'

'Aye, Captain.'

A salt-crusted rag was quickly wrapped about Karsa's lower face, making it difficult to breathe.

'Don't suffocate him, you idiots.'

'Aye, sir.'

The knots were loosened, the cloth pulled down to beneath his nose.

The captain wheeled. 'Now, what in Mael's name are you all standing around for?'

As the workers all scattered, the captain thumping away, Torvald slowly climbed to his feet. 'Sorry, Karsa,' he mumbled through split lips. 'I'll get that off you, I promise. It may take a little time, alas. And when I do, friend, *please*, don't be smiling . . .'

Why have you come to me, Karsa Orlong, son of Synyg, grandson of Pahlk?

One presence, and six. Faces that might have been carved from rock, barely visible through a swirling haze. One, and six.

'I am before you, Urugal,' Karsa said, a truth that left him confused.

You are not. Only your mind, Karsa Orlong. It has fled your mortal prison.

'Then, I have failed you, Urugal.'

Failed. Yes. You have abandoned us and so in turn we must abandon you. We must seek another, one of greater strength. One who does not accept surrender. One who does not flee. In you, Karsa Orlong, our faith was misplaced.

The haze thickened, dull colours flashing through it. He found himself standing atop a hill that shifted and crunched beneath him. Chains stretched out from his wrists, down the slopes on all sides. Hundreds of chains, reaching out into the rainbow mists, and at the unseen ends of each one, there was movement. Looking down, Karsa saw bones beneath his feet. Teblor. Lowlander. The entire hill was naught but bones.

The chains slackened suddenly.

Movement in the mists, drawing closer from every direction.

Terror surged through Karsa.

Corpses, many of them headless, staggered into view. The chains that held the horrifying creatures to Karsa penetrated their chests through gaping holes. Withered, long-nailed hands reached towards him. Stumbling on the slopes, the apparitions began climbing.

Karsa struggled, seeking to flee, but he was surrounded. The very bones at his feet held him fast, clattering and shifting tighter about his ankles.

A hiss, a susurration of voices through rotting throats. *'Lead us, Warleader . . .'*

He shrieked.

'Lead us, Warleader.'

Climbing closer, arms reaching up, nails clawing the air—

A hand closed about his ankle.

Karsa's head snapped back, struck wood with a resounding

crunch. He gulped air that slid like sand down his throat, choking him. Eyes opening, he saw before him the gently pitching decks of the ship, figures standing motionless, staring at him.

He coughed behind his gag, each convulsion a rage of fire in his lungs. His throat felt torn, and he realized that he had been screaming. Enough to spasm his muscles so they now clenched tight, cutting off the flow of his air passages.

He was dying.

The whisper of a voice deep in his mind: *Perhaps we will not abandon you, yet. Breathe, Karsa Orlong. Unless, of course, you wish to once more meet your dead.*

Breathe.

Someone snatched the gag from his mouth. Cold air flooded his lungs.

Through watering eyes, Karsa stared down at Torvald Nom. The Daru was barely recognizable, so dark was his skin, so thick and matted his beard. He had used the very chains holding Karsa to climb up within reach of the gag, and was now shouting unintelligible words the Teblor barely heard – words flung back at the frozen, fear-stricken Malazans.

Karsa's eyes finally made note of the sky beyond the ship's prow. There were colours there, amidst churning clouds, flashing and blossoming, swirls bleeding out from what seemed huge, open wounds. The storm – if that was what it was – commanded the entire sky ahead. And then he saw the chains, snapping down through the clouds to crack thunderously on the horizon. Hundreds of chains, impossibly huge, black, whipping in the air with explosions of red dust, crisscrossing the sky. Horror filled his soul.

There was no wind. The sails hung limp. The ship lolled on lazy, turgid seas. And the storm was coming.

A sailor approached with a tin cup filled with water, lifted it up to Torvald, who took it and brought it to Karsa's scabbed, crusted lips. The brackish liquid entered his mouth, burning like acid. He drew his head away from the cup.

Torvald was speaking in low tones, words that slowly grew comprehensible to Karsa. '. . . long lost to us. Only your beating heart and the rise and fall of your chest told us you still lived. It has been weeks and weeks, my friend. You'd keep hardly anything down. There's almost nothing left of you – you're showing bones where no bones should be.

'And then this damned becalming. Day after day. Not a cloud in the sky . . . until three bells past. Three bells, when you stirred, Karsa Orlong. When you tilted your head back and began screaming behind your gag. Here, more water – you must drink.

'Karsa, they're saying you've called this storm. Do you understand? They want you to send it away – they'll do anything, they'll unchain you, set you free. Anything, friend, anything at all – just send this unholy storm away. Do you understand?'

Ahead, he could see now, the seas were exploding with each lash of the black, monstrous chains, twisting spouts of water skyward as each chain retreated upward once more. The billowing, heaving clouds seemed to lean forward over the ocean, closing on their position from all sides now.

Karsa saw the Malazan captain descend from the foredeck, the blue-tinged skin on his face a sickly greyish hue. 'This is no Mael-blessed squall, Daru, meaning it don't belong.' He jerked a trembling finger at Karsa. 'Tell him he's running out of time. Tell him to send it away. Once he does that, we can negotiate. Tell him, damn you!'

'I *have* been, Captain!' Torvald retorted. 'But how in Hood's name do you expect him to send *anything* away when I'm not even sure he knows where he is? Worse, we don't even know for sure if he's responsible!'

'Let's see, shall we?' The captain spun round, gestured. A score of crewmen rushed forward, axes in hand.

Torvald was dragged down and thrown to the deck.

The axes chopped through the heavy ropes binding the platform to the mast. More crew came forward then. A ramp was laid out, angled up to the starboard gunnel. Log rollers were positioned beneath the platform as it was roughly lowered.

'Wait!' Torvald cried out. 'You can't—'

'We can,' the captain growled.

'At least unchain him!'

'Not a chance, Torvald.' The captain grabbed a passing sailor by the arm. 'Find everything this giant owned – all that stuff confiscated from the slavemaster. It's all going with him. Hurry, damn you!'

Chains ripped the seas on all sides close enough to lift spray over the ship, each detonation causing hull, masts and rigging to tremble.

Karsa stared up at the tumbling stormclouds as the platform was dragged along the rollers, up the ramp.

'Those chains will sink it!' Torvald said.

'Maybe, maybe not.'

'What if it lands wrong way up?'

'Then he drowns, and Mael can have him.'

'Karsa! Damn you! Cease playing your game of mindlessness! Say something!'

The warrior croaked out two words, but the noise that came from his lips was unintelligible even to him.

'What did he say?' the captain demanded.

'I don't know!' Torvald screamed. 'Karsa, damn you, try again!'

He did, yielding the same guttural noise. He began repeating the same two words, over and over again, as the sailors pushed and pulled the platform up onto the gunnel until it was balanced precariously, half over the deck, half over the sea.

Directly above them, as he uttered his two words once more, Karsa watched the last patch of clear sky vanish, like the closing of a tunnel mouth. A sudden plunge into darkness, and Karsa knew it was too late, even as, in the sudden terror-stricken silence, his words came out clear and audible.

'Go *away*.'

From overhead, chains snapped down, massive, plunging, reaching directly for – it seemed – Karsa's own chest.

A blinding flash, a detonation, the splintering crackle of masts toppling, spars and rigging crashing down. The entire ship was falling away beneath Karsa, beneath the platform itself, which slid wildly down the length of the gunnel before crunching against the foredeck railing, pivoting, then plunging for the waves below.

He stared down at the water's sickly green, heaving surface.

The entire platform shuddered in its fall as the cargo ship's hull rolled up and struck its edge.

Karsa caught an upside-down glimpse of the ship – its deck torn open by the impact of the huge chains, its three masts gone, the twisted forms of sailors visible in the wreckage – then he was staring up at the sky, at a virulent, massive wound directly overhead.

A fierce impact, then darkness.

His eyes opened to a faint gloom, the desultory lap of waves, the sodden boards beneath him creaking as the platform rocked to someone else's movement. Thumps; low, gasping mutters.

The Teblor groaned. The joints of every limb felt torn inside.

'Karsa?' Torvald Nom crawled into view.

'What – what has happened?'

The shackles remained on the Daru's wrists, the chains connected on the other end to arm-length, roughly broken fragments of the deck. 'Easy for you, sleeping through all the hard work,' he grumbled as he moved into a sitting position, pulling his arms around his knees. 'This sea's a lot colder than you'd think, and these chains didn't help. I've nearly drowned a dozen times, but you'll be glad to know we now have three water casks and a bundle of something that might be food – I've yet to untie its bindings. Oh, and your sword and armour, both of which float, of course.'

The sky overhead looked unnatural, luminous grey shot through with streaks of darker pewter, and the water smelled of clay and silts. 'Where are we?'

'I was hoping you'd know. It's pretty damned clear to me that you called that storm down on us. That's the only explanation for what happened—'

'I called nothing.'

'Those chains of lightning, Karsa – not one missed its target. Not a single Malazan was left standing. The ship was falling apart – your platform had landed right-side up and was drifting away. I was still working free when Silgar and three of his men climbed out of the hold, dragging their chains with them – the hull was riven through, coming apart all around the bastards. Only one had drowned.'

'I am surprised they didn't kill us.'

'You were out of reach, at least to start with. Me, they threw overboard. A short while later, after I'd made it to this platform, I saw them in the lone surviving dory. They were rounding the sinking wreck, and I knew they were coming for us. Then, somewhere on the other side of the ship, beyond my sight, something must have happened, because they never reappeared. They vanished, dory and all. The ship then went down, though a lot of stuff has been coming back up. So, I've been resupplying. Collecting rope and wood, too – everything I could drag over here. Karsa, your platform is slowly sinking. None of the water casks are full, so that's added some buoyancy, and I'll be slipping more planks and boards under it, which should help. Even so . . .'

'Break my chains, Torvald Nom.'

The Daru nodded, then ran a hand through his dripping, tangled hair. 'I've checked on that, friend. It will take some work.'

'Is there land about?'

Torvald glanced over at the Teblor. 'Karsa, this isn't the Meningalle Ocean. We're somewhere else. Is there land nearby? None in sight. I overheard Silgar talking about a warren, which is one of those paths a sorcerer uses. He said he thought we'd all entered one. There may be no land here. None at all. Hood knows there's no wind and we don't seem to be moving in any direction – the wreckage of the ship is still all around us. In fact, it almost pulled us under with it. Also, this sea is fresh water – no, I wouldn't want to drink it. It's full of silt. No fish. No birds. No signs of life anywhere.'

'I need water. Food.'

Torvald crawled over to the wrapped bundle he had retrieved. 'Water, we have. Food? No guarantees. Karsa, did you call upon your gods or something?'

'No.'

'What started you screaming like that, then?'

'A dream.'

'A dream?'

'Yes. Is there food?'

'Uh, I'm not sure, it's mostly padding . . . around a small wooden box.'

Karsa listened to ripping sounds as Torvald pulled away the padding. 'There's a mark branded on it. Looks . . . Moranth, I think.' The lid was pried free. 'More padding, and a dozen clay balls . . . with wax plugs on them – oh, Beru fend—' The Daru backed away from the package. 'Hood's dripping tongue. I think I know what these are. Never seen one, but I've heard about them – who hasn't? Well . . .' He laughed suddenly. 'If Silgar reappears and comes after us, he's in for a surprise. So's anyone else who might mean trouble.' He edged forward again and carefully replaced the padding, then the lid.

'What have you found?'

'Alchemical munitions. Weapons of war. You throw them, preferably as far as you can. The clay breaks and the chemicals within explode. What you don't want to happen is have one break in your hand, or at your feet. Because then you're dead. The Malazans have been using these in the Genabackan campaign.'

'Water, please.'

'Right. There's a ladle here . . . somewhere . . . found it.'

A moment later Torvald hovered over Karsa, and the Teblor drank, slowly, all the water the ladle contained.

'Better?'

'Yes.'

'More?'

'Not yet. Free me.'

'I need to get back into the water first, Karsa. I need to push some planks under this raft.'

'Very well.'

There seemed to be no day and no night in this strange place; the sky shifted hue occasionally, as if jostled by high, remote winds, the streaks of pewter twisting and stretching, but there was no change otherwise. The air surrounding the raft remained motionless, damp and cool and strangely thick.

The flanges anchoring Karsa's chains were on the underside, holding him in place in a fashion identical to that in the slave trench at Silver Lake. The shackles themselves had been welded shut. Torvald's only recourse was to attempt to widen the holes in the planks where the chains went through, using an iron buckle to dig at the wood.

Months of imprisonment had left him weakened, forcing frequent rests, and the buckle made a bloody mess of his hands, but once begun the Daru would not relent. Karsa measured the passing of time by the rhythmic crunching and scraping sounds, noting how each pause to rest stretched longer, until Torvald's breathing told him the Daru had fallen into an exhausted sleep. Then, the Teblor's only company was the sullen lap of water as it slipped back and forth across the platform.

For all the wood positioned beneath it, the raft was still sinking, and Karsa knew that Torvald would not be able to free him in time.

He had never before feared death. But now, he knew that

Urugal and the other Faces in the Rock would abandon his soul, would leave it to the hungry vengeance of those thousands of ghastly corpses. He knew his dream had revealed to him a fate that was real, and inevitable. And inexplicable. Who had set such horrid creatures upon him? Undead Teblor, undead lowlander, warrior and child, an army of corpses, all chained to him. Why?

Lead us, Warleader.

Where?

And now, he would drown. Here, in this unknown place, far from his village. His claims to glory, his vows, all now mocking him, whispering a chorus of muted creaks, soft groans . . .

'Torvald.'

'Uh . . . what? What is it?'

'I hear new sounds—'

The Daru sat up, blinking crusted silt from his eyes. He looked around. 'Beru fend!'

'What do you see?'

The Daru's gaze was fixed on something beyond Karsa's head. 'Well, it seems there's currents here after all, though which of us has done the moving? Ships, Karsa. A score or more of them, all dead in the water, like us. Floating wrecks. No movement on them . . . that I can see as yet. Looks like there was a battle. With plenty of sorcery being flung back and forth . . .'

Some indiscernible shift drew the ghostly flotilla into Karsa's view, an image on its side to his right. There were two distinct styles of craft. Twenty or so were low and sleek, the wood stained mostly black, though where impacts and collisions and other damage had occurred the cedar's natural red showed like gaping wounds. Many of these ships sat low in the water, a few with their decks awash. They were single-masted, square-sailed, the torn and shredded sails also black, shimmering in the pellucid light. The remaining six ships were larger, high-decked and three-masted. They had been fashioned from a wood that was true black – not stained – as was evinced from the gashes and splintered planks marring the broad, bellied hulls. Not one of these latter ships sat level in the water; all leaned one way or the other, two of them at very steep angles.

'We should board a few,' Torvald said. 'There will be tools, maybe even weapons. I could swim over – there, that raider. It's not yet awash, and I see lots of wreckage.'

Karsa sensed the Daru's hesitation. 'What is wrong? Swim.'

'Uh, I am a little concerned, friend. I seem to have not much strength left, and these chains on me . . .'

The Teblor said nothing for a moment, then he grunted. 'So be it. No more can be asked of you, Torvald Nom.'

The Daru slowly turned to regard Karsa. 'Compassion, Karsa Orlong? Is it helplessness that has brought you to this?'

'Too many empty words from you, lowlander,' the Teblor sighed. 'There are no gifts that come from being—'

A soft splash sounded, then sputtering and thrashing – the sputtering turning into laughter. Torvald, now alongside the raft, moved into Karsa's line of sight. 'Now we know why those ships are canted so!' And the Teblor saw that Torvald was standing, the water lapping around his upper chest. 'I can drag us over, now. This also tells us we're the ones who've been drifting. And there's something else.'

'What?'

The Daru had begun pulling the raft along, using Karsa's chains. 'These ships all grounded during the battle – I think a lot of the hand to hand fighting was actually between ships, chest-deep in water.'

'How do you know this?'

'Because there's bodies all around me, Karsa Orlong. Against my shins, rolling about on the sands – it's an unpleasant feeling, let me tell you.'

'Pull one up. Let us see these combatants.'

'All in good time, Teblor. We're almost there. Also,

these bodies, they're, uh, rather soft. We might find something more recognizable if there's any on the ship itself. Here' – there was a bump – 'we're alongside. A moment, while I climb aboard.'

Karsa listened to the Daru's grunts and gasps, the slipping scrabble of his bare feet, the rustle of chains, finally followed by a muted thud.

Then silence.

'Torvald Nom?'

Nothing.

The raft's end beyond Karsa's head bumped alongside the raider's hull, then began drifting along it. Cool water flowed across the surface, and Karsa recoiled at the contact, but could do nothing as it seeped beneath him. 'Torvald Nom!'

His voice strangely echoed.

No reply.

Laughter rumbled from Karsa, a sound oddly disconnected from the Teblor's own will. In water that, had he been able to stand, would likely rise no higher than his hips, he would drown. Assuming there would be time for that. Perhaps Torvald Nom had been slain – it would be a bizarre battle if there had been no survivors – and even now, beyond his sight, the Teblor was being looked down upon, his fate hanging in the balance.

The raft edged near the ship's prow.

A scuffling sound, then, 'Where? Oh.'

'Torvald Nom?'

Footsteps, half-stumbling, moved alongside from the ship's deck. 'Sorry, friend. I think I must have passed out. Were you laughing a moment ago?'

'I was. What have you found?'

'Not much. Yet. Bloodstains – dried. Trails through it. This ship has been thoroughly stripped. Hood below – you're sinking!'

'And I do not think you will be able to do anything about it, lowlander. Leave me to my fate. Take the water, and my weapons—'

But Torvald had reappeared, rope in his hand, sliding down over the gunnel near the high prow and back into the water. Breathing hard, he fumbled with the rope for a moment before managing to slip it underneath the chains. He then drew it along and repeated the effort on the other side of the raft. A third time, down near Karsa's left foot, then a fourth loop opposite.

The Teblor could feel the wet, heavy rope being dragged through the chains. 'What are you doing?'

Torvald made no reply. Still trailing the rope, he climbed back onto the ship. There was another long stretch of silence, then Karsa heard movement once more, and the rope slowly tautened.

Torvald's head and shoulders moved into view. The lowlander was deathly pale. 'Best I could do, friend. There may be some more settling, but hopefully not much. I will check again on you in a little while. Don't worry, I won't let you drown. I'm going to do some exploring right now – the bastards couldn't have taken *everything*.'

He vanished from Karsa's line of sight.

The Teblor waited, racked with shivering as the sea slowly embraced him. The level had reached his ears, muting all sounds other than the turgid swirl of water. He watched the four lengths of rope slowly growing tighter above him.

It was difficult to recall a time when his limbs had been free to move without restraint, when his raw, suppurating wrists had not known the implacable iron grip of shackles, when he had not felt – deep in his withered body – a vast weakness, a frailty, his blood flowing as thin as water. He closed his eyes and felt his mind falling away.

Away . . .

Urugal, I stand before you once more. Before these faces in the rock, before my gods. Urugal—

'I see no Teblor standing before me. I see no warrior wading through his enemies, harvesting souls. I do not see the dead piled high on the ground, as numerous as a herd of bhederin driven

193

over a cliff. Where are my gifts? Who is this who claims to serve me?'

Urugal. You are a bloodthirsty god—

'A truth a Teblor warrior revels in!'

As I once did. But now, Urugal, I am no longer so sure—

'Who stands before us? Not a Teblor warrior! Not a servant of mine!'

Urugal. What are these 'bhederin' you spoke of? What are these herds? Where among the lands of the Teblor—

'Karsa!'

He flinched. Opened his eyes.

Torvald Nom, a burlap sack over one shoulder, was climbing back down. His feet made contact with the raft, pushing it a fraction deeper. Water stung the outside corners of Karsa's eyes.

The sack made numerous clunking sounds as the Daru set it down and reached inside. 'Tools, Karsa! A ship-wright's tools!' He drew forth a chisel and an iron-capped mallet.

The Teblor felt his heart begin pounding hard in his chest.

Torvald set the chisel against a chain link, then began hammering.

A dozen swings, the concussions pealing loudly in the still, murky air, then the chain snapped. Its own weight swiftly dragged it through the iron ring of Karsa's right wrist shackle. Then, with a soft rustle, it was gone beneath the sea's surface. Agony lanced through his arm as he attempted to move it. The Teblor grunted, even as consciousness slipped away.

He awoke to the sounds of hammering, down beside his right foot, and thundering waves of pain, through which he heard, dimly, Torvald's voice.

'. . . heavy, Karsa. You'll need to do the impossible. You'll need to climb. That means rolling over, getting onto your hands and knees. Standing. Walking – oh, Hood, you're right, I'll need to think of something else. No food anywhere on this damned ship.' There was a loud crack, then the hiss of a chain falling away. 'That's it, you're free. Don't worry, I've retied the ropes to the platform itself – you won't sink. Free. How's it feel? Never mind – I'll ask that a few days from now. Even so, you're free, Karsa. I promised, didn't I? Let it not be said that Torvald Nom doesn't hold to his – well, uh, let it not be said that Torvald Nom isn't afraid of new beginnings.'

'Too many words,' Karsa muttered.

'Aye, far too many. Try moving, at least.'

'I am.'

'Bend your right arm.'

'I am trying.'

'Shall I do it for you?'

'Slowly. Should I lose consciousness, do not cease. And do the same for the remaining limbs.'

He felt the lowlander's hands grip his right arm, at the wrist and above the elbow, then, once again, mercifully, blackness swallowed him.

When he came to once more, bundles of sodden cloth had been propped beneath his head, and he was lying on his side, limbs curled. There was dull pain in every muscle, every joint, yet it seemed strangely remote. He slowly lifted his head.

He was still on the platform. The ropes that held it to the ship's prow had prevented it from sinking further. Torvald Nom was nowhere in sight.

'I call upon the blood of the Teblor,' Karsa whispered. 'All that is within me must be used now to heal, to gift me strength. I am freed. I did not surrender. The warrior remains. He remains . . .' He tried to move his arms. Throbs of pain, sharp, but bearable. He shifted his legs, gasped at the agony flaring in his hips. A moment of light-headedness, threatening oblivion once again . . . that then passed.

He tried to push himself to his hands and knees. Every minuscule shift was torture, but he refused to surrender to it. Sweat streamed down his limbs. Waves of trembling washed through him. Eyes squeezed shut, he struggled on.

He had no idea how much time had passed, but then he was sitting, the realization arriving with a shock. He was sitting, his full weight on his haunches, and the pain was fading. He lifted his arms, surprised and a little frightened by their looseness, horrified by their thinness.

As he rested, he looked about. The shattered ships remained, detritus clumped in makeshift rafts between them. Tattered sails hung in shrouds from the few remaining masts. The prow looming beside him held panels crowded with carvings: figures, locked in battle. The figures were long-limbed, standing on versions of ships closely resembling the raiders on all sides. Yet the enemy in these reliefs were not, it seemed, the ones the ship's owners had faced here, for the craft they rode in were, if anything, smaller and lower than the raiders. The warriors looked much like Teblor, thick-limbed, heavily muscled, though in stature shorter than their foes.

Movement in the water, a gleaming black hump, spike-finned, rising into view then vanishing again. All at once, more appeared, and the surface of the water between the ships was suddenly aswirl. There was life in this sea after all, and it had come to feed.

The platform lurched beneath Karsa, throwing him off balance. His left arm shot out to take his weight as he began toppling. A jarring impact, excruciating pain – but the arm held.

He saw a bloated corpse roll up into view alongside the raft, then a black shape, a broad, toothless mouth, gaping wide, sweeping up and around the corpse, swallowing it whole. A small grey eye behind a spiny whisker flashed into sight as the huge fish swept past. The eye swivelled to track him, then the creature was gone.

Karsa had not seen enough of the corpse to judge whether it was a match to him in size, or to the Daru,

Torvald Nom. But the fish could have taken Karsa as easily as it had the corpse.

He needed to stand. Then, to climb.

And – as he watched another massive black shape break the surface alongside another ship, a shape almost as long as the ship itself – he would have to do it quickly.

He heard footsteps from above, then Torvald Nom was at the gunnel beside the prow. 'We've got to – oh, Beru bless you, Karsa! Can you stand up? You've no choice – these catfish are bigger than sharks and likely just as nasty. There's one – just rolled up behind you – it's circling, it knows you're there! Stand up, use the ropes!'

Nodding, Karsa reached up for the nearest stretch of rope.

An explosion of water behind him. The platform shuddered, wood splintering – Torvald screamed a warning – and Karsa knew without looking back over his shoulder that one of the creatures had just risen up, had just thrown itself bodily onto the raft, splitting it in two.

The rope was in his hand. He gripped hard as the sloshing surface beneath him seemed to vanish. A flood of water around his legs, rising to his hips. Karsa closed his other hand on the same rope.

'Urugal! Witness!'

He drew his legs from the foaming water, then, hand over hand, climbed upward. The rope swung free of the platform's fragments, threw him against the ship's hull. He grunted at the impact, yet would not let go.

'Karsa! Your legs!'

The Teblor looked down, saw nothing but a massive mouth, opened impossibly wide, rising up beneath him.

Hands closed on his wrists. Screaming at the pain in his shoulders and hips, Karsa pulled himself upward in a single desperate surge.

The mouth snapped shut in a spray of milky water.

Knees cracking against the gunnel, Karsa scrambled wildly for a moment, then managed to shift his weight over the rail, drawing his legs behind him, to sprawl with a heavy thump on the deck.

Torvald's shrieks continued unabated, forcing the Teblor to roll over – to see the Daru fighting to hold on to what appeared to be some kind of harpoon. Torvald's shouts, barely comprehensible, seemed to be referring to a line. Karsa glanced about, until he saw that the harpoon's butt-end held a thin rope, which trailed down to a coiled pile almost within the Teblor's reach. Groaning, he scrabbled towards it. He found the end, began dragging it towards the prow.

He pulled himself up beside it, looped the line over and around, once, twice – then there was a loud curse from Torvald, and the coil began playing out. Karsa threw the line around one more time, then managed something like a half-hitch.

He did not expect the thin rope to hold. He ducked down beneath it as the last of the coil was snatched from his hands, thrumming taut.

The galley creaked, the prow visibly bending, then the ship lurched into motion, shuddering as it was dragged along the sandy bottom.

Torvald scrambled up beside Karsa. 'Gods below, I didn't think – let's hope it holds!' he gasped. 'If it does, we won't go hungry for a long while, no, not a long while!' He slapped Karsa on the back, then pulled himself up to the prow. His wild grin vanished. 'Oh.'

Karsa rose.

The harpoon's end was visible directly ahead, cutting a V through the choppy waves – heading directly for one of the larger, three-masted ships. The grinding sound suddenly ceased beneath the raider, and the craft surged forward.

'To the stern, Karsa! To the stern!'

Torvald made a brief effort to drag Karsa, then gave up with a curse, running full tilt for the galley's stern.

Weaving, fighting waves of blackness, the Teblor

staggered after the Daru. 'Could you not have speared a smaller one?'

The impact sent them both sprawling. A terrible splitting sound reverberated down the galley's spine, and all at once there was water everywhere, foaming up from the hatches, sweeping in from the sides. Planks from the hull on both sides parted like groping fingers.

Karsa found himself thrashing about in waist-deep water. Something like a deck remained beneath him, and he managed to struggle upright. And, bobbing wildly directly in front of him, was his original bloodsword. He snatched at it, felt his hand close about the familiar grip. Exultation soared through him, and he loosed an Uryd warcry.

Torvald sloshed into view beside him. 'If that didn't freeze that fish's tiny heart, nothing will. Come on, we need to get onto that other damned ship. There's more of those bastards closing in all around us.'

They struggled forward.

The ship they had broadsided had been leaning in the other direction. The galley had plunged into its hull, creating a massive hole before itself shattering, the prow with its harpoon line snapping off and vanishing within the ship's lower decks. It was clear that the huge ship was solidly grounded, nor had the collision dislodged it.

As they neared the gaping hole, they could hear wild thrashing from somewhere within, deep in the hold.

'Hood take me!' Torvald muttered in disbelief. 'That thing went through the hull first. Well, at least we're not fighting a creature gifted with genius. It's trapped down there, is my guess. We should go hunting—'

'Leave that to me,' Karsa growled.

'You? You can barely stand—'

'Even so, I will kill it.'

'Well, can't I watch?'

'If you insist.'

There were three decks within the ship's hull, in so far as they could see, the bottom one comprising the hold itself, the other two scaled to suit tall lowlanders. The hold had been half-filled with cargo, which was now tumbling out in the backwash – bundles, bales and casks.

Karsa plunged into waist-deep water, making for the thrashing sounds deeper within. He found the huge fish writhing on the second level, in sloshing, foaming water that barely covered the Teblor's ankles. Spears of splintered wood jutted from the fish's enormous head, blood streaming out to stain the foam pink. It had rolled onto its side, revealing a smooth, silvery underbelly.

Clambering across to the creature, Karsa drove his sword into its abdomen. The huge tail twisted round, struck him with the strength of a destrier's kick. He was suddenly in the air, then the curved wall of the hull struck his back.

Stunned by the impact, the Teblor slumped in the swirling water. He blinked the drops from his eyes, then, unmoving in the gloom, watched the fish's death-throes.

Torvald climbed into view. 'You're still damned fast, Karsa – left me behind. But I see you've done the deed. There's food among these supplies . . .'

But Karsa heard no more, as unconsciousness took him once again.

He awoke to the stench of putrefying flesh that hung heavy in the still air. In the half-light, he could just make out the body of the dead fish opposite him, its belly slit open, a pallid corpse partially tumbled out. There was the distant sound of movement somewhere above him.

Well beyond the fish and to the right, steep steps were visible, leading upward.

Fighting to keep from gagging, Karsa collected his sword and began crawling towards the stairs.

He eventually emerged onto the midship's deck. Its sorcery-scarred surface was sharply canted, sufficient to make traverse difficult. Supplies had been collected and were piled against the downside railing, where ropes trailed over the side. Pausing near the hatch to regain his breath,

Karsa looked around for Torvald Nom, but the Daru was nowhere in sight.

Magic had ripped deep gouges across the deck. There were no bodies visible anywhere, no indications of the nature of the ship's owners. The black wood – which seemed to emanate darkness – was of a species the Teblor did not recognize, and it was devoid of any ornamentation, evoking pragmatic simplicity. He found himself strangely comforted.

Torvald Nom clambered into view from the downside rail. He had managed to remove the chains attached to his shackles, leaving only the black iron bands on wrists and ankles. He was breathing hard.

Karsa pushed himself upright, leaning on the sword's point for support.

'Ah, my giant friend, with us once more!'

'You must find my weakness frustrating,' Karsa grumbled.

'To be expected, all things considered,' Torvald said, moving among the supplies now. 'I've found food. Come and eat, Karsa, while I tell you of my discoveries.'

The Teblor slowly made his way down the sloping deck.

Torvald drew out a brick-shaped loaf of dark bread. 'I've found a dory, and oars to go along with a sail, so we won't remain victims to this endless calm. We've water for a week and a half, if we're sparing, and we won't go hungry no matter how fast your appetite comes back . . .'

Karsa took the bread from the Daru's hand and began tearing off small chunks. His teeth felt slightly loose, and he was not confident of attempting anything beyond gentle chewing. The bread was rich and moist, filled with morsels of sweet fruit and tasting of honey. His first swallow left him struggling to keep it down. Torvald handed him a skin filled with water, then resumed his monologue.

'The dory's got benches enough for twenty or so – spacious for lowlanders but we'll need to knock one loose to give your legs some room. If you lean over the gunnel you can see it for yourself. I've been busy loading what we'll need. We could explore some of the other ships if you like, though we've more than enough—'

'No need,' Karsa said. 'Let us leave this place as quickly as possible.'

Torvald's eyes narrowed on the Teblor for a moment, then the Daru nodded. 'Agreed. Karsa, you say you did not call upon that storm. Very well. I shall have to believe you – that you've no recollection of having done so, in any case. But I was wondering, this cult of yours, these Seven Faces in the Rock or however they're called. Do they claim a warren for themselves? A realm other than the one you and I live in, where they exist?'

Karsa swallowed another mouthful of bread. 'I had heard nothing of these warrens you speak of, Torvald Nom. The Seven dwell in the rock, and in the dreamworld of the Teblor.'

'Dreamworld . . .' Torvald waved a hand. 'Does any of this look like that dreamworld, Karsa?'

'No.'

'What if it had been . . . flooded?'

Karsa scowled. 'You remind me of Bairoth Gild. Your words make no sense. The Teblor dreamworld is a place of no hills, where mosses and lichens cling to half-buried boulders, where snow makes low dunes sculpted by cold winds. Where strange brown-haired beasts run in packs in the distance . . .'

'Have you visited it yourself, then?'

Karsa shrugged. 'These are descriptions given by the shamans.' He hesitated, then said, 'The place I visited . . .' He trailed off, then shook his head. 'Different. A place of . . . of coloured mists.'

'Coloured mists. And were your gods there?'

'You are not Teblor. I have no need to tell you more. I have spoken too much already.'

'Very well. I was just trying to determine where we were.'

'We are on a sea, and there is no land.'

'Well, yes. But which sea? Where's the sun? Why is there no night? No wind? Which direction shall we choose?'

'It does not matter which direction. Any direction.' Karsa rose from where he had been sitting on a bale. 'I have eaten enough for now. Come, let us finish loading, and then leave.'

'As you say, Karsa.'

He felt stronger with each passing day, lengthening his turns at the oars each time he took over from Torvald Nom. The sea was shallow, and more than once the dory ground up onto shoals, though fortunately these were of sand and so did little to damage the hull. They had seen nothing of the huge catfish, nor any other life in the water or in the sky, though the occasional piece of driftwood drifted past, devoid of bark or leaf.

As Karsa's strength returned, their supply of food quickly dwindled, and though neither spoke of it, despair had become an invisible passenger, a third presence that silenced the Teblor and the Daru, that shackled them as had their captors of old, and the ghostly chains grew heavier.

In the beginning they had marked out days based on the balance of sleep and wakefulness, but the pattern soon collapsed as Karsa took to rowing through Torvald's periods of sleep in addition to relieving the weary Daru at other times. It became quickly evident that the Teblor required less rest, whilst Torvald seemed to need ever more.

They were down to the last cask of water, which held only a third of its capacity. Karsa was at the oars, pulling the undersized sticks in broad, effortless sweeps through the murky swells. Torvald lay huddled beneath the sail, restless in his sleep.

The ache was almost gone from Karsa's shoulders, though pain lingered in his hips and legs. He had fallen into a pattern of repetition empty of thought, unaware of the passage of time, his only concern that of maintaining a straight course – as best as he could determine, given the lack of reference points. He had naught but the dory's own wake to direct him.

Torvald's eyes opened, bloodshot and red-rimmed. He had long ago lost his loquaciousness. Karsa suspected the man was sick – they'd not had a conversation in some time. The Daru slowly sat up.

Then stiffened. 'We've company,' he said, his voice cracking.

Karsa shipped the oars and twisted round in his seat. A large, three-masted, black ship was bearing down on them, twin banks of oars flashing dark over the milky water. Beyond it, on the horizon's very edge, ran a dark, straight line. The Teblor collected his sword then slowly stood.

'That's the strangest coast I've ever seen,' Torvald muttered. 'Would that we'd reached it without the company.'

'It is a wall,' Karsa said. 'A straight wall, before which lies some kind of beach.' He returned his gaze to the closing ship. 'It is like those that had been beset by the raiders.'

'So it is, only somewhat bigger. Flagship, is my guess, though I see no flag.'

They could see figures now, crowding the high forecastle. Tall, though not as tall as Karsa, and much leaner.

'Not human,' Torvald muttered. 'Karsa, I do not think they will be friendly. Just a feeling, mind you. Still . . .'

'I have seen one of them before,' the Teblor replied. 'Half spilled out from the belly of the catfish.'

'That beach is rolling with the waves, Karsa. It's flotsam. Must be two, three thousand paces of it. The wreckage of an entire world. As I suspected, this sea doesn't belong here.'

'Yet there are ships.'

'Aye, meaning they don't belong here, either.'

Karsa shrugged his indifference to that observation. 'Have you a weapon, Torvald Nom?'

'A harpoon . . . and a mallet. You will not try to talk first?'

Karsa said nothing. The twin banks of oars had lifted

from the water and now hovered motionless over the waves as the huge ship slid towards them. The oars dipped suddenly, straight down, the water churning as the ship slowed, then came to a stop.

The dory thumped as it made contact with the hull on the port side, just beyond the prow.

A rope ladder snaked down, but Karsa, his sword slung over a shoulder, was already climbing up the hull, there being no shortage of handholds. He reached the forecastle rail and swung himself up and over it. His feet found the deck and he straightened.

A ring of grey-skinned warriors faced him. Taller than lowlanders, but still a head shorter than the Teblor. Curved sabres were scabbarded to their hips, and much of their clothing was made of some kind of hide, short-haired, dark and glistening. Their long brown hair was intricately braided, hanging down to frame angular, multihued eyes. Behind them, down amidships, there was a pile of severed heads, a few lowlander but most similar in features to the grey-skinned warriors, though with skins of black.

Ice rippled up Karsa's spine as he saw countless eyes among those severed heads shift towards him.

One of the grey-skinned warriors snapped something, his expression as contemptuous as his tone.

Behind Karsa, Torvald reached the railing.

The speaker seemed to be waiting for some sort of response. As the silence stretched, the faces on either side twisted into sneers. The spokesman barked out a command, pointed to the deck.

'Uh, he wants us to kneel, Karsa,' Torvald said. 'I think maybe we should—'

'I would not kneel when chained,' Karsa growled. 'Why would I do so now?'

'Because I count sixteen of them – and who knows how many more are below. And they're getting angrier—'

'Sixteen or sixty,' Karsa cut in. 'They know nothing of fighting Teblor.'

'How can you—'

Karsa saw two warriors shift gauntleted hands towards sword-grips. The bloodsword flashed out, cut a sweeping horizontal slash across the entire half-circle of grey-skinned warriors. Blood sprayed. Bodies reeled, sprawled backward, tumbling over the low railing and down to the mid-deck.

The forecastle was clear apart from Karsa and, a pace behind him, Torvald Nom.

The seven warriors who had been on the mid-deck drew back as one, then, unsheathing their weapons, they edged forward.

'They were within my reach,' Karsa answered the Daru's question. 'That is how I know they know nothing of fighting a Teblor. Now, witness while I take this ship.' With a bellow he leapt down into the midst of the enemy.

The grey-skinned warriors were not lacking in skill, yet it availed them naught. Karsa had known the loss of freedom; he would not accept such again. The demand to kneel before these scrawny, sickly creatures had triggered in him seething fury.

Six of the seven warriors were down; the last one, shouting, had turned about and was running towards the doorway at the other end of the mid-deck. He paused long enough to drag a massive harpoon from a nearby rack, spinning and flinging it at Karsa.

The Teblor caught it in his left hand.

He closed on the fleeing man, cutting him down at the doorway's threshold. Ducking and reversing the weapons in his hands – the harpoon now in his right and the bloodsword in his left – he plunged into the gloom of the passage beyond the doorway.

Two steps down, into a wide galley with a wooden table in its centre. A second doorway at the opposite end, a narrow passage beyond, lined by berths, then an ornate door that squealed as Karsa shoved it aside.

Four attackers, a fury of blows exchanged, Karsa blocking with the harpoon and counter-attacking with the bloodsword. In moments, four broken bodies dying on the cabin's gleaming wooden floor. A fifth figure, seated in a chair on the other side of the room, hands raised, sorcery swirling into the air.

With a snarl, Karsa surged forward. The magic flashed, sputtered, then the harpoon's point punched into the figure's chest, tore through and drove into the chair's wood backing. A look of disbelief frozen on the grey face, eyes locking with Karsa's own one last time, before all life left them.

'Urugal! Witness a Teblor's rage!'

Silence following his ringing words, then the slow pat of blood dripping from the sorcerer's chair onto the rug. Something cold rippled through Karsa, the breath of someone unknown, nameless, but filled with rage. Growling, he shrugged it off, then looked around. High-ceilinged for lowlanders, the ship's cabin was all of the same black wood. Oil lanterns glimmered from sconces on the walls. On the table were maps and charts, the drawings on them illegible as far as the Teblor was concerned.

A sound from the doorway.

Karsa turned.

Torvald Nom stepped within, scanning the sprawled corpses, then fixing his gaze on the seated figure with the spear still impaling it. 'You needn't worry about the oarsmen,' he said.

'Are they slaves? Then we shall free them.'

'Slaves?' Torvald shrugged. 'I don't think so. They wear no chains, Karsa. Mind you, they have no heads, either. As I said, I don't think we have to concern ourselves with them.' He strode forward to examine the maps on the table. 'Something tells me these hapless bastards you just killed were as lost as us—'

'They were the victors in the battle of the ships.'

'Little good it did them.'

Karsa shook the blood from his sword, drew a deep breath. 'I kneel to no-one.'

'I could've knelt twice and that might have satisfied them. Now, we're as ignorant as we were before seeing this ship. Nor can the two of us manage a craft of this size.'

'They would have done to us as was done to the oarsmen,' Karsa asserted.

'Possibly.' He swung his attention on one of the corpses at his feet, slowly crouched. 'Barbaric-looking, these ones – uh, by Daru standards, that is. Sealskin – true seafarers, then – and strung claws and teeth and shells. The one in the captain's chair was a mage?'

'Yes. I do not understand such warriors. Why not use swords or spears? Their magic is pitiful, yet they seem so sure of it. And look at his expression—'

'Surprised, yes,' Torvald murmured. He glanced back at Karsa. 'They're confident because sorcery usually works. Most attackers don't survive getting hit by magic. It rips them apart.'

Karsa made his way back to the doorway. After a moment Torvald followed.

They returned to the mizzen deck. Karsa began stripping the corpses lying about, severing ears and tongues before tossing the naked bodies overboard.

The Daru watched for a time, then he moved to the decapitated heads. 'They've been following everything you do,' he said to Karsa, 'with their eyes. It's too much to bear.' He removed the hide wrapping of a nearby bundle and folded it around the nearest severed head, then tied it tight. 'Darkness would better suit them, all things considered . . .'

Karsa frowned. 'Why do you say that, Torvald Nom? Which would you prefer, the ability to see things around you, or darkness?'

'These are Tiste Andii, apart from a few – and those few look far too much like me.'

'Who are these Tiste Andii?'

'Just a people. There are some fighting in Caladan Brood's liberation army on Genabackis. An ancient people, it's said. In any case, they worship Darkness.'

Karsa, suddenly weary, sat down on the steps leading to the forecastle. 'Darkness,' he muttered. 'A place where one is left blind – a strange thing to worship.'

'Perhaps the most realistic worship of all,' the Daru replied, wrapping another severed head. 'How many of us bow before a god in the desperate hope that we can somehow shape our fate? Praying to that familiar face pushes away our terror of the unknown – the unknown being the future. Who knows, maybe these Tiste Andii are the only ones among us all who see the truth, the truth being oblivion.' Keeping his eyes averted, he carefully gathered another black-skinned, long-haired head. 'It's a good thing these poor souls have no throats left to utter sounds, else we find ourselves in a ghastly debate.'

'You doubt your own words, then.'

'Always, Karsa. On a more mundane level, words are like gods – a means of keeping the terror at bay. I will likely have nightmares about this until my aged heart finally gives out. An endless succession of heads, with all-too-cognizant eyes, to wrap up in sealskin. And with each one I tie up, *pop!* Another appears.'

'Your words are naught but foolishness.'

'Oh, and how many souls have *you* delivered unto darkness, Karsa Orlong?'

The Teblor's eyes narrowed. 'I do not think it was darkness that they found,' he replied quietly. After a moment, he looked away, struck silent by a sudden realization. A year ago he would have killed someone for saying what Torvald had just said, had he understood its intent to wound – which in itself was unlikely. A year ago, words had been blunt, awkward things, confined within a simple, if slightly mysterious world. But that flaw had been Karsa's alone – not a characteristic of the Teblor in general – for Bairoth Gild had flung many-edged words at Karsa, a constant source of amusement for the clever warrior though probably dulled by Karsa's own unawareness of their intent.

Torvald Nom's endless words – but no, more than just

that – all that Karsa had experienced since leaving his village – had served as instruction on the complexity of the world. Subtlety had been a venomed serpent slithering unseen through his life. Its fangs had sunk deep many times, yet not once had he become aware of their origin; not once had he even understood the source of the pain. The poison itself had coursed deep within him, and the only answer he gave – when he gave one at all – was of violence, often misdirected, a lashing out on all sides.

Darkness, and living blind. Karsa returned his gaze to the Daru kneeling and wrapping severed heads, there on the mizzen deck. *And who has dragged the cloth from my eyes? Who has awakened Karsa Orlong, son of Synyg? Urugal?* No, not Urugal. He knew that for certain, for the otherworldly rage he had felt in the cabin, that icy breath that had swept through him – that had belonged to his god. A fierce displeasure – to which Karsa had found himself oddly ... indifferent.

The Seven Faces in the Rock never spoke of freedom. The Teblor were their servants. *Their slaves.*

'You look unwell, Karsa,' Torvald said, approaching. 'I am sorry for my last words—'

'There is no need, Torvald Nom,' Karsa said, rising. 'We should return to our—'

He stopped as the first splashes of rain struck him, then the deck on all sides. Milky, slimy rain.

'Uh!' Torvald grunted. 'If this is a god's spit, he's decidedly unwell.'

The water smelled foul, rotten. It quickly coated the ship decks, the rigging and tattered sails overhead, in a thick, pale grease.

Swearing, the Daru began gathering foodstuffs and watercasks to load into their dory below. Karsa completed one last circuit of the decks, examining the weapons and armour he had pulled from the grey-skinned bodies. He found the rack of harpoons and gathered the six that remained.

The downpour thickened, creating murky, impenetrable walls on all sides of the ship. Slipping in the deepening muck, Karsa and Torvald quickly resupplied the dory, then pushed out from the ship's hull, the Teblor at the oars. Within moments the ship was lost from sight, and around them the rain slackened. Five sweeps of the oars and they were out from beneath it entirely, once again on gently heaving seas under a pallid sky. The strange coastline was visible ahead, slowly drawing closer.

On the forecastle of the massive ship, moments after the dory with its two passengers slipped behind the screen of muddy rain, seven almost insubstantial figures rose from the slime. Shattered bones, gaping wounds bleeding nothing, the figures weaved uncertainly in the gloom, as if barely able to maintain their grip on the scene they had entered.

One of them hissed with anger. 'Each time we seek to draw the knot tight—'

'He cuts it,' another finished in a wry, bitter tone.

A third one stepped down to the mizzen deck, kicked desultorily at a discarded sword. 'The failure belonged to the Tiste Edur,' this one pronounced in a rasping voice. 'If punishment must be enacted, it should be in answer to their arrogance.'

'Not for us to demand,' the first speaker snapped. 'We are not the masters in this scheme—'

'Nor are the Tiste Edur!'

'Even so, and we are each given particular tasks. Karsa Orlong survives still, and he must be our only concern—'

'He begins to know doubts.'

'None the less, his journey continues. It falls to us, now, with what little power we are able to extend, to direct his path onward.'

'We've had scant success thus far!'

'Untrue. The Shattered Warren stirs awake once more. The broken heart of the First Empire begins to bleed – less than a trickle at the moment, but soon it will become a flood. We need only set our chosen warrior upon the proper current . . .'

'And is that within our power, limited as it still remains?'

'Let us find out. Begin the preparations. Ber'ok, scatter that handful of otataral dust in the cabin – the Tiste Edur sorcerer's warren remains open and, in this place, it will quickly become a wound . . . a growing wound. The time has not yet come for such unveilings.'

The speaker then lifted its mangled head and seemed to sniff the air. 'We must work quickly,' it announced after a moment. 'I believe we are being hunted.'

The remaining six turned to face the speaker, who nodded in answer to their silent question. 'Yes. There are kin upon our trail.'

The wreckage of an entire land had drawn up alongside the massive stone wall. Uprooted trees, rough-hewn logs, planks, shingles and pieces of wagons and carts were visible amidst the detritus. The verges were thick with matted grasses and rotted leaves, forming a broad plain that twisted, rose and fell on the waves. The wall was barely visible in places, so high was the flotsam, and the level of the water beneath it.

Torvald Nom was positioned at the bow whilst Karsa rowed. 'I don't know how we'll get to that wall,' the Daru said. 'You'd better back the oars now, friend, lest we ground ourselves on that mess – there's catfish about.'

Karsa slowed the dory. They drifted, the hull nudging the carpet of flotsam. After a few moments it became apparent that there was a current, pulling their craft along the edge.

'Well,' Torvald muttered, 'that's a first for this sea. Do you think this is some sort of tide?'

'No,' Karsa replied, his gaze tracking the strange shoreline in the direction of the current. 'It is a breach in the wall.'

'Oh. Can you see where?'

'Yes, I think so.'

The current was tugging them along faster, now.

Karsa continued, 'There is an indentation in the shoreline, and many trees and logs jammed where the wall should be – can you not hear the roar?'

'Aye, now I can.' Tension rode the Daru's words. He straightened at the bow. 'I see it. Karsa, we'd better—'

'Yes, it is best we avoid this.' The Teblor repositioned himself at the oars. He drew the dory away from the verge. The hull tugged sluggishly beneath them, began twisting. Karsa leaned his weight into each sweep, struggling to regain control. The water swirled around them.

'Karsa!' Torvald shouted. 'There's people – near the breach! I see a wrecked boat!'

The breach was on the Teblor's left as he pulled the dory across the current. He looked to where Torvald was pointing, and, after a moment, he bared his teeth. 'The slavemaster and his men.'

'They're waving us over.'

Karsa ceased sweeping with his left oar. 'We cannot defeat this current,' he announced, swinging the craft around. 'The further out we proceed, the stronger it becomes.'

'I think that's what happened to Silgar's boat – they managed to ground it just this side of the mouth, stoving it in, in the process. We should try to avoid a similar fate, Karsa, if we can, that is.'

'Then keep an eye out for submerged logs,' the Teblor said as he angled the dory closer to shore. 'Also, are the lowlanders armed?'

'Not that I can see,' Torvald replied after a moment. 'They look to be in, uh, in pretty bad condition. They're perched on a small island of logs. Silgar, and Damisk, and one other . . . Borrug, I think. Gods, Karsa, they're starved.'

'Take a harpoon,' the Teblor growled. 'That hunger could well drive them to desperation.'

'A touch shoreward, Karsa, we're almost there.'

There was a soft crunch from the hull, then a grinding, stuttering motion as the current sought to drag them along the verge. Torvald clambered out, ropes in one hand and harpoon in the other. Beyond him, Karsa saw as he turned about, huddled the three Nathii lowlanders, making no move to help and, if anything, drawing back as far as they could manage on the tangled island. The breach's roar was a still-distant thundering, though closer at hand were ominous cracks, tearing and shifting noises – the logjam was coming loose.

Torvald made fast the dory with a skein of lines tied to various branches and roots. Karsa stepped ashore, drawing his bloodsword, his eyes levelling on Silgar.

The slavemaster attempted to retreat further.

Near the three emaciated lowlanders lay the remains of a fourth, his bones picked clean.

'Teblor!' Silgar implored. 'You must listen to me!'

Karsa slowly advanced.

'I can save us!'

Torvald tugged at Karsa's arm. 'Wait, friend, let's hear the bastard.'

'He will say anything,' Karsa growled.

'Even so—'

Damisk Greydog spoke. 'Karsa Orlong, listen! This island is being torn apart – we all need your boat. Silgar's a mage – he can open a portal. But not if he's drowning. Understand? He can take us from this realm!'

'Karsa,' Torvald said, weaving as the logs shifted under him, his grip on the Teblor's arm tightening.

Karsa looked down at the Daru beside him. 'You trust Silgar?'

'Of course not. But we've no choice – we'd be unlikely to survive plunging through that breach in the dory. We don't even know this wall's height – the drop on the other side could be endless. Karsa, we're armed and they're not – besides, they're too weak to cause us trouble, you can see that, can't you?'

Silgar screamed as a large section of the logjam sank away immediately behind him.

Scowling, Karsa sheathed his sword. 'Begin untying the boat, Torvald.' He waved at the lowlanders. 'Come, then. But know this, Slavemaster, any sign of treachery from you and your friends will be picking your bones next.'

Damisk, Silgar and Borrug scrambled forward.

The entire section of flotsam was pulling away, breaking up along its edges as the current swept it onward. Clearly, the breach was expanding, widening to the pressure of an entire sea.

Silgar climbed in and crouched down beside the dory's prow. 'I shall open a portal,' he announced, his voice a rasp. 'I can only do so but once—'

'Then why didn't you leave a long time ago?' Torvald demanded, as he slipped the last line loose and clambered back aboard.

'There was no path before – out on the sea. But now, here – someone has opened a gate. Close. The fabric is . . . weakened. I've not the skill to do such a thing myself. But I can follow.'

The dory scraped free of the crumbling island, swung wildly into the sweeping current. Karsa pushed and pulled with the oars to angle their bow into the torrential flow.

'Follow?' Torvald repeated. 'Where?'

To that Silgar simply shook his head.

Karsa abandoned the oars and made his way to the stern, taking the tiller in both hands.

They rode the tumbling, churning sea of wreckage towards the breach. Where the wall had given way there was an ochre cloud of mist as vast and high as a thunderhead. Beyond it, there seemed to be nothing at all.

Silgar was making gestures with both hands, snapping them out as would a blind man seeking a door latch. Then he jabbed a finger to the right. 'There!' he shrieked, swinging a wild look on Karsa. 'There! Angle us there!'

The place Silgar pointed towards looked no different

from anywhere else. Immediately beyond it, the water simply vanished – a wavering line that was the breach itself. Shrugging, Karsa pushed on the tiller. Where they went over mattered little to him. If Silgar failed they would plunge over, falling whatever distance, to crash amidst a foaming maelstrom that would kill them all.

He watched as everyone but Silgar hunkered down, mute with terror.

The Teblor smiled. 'Urugal!' he bellowed, half rising as the dory raced for the edge.

Darkness swallowed them.

And then they were falling.

A loud, explosive crack. The tiller's handle split under Karsa's hands, then the stern hammered into him from behind, throwing the Teblor forward. He struck water a moment later, the impact making him gasp – taking in a mouthful of salty sea – before plunging into the chill blackness.

He struggled upward until his head broke the surface, but there was no lessening of the darkness, as if they'd fallen down a well, or had appeared within a cave. Nearby, someone was coughing helplessly, whilst a little farther off another survivor was thrashing about.

Wreckage brushed up against Karsa. The dory had shattered, though the Teblor was fairly certain that the fall had not been overly long – they had arrived at a height of perhaps two adult warriors combined. Unless the boat had struck something, it should have survived.

'Karsa!'

Still coughing, Torvald Nom arrived alongside the Teblor. The Daru had found the shaft of one of the oars, over which he had draped his arms. 'What in Hood's name do you think happened?'

'We passed through that sorcerous gate,' Karsa explained. 'That should be obvious, for we are now somewhere else.'

'Not as simple as that,' Torvald replied. 'The blade of this oar – here, look at the end.'

216

Finding himself comfortably buoyant in this salty water, it took only a moment for Karsa to swim to the end of the shaft. It had been cut through, as if by a single blow from an iron sword such as the lowlanders used. He grunted.

The distant thrashing sounds had drawn closer. From much farther away, Damisk's voice called out.

'Here!' Torvald shouted back.

A shape loomed up beside them. It was Silgar, clinging to one of the water casks.

'Where are we?' Karsa asked the slavemaster.

'How should I know?' the Nathii snapped. 'I did not fashion the gate, I simply made use of it – and it had mostly closed, which is why the floor of the boat did not come with us. It was sheared clean off. None the less, I believe we are in a sea, beneath an overcast sky. Were there no ambient light, we'd not be able to see each other right now. Alas, I can hear no coast, though it's so calm there might be no waves to brush the shoreline.'

'Meaning we could be within a dozen strokes and not know it.'

'Yes. Fortunately for us, it is a rather warm sea. We must simply await dawn—'

'Assuming there is one,' Torvald said.

'There is,' Silgar asserted. 'Feel the layers in this water. It's colder down where our feet are. So a sun has looked down upon this sea, I am certain of it.'

Damisk swam into view, struggling with Borrug, who seemed to be unconscious. As he reached out to take hold of the water cask Silgar pushed him back, then kicked himself further away.

'Slavemaster!' Damisk gasped.

'This cask barely holds my weight as it is,' Silgar hissed. 'It's near filled with fresh water – which we're likely to need. What is the matter with Borrug?'

Torvald moved along to give Damisk a place at the oar shaft. The tattooed guard attempted to drape Borrug's arms over it as well and Torvald drew closer once more to help.

'I don't know what's wrong with him,' Damisk said. 'He may have struck his head, though I can find no wound. He was babbling at first, floundering about, then he simply fell unconscious and nearly slipped under. I was lucky to reach him.'

Borrug's head kept lolling beneath the surface.

Karsa reached out and collected the man's wrists. 'I will take him,' he snarled, turning about and dragging the man's arms around his neck.

'A light!' Torvald suddenly shouted. 'I saw a light – there!'

The others swung round.

'I see nothing,' Silgar growled.

'I did,' Torvald insisted. 'It was dim. Gone now. But I saw it—'

'Likely an overwrought imagination,' Silgar said. 'Had I the strength, I'd open my warren—'

'I know what I saw,' the Daru said.

'Lead us, then, Torvald Nom,' Karsa said.

'It could be in the wrong direction!' Silgar hissed. 'We are safer to wait—'

'Then wait,' Karsa replied.

'I have the fresh water, not you—'

'A good point. I shall have to kill you, then, since you have decided to stay here. We might need that water, after all. You won't, because you will be dead.'

'Teblor logic,' Torvald chuckled, 'is truly wonderful.'

'Very well, I will follow,' Silgar said.

The Daru set off at a slow but steady pace, kicking beneath the surface as he pulled the oar shaft along. Damisk kept one hand on the length of wood, managing a strange motion with his legs that resembled that of a frog.

Gripping Borrug's wrists in one hand, Karsa moved into their wake. The unconscious lowlander's head rested on his right shoulder, his knees bumping against the Teblor's thighs.

Off to one side, feet thrashing, Silgar propelled the water

cask along. Karsa could see that the cask was far less filled than the slavemaster had claimed – it could have easily borne them all.

The Teblor himself felt no need. He was not particularly tired, and it seemed that he possessed a natural buoyancy superior to that of the lowlanders. With each indrawn breath, his shoulders, upper arms and the upper half of his chest rose above the water. And apart from Borrug's knees constantly fouling Karsa's kicking, the lowlander's presence was negligible . . .

There was, he realized, something odd about those knees. He paused, reached down.

Both legs were severed clean just beneath the kneecaps, the water warm in their immediate wakes.

Torvald had glanced back. 'What's wrong?' he asked.

'Do you think there are catfish in these waters?'

'I doubt it,' the Daru replied. 'That was fresh water, after all.'

'Good,' Karsa grunted, resuming his swim.

There was no recurrence of the light Torvald had seen. They continued on in the unrelieved darkness, through perfectly calm water.

'This is foolish,' Silgar pronounced after a time. 'We exhaust ourselves for no purpose—'

Torvald called, 'Karsa, why did you ask about the catfish?'

Something huge and rough-skinned rose up to land on Karsa's back, its massive weight driving him under. Borrug's wrists were torn from his grip, the arms whipping back and vanishing. Pushed more than a warrior's height beneath the surface, Karsa twisted round. One of his kicking feet collided with a solid, unyielding body. He used the contact to propel himself away and back towards the surface.

Even as he reached it – bloodsword in his hands – he saw, less than a body length distant, an enormous grey fish, its jagged-toothed mouth closing about the little that remained visible of Borrug. Lacerated head, shoulders and flopping arms. The fish's wide head thrashed wildly back and forth, its strange saucer-like eyes flashing as if lit from within.

There was screaming behind Karsa and he turned. Both Damisk and Silgar were kicking wildly in an effort to escape. Torvald was on his back, the oar held tight in his hands, his legs kicking beneath the surface – he alone was making no noise, though his face was twisted with fear.

Karsa faced the fish once more. It seemed to be having trouble swallowing Borrug – one of the man's arms was lodged crossways. The fish itself was positioned close to vertical in the water, ripping its head back and forth.

Growling, Karsa swam towards it.

Borrug's arm came free even as the Teblor arrived, the corpse disappearing within the maw. Taking a deep breath and kicking hard, Karsa half rose out of the water, his bloodsword a curving spray as it chopped down into the fish's snout.

Warm blood spattered Karsa's forearms.

The fish seemed to fling its entire body backward.

Karsa lunged closer, closing his legs around the creature's body just beneath the flanking flippers. The fish twisted away at the contact, but could not drag itself free of Karsa's tightening grip.

The Teblor reversed his sword and plunged it deep into the beast's belly, ripped it downward.

The water was suddenly hot with blood and bile. The fish's body became a dead weight, dragging Karsa downward. He sheathed his sword; then, as he and the fish sank beneath the surface, he reached down into the gaping wound. One hand closed on the thigh of Borrug – a shredded mass of flesh – and the fingers dug in to close around bone.

Karsa pulled the lowlander through a cloud of milky, eye-stinging fluid, then, drawing the body with him, returned to the surface.

Torvald was shouting now. Turning, Karsa saw the Daru,

standing in waist-deep water, both arms waving. Near him, Silgar and Damisk were wading their way onto some kind of shore.

Dragging Borrug with him, Karsa made his way forward. A half-dozen strokes and his feet thumped and scraped on a sandy bottom. He stood, still holding one of Borrug's legs. Moments later, he was on the beach.

The others sat or knelt on the pale strip of sand, regaining their breaths.

Dropping the body onto the beach, Karsa remained standing, his head tilted back as he sniffed the warm, sultry air. There was heavy, lush foliage beyond the strand's shell-cluttered high-tide line. The buzz and whine of insects, a faint rustle as something small moved across dry seaweed.

Torvald crawled close. 'Karsa, the man's dead. He was dead when the shark took him—'

'So that was a shark. The sailors on the Malazan ship spoke of sharks.'

'Karsa, when a shark swallows someone you don't go after the poor bastard. He's finished—'

'He was in my care,' Karsa rumbled. 'The shark had no right to him, whether he was dead or alive.'

Silgar was on his feet a few paces away. At Karsa's words he laughed, the sound high-pitched, then said, 'From a shark's belly to seagulls and crabs! Borrug's pathetic spirit no doubt thanks you, Teblor!'

'I have delivered the lowlander,' Karsa replied, 'and now return him to your care, Slavemaster. If you wish to leave him for seagulls and crabs, that is for you to decide.' He faced the dark sea once more, but could see no sign of the dead shark.

'No-one would believe me,' Torvald muttered.

'Believe what, Torvald Nom?'

'Oh, I was imagining myself as an old man, years from now, sitting in Quip's Bar in Darujhistan, telling this tale. I saw it with my own eyes, and even I am having trouble believing it. You were halfway out of the water when you swung that sword down – helps having four lungs, I suppose. Even so . . .' he shook his head.

Karsa shrugged. 'The catfish were worse,' he said. 'I did not like the catfish.'

'I suggest,' Silgar called out, 'we get some sleep. Come the dawn, we will discover what there is to discover of this place. For now, thank Mael that we are still alive.'

'Forgive me,' Torvald said, 'but I'd rather give thanks to a stubborn Teblor warrior than to any sea god.'

'Then your faith is sorely misplaced,' the slavemaster sneered, turning away.

Torvald slowly climbed upright. 'Karsa,' he murmured, 'you should know that Mael's chosen beast of the sea is the shark. I've no doubt at all that Silgar was indeed praying hard while we were out there.'

'It does not matter,' Karsa replied. He drew a deep breath of jungle-scented air, slowly released it. 'I am on land, and I am free, and now I shall walk along this beach, and so taste something of this new land.'

'I will join you, then, friend, for I believe the light I saw was to our right, slightly above this beach, and I would investigate.'

'As you like, Torvald Nom.'

They began walking along the strand.

'Karsa, neither Silgar nor Damisk possesses a shred of decency. I, however, do. A small shred, granted, but one none the less. Thus: thank you.'

'We have saved each other's lives, Torvald Nom, and so I am pleased to call you friend, and to think of you as a warrior. Not a Teblor warrior, of course, but a warrior even so.'

The Daru said nothing for a long time. They had moved well out of sight of Silgar and Damisk. The shelf of land to their right was rising in layers of pale stone, the wave-sculpted wall webbed with creepers from the thick growth clinging to the overhang. A break in the clouds overhead cast faint starlight down, reflecting on the virtually motionless water on their left. The sand underfoot was giving way to smooth, undulating stone.

Torvald touched Karsa's arm and stopped, pointing upslope. 'There,' he whispered.

The Teblor softly grunted. A squat, misshapen tower rose above the tangle of brush. Vaguely square and sharply tapering to end at a flat roof, the tower hunched over the beach, a gnarled black mass. Three-quarters of the way up its seaward-facing side was a deeply inset triangular window. Dull yellow light outlined the shutter's warped slats.

A narrow footpath was visible winding down to the shore, and nearby – five paces beyond the high tide line – lay the collapsed remnants of a fisherboat, the sprung ribs of the hull jutting out to the sides wrapped in seaweed and limned in guano.

'Shall we pay a visit?' Torvald asked.

'Yes,' Karsa replied, walking towards the footpath.

The Daru quickly moved up beside him. 'No trophies, though, right?'

Shrugging, the Teblor said, 'That depends on how we are received.'

'Strangers on a desolate beach, one of them a giant with a sword almost as tall as me. In the dead of night. Pounding on the door. If we're met with open arms, Karsa, it will be a miracle. Worse yet, there's not much likelihood of us sharing a common language—'

'Too many words,' Karsa cut in.

They had reached the base of the tower. There was no entrance on the seaward side. The trail curved round to the other side, a well-trod path of limestone dust. Huge slabs of the yellow rock lay in heaps – many of them appearing to have been dragged in from other places and bearing chisel and cut marks. The tower itself was constructed of identical material, though its gnarled aspect remained a mystery until Karsa and Torvald drew closer.

The Daru reached out and ran his fingers along one of

223

the cornerstones. 'This tower is nothing but fossils,' he murmured.

'What are fossils?' Karsa asked, studying the strange shapes embedded in the stone.

'Ancient life, turned to stone. I imagine scholars have an explanation for how such transformation occurred. Alas, my education was sporadic and, uh, poorly received. Look, this one – it's a massive shell of some sort. And there, those look like vertebrae, from some snake-like beast . . .'

'They are naught but carvings,' Karsa asserted.

A deep rumbling laugh made them swing round. The man standing at the bend in the path ten paces ahead was huge by lowlander standards, his skin so dark as to seem black. He wore no shirt, only a sleeveless vest of heavy mail stiffened by rust. His muscles were vast, devoid of fat, making his arms, shoulders and torso look like they had been fashioned of taut ropes. He wore a belted loincloth of some colourless material. A hat that seemed made of the torn remnant of a hood covered his head, but Karsa could see thick, grey-shot beard covering the lower half of the man's face.

No weapons were visible, not even a knife. His teeth flashed in a smile. 'Screams from the sea, and now a pair of skulkers jabbering in Daru in my tower's front yard.' His head tilted upward slightly to regard Karsa for a moment. 'At first I'd thought you a Fenn, but you're no Fenn, are you?'

'I am Teblor—'

'Teblor! Well, lad, you're a long way from home, aren't you?'

Torvald stepped forward. 'Sir, your command of Daru is impressive, though I am certain I detect a Malazan accent. More, by your colour, I'd hazard you are Napan. Are we then on Quon Tali?'

'You don't know?'

'Alas, sir, I am afraid not.'

The man grunted, then turned back up the trail, 'Carvings, ha!'

Torvald glanced back at Karsa, then, with a shrug, set off after the man.

Karsa followed.

The door was situated on the inland side. The path forked in front of it, one trail leading to the tower and the other to a raised road that ran parallel to the coastline, beyond which was a dark band of forest.

The man pushed open the door and ducked inside.

Both Torvald and Karsa had involuntarily paused at the fork, staring up at the enormous stone skull that formed the lintel above the low doorway. It was as long as the Teblor was tall, running the entire width of the wall. The rows of dagger-like teeth dwarfed even that of a grey bear.

The man reappeared. 'Aye, impressive, isn't it? I've collected most of the bastard's body, too – I should've guessed it would be bigger than I'd first thought, but it was the forearms I found, you see, and they're puny, so there I was picturing a beast no taller than you, Teblor, but with a head of equal size. No wonder they died out, I told myself. Of course, it's mistakes like these that teach a man to be humble, and Hood knows, this one's humbled me good. Come inside; I'm brewing some tea.'

Torvald grinned up at Karsa. 'See what happens when you live alone?'

The two entered the tower.

And were stunned by what awaited them. The tower was hollow, with only a flimsy scaffold projecting out from the seaside wall, just below the lone window. The floor was a thick, crunching carpet of stone chips. Weathered poles reared up on all sides at various angles, joined by cross-beams here and there and festooned with ropes. This wooden framework surrounded the lower half of a stone skeleton, standing upright on two thick-boned legs – reminiscent of a bird's – with three-toed, hugely taloned feet. The tail was a chain of vertebrae, snaking up one of the walls.

The man was seated near a brick-lined hearth beneath

the scaffold, stirring one of the two pots resting in the coals. 'See my problem? I built the tower thinking there'd be plenty of room to reconstruct this leviathan. But I kept uncovering more and more of those Hood-damned ribs – I can't even attach the shoulder blades, much less the fore-arms, neck and head. I was planning on dismantling the tower eventually, anyway, so I could get at the skull. But now all my plans are awry, and I'm going to have to extend the roof, which is tricky. Damned tricky.'

Karsa moved over to the hearth, bent down to sniff at the other pot, wherein a thick, soupy liquid bubbled.

'Wouldn't try that,' the man said. 'It's what I use to fix the bones together. Sets harder than the stone itself, takes any weight once it's cured.' He found some extra clay cups and ladled the herbal tea into them. 'Makes good dishware, too.'

Torvald dragged his eyes from the huge skeleton looming over them and approached to collect his cup. 'I am named Torvald Nom—'

'Nom? Of the House of Nom? Darujhistan? Odd, I'd figured you for a bandit – before you became a slave, that is.'

Torvald threw Karsa a grimace. 'It's these damned shackle scars – we need a change of clothes, something with long sleeves. And moccasins that go up to the knees.'

'Plenty of escaped slaves about,' the Napan said, shrugging. 'I wouldn't worry too much about it.'

'Where are we?'

'North coast of Seven Cities. The sea yonder is the Otataral Sea. The forest covering this peninsula is called the A'rath. Nearest city is Ehrlitan, about fifteen days on foot west of here.'

'And what is your name, if I may ask?'

'Well, Torvald Nom, there's no easy answer to that question. Locally, I'm known as Ba'ienrok, which is Ehrlii for "Keeper". Beyond that, in the fierce and unpleasant world, I'm not known at all, except as someone who died long ago, and that's how I plan on keeping it. So, Ba'ienrok or Keeper, take your pick.'

'Keeper, then. What is in this tea? There are flavours I do not recognize, and from someone born and raised in Darujhistan, that detail alone is close to impossible.'

'A collection of local plants,' Keeper replied. 'Don't know their names, don't know their properties, but I like their taste. I long ago weeded out the ones that made me sick.'

'Delighted to hear that,' Torvald said. 'Well, you seem to know a lot about that fierce and unpleasant world out there. Daru, Teblor . . . That wrecked boat down below, was that yours?'

Keeper slowly rose. 'Now you're making me nervous, Torvald. It's not good when I get nervous.'

'Uh, I'll ask no more questions, then.'

Keeper jabbed a fist against Torvald's shoulder, rocking the Daru back a step. 'Wise choice, lad. I think I can get along with you, though I'd feel better if your silent friend said a thing or two.'

Rubbing at his shoulder, Torvald turned to Karsa.

The Teblor bared his teeth. 'I have nothing to say.'

'I like men with nothing to say,' Keeper said.

'Lucky for you,' Karsa growled. 'For you would not wish me as an enemy.'

Keeper refilled his cup. 'I've had worse than you, Teblor, in my day. Uglier and bigger and meaner. Of course, they're mostly all dead, now.'

Torvald cleared his throat. 'Alas, age takes us all, eventually.'

'That it does, lad,' Keeper said. 'Too bad none of them had the chance to see for themselves. Now, I expect you're hungry. But to eat my food, you've got to do something to earn it first. And that means helping me dismantle the roof. Shouldn't take more than a day or two.'

Karsa looked around. 'I will not work for you. Digging up bones and putting them together is a waste of time. It is pointless.'

Keeper went perfectly still. 'Pointless?' He barely breathed the word.

'It's that woeful streak of Teblor pragmatism,' Torvald said hastily. 'That and a warrior's blunt manners, which often come across as unintentionally rude—'

'Too many words,' Karsa cut in. 'This man wastes his life with stupid tasks. When I decide I am hungry, I will take food.'

Though the Teblor was anticipating a violent reaction from Keeper, and though Karsa's hand was close to the grip of his bloodsword, he was unable to avoid the blurred fist that lashed out, connecting with his lower ribs on his right side. Bones cracked. The air in his lungs exploded outward. Sagging, Karsa staggered back, incapable of drawing breath, a flood of pain darkening his vision.

He had never been hit so hard in his life. Not even Bairoth Gild had managed to deliver such a blow. Even as consciousness slipped from him, he swung a look of astonished, unfeigned admiration on Keeper. Then he collapsed.

When he awoke, sunlight was streaming through the open doorway. He found himself lying in the stone chips. The air was filled with mortar dust, descending from above. Groaning with the pain of cracked ribs, Karsa slowly sat up. He could hear voices from up near the tower's ceiling.

The bloodsword still hung from its straps on his back. The Teblor leaned against the stone leg bones of the skeleton as he climbed to his feet. Glancing up, he saw Torvald and Keeper, balanced in the wood framework directly beneath the ceiling, which had already been partly dismantled. The Daru looked down.

'Karsa! I would invite you up but I suspect this scaffold wouldn't manage your weight. We've made good progress in any case—'

Keeper interrupted with, 'It'll take his weight. I winched up the entire spine and that weighs a lot more than a lone Teblor. Get up here, lad, we're ready to start on the walls.'

Karsa probed the vaguely fist-shaped bruise covering his lower ribs on his right side. It was painful to draw breath; he was unsure whether he would be able to climb, much less work. At the same time, he was reluctant to show weakness, particularly to that muscle-knotted Napan. Grimacing, he reached up to the nearest crossbeam.

The climb was agonizing, torturously slow. High above, the two lowlanders watched in silence. By the time Karsa reached the walkway beneath the ceiling, dragging himself alongside Keeper and Torvald, he was sheathed in sweat.

Keeper was staring at him. 'Hood take me,' he muttered, 'I was surprised that you managed to stand at all, Teblor. I know that I broke ribs – damn' – he lifted a splinted, bandage-swathed hand – 'I broke bones of my own. It's my temper, you see. It's always been a problem. I don't take insults too well. Best just sit there – we'll manage.'

Karsa sneered. 'I am of the Uryd tribe. Think you that a lowlander's tap concerns me?' He straightened. The ceiling had been a single slab of limestone, slightly projecting beyond the walls. Its removal had involved chiselling away the mortar at the joins, then simply sliding it to one side until it toppled, crashing into pieces down at the foot of the tower. The mortar around the wall's large, rough blocks had been cut away down to the edge of the scaffold. Karsa set his shoulder against one side and pushed.

Both men snatched at the bloodsword's straps as the Teblor toppled forward, a huge section of wall vanishing in front of him. A thunderous concussion from below shook the tower. There was a moment when it seemed that Karsa's weight would drag all three of them over, then Keeper hooked a leg around a pole, grunting as the straps drew taut at the end of one arm. All hung in balance for a heartbeat, then the Napan slowly curled his arm, drawing Karsa back onto the platform.

The Teblor could do nothing to help – he had come close to fainting when he had pushed the stones over, and pain roared through his skull. He slowly sank to his knees.

Gasping, Torvald pulled his hands free of the straps, sat down on the warped boards with a thump.

Keeper laughed. 'Well, that was easy. Good enough, you've both earned breakfast.'

Torvald coughed, then said to Karsa, 'In case you were wondering, I went back down to the beach at dawn, to retrieve Silgar and Damisk. But they weren't where we'd left them. I don't think the slavemaster planned on travelling with us – he likely feared for his life in your company, Karsa, which you have to admit is not entirely unreasonable. I followed their tracks up onto the coast road. They had headed west, suggesting that Silgar knew more of where we are than he'd let on. Fifteen days to Ehrlitan, which is a major port. If they'd gone east, it would have been a month or more to the nearest city.'

'You talk too much,' Karsa said.

'Aye,' Keeper agreed, 'he does. You two have had quite a journey – I now know more of it than I'd care to. No cause for worry, though, Teblor. I only believed half of it. Killing a shark, well, the ones that frequent this coast are the big ones, big enough to prove too much for the dhenrabi. All the small ones get eaten, you see. I've yet to see one off-shore here that's less than twice your height in length, Teblor. Splitting one's head open with a single blow? With a wooden sword? In deep water? And what's that other one? Catfish big enough to swallow a man whole? Hah, a good one.'

Torvald stared at the Napan. 'Both true. As true as a flooded world and a ship with headless Tiste Andii at the oars!'

'Well, I believe all that, Torvald. But the shark and the catfish? Do you take me for a fool? Now, let's climb down and cook up a meal. Let me get a harness on you, Teblor, in case you decide to go to sleep halfway down. We'll follow.'

The flatfish that Keeper cut up and threw into a broth of starchy tubers had been smoked and salted. By the time

Karsa finished his two helpings he was desperately thirsty. Keeper directed them to a natural spring close to the tower, where both he and Torvald went to drink deep of the sweet water.

The Daru then splashed his face and settled down with his back to a fallen palm tree. 'I have been thinking, friend,' he said.

'You should do more of that, instead of talking, Torvald Nom.'

'It's a family curse. My father was even worse. Oddly enough, some lines of the Nom House are precisely opposite – you couldn't get a word out of them even under torture. I have a cousin, an assassin—'

'I thought you had been thinking.'

'Oh, right. So I was. Ehrlitan. We should head there.'

'Why? I saw nothing of value in any of the cities we travelled through on Genabackis. They stink, they're too loud, and the lowlanders scurry about like cliff-mice.'

'It's a port, Karsa. A Malazan port. That means there are ships setting out from it, heading for Genabackis. Isn't it time to go home, friend? We could work for our passage. Me, I'm ready to enter the embrace of my dear family, the long-lost child returned, wiser, almost reformed. As for you, I'd think your tribe would be, uh, delighted to have you back. You've knowledge now, and they are in dire need of that, unless you want what happened to the Sunyd to happen to the Uryd.'

Karsa frowned at the Daru for a moment, then he looked away. 'I shall indeed return to my people. One day. But Urugal guides my steps still – I can feel him. Secrets have power so long as they remain secret. Bairoth Gild's words, to which I gave little thought at the time. But now, that has changed. I am changed, Torvald Nom. Mistrust has taken root in my soul, and when I find Urugal's stone face in my mind, when I feel his will warring with my own, I feel my own weakness. Urugal's power over me lies in what I do not know, in secrets – secrets my own god would keep from me. I have ceased fighting this war within my soul. Urugal guides me and I follow, for our journey is to truth.'

Torvald studied the Teblor with lidded eyes. 'You may not like what you find, Karsa.'

'I suspect you are right, Torvald Nom.'

The Daru stared for a moment longer, then he climbed to his feet and brushed sand from his ragged tunic. 'Keeper has the opinion that it isn't safe around you. He says it's as if you're dragging a thousand invisible chains behind you, and whatever's on the ends of each one of them is filled with venom.'

Karsa felt his blood grow cold within him.

Torvald must have noted a change in the Teblor's expression, for he raised both hands. 'Wait! He only spoke in passing, it was nothing really, friend. He was simply telling me to be careful in your company – as if I didn't already know that. You are Hood's own lodestone – to your enemies, that is. In any case, Karsa, I'd advise you not to cross that man. Pound for pound he's the strongest man I've ever met – and that includes you. Besides, while you've regained some of your old strength, you've a half-dozen broken ribs—'

'Enough words, Torvald Nom. I do not intend to attack Keeper. His vision troubles me, that is all. For I have shared it, in my dreams. Now you understand why I must seek out the truth.'

'Very well.' Torvald lowered his hands, then sighed. 'Still, I'd advise Ehrlitan. We need clothes and—'

'Keeper spoke the truth when he said I am dangerous to be around, Torvald Nom. And that danger is likely to increase. I will join you on the journey to Ehrlitan. Then, I will see to it that you find a ship, so that you may return to your family. When this is done, we shall part ways. I shall, however, keep the truth of your friendship with me.'

The Daru grinned. 'It's settled, then. Ehrlitan. Come, let us return to the tower, so we may give our thanks to Keeper for his hospitality.'

They began making their way along the trail. 'Rest assured,' Torvald continued, 'that I shall hold the truth of your friendship in me as well, though it's a truth no-one else is likely to believe.'

'Why is that?' Karsa asked.

'I was never very good at acquiring friends. Acquaintances, minions and the like – that was easy. But my big mouth—'

'Sends potential friends fleeing. Yes, I understand. Clearly.'

'Ah, now I see. You want to throw me on the first ship just to get away from me.'

'There is that,' Karsa replied.

'In keeping with the pathetic state of my life, it makes sense all right.'

After a moment, as they rounded a bend and came within sight of the tower, Karsa scowled and said, 'Making light of words is still difficult—'

'All that talk of friendship made for a momentary discomfort. You did well to slide away from it.'

'No, for what I would say is this. On the ship, when I hung in chains from the mast, you were my only hold on this world. Without you and your endless words, Torvald Nom, the madness I had feigned would have become a madness in truth. I was a Teblor warleader. I was needed, but I myself did not need. I had followers, but not allies, and only now do I understand the difference. And it is vast. And from this, I have come to understand what it is to possess regrets. Bairoth Gild. Delum Thord. Even the Rathyd, whom I have greatly weakened. When I return on my old path, back into the lands of the Teblor, there are wounds that I shall need to mend. And so, when you say it is time to return to your family, Torvald Nom, I understand and my heart is gladdened.'

Keeper was sitting on a three-legged stool outside the tower's doorway. A large sack with shoulder-straps rested at his feet, along with two stoppered gourds glittering with condensation. He had in his unbandaged hand a small bag, which he tossed towards Torvald as the two men arrived.

The bag jingled as the Daru caught it. Brows lifting, Torvald asked, 'What—'

'Silver jakatas, mostly,' Keeper said. 'Some local coin, too, but those are of very high denomination, so be careful of showing them. Ehrlitan's cutpurses are legendary.'

'Keeper—'

The Napan waved a hand. 'Listen, lad. When a man arranges his own death, he needs to plan ahead. A life of anonymity doesn't come as cheap as you'd imagine. I emptied half of Aren's treasury a day before my tragic drowning. Now, you might manage to kill me and try to find it, but it'd be hopeless. So thank me for my generosity and get on your way.'

'One day,' Karsa said, 'I shall return here and repay you.'

'For the coin or the broken ribs?'

The Teblor simply smiled.

Keeper laughed, then rose and ducked through the doorway. A moment later, they could hear him climbing the frame.

Torvald collected the pack, drawing the straps over his shoulders, then handed one of the gourds to Karsa.

They set off down the road.

CHAPTER FOUR

'Has a drowned Napan's body ever surfaced?'

Empress Laseen to High Mage Tayschrenn
(following the Disappearances)
Life of Empress Laseen
Abelard

There were villages on the coastal road, usually set on the inland side, as if the inhabitants sought nothing from the sea. A scattering of adobe dwellings, flimsy corrals, goats, dogs and dark-skinned figures hidden within swaths of full-length, sun-bleached cloth. Shadowed faces tracked the Teblor and the Daru from doorways but otherwise made no move.

On the fourth day, in the fifth of such villages, they found a merchant's wagon drawn up in the virtually empty market square, and Torvald managed to purchase, for a handful of silver, an antique sword, top-heavy and sharply curved. The merchant had bolts of cloth for sale as well, but nothing already made into clothing. The sword's handle fell apart shortly afterwards.

'I need to find a wood-carver,' Torvald said after a lengthy and rather elaborate string of curses. They were once more walking down the road, the sun overhead fiercely hot in a cloudless sky. The forest had thinned to either side, low, straggly and dusty, allowing them a view of the turquoise water of the Otataral Sea to their right, and the dun tones of the undulating horizon inland. 'And I'd swear that merchant understood Malazan – even as bad as I speak it. He just wouldn't admit to that fact.'

Karsa shrugged. 'The Malazan soldiers in Genabaris said the Seven Cities was going to rebel against their occupiers. This is why the Teblor do not make conquests. Better that the enemy keeps its land, so that we may raid again and again.'

'Not the imperial way,' the Daru responded, shaking his head. 'Possession and control, the two are like insatiable hungers for some people. Oh, no doubt the Malazans have thought up countless justifications for their wars of expansion. It's well known that Seven Cities was a rat's warren of feuds and civil wars, leaving most of the population suffering and miserable and starving under the heels of fat warlords and corrupt priest-kings. And that, with the Malazan conquest, the thugs ended up spiked to the city walls or on the run. And the wilder tribes no longer sweep down out of the hills to deliver mayhem on their more civilized kin. And the tyranny of the priesthoods was shattered, putting an end to human sacrifice and extortion. And of course the merchants have never been richer, or safer on these roads. So, all in all, this land is rife for rebellion.'

Karsa stared at Torvald for a long moment, then said, 'Yes, I can see how that would be true.'

The Daru grinned. 'You're learning, friend.'

'The lessons of civilization.'

'Just so. There's little value in seeking to find reasons for why people do what they do, or feel the way they feel. Hatred is a most pernicious weed, finding root in any kind of soil. It feeds on itself.'

'With words.'

'Indeed, with words. Form an opinion, say it often enough and pretty soon everyone's saying it right back at you, and then it becomes a conviction, fed by unreasoning anger and defended with weapons of fear. At which point, words become useless and you're left with a fight to the death.'

Karsa grunted. 'A fight beyond death, I would say.'

'True enough. Generation after generation.'

'Are all the people of Darujhistan like you, Torvald Nom?'

'More or less. Contentious bastards. We thrive on argument, meaning we never go past the stage of using words. We love words, Karsa, as much as you love cutting off heads and collecting ears and tongues. Walk down any street, in any district, and everyone you speak to will have a different opinion, no matter what the subject. Even the possibility of being conquered by the Malazans. I was thinking a moment ago – that shark, choking on Borrug's body. I suspect, should Darujhistan ever become part of the Malazan Empire, the empire will be like that shark, and Darujhistan like Borrug. We'll choke the beast that swallows us.'

'The shark did not choke for very long.'

'That's because Borrug was too dead to say anything about it.'

'An interesting distinction, Torvald Nom.'

'Well of course. Us Daru are a subtle folk.'

They were approaching another village, this one distinct from the others they had walked through for having a low stone wall encircling it. Three large limestone buildings rose from its centre. Nearby was a pen crowded with goats, loudly complaining in the heat.

'You'd think they'd be out wandering,' Torvald commented as they came closer.

'Unless they are about to be slaughtered.'

'All of them?'

Karsa sniffed the air. 'I smell horses.'

'I don't see any.'

The road narrowed at the wall, spanning a trench before passing through a crumbling, leaning arch. Karsa and

Torvald crossed the bridge and passed under the arch, emerging onto the village's main street.

There was no-one in sight. Not entirely unusual, as the locals usually retreated into their homes at the Teblor's arrival, although in this case the doors of those dwellings were firmly shut, the windows shuttered.

Karsa drew his bloodsword. 'We have walked into an ambush,' he said.

Torvald sighed. 'I think you are right.' He had wrapped his sword's tang in spare leather strapping taken from the pack – a temporary and not entirely successful effort to make the weapon useful. The Daru now slid the scimitar from its cracked wooden scabbard.

At the far end of the street, beyond the large buildings, horsemen now appeared. A dozen, then two, then three. They were covered from head to toe in loose, dark blue clothing, their faces hidden behind scarves. Short, recurved bows, arrows nocked, were trained on Karsa and Torvald.

Horse hoofs from behind made them turn, to see a score more riders coming through the archway, some with bows, others with lances.

Karsa scowled. 'How effective are those tiny bows?' he asked the Daru beside him.

'Sufficient to punch arrows through chain,' Torvald replied, lowering his sword. 'And we're wearing no armour in any case.'

A year ago and Karsa would have attacked none the less. Now, he simply reslung his bloodsword.

The riders behind them closed, then dismounted. A number approached with chains and shackles.

'Beru fend,' Torvald muttered, 'not again.'

Karsa shrugged.

Neither resisted as the shackles were fitted onto their wrists and ankles. There was some difficulty in dealing with the Teblor in this matter – when the shackles clicked into place, they were so tight as to cut off the blood flow to Karsa's hands and feet.

Torvald, watching, said in Malazan, 'Those will need to be changed, lest he lose his appendages—'

'Hardly a consideration,' said a familiar voice from the entrance to one of the larger buildings. Silgar, trailed by Damisk, emerged onto the dusty street. 'You will indeed lose your hands and feet, Karsa Orlong, which should effectively put an end to the threat you pose. Of course, that will do much to diminish your value as a slave, but I am prepared to accept the loss.'

'Is this how you repay saving your miserable lives?' Torvald demanded.

'Why, yes, it is. Repayment. For the loss of most of my men. For the arrest by the Malazans. For countless other outrages which I won't bother listing, since these dear Arak tribesmen are rather far from home, and, given that they're somewhat less than welcome in this territory, they are impatient to depart.'

Karsa could no longer feel his hands and feet. As one of the Arak tribesmen pushed him forward he stumbled, then fell to his knees. A thick knout cracked into the side of his head. Sudden rage gripped the Teblor. He lashed out his right arm, ripping the chain from an Arak's hands, and swung it full into the face of his attacker. The man screamed.

The others closed in then, wielding their knouts – clubs made from black, braided hair – until Karsa fell senseless to the ground.

When he finally regained consciousness, it was dusk. He had been tied to some sort of travois, which was in the process of being unhitched from a train of long-legged, lean horses. Karsa's face was a mass of bruises, his eyes almost swollen shut, his tongue and the inside of his mouth cut and nicked by his own teeth. He looked down at his hands. They were blue, the fingertips darkening to black. They were dead weights at the ends of his limbs, as were his feet.

The tribesmen were making camp a short distance from the coastal road. To the west, at the horizon's very edge, was the dull yellow glow of a city.

A half-dozen small, virtually smokeless fires had been lit by the Arak, using some sort of dung for fuel. Karsa saw, twenty paces distant, the slavemaster and Damisk seated among a group of the tribesmen. The hearth closest to the Teblor was being used to cook suspended skewers of tubers and meat.

Torvald sat nearby, working on something in the gloom. None of the Arak seemed to be paying the two slaves any attention.

Karsa hissed.

The Daru glanced over. 'Don't know about you,' he whispered, 'but I'm damned hot. Got to get out of these clothes. I'm sure you are as well. I'll come over and help you in a moment.' There was the faint sound of ripping seams. 'At last,' Torvald murmured, dragging his tunic free. Naked, he began edging closer to Karsa. 'Don't bother trying to say anything, friend. I'm surprised you can even breathe, with the way they beat you. In any case, I need your clothes.'

He came up alongside the Teblor, spared a glance towards the tribesmen – none of whom had noticed him – then reached up and began tugging at Karsa's tunic. There was but a single seam, and it had already been stretched and sundered in places. As he worked, Torvald continued whispering. 'Small fires. Smokeless. Camping in a basin, despite the insects. Talking in mumbles, very quiet. And Silgar's words earlier, that stupid gloat – had the Arak understood him they would probably have skinned the idiot on the spot. Well, from his stupidity was born my brilliance, as you'll soon see. It'll likely cost me my life, but I swear I'll be here even as a ghost, just to see what comes. Ah, done. Stop shivering, you're not helping things at all.'

He pulled the tattered tunic from Karsa, then took it with him back to his original position. He then tore handfuls of grasses from the ground, until he had two large piles. Bundling both pieces of tunic, he then stuffed them with the grass. Flashing Karsa a grin, he crawled over to the nearest hearth, bundles in tow.

He pushed them up against the glowing fragments of dung, then retreated.

Karsa watched as first one caught fire, then the other. Flames flared into the night, a roar of sparks and snake-like blades of grass lifting high.

Shouts from the Arak, figures rushing over, scrambling for handfuls of earth, but there was little of that in the basin, only pebbles and hard, sun-dried clay. Horse-blankets were found, thrown over the roaring flames.

The panic that then swept through the tribesmen left the two slaves virtually ignored, as the Arak rushed to break camp, repack supplies, saddle their horses. Through it all, Karsa heard a single word repeated numerous times, a word filled with fear.

Gral.

Silgar appeared as the Arak gathered their horses. His face was filled with fury. 'For that, Torvald Nom, you have just forfeited your life—'

'You won't make it to Ehrlitan,' the Daru predicted with a hard grin.

Three tribesmen were approaching, hook-bladed knives in their hands.

'I will enjoy watching your throat cut,' Silgar said.

'The Gral have been after these bastards all this time, Slavemaster. Hadn't you realized that? Now, I've never heard of the Gral, but your Arak friends have one and all pissed onto their hearths, and even a Daru like me knows what that means – they don't expect to live through the night, and not one of them wants to spill his bladder when he dies. Seven Cities taboo, I gather—'

The first Arak reached Torvald, one hand snapping out to take the Daru by the hair, pushing Torvald's head back and lifting the knife.

The ridgeline behind the Arak was suddenly swarming with dark figures, silently sweeping down into the camp.

The night was broken by screams.

The Arak crouched before Torvald snarled and tore the knife across the Daru's throat. Blood spattered the hard clay. Straightening, the tribesman wheeled to run for his horse. He managed not a single step, for a half-dozen shapes came out of the darkness, silent as wraiths. There was a strange whipping sound, and Karsa saw the Arak's head roll from his shoulders. His two companions were both down.

Silgar was already fleeing. As a figure rose before him, he lashed out. A wave of sorcery struck the attacker, dropped the man to the ground, where he writhed in the grip of crackling magic for a moment, before his flesh exploded.

Ululating cries pealed through the air. The same whipping sound sang in the darkness from all sides. Horses screamed.

Karsa dragged his gaze from the scene of slaughter and looked over at Torvald's slumped body. To his amazement, the Daru was still moving, feet kicking furrows in the pebbles, both hands up at his throat.

Silgar returned to Karsa's position, his lean face gleaming with sweat. Damisk appeared behind him and the slave-master gestured the tattooed guard forward.

Damisk held a knife. He quickly cut at the bindings holding Karsa to the travois. 'No easy out for you,' he hissed. 'We're leaving. By warren, and we're taking you with us. Silgar's decided to make you his plaything. A lifetime of torture—'

'Enough babbling!' Silgar snapped. 'They're almost all dead! Hurry!'

Damisk cut the last rope.

Karsa laughed, then managed to form words. 'What would you have me do now? Run?'

Snarling, Silgar moved closer. There was a flare of blue light, then the three of them were plunging into fetid, warm water.

Unable to swim, the weight of his chains dragging him down, Karsa sank into the midnight depths. He felt a tug on his chains, then saw a second flash of lurid light.

His head, then his back, struck hard cobbles. Dazed, he rolled onto his side. Silgar and Damisk, both coughing, knelt nearby. They were on a street, flanked on one side by enormous warehouses, and on the other by stone jetties and moored ships. At the moment, there was no-one else in sight.

Silgar spat, then said, 'Damisk, get those shackles off him – he bears no criminal brand, so the Malazans won't see him as a slave. I won't be arrested again – not after all this. The bastard is ours, but we've got to get him off the street. We've got to hide.'

Karsa watched Damisk crawl to his side, fumbling with keys. Watched as the Nathii unlocked the shackles on his wrists, then his ankles. A moment later, the pain struck as blood flowed back into near-dead flesh. The Teblor screamed.

Silgar unleashed magic once more, a wave that descended on the Teblor like a blanket – that he tore off with unthinking ease, his shrieks slicing into the night air, echoing back from nearby buildings, ringing out across the crowded harbour.

'You there!' Malazan words, a bellow, then the swiftly approaching clash and clatter of armoured soldiers.

'An escaped slave, sirs!' Silgar said hastily. 'We have – as you can see – just recaptured him—'

'Escaped slave? Let's see his brand—'

The last words Karsa registered, as the pain in his hands and feet sent him plummeting into oblivion.

He awoke to Malazan words being spoken directly above him. '... extraordinary. I've never seen natural healing such as this. His hands and feet – those shackles were on for some time, Sergeant. On a normal man I'd be cutting them off right now.'

Another voice spoke, 'Are all Fenn such as this one?'

'Not that I've ever heard. Assuming he's Fenn.'

'Well, what else would he be? He's as tall as two Dal Honese put together.'

'I wouldn't know, Sergeant. Before I was posted here, the only place I knew well was six twisting streets in Li Heng. Even the Fenn was just a name and some vague description about them being giants. Giants no-one's seen for decades at that. The point is, this slave was in bad shape when you first brought him in. Beaten pretty fierce, and someone punched him in the ribs hard enough to crack bones – wouldn't want to cross whoever that was. For all that, the swelling's already down on his face – despite what I've just done to it – and the bruises are damned near fading in front of our eyes.'

Continuing to feign unconsciousness, Karsa listened to the speaker stepping back, then the sergeant asking, 'So the bastard's not in danger of dying, then.'

'Not that I can see.'

'Good enough, Healer. You can return to the barracks.'

'Aye, sir.'

Various movement, boots on flagstones, the clang of an iron-barred door; then, as these echoes dwindled, the Teblor heard, closer by, the sound of breathing.

In the distance there was some shouting, faint and muted by intervening walls of stone, yet Karsa thought he recognized the voice as belonging to the slavemaster, Silgar. The Teblor opened his eyes. A low, smoke-stained ceiling – not high enough to permit him to stand upright. He was lying on a straw-littered, greasy floor. There was virtually no light, apart from a dim glow reaching in from the walkway beyond the barred door.

His face hurt, a strange stinging sensation prickling on his cheeks, forehead and along his jaw.

Karsa sat up.

There was someone else in the small, windowless cell, hunched in a dark corner. The figure grunted and said something in one of the languages of the Seven Cities.

A dull ache remained in Karsa's hands and feet. The inside of his mouth was dry and felt burnt, as if he'd just swallowed hot sand. He rubbed at his tingling face.

A moment later the man tried Malazan, 'You'd likely understand me if you were Fenn.'

'I understand you, but I am not one of these Fenn.'

'I said it sounds like your master isn't enjoying his stay in the stocks.'

'He has been arrested?'

'Of course. The Malazans like arresting people. You'd no brand. At the time. Keeping you as a slave is therefore illegal under imperial law.'

'Then they should release me.'

'Little chance of that. Your master confessed that you were being sent to the otataral mines. You were on a ship out of Genabaris that you'd cursed, said curse then leading to the ship's destruction and the deaths of the crew and the marines. The local garrison is only half-convinced by that tale, but that's sufficient – you're on your way to the island. As am I.'

Karsa rose. The low ceiling forced him to stand hunched over. He made his way, hobbling, to the barred door.

'Aye, you could probably batter it down,' the stranger said. 'But then you'll be cut down before you manage three steps from this gaol. We're in the middle of the Malazan compound. Besides, we're about to be taken outside in any case, to join the prisoners' line chained to a wall. In the morning, they'll march us down to the imperial jetty and load us onto a transport.'

'How long have I been unconscious?'

'The night you were carried in, the day after, the next night. It's now midday.'

'And the slavemaster has been in the stocks all this time?'

'Most of it.'

'Good,' Karsa growled. 'What of his companion? The same?'

'The same.'

'And what crime have you committed?' Karsa asked.

'I consort with dissidents. Of course,' he added, 'I am innocent.'

'Can you not prove that?'

'Prove what?'

'Your innocence.'

'I could if I was.'

The Teblor glanced back at the figure crouched in the corner. 'Are you, by any chance, from Darujhistan?'

'Darujhistan? No, why do you ask?'

Karsa shrugged. He thought back to Torvald Nom's death. There was a coldness surrounding the memory, but he could sense all that it held at bay. The time for surrender, however, was not now.

The barred door was set in an iron frame, the frame fixed to the stone blocks with large iron bolts. The Teblor gave it a shake. Dust sifted out from around the bolts, pattered onto the floor.

'I see you're a man who ignores advice,' the stranger observed.

'These Malazans are careless.'

'Overconfident, I'd suggest. Then again, perhaps not. They've had dealings with Fenn, with Trell, Barghast – a whole host of oversized barbarians. They're tough, and sharper than they let on. They put an otataral anklet on that slavemaster – no magic from him any more—'

Karsa turned. 'What is this "otataral" everyone speaks of?'

'A bane to magic.'

'And it must be mined.'

'Yes. It's usually a powder, found in layers, like sandstone. Resembles rust.'

'We scrape a red powder from cliffsides to make our blood-oil,' the Teblor murmured.

'What is blood-oil?'

'We rub it into our swords, and into our armour. To bring on battle madness, we taste it.'

The stranger was silent for a moment, though Karsa

246

could feel the man's eyes on him. 'And how well does magic work against you?'

'Those who attack me with sorcery usually reveal surprise on their faces . . . just before I kill them.'

'Well now, that is interesting. It is believed that otataral is only found on the single large island east of here. The empire controls its production. Tightly. Their mages learned the hard way during the conquest, in the battles before the T'lan Imass got involved. If not for the T'lan Imass, the invasion would have failed. I have some more advice for you. Reveal nothing of this to the Malazans. If they discover there is another source of otataral, a source they do not control, well, they will send into your home-land – wherever that is – every regiment they possess. They will crush your people. Utterly.'

Karsa shrugged. 'The Teblor have many enemies.'

The stranger slowly sat straighter. 'Teblor? That is what you call yourselves? *Teblor?*' After a moment, he leaned back again, and softly laughed.

'What do you find so amusing?'

An outer door clanged open, and Karsa stepped back from the barred door as a squad of soldiers appeared. The three at the front had unsheathed their swords, while the four behind them held large, cocked crossbows. One of the swordsmen stepped up to the door. He paused upon seeing Karsa. 'Careful,' he called to his companions, 'the savage has awakened.' He studied the Teblor and said, 'Do nothing stupid, Fenn. It matters nothing to us whether you live or die – the mines are crowded enough for them not to miss you. Understand me?'

Karsa bared his teeth, said nothing.

'You there, in the corner, on your feet. It's time for some sunshine.'

The stranger slowly straightened. He was wearing little more than rags. Lean and dark-skinned, his eyes were a startling light blue. 'I demand a proper trial, as is my right under imperial law.'

The guardsman laughed. 'Give it up. You've been identified. We know precisely who you are. Aye, your secret organization is not as seamless as you might think. Betrayed by one of your own – how does that feel? Let's go, you come out first. Jibb, you and Gullstream keep your crossbows on that Fenn – I don't like his smile. Especially now,' he added.

'Oh look,' another soldier said, 'you've confused the poor ox. Bet he doesn't even know his entire face is one big tattoo. Scrawl did good work, though. Best I've seen in a long while.'

'Right,' another drawled, 'and how many escaped prisoner tattoos have you seen, Jibb?'

'Just one, and it's a work of art.'

The source of the stinging sensation on Karsa's face was revealed now. He reached up, seeking to feel something of the pattern, and slowly began tracing lines of slightly raised, damp strips of raw skin. They were not contiguous. He could make no sense of what the tattoo portrayed.

'Shattered,' the other prisoner said as he walked over to the door, which the first guard unlocked and swung open. 'The brand makes your face look like it's been shattered.'

Two guards escorted the man outside, whilst the others, nervously eyeing Karsa, waited for their return. One of the crossbowmen, whose high forehead revealed white blotches – leading the Teblor to speculate that he was the one named Gullstream – leaned back against the opposite wall and said, 'I don't know, I'm thinking Scrawl made it too big – he was ugly enough to start with, now he looks damned terrifying.'

'So what?' another guard drawled. 'There's plenty of hill-grubbing savages that carve up their own faces to frighten weak-kneed recruits like you, Gullstream. Barghast and Semk and Khundryl, but they all break against a Malazan legion just the same.'

'Well, ain't none of them being routed these days, though, are they?'

'That's only because the Fist's cowering in his keep and

wants us all to put 'im to bed every night. Nobleborn officers – what do you expect?'

'Might change when the reinforcements arrive,' Gullstream suggested. 'The Ashok Regiment knows these parts—'

'And that's the problem,' the other retorted. 'If this rebellion actually happens this time, who's to say they won't turn renegade? We could get smilin' throats in our own barracks. It's bad enough with the Red Blades stirrin' things up in the streets . . .'

The guards returned.

'You, Fenn, now it's your turn. Make it easy for us and it'll be easy for you. Walk. Slow. Not too close. And trust me, the mines ain't so bad, considering the alternatives. All right, come forward now.'

Karsa saw no reason to give them trouble.

They emerged onto a sunlit compound. Thick, high walls surrounded the broad parade ground. A number of squat, solid-looking buildings projected out from three of the four walls; along the fourth wall there was a line of prisoners shackled to a heavy chain that ran its entire length, bolted to the foundation stones at regular intervals. Near the heavily fortified gate was a row of stocks, of which only two were occupied – Silgar and Damisk. On the slave-master's right ankle there glinted a copper-coloured ring.

Neither man had lifted his head at Karsa's appearance, and the Teblor considered shouting to attract their attention; instead, he simply bared his teeth at seeing their plight. As the guards escorted him to the line of chained prisoners, Karsa turned to the one named Jibb and spoke in Malazan. 'What will be the slavemaster's fate?'

The man's helmed head jerked up in surprise. Then he shrugged. 'Ain't been decided yet. He claims to be rich back in Genabackis.'

Karsa sneered. 'He can buy his way out from his crimes, then.'

'Not under imperial law – if they're serious crimes, that

is. Might be he'll just be fined. He may be a merchant who deals in flesh, but he's still a merchant. Always best to bleed 'em where it hurts most.'

'Enough jawing, Jibb,' another guard growled.

They approached one end of the line, where oversized shackles had been attached. Once more, Karsa found himself in irons, though these were not tight enough to cause him pain. The Teblor noted that he was beside the blue-eyed native.

The squad checked the fittings one more time, then marched away.

There was no shade, though buckets of well-water had been positioned at intervals down the line. Karsa remained standing for a time, then finally settled down to sit with his back against the wall, matching the position of most of the other prisoners. There was little in the way of conversation as the day slowly dragged on. Towards late afternoon shade finally reached them, though the relief was momentary, as biting flies soon descended.

As the sky darkened overhead, the blue-eyed native stirred, then said in a low voice, 'Giant, I have a proposal for you.'

Karsa grunted. 'What?'

'It's said that the mining camps are corrupt, meaning one can carve out favours – make life easier. The kind of place where it pays to have someone guarding your back. I suggest a partnership.'

Karsa thought about it, then he nodded. 'Agreed. But if you attempt to betray me, I will kill you.'

'I could see no other answer to betrayal,' the man said.

'I am done talking,' Karsa said.

'Good, so am I.'

He thought to ask the man's name, but there would be time enough for that later. For now, he was content to stretch the silence, to give space for his thoughts. It seemed Urugal was willing him to these otataral mines after all. Karsa would have preferred a more direct – a simpler –

journey, such as the one the Malazans had originally intended. *Too many blood-soaked digressions, Urugal. Enough.*

Night arrived. A pair of soldiers appeared with lanterns and sauntered down the line of prisoners, checking the fetters one more time, before heading off to the barracks. From where he slumped, Karsa could see a handful of soldiers stationed at the gate, whilst at least one patrolled the walkway along each wall. Two more stood outside the steps of the headquarters.

The Teblor settled his head against the stone wall and closed his eyes.

Some time later he opened them again. He had slept. The sky was overcast, the compound a mottled pattern of light and darkness. Something had awoken him. He made to stand but a hand stayed him. He looked over to see the native huddled motionless beside him – head lowered as if still asleep. The hand on the Teblor's arm tightened a moment, then withdrew.

Frowning, Karsa settled back. And then he saw.

The guards at the gate were gone, as were those outside the headquarters. Along the wall walkways . . . no-one.

Then, alongside a nearby building – movement, a figure sliding through shadows in silence, followed by another, padding along with far less stealth, one gloved hand reaching up to steady itself every now and then.

The two were making directly for Karsa.

Swathed in black cloth, the lead figure halted a few paces from the wall. The other moved up alongside it, then edged past. Hands lifted, slipped back a black hood—

Torvald Nom.

Bloodstained bandages encircling his neck, the face above it deathly pale and gleaming with sweat, but the Daru was grinning.

He drew up to Karsa's side. 'Time to go, friend,' he whispered, raising something that looked very much like a shackle key.

'Who is with you?' Karsa whispered back.

'Oh, a motley collection indeed. Gral tribesmen here doing the sneaky work, and agents from their main trading partner here in Ehrlitan . . .' His eyes glittered. 'The House of Nom, no less. Oh, aye, the thread of blood between us is thin as a virgin's hair, but it is being honoured none the less. Indeed, with delighted vigour. Now, enough words – as you are wont to say – we don't want to wake anyone else—'

'Too late,' murmured the man chained beside Karsa.

The Gral behind Torvald moved forward, but halted at a strange, elaborate series of gestures from the prisoner.

Torvald grunted. 'That damned silent language.'

'It is agreed,' the prisoner said. 'I will be going with you.'

'And if you wasn't, you'd be sounding the alarm.'

The man said nothing.

After a moment, Torvald shrugged. 'So be it. All this talk and I'm surprised everyone else in this line isn't awake—'

'They would be, only they're all dead.' The prisoner beside Karsa slowly straightened. 'No-one likes criminals. Gral have a particular hatred for them, it seems.'

A second tribesman, who had been moving along the line, reached them. A large, curved knife was in one hand, slick with blood. More hand gestures, then the newcomer sheathed his weapon.

Muttering under his breath, Torvald crouched to unlock Karsa's shackles.

'You are as hard to kill as a Teblor,' Karsa murmured.

'Thank Hood that Arak was distracted at the time. Even so, if not for the Gral, I'd have bled to death.'

'Why did they save you?'

'The Gral like to ransom people. Of course, if they turn out worthless, they kill them. The trading partnership with the House of Nom took precedence over all that, of course.'

Torvald moved on to the other prisoner.

Karsa stood, rubbing his wrists. 'What kind of trade?'

The Daru flashed a grin. 'Brokering the ransoms.'

Moments later they were moving through the darkness

towards the front gate, skirting the patches of light. Near the gatehouse a half-dozen bodies had been dragged up against the wall. The ground was soaked black with blood.

Three more Gral joined them. One by one, the group slipped through the gateway and into the street beyond. They crossed to an alley and made their way down to the far end, where they halted.

Torvald laid a hand on Karsa's arm. 'Friend, where would you go now? My own return to Genabackis will be delayed awhile. My kin here have embraced me with open arms – a unique experience for me, and I plan on savouring it. Alas, the Gral won't take you – you're too recognizable.'

'He will come with me,' the blue-eyed native said. 'To a place of safety.'

Torvald looked up at Karsa, brows rising.

The Teblor shrugged. 'It is clear that I cannot be hidden in this city; nor will I further endanger you or your kin, Torvald Nom. If this man proves unworthy I need only kill him.'

'How long until the compound guards are changed?' the blue-eyed man asked.

'A bell at least, so you will have plenty—'

Sudden alarms shattered the night, from the direction of the Malazan garrison.

The Gral seemed to vanish before Karsa's eyes, so quickly did they scatter. 'Torvald Nom, for all you have done for me, I thank you—'

The Daru scurried over to a pile of rubbish in the alley. He swept it aside, then lifted into view Karsa's bloodsword. 'Here, friend.' He tossed the sword into the Teblor's hands. 'Come to Darujhistan in a few years' time.'

A final wave, then the Daru was gone.

The blue-eyed man – who had collected a sword from one of the dead guards – now gestured. 'Stay close. There are ways out of Ehrlitan the Malazans know nothing of. Follow, and quietly.'

He set off. Karsa slipped into his wake.

Their route twisted through the lower city, down countless alleys, some so narrow that the Teblor was forced to
sidle sideways along their crooked lengths. Karsa had
thought that his guide would lead them towards the docks,
or perhaps the outer walls facing onto the wasteland to the
south. Instead, they climbed towards the single massive hill
at Ehrlitan's heart, and before long were moving through
the rubble of countless collapsed buildings.

They arrived at the battered base of a tower, the native
not hesitating as he ducked in through the gaping, dark
doorway. Following, Karsa found himself in a cramped
chamber, its floor uneven with heaved flagstones. A second
portal was barely visible opposite the entrance, and at its
threshold the man paused.

'Mebra!' he hissed.

There was movement, then: 'Is it you? Dryjhna bless us,
I had heard that you had been captured – ah, the alarms
down below . . . well done—'

'Enough of that. Do the provisions remain in the
tunnels?'

'Of course! Always. Including your own cache—'

'Good, now move aside. I've someone with me.'

Beyond the portal was a rough series of stone steps,
descending into even deeper darkness. Karsa sensed the
man Mebra's presence as he edged past, heard his sharp
intake of breath.

The blue-eyed man below the Teblor halted suddenly.
'Oh, and Mebra, tell no-one you have seen us – not even
your fellow servants to the cause. Understand?'

'Of course.'

The two fugitives continued on, leaving Mebra
behind. The stairs continued down, until Karsa had
begun to think that they were approaching the bowels of
the earth. When it finally levelled out, the air was
heavy with damp, smelling of salt, and the stones underfoot
were wet and streaked in slime. At the tunnel's mouth
a number of niches had been carved into the limestone

walls, each one holding leather packs and travel gear.

Karsa watched as his companion strode quickly to one niche in particular. After a moment's examination, he dropped the Malazan sword he had been carrying and drew forth a pair of objects that moved with the sound of rustling chain.

'Take that food-pack,' the man instructed, nodding towards a nearby niche. 'And you will find a telaba or two – clothes – and weapon-belts and harnesses – leave the lanterns, the tunnel ahead is long but has no branches.'

'Where does it lead?'

'Out,' the man replied.

Karsa fell silent. He disliked the extent to which his life was in this native's hands, but it seemed that, for the time being, there was nothing he could do about it. Seven Cities was a stranger place than even the Genabackan cities of Malyntaeas and Genabaris. The lowlanders filled this world like vermin – more tribes than the Teblor had thought possible, and it was clear that none liked each other. While that was a sentiment Karsa well understood – for tribes should dislike each other – it was also obvious that, among the lowlanders, there was no sense of any other sort of loyalty. Karsa was Uryd, but he was also Teblor. The lowlanders seemed so obsessed with their differences that they had no comprehension of what unified them.

A flaw that could be exploited.

The pace set by Karsa's guide was fierce, and though most of the damage done to the Teblor was well along in healing, his reserves of strength and stamina were not what they had once been. After a time, the distance between the two began to lengthen, and eventually Karsa found himself travelling alone through the impenetrable darkness, one hand on the rough-hewn wall to his right, hearing only the sounds of his own passage. The air was no longer damp, and he could taste dust in his mouth.

The wall suddenly vanished under his hand. Karsa stumbled, drew to a halt.

'You did well,' the native said from somewhere on the Teblor's left. 'Running hunched over as you had to be . . . not an easy task. Look up.'

He did, and slowly straightened. There were stars overhead.

'We're in a gully,' the man continued. 'It will be dawn before we climb out of it. Then it's five, maybe six days across the Pan'potsun Odhan. The Malazans will be after us, of course, so we will have to be careful. Rest awhile. Drink some water – the sun is a demon and will steal your life if it can. Our route will take us from one place of water to the next, so we need not suffer.'

'You know this land,' Karsa said. 'I do not.' He raised his sword. 'But know this, I will not be taken prisoner again.'

'That's the spirit,' the lowlander replied.

'That is not what I meant.'

The man laughed. 'I know. If you so wish it, once we are clear of this gully you may go in any direction you like. What I have offered you is the best chance of surviving. There is more than recapture by the Malazans to worry about in this land. Travel with me, and you shall learn how to survive. But as I said, the choice is yours. Now, shall we proceed?'

Dawn arrived to the world above before the two fugitives reached the end of the gully. While they could see bright blue sky overhead, they continued walking through chill shadows. The means of exit was marked by a tumbled scree of boulders where a past flood had undercut one wall sufficiently to trigger a collapse.

Clambering up the slope, they emerged onto a heat-blasted land of weathered crags, sand-filled riverbeds, cacti and thorny bushes, the sun blindingly bright, making the air shimmer in all directions. There was no-one in sight, nor was there any sign that the area was inhabited by anything other than wild creatures.

The lowlander led Karsa southwestward, their route

circuitous, making use of every form of cover available and avoiding ridges or hilltops that would set them against the sky. Neither spoke, saving their breath in the enervating heat as the day stretched on.

Late in the afternoon, the lowlander halted suddenly and turned. He hissed a curse in his native language, then said, 'Horsemen.'

Karsa swung round, but could see no-one in the desolate landscape behind them.

'Feel them underfoot,' the man muttered. 'So, Mebra has turned. Well, one day I will answer that betrayal.'

And now Karsa could sense, through the callused soles of his bared feet, the tremble of distant horse hoofs. 'If you'd suspected this Mebra why did you not kill him?'

'If I killed everyone I was suspicious about I'd have scant company. I needed proof, and now I have it.'

'Unless he told someone else.'

'Then he's either a traitor or stupid – both lead to the same fatal consequence. Come, we need to make this a challenge for the Malazans.'

They set off. The lowlander was unerring in choosing paths that left no footprints or other signs of passage. Despite this, the sound of the riders drew ever nearer. 'There's a mage among them,' the lowlander muttered as they raced across yet another stretch of bedrock.

'If we can avoid them until nightfall,' Karsa said, 'then I shall become the hunter and they the hunted.'

'There's at least twenty of them. We're better off using the darkness to stretch the distance between us. See those mountains to the southwest? That is our destination. If we can reach the hidden passes, we will be safe.'

'We cannot outrun horses,' Karsa growled. 'Come dark, I will be done running.'

'Then you attack alone, for it will mean your death.'

'Alone. That is well. I need no lowlander getting underfoot.'

* * *

The plunge into night was sudden. Just before the last light failed, the two fugitives, slipping onto a plain crowded with enormous boulders, finally caught sight of their pursuers. Seventeen riders, three spare horses. All but two of the Malazans were in full armour, helmed and armed with either lances or crossbows. The other two riders were easily recognizable to Karsa. Silgar and Damisk.

Karsa suddenly recalled that, the night of their escape from the compound, the stocks had been empty. He'd thought little of it at the time, assuming that the two prisoners had been taken inside for the night.

The pursuers had not seen the two fugitives, who quickly moved behind the cover of the boulders.

'I have led them to an old campground,' the lowlander at Karsa's side whispered. 'Listen. They're making camp. The two who weren't soldiers—'

'Yes. The slavemaster and his guard.'

'They must have taken that otataral anklet off him. He wants you badly, it seems.'

Karsa shrugged. 'And he will find me. Tonight. I am done with those two. Neither will see the dawn, this I swear before Urugal.'

'You cannot attack two squads on your own.'

'Then consider it a diversion and make good your escape, lowlander.' With that the Teblor swung about and made his way towards the Malazan camp.

He was not interested in waiting for them to settle. The crossbowmen had ridden all day with their weapons cocked. They would probably be replacing the wrapped cords at this very moment, assuming they followed the practice that Karsa had seen among the squads of the Ashok Regiment. Others would be removing saddles and tending to the horses, whilst most of the remaining soldiers would be preparing to cook meals and raise tents. At most, there would be two or three guards establishing a picket around the camp.

Karsa paused behind a huge boulder just beyond the

Malazans. He could hear them setting up their position for the night. The Teblor collected a handful of sand and dried the sweat from his palms, then he hefted his blood-sword in his right hand and edged forward.

Three fires had been lit using dung, the hearths ringed with large rocks to cut the light cast out by the flickering flames. The horses stood within a rope corral, three soldiers moving among them. A half-dozen crossbowmen sat nearby, their weapons dismantled on their laps. Two guards stood facing the plain of boulders, one positioned slightly behind the other. The soldier closest to Karsa held a drawn short-sword and a round shield, his companion six paces behind him a short bow, arrow nocked.

There were, in fact, more guards at the pickets than Karsa would have liked, one visible on each other flank of the encampment. The bowman was so positioned as to permit him a field of fire for every one of them.

Crouched before a firepit near the centre of the camp were Silgar, Damisk and a Malazan officer, the latter with his back to Karsa.

The Teblor silently worked his way around the boulder. The guard closest to him was looking to the left at the moment. Five paces to close in a charge. The bowman had turned in his restless scanning towards the guard at the far end of the camp.

Now.

The helmed head was swinging back, the weathered face pale beneath its rim.

And then Karsa was alongside him, his left hand snapping out to close around the man's throat. Cartilage collapsed with a dry popping sound.

Enough to make the bowman whirl.

Had his attacker the short legs of a lowlander, he would have had a chance to loose his arrow. As it was, he barely had time to draw before the Teblor reached him.

The man's mouth opened to shout as he tensed to throw himself backward. Karsa's sword flashed outward, sending the helmed head tumbling from shoulders. Armour clattered behind him as the corpse fell to the ground.

Faces swung round. Shouts rang through the night.

Three soldiers rose from a hearth directly in front of the Teblor. Short-swords hissed from scabbards. One Malazan threw himself into Karsa's path in an effort to give his companions time to find their shields. A brave and fatal gesture, for his weapon's reach was no match for the blood-sword. The man shrieked as he lost both forearms to a vicious lateral slash.

One of the next two Malazans had managed to ready his round shield, raising it into the path of Karsa's downward swing. The bronze-banded wood exploded at the impact, the arm holding it shattering beneath it. As the soldier crumpled, the Teblor leapt over him, quickly cutting down the third man.

A blaze of pain along the top of his right thigh as a lance ripped a path to thrum into the dusty ground behind him. Wheeling, he whipped his blade around in time to bat aside another lance which had been about to strike his chest.

Footsteps rushing him from behind and to the left – one of the picket guards – while directly before him, three paces distant, stood Silgar, Damisk and the Malazan officer. The slavemaster's face was twisted with terror, even as sorcery rose into a writhing wave in front of him, then roared towards Karsa.

The magic struck him at the precise moment that the picket guard arrived. Sorcery engulfed them both. The Malazan's scream ripped through the air. Grunting at the writhing, ghostly tendrils seeking to snare him in place, Karsa surged through it – and came face to face with the slavemaster.

Damisk had already fled. The officer had thrown himself to one side, deftly ducking beneath Karsa's side-swing.

Silgar threw his hands up.

Karsa cut them off.

The slavemaster reeled back.

The Teblor chopped down, severing Silgar's right leg just above the ankle. The man toppled onto his upper shoulders, legs in the air. A fourth swing sent the left foot spinning.

Two soldiers rushed Karsa from his right, a third one trailing.

A bellowed command rang through the night, and the Teblor – weapon readied – was surprised to see the three men peel away. By his count there were five others, as well as the officer and Damisk. He spun, glaring, but there was no-one – just the sounds of boots retreating into the darkness. He looked to where the horses had been corralled – the animals were gone.

A lance darted towards him. Snarling, Karsa splintered it as the back of his bloodsword deflected it to one side. He paused, then padded over to Silgar. The slavemaster had curled into a tight ball. Blood flowed from the four stumps. Karsa picked him up by his silk belt and carried him back to the plain of boulders.

As he moved around the first of the massive rocks a voice spoke low and clear from the shadows. 'This way.'

The Teblor grunted. 'You were supposed to have fled.'

'They will regroup, but without the mage we should be able to elude them.'

Karsa followed his companion deeper into the studded plain, then, after fifty or so paces, the man stopped and turned to the Teblor.

'Of course, with your prize leaving a trail of blood, there will be little trouble in following us. Do something with him now.'

Karsa dropped Silgar to the ground, kicked him onto his back. The slavemaster was unconscious.

'He will bleed to death,' the lowlander said. 'You have your revenge. Leave him here to die.'

Instead, the Teblor began cutting strips from Silgar's telaba, tying them tight about the stumps at the ends of his arms and legs.

'There will still be some leakage—'

'Which we shall have to live with,' Karsa growled. 'I am not yet done with this man.'

'What value senseless torture?'

Karsa hesitated, then he sighed. 'This man enslaved an entire tribe of Teblor. The Sunyd's spirit is broken. The slavemaster is not as a soldier – he has not earned swift death. He is as a mad dog, to be driven into a hut and killed—'

'So kill him.'

'I shall . . . once I have driven him mad.'

Karsa lifted Silgar once more, throwing him over a shoulder. 'Lead us on, lowlander.'

Hissing under his breath, the man nodded.

Eight days later, they reached the hidden pass through the Pan'potsun Mountains. The Malazans had resumed their pursuit, but had not been seen since two days past, indicating that the efforts to evade them had succeeded.

They ascended the steep, rocky trail through the course of the day. Silgar was still alive, fevered and only periodically aware. He had been gagged to prevent him making any sounds. Karsa carried him on his shoulder.

Shortly before dusk they reached the summit, and came to the southwest edge. The path wound down into a shadowed plain. At the crest they sat down to rest.

'What lies beyond?' Karsa asked as he dropped Silgar to the ground. 'I see naught but a wasteland of sand below.'

'And so it is,' his companion replied in a reverent tone. 'And in its heart, the one I serve.' He glanced over at Karsa. 'She will, I think, be interested in you . . .' he smiled, '*Teblor*.'

Karsa scowled. 'Why does the name of my people amuse you so?'

'Amuse? More like *appals*. The Fenn had fallen far from their past glories, yet they remembered enough to know their old name. You cannot even make that claim. Your kind walked this earth when the T'lan Imass were still flesh. From your blood came the Barghast and the Trell. You are Thelomen Toblakai.'

'These are names I do not know,' Karsa growled, 'even as I do not know yours, lowlander.'

The man returned his gaze to the dark lands below. 'I am named Leoman. And the one I serve, the Chosen One to whom I will deliver you, she is Sha'ik.'

'I am no-one's servant,' Karsa said. 'This Chosen One, she dwells in the desert before us?'

'In its very heart, Toblakai. In Raraku's very heart.'

BOOK TWO

COLD IRON

There are folds in this shadow . . .
hiding entire worlds.

Call to Shadow
Felisin

CHAPTER FIVE

Woe to the fallen
in the alleys of Aren . . .

Anonymous

A single kick from the burly soldier in the lead sent the flimsy door crashing inward. He disappeared into the gloom beyond, followed by the rest of his squad. From within came shouts, the sound of crashing furniture.

Gamet glanced over at Commander Blistig.

The man shrugged. 'Aye, the door was unlocked – it's an inn, after all, though such a lofty title for this squalid pit is stretching things somewhat. Even so, it's a matter of achieving the proper effect.'

'You misunderstood me,' Gamet replied. 'I simply cannot believe that your soldiers found him *here*.'

Unease flitted across Blistig's solid, broad features. 'Aye, well, we've rounded up others in worse places, Fist. It's what comes of—' he squinted up the street, 'of broken hearts.'

Fist. The title still clambers into my gut like a starving crow. Gamet frowned. 'The Adjunct has no time for broken-hearted soldiers, Commander.'

'It was unrealistic to arrive here expecting to stoke the fires of vengeance. Can't stoke cold ashes, though don't take me wrong, I wish her the Lady's luck.'

'Rather more is expected of you than that,' Gamet said drily.

The streets were virtually deserted at this time of day, the afternoon heat oppressive. Of course, even at other times, Aren was not as it once had been. Trade from the north had ceased. Apart from Malazan warships and transports, and a few fisherboats, the harbour and river mouth were empty. This was, Gamet reflected, a scarred populace.

The squad was re-emerging from the inn, carrying with them a rag-clad, feebly struggling old man. He was smeared in vomit, the little hair he had left hanging like grey strings, his skin patched and grey with filth. Cursing at the stench, the soldiers of Blistig's Aren Guard hurried their burden towards the cart's bed.

'It was a miracle we found him at all,' the commander said. 'I truly expected the old bastard to up and drown himself.'

Momentarily unmindful of his new title, Gamet turned and spat onto the cobbles. 'This situation is contemptible, Blistig. Damn it, *some* semblance of military decorum – of *control*, Hood take me – should have been possible . . .'

The commander stiffened at Gamet's tone. The guards gathered at the back of the cart all turned at his words.

Blistig stepped close to the Fist. 'You listen to me and listen well,' he growled under his breath, a tremble shivering across his scarred cheeks, his eyes hard as iron. 'I stood on the damned wall and *watched*. As did every one of my soldiers. Pormqual running in circles like a castrated cat – that historian and those two Wickan children wailing with grief. I watched – we all watched – as Coltaine and his Seventh were cut down before our very eyes. And if that wasn't enough, the High Fist then marched out his army and ordered them to disarm! If not for one of my captains delivering intelligence concerning Mallick Rel being an agent of Sha'ik's, my Guard would have died with them. Military decorum? Go to Hood with your military decorum, Fist!'

Gamet stood unmoving at the commander's tirade. It was not the first time that he'd felt the snap of this man's temper. Since he had arrived with Adjunct Tavore's retinue, and was given the liaison role that took him to the forefront of dealing with the survivors of the Chain of Dogs – both those who had come in with the historian Duiker, and those who had awaited them in the city – Gamet had felt under siege. The rage beneath the mantle of propriety erupted again and again. Hearts not simply broken, but shattered, torn to pieces, trampled on. The Adjunct's hope of resurrecting the survivors – making use of their local experience to steady her legions of untested recruits – was, to Gamet, seeming more and more unrealistic with each day that passed.

It was also clear that Blistig cared little that Gamet made daily reports to the Adjunct, and could reasonably expect his tirades to have been passed on to Tavore, in culpable detail. The commander was doubly fortunate, therefore, that Gamet had as yet said nothing of them to the Adjunct, exercising extreme brevity in his debriefings and keeping personal observations to the minimum.

As Blistig's words trailed away, Gamet simply sighed and approached the cart to look down on the drunken old man lying on its bed. The soldiers backed away a step – as if the Fist carried a contagion.

'So,' Gamet drawled, 'this is Squint. The man who killed Coltaine—'

'Was a mercy,' one of the guards snapped.

'Clearly, Squint does not think so.'

There was no reply to that. Blistig arrived at the Fist's side. 'All right,' he said to his squad, 'take him and get him cleaned up – and under lock and key.'

'Aye, sir.'

Moments later the cart was being pulled away.

Gamet faced Blistig once more. 'Your rather unsubtle plan of getting yourself stripped of rank, shackled in irons, and sent back to Unta on the first ship, will not succeed,

Commander. Neither the Adjunct, nor I, care one whit for your fragile state. We are preparing to fight a war, and for that you will be needed. You and every one of your crumple-faced soldiers.'

'Better we'd died with the rest—'

'But you did not. We have three legions of recruits, Commander. Wide-eyed and young but ready to shed Seven Cities blood. The question is, what do you and your soldiers intend to show them?'

Blistig glared. 'The Adjunct makes the captain of her House Guard into a Fist, and I'm supposed to—'

'Fourth Army,' Gamet snapped. 'In the 1st Company at its inception. The Wickan Wars. Twenty-three years' service, Commander. I knew Coltaine when you were still bouncing on your mother's knee. I took a lance through the chest but proved too stubborn to die. My commander was kind enough to retire me to what he figured was a safe position back in Unta. Aye, captain of the guard in the House of Paran. But I'd damn well earned it!'

After a long moment, a wry grin twisted Blistig's mouth. 'So you're as happy to be here as I am.'

Gamet grimaced, made no reply.

The two Malazans returned to their horses.

Swinging himself onto the saddle, Gamet said, 'We're expecting the last transport of troops from Malaz Island some time today. The Adjunct wants all the commanders assembled in her council chambers at the eighth bell.'

'To what end?' Blistig asked.

If I had my way, to see you drawn and quartered. 'Just be there, Commander.'

The vast mouth of the Menykh River was a brown, turgid swirl that reached half a league out into Aren Bay. Leaning on the transport's starboard railing just behind the fore-castle, Strings studied the roiling water below, then lifted his gaze to the city on the river's north shore.

He rubbed at the bristles on his long jaw. The rusty hue

of his beard in youth had given way now to grey . . . which was a good thing as far as he was concerned.

The city of Aren had changed little in the years since he had last seen it, barring the paucity of ships in the harbour. The same pall of smoke hanging over it, the same endless stream of sewage crawling the currents into the Seeker's Deep – through which the broad-beamed, sluggish transport now sailed.

The newly issued leather cap chafed the back of his neck; it had damned near broken his heart to discard his old one, along with his tattered leather surcoat, and the sword-belt he'd stripped from a Falah'dan guard who no longer needed it. In fact, he had retained but one possession from his former life, buried down in the bottom of his kit bag in his berth below decks, and he had no intention of permitting its discovery by anyone.

A man came alongside him, leaned casually on the rail and stared out over the water to the city drawing ever nearer.

Strings offered no greeting. Lieutenant Ranal embodied the worst of Malazan military command. Nobleborn, commission purchased in the city of Quon, arrogant and inflexible and righteous and yet to draw a sword in anger. A walking death sentence to his soldiers, and it was the Lord's luck that Strings was one of those soldiers.

The lieutenant was a tall man, his Quon blood the purest it could be; fair-skinned, fair-haired, his cheekbones high and wide, his nose straight and long, his mouth full. Strings had hated him on sight.

'It is customary to salute your superior,' Ranal said with affected indifference.

'Saluting officers gets them killed, sir.'

'Here on a transport ship?'

'Just getting into the habit,' Strings replied.

'It has been plain from the start that you have done this before, soldier.' Ranal paused to examine the supple, black knuckles of his gloved hands. 'Hood knows, you're old enough to be the father of most of those marines sitting on the deck behind us. The recruiting officer sent you straight through – you've not trained or sparred once, yet here I am, expected to accept you as one of my soldiers.'

Strings shrugged, said nothing.

'That recruiting officer,' Ranal went on after a moment, his pale blue eyes fixed on the city, 'said she saw from the start what you'd been trying to hide. Oddly, she considered it – you, to be more precise – a valuable resource, even so much as to suggesting I make you a sergeant. Do you know why I find that odd?'

'No, sir, but I am sure you will tell me.'

'Because I think you were a deserter.'

Strings leaned far forward and spat down into the water. 'I've met more than a few, and they've all got their reasons and no two of them alike. But there's one thing they all have in common.'

'And what is that?'

'You'll never find them in an enlistment line, Lieutenant. Enjoy the view, sir.' He turned away and wandered back to where the other marines sprawled on the midship deck. Most had long since recovered from their seasickness, yet their eagerness to disembark was palpable. Strings sat down, stretched out his legs.

'Lieutenant wants your head on a plate,' a voice murmured beside him.

Strings sighed and closed his eyes, lifting his face to the afternoon sun. 'What the lieutenant wants and what he gets ain't the same thing, Koryk.'

'What he'll get is the bunch of us right here,' the Seti half-blood replied, rolling his broad shoulders, strands of his long black hair whipping across his flat-featured face.

'The practice is to mix recruits with veterans,' Strings said. 'Despite everything you've heard, there's survivors of the Chain of Dogs in yon city over there. A whole shipload of wounded marines and Wickans made it through, I've heard. And there's the Aren Guard, and the Red Blades. A number of coastal marine ships straggled in as well. Finally, there's Admiral Nok's fleet, though I imagine he'll want to keep his own forces intact.'

'What for?' another recruit asked. 'We're heading for a desert war, aren't we?'

Strings glanced over at her. Frighteningly young, reminding him of another young woman who'd marched alongside him a while ago. He shivered slightly, then said, 'The Adjunct would have to be a fool to strip the fleet. Nok's ready to begin the reconquest of the coast cities – he could've started months ago. The empire needs secure ports. Without them we're finished on this continent.'

'Well,' the young woman muttered, 'from what *I've* heard, this Adjunct might be just what you said, old man. Hood knows, she's nobleborn, ain't she?'

Strings snorted, but said nothing, closing his eyes once more. He was worried the lass might be right. Then again, this Tavore was sister to Captain Paran. And Paran had shown some spine back in Darujhistan. At the very least, he was no fool.

'Where'd you get the name "Strings", anyway?' the young woman asked after a moment.

Fiddler smiled. 'That tale's too long to tell, lass.'

Her gauntlets thudded down onto the tabletop, raising a cloud of dust. Armour rustling, sweat soaking the under-padding between her breasts, she unstrapped her helmet and – as the wench arrived with the tankard of ale – dragged out the rickety chair and sat down.

Street urchin messenger. Delivering a small strip of green silk which bore, written in a fine hand, the Malazan words: *Dancer's Tavern, dusk.* Lostara Yil was more irritated than intrigued.

The interior of Dancer's Tavern consisted of a single room, the four walls making some ancient claim to white-washed plaster, remnants of which now clung to the adobe bricks in misshapen, wine-stained patches, like a map of a

273

drunkard's paradise. The low ceiling was rotting before the very eyes of owner and patron, dust sifting down in clouds lit by the low sun that cast streams of light through the front window's shutters. Already, the foam-threaded surface of the ale in the tankard before her sported a dull sheen.

There were but three other patrons, two bent over a game of slivers at the table closest to the window, and a lone, mumbling, semi-conscious man slumped against the wall beside the piss trench.

Although early, the Red Blade captain was already impatient to see an end to this pathetic mystery, if mystery it was meant to be. She'd needed but a moment to realize who it was who had set up this clandestine meeting. And while a part of her was warmed by the thought of seeing him again – for all his affectations and airs he was handsome enough – she had sufficient responsibilities to wrestle with as Tene Baralta's aide. Thus far, the Red Blades were being treated as a company distinct from the Adjunct's punitive army, despite the fact that there were few soldiers available with actual fighting experience . . . *and even fewer with the backbone to put that experience to use.*

The disordered apathy rife in Blistig's Aren Guard was not shared by the Red Blades. Kin had been lost in the Chain of Dogs, and that would be answered.

If . . .

The Adjunct was Malazan – an unknown to Lostara and the rest of the Red Blades; even Tene Baralta, who had met her face to face on three occasions, remained unable to gauge her, to take her measure. Did Tavore trust the Red Blades?

Maybe the truth is already before us. She's yet to give our company anything. Are we part of her army? Will the Red Blades be permitted to fight the Whirlwind?

Questions without answers.

And here she sat, wasting time—

The door swung open.

A shimmering grey cloak, green-tinted leathers, dark,

sun-burnished skin, a wide, welcoming smile. 'Captain Lostara Yil! I am delighted to see you again.' He strode over, dismissing the approaching serving wench with a casual wave of one gloved hand. Settling into the chair opposite her, he raised two crystal goblets that seemed to appear from nowhere and set them on the dusty table. A black bottle, long-necked and glistening, followed. 'I strongly advise against the local ale in this particular establishment, my dear. This vintage suits the occasion far better. From the sun-drenched south slopes of Gris, where grow the finest grapes this world has seen. Is mine an informed opinion, you are wondering? Most assuredly so, lass, since I hold a majority interest in said vineyards—'

'What is it you want with me, Pearl?'

He poured the magenta-hued wine into the goblets, his smile unwavering. 'Plagued as I am with sentimentality, I thought we might raise our glasses to old times. Granted, they were rather harrowing times; none the less, we survived, did we not?'

'Oh yes,' Lostara replied. 'And you went your way, on to greater glory no doubt. Whilst I went mine – straight into a cell.'

The Claw sighed. 'Ah well, poor Pormqual's advisers failed him dearly, alas. But I see now that you and your fellow Red Blades are free once more, your weapons returned to you, your place in the Adjunct's army secure—'

'Not quite.'

Pearl arched an elegant brow.

Lostara collected the goblet and drank a mouthful, barely noticing its taste. 'We have had no indication of the Adjunct's wishes towards us.'

'How strange!'

Scowling, the captain said, 'Enough games – you surely know far more about it than we do—'

'Alas, I must disabuse you of that notion. The new Adjunct is as unfathomable to me as she is to you. My failure was in making assumptions that she would hasten to

275

repair the damage done to your illustrious company. To leave unanswered the question of the Red Blades' loyalty . . .' Pearl sipped wine, then leaned back. 'You have been released from the gaols, your weapons returned to you – have you been barred from leaving the city? From headquarters?'

'Only her council chambers, Pearl.'

The Claw's expression brightened. 'Ah, but in that you are not alone, my dear. From what I have heard, apart from the select few who have accompanied her from Unta, the Adjunct has hardly spoken with anyone at all. I believe, however, that the situation is about to change.'

'What do you mean?'

'Why, only that there will be a council of war tonight, one to which your commander, Tene Baralta, has no doubt been invited, as well as Commander Blistig and a host of others whose appearance will likely surprise one and all.' He fell silent then, his green eyes holding on her.

Lostara slowly blinked. 'That being the case, I must needs return to Tene Baralta—'

'A fair conclusion, lass. Unfortunately wrong, I am afraid.'

'Explain yourself, Pearl.'

He leaned forward once more and topped up her drink. 'Delighted to. As recalcitrant as the Adjunct has been, I did manage to have occasion to present to her a request, which she has approved.'

Lostara's voice was flat. 'What kind of request?'

'Well, sentimentality is my curse, as I mentioned earlier. Fond are my memories of you and me working together. So fond, in fact, that I have requested you as my, uhm, my aide. Your commander has of course been informed—'

'I am a captain in the Red Blades!' Lostara snapped. 'Not a Claw, not a spy, not a mur—' She bit the word back.

Pearl's eyes widened. 'I am deeply hurt. But magnanimous enough this evening to excuse your ignorance. Whilst you may find no distinction between the art of assassination and the crude notion of murder, I assure you that one exists. Be that as it may, permit me to allay your fears – the task awaiting you and me will not involve the ghastlier side of my calling. No indeed, lass, my need for you in this upcoming endeavour depends entirely upon two of your numerous qualities. Your familiarity as a native of Seven Cities, for one. And the other – even more vital – your unquestioned loyalty to the Malazan Empire. Now, while you could in no way argue the veracity of the former, it now falls to you to reassert your claim to the latter.'

She stared at him for a long moment, then slowly nodded. 'I see. Very well, I am at your disposal.'

Pearl smiled once more. 'Wonderful. My faith in you was absolute.'

'What is this mission we are to embark upon?'

'Details will be forthcoming once we have our personal interview with the Adjunct this evening.'

She straightened. 'You have no idea, do you?'

His smile broadened. 'Exciting, yes?'

'So you don't know if it will involve assassination—'

'Assassination? Who knows? But murder? Assuredly not. Now, drink up, lass. We must needs march to the palace of the late High Fist. I have heard that the Adjunct has little toleration for tardiness.'

Everyone had arrived early. Gamet stood near the door through which the Adjunct would appear, his back to the wall, his arms crossed. Before him, stationed in the long, low-ceilinged council chamber, were the three commanders who had been assembled for this evening's first set of meetings. The next few bells, with all the orchestration directing them, promised to be interesting. None the less, the once-captain of House Paran was feeling somewhat intimidated.

He had been a common soldier years back, not one to find himself in councils of war. There was little comfort in this new mantle of Fist, for he knew that merit had had nothing to do with acquiring the title. Tavore knew him, had grown used to commanding him, to leaving to him the tasks of organization, the arranging of schedules . . . but for a noble household. Yet it seemed she intended to use him in an identical manner, this time for the entire Fourteenth Army. Which made him an administrator, not a Fist. A fact of which no-one present in this room was unaware.

He was unused to the embarrassment he felt, and recognized that the bluster he often displayed was nothing more than a knee-jerk reaction to his own sense of inadequacy. For the moment, however, he did not feel capable of managing even so much as diffidence, much less bluster.

Admiral Nok was standing a half-dozen paces away, in quiet conversation with the imposing commander of the Red Blades, Tene Baralta. Blistig sat sprawled in a chair at the far end of the map table, farthest from where the Adjunct would seat herself once the meeting commenced.

Gamet's eyes were drawn again and again to the tall admiral. Apart from Dujek Onearm, Nok was the last of the commanders from the Emperor's time. *The only admiral who didn't drown.* With the sudden deaths of the Napan brothers, Urko and Crust, Nok had been given overall command of the imperial fleets. The Empress had sent him and a hundred and seven of his ships to Seven Cities when the rumours of rebellion had reached fever pitch. Had the High Fist in Aren not effectively impounded that fleet in the harbour, Coltaine's Chain of Dogs could have been prevented; indeed, the rebellion might well be over. Now, the task of reconquest promised to be a drawn-out, bloody endeavour. Whatever feelings the admiral might have regarding all that had occurred and all that was likely to come, he gave no outward indication, his expression remaining cold and impersonal.

Tene Baralta had his own grievances. The Red Blades had been charged with treason by Pormqual, even as one of their companies fought under Coltaine's command – fought, and was annihilated. Blistig's first order once the

High Fist left the city had been their release. As with the survivors of the Chain of Dogs and the Aren Guard, the Adjunct had inherited their presence. The question of what to do with them – what to do with them all – was about to be answered.

Gamet wished he could allay their concerns, but the truth was, Tavore had never been free with her thoughts. The Fist had no idea what this evening would bring.

The door opened.

As was her style, Tavore's clothes were well made, but plain and virtually colourless. A match to her eyes, to the streaks of grey in her reddish, short-cropped hair, to her unyielding, unprepossessing features. She was tall, somewhat broad in the hips, her breasts slightly oversized for her frame. The otataral sword of her office was scabbarded at her belt – the only indication of her imperial title. A half-dozen scrolls were tucked under one arm.

'Stand or sit as you like,' were her first words as she strode to the High Fist's ornate chair.

Gamet watched Nok and Tene Baralta move to chairs at the table, then followed suit.

Back straight, the Adjunct sat. She set the scrolls down. 'The disposition of the Fourteenth Army is the subject of this meeting. Remain in our company, Admiral Nok, please.' She reached for the first scroll and slipped its ties. 'Three legions. The 8th, 9th and 10th. Fist Gamet shall command the 8th. Fist Blistig, the 9th, and Fist Tene Baralta, the 10th. The choice of officers under each respective command is at the discretion of each Fist. I advise you to select wisely. Admiral Nok, detach Commander Alardis from your flagship. She is now in charge of the Aren Guard.' Without pause she reached for a second scroll. 'As to the survivors of the Chain of Dogs and sundry unattached elements at our disposal, their units are now dissolved. They have been reassigned and dispersed throughout the three legions.' She finally looked up – and if she took note of the shock on the faces that Gamet saw, a shock he shared, she hid it well. 'In three days' time, I will review your troops. That is all.'

In numbed silence, the four men slowly rose.

The Adjunct gestured at the two scrolls she had laid out. 'Fist Blistig, take these please. You and Tene Baralta might wish to reconvene in one of the side chambers, in order to discuss the details of your new commands. Fist Gamet, you can join them later. For now, remain with me. Admiral Nok, I wish to speak with you privately later this evening. Please ensure that you are at my disposal.'

The tall, elderly man cleared his throat. 'I shall be in the mess hall, Adjunct.'

'Very good.'

Gamet watched the three men depart.

As soon as the doors closed, the Adjunct rose from her chair. She walked over to the ancient, woven tapestries running the length of one of the walls. 'Extraordinary patterns, Gamet, don't you think? A culture obsessed with intricacies. Well,' she faced him, 'that was concluded with unexpected ease. It seems we have a few moments before our next guests.'

'I believe they were all too shocked to respond, Adjunct. The imperial style of command usually includes discussion, argument, compromise—'

Her only reply was a brief half-smile, then she returned her attention to the weavings. 'What officers will Tene Baralta choose, do you imagine?'

'Red Blades, Adjunct. How the Malazan recruits will take—'

'And Blistig?'

'Only one seemed worthy of his rank – and he's now in the Aren Guard and so not available to Blistig,' Gamet replied. 'A captain, Keneb—'

'Malazan?'

'Yes, though stationed here in Seven Cities. He lost his troops, Adjunct, to the renegade, Korbolo Dom. It was Keneb who warned Blistig about Mallick Rel—'

'Indeed. So, apart from Captain Keneb?'

Gamet shook his head. 'I feel for Blistig at the moment.'

'Do you?'

'Well, I didn't say *what* I was feeling, Adjunct.'

She faced him again. 'Pity?'

'Some of that,' he allowed after a moment.

'Do you know what bothers Blistig the most, Fist?'

'Witnessing the slaughter—'

'He may well claim that and hope that you believe it, but you are wrong to do so. Blistig disobeyed a High Fist's order. He stands before me, his new commander, and believes I hold no faith in him. From that, he concludes that it would be best for everyone concerned if I were to send him to Unta, to face the Empress.' She turned away again, was silent.

Gamet's thoughts raced, but he finally had to conclude that Tavore's thoughts proceeded on levels too deep for him to fathom. 'What is it you wish me to tell him?'

'You think I wish you to tell him something from me? Very well. He may have Captain Keneb.'

A side door swung open and Gamet turned to see three Wickans enter. Two were children, the third one not much older. While the Fist had yet to meet them, he knew who they must be. *Nether and Nil. The witch and the warlock. And the lad with them is Temul, the eldest among the warrior youths Coltaine sent with the historian.*

Only Temul seemed pleased at having been summoned into the Adjunct's presence. Nil and Nether were both unkempt, their feet bare and almost grey with layers of dirt. Nether's long black hair hung in greasy ropes. Nil's deerhide tunic was scarred and torn. Both held expressions of disinterest. In contrast, Temul's war gear was immaculate, as was the mask of deep red face paint denoting his grief, and his dark eyes glittered like sharp stones as he drew himself to attention before the Adjunct.

But Tavore's attention was on Nil and Nether. 'The Fourteenth Army lacks mages,' she said. 'Therefore, you will now be acting in that capacity.'

'No, Adjunct,' Nether replied.

'This matter is not open for discussion—'

Nil spoke. 'We want to go home,' he said. 'To the Wickan plains.'

The Adjunct studied them for a moment, then, gaze unwavering, said, 'Temul, Coltaine placed you in charge of the Wickan youths from the three tribes present in the Chain of Dogs. What is the complement?'

'Thirty,' the youth replied.

'And how many Wickans were among the wounded delivered by ship to Aren?'

'Eleven survived.'

'Thus, forty-one in all. Are there any warlocks among your company?'

'No, Adjunct.'

'When Coltaine sent you with the historian Duiker, did he attach warlocks to your company at that time?'

Temul's eyes flicked to Nil and Nether for a moment, then his head jerked in a nod. 'Yes.'

'And has your company been officially dissolved, Temul?'

'No.'

'In other words, Coltaine's last command to you still obtains.' She addressed Nil and Nether once more. 'Your request is denied. I have need of both you and Captain Temul's Wickan lancers.'

'We can give you nothing,' Nether replied.

'The warlock spirits within us are silent,' Nil added.

Tavore slowly blinked as she continued to regard them. Then she said, 'You shall have to find a means of awakening them once more. The day we close to battle with Sha'ik and the Whirlwind, I expect you to employ your sorcery to defend the legions. Captain Temul, are you the eldest among the Wickans in your company?'

'No, Adjunct. There are four warriors of the Foolish Dog, who were on the ship bearing the wounded.'

'Do they resent your command?'

The youth drew himself straighter. 'They do not,' he

replied, his right hand settling on the grip of one of his long knives.

Gamet winced and looked away.

'You three are dismissed,' the Adjunct said after a moment.

Temul hesitated, then spoke. 'Adjunct, my company wishes to fight. Are we to be attached to the legions?'

Tavore tilted her head. 'Captain Temul, how many summers have you seen?'

'Fourteen.'

The Adjunct nodded. 'At present, Captain, our mounted troops are limited to a company of Seti volunteers, five hundred in all. In military terms, they are light cavalry at best, scouts and outriders at worst. None have seen battle, and none are much older than you. Your own command consists of forty Wickans, all but four younger than you. For our march northward, Captain Temul, your company will be attached to my entourage. As bodyguards. The ablest riders among the Seti will act as messengers and scouts. Understand, I have not the forces to mount a cavalry engagement. The Fourteenth Army is predominantly infantry.'

'Coltaine's tactics—'

'This is no longer Coltaine's war,' Tavore snapped.

Temul flinched as if struck. He managed a stiff nod, then turned on his heel and departed the chamber. Nil and Nether followed a moment later.

Gamet let out a shaky breath. 'The lad wanted to bring good news to his Wickans.'

'To silence the grumbling from the four Foolish Dog warriors,' the Adjunct said, her voice still holding a tone of irritation. 'Aptly named indeed. Tell me, Fist, how do you think the discussion between Blistig and Tene Baralta is proceeding at this moment?'

The old veteran grunted. 'Heatedly, I would imagine, Adjunct. Tene Baralta likely expected to retain his Red Blades as a discrete regiment. I doubt he has much

283

interest in commanding four thousand Malazan recruits.'

'And the admiral, who waits below in the mess hall?'

'To that, I have no idea, Adjunct. His taciturnity is legend.'

'Why, do you think, did he not simply usurp High Fist Pormqual? Why did he permit the annihilation of Coltaine and the Seventh, then of the High Fist's own army?'

Gamet could only shake his head.

Tavore studied him for another half-dozen heartbeats, then slowly made her way to the scrolls lying on the table-top. She drew one out and removed its ties. 'The Empress never had cause to question Admiral Nok's loyalty.'

'Nor Dujek Onearm's,' Gamet muttered under his breath.

She heard and looked up, then offered a tight, momentary smile. 'Indeed. One meeting remains to us.' Tucking the scroll under one arm, she strode towards a small side door. 'Come.'

The room beyond was low-ceilinged, its walls virtually covered in tapestries. Thick rugs silenced their steps as they entered. A modest round table occupied the centre, beneath an ornate oil lamp that was the only source of light. There was a second door opposite, low and narrow. The table was the chamber's sole piece of furniture.

Tavore dropped the scroll onto its battered top as Gamet shut the door behind him. When he turned he saw that she was facing him. There was a sudden vulnerability in her eyes that triggered a clutching anxiety in his gut – for it was something he had never before seen from this daughter of House Paran. 'Adjunct?'

She broke the contact, visibly recovered. 'In this room,' she quietly said, 'the Empress is not present.'

Gamet's breath caught, then he jerked his head in a nod.

The smaller door opened, and the Fist turned to see a tall, almost effeminate man, clothed in grey, a placid smile on his handsome features as he took a step into the chamber. An armoured woman followed – an officer of the Red Blades. Her skin was dark and tattooed in Pardu style, her eyes black and large, set wide above high cheekbones, her nose narrow and aquiline. She seemed anything but pleased, her gaze fixing on the Adjunct with an air of calculating arrogance.

'Close the door behind you, Captain,' Tavore said to the Red Blade.

The grey-clad man was regarding Gamet, his smile turning faintly quizzical. 'Fist Gamet,' he said. 'I imagine you are wishing you were still in Unta, that bustling heart of the empire, arguing with horse-traders on behalf of House Paran. Instead, here you are, a soldier once more—'

Gamet scowled and said, 'I am afraid I do not know you—'

'You may call me Pearl,' the man replied, hesitating on the name as if its revelation was the core of some vast joke of which only he was aware. 'And my lovely companion is Captain Lostara Yil, late of the Red Blades but now – happily – seconded into my care.' He swung to the Adjunct and elaborately bowed. 'At your service.'

Gamet could see Tavore's expression tighten fractionally. 'That remains to be seen.'

Pearl slowly straightened, the mockery in his face gone. 'Adjunct, you have quietly – *very* quietly – arranged this meeting. This stage has no audience. While I am a Claw, you and I are both aware that I have – lately – incurred my master Topper's – and the Empress's – displeasure, resulting in my hasty journey through the Imperial Warren. A temporary situation, of course, but none the less, the consequence is that I am at something of a loose end at the moment.'

'Then one might conclude,' the Adjunct said carefully, 'that you are available, as it were, for a rather more . . . private enterprise.'

Gamet shot her a glance. *Gods below! What is this about?*

'One might,' Pearl replied, shrugging.

There was silence, broken at last by the Red Blade,

Lostara Yil. 'I am made uneasy by the direction of this conversation,' she grated. 'As a loyal subject of the empire—'

'Nothing of what follows will impugn your honour, Captain,' the Adjunct replied, her gaze unwavering on Pearl. She added nothing more.

The Claw half smiled then. 'Ah, now you've made me curious. I delight in being curious, did you know that? You fear that I will bargain my way back into Laseen's favour, for the mission you would propose to the captain and me is, to be precise, not on behalf of the Empress, nor, indeed, of the empire. An extraordinary departure from the role of Imperial Adjunct. Unprecedented, in fact.'

Gamet took a step forward, 'Adjunct—'

She raised a hand to cut him off. 'Pearl, the task I would set to you and the captain may well contribute, ultimately, to the well-being of the empire—'

'Oh well,' the Claw smiled, 'that is what a good imagination is for, isn't it? One can scrape patterns in the blood no matter how dried it's become. I admit to no small skill in attributing sound justification for whatever I've just done. By all means, proceed—'

'Not yet!' Lostara Yil snapped, her exasperation plain. 'In serving the Adjunct I expect to serve the empire. She is the will of the Empress. No other considerations are permitted her—'

'You speak true,' Tavore said. She faced Pearl again. 'Claw, how fares the Talon?'

Pearl's eyes went wide and he almost rocked back a step. 'They no longer exist,' he whispered.

The Adjunct frowned. 'Disappointing. We are all, at the moment, in a precarious position. If you are to expect honesty from me, then can I not do so in return?'

'They remain,' Pearl muttered, distaste twisting his features. 'Like bot-fly larvae beneath the imperial hide. When we probe, they simply dig deeper.'

'They none the less serve a certain . . . function,' Tavore

said. 'Unfortunately, not as competently as I would have hoped.'

'The Talons have found support among the nobility?' Pearl asked, a sheen of sweat now visible on his high brow.

The Adjunct's shrug was almost indifferent. 'Does that surprise you?'

Gamet could almost see the Claw's thoughts racing. Racing on, and on, his expression growing ever more astonished and . . . dismayed. 'Name him,' he said.

'Baudin.'

'He was assassinated in Quon—'

'The father was. Not the son.'

Pearl suddenly began pacing in the small chamber. 'And this son, how much like the bastard who spawned him? Baudin Elder left Claw corpses scattered in alleys throughout the city. The hunt lasted four entire nights . . .'

'I had reason to believe,' Tavore said, 'that he was worthy of his father's name.'

Pearl's head turned. 'But no longer?'

'I cannot say. I believe, however, that his mission has gone terribly wrong.'

The name slipped from Gamet's lips unbidden but with a certainty heavy as an anchor-stone: 'Felisin.'

He saw the wince in Tavore's face, before she turned away from all three of them to study one of the tapestries.

Pearl seemed far ahead in his thoughts. 'When was contact lost, Adjunct? And where?'

'The night of the Uprising,' she replied, her back to them still. 'The mining camp called Skullcup. But there had been a . . . a loss of control for some weeks before then.' She gestured at the scroll on the table. 'Details, potential contacts. Burn the scroll once you have completed reading it, and scatter the ashes in the bay.' She faced them suddenly. 'Pearl. Captain Lostara Yil. Find Felisin. Find my sister.'

The roar of the mob rose and fell in the city beyond the estate's walls. It was the Season of Rot in Unta, and, in the minds of thousands of denizens, that rot was being excised. The dreaded Cull had begun.

Captain Gamet stood by the gatehouse, flanked by three nervous guards. The estate's torches had been doused, the house behind them dark, its windows shuttered. And within that massive structure huddled the last child of Paran, her parents gone since the arrests earlier that day, her brother lost and presumably dead on a distant continent, her sister – her sister . . . madness had come once again to the empire, with the fury of a tropical storm . . .

Gamet had but twelve guards, and three of those had been hired in the last few days, when the stillness of the air in the streets had whispered to the captain that the horror was imminent. No proclamations had been issued, no imperial edict to fire-lick the commoners' greed and savagery into life. There were but rumours, racing through the city's streets, alleys and market rounds like dust-devils. 'The Empress is displeased.' 'Behind the rot of the imperial army's incompetent command, you will find the face of the nobility.' 'The purchase of commissions is a plague threatening the entire empire. Is it any wonder the Empress is displeased?'

A company of Red Blades had arrived from Seven Cities. Cruel killers, incorruptible and far removed from the poison of noble coin. It was not difficult to imagine the reason behind their appearance.

The first wave of arrests had been precise, almost understated. Squads in the dead of night. There had been no skirmishes with house guards, no estates forewarned to purchase time to raise barricades, or even flee the city.

And Gamet thought he knew how such a thing came to pass.

Tavore was now the Adjunct to the Empress. Tavore knew . . . her kind.

The captain sighed, then strode forward to the small inset door at the gate. He drew the heavy bolt, let the iron bar drop with a clank. He faced the three guards. 'Your services are no longer required. In the murder hole you'll find your pay.'

Two of the three armoured men exchanged a glance, then, one of them shrugging, they walked to the door. The third man had not moved. Gamet recalled that he'd given his name as Kollen – a Quon name and a Quon accent. He had been hired more for his imposing presence than anything else, though Gamet's practised eye had detected a certain . . . confidence, in the way the man wore his armour, seemingly indifferent to its weight, hinting at a martial grace that belonged only to a professional soldier. He knew next to nothing of Kollen's past, but these were desperate times, and in any case none of the three new hirelings had been permitted into the house itself.

In the gloom beneath the gatehouse lintel, Gamet now studied the motionless guard. Through the tidal roar of the rampaging mob that drew ever closer came shrill screams, lifting into the night a despairing chorus. 'Make this easy, Kollen,' he said quietly. 'There are four of my men twenty paces behind you, crossbows cocked and fixed on your back.'

The huge man tilted his head. 'Nine of you. In less than a quarter-bell several hundred looters and murderers will come calling.' He slowly looked around, as if gauging the estate's walls, the modest defences, then returned his steady gaze to Gamet.

The captain scowled. 'No doubt you would have made it even easier for them. As it is, we might bloody their noses enough to encourage them to seek somewhere else.'

'No, you won't, Captain. Things will simply get . . . messier.'

'Is this how the Empress simplifies matters, Kollen? An unlocked gate. Loyal guards cut down from behind. Have you honed your knife for my back?'

'I am not here at the behest of the Empress, Captain.'

Gamet's eyes narrowed.

'No harm is to come to her,' the man went on after a moment. 'Provided I have your full co-operation. But we are running out of time.'

'This is Tavore's answer? What of her parents? There was

nothing to suggest that their fate would be any different from that of the others who'd been rounded up.'

'Alas, the Adjunct's options are limited. She is under some . . . scrutiny.'

'What is planned for Felisin, Kollen – or whoever you are?'

'A brief stint in the otataral mines—'

'What!?'

'She will not be entirely alone. A guardian will accompany her. Understand, Captain, it is this, or the mob outside.'

Nine loyal guards cut down, blood on the floors and walls, a handful of servants overwhelmed at flimsy barricades outside the child's bedroom door. Then, for the child . . . no-one. 'Who is this "guardian", then, Kollen?'

The man smiled. 'Me, Captain. And no, my true name is not Kollen.'

Gamet stepped up to him, until their faces were but a hand's width apart. 'If any harm comes to her, I will find you. And I don't care if you're a Claw—'

'I am not a Claw, Captain. As for harm coming to Felisin, I regret to say that there will be some. It cannot be helped. We must hope she is resilient – it is a Paran trait, yes?'

After a long moment, Gamet stepped back, suddenly resigned. 'Do you kill us now or later?'

The man's brows rose. 'I doubt I could manage that, given those crossbows levelled behind me. No, but I am to ask that you now escort me to a safe house. At all costs, we must not permit the child to fall into the mob's hands. Can I rely upon your help in this, Captain?'

'Where is this safe house?'

'On the Avenue of Souls . . .'

Gamet grimaced. Judgement's Round. To the chains. Oh, Beru guard you, lass. He strode past Kollen. 'I will awaken her.'

Pearl stood at the round table, leaning on both hands, his head lowered as he studied the scroll. The Adjunct had departed half a bell past, her Fist on her heels like a misshapen shadow. Lostara waited, arms crossed, with her back against the door through which Tavore and Gamet had left. She had held silent during the length of Pearl's perusal of the scroll, her anger and frustration growing with each passing moment.

Finally, she'd had enough. 'I will have no part of this. Return me to Tene Baralta's command.'

Pearl did not look up. 'As you wish, my dear,' he murmured, then added: 'Of course I will have to kill you at some point – certainly before you report to your commander. It's the hard rules of clandestine endeavours, I regret to say.'

'Since when are you at the Adjunct's beck and call, Pearl?'

'Why,' he glanced up and met her gaze, 'ever since she unequivocally reasserted her loyalty to the Empress, of course.' He returned his attention to the scroll.

Lostara scowled. 'I'm sorry, I think I missed that part of the conversation.'

'Not surprising,' Pearl replied, 'since it resided *in between* the words actually spoken.' He smiled at her. 'Precisely where it belonged.'

With a hiss, Lostara began pacing, struggled against an irrational desire to take a knife blade to these damned tapestries and their endless scenes of past glories. 'You will have to explain, Pearl,' she growled.

'And will that relieve your conscience sufficiently to return you to my side? Very well. The resurgence of the noble class in the chambers of imperial power has been uncommonly swift. Indeed, one might say unnaturally so. Almost as if they were receiving help – but *who*? we wondered. Oh, absurd rumours of the return of the Talons persisted. And every now and then some poor fool who'd been arrested for something completely unrelated went and confessed to being a Talon, but they were young, caught up in romantic notions and the lure of cults and whatnot. They might well call themselves Talons, but they did not even come close to the real organization, to Dancer's own – of which many of us Claw possessed firsthand experience.

'In any case, back to the matter at hand. Tavore is of noble blood, and it's now clear that a truly covert element of Talons has returned to plague us, and has been making use of the nobility. Placing sympathetic agents in the military and administration – a mutually profitable infiltration. But Tavore is now the Adjunct, and as such, her old ties, her old loyalties, must needs be severed.' Pearl paused to tap a finger on the laid-out scroll before him. 'She has given us the Talons, Captain. We will find this Baudin Younger, and from him we will unravel the entire organization.'

Lostara said nothing for a long moment. 'In a sense, then,' she said, 'our mission is not extraneous to the interests of the empire after all.'

Pearl flashed a smile.

'But if so,' Lostara continued, 'why didn't the Adjunct just say so?'

'Oh, I think we can leave that question unanswered for the time being—'

'No, I would have it answered now!'

Pearl sighed. 'Because, my dear, for Tavore, the surrendering of the Talons is secondary to our finding Felisin. And that *is* extraneous, and not only extraneous, but also damning. Do you think the Empress would smile upon this clever little scheme, the lie behind this all-too-public demonstration of the new Adjunct's loyalty? Sending her sister to the otataral mines! Hood take us all, that's a hard woman! The Empress has chosen well, has she not?'

Lostara grimaced. *Chosen well . . . based on what, though?* 'Indeed she has.'

'Aye, I agree. It's a fair exchange in any case – we save Felisin and are rewarded with a principal agent of the Talons. The Empress will no doubt wonder what we were doing out on the Otataral Isle in the first place—'

'You will have to lie to her, won't you?'

Pearl's smile broadened. 'We both will, lass. As would the Adjunct, and Fist Gamet if it came to that. Unless, of course, I take what the Adjunct has offered me. Offered me personally, that is.'

Lostara slowly nodded. 'You are at a loose end. Yes. Out of favour with the Clawmaster and the Empress. Eager to make reparations. An independent mission – you somehow latched onto the rumour of a true Talon, and set off on his trail. Thus, the credit for unravelling the Talons is to be yours, and yours alone.'

'Or ours,' Pearl corrected. 'If you so desire.'

She shrugged. 'We can decide that later. Very well, Pearl. Now,' she moved to his side, 'what are these details with which the Adjunct has so kindly provided us?'

Admiral Nok had been facing the hearth, his gaze on its cold ashes. At the sound of the door opening, he slowly turned, his expression as impassive as ever.

'Thank you,' the Adjunct said, 'for your patience.'

The admiral said nothing, his level gaze shifting to Gamet for a moment.

The midnight bell's muted echoes were only now fading. The Fist was exhausted, feeling fragile and scattered, unable to meet Nok's eyes for very long. This night, he'd been little more than the Adjunct's pet, or worse, a familiar. Tacitly conjoined with her plans within plans, bereft of even so much as the illusion of a choice. When Tavore had first drawn him into her entourage – shortly after Felisin's arrest – Gamet had briefly considered slipping away, vanishing in the time-honoured tradition of Malazan soldiers who found themselves in unwelcome circumstances. But he hadn't, and his reasons for joining the Adjunct's core of advisers – not that they were ever invited to *advise* – had, upon ruthless self-reflection, proved less than laudable. He had been driven by macabre curiosity. Tavore had ordered the arrests of her parents, had sent her younger sister into the horrors of the otataral mines. *For her career's sake.* Her brother, Paran, had in some way been disgraced on Genabackis. He had subsequently deserted. *An embarrassment, granted, but surely not sufficient to warrant Tavore's reaction. Unless . . .* There were rumours that the lad had been an agent of Adjunct Lorn's, and that his desertion had led, ultimately, to the woman's death in Darujhistan. Yet, if that were true, then why did the Empress turn her royal gaze upon another child of the House of Paran? Why make *Tavore* the new Adjunct?

'Fist Gamet.'

He blinked. 'Adjunct?'

'Seat yourself, please. I would have some final words with you, but they can wait for the time being.'

Nodding, Gamet glanced around until he spied the lone high-backed chair set against one of the small room's walls. It looked anything but comfortable, which was probably an advantage, given his weariness. Ominous creaks sounded when he settled into the chair and he grimaced. 'No wonder Pormqual didn't send this one off with all the rest,' he muttered.

'It is my understanding,' Nok said, 'that the transport ship in question sank in the harbour of Malaz City, taking the late High Fist's loot with it.'

Gamet's wiry brows rose. 'All that way . . . just to sink in the harbour? What happened?'

The admiral shrugged. 'None of the crew reached the shore to tell the tale.'

None?

Nok seemed to note his scepticism, for he elaborated, 'Malaz Harbour is well known for its sharks. A number of dories were found, all awash but otherwise empty.'

The Adjunct had, uncharacteristically, been permitting the exchange to continue, leading Gamet to wonder if Tavore had sensed a hidden significance to the mysterious loss of the transport ship. Now she spoke. 'It remains, then, a peculiar curse – unexplained founderings, empty dories, lost crews. Malaz Harbour is indeed notorious for its sharks, particularly since they seem uniquely capable of eating victims whole, leaving no remnants whatsoever.'

'There are sharks that can do just that,' Nok replied. 'I know of at least twelve ships on the muddy bottom of the harbour in question—'

'Including the *Twisted*,' the Adjunct drawled, 'the old emperor's flagship, which mysteriously slipped its moorings the night after the assassinations, then promptly plummeted into the deeps, taking its resident demon with it.'

'Perhaps it likes company,' Nok observed. 'The island's fishermen all swear the harbour's haunted, after all. The frequency with which nets are lost—'

'Admiral,' Tavore cut in, her eyes resting on the dead hearth, 'there is you, and three others. All who are left.'

Gamet slowly straightened in his chair. *Three others. High Mage Tayschrenn, Dujek Onearm, and Whiskeyjack. Four . . . gods, is that all now? Tattersail, Bellurdan, Nightchill, Duiker . . . so many fallen—*

Admiral Nok was simply studying the Adjunct. He had stood against the wrath of the Empress, first with Cartheron Crust's disappearance, then Urko's and Ameron's. Whatever answers he had given, he had done so long ago.

'I do not speak for the Empress,' Tavore said after a moment. 'Nor am I interested in . . . details. What interests me is . . . a matter of personal . . . curiosity. I would seek to understand, Admiral, why they abandoned her.'

There was silence, filling the room, growing towards something like an impasse. Gamet leaned back and closed his eyes. *Ah, lass, you ask questions of . . . of loyalty, as would someone who has never experienced it. You reveal to this admiral what can only be construed as a critical flaw. You command the Fourteenth Army, Adjunct, yet you do so in isolation, raising the very barricades you must needs take down if you would truly lead. What does Nok think of this, now? Is it any wonder he does not—*

'The answer to your question,' the admiral said, 'lies in what was both a strength and a flaw of the Emperor's . . . family. The family that he gathered to raise an empire. Kellanved began with but one companion – Dancer. The two then hired a handful of locals in Malaz City and set about conquering the criminal element in the city – I should point out, that criminal element happened to rule the entire island. Their target was Mock, Malaz Island's unofficial ruler. A pirate, and a cold-blooded killer.'

'Who were these first hirelings, Admiral?'

'Myself, Ameron, Dujek, a woman named Hawl – my wife. I had been First Mate to a corsair that worked the sea lanes around the Napan Isles – which had just been annexed by Unta and were providing a staging point for the Untan king's planned invasion of Kartool. We'd taken a beating and had limped into Malaz Harbour, only to have the ship and its crew arrested by Mock, who was negotiating a trade of prisoners with Unta. Only Ameron and Hawl and I escaped. A lad named Dujek discovered where we were holed up and he delivered us to his new employers. Kellanved and Dancer.'

'Was this before they were granted entry into the Deadhouse?' Gamet asked.

'Aye, but only just. Our residency in the Deadhouse rewarded us with – as is now clearly evident – certain gifts. Longevity, immunity to most diseases, and . . . other things. The Deadhouse also provided us with an unassailable base of operations. Dancer later bolstered our numbers by recruiting among the refugee Napans who'd fled the conquest: Cartheron Crust and his brother, Urko. And Surly – Laseen. Three more men were to follow shortly thereafter. Toc Elder, Dassem Ultor – who was, like Kellanved, of Dal Honese blood – and a renegade High Septarch of the D'rek Cult, Tayschrenn. And finally, Duiker.' He half smiled at Tavore. 'The family. With which Kellanved conquered Malaz Island. Swiftly done, with minimal losses . . .'

Minimal . . . 'Your wife,' Gamet said.

'Yes, her.' After a long moment, he shrugged and continued, 'To answer you, Adjunct. Unknown to the rest of us, the Napans among us were far more than simple refugees. Surly was of the royal line. Crust and Urko had been captains in the Napan fleet, a fleet that would have likely repelled the Untans if it hadn't been virtually destroyed by a sudden storm. As it turned out, theirs was a singular purpose – to crush the Untan hegemony – and they planned on using Kellanved to achieve that. In a sense, that was the first betrayal within the family, the first fissure. Easily healed, it seemed, since Kellanved already possessed imperial ambitions, and of the two major rivals on the mainland, Unta was by far the fiercest.'

'Admiral,' Tavore said, 'I see where this leads. Surly's assassination of Kellanved and Dancer shattered that family irrevocably, but that is precisely where my understanding falters. Surly had taken the Napan cause to its penultimate conclusion. Yet it was not you, not Tayschrenn, Duiker, Dassem Ultor or Toc Elder who . . . disappeared. It was . . . *Napans.*'

'Barring Ameron,' Gamet pointed out.

The admiral's lined face stretched as he bared his teeth in a humourless grin. 'Ameron was half-Napan.'

'So it was only the *Napans* who deserted the new Empress?' Gamet stared up at Nok, now as confused as Tavore. 'Yet Surly was of the *royal* Napan line?'

Nok said nothing for a long time, then he sighed. 'Shame is a fierce, vigorous poison. To now serve the new Empress . . . complicity and damnation. Crust, Urko and Ameron were not party to the betrayal . . . but who would believe them? Who could not help but see them as party to the murderous plot? Yet, in truth,' his eyes met Tavore's, 'Surly had included none of us in her scheme – she could not afford to. She had the Claw, and that was all she needed.'

'And where were the Talons in all this?' Gamet asked, then cursed himself – *ah, gods, too tired—*

Nok's eyes widened for the first time that night. 'You've a sharp memory, Fist.'

Gamet clamped his jaws tight, sensing the Adjunct's hard stare fixing on him.

The admiral continued, 'I am afraid I have no answer to that. I was not in Malaz City on that particular night; nor have I made enquiries to those who were. The Talons essentially vanished with Dancer's death. It was widely believed that the Claw had struck them down in concert with the assassinations of Dancer and the Emperor.'

The Adjunct's tone was suddenly curt. 'Thank you, Admiral, for your words this night. I will keep you no longer.'

The man bowed, then strode from the room.

Gamet waited with held breath, ready for her fiercest castigation. Instead, she simply sighed. 'You have much work ahead of you, Fist, in assembling your legion. Best retire now.'

'Adjunct,' he acknowledged, pushing himself to his feet. He hesitated, then with a nod strode to the door.

'Gamet.'

He turned. 'Yes?'

'Where is T'amber?'

'She awaits you in your chambers, Adjunct.'

'Very well. Goodnight, Fist.'

'And to you, Adjunct.'

Buckets of salt water had been sloshed across the cobbled centre aisle of the stables, which had the effect of damping the dust and sending the biting flies into a frenzy, as well as making doubly rank the stench of horse piss. Strings, standing just within the doors, could already feel his sinuses stinging. His searching gaze found four figures seated on bound rolls of straw near the far end. Scowling, the Bridgeburner shifted the weight of the pack on his shoulder, then headed over.

'Who was the bright spark missing the old smells of home?' he drawled as he approached.

The half-Seti warrior named Koryk grunted, then said, 'That would be Lieutenant Ranal, who then had a quick excuse to leave us for a time.' He'd found a flap of hide from somewhere and was cutting long strands from it with a thin-bladed pig-sticker. Strings had seen his type before, obsessed with tying things down, or worse, tying things to their bodies. Not just fetishes, but loot, extra equipment, tufts of grass or leafy branches depending on the camouflage being sought. In this case, Strings half expected to see twists of straw sprouting from the man.

For centuries the Seti had fought a protracted war with the city-states of Quon and Li Heng, defending the barely inhabitable lands that had been their traditional home. Hopelessly outnumbered and perpetually on the run, they had learned the art of hiding the hard way. But the Seti lands had been pacified for sixty years now; almost three generations had lived in that ambivalent, ambiguous border that was the edge of civilization. The various tribes had dissolved into a single, murky nation, with mixed-bloods coming to dominate the population. What had befallen them had been the impetus, in fact, for Coltaine's rebellion and the Wickan Wars – for Coltaine had clearly seen that a similar fate awaited his own people.

It was not, Strings had come to believe, a question of right and wrong. Some cultures were inward-looking. Others were aggressive. The former were rarely capable of mustering a defence against the latter, not without meta-morphosing into some other thing, a thing twisted by the exigencies of desperation and violence. The original Seti had not even ridden horses. Yet now they were known as horse warriors, a taller, darker-skinned and more morose kind of Wickan.

Strings knew little of Koryk's personal history, but he felt he could guess. Half-bloods did not lead pleasant lives. That Koryk had chosen to emulate the old Seti ways, whilst joining the Malazan army as a marine rather than a horse warrior, spoke tomes of the clash in the man's scarred soul.

Setting down his pack, Strings stood before the four recruits. 'As much as I hate to confess it, I am now your sergeant. Officially, you're 4th Squad, one of three squads under Lieutenant Ranal's command. The 5th and 6th squads are supposedly on their way over from the tent city west of Aren. We're all in the 9th Company, which consists of three squads of heavy infantry, three of marines, and eighteen squads of medium infantry. Our commander is a man named Captain Keneb – and no, I've not met him and know nothing of him. Nine companies in all, making up the 8th Legion – us. The 8th is under the command of Fist Gamet, who I gather is a veteran who'd retired to the Adjunct's household before she became the Adjunct.' He paused, grimacing at the slightly glazed faces before him. 'But never mind all that. You're in the 4th Squad. We've got one more coming, but even with that one we're under-manned as a squad, but so are all the others and before you ask, I ain't privy to the reasons for that. Now, any questions yet?'

Three men and one young woman sat in silence, staring up at him.

Strings sighed, and pointed to the nondescript soldier sitting to Koryk's left. 'What's your name?' he asked.

A bewildered look, then, 'My real name, Sergeant, or the one the drill sergeant in Malaz City gave me?'

By the man's accent and his pale, stolid features, Strings knew him as being from Li Heng. That being the case, his real name was probably a mouthful: nine, ten or even fifteen names all strung together. 'Your new one, soldier.'

'Tarr.'

Koryk spoke up. 'If you'd seen him on the training ground, you'd understand. Once he's planted his feet behind that shield of his, you could hit him with a battering ram and he won't budge.'

Strings studied Tarr's placid, pallid eyes. 'All right. You're now Corporal Tarr—'

The woman, who'd been chewing on a straw, suddenly

choked. Coughing, spitting out pieces of the straw, she glared up at Strings with disbelief. 'What? Him? He never says nothing, never does nothing unless he's told, never—'

'Glad to hear all that,' Strings cut in laconically. 'The perfect corporal, especially that bit about not talking.'

The woman's expression tightened, then unveiled a small sneer as she looked away in feigned disinterest.

'And what is your name, soldier?' Strings asked her.

'My real name—'

'I don't care what you used to be called. None of you. Most of us get new ones and that's just the way it is.'

'I didn't,' Koryk growled.

Ignoring him, Strings continued, 'Your name, lass?'

Sour contempt at the word *lass*.

'Drill sergeant named her Smiles,' Koryk said.

'Smiles?'

'Aye. She never does.'

Eyes narrowing, Strings swung to the last soldier, a rather plain young man wearing leathers but no weapon. 'And yours?'

'Bottle.'

'Who was your drill sergeant?' he demanded to the four recruits.

Koryk leaned back as he replied, 'Braven Tooth—'

'Braven Tooth! That bastard's still alive?'

'It was hard to tell at times,' Smiles muttered.

'Until his temper snapped,' Koryk added. 'Just ask Corporal Tarr there. Braven Tooth spent near two bells pounding on him with a mace. Couldn't get past the shield.'

Strings glared at his new corporal. 'Where'd you learn that skill?'

The man shrugged. 'Don't know. Don't like getting hit.'

'Well, do you ever counter-attack?'

Tarr frowned. 'Sure. When they're tired.'

Strings was silent for a long moment. Braven Tooth – he was dumbfounded. The bastard was grizzled back when . . .

when the whole naming thing began. It had been Braven who'd started it. Braven who'd named most of the Bridgeburners. Whiskeyjack. Trotts, Mallet, Hedge, Blend, Picker, Toes . . . Fiddler himself had avoided a new name through his basic training; it had been Whiskeyjack who'd named him, on that first ride through Raraku. He shook his head, glanced sidelong at Tarr. 'You should be a heavy infantryman, Corporal, with a talent like that. The marines are supposed to be fast, nimble – avoiding the toe-to-toe whenever possible or, if there's no choice, making it quick.'

'I'm good with a crossbow,' Tarr said, shrugging.

'And a fast loader,' Koryk added. 'It was that that made Braven decide to make him a marine.'

Smiles spoke. 'So who named Braven Tooth, Sergeant?'

I did, after the bastard left one of his in my shoulder the night of the brawl. The brawl we all later denied happening. Gods, so many years ago, now . . . 'I have no idea,' he said. He shifted his attention back to the man named Bottle. 'Where's your sword, soldier?'

'I don't use one.'

'Well, what do you use?'

The man shrugged. 'This and that.'

'Well, Bottle, someday I'd like to hear how you got through basic training without picking up a weapon – no, not now. Not tomorrow either, not even next week. For now, tell me what I should be using you for.'

'Scouting. Quiet work.'

'As in sneaking up behind someone. What do you do then? Tap him on the shoulder? Never mind.' *This man smells like a mage to me, only he doesn't want to advertise it. Fine, be that way, we'll twist it out of you sooner or later.*

'I do the same kind of work,' Smiles said. She settled a forefinger on the pommel of one of the two thin-bladed knives at her belt. 'But I finish things with these.'

'So there's only two soldiers in this outfit who can actually fight toe-to-toe?'

'You said one more's coming,' Koryk pointed out.

'We can all handle crossbows,' Smiles added. 'Except for Bottle.'

They heard voices from outside the commandeered stables, then figures appeared in the doorway, six in all, burdened with equipment. A deep voice called, 'You put the latrine trench *outside* the barracks, for Hood's sake! Bastards don't teach ya anything these days?'

'Compliments of Lieutenant Ranal,' Strings said.

The soldier who'd spoken was in the lead as the squad approached. 'Right. Met him.'

Aye, nothing more need be said on that. 'I'm Sergeant Strings – we're the 4th.'

'Well hey,' a second soldier said, grinning through his bushy red beard, 'someone can count after all. These marines are full of surprises.'

'Fifth,' the first soldier said. There was a strange, burnished cast to the man's skin, making Strings doubt his initial guess that he was Falari. Then he noted an identical sheen to the red-bearded soldier, as well as on a much younger man. 'I'm Gesler,' the first soldier added. 'Temporarily sergeant of this next-to-useless squad.'

The red-bearded man dropped his pack to the floor. 'We was coastal guards, me and Gesler and Truth. I'm Stormy. But Coltaine made us marines—'

'Not Coltaine,' Gesler corrected. 'Captain Lull, it was, Queen harbour his poor soul.'

Strings simply stared at the two men.

Stormy scowled. 'Got a problem with us?' he demanded, face darkening.

'Adjutant Stormy,' Strings muttered. 'Captain Gesler. Hood's rattling bones—'

'We ain't none of those things any more,' Gesler said. 'Like I said, I'm now a sergeant, and Stormy's my corporal. And the rest here . . . there's Truth, Tavos Pond, Sands and Pella. Truth's been with us since Hissar, and Pella was a camp guard at the otataral mines – only a handful survived the uprising there, from what I gather.'

'Strings, is it?' Stormy's small eyes had narrowed suspiciously. He nudged his sergeant. 'Hey, Gesler, think we should have done that? Changed our names, I mean. This Strings here is Old Guard as sure as I'm a demon in my dear father's eye.'

'Let the bastard keep whatever name he wants,' Gesler muttered. 'All right, squad, find some place to drop your stuff. The 6th should be showing up any time, and the lieutenant, too. Word is, we're all being mustered out to face the Adjunct's lizard eyes in a day or two.'

The soldier Gesler had named Tavos Pond – a tall, dark, moustached man who was probably Korelri – spoke up. 'So we should polish our equipment, Sergeant?'

'Polish whatever you like,' the man replied disinterestedly, 'just not in public. As for the Adjunct, if she can't handle a few scuffed up soldiers then she won't last long. It's a dusty world out there, and the sooner we blend in the better.'

Strings sighed. He was feeling more confident already. He faced his own soldiers. 'Enough sitting on that straw. Start spreading it out to soak up this horse piss.' He faced Gesler again. 'A word with you in private?'

The man nodded. 'Let's head back outside.'

Moments later the two men stood on the cobbled courtyard of the estate that had once housed a well-off local merchant and was now the temporary bivouac for Ranal's squads. The lieutenant had taken the house proper for himself, leaving Strings wondering what the man did with all those empty rooms.

They said nothing for a moment, then Strings grinned. 'I can picture Whiskeyjack's jaw dropping – the day I tell him you was my fellow sergeant in the new 8th Legion.'

Gesler scowled. 'Whiskeyjack. He was busted down to sergeant before I was, the bastard. Mind you, I then made corporal, so I beat him after all.'

'Except now you're a sergeant again. While Whiskeyjack's an outlaw. Try beating that.'

'I just might,' Gesler muttered.

'Got concerns about the Adjunct?' Strings quietly asked. The courtyard was empty, but even so . . .

'Met her, you know. Oh, she's as cold as Hood's forked tongue. She impounded my ship.'

'You had a ship?'

'By rights of salvage, aye. I was the one who brought Coltaine's wounded to Aren. And that's the thanks I get.'

'You could always punch her in the face. That's what you usually end up doing to your superiors, sooner or later.'

'I could at that. I'd have to get past Gamet, of course. The point I was making is this: she's never commanded anything more than a damned noble household, and here she's been handed three legions and told to reconquer an entire subcontinent.' He glanced sidelong at Strings. 'There wasn't many Falari made it into the Bridgeburners. Bad timing, I think, but there was one.'

'Aye, and I'm him.'

After a moment, Gesler grinned and held out his hand. 'Strings. Fiddler. Sure.'

They clasped wrists. To Strings, the other man's hand and arm felt like solid stone.

'There's an inn down the street,' Gesler continued. 'We need to swap stories, and I guarantee you, mine's got yours beat by far.'

'Oh, Gesler,' Strings sighed, 'I think you're in for a surprise.'

CHAPTER SIX

We came within sight of the island, close enough to
gaze into the depths through the ancient cedars and
firs. And it seemed there was motion within that
gloom, as if the shadows of long dead and long
fallen trees still remained, swaying and shifting on
ghostly winds . . .

Quon Sea Charting Expedition of
1127 Burn's Sleep, Drift Avalii

Hedoranas

The journey home had been enough, if only to return
one last time to the place of beginnings, to
crumbled reminiscences amidst sea-thrust coral
sands above the tide line, the handful of abandoned shacks
battered by countless storms into withered skeletons of
wood. Nets lay buried in glistening drifts blinding white in
the harsh sunlight. And the track that had led down from
the road, overgrown now with wind-twisted grasses . . . no
place from the past survived unchanged, and here, in this
small fisher village on the coast of Itko Kan, Hood had
walked with thorough and absolute deliberation, leaving
not a single soul in his wake.

Barring the one man who had now returned. And the
daughter of that man, who had once been possessed by a
god.

And in the leaning shack that had once housed them
both – its frond-woven roof long since stripped away – with

the broad, shallow-draught fisherboat close by now showing but a prow and a stern, the rest buried beneath the coral sand, the father had laid himself down and slept.

Crokus had awakened to soft weeping. Sitting up, he had seen Apsalar kneeling beside the still form of her father. There were plenty of footprints on the floor of the shack from the previous evening's random explorations, but Crokus noted one set in particular, prints large and far apart yet far too lightly pressed into the damp sand. A silent arrival in the night just past, crossing the single chamber to stand square-footed beside Rellock. Where it had gone after that left no markings in the sand.

A shiver rippled through the Daru. It was one thing for an old man to die in his sleep, but it was another for Hood himself – or one of his minions – to physically arrive to collect the man's soul.

Apsalar's grief was quiet, barely heard above the hiss of waves on the beach, the faint whistle of the wind through the warped slats in the shack's walls. She knelt with bowed head, face hidden beneath her long black hair that hung so appropriately like a shawl. Her hands were closed around her father's right hand.

Crokus made no move towards her. In the months of their travelling together, he had come, perversely, to know her less and less. Her soul's depths had become unfathomable, and whatever lay at its heart was otherworldly and . . . not quite human.

The god that had possessed her – Cotillion, the Rope, Patron of Assassins within the House of Shadow – had been a mortal man, once, the one known as Dancer who had stood at the Emperor's side, who had purportedly shared Kellanved's fate at Laseen's hands. Of course, neither had died in truth. Instead, they had ascended. Crokus had no idea how such a thing could come to be. Ascendancy was but one of the countless mysteries of the world, a world where uncertainty ruled all – god and mortal alike – and its rules were impenetrable. But, it seemed to him, to ascend was also to *surrender*. Embracing what to all intents and purposes could be called immortality, was, he had begun to believe, presaged by a turning away. Was it not a mortal's fate – fate, he knew, was the wrong word, but he could think of no other – was it not a mortal's fate, then, to embrace life itself, as one would a lover? Life, with all its fraught, momentary fragility.

And could life not be called a mortal's first lover? A lover whose embrace was then rejected in that fiery crucible of ascendancy?

Crokus wondered how far she had gone down that path – for it was a path she was surely on, this beautiful woman no older than him, who moved in appalling silence, with a killer's terrible grace, this temptress of death.

The more remote she grew, the more Crokus felt himself drawn forward, to that edge within her. The lure to plunge into that darkness was at times overwhelming, could, at a moment's thought, turn frantic the beat of his heart and fierce the fire of the blood in his veins. What made the silent invitation so terrifying to him was the seeming indifference with which she offered it to him.

As if the attraction itself was . . . self-evident. Not worth even acknowledging. Did Apsalar want him to walk at her side on this path to ascendancy – if that was what it was? Was it Crokus she wanted, or simply . . . somebody, anybody?

The truth was this: he had grown afraid to look into her eyes.

He rose from his bedroll and quietly made his way outside. There were fisherboats out on the shoals, white sails taut like enormous shark fins plying the sea beyond the breakers. The Hounds had once torn through this area of the coast, leaving naught but corpses, but people had returned – there if not here. Or perhaps they had *been* returned, forcibly. The land itself had no difficulty absorbing spilled blood; its thirst was indiscriminate, true to the nature of land everywhere.

Crokus crouched down and collected a handful of white sand. He studied the coral pebbles as they slipped down between his fingers. *The land does its own dying, after all. And yet, these are truths we would escape, should we proceed down this path. I wonder, does fear of dying lie at the root of ascendancy?*

If so, then he would never make it, for, somewhere in all that had occurred, all that he had survived in coming to this place, Crokus had lost that fear.

He sat down, resting his back against the trunk of a massive cedar that had been thrown up onto this beach – roots and all – and drew out his knives. He practised a sequenced shift of grips, each hand reversing the pattern of the other, and stared down until the weapons – and his fingers – became little more than blurs of motion. Then he lifted his head and studied the sea, its rolling breakers in the distance, the triangular sails skidding along beyond the white line of foam. He made the sequence in his right hand random. Then did the same for his left.

Thirty paces down the beach waited their single-masted runner, its magenta sail reefed, its hull's blue, gold and red paint faint stains in the sunlight. A Korelri craft, paid in debt to a local bookmaker in Kan – for an alley in Kan had been the place where Shadowthrone had sent them, not to the road above the village as he had promised.

The bookmaker had paid the debt in turn to Apsalar and Crokus for a single night's work that had proved, for Crokus, brutally horrifying. It was one thing to practise passes with the blades, to master the deadly dance against ghosts of the imagination, but he had killed two men that night. Granted, they were murderers, in the employ of a man who was making a career out of extortion and terror. Apsalar had shown no compunction in cutting his throat, no qualms at the spray of blood that spotted her gloved hands and forearms.

There had been a local with them, to witness the veracity of the night's work. In the aftermath, as he stood in the doorway and stared down at the three corpses, he'd lifted his head and met Crokus's eyes. Whatever he saw in them had drained the blood from the man's face.

By morning Crokus had acquired a new name. Cutter.

At first he had rejected it. The local had misread all that had been revealed behind the Daru's eyes that night. Nothing fierce. The barrier of shock, fast crumbling to self-condemnation. Murdering killers was still murder, the act like the closing of shackles between them all, joining a line of infinite length, one killer to the next, a procession from which there was no escape. His mind had recoiled from the name, recoiled from all that it signified.

But that had proved a short-lived rectitude. The two murderers had died indeed – at the hands of the man named Cutter. Not Crokus, not the Daru youth, the cut-purse – who had vanished. Vanished, probably never to be seen again.

The delusion held a certain comfort, as cavernous at its core as Apsalar's embrace at night, but welcome all the same.

Cutter would walk her path.

Aye, the Emperor had Dancer, yes? A companion, for a companion was what was needed. Is needed. Now, she has Cutter. Cutter of the Knives, who dances in his chains as if they were weightless threads. Cutter, who, unlike poor Crokus, knows his place, knows his singular task – to guard her back, to match her cold precision in the deadly arts.

And therein resided the final truth. Anyone could become a killer. Anyone at all.

She stepped out of the shack, wan but dry-eyed.

He sheathed his knives in a single, fluid motion, rose to his feet and faced her.

'Yes,' she said. 'What now?'

Broken pillars of mortared stone jutted from the undulating vista. Among the half-dozen or so within sight, only two rose as tall as a man, and none stood straight. The plain's strange, colourless grasses gathered in tufts around their bases, snarled and oily in the grey, grainy air.

As Kalam rode into their midst, the muted thunder of his horse's hoofs seemed to bounce back across his path, the echoes multiplying until he felt as if he was riding at the head of a mounted army. He slowed his charger's canter, finally reining in beside one of the battered columns.

These silent sentinels felt like an intrusion on the solitude he had been seeking. He leaned in his saddle to study the one nearest him. It looked old, old in the way of so many things within the Warren of Shadow, forlorn with an air of abandonment, defying any chance he might have of discerning its function. There were no intervening ruins, no foundation walls, no cellar pits or other angular pocks in the ground. Each pillar stood alone, unaligned.

His examination settled on a rusted ring set into the stone near the base, from which depended a chain of seized links vanishing into the tufts of grass. After a moment, Kalam dismounted. He crouched down, reaching out to close his hand on the chain. A slight upward tug. The desiccated hand and forearm of some hapless creature lifted from the grasses. Dagger-length talons, four fingers and two thumbs.

The rest of the prisoner had succumbed to the roots, was half buried beneath dun-coloured, sandy soil. Pallid yellow hair was entwined among the grass blades.

The hand suddenly twitched.

Disgusted, Kalam released the chain. The arm dropped back to the ground. A faint, subterranean keening sound rose from the base of the pillar.

Straightening, the assassin returned to his horse.

Pillars, columns, tree stumps, platforms, staircases leading nowhere, and for every dozen there was one among them holding a prisoner. None of whom seemed capable of dying. Not entirely. Oh, their minds had died – most of them – long ago. Raving in tongues, murmuring senseless incantations, begging forgiveness, offering bargains, though not one had yet – within Kalam's hearing – proclaimed its own innocence.

As if mercy could be an issue without it. He nudged his horse forward once more. This was not a realm to his liking. Not that he'd in truth had much choice in the matter. Bargaining with gods was – for the mortal involved – an exercise in self-delusion. Kalam would rather leave Quick Ben to play games with the rulers of this warren – the wizard had the advantage of enjoying the challenge – no, it was more than that. Quick Ben had left so many knives in so many backs – none of them fatal but none the less sure to sting when tugged, and it was that tugging the wizard loved so much.

The assassin wondered where his old friend was right now. There'd been trouble – *nothing new there* – and, since then, naught but silence. And then there was Fiddler. The fool had re-enlisted, for Hood's sake!

Well, at least they're doing something. Not Kalam, oh no, not Kalam. Thirteen hundred children, resurrected on a whim. Shining eyes following his every move, mapping his every step, memorizing his every gesture – what could he teach them? The art of mayhem? As if children needed help in that.

A ridge lay ahead. He reached the base and brought his horse into a gentle canter up the slope.

Besides, Minala seemed to have it all under control. A natural born tyrant, she was, both in public and in private amidst the bedrolls in the half-ruined hovel they shared. And oddly enough, he'd found he was not averse to tyranny. In principle, that is. Things had a way of actually working when someone capable and implacable took charge. And he'd had enough experience taking orders to not chafe at her position of command. Between her and the aptorian demoness, a certain measure of control was being maintained, a host of life skills were being inculcated . . . *stealth, tracking, the laying of ambushes, the setting of traps for game both two- and four-legged, riding, scaling walls, freezing in place, knife throwing and countless other weapon skills, the weapons themselves donated by the warren's mad rulers – half of them cursed or haunted or fashioned for entirely unhuman hands.* The children took to such training with frightening zeal, and the gleam of pride in Minala's eyes left the assassin . . . chilled.

An army in the making for Shadowthrone. An alarming prospect, to say the least.

He reached the ridge. And suddenly reined in.

An enormous stone gate surmounted the hill opposite, twin pillars spanned by an arch. Within it, a swirling grey wall. On this side of the gate, the grassy summit flowed with countless, sourceless shadows, as if they were somehow tumbling out from the portal, only to swarm like lost wraiths around its threshold.

'Careful,' a voice murmured beside Kalam.

He turned to see a tall, hooded and cloaked figure standing a few paces away, flanked by two Hounds. Cotillion, and his favoured two, Rood and Blind. The beasts sat on their scarred haunches, lurid eyes – seeing and unseeing – on the portal.

'Why should I be careful?' the assassin asked.

'Oh, the shadows at the gate. They've lost their masters . . . but anyone will do.'

'So this gate is sealed?'

The hooded head slowly turned. 'Dear Kalam, is this a flight from our realm? How . . . ignoble.'

'I said nothing to suggest—'

'Then why does your shadow stretch so yearningly forward?'

Kalam glanced down at it, then scowled. 'How should I know? Perhaps it considers its chances better in yonder mob.'

'Chances?'

'For excitement.'

'Ah. Chafing, are you? I would never have guessed.'

'Liar,' Kalam said. 'Minala has banished me. But you

313

already know that, which is why you've come to find me.'

'I am the Patron of Assassins,' Cotillion said. 'I do not mediate marital disputes.'

'Depends on how fierce they get, doesn't it?'

'Are you ready to kill each other, then?'

'No. I was only making a point.'

'Which was?'

'What are you doing here, Cotillion?'

The god was silent for a long moment. 'I have often wondered,' he finally said, 'why it is that you, an assassin, offer no obeisance to your patron.'

Kalam's brows rose. 'Since when have you expected it? Hood take us, Cotillion, if it was fanatical worshippers you hungered for, you should never have looked to assassins. By our very natures, we're antithetical to the notion of subservience – as if you weren't already aware of that.' His voice trailed off, and he turned to study the shadow-wreathed figure standing beside him. 'Mind you, you stood at Kellanved's side, through to the end. Dancer, it seems, knew both loyalty and servitude . . .'

'Servitude?' There was a hint of a smile in the tone.

'Mere expedience? That seems difficult to countenance, given all that the two of you went through. Out with it, Cotillion, what is it you're asking?'

'Was I asking something?'

'You want me to . . . serve you, as would a minion his god. Some probably disreputable mission. You need me for something, only you've never learned how to *ask*.'

Rood slowly rose from his haunches, then stretched, long and languorous. The massive head then swung round, lambent eyes settling on Kalam.

'The Hounds are troubled,' Cotillion murmured.

'I can tell,' the assassin replied drily.

'I have certain tasks before me,' the god continued, 'that will consume much of my time for the near future. Whilst at the same time, certain other . . . activities . . . must be undertaken. It is one thing to find a loyal subject, but another entirely to find one conveniently positioned, as it were, to be of practical use—'

Kalam barked a laugh. 'You went fishing for faithful servants and found your subjects wanting.'

'We could argue interpretation all day,' Cotillion drawled.

There was a detectable irony in the god's voice that pleased Kalam. In spite of his wariness, he admitted that he actually liked Cotillion. *Uncle* Cotillion, as the child Panek called him. Certainly, between the Patron of Assassins and Shadowthrone, only the former seemed to possess any shred of self-examination – and thus was actually *capable* of being humbled. Even if the likelihood was in truth remote. 'Agreed,' Kalam replied. 'Very well, Minala has no interest in seeing my pretty face for a time. Leaving me free, more or less—'

'And without a roof over your head.'

'Without a roof over my head, aye. Fortunately it never seems to rain in your realm.'

'Ah,' Cotillion murmured, 'my realm.'

Kalam studied Rood. The beast had not relinquished its steady stare. The assassin was growing nervous under that unwavering attention. 'Is your claim – yours and Shadowthrone's – being contested?'

'Difficult to answer,' Cotillion murmured. 'There have been . . . trembles. Agitation . . .'

'As you said, the Hounds are troubled.'

'They are indeed.'

'You wish to know more of your potential enemy.'

'We would.'

Kalam studied the gate, the swirling shadows at its threshold. 'Where would you have me begin?'

'A confluence to your own desires, I suspect.'

The assassin glanced at the god, then slowly nodded.

In the half-light of dusk, the seas grew calm, gulls wheeling in from the shoals to settle on the beach. Cutter had built a fire from driftwood, more from the need to be doing something than seeking warmth, for the Kanese coast was subtropical, the breeze sighing down off the verge faint and sultry. The Daru had collected water from the spring near the trail head and was now brewing tea. Overhead, the first stars of night flickered into life.

Apsalar's question earlier that afternoon had gone unanswered. Cutter was not yet ready to return to Darujhistan, and he felt nothing of the calm he'd expected to follow the completion of their task. Rellock and Apsalar had, finally, returned to their home, only to find it a place haunted by death, a haunting that had slipped its fatal flavour into the old man's soul, adding yet one more ghost to this forlorn strand. There was, now, nothing for them here.

Cutter's own experience here in the Malazan Empire was, he well knew, twisted and incomplete. A single vicious night in Malaz City, followed by three tense days in Kan that closed with yet more assassinations. The empire was a foreign place, of course, and one could expect a certain degree of discord between it and what he was used to in Darujhistan, but if anything what he had seen of daily life in the cities suggested a stronger sense of lawfulness, of order and calm. Even so, it was the smaller details that jarred his sensibilities the most, that reinforced the fact that he was a stranger.

Feeling vulnerable was not a weakness he shared with Apsalar. She seemed possessed of absolute calm, an ease, no matter where she was – the confidence of the god who once possessed her had left something of a permanent imprint on her soul. *Not just confidence.* He thought once more of the night she had killed the man in Kan. *Deadly skills, and the icy precision necessary when using them.* And, he recalled with a shiver, many of the god's own memories remained with her, reaching back to when the god had been a mortal man, had been Dancer. Among those, the night of the assassinations – when the woman who would become

Empress had struck down the Emperor . . . and Dancer.

She had revealed that much, at least, a revelation devoid of feeling, of sentiment, delivered as casually as a comment about the weather. Memories of biting knives, of dust-covered blood rolling like pellets across a floor . . .

He removed the pot from the coals, threw a handful of herbs into the steaming water.

She had gone for a walk, westward along the white beach. Even as dusk settled, he had lost sight of her, and he had begun to wonder if she was ever coming back.

A log settled suddenly, flinging sparks. The sea had grown entirely dark, invisible; he could not even hear the lap of the waves beyond the crackling fire. A cooler breath rode the breeze.

Cutter slowly rose, then spun round to face inland as something moved in the gloom beyond the fire's light. 'Apsalar?'

There was no reply. A faint thumping underfoot, as if the sands trembled to the passage of something huge . . . huge and four-legged.

The Daru drew out his knives, stepping away from the flickering light.

Ten paces away, at a height to match his own, he saw two glowing eyes, set wide, gold and seemingly depthless. The head and the body beneath it were darker stains in the night, hinting at a mass that left Cutter cold.

'Ah,' a voice said from the shadows to his left, 'the Daru lad. Blind has found you, good. Now, where is your companion?'

Cutter slowly sheathed his weapons. 'That damned Hound gave me a start,' he muttered. 'And if it's blind, why is it looking straight at me?'

'Well, her name is something of a misnomer. She sees, but not as we see.' A cloaked figure stepped into the fire-light. 'Do you know me?'

'Cotillion,' Cutter replied. 'Shadowthrone is much shorter.'

'Not that much, though perhaps in his affectations he exaggerates certain traits.'

'What do you want?'

'I would speak with Apsalar, of course. There is the smell of death here . . . recent, that is—'

'Rellock. Her father. In his sleep.'

'Unfortunate.' The god's hooded head turned, as if scanning the vicinity, then swung back to face Cutter. 'Am I your patron now?' he asked.

He wanted to answer *no*. He wanted to back away, to flee the question and all his answer would signify. He wanted to unleash vitriol at the suggestion. 'I believe you might be at that, Cotillion.'

'I am . . . pleased, Crokus.'

'I am now named Cutter.'

'Far less subtle, but apt enough, I suppose. Even so, there was the hint of deadly charm in your old Daru name. Are you sure you will not reconsider?'

Cutter shrugged, then said, 'Crokus had no . . . patron god.'

'Of course. And one day, a man will arrive in Darujhistan. With a Malazan name, and no-one will know him, except perhaps by reputation. And he will eventually hear tales of the young Crokus, a lad so instrumental in saving the city on the night of the Fete, all those years ago. Innocent, unsullied Crokus. So be it . . . Cutter. I see you have a boat.'

The change of subject startled him slightly, then he nodded. 'We have.'

'Sufficiently provisioned?'

'More or less. Not for a long voyage, though.'

'No, of course not. Why should it be? May I see your knives?'

Cutter unsheathed them and passed them across to the god, pommels forward.

'Decent blades,' Cotillion murmured. 'Well balanced. Within them are the echoes of your skill, the taste of blood. Shall I bless them for you, Cutter?'

'If the blessing is without magic,' the Daru replied.

'You desire no sorcerous investment?'

'No.'

'Ah. You would follow Rallick Nom's path.'

Cutter's eyes narrowed. *Oh, yes, he would recall him. When he saw through Sorry's eyes, at the Phoenix Inn, perhaps. Or maybe Rallick acknowledged his patron . . . though I find that difficult to believe.* 'I think I would have trouble following that path, Cotillion. Rallick's abilities are . . . were—'

'Formidable, yes. I do not think you need use the past tense when speaking of Rallick Nom, or Vorcan for that matter. No, I've no news . . . simply a suspicion.' He handed the knives back. 'You underestimate your own skills, Cutter, but perhaps that is for the best.'

'I don't know where Apsalar's gone,' Cutter said. 'I don't know if she's coming back.'

'As it has turned out, her presence has proved less vital than expected. I have a task for you, Cutter. Are you amenable to providing a service to your patron?'

'Isn't that expected?'

Cotillion was silent for a moment, then he laughed softly. 'No, I shall not take advantage of your . . . in-experience, though I admit to some temptation. Shall we begin things on a proper footing? Reciprocity, Cutter. A relationship of mutual exchanges, yes?'

'Would that you had offered the same to Apsalar.' Then he clamped his jaw shut.

But Cotillion simply sighed. 'Would that I had. Consider this new tact the consequence of difficult lessons.'

'You said reciprocity. What will I receive in return for providing this service?'

'Well, since you'll not accept my blessing or any other investment, I admit to being at something of a loss. Any suggestions?'

'I'd like some questions answered.'

'Indeed.'

'Yes. Such as, why did you and Shadowthrone scheme to destroy Laseen and the empire? Was it just a desire for revenge?'

The god seemed to flinch within his robes, and Cutter felt unseen eyes harden. 'Oh my,' Cotillion drawled, 'you force me to reconsider my offer.'

'I would know,' the Daru pressed on, 'so I can understand what you did . . . did to Apsalar.'

'You demand that your patron god justify his actions?'

'It wasn't a demand. Just a question.'

Cotillion said nothing for a long moment.

The fire was slowly dying, embers pulsing with the breeze. Cutter sensed the presence of a second Hound somewhere in the darkness beyond, moving restlessly.

'Necessities,' the god said quietly. 'Games are played, and what may appear precipitous might well be little more than a feint. Or perhaps it was the city itself, Darujhistan, that would serve our purposes better if it remained free, independent. There are layers of meaning behind every gesture, every gambit. I will not explain myself any further than that, Cutter.'

'Do – do you regret what you did?'

'You are indeed fearless, aren't you? Regret? Yes. Many, many regrets. One day, perhaps, you will see for yourself that regrets are as nothing. The value lies in how they are answered.'

Cutter slowly turned and stared out into the darkness of the sea. 'I threw Oponn's coin into the lake,' he said.

'And do you now regret the act?'

'I'm not sure. I didn't like their . . . attention.'

'I am not surprised,' Cotillion muttered.

'I have one more request,' Cutter said, facing the god again. 'This task you shall set me on – if I am assailed during it, can I call upon Blind?'

'The Hound?' The astonishment was clear in Cotillion's voice.

'Aye,' Cutter replied, his gaze now on the huge beast. 'Her attention . . . comforts me.'

'That makes you rarer than you could imagine, mortal. Very well. If the need is dire, call upon her and she will come.'

Cutter nodded. 'Now, what would you have me do on your behalf?'

The sun had cleared the horizon when Apsalar returned. After a few hours' sleep, Cutter had risen to bury Rellock above the tide line. He was checking the boat's hull one last time when a shadow appeared alongside his own.

'You had visitors,' she said.

He squinted up at her, studied her dark, depthless eyes. 'Aye.'

'And do you now have an answer to my question?'

Cutter frowned, then he sighed and nodded. 'I do. We're to explore an island.'

'An island? Is it far?'

'Middling, but getting farther by the moment.'

'Ah. Of course.'

Of course.

Overhead, gulls cried in the morning air on their way out to sea. Beyond the shoals, their white specks followed the wind, angling southwestward.

Cutter set his shoulder to the prow and pushed the craft back out onto the water. Then he clambered aboard. Apsalar joined him, making her way to the tiller.

What now? A god had given him his answer.

There had been no sunset in the realm the Tiste Edur called the Nascent for five months. The sky was grey, the light strangely hued and diffuse. There had been a flood, and then rains, and a world had been destroyed.

Even in the wreckage, however, there was life.

A score of broad-limbed catfish had clambered onto the mud-caked wall, none less than two man-lengths from

321

blunt head to limp tail. They were well-fed creatures, their silvery-white bellies protruding out to the sides. Their skins had dried and fissures were visible in a latticed web across their dark backs. The glitter of their small black eyes was muted beneath the skin's crinkled layer.

And it seemed those eyes were unaware of the solitary T'lan Imass standing over them.

Echoes of curiosity still clung to Onrack's tattered, desiccated soul. Joints creaking beneath the knotted ropes of ligaments, he crouched beside the nearest catfish. He did not think the creatures were dead. Only a short time ago, these fish had possessed no true limbs. He was witness, he suspected, to a metamorphosis.

After a moment, he slowly straightened. The sorcery that had sustained the wall against the vast weight of the new sea still held along this section. It had crumbled in others, forming wide breaches and foaming torrents of silt-laden water rushing through to the other side. A shallow sea was spreading out across the land on that side. There might come a time, Onrack suspected, when fragments of this wall were this realm's only islands.

The sea's torrential arrival had caught them unawares, scattering them in its tumbling maelstrom. Other kin had survived, the T'lan Imass knew, and indeed some had found purchase on this wall, or on floating detritus, sufficient to regain their forms, to link once more so that the hunt could resume.

But Kurald Emurlahn, fragmented or otherwise, was not amenable to the T'lan Imass. Without a Bonecaster beside him, Onrack could not extend his Tellann powers, could not reach out to his kin, could not inform them that he had survived. For most of his kind, that alone would have been sufficient cause for . . . surrender. The roiling waters he had but recently crawled from offered true oblivion. Dissolution was the only escape possible from this eternal ritual, and even among the Logros – Guardians of the First Throne itself – Onrack knew of kin who had chosen that path. Or worse . . .

The warrior's contemplation of choosing an end to his existence was momentary. In truth, he was far less haunted by his immortality than most T'lan Imass.

There was always something else to see, after all.

He detected movement beneath the skin of the nearest catfish, vague hints of contraction, of emerging awareness. Onrack drew forth his two-handed, curved obsidian sword. Most things he stumbled upon usually had to be killed. Occasionally in self-defence, but often simply due to an immediate and probably mutual loathing. He had long since ceased questioning why this should be so.

From his massive shoulders hung the rotted skin of an enkar'al, pebbled and colourless. It was a relatively recent acquisition, less than a thousand years old. Another example of a creature that had hated him on first sight. Though perhaps the black rippled blade swinging at its head had tainted its response.

It would be some time, Onrack judged, before the beast crawled out from its skin. He lowered his weapon and stepped past it. The Nascent's extraordinary, continent-spanning wall was a curiosity in itself. After a moment, the warrior decided to walk its length. Or at least, until his passage was blocked by a breach.

He began walking, hide-wrapped feet scuffing as he dragged them forward, the point of the sword inscribing a desultory furrow in the dried clay as it trailed from his left hand. Clumps of mud clung to his ragged hide shirt and the leather straps of his weapon harness. Silty, soupy water had seeped into the various gashes and punctures on his body and now leaked in trickling runnels with every heavy step he took. He had possessed a helm once, an impressive trophy from his youth, but it had been shattered at the final battle against the Jaghut family in the Jhag Odhan. A single crossways blow that had also shorn away a fifth of his skull, parietal and temporal, on the right side. Jaghut women had deceptive strength and admirable ferocity, especially when cornered.

The sky above him had a sickly cast, but one he had already grown used to. This fragment of the long-fractured Tiste Edur warren was by far the largest he had come across, larger even than the one that surrounded Tremorlor, the Azath Odhanhouse. And this one had known a period of stability, sufficient for civilizations to arise, for savants of sorcery to begin unravelling the powers of Kurald Emurlahn, although those inhabitants had not been Tiste Edur.

Idly, Onrack wondered if the renegade T'lan Imass he and his kin pursued had somehow triggered the wound that had resulted in the flooding of this world. It seemed likely, given its obvious efficacy in obscuring their trail. Either that, or the Tiste Edur had returned, to reclaim what had once been theirs.

Indeed, he could smell the grey-skinned Edur – they had passed this way, and recently, arriving from another warren. Of course, the word 'smell' had acquired new meaning for the T'lan Imass in the wake of the Ritual. Mundane senses had for the most part withered along with flesh. Through the shadowed orbits of his eyes, for example, the world was a complex collage of dull colours, heat and cold and often measured by an unerring sensitivity to motion. Spoken words swirled in mercurial clouds of breath – if the speaker lived, that is. If not, then it was the sound itself that was detectable, shivering its way through the air. Onrack sensed sound as much by sight as by hearing.

And so it was that he became aware of a warm-blooded shape lying a short distance ahead. The wall here was slowly failing. Water spouted in streams from fissures between the bulging stones. Before long, it would give way entirely.

The shape did not move. It had been chained in place.

Another fifty paces and Onrack reached it.

The stench of Kurald Emurlahn was overpowering, faintly visible like a pool enclosing the supine figure, its surface rippling as if beneath a steady but thin rain. A deep ragged scar marred the prisoner's broad brow beneath a hairless pate, the wound glowing with sorcery. There had been a metal tongue to hold down the man's tongue, but that had dislodged, as had the straps wound round the figure's head.

Slate-grey eyes stared up, unblinking, at the T'lan Imass.

Onrack studied the Tiste Edur for a moment longer, then he stepped over the man and continued on.

A ragged, withered voice rose in his wake. 'Wait.'

The undead warrior paused and glanced back.

'I – I would bargain. For my freedom.'

'I am not interested in bargains,' Onrack replied in the Edur language.

'Is there nothing you desire, warrior?'

'Nothing you can give me.'

'Do you challenge me, then?'

Tendons creaking, Onrack tilted his head. 'This section of the wall is about to collapse. I have no wish to be here when it does.'

'And you imagine that I do?'

'Considering your sentiments on the matter is a pointless effort on my part, Edur. I have no interest in imagining myself in your place. Why would I? You are about to drown.'

'Break my chains, and we can continue this discussion in a safer place.'

'The quality of this discussion has not earned such an exercise,' Onrack replied.

'I would improve it, given the time.'

'This seems unlikely.' Onrack turned away.

'Wait! I can tell you of your enemies!'

Slowly, the T'lan Imass swung round once more. 'My enemies? I do not recall saying that I had any, Edur.'

'Oh, but you do. I should know. I was once one of them, and indeed that is why you find me here, for I am your enemy no longer.'

'You are now a renegade among your own kind, then,' Onrack observed. 'I have no faith in traitors.'

'To my own kind, T'lan Imass, I am not the traitor. That epithet belongs to the one who chained me here. In any case, the question of faith cannot be answered through negotiation.'

'Should you have made that admission, Edur?'

The man grimaced. 'Why not? I would not deceive you.'

Now, Onrack was truly curious. 'Why would you not deceive me?'

'For the very cause that has seen me Shorn,' the Edur replied. 'I am plagued by the need to be truthful.'

'That is a dreadful curse,' the T'lan Imass said.

'Yes.'

Onrack lifted his sword. 'In this case, I admit to possessing a curse of my own. Curiosity.'

'I weep for you.'

'I see no tears.'

'In my heart, T'lan Imass.'

A single blow shattered the chains. With his free right hand, Onrack reached down and clutched one of the Edur's ankles. He dragged the man after him along the top of the wall.

'I would rail at the indignity of this,' the Tiste Edur said as he was pulled onward, step by scuffing step, 'had I the strength to do so.'

Onrack made no reply. Dragging the man with one hand, his sword with the other, he trudged forward, his progress eventually taking them past the area of weakness on the wall.

'You can release me now,' the Tiste Edur gasped.

'Can you walk?'

'No, but—'

'Then we shall continue like this.'

'Where are you going, then, that you cannot afford to wait for me to regain my strength?'

'Along this wall,' the T'lan Imass replied.

There was silence between them for a time, apart from the creaks from Onrack's bones, the rasp of his hide-wrapped feet, and the hiss and thump of the Tiste Edur's body and limbs across the mud-layered stones. The detritus-filled sea remained unbroken on their left, a festering marshland on their right. They passed between and around another dozen catfish, these ones not quite as large yet fully as limbed as the previous group. Beyond them, the wall stretched on unbroken to the horizon.

In a voice filled with pain, the Tiste Edur finally spoke again. 'Much more ... T'lan Imass ... and you'll be dragging a corpse.'

Onrack considered that for a moment, then he halted his steps and released the man's ankle. He slowly swung about.

Groaning, the Tiste Edur rolled himself onto his side. 'I assume,' he gasped, 'you have no food, or fresh water.'

Onrack lifted his gaze, back to the distant humps of the catfish. 'I suppose I could acquire some. Of the former, that is.'

'Can you open a portal, T'lan Imass? Can you get us out of this realm?'

'No.'

The Tiste Edur lowered his head to the clay and closed his eyes. 'Then I am as good as dead in any case. None the less, I appreciate your breaking my chains. You need not remain here, though I would know the name of the warrior who showed me what mercy he could.'

'Onrack. Clanless, of the Logros.'

'I am Trull Sengar. Also clanless.'

Onrack stared down at the Tiste Edur for a while. Then the T'lan Imass stepped over the man and set off, retracing their path. He arrived among the catfish. A single chop downward severed the head of the nearest one.

The slaying triggered a frenzy among the others. Skin split, sleek four-limbed bodies tore their way free. Broad, needle-fanged heads swung towards the undead warrior in their midst, tiny eyes glistening. Loud hisses from all sides. The beasts moved on squat, muscular legs, three-toed feet thickly padded and clawed. Their tails were short, extending in a vertical fin back up their spines.

They attacked as would wolves closing on wounded prey.

Obsidian blade flashed. Thin blood sprayed. Heads and limbs flopped about.

One of the creatures launched itself into the air, huge mouth closing over Onrack's skull. As its full weight descended, the T'lan Imass felt his neck vertebrae creak and grind. He fell backward, letting the animal drag him down.

Then he dissolved into dust.

And rose five paces away to resume his killing, wading among the hissing survivors. A few moments later they were all dead.

Onrack collected one of the corpses by its hind foot and, dragging it, made his way back to Trull Sengar.

The Tiste Edur was propped up on one elbow, his flat eyes fixed on the T'lan Imass. 'For a moment,' he said, 'I thought I was having the strangest dream. I saw you, there in the distance, wearing a huge, writhing hat. That then ate you whole.'

Onrack pulled the body up alongside Trull Sengar. 'You were not dreaming. Here. Eat.'

'Might we not cook it?'

The T'lan Imass strode to the seaside edge of the wall. Among the flotsam were the remnants of countless trees, from which jutted denuded branches. He climbed down onto the knotted detritus, felt it shift and roll unsteadily beneath him. It required but a few moments to snap off an armful of fairly dry wood, which he threw back up onto the wall. Then he followed.

He felt the Tiste Edur's eyes on him as he prepared a hearth.

'Our encounters with your kind,' Trull said after a moment, 'were few and far between. And then, only after your . . . ritual. Prior to that, your people fled from us at first sight. Apart from those who travelled the oceans with the Thelomen Toblakai, that is. Those ones fought us. For centuries, before we drove them from the seas.'

'The Tiste Edur were in my world,' Onrack said as he drew out his spark stones, 'just after the coming of the Tiste Andii. Once numerous, leaving signs of passage in the snow, on the beaches, in deep forests.'

'There are far fewer of us now,' Trull Sengar said. 'We came here – to this place – from Mother Dark, whose children had banished us. We did not think they would pursue, but they did. And upon the shattering of this warren, we fled yet again – to your world, Onrack. Where we thrived . . .'

'Until your enemies found you once more.'

'Yes. The first of those were . . . fanatical in their hatred. There were great wars – unwitnessed by anyone, fought as they were within darkness, in hidden places of shadow. In the end, we slew the last of those first Andii, but were broken ourselves in the effort. And so we retreated into remote places, into fastnesses. Then, more Andii came, only these seemed less . . . interested. And we in turn had grown inward, no longer consumed with the hunger of expansion—'

'Had you sought to assuage that hunger,' Onrack said as the first wisps of smoke rose from the shredded bark and twigs, 'we would have found in you a new cause, Edur.'

Trull was silent, his gaze veiled. 'We had forgotten it all,' he finally said, settling back to rest his head once more on the clay. 'All that I have just told you. Until a short while ago, my people – the last bastion, it seems, of the Tiste Edur – knew almost nothing of our past. Our long, tortured history. And what we knew was in fact false. If only,' he added, 'we had remained ignorant.'

Onrack slowly turned to gaze at the Edur. 'Your people no longer look inward.'

'I said I would tell you of your enemies, T'lan Imass.'

'You did.'

'There are your kind, Onrack, among the Tiste Edur. In league with our new purpose.'

'And what is this purpose, Trull Sengar?'

The man looked away, closed his eyes. 'Terrible, Onrack. A terrible purpose.'

The T'lan Imass warrior swung to the corpse of the creature he had slain, drew forth an obsidian knife. 'I am familiar with terrible purposes,' he said as he began cutting meat.

'I shall tell you my tale now, as I said I would. So you understand what you now face.'

'No, Trull Sengar. Tell me nothing more.'

'But why?'

Because your truth would burden me. Force me to find my kin once more. Your truth would chain me to this world – to my world, once more. And I am not ready for that. 'I am weary of your voice, Edur,' he replied.

The beast's sizzling flesh smelled like seal meat.

A short time later, while Trull Sengar ate, Onrack moved to the edge of the wall facing onto the marsh. The flood waters had found old basins in the landscape, from which gases now leaked upward to drift in pale smears over the thick, percolating surface. Thicker fog obscured the horizon, but the T'lan Imass thought he could sense a rising of elevation, a range of low, humped hills.

'It's getting lighter,' Trull Sengar said from where he lay beside the hearth. 'The sky is glowing in places. There . . . and there.'

Onrack lifted his head. The sky had been an unrelieved sea of pewter, darkening every now and then to loose a deluge of rain, though that had grown more infrequent of late. But now rents had appeared, ragged-edged. A swollen orb of yellow light commanded one entire horizon, the wall ahead seeming to drive towards its very heart; whilst directly overhead hung a smaller circle of blurred fire, this one rimmed in blue.

'The suns return,' the Tiste Edur murmured. 'Here, in the Nascent, the ancient twin hearts of Kurald Emurlahn live on. There was no way of telling, for we did not rediscover this warren until after the Breach. The flood waters must have brought chaos to the climate. And destroyed the civilization that existed here.'

Onrack looked down. 'Were they Tiste Edur?'

The man shook his head. 'No, more like your descendants, Onrack. Although the corpses we saw here along the wall were badly decayed.' Trull grimaced. 'They are as vermin, these humans of yours.'

'Not mine,' Onrack replied.

'You feel no pride, then, at their insipid success?'

The T'lan Imass cocked his head. 'They are prone to mistakes, Trull Sengar. The Logros have killed them in their thousands when the need to reassert order made doing so necessary. With ever greater frequency they annihilate themselves, for success breeds contempt for those very qualities that purchased it.'

'It seems you've given this some thought.'

Onrack shrugged in a clatter of bones. 'More than my kin, perhaps, the edge of my irritation with humankind remains jagged.'

The Tiste Edur was attempting to stand, his motions slow and deliberate. 'The Nascent required ... cleansing,' he said, his tone bitter, 'or so it was judged.'

'Your methods,' Onrack said, 'are more extreme than what the Logros would choose.'

Managing to totter upright, Trull Sengar faced the T'lan Imass with a wry grin. 'Sometimes, friend, what is begun proves too powerful to contain.'

'Such is the curse of success.'

Trull seemed to wince at the words, and he turned away. 'I must needs find fresh, clean water.'

'How long had you been chained?'

The man shrugged. 'Long, I suppose. The sorcery within the Shorning was designed to prolong suffering. Your sword severed its power, and now the mundane requirements of the flesh return.'

The suns were burning through the clouds, their

combined heat filling the air with humidity. The overcast was shredding apart, vanishing before their very eyes. Onrack studied the blazing orbs once more. 'There has been no night,' he said.

'Not in the summer, no. The winters, it's said, are another matter. At the same time, with the deluge I suspect it is fruitless to predict what will come. Personally, I have no wish to find out.'

'We must leave this wall,' the T'lan Imass said after a moment.

'Aye, before it collapses entirely. I think I can see hills in the distance.'

'If you have the strength, clasp your arms about me,' Onrack said, 'and I will climb down. We can skirt the basins. If any local animals survived, they will be on higher ground. Do you wish to collect and cook more from this beast?'

'No. It is less than palatable.'

'That is not surprising, Trull Sengar. It is a carnivore, and has fed long on rotting flesh.'

The ground was sodden underfoot when they finally reached the base of the wall. Swarms of insects rose around them, closing on the Tiste Edur with frenzied hunger. Onrack allowed his companion to set the pace as they made their way between the water-filled basins. The air was humid enough to sheathe their bodies, soaking through the clothing they wore. Although there was no wind at ground level, the clouds overhead had stretched into streamers, racing to overtake them then scudding on to mass against the range of hills, where the sky grew ever darker.

'We are heading right towards a squall,' Trull muttered, waving his arms about to disperse the midges.

'When it breaks, this land will flood,' Onrack noted. 'Are you capable of increasing your pace?'

'No.'

'Then I shall have to carry you.'

'Carry, or drag?'

'Which do you prefer?'

'Carrying seems somewhat less humiliating.'

Onrack returned his sword to its loop in the shoulder harness. Though the warrior was judged tall among his own kind, the Tiste Edur was taller, by almost the length of a forearm. The T'lan Imass had the man sit down on the ground, knees drawn up, then Onrack squatted and slipped one arm beneath Trull's knees, the other below his shoulder blades. Tendons creaking, the warrior straightened.

'There's fresh gouges all around your skull, or what's left of it at any rate,' the Tiste Edur noted.

Onrack said nothing. He set forth at a steady jog.

Before long a wind arrived, tumbling down from the hills, growing to such force that the T'lan Imass had to lean forward, his feet thumping along the gravel ridges between the pools.

The midges were quickly swept away.

There was, Onrack realized, a strange regularity to the hills ahead. There were seven in all, arrayed in what seemed a straight line, each of equal height though uniquely misshapen. The storm clouds were piling well behind them, corkscrewing in bulging columns skyward above an enormous range of mountains.

The wind howled against Onrack's desiccated face, snapped at the strands of his gold-streaked hair, thrummed with a low-pitched drone through the leather strips of his harness. Trull Sengar was hunched against him, head ducked away from the shrieking blast.

Lightning bridged the heaving columns, the thunder long in reaching them.

The hills were not hills at all. They were edifices, massive and hulking, constructed from a smooth black stone, seemingly each a single piece. Twenty or more man-lengths high. Dog-like beasts, broad-skulled and small-eared, thickly muscled, heads lowered towards the two travellers and the distant wall behind them, the vast pits of their eyes faintly gleaming a deep, translucent amber.

Onrack's steps slowed.

But did not halt.

The basins had been left behind, the ground underfoot slick with wind-borne rain but otherwise solid. The T'lan Imass angled his approach towards the nearest monument. As they came closer, they moved into the statue's lee.

The sudden falling off of the wind was accompanied by a cavernous silence, the wind to either side oddly mute and distant. Onrack set Trull Sengar down.

The Tiste Edur's bewildered gaze found the edifice rearing before them. He was silent, slow to stand as Onrack moved past him.

'Beyond,' Trull quietly murmured, 'there should be a gate.'

Pausing, Onrack slowly swung round to study his companion. 'This is your warren,' he said after a moment. 'What do you sense of these . . . monuments?'

'Nothing, but I know what they are meant to represent . . . as do you. It seems the inhabitants of this realm made them into their gods.'

To that, Onrack made no reply. He faced the massive statue once more, head tilting as his gaze travelled upward, ever upward. To those gleaming, amber eyes.

'There will be a gate,' Trull Sengar persisted behind him. 'A means of leaving this world. Why do you hesitate, T'lan Imass?'

'I hesitate in the face of what you cannot see,' Onrack replied. 'There are seven, yes. But two of them are . . . alive.' He hesitated, then added, 'And this is one of them.'

CHAPTER SEVEN

An army that waits is soon an army at war with itself.
Kellanved

The world was encircled in red. the hue of old blood, of iron rusting on a battlefield. It rose in a wall like a river turned on its side, crashing confused and uncertain against the rough cliffs that rose broken-toothed around the rim of Raraku. The Holy Desert's most ancient guardians, those bleached limestone crags, now withering beneath the ceaseless storm of the Whirlwind, the raging goddess who could countenance no rival to her dominion. Who would devour the cliffs themselves in her fury.

Whilst the illusion of calm lay within her heart.

The old man who had come to be known as Ghost Hands slowly clambered his way up the slope. His ageing skin was deep bronze, his tattooed, blunt and wide face as creased as a wind-clawed boulder. Small yellow flowers cloaked the ridge above him, a rare blossoming of the low-growing desert plant the local tribes called *hen'bara*. When dried, the flowers made a heady tea, mender of grief, balm against pain in a mortal soul. The old man scrabbled and scraped his way up the slope with something like desperation.

No life's path is bloodless. Spill that of those blocking your path. Spill your own. Struggle on, wade the growing torrent with all the frenzy that is the brutal unveiling of self-preservation. The macabre dance in the tugging currents held no artistry, and to pretend otherwise was to sink into delusion.

Delusions. Heboric Light Touch, once priest of Fener, possessed no more delusions. He had drowned them one by one with his own hands long ago. His hands – his Ghost Hands – had proved particularly capable of such tasks. Whisperers of unseen powers, guided by a mysterious, implacable will. He knew that he had no control over them, and so held no delusions. How could he?

Behind him, in the vast flat where tens of thousands of warriors and their followers were encamped amidst a city's ruins, such clear-eyed vision was absent. The army was the strong hands, now at rest but soon to raise weapons, guided by a will that was anything but implacable, a will that was drowning in delusions. Heboric was not only different from all those below – he was their very opposite, a sordid reflection in a mangled mirror.

Hen'bara's gift was dreamless sleep at night. The solace of oblivion.

He reached the ridge, breathing hard from the exertion, and settled down among the flowers for a moment to rest. Ghostly hands were as deft as real ones, though he could not see them – not even as the faint, mottled glow that others saw. Indeed, his vision was failing him in all things. It was an old man's curse, he believed, to witness the horizons on all sides drawing ever closer. Even so, while the carpet of yellow surrounding him was little more than a blur to his eyes, the spicy fragrance filled his nostrils and left a palpable taste on his tongue.

The desert sun's heat was bludgeoning, oppressive. It had a power of its own, transforming the Holy Desert into a prison, pervasive and relentless. Heboric had grown to despise that heat, to curse Seven Cities, to cultivate an abiding hatred for its people. And he was trapped among them, now. The Whirlwind's barrier was indiscriminate, impassable both to those on the outside and those within – at the discretion of the Chosen One.

Movement to one side, the blur of a slight, dark-haired figure. Who then settled down beside him.

Heboric smiled. 'I thought I was alone.'

'We are both alone, Ghost Hands.'

'Of that, Felisin, neither of us needs reminding.' *Felisin Younger, but that is a name I cannot speak out loud. The mother who adopted you, lass, has her own secrets.* 'What is that you have in your hands?'

'Scrolls,' the girl replied. 'From Mother. She has, it seems, rediscovered her hunger for writing poetry.'

The tattooed ex-priest grunted, 'I thought it was a love, not a hunger.'

'You are not a poet,' she said. 'In any case, to speak plainly is a true talent; to bury beneath obfuscation is a poet's calling these days.'

'You are a brutal critic, lass,' Heboric observed.

'*Call to Shadow*, she has called it. Or, rather, she continues a poem her own mother began.'

'Ah, well, Shadow is a murky realm. Clearly she has chosen a style to match the subject, perhaps to match that of her own mother.'

'Too convenient, Ghost Hands. Now, consider the name by which Korbolo Dom's army is now called. *Dogslayers*. That, old man, is poetic. A name fraught with diffidence behind its proud bluster. A name to match Korbolo Dom himself, who stands square-footed in his terror.'

Heboric reached out and plucked the first flower head. He held it to his nose a moment before dropping it into the leather bag at his belt. '"Square-footed in his terror." An arresting image, lass. But I see no fear in the Napan. The Malazan army mustering in Aren is nothing but three paltry legions of recruits. Commanded by a woman devoid of any relevant experience. Korbolo Dom has no reason to be afraid.'

The young girl's laugh was a trill that seemed to cut an icy path through the air. 'No reason, Ghost Hands? Many reasons, in fact. Shall I list them? Leoman. Toblakai.

Bidithal. L'oric. Mathok. And, the one he finds most terrifying of all: Sha'ik. My mother. The camp is a snake-pit, seething with dissent. You have missed the last spitting frenzy. Mother has banished Mallick Rel and Pullyk Alar. Cast them out. Korbolo Dom loses two more allies in the power struggle—'

'There is no power struggle,' Heboric growled, tugging at a handful of flowers. 'They are fools to believe that one is possible. Sha'ik has thrown those two out because treachery flows in their veins. She is indifferent to Korbolo Dom's feelings about it.'

'He believes otherwise, and that conviction is more important than what might or might not be true. And how does Mother respond to the aftermath of her pronouncements?' Felisin swiped the plants before her with the scrolls. 'With poetry.'

'The gift of knowledge,' Heboric muttered. 'The Whirlwind Goddess whispers in the Chosen One's ear. There are secrets within the Warren of Shadow, secrets containing truths that are relevant to the Whirlwind itself.'

'What do you mean?'

Heboric shrugged. His bag was nearly full. 'Alas, I possess my own prescient knowledge.' *And little good it does me.* 'The sundering of an ancient warren scattered fragments throughout the realms. The Whirlwind Goddess possesses power, but it was not her own, not at first. Just one more fragment, wandering lost and in pain. What was the goddess, I wonder, when she first stumbled onto the Whirlwind? Some desert tribe's minor deity, I suspect. A spirit of the summer wind, protector of some whirlpool spring, possibly. One among many, without question. Of course, once she made that fragment her own, it did not take long for her to destroy her old rivals, to assert complete, ruthless domination over the Holy Desert.'

'A quaint theory, Ghost Hands,' Felisin drawled. 'But it speaks nothing of the Seven Holy Cities, the Seven Holy Books, the prophecy of Dryjhna the Apocalyptic.'

Heboric snorted. 'Cults feed upon one another, lass. Whole myths are co-opted to fuel the faith. Seven Cities was born of nomadic tribes, yet the legacy preceding them was that of an ancient civilization, which in turn rested uneasy on the foundations of a still older empire – the First Empire of the T'lan Imass. That which survives in memory or falters and fades away is but chance and circumstance.'

'Poets may know hunger,' she commented drily, 'but historians devour. And devouring murders language, makes of it a dead thing.'

'Not the historian's crime, lass, but the critic's.'

'Why quibble? Scholars, then.'

'Are you complaining that my explanation destroys the mysteries of the pantheon? Felisin, there are more worthy things to wonder at in this world. Leave the gods and goddesses to their own sickly obsessions.'

Her laugh struck through him again. 'Oh, you are amusing company, old man! A priest cast out by his god. An historian once gaoled for his theories. A thief with nothing left worth stealing. I am not the one in need of wonder.'

He heard her climb to her feet. 'In any case,' she continued, 'I was sent to find you.'

'Oh? Sha'ik seeks more advice that she will no doubt ignore?'

'Not this time. Leoman.'

Heboric scowled. *And where Leoman is, so too will be Toblakai. The slayer's only quality his holding to his vow to never again speak to me. Still, I will feel his eyes upon me. His killer's eyes. If there's anyone in the camp who should be banished . . .* He slowly clambered upright. 'Where will I find him?'

'In the pit temple,' she replied.

Of course. And what, dear lass, were you doing in Leoman's company?

'I would take you by hand,' Felisin added, 'but I find their touch far too poetic.'

She walked at his side, back down the slope, between the two vast kraals which were empty at the moment – the goats and sheep driven to the pastures east of the ruins for the day. They passed through a wide breach in the dead city's wall, intersecting one of the main avenues that led to the jumble of sprawling, massive buildings of which only foundations and half-walls remained, that had come to be called the Circle of Temples.

Adobe huts, yurts and hide tents fashioned a modern city on the ruins. Neighbourhood markets bustled beneath wide, street-length awnings, filling the hot air with countless voices and the redolent aromas of cooking. Local tribes, those that followed their own war chief, Mathok – who held a position comparable to general in Sha'ik's command – mingled with Dogslayers, with motley bands of renegades from cities, with cut-throat bandits and freed criminals from countless Malazan garrison gaols. The army's camp followers were equally disparate, a bizarre self-contained tribe that seemed to wander a nomadic round within the makeshift city, driven to move at the behest of hidden vagaries no doubt political in nature. At the moment, some unseen defeat had them more furtive than usual – old whores leading scores of mostly naked, thin children, weapon smiths and tack menders and cooks and latrine diggers, widows and wives and a few husbands and fewer still fathers and mothers . . . threads linked most of them to the warriors in Sha'ik's army, but they were tenuous at best, easily severed, often tangled into a web of adultery and bastardy.

The city was a microcosm of Seven Cities, in Heboric's opinion. Proof of all the ills the Malazan Empire had set out to cure as conquerors then occupiers. There seemed few virtues to the freedoms to which the ex-priest had been witness, here in this place. Yet he suspected he was alone in his traitorous thoughts. *The empire sentenced me a criminal, yet I remain Malazan none the less. A child of the empire, a reawakened devotee to the old emperor's 'peace by the sword'.*

So, dear Tavore, lead your army to this heart of rebellion, and cut it dead. I'll not weep for the loss.

The Circle of Temples was virtually abandoned compared to the teeming streets the two had just passed through. The home of old gods, forgotten deities once worshipped by a forgotten people who left little behind apart from crumbling ruins and pathways ankle-deep in dusty potsherds. Yet something of the sacred still lingered for some, it seemed, for it was here where the most decrepit of the lost found meagre refuge.

A scattering of minor healers moved among these destitute few – the old widows who'd found no refuge as a third or even fourth wife to a warrior or merchant, fighters who'd lost limbs, lepers and other diseased victims who could not afford the healing powers of High Denul. There had once numbered among these people abandoned children, but Sha'ik had seen to an end to that. Beginning with Felisin, she had adopted them all – her private retinue, the Whirlwind cult's own acolytes. By Heboric's last cursory measure, a week past, they had numbered over three thousand, in ages ranging from newly weaned to Felisin's age – close to Sha'ik's own, true age. To all of them, she was Mother.

It had not been a popular gesture. The pimps had lost their lambs.

In the centre of the Circle of Temples was a broad, octagonal pit, sunk deep into the layered limestone, its floor never touched by the sun, cleared out now of its resident snakes, scorpions and spiders and reoccupied by Leoman of the Flails. Leoman, who had once been Elder Sha'ik's most trusted bodyguard. But the reborn Sha'ik had delved deep into the man's soul, and found it empty, bereft of faith, by some flaw of nature inclined to disavow all forms of certainty. The new Chosen One had decided she could not trust this man – not at her side, at any rate. He had been seconded to Mathok, though it seemed that the position involved few responsibilities. While Toblakai remained as Sha'ik's personal guardian, the giant with the shattered tattoo on his face had not relinquished his friendship with Leoman and was often in the man's sour company.

There was history between the two warriors, of which Heboric was certain he sensed but a fraction. They had once shared a chain as prisoners of the Malazans, it was rumoured. Heboric wished the Malazans had shown less mercy in Toblakai's case.

'I will leave you now,' Felisin said at the pit's brick-lined edge. 'When next I desire to clash views with you, I will seek you out.'

Grimacing, Heboric nodded and began making his way down the ladder. The air around him grew cooler in layers as he descended into the gloom. The smell of durhang was sweet and heavy – one of Leoman's affectations, leading the ex-priest to wonder if young Felisin was following her mother's path more closely than he had suspected.

The limestone floor was layered in rugs now. Ornate furniture – the portable kind wealthy travelling merchants used – made the spacious chamber seem crowded. Wood-framed screens stood against the walls here and there, the stretched fabric of their panels displaying woven scenes from tribal mythology. Where the walls were exposed, black and red ochre paintings from some ancient artist transformed the smooth, rippled stone into multi-layered vistas – savannas where transparent beasts roamed. For some reason these images remained clear and sharp to Heboric's eyes, whispering memories of movement ever on the edges of his vision.

Old spirits wandered this pit, trapped for eternity by its high, sheer walls. Heboric hated this place, with all its spectral laminations of failure, of worlds long extinct.

Toblakai sat on a backless divan, rubbing oil into the blade of his wooden sword, not bothering to look up as Heboric reached the base of the ladder. Leoman lay sprawled among cushions near the wall opposite.

'Ghost Hands,' the desert warrior called in greeting. 'You have hen'bara? Come, there is a brazier here, and water—'

'I reserve that tea for just before I go to bed,' Heboric replied, striding over. 'You would speak with me, Leoman?'

'Always, friend. Did not the Chosen One call us her sacred triangle? We three, here in this forgotten pit? Or perhaps I have jumbled my words, and should reverse my usage of "sacred" and "forgotten"? Come, sit. I have herbal tea, the kind that makes one wakeful.'

Heboric sat down on a cushion. 'And what need have we to be wakeful?'

Leoman's smile was loose, telling Heboric that durhang had swept away his usual reticence. 'Dear Ghost Hands,' the warrior murmured, 'it is the need of the *hunted*. It is the gazelle with its nose to the ground that the lion sups with, after all.'

The ex-priest's brows rose. 'And who is stalking us now, Leoman?'

Leaning back, Leoman replied, 'Why, the Malazans, of course. Who other?'

'Why, most certainly then we must talk,' Heboric said in mock earnestness. 'I had no idea, after all, that the Malazans were planning on doing us harm. Are you certain of your information?'

Toblakai spoke to Leoman. 'As I have told you before, this old man should be killed.'

Leoman laughed. 'Ah, my friend, now that you are the only one of us three who still has the Chosen One's ear . . . as it were . . . I would suggest you relinquish that subject. She has forbidden it and that is that. Nor am I inclined to agree with you in any case. It is an old refrain that needs burying.'

'Toblakai hates me because I see too clearly what haunts his soul,' Heboric said. 'And, given his vow to not speak to me, his options for dialogue are sadly limited.'

'I applaud your empathy, Ghost Hands.'

Heboric snorted. 'If there is to be subject to this meeting,

Leoman, let's hear it. Else I'll make my way back to the light.'

'That would prove a long journey,' the warrior chuckled. 'Very well. Bidithal is back to his old ways.'

'Bidithal, the High Mage? What "old ways"?'

'His ways with children, Heboric. Girls. His unpleasant . . . hungers. Sha'ik is not all-knowing, alas. Oh, she knows Bidithal's old predilections – she experienced them first-hand when she was Sha'ik Elder, after all. But there are close to a hundred thousand people in this city, now. A few children vanishing every week . . . easily passing virtually unnoticed. Mathok's people, however, are by nature watchful.'

Heboric scowled. 'And what would you have me do about it?'

'Are you disinterested?'

'Of course not. But I am one man, without, as you say, a voice. While Bidithal is one of the three sworn to Sha'ik, one of her most powerful High Mages.'

Leoman began making tea. 'We share a certain loyalty, friend,' he murmured, 'the three of us here. With a certain child.' He looked up then, leaning close as he set the pot of water on the brazier's grate, his veiled blue eyes fixing on Heboric. 'Who has caught Bidithal's eye. But that attention is more than simply sexual. Felisin is Sha'ik's chosen heir – we can all see that, yes? Bidithal believes she must be shaped in a manner identical to her mother – when her mother was Sha'ik Elder, that is. The child must follow the mother's path, Bidithal believes. As the mother was broken inside, so too must the child be broken inside.'

Cold horror filled Heboric at Leoman's words. He snapped a glare at Toblakai. 'Sha'ik must be told of this!'

'She has,' Leoman said. 'But she needs Bidithal, if only to balance the schemes of Febryl and L'oric. The three despise each other, naturally. She has been told, Ghost Hands, and so she tasks us three in turn to be . . . watchful.'

'How in Hood's name am I supposed to be watchful?'

Heboric snapped. 'I am damned near blind! Toblakai! Tell Sha'ik to take that wrinkled bastard and flay him alive, never mind Febryl and L'oric!'

The huge savage bared his teeth at Leoman. 'I hear a lizard hissing from under its rock, Leoman of the Flails. Such bravado is quickly ended with the heel of a boot.'

'Ah,' Leoman sighed to Heboric, 'alas, Bidithal is not the problem. Indeed, he may prove Sha'ik's saviour. Febryl schemes betrayal, friend. Who are his co-conspirators? Unknown. Not L'oric, that's for certain – L'oric is by far the most cunning of the three, and so not a fool by any measure. Yet Febryl needs allies among the powerful. Is Korbolo Dom in league with the bastard? We don't know. Kamist Reloe? His two lieutenant mages, Henaras and Fayelle? Even if they all were, Febryl would still need Bidithal – either to stand aside and do nothing, or to join.'

'Yet,' Toblakai growled, 'Bidithal is loyal.'

'In his own way,' Leoman agreed. 'And he knows that Febryl is planning treachery, and now but awaits the invitation. Whereupon he will tell Sha'ik.'

'And all the conspirators will then die,' Toblakai said.

Heboric shook his head. 'And what if those conspirators comprise her *entire* command?'

Leoman shrugged, then began pouring tea. 'Sha'ik has the Whirlwind, friend. To lead the armies? She has Mathok. And me. And L'oric will remain, that is certain. Seven take us, Korbolo Dom is a liability in any case.'

Heboric was silent for a long moment. He made no move when with a gesture Leoman invited him to partake of the tea. 'And so the lie is revealed,' he finally murmured. 'Toblakai has told Sha'ik nothing. Not him, nor Mathok, nor you, Leoman. This is your way of getting back into power. Crush a conspiracy and thereby eliminate all your rivals. And now, you invite me into the lie.'

'Not a great lie,' Leoman replied. 'Sha'ik has been informed that Bidithal hunts children once more . . .'

'But not Felisin in particular.'

'The Chosen One must not let her personal loyalties place the entire rebellion at risk. She would act too quickly—'

'And you think I give a damn about this rebellion, Leoman?'

The warrior smiled as he leaned back on the cushions. 'You care about nothing, Heboric. Not even yourself. But no, that is not true, is it? There is Felisin. There is the child.'

Heboric climbed to his feet. 'I am done here.'

'Go well, friend. Know that your company is always welcome here.'

The ex-priest made his way towards the ladder. Reaching it, he paused. 'And here I'd been led to believe that the snakes were gone from this pit.'

Leoman laughed. 'The cool air but makes them ... dormant. Be careful on that ladder, Ghost Hands.'

After the old man had left, Toblakai sheathed his sword and rose. 'He will head straight to Sha'ik,' he pronounced.

'Will he?' Leoman asked, then shrugged. 'No, I think not. Not to Sha'ik ...'

Of all the temples of the native cults in Seven Cities, only the ones raised in the name of a particular god displayed an architectural style that could be seen to echo the ancient ruins in the Circle of Temples. And so, in Heboric's mind, there was nothing accidental to Bidithal's choice of abode. Had the foundations of the temple the High Mage now occupied still held aloft walls and ceiling, it would be seen to be a low, strangely elongated dome, buttressed by half-arches like the ribs of a vast sea-creature, or perhaps the skeletal framework of a longship. The tent-cloth covering the withered and crumbled remnants was affixed to the few surviving upright wings. These wings and the floor plan gave sufficient evidence of what the temple had originally looked like; and in the Seven Holy Cities and among its more populated lesser kin, a certain extant temple could be found that closely resembled this ruin in style.

And in these truths, Heboric suspected a mystery. Bidithal had not always been a High Mage. Not in title in any case. In the Dhobri language, he had been known as Rashan'ais. The archpriest of the cult of Rashan, which had existed in Seven Cities long before the Throne of Shadow had been reoccupied. In the twisted minds of humanity, it seemed, there was nothing objectionable about worshipping an empty throne. *No stranger than kneeling before the Boar of Summer, before a god of war.*

The cult of Rashan had not taken well the ascension of Ammanas – Shadowthrone – and the Rope into positions of penultimate power within the Warren of Shadow. Though Heboric's knowledge of the details was sketchy at best, it seemed that the cult had torn itself apart. Blood had been spilled within temple walls, and in the aftermath of desecrating murder, only those who acknowledged the mastery of the new gods remained among the devotees. To the wayside, bitter and licking deep wounds, the banished slunk away.

Men like Bidithal.

Defeated but, Heboric suspected, not yet finished. *For it is the Meanas temples of Seven Cities that most closely mimic this ruin in architectural style . . . as if a direct descendant of this land's earliest cults . . .*

Within the Whirlwind, the cast-out Rashan'ais had found refuge. Further proof of his belief that the Whirlwind was but a fragment of a shattered warren, and that shattered warren was Shadow. *And if that is indeed the case, what hidden purpose holds Bidithal to Sha'ik? Is he truly loyal to Dryjhna the Apocalyptic, to this holy conflagration in the name of liberty?* Answers to such questions were long in coming, if at all. The unknown player, the unseen current beneath this rebellion – indeed, beneath the Malazan Empire itself – was the new ruler of Shadow and his deadly companion. *Ammanas Shadowthrone, who was Kellanved – emperor of*

Malaz and conqueror of Seven Cities. Cotillion, who was Dancer – master of the Talon and the empire's deadliest assassin, deadlier even than Surly. Gods below, something breathes there . . . I now wonder, whose war is this?

Distracted by such troubling thoughts as he made his way to Bidithal's abode, it was a moment before Heboric realized that his name had been called. Eyes straining to focus as he searched for the originator of that call, he was suddenly startled by a hand settling on his shoulder.

'My apologies, Ghost Hands, if I frightened you.'

'Ah, L'oric,' Heboric replied, finally recognizing the tall, white-robed figure standing beside him. 'These are not your usual haunts, are they?'

A slightly pained smile. 'I regret that my presence is seen as a haunting – unless of course your use of the word was unmindful.'

'Careless, you mean. It was. I have been in the company of Leoman, inadvertently breathing fumes of durhang. What I meant was, I rarely see you in these parts, that is all.'

'Thus explaining your perturbed expression,' L'oric murmured.

Meeting you, the durhang or Leoman? The tall mage – one of Sha'ik's three – was not by nature approachable, nor given to drama. Heboric had no idea which warren the man employed in his sorceries. Perhaps Sha'ik alone knew.

After a moment, the High Mage resumed, 'Your route suggests a visit to a certain resident here in the Circle. Further, I sense a storm of emotions stirring around you, which could lead one to surmise the impending encounter will prove tumultuous.'

'You mean we might argue, Bidithal and I,' Heboric growled. 'Well yes, that's damned likely.'

'I myself have but recently departed his company,' L'oric said. 'Perhaps a warning? He is much agitated over something, and so short of temper.'

'Perhaps it was something you said,' Heboric ventured.

'Entirely possible,' the mage conceded. 'And if so, then I apologize.'

'Fener's tusks, L'oric, what are you doing in this damned army of vipers?'

Again the pained smile, then a shrug. 'Mathok's tribes have among them women and men who dance with flare-necked vipers – such as are sometimes found where grasses grow deep. It is a complicated and obviously dangerous dance, yet one possessed of a certain charm. There are attractions to such exercise.'

'You enjoy taking risks, even with your life.'

'I might in turn ask why are you here, Heboric? Do you seek to return to your profession as historian, thus ensuring that the tale of Sha'ik and the Whirlwind will be told? Or are you indeed ensnared with loyalties to the noble cause of liberty? Surely, you cannot say you are both, can you?'

'I was a middling historian at best, L'oric,' Heboric muttered, reluctant to elaborate on his reasons for remaining – none of which had any real relevance, since Sha'ik was not likely to let him leave in any case.

'You are impatient with me. I will leave you to your task, then.' L'oric made a slight bow as he stepped back.

Watching the man walk away, Heboric stood motionless for a moment longer, then he resumed his journey. Bidithal was agitated, was he? An argument with L'oric, or something behind the veil? The High Mage's dwelling was before him now, the tent walls and peaked ceiling sun-faded and smoke-stained, a dusty smear of mottled magenta squatting above the thick foundation stones. Huddled just outside the flap entrance was a sunburned, filthy figure, mumbling in some foreign language, face hidden beneath long greasy strands of brown hair. The figure had no hands and no feet, the stumps showing old scar tissue yet still suppurating a milky yellow discharge. The man was using one of his wrist stumps to draw broad patterns in the thick dust, surrounding himself in linked chains, round and round, each pass obscuring what had been made before.

This one belongs to Toblakai. His master work – Sulgar? *Silgar. The Nathii.* The man was one of the many crippled, diseased and destitute inhabitants of the Circle of Temples. Heboric wondered what had drawn him to Bidithal's tent.

He arrived at the entrance. In tribal fashion, the flap was tied back, the customary expansive gesture of invitation, the message one of ingenuousness. As he ducked to step through, Silgar stirred, head snapping up.

'Brother of mine! I've seen you before, yes! Maimed – we are kin!' The language was a tangled mix of Nathii, Malazan and Ehrlii. The man's smile revealed a row of rotting teeth. 'Flesh and spirit, yes? We are, you and I, the only honest mortals here!'

'If you say so,' Heboric muttered, striding into Bidithal's home. Silgar's cackle followed him in.

No effort had been made to clean the sprawling chamber within. Bricks and rubble lay scattered across a floor of sand, broken mortar and potsherds. A half-dozen pieces of furniture were positioned here and there in the cavernous space. There was a large, low bed, wood-slatted and layered in thin mattresses. Four folding merchant chairs of the local three-legged kind faced onto the bed in a ragged row, as if Bidithal was in the habit of addressing an audience of acolytes or students. A dozen small oil lamps crowded the surface of a small table nearby.

The High Mage had his back to Heboric and most of the long chamber. A torch, fixed to a spear that had been thrust upright, its base mounded with stones and rubble, stood slightly behind Bidithal's left shoulder, casting the man's own shadow onto the tent wall.

A chill rippled through Heboric, for it seemed the High Mage was conversing in a language of gestures with his own shadow. *Cast out in name only, perhaps. Still eager to play with Meanas. In the Whirlwind's name, or his own?* 'High Mage,' the ex-priest called.

The ancient, withered man slowly turned. 'Come to me,' he rattled, 'I would experiment.'

350

'Not the most encouraging invitation, Bidithal.' But Heboric approached none the less.

Bidithal waved impatiently. 'Closer! I would see if your ghostly hands cast shadows.'

Heboric halted, stepped back with a shake of his head. 'No doubt you would, but I wouldn't.'

'Come!'

'No.'

The dark wrinkled face twisted into a scowl, black eyes glittering. 'You are too eager to protect your secrets.'

'And you aren't?'

'I serve the Whirlwind. Nothing else is important—'

'Barring your appetites.'

The High Mage cocked his head, then made a small, almost effeminate wave with one hand. 'Mortal necessities. Even when I was Rashan'ais, we saw no imperative to turn away from the pleasures of the flesh. Indeed, the inter-weaving of the shadows possesses great power.'

'And so you raped Sha'ik when she was but a child. And scourged from her all future chance at such pleasures as you now espouse. I see little logic in that, Bidithal – only sickness.'

'My purposes are beyond your ability to comprehend, Ghost Hands,' the High Mage said with a smirk. 'You cannot wound me with such clumsy efforts.'

'I'd been given to understand you were agitated, discomfited.'

'Ah, L'oric. Another stupid man. He mistook excitement for agitation, but I will say no more of that. Not to you.'

'Allow me to be equally succinct, Bidithal.' Heboric stepped closer. 'If you even so much as look in Felisin's direction, these hands of mine will twist your head from your neck.'

'Felisin? Sha'ik's dearest? Do you truly believe she is a virgin? Before Sha'ik returned, the child was a waif, an orphan in the camp. None cared a whit about her—'

'None of which matters,' Heboric said.

The High Mage turned away. 'Whatever you say, Ghost Hands. Hood knows, there are plenty of others—'

'All now under Sha'ik's protection. Do you imagine she will permit such abuses from you?'

'You shall have to ask her that yourself,' Bidithal replied. 'Now leave me. You are guest no longer.'

Heboric hesitated, barely resisting an urge to kill the man now, this instant. *Would it even be pre-emptive? Has he not as much as admitted to his crimes? But this was not a place of Malazan justice, was it? The only law that existed here was Sha'ik's. Nor will I be alone in this. Even Toblakai has vowed protection over Felisin. But what of the other children? Why does Sha'ik tolerate this, unless it is as Leoman has said. She needs Bidithal. Needs him to betray Febryl's plotting.*

Yet what do I care for all of that? This . . . creature does not deserve to live.

'Contemplating murder?' Bidithal murmured, his back turned once more, his own shadow dancing on its own on the tent wall. 'You would not be the first, nor, I suspect, the last. I should warn you, however, this temple is newly resanctified. Take another step towards me, Ghost Hands, and you will see the power of that.'

'And you believe Sha'ik will permit you to kneel before Shadowthrone?'

The man whirled, his face black with rage. 'Shadowthrone? That . . . *foreigner*? The roots of Meanas are found in an elder warren! Once ruled by—' he snapped his mouth shut, then smiled, revealing dark teeth. 'Not for you. Oh no, not for you, ex-priest. There are purposes within the Whirlwind – your existence is tolerated but little more than that. Challenge me, Ghost Hands, and you will know holy wrath.'

Heboric's answering grin was hard. 'I've known it before, Bidithal. Yet I remain. Purposes? Perhaps mine is to block your path. I'd advise you to think on that.'

Stepping outside once more, he paused briefly, blinking in the harsh sunlight. Silgar was nowhere to be seen, yet he had completed an elaborate pattern in the dust around Heboric's moccasins. Chains, surrounding a figure with stumps instead of hands ... yet footed. The ex-priest scowled, kicking through the image as he set forth.

Silgar was no artist. Heboric's own eyes were bad. Perhaps he'd seen only what his fears urged – it had been Silgar himself within the circle of chains the first time, after all. In any case, it was not important enough to make him turn back for a second look. Besides, his own steps had no doubt left it ruined.

None of which explained the chill that clung to him as he walked beneath the searing sun.

The vipers were writhing in their pit, and he was in their midst.

The old scars of ligature damage made his ankles and wrists resemble segmented tree trunks, each pinched width encircling his limbs to remind him of those times, of every shackle that had snapped shut, every chain that had held him down. In his dreams, the pain reared like a thing alive once more, weaving mesmerizing through a tumult of confused, distraught scenes.

The old Malazan with no hands and the shimmering, near solid tattoo had, despite his blindness, seen clearly enough, seen those trailing ghosts, the wind-moaning train of deaths that stalked him day and night now, loud enough in Toblakai's mind to drown out the voice of Urugal, close enough to obscure his god's stone visage behind veil after veil of mortal faces – each and every one twisted with the agony and fear that carved out the moment of dying. Yet the old man had not understood, not entirely. The children among those victims – children in terms of recently birthed, as the lowlanders used the word – had not all fallen to the bloodwood sword of Karsa Orlong. They were, one and all, the progeny that would never be, the bloodlines severed in the trophy-cluttered cavern of the Teblor's history.

Toblakai. A name of past glories, of a race of warriors who had stood alongside mortal Imass, alongside cold-miened Jaghut and demonic Forkrul Assail. A name by which Karsa Orlong was now known, as if he alone was the inheritor of elder dominators in a young, harsh world. Years ago, such a thought would have filled his chest with fierce, bloodthirsty pride. Now it racked him like a desert cough, weakened him deep in his bones. He saw what no-one else saw, that his new name was a title of polished, blinding irony.

The Teblor were long fallen from Thelomen Toblakai. Mirrored reflections in flesh only. Kneeling like fools before seven blunt-featured faces carved into a cliffside. Valley dwellers, where every horizon was almost within reach. Victims of brutal ignorance – for which no-one else could be blamed – entwined with deceit, for which Karsa Orlong would seek a final accounting.

He and his people had been wronged, and the warrior who now strode between the dusty white boles of a long-dead orchard would, one day, give answer to that.

But the enemy had so many faces . . .

Even alone, as he was now, he longed for solitude. But it was denied him. The rattle of chains was unceasing, the echoing cries of the slain endless. Even the mysterious but palpable power of Raraku offered no surcease – Raraku itself, not the Whirlwind, for Toblakai knew that the Whirlwind was like a child to the Holy Desert's ancient presence, and it touched him naught. Raraku had known many such storms, yet it weathered them as it did all things, with untethered skin of sand and the solid truth of stone. Raraku was its own secret, the hidden bedrock that held the warrior in this place. From Raraku, Karsa believed, he would find his own truth.

He had knelt before Sha'ik Reborn, all those months ago. The young woman with the Malazan accent who'd stumbled into view half carrying her tattooed, handless pet. Knelt, not in servitude, not from resurrected faith, but in relief. Relief, that the waiting had ended, that he would be able to drag Leoman away from that place of failure and death. They had seen Sha'ik Elder murdered while under their protection. A defeat that had gnawed at Karsa. Yet he could not deceive himself into believing that the new Chosen One was anything but a hapless victim that the insane Whirlwind Goddess had simply plucked from the wilderness, a mortal tool that would be used with merciless brutality. That she had proved a willing participant in her own impending destruction was equally pathetic in Karsa's eyes. Clearly, the scarred young woman had her own reasons, and seemed eager for the power.

Lead us, Warleader.

The words laughed bitterly through his thoughts as he wandered through the grove – the city almost a league to the east, the place where he now found himself a remnant outskirt of some other town. Warleaders needed such forces gathered around them, arrayed in desperate defence of self-delusion, of headlong singlemindedness. The Chosen One was more like Toblakai than she imagined, or, rather, a younger Toblakai, a Teblor commanding slayers – an army of two with which to deliver mayhem.

Sha'ik Elder had been something else entirely. She had lived long through her haunting, her visions of Apocalypse that had tugged and jerked her bones ever onward as if they were string-tied sticks. And she had seen truths in Karsa's soul, had warned him of the horrors to come – not in specific terms, for like all seers she had been cursed with ambiguity – but sufficient to awaken within Karsa a certain . . . watchfulness.

And, it seemed, he did little else these days but *watch*. As the madness that was the soul of the Whirlwind Goddess seeped out like poison in the blood to infect every leader among the rebellion. Rebellion . . . oh, there was truth enough in that. But the enemy was not the Malazan Empire. *It is sanity itself that they are rebelling against. Order. Honourable conduct. 'Rules of the common', as Leoman called them, even as his consciousness sank beneath the opaque fumes of durhang. Yes, I would well understand his flight, were I to believe what he would present to us all – the drifting layers of smoke in his pit, the sleepy look in his eyes, the slurred words . . . ah, but Leoman, I have never witnessed you actually partake of the drug. Only its apparent aftermath, the evidence scattered all about, and the descent into sleep that seems perfectly timed whenever you wish to close a conversation, end a certain discourse . . .*

Like him, Karsa suspected, Leoman was biding his time.

Raraku waited with them. Perhaps, *for* them. The Holy Desert possessed a gift, yet it was one that few had ever recognized, much less accepted. A gift that would arrive unseen, unnoticed at first, a gift too old to find shape in words, too formless to grasp in the hands as one would a sword.

Toblakai, once a warrior of forest-cloaked mountains, had grown to love this desert. The endless tones of fire painted on stone and sand, the bitter-needled plants and the countless creatures that crawled, slithered or scampered, or slipped through night-air on silent wings. He loved the hungry ferocity of these creatures, their dancing as prey and predator a perpetual cycle inscribed on the sand and beneath the rocks. And the desert in turn had reshaped Karsa, weathered his skin dark, stretched taut and lean his muscles, thinned his eyes to slits.

Leoman had told him much of this place, secrets that only a true inhabitant would know. The ring of ruined cities, harbours one and all, the old beach ridges with their natural barrows running for league upon league. Shells that had turned hard as stone and would sing low and mournful in the wind – Leoman had presented him with a gift of these, a vest of hide on which such shells had been affixed, armour that moaned in the endless, ever-dry winds. There were hidden springs in the wasteland, cairns and caves where an ancient sea-god had been worshipped. Remote basins that would, every few years, be stripped of sand to reveal long, high-prowed ships of petrified wood that was crowded with carvings – a long-dead fleet revealed beneath starlight only to be buried once more the following day. In other places, often behind the beach ridges, the forgotten mariners had placed cemeteries, using hollowed-out cedar trunks to hold their dead kin – all turned to stone, now, claimed by the implacable power of Raraku.

Layer upon countless layer, the secrets were unveiled by the winds. Sheer cliffs rising like ramps, in which the fossil skeletons of enormous creatures could be seen. The stumps of cleared forests, hinting of trees as large as any Karsa had known from his homeland. The columnar pilings of docks and piers, anchor-stones and the open cavities of tin mines, flint quarries and arrow-straight raised roads, trees that grew entirely underground, a mass of roots stretching out for leagues, from which the ironwood of Karsa's new sword had been carved – his bloodsword having cracked long ago.

Raraku had known Apocalypse first-hand, millennia past, and Toblakai wondered if it truly welcomed its return. Sha'ik's goddess stalked the desert, her mindless rage the shriek of unceasing wind along its borders, but Karsa wondered at the Whirlwind's manifestation – just whose was it? Cold, disconnected rage, or a savage, unbridled argument?

Did the goddess war with the desert?

Whilst, far to the south in this treacherous land, the Malazan army prepared to march.

As he approached the heart of the grove – where a low altar of flatstones occupied a small clearing – he saw a slight, long-haired figure, seated on the altar as if it was no more than a bench in an abandoned garden. A book was in her lap, its cracked skin cover familiar to Toblakai's eyes.

She spoke without turning round. 'I have seen your tracks in this place, Toblakai.'

'And I yours, Chosen One.'

'I come here to wonder,' she said as he walked into view around the altar to stand facing her.

As do I.

'Can you guess what it is I wonder about?' she asked.

'No.'

The almost-faded pocks of bloodfly scars only showed themselves when she smiled. 'The gift of the goddess . . .' the smile grew strained, 'offers only destruction.'

He glanced away, studied the nearby trees. 'This grove will resist in the way of Raraku,' he rumbled. 'It is stone. And stone holds fast.'

'For a while,' she muttered, her smile falling away. 'But there remains that within me that urges . . . creation.'

'Have a baby.'

Her laugh was almost a yelp. 'Oh, you hulking fool, Toblakai. I should welcome your company more often.'

Then why do you choose not to?

She waved a small hand at the book in her lap. 'Dryjhna was an author who, to be gracious, lived with malnourished talent. There are naught but bones in this tome, I am afraid. Obsessed with the taking of life, the annihilation of order. Yet not once does he offer anything in its stead. There is no rebirth among the ashes of his vision, and that saddens me. Does it sadden you, Toblakai?'

He stared down at her for a long moment, then said, 'Come.'

Shrugging, she set the book down on the altar and rose, straightening the plain, worn, colourless telaba that hung loose over her curved body.

He led her into the rows of bone-white trees. She followed in silence.

Thirty paces, then another small clearing, this one ringed tight in thick, petrified boles. A squat, rectangular mason's chest sat in the skeletal shade cast down by the branches – which had remained intact down to the very twigs. Toblakai stepped to one side, studied her face as she stared in silence at his works-in-progress.

Before them, the trunks of two of the trees ringing the clearing had been reshaped beneath chisel and pick. Two warriors stared out with sightless eyes, one slightly shorter than Toblakai but far more robust, the other taller and thinner.

He saw that her breath had quickened, a slight flush on her cheeks. 'You have talent . . . rough, but driven,' she murmured without pulling her eyes from their study. 'Do you intend to ring the entire clearing with such formidable warriors?'

'No. The others will be . . . different.'

Her head turned at a sound. She stepped quickly closer to Karsa. 'A snake.'

He nodded. 'There will be more, coming from all sides. The clearing will be filled with snakes, should we choose to remain here.'

'Flare-necks.'

'And others. They won't bite or spit, however. They never do. They come . . . to watch.'

She shot him a searching glance, then shivered slightly. 'What power manifests here? It is not the Whirlwind's—'

'No. Nor do I have a name for it. Perhaps the Holy Desert itself.'

She slowly shook her head to that. 'I think you are wrong. The power, I believe, is yours.'

He shrugged. 'We shall see, when I have done them all.'

'How many?'

'Besides Bairoth and Delum Thord? Seven.'

She frowned. 'One for each of the Holy Protectors?'

No. 'Perhaps. I have not decided. These two you see, they were my friends. Now dead.' He paused, then added, 'I had but two friends.'

She seemed to flinch slightly at that. 'What of Leoman? What of Mathok? What of . . . me?'

'I have no plans on carving your likenesses here.'

'That is not what I meant.'

I know. He gestured at the two Teblor warriors. 'Creation, Chosen One.'

359

'When I was young, I wrote poetry, in the path that my mother already walked. Did you know that?'

He smiled at the word 'young' but replied in all seriousness, 'No, I did not.'

'I . . . I have resurrected the habit.'

'May it serve you well.'

She must have sensed something of the blood-slick edge underlying his statement, for her expression tightened. 'But that is never its purpose, is it. To *serve*. Or to yield satisfaction – self-satisfaction, I mean, since the other kind but follows as a returning ripple in a well—'

'Confusing the pattern.'

'As you say. It is far too easy to see you as a knot-browed barbarian, Toblakai. No, the drive to create is something other, isn't it? Have you an answer?'

He shrugged. 'If one exists, it will only be found in the search – and searching is at creation's heart, Chosen One.'

She stared at the statues once more. 'And what are you searching for? With these . . . old friends?'

'I do not know. Yet.'

'Perhaps they will tell you, one day.'

The snakes surrounded them by the hundreds now, slithering unremarked by either over their feet, around their ankles, heads lifting again and again to flick tongues towards the carved trunks.

'Thank you, Toblakai,' Sha'ik murmured. 'I am humbled . . . and revived.'

'There is trouble in your city, Chosen One.'

She nodded. 'I know.'

'Are you the calm at its heart?'

A bitter smile twisted her lips as she turned away. 'Will these serpents permit us to leave?'

'Of course. But do not step. Instead, shuffle. Slowly. They will open for you a path.'

'I should be alarmed by all this,' she said as she edged back on their path.

But it is the least of your worries, Chosen One. 'I

will keep you apprised of developments, if you wish.'

'Thank you, yes.'

He watched her make her way out of the clearing. There were vows wrapped tight around Toblakai's soul. Slowly constricting. Some time soon, something would break. He knew not which, but if Leoman had taught him one thing, it was patience.

When she was gone, the warrior swung about and approached the mason's chest.

Dust on the hands, a ghostly patina, tinted faintly pink by the raging red storm encircling the world.

The heat of the day was but an illusion in Raraku. With the descent of darkness, the desert's dead bones quickly cast off the sun's shimmering, fevered breath. The wind grew chill and the sands erupted with crawling, buzzing life, like vermin emerging from a corpse. Rhizan flitted in a frenzied wild hunt through the clouds of capemoths and chigger fleas above the tent city sprawled in the ruins. In the distance desert wolves howled as if hunted by ghosts.

Heboric lived in a modest tent raised around a ring of stones that had once provided the foundation for a granary. His abode was situated well away from the settlement's centre, surrounded by the yurts of one of Mathok's desert tribes. Old rugs covered the floor. Off to one side a small table of piled bricks held a brazier, sufficient for cooking if not warmth. A cask of well-water stood nearby, flavoured with amber wine. A half-dozen flickering oil lamps suffused the interior with yellow light.

He sat alone, the pungent aroma of the hen'bara tea sweet in the cooling air. Outside, the sounds of the settling tribe offered a comforting background, close enough and chaotic enough to keep scattered and random his thoughts. Only later, when sleep claimed all those around him, would the relentless assault begin, the vertiginous visions of a face of jade, so massive it challenged comprehension. Power both alien and earthly, as if born of a natural force never meant to be altered. Yet altered it had been, shaped, cursed sentient. A giant buried in otataral, held motionless in an eternal prison.

Who could now touch the world beyond, with the ghosts of two human hands – hands that had been claimed then abandoned by a god.

But was it Fener who abandoned me, or did I abandon Fener? Which of us, I wonder, is more . . . exposed?

This camp, this war – this *desert* – all had conspired to ease the shame of his hiding. Yet one day, Heboric knew, he would have to return to that dreaded wasteland from his past, to the island where the stone giant waited. Return. *But to what end?*

He had always believed that Fener had taken his severed hands into keeping, to await the harsh justice that was the Tusked One's right. A fate that Heboric had accepted, as best he could. But it seemed there was to be no end to the betrayals a single once-priest could commit against his god. Fener had been dragged from his realm, left abandoned and trapped on this world. Heboric's severed hands had found a new master, a master possessed of such immense power that it could war with otataral itself. Yet it did not belong. The giant of jade, Heboric now believed, was an intruder, sent here from another realm for some hidden purpose.

And, instead of completing that purpose, someone had imprisoned it.

He sipped at his tea, praying that its narcotic would prove sufficient to deaden the sleep to come. It was losing its potency, or, rather, he was becoming inured to its effects.

The face of stone beckoned.

The face that was trying to speak.

There was a scratching at the tent flap, then it was pulled aside.

Felisin entered. 'Ah, still awake. Good, that will make this easier. My mother wants you.'

'Now?'

'Yes. There have been events in the world beyond.

Consequences to be discussed. Mother seeks your wisdom.'

Heboric cast a mournful glance at the clay cup of steaming tea in his invisible hands. It was little more than flavoured water when cold. 'I am uninterested in events in the world beyond. If she seeks wise words from me, she will be disappointed.'

'So I argued,' Felisin Younger said, an amused glint in her eyes. 'Sha'ik insists.'

She helped him don a cloak then led him outside, one of her hands light as a capemoth on his back.

The night was bitter cold, tasting of settling dust. They set out along the twisting alleyways between the yurts, walking in silence.

They passed the raised dais where Sha'ik Reborn had first addressed the mob, then through the crumbled gateposts leading to the huge, multi-chambered tent that was the Chosen One's palace. There were no guards as such, for the goddess's presence was palpable, a pressure in the chill air.

There was little warmth in the first room beyond the tent flap, but with each successive curtain that they parted and stepped through, the temperature rose. The palace was a maze of such insulating chambers, most of them empty of furniture, offering little in the way of distinguishing one from another. An assassin who proceeded this far, somehow avoiding the attention of the goddess, would quickly get lost. The approach to where Sha'ik resided followed its own torturous, winding route. Her chambers were not central, not at the heart of the palace as one might expect.

With his poor vision and the endless turns and twists, Heboric was quickly confused; he had never determined the precise location of their destination. He was reminded of the escape from the mines, the arduous journey to the island's west coast – it had been Baudin in the lead, Baudin whose sense of direction had proved unerring, almost uncanny. Without him, Heboric and Felisin would have died.

A Talon, no less. Ah, Tavore, you were not wrong to place your faith in him. It was Felisin who would not co-operate. You should have anticipated that. Well, sister, you should have anticipated a lot of things . . .

But not this.

They entered the square, low-ceilinged expanse that the Chosen One – *Felisin Elder, child of the House of Paran* – had called her Throne Room. And indeed there was a dais, once the pedestal for a hearth, on which was a tall-backed chair of sun-bleached wood and padding. In councils such as these, Sha'ik invariably positioned herself in that makeshift throne; nor would she leave it while her advisers were present, not even to peruse the yellowed maps the commanders were wont to lay out on the hide-covered floor. Apart from Felisin Younger, the Chosen One was the smallest person there.

Heboric wondered if Sha'ik Elder had suffered similar insecurities. He doubted it.

The room was crowded; among the army's leaders and Sha'ik's select, only Leoman and Toblakai were absent. There were no other chairs, although cushions and pillows rested against the base of three of the four tent walls, and it was on these that the commanders sat. Felisin at his side, Heboric made his way to the far side, Sha'ik's left, and took his place a few short paces from the dais, the young girl settling down beside him.

Some permanent sorcery illuminated the chamber, the light somehow warming the air as well. Everyone else was in their allotted place, Heboric noted. Though they were little more than blurs in his eyes, he knew them all well enough. Against the wall opposite the throne sat the half-blood Napan, Korbolo Dom, shaved hairless, his dusty blue skin latticed in scars. On his right, the High Mage Kamist Reloe, gaunt to the point of skeletal, his grey hair cut short to stubble, a tight-curled iron beard reaching up to prominent cheekbones above which glittered sunken eyes. On Korbolo's left sat Henaras, a witch from some desert tribe that had, for unknown reasons, banished her. Sorcery kept her youthful in appearance, the heavy languor in her dark eyes the product of diluted Tralb, a poison drawn from a local snake, which she imbibed to inure her against assassination. Beside her was Fayelle, an obese, perpetually nervous woman of whom Heboric knew little.

Along the wall opposite the ex-priest were L'oric, Bidithal and Febryl, the latter shapeless beneath an over-sized silk telaba, its hood opened wide like the neck of a desert snake, tiny black eyes glittering out from its shadow. Beneath those eyes gleamed twin fangs of gold, capping his upper canines. They were said to hold Emulor, a poison rendered from a certain cactus that gifted not death, but permanent dementia.

The last commander present was on Felisin's left. Mathok. Beloved of the desert tribes, the tall, black-skinned warrior possessed an inherent nobility, but it was the kind that seemed to irritate everyone around him, barring perhaps Leoman who appeared to be indifferent to the war chief's grating personality. There was, in fact, little to give cause to the dislike, for Mathok was ever courteous, even congenial, quick to smile – *perhaps too quick at that, as if the man dismissed everyone as not worth taking seriously.* With the exception of the Chosen One, of course.

As Heboric settled, Sha'ik murmured, 'Are you with us this evening, Ghost Hands?'

'Well enough,' he replied.

An undercurrent of tense excitement was in her voice, 'You had better be, old man. There have been . . . startling developments. Distant catastrophes have rocked the Malazan Empire . . .'

'How long ago?' Heboric asked.

Sha'ik frowned at the odd question, but Heboric did not elaborate. 'Less than a week. The warrens have been shaken, one and all, as if by an earthquake. Sympathizers of the rebellion remain in Dujek Onearm's army, delivering to us the details.' She gestured to L'oric. 'I've no wish to talk all night. Elaborate on the events, L'oric, for the benefit of Korbolo, Heboric, and whoever else knows nothing of all that has occurred.'

The man tilted his head. 'Delighted to, Chosen One. Those of you who employ warrens will no doubt have felt the repercussions, the brutal reshaping of the pantheon. But what specifically happened? The first answer, simply, is usurpation. Fener, Boar of Summer, has, to all intents and purposes, been ousted as the pre-eminent god of war.' He was merciful enough to not glance at Heboric. 'In his place, the once First Hero, Treach. The Tiger of Summer—'

Ousted. The fault is mine and mine alone.

Sha'ik's eyes were shining, fixed on Heboric. The secrets they shared taut between them, crackling yet unseen by anyone else.

L'oric would have continued, but Korbolo Dom interrupted the High Mage. 'And what is the significance of that to us? War needs no gods, only mortal contestants, two enemies and whatever reasons they invent in order to justify killing each other.' He paused, smiling at L'oric, then shrugged. 'All of which satisfies me well enough.'

His words had pulled Sha'ik's gaze from Heboric. An eyebrow rising, she addressed the Napan. 'And what are your reasons, specifically, Korbolo Dom?'

'I like killing people. It is the one thing I am very good at.'

'Would that be people in general?' Heboric asked him. 'Or perhaps you meant the enemies of the Apocalypse.'

'As you say, Ghost Hands.'

There was a moment of general unease, then L'oric cleared his throat and said, 'The usurpation, Korbolo Dom, is the one detail that a number of mages present may already know. I would lead us, gently, towards the less well known developments on far-away Genabackis. Now, to continue. The pantheon was shaken yet again – by the sudden, unexpected taking of the Beast Throne by Togg and Fanderay, the mated Elder Wolves that had seemed eternally cursed to never find each other – riven apart as they were by the Fall of the Crippled God. The full effect of this reawakening of the ancient Hold of the Beast is yet to be realized. All I would suggest, personally, is to those Soletaken and D'ivers among us: 'ware the new occupants of the Beast Throne. They may well come to you, eventually, to demand that you kneel before them.' He smiled. 'Alas, all those poor fools who followed the Path of the Hand. The game was won far, far away—'

'We were the victims,' Fayelle murmured, 'of deception. By minions of Shadowthrone, no less, for which there will one day be a reckoning.'

Bidithal smiled at her words, but said nothing.

L'oric's shrug affected indifference. 'As to that, Fayelle, my tale is far from done. Allow me, if you will, to shift to mundane – though if anything even more important – events. A very disturbing alliance had been forged on Genabackis, to deal with a mysterious threat called the Pannion Domin. Onearm's Host established an accord with Caladan Brood and Anomander Rake. Supplied by the supremely wealthy city of Darujhistan, the joined armies marched off to wage war against the Domin. We were, truth be told, relieved by this event from a short-term perspective, though we recognized that in the long term such an alliance was potentially catastrophic to the cause of the rebellion here in Seven Cities. Peace on Genabackis would, after all, free Dujek and his army, leaving us with the potential nightmare of Tavore approaching from the south, and Dujek and his ten thousand disembarking at Ehrlitan then marching down from the north.'

'An unpleasant thought,' Korbolo Dom growled. 'Tavore alone will not cause us much difficulty. But the High Fist and his ten thousand . . . that's another matter. Granted, most of the soldiers are from Seven Cities, but I would not cast knuckles on the hope that they would switch sides. Dujek owns them body and soul—'

'Barring a few spies,' Sha'ik said, her voice strangely flat.

'None of whom would have contacted us,' L'oric said, 'had things turned out . . . differently.'

'A moment, please,' young Felisin cut in. 'I thought that Onearm and his host had been outlawed by the Empress.'

'Thus permitting him to forge the alliance with Brood and Rake,' L'oric explained. 'A convenient and temporary ploy, lass.'

'We don't want Dujek on our shores,' Korbolo Dom said. 'Bridgeburners. Whiskeyjack, Quick Ben, Kalam, Black Moranth and their damned munitions—'

'Permit me to ease your pattering heart, Commander,' L'oric murmured. 'We shall not see Dujek. Not anytime soon, at any rate. The Pannion War proved . . . devastating. The ten thousand lost close to seven thousand of their number. The Black Moranth were similarly mauled. Oh, they won, in the end, but at such a cost. The Bridgeburners . . . gone. Whiskeyjack . . . dead.'

Heboric slowly straightened. The room was suddenly cold.

'And Dujek himself,' L'oric went on, 'a broken man. Is this news pleasing enough? There is this: the scourge that is the T'lan Imass is no more. They have departed, one and all. No more will their terrors be visited upon the innocent citizens of Seven Cities. Thus,' he concluded, 'what has the Empress left? Adjunct Tavore. An extraordinary year for the empire. Coltaine and the Seventh, the Aren Legion, Whiskeyjack, the Bridgeburners, Onearm's Host – we will be hard-pressed to best that.'

'But we shall,' Korbolo Dom laughed, both hands closed into pale-knuckled fists. 'Whiskeyjack! Dead! Ah, blessings to Hood this night! I shall make sacrifice before his altar! And Dujek – oh, his spirit will have been broken indeed. Crushed!'

'Enough gloating,' Heboric growled, sickened.

Kamist Reloe was leaning far forward, 'L'oric!' he hissed. 'What of Quick Ben?'

'He lives, alas. Kalam did not accompany the army –

no-one knows where he has gone. There were but a hand-ful of survivors from the Bridgeburners, and Dujek disbanded them and had them listed as casualties—'

'*Who lived?*' Kamist demanded.

L'oric frowned. 'A handful, as I said. Is it important?'

'Yes!'

'Very well.' L'oric glanced over at Sha'ik. 'Chosen One, do you permit me to make contact once more with my servant in that distant army? It will be but a few moments.'

She shrugged. 'Proceed.' Then, as L'oric lowered his head, she slowly leaned back in her chair. 'Thus. Our enemy has faced irreparable defeat. The Empress and her dear empire reel from the final gush of life-blood. It falls to us, then, to deliver the killing blow.'

Heboric suspected he was the only one present who heard the hollowness of her words.

Sister Tavore stands alone, now.

And alone is what she prefers. Alone is the state in which she thrives. Ah, lass, you would pretend to excitement at this news, yet it has achieved the very opposite for you, hasn't it. Your fear of sister Tavore has only deepened.

Freezing you in place.

L'oric began speaking without raising his head. 'Blend. Toes. Mallet. Spindle. Sergeant Antsy. Lieutenant Picker . . . Captain Paran.'

There was a thump from the high-backed chair as Sha'ik's head snapped back. All colour had left her face, the only detail Heboric could detect with his poor eyes, but he knew the shock that would be written on those features. A shock that rippled through him as well, though it was but the shock of recognition – not of what it portended for this young woman seated on this throne.

Unmindful, L'oric continued, 'Quick Ben has been made High Mage. It is believed the surviving Bridgeburners departed by warren to Darujhistan, though my spy is in fact uncertain of that. Whiskeyjack and the fallen Bridgeburners . . . were interred . . . in Moon's Spawn, which has – gods below! Abandoned! The Son of Darkness has abandoned Moon's Spawn!' He seemed to shiver then, and slowly looked up, blinking rapidly. A deep breath, loosed raggedly. 'Whiskeyjack was killed by one of Brood's commanders. Betrayal, it seemed, plagued the alliance.'

'Of course it did,' Korbolo Dom sneered.

'We must consider Quick Ben,' Kamist Reloe said, his hands wringing together incessantly on his lap. 'Will Tayschrenn send him to Tavore? What of the remaining three thousand of Onearm's Host? Even if Dujek does not lead them—'

'They are broken in spirit,' L'oric said. 'Hence, the wavering souls among them who sought me out.'

'And where is Kalam Mekhar?' Kamist hissed, inadvertently glancing over his shoulder then starting at his own shadow on the wall.

'Kalam Mekhar is nothing without Quick Ben,' Korbolo Dom snarled. 'Even less now that his beloved Whiskeyjack is dead.'

Kamist rounded on his companion. 'And what if Quick Ben is reunited with that damned assassin? What then?'

The Napan shrugged. 'We didn't kill Whiskeyjack. Their minds will be filled with vengeance for the slayer among Brood's entourage. Do not fear what will never come to pass, old friend.'

Sha'ik's voice rang startlingly through the room. 'Everyone out but Heboric! Now!'

Blank looks, then the others rose.

Felisin Younger hesitated. 'Mother?'

'You as well, child. Out.'

L'oric said, 'There is the matter of the new House and all it signifies, Chosen—'

'Tomorrow night. We will resume the discussion then. Out!'

A short while later Heboric sat alone with Sha'ik. She stared down at him in silence for some time, then rose suddenly and stepped down from the dais. She fell to her knees in front of Heboric, sufficiently close for him to focus on her face. It was wet with tears.

'My brother lives!' she sobbed.

And suddenly she was in his arms, face pressed against his shoulders as shudders heaved through her small, fragile frame.

Stunned, Heboric remained silent.

She wept for a long, long time, and he held her tight, unmoving, as solid as he could manage. And each time the vision of his fallen god rose before his mind's eye, he ruthlessly drove it back down. The child in his arms – for child she was, once more – cried in nothing other than the throes of salvation. She was no longer alone, no longer alone with only her hated sister to taint the family's blood.

For that – for the need his presence answered – his own grief would wait.

CHAPTER EIGHT

Among the untried recruits of the Fourteenth Army, fully
half originated from the continent of Quon Tali, the very
centre of the empire. Young and idealistic, they stepped onto
blood-soaked ground, in the wake of the sacrifices made by
their fathers and mothers, their grandfathers and
grandmothers. It is the horror of war that, with each newly
arrived generation, the nightmare is reprised by innocents.

The Sha'ik Rebellion, Illusions of Victory
Imrygyn Tallobant

Adjunct Tavore stood alone in front of four
thousand milling, jostling soldiers, while officers
bellowed and screamed through the press, their
voices hoarse with desperation. Pikes wavered and flashed
blinding glares through the dusty air of the parade ground
like startled birds of steel. The sun was a raging fire
overhead.

Fist Gamet stood twenty paces behind her, tears in his
eyes as he stared at Tavore. A pernicious wind was sweeping the dust cloud directly towards the Adjunct. In
moments she was engulfed. Yet she made no move, her
back straight, her gloved hands at her sides.

No commander could be more alone than she was now.
Alone, and helpless.

*And worse. This is my legion. The 8th. The first to assemble,
Beru fend us all.*

But she had ordered that he remain where he was, if only

to spare him the humiliation of trying to impose some kind of order on his troops. She had, instead, taken that humiliation upon herself. And Gamet wept for her, unable to hide his shame and grief.

Aren's parade ground was a vast expanse of hard-packed, almost white earth. Six thousand fully armoured soldiers could stand arrayed in ranks with sufficient avenues between the companies for officers to conduct their review. The Fourteenth Army was to assemble before the scrutiny of Adjunct Tavore in three phases, a legion at a time. Gamet's 8th had arrived in a ragged, dissolving mob over two bells past, every lesson from every drill sergeant lost, the few veteran officers and non-coms locked in a titanic struggle with a four-thousand-headed beast that had forgotten what it was.

Gamet saw Captain Keneb, whom Blistig had graciously given him to command the 9th Company, battering at soldiers with the flat of his blade, forcing them into a line that broke up in his wake as other soldiers pressed forward from behind. There were some old soldiers in that front row, trying to dig in their heels – sergeants and corporals, red-faced with sweat streaming from beneath their helms.

Fifteen paces behind Gamet waited the other two Fists, as well as the Wickan scouts under the command of Temul. Nil and Nether were there as well, although, mercifully, Admiral Nok was not – for the fleet had sailed.

Impulses at war within him, Gamet trembled, wanting to be elsewhere – anywhere – and wanting to drag the Adjunct with him. Failing that, wanting to step forward, defying her direct order, to take position at her side.

Someone came alongside him. A heavy leather sack thumped into the dust, and Gamet turned to see a squat soldier, blunt-featured beneath a leather cap, wearing barely half of a marine's standard issue of armour – a random collection of boiled leather fittings – over a threadbare, stained uniform, the magenta dye so faded as to be mauve. No insignia was present. The man's scarred, pitted face stared impassively at the seething mob.

Gamet swung further round to see an additional dozen decrepit men and women, each standing an arm's reach from the one in front, wearing unrepaired, piecemeal armour and carrying an assortment of weapons – few of which were Malazan.

The Fist addressed the man in the lead. 'And who in Hood's name are you people?'

'Sorry we was late,' the soldier grunted. 'Then again,' he added, 'I could be lying.'

'Late? Which squads? What companies?'

The man shrugged. 'This and that. We was in Aren gaol. Why was we there? This and that. But now we're here, sir. You want these children quelled?'

'If you can manage that, soldier, I'll give you a command of your own.'

'No you won't. I killed an Untan noble here in Aren. Name of Lenestro. Snapped his neck with these two hands.'

Through the clouds of dust before them, a sergeant had clawed free of the mob and was approaching Adjunct Tavore. For a moment Gamet was terrified that he would, insanely, cut her down right there, but the man sheathed his short-sword as he drew up before her. Words were exchanged.

The Fist made a decision. 'Come with me, soldier.'

'Aye, sir.' The man reached down and collected his kit bag.

Gamet led him to where Tavore and the sergeant stood. An odd thing happened then. There was a grunt from the veteran at the Fist's side, even as the wiry, red-and-grey-bearded sergeant's eyes flickered past the Adjunct and fixed on the soldier. A sudden broad grin, then a quick succession of gestures – a hand lifting, as if holding an invisible rock or ball, then the hand flipping, index finger inscribing a circle, followed by a jerk of the thumb towards the east, concluded with a shrug. In answer to all this, the soldier from the gaol gave his kit bag a shake.

The sergeant's blue eyes widened.

They arrived, coming alongside the Adjunct, who swung a blank gaze on Gamet.

'Your pardon, Adjunct,' the Fist said, and would have added more, but Tavore raised a hand and made to speak.

She didn't get a chance.

The soldier at Gamet's side spoke to the sergeant. 'Draw us a line, will ya?'

'I'll do just that.'

The sergeant pivoted and returned to the heaving ranks.

Tavore's eyes had snapped to the soldier, but she said nothing, for the man had set his bag down, drawn back its flap, and was rummaging inside it.

Five paces in front of the legion's uneven ranks, the sergeant once more drew his sword, then drove its blunt tip into the dust and set off, inscribing a sharp furrow in the ground.

Draw us a line, will ya?

The soldier crouched over his kit bag looked up suddenly. 'You two still here? Go back to them Wickans, then all of you pull back another thirty, forty paces. Oh, and get them Wickans off their horses and a tight grip on the reins, and all of ya, take for yourselves a wide stance. Then when I give the signal, plug your ears.'

Gamet flinched as the man began withdrawing a succession of clay balls from his bag. *The bag . . . that thumped down beside me not fifty heartbeats ago. Hood's breath!*

'What is your name, soldier?' Adjunct Tavore rasped.

'Cuttle. Now, better get moving, lass.'

Gamet reached out and touched her shoulder. 'Adjunct, those are—'

'I know what they are,' she snapped. 'And this man's liable to kill fifty of my soldiers—'

'Right now, lady,' Cuttle growled as he drew out a folding shovel, 'you ain't got any. Now take it from me, that otataral blade at your comely hip ain't gonna help you one bit if you decide to stand here. Pull 'em all back, and leave the rest to me and the sergeant.'

'Adjunct,' Gamet said, unable to keep the pleading from his tone.

She shot him a glare, then wheeled. 'Let us be about it, then, Fist.'

He let her take the lead, paused after a few paces to glance back. The sergeant had rejoined Cuttle, who had managed to dig a small hole in what seemed an absurdly short time.

'Cobbles down there!' The sergeant nodded. 'Perfect!'

'About what I figured,' Cuttle replied. 'I'll angle these crackers, with the cusser a hand's width deeper—'

'Perfect. I'd have done the same if I'd thought to bring some with me—'

'You supplied?'

'Well enough.'

'What I got here in my bag are the last.'

'I can mend that, Cuttle.'

'For that, Fid—'

'Strings.'

'For that, Strings, you've earned a kiss.'

'I can't wait.'

Gamet pulled himself away with a shake of his head. *Sappers.*

The explosion was a double thump that shook the earth, cobbles punching free of the overburden of dust – which had leapt skyward – to clack and clash in a maelstrom of stone chips and slivers. Fully a third of the legion were thrown from their feet, taking down others with them.

Astonishingly, none seemed fatally injured, as if Cuttle had somehow directed the force of the detonation downward and out under the cobbles.

As the last rubble pattered down, Adjunct Tavore and Gamet moved forward once again.

Facing the silenced mob, Cuttle stood with a sharper

held high in one hand. In a bellowing voice, he addressed the recruits. 'Next soldier who moves gets this at his feet, and if you think my aim ain't any good, try me! Now, sergeants and corporals! Up nice and slow now. Find your squads. You up here in front, Sergeant Strings here has drawn us a tidy nice line – all right, so it's a bit messy right now so he's drawing it again – walk up to it easy like, toes a finger's width away from it, boots square! We're gonna do this right, or people are going to *die*.'

Sergeant Strings was moving along the front line now, ensuring the line was held, spreading soldiers out. Officers were shouting once more, though not as loud as before, since the recruits remained silent. Slowly, the legion began taking shape.

Those recruits were indeed silent, and . . . watchful, Gamet noted as he and the Adjunct returned to close to their original position – the gaping, smoking crater off to one side. Watchful . . . of the madman with the sharper held high above his head. After a moment, the Fist moved up to stand beside Cuttle.

'You killed a nobleman?' he asked in a low voice, studying the assembling ranks.

'Aye, Fist. I did.'

'Was he on the Chain of Dogs?'

'He was.'

'As were you, Cuttle.'

'Until I took a spear through a shoulder. Went with the others on the *Silanda*. Missed the final argument, I did. Lenestro was . . . second best. I wanted Pullyk Alar to start, but Alar's run off with Mallick Rel. I want both of them, Fist. Maybe they think the argument's over, but not for me.'

'I'd be pleased if you took me up on that offer of command,' Gamet said.

'No thanks, sir. I'm already assigned to a squad. Sergeant Strings's squad, in fact. Suits me fine.'

'Where do you know him from?'

Cuttle glanced over, his eyes thinned to slits.

Expressionless, he said, 'Never met him before today, sir. Now, if you'll excuse me, I owe him a kiss.'

Less than a quarter-bell later, Fist Gamet's 8th Legion stood motionless in tight, even ranks. Adjunct Tavore studied them from where she stood at Gamet's side, but had yet to speak. Cuttle and Sergeant Strings had rejoined the 9th Company's 4th squad.

Tavore seemed to reach some decision. A gesture behind her brought Fists Tene Baralta and Blistig forward. Moments later they came up alongside Gamet and halted. The Adjunct's unremarkable eyes fixed on Blistig. 'Your legion waits in the main avenue beyond?'

The red-faced man nodded. 'Melting in the heat, Adjunct. But that cusser going off settled them down.'

Her gaze shifted to the Red Blade. 'Fist Baralta?'

'Calmed, Adjunct.'

'When I dismiss the 8th and they depart the parade ground, I suggest the remaining soldiers enter by company. Each company will then take position and when they are ready the next one follows. It may take longer, but at the very least we will not have a repetition of the chaos we have just witnessed. Fist Gamet, are you satisfied with the assemblage of your troops?'

'Well enough, Adjunct.'

'As am I. You may now—'

She got no further, seeing that the attention of the three men standing before her had slipped past, over her shoulder; and from the four thousand soldiers standing at attention, there was sudden, absolute silence – not a rustle of armour, not a cough. For the 8th had drawn a single breath, and now held it.

Gamet struggled to maintain his expression, even as Tavore raised an eyebrow at him. Then she slowly turned.

The toddler had come from nowhere, unseen by any until he arrived to stand in the very spot where the Adjunct had first stood, his oversized rust-red telaba trailing like a royal train. Blond hair a tangled shock above a deeply tanned, cherubic face smeared with dirt, the child faced the ranks of soldiers with an air of unperturbed calculation.

A strangled cough from among the soldiers, then someone stepped forward.

Even as the man emerged from the front line, the toddler's eyes found him. Both arms, buried in sleeves, reached out. Then one sleeve slipped back, revealing the tiny hand, and in that hand there was a bone. A human longbone. The man froze in mid-step.

The air above the parade ground seemed to hiss like a thing alive with the gasps of four thousand soldiers.

Gamet fought down a shiver, then spoke to the man. 'Captain Keneb,' he said loudly, struggling to swallow a welling dread, 'I suggest you collect your lad. Now, before he, uh, starts screaming.'

Face flushed, Keneb threw a shaky salute then strode forward.

'Neb!' the toddler shouted as the captain gathered him up.

Adjunct Tavore snapped, 'Follow me!' to Gamet, then walked to the pair. 'Captain Keneb, is it?'

'Your p-pardon, Adjunct. The lad has a nurse but seems determined to slip through her grasp at every opportunity – there's a blown graveyard behind the—'

'Is he yours, Captain?' Tavore demanded, her tone brittle.

'As good as, Adjunct. An orphan from the Chain of Dogs. The historian Duiker placed him into my care.'

'Has he a name?'

'Grub.'

'Grub?'

Keneb's shrug was apologetic. 'For now, Adjunct. It well suits him—'

'And the 8th. Yes, I see that. Deliver him to your hired nurse, Captain. Then, tomorrow, fire her and hire a better

379

one . . . or three. Will the child accompany the army?'

'He has no-one else, Adjunct. There will be other families among the camp followers—'

'I am aware of that. Be on your way, Captain Keneb.'

'I – I am sorry, Adjunct—'

But she was already turning away, and only Gamet heard her sigh and murmur, 'It is far too late for that.'

And she was right. Soldiers – even recruits – recognized an omen when it arrived. *A child in the very boot prints of the woman who would lead this army. Raising high a sun-bleached thigh bone.*

Gods below . . .

'Hood's balls skewered on a spit.'

The curse was spoken as a low growl, in tones of disgust.

Strings watched Cuttle set his bag down and slide it beneath the low flatboard bed. The stable that had been transformed into a makeshift barracks held eight squads now, the cramped confines reeking of fresh sweat . . . and stark terror. At the back wall's urine hole someone was being sick.

'Let's head outside, Cuttle,' Strings said after a moment. 'I'll collect Gesler and Borduke.'

'I'd rather go get drunk,' the sapper muttered.

'Later, we'll do just that. But first, we need to have a small meeting.'

Still the other man hesitated.

Strings rose from his cot and stepped close. 'Aye, it's that important.'

'All right. Lead on . . . Strings.'

As it turned out, Stormy joined the group of veterans that pushed silently past ashen-faced recruits – many of them with closed eyes and mouthing silent prayers – and headed out into the courtyard.

It was deserted, Lieutenant Ranal – who had proved pathetically ineffective at the assembly – having fled into the main house the moment the troop arrived.

All eyes were on Strings. He in turn studied the array of grim expressions around him. There was no doubt among them concerning the meaning of the omen, and Strings was inclined to agree. *A child leads us to our deaths. A leg bone to signify our march, withered under the curse of the desert sun. We've all lived too long, seen too much, to deceive ourselves of this one brutal truth: this army of recruits now see themselves as already dead.*

Stormy's battered, red-bearded face finally twisted into an expression too bitter to be wry. 'If you're going to say that us here have a hope at Hood's gate in fighting the tide, Strings, you've lost your mind. The lads and lasses in there ain't unique – the whole damned three legions—'

'I know,' Strings cut in. 'We ain't none of us stupid. Now, all I'm asking is for a spell of me talking. Me talking. No interruptions. I'll tell you when I'm done. Agreed?'

Borduke turned his head and spat. 'You're a Hood-damned Bridgeburner.'

'Was. Got a problem with that?'

The sergeant of the 6th squad grinned. 'What I meant by that, Strings, is that for you I'll listen. As you ask.'

'Same with us,' Gesler muttered, Stormy nodding agreement at his side.

Strings faced Cuttle. 'And you?'

'Only because it's you and not Hedge, Fiddler. Sorry. *Strings.*'

Borduke's eyes widened in recognition of the name. He spat a second time.

'Thank you.'

'Don't thank us yet,' Cuttle said, but took the edge off with a slight smile.

'All right, I'll start with a story. Has to do with Nok, the admiral, though he wasn't an admiral back then, just the commander of six dromons. I'd be surprised if any of you have heard this story but if you have don't say nothing – but its relevance here should have occurred to you already. Six dromons. On their way to meet the Kartool fleet, three pirate galleys, which had each been blessed by the island's priests of D'rek. The Worm of Autumn. Yes, you all know D'rek's other name, but I said it for emphasis. In any case, Nok's fleet had stopped at the Napan Isles, went up the mouth of Koolibor River to drag barrels – drawing fresh water. What every ship did when heading out to Kartool or beyond on the Reach. Six ships, each drawing water, storing the barrels below decks.

'Half a day out of the Napan Isles, the first barrel was broached, by a cook's helper, on the flagship. And straight out through the hole came a snake. A paralt, up the lad's arm. Sank both fangs into his left eye. Screaming, he ran out on deck, the snake with its jaws wide and holding tight, writhing around. Well, the lad managed two steps before he died, then he went down, already white as a sun-bleached yard. The snake was killed, but as you can imagine, it was too late.

'Nok, being young, just shrugged the whole event off, and when word spread and sailors and marines started dying of thirst – in ships loaded with barrels of fresh water that no-one would dare open – he went and did the obvious thing. Brought up another barrel. Breached it with his own hands.' Strings paused. He could see that no-one else knew the tale. Could see that he had their attention.

'The damned barrel was full of snakes. Spilling out onto the deck. A damned miracle Nok wasn't bitten. It was just starting dry season, you see. The paralts' season in the river was ending. The waters fill with them as they head down to the river mouth on their way out to sea. Every single barrel on those six dromons held snakes.

'The fleet never closed to do battle with the Kartoolians. By the time it made it back to Nap, half of the complement was dead of thirst. All six ships were holed outside the harbour, packed with offerings to D'rek, the Worm of Autumn, and sent to the deep. Nok had to wait until the next year to shatter Kartool's paltry fleet. Two months after that, the island was conquered.' He fell silent for a moment, then shook his head. 'No, I'm not finished. That was a story, a story of how to do things wrong. You don't destroy an omen by fighting it. No, you do the opposite. You swallow it whole.'

Confused expressions. Gesler's was the first to clear and at the man's grin – startling white in his bronze-hued face – Strings slowly nodded, then said, 'If we don't close both hands on this omen, we're all nothing more than pall-bearers to those recruits in there. To the whole damned army.

'Now, didn't I hear that captain mention something about a nearby cemetery? Blown clear, the bones exposed to all. I suggest we go find it. Right now. All right, I'm finished talking.'

'That was a damned thigh bone,' Stormy growled.

Gesler stared at his corporal.

'We march in two days' time.'

Before anything else happens, Gamet silently added to the Adjunct's announcement. He glanced over at Nil and Nether where they sat side by side on the bench against the wall. Both racked with shivers, the aftermath of the omen's power leaving them huddled and pale.

Mysteries stalked the world. Gamet had felt their chill breath before, a reverberation of power that belonged to no god, but existed none the less. As implacable as the laws of nature. Truths beneath the bone. To his mind, the Empress would be better served by the immediate disbanding of the Fourteenth Army. A deliberate and thorough breaking up of the units with reassignments throughout the empire, the wait of another year for another wave of recruits.

Adjunct Tavore's next words to those gathered in the chamber seemed to speak directly to Gamet's thoughts. 'We cannot afford it,' she said, uncharacteristically pacing. 'The Fourteenth cannot be defeated before it sets foot outside Aren. The entire subcontinent will be irretrievably lost if that happens. Better we get annihilated in Raraku. Sha'ik's forces will have at least been reduced.

'Two days.

'In the meantime, I want the Fists to call their officers together, rank of lieutenant and higher. Inform them I will be visiting each company in person, beginning tonight. Give no indication of which one I will visit first – I want them all alert. Apart from guard postings, every soldier is restricted to barracks. Keep a particular eye on veterans. They will want to get drunk, and stay drunk, if they can. Fist Baralta, contact Orto Setral and have him assemble a troop of Red Blades. They're to sweep the settlement of the camp followers and confiscate all alcohol and durhang or whatever else the locals possess that deadens the senses. Then establish a picket round that settlement. Any questions? Good. You are all dismissed. Gamet, send for T'amber.'

'Aye, Adjunct.' *Uncharacteristically careless. That perfumed lover of yours has been kept from the sights of everyone here but me. They know, of course. Even so . . .*

Outside in the hallway, Blistig exchanged a nod with Baralta then gripped Gamet's upper arm. 'With us, if you please.'

Nil and Nether shot them a glance then hurried off.

'Take that damned hand off me,' Gamet said quietly. 'I can follow without your help, Blistig.'

The grip fell away.

They found an empty room, once used to store items on hooks fixed three-quarters of the way up all four walls. The air smelled of lanolin.

'Time's come,' Blistig said without preamble. 'We cannot march in two days' time, Gamet, and you know it. We cannot march at all. There will be a mutiny at worst, at best an endless bleeding of desertions. The Fourteenth is finished.'

The satisfied gleam in the man's eyes triggered a boiling rage in Gamet. He struggled for a moment then managed to clamp down on his emotions, sufficient to lock gazes with Blistig and ask, 'Was that child's arrival set up between you and Keneb?'

Blistig recoiled as if struck, then his face darkened. 'What do you take me for—'

'Right now,' Gamet snapped, 'I am not sure.'

The once-commander of the Aren garrison tugged the peace-loop from his sword's hilt, but Tene Baralta stepped between the two men, armour clanking. Taller and broader than either Malazan, the dusk-skinned warrior reached out to set a gloved hand on each chest, then slowly pushed the men apart. 'We are here to reach agreement, not kill one another,' he rumbled. 'Besides,' he added, facing Blistig, 'Gamet's suspicion had occurred to me as well.'

'Keneb would not do such a thing,' Blistig rasped, 'even if you two imagine that I might.'

A worthy answer.

Gamet pulled away and strode to face the far wall, back to the others. His mind raced, then he finally shook his head. Without turning round, he said, 'She asked for two days—'

'Asked? I heard an order—'

'Then you were not listening carefully enough, Blistig. The Adjunct, young and untested though she may be, is not a fool. She sees what you see – what we all see. But she has asked for two days. Come the moment to march . . . well, a final decision will become obvious, either way, at that moment. Trust her.' He swung round. 'For this and this alone, if need be. Two days.'

After a long moment, Baralta nodded. 'So be it.'

'Very well,' Blistig allowed.

Beru bless us. As Gamet made to leave, Tene Baralta touched his shoulder. 'Fist,' he said, 'what is the situation with this . . . this T'amber? Do you know? Why is the Adjunct being so . . . cagey? Women who take women for lovers – the only crime is the loss to men, and so it has always been.'

'Cagey? No, Tene Baralta. Private. The Adjunct is simply a private woman.'

The ex-Red Blade persisted, 'What is this T'amber like?

Does she exercise undue influence on our commander?'

'I have no idea, to answer your latter question. What is she like? She was a concubine, I believe, in the Grand Temple of the Queen of Dreams, in Unta. Other than that, my only words with her have been at the Adjunct's behest. Nor is T'amber particularly talkative . . .' *And that is an understatement of prodigious proportions. Beautiful, aye, and remote. Has she undue influence over Tavore? I wish I knew.* 'And speaking of T'amber, I must leave you now.'

At the door he paused and glanced back at Blistig. 'You gave good answer, Blistig. I no longer suspect you.'

In reply, the man simply nodded.

Lostara Yil placed the last of her Red Blade accoutrements into the chest then lowered the lid and locked it. She straightened and stepped back, feeling bereft. There had been a vast comfort in belonging to that dreaded company. That the Red Blades were hated by their tribal kin, reviled in their own land, had proved surprisingly satisfying. For she hated them in turn.

Born a daughter instead of the desired son in a Pardu family, as a child she had lived on the streets of Ehrlitan. It had been common practice – before the Malazans came with their laws for families – among many tribes to cast out their unwanted children once they reached the fifth year of life. Acolytes from numerous temples – followers of mystery cults – regularly rounded up such abandoned children. No-one knew what was done with them. The hopeful among the rough circle of fellow urchins Lostara had known had believed that, among the cults, there could be found a kind of salvation. Schooling, food, safety, all leading to eventually becoming an acolyte in turn. But the majority of children suspected otherwise. They'd heard tales of – or had themselves seen – the occasional nightly foray of shrouded figures emerging from the backs of temples, wending down alleyways with a covered cart, on their way to the crab-infested tidal pools east of the city, pools not so deep that one could not see the glimmer of small picked bones at the bottom.

One thing all could agree on. The hunger of the temples was insatiable.

Optimistic or pessimistic, the children of Ehrlitan's streets did all they could to evade the hunters with their nets and pole-ropes. A life could be eked out, a kind of freedom won, bitter though it might be.

Midway through her seventh year, Lostara was dragged down to the greasy cobbles by an acolyte's net. Her shrieks went unheeded by the citizens who stepped aside as the silent priest dragged his prize back to the temple. Impassive eyes met hers every now and then on that horrible journey, and those eyes Lostara would never forget.

Rashan had proved less bloodthirsty than most of the other cults in the habit of hunting children. She had found herself among a handful of new arrivals, all tasked with maintenance of the temple grounds, destined, it seemed, for a lifetime of menial servitude. The drudgery continued until her ninth year, when for reasons unknown to Lostara she was selected for schooling in the Shadow Dance. She had caught rare and brief glimpses of the dancers – a hidden and secretive group of men and women for whom worship was an elaborate, intricate dance. Their only audience were priests and priestesses – none of whom would watch the actual dancers, only their shadows.

You are nothing, child. Not a dancer. Your body is in service to Rashan, and Rashan is this realm's manifestation of Shadow, the drawing of darkness to light. When you dance, it is not you that is watched. It is the shadow your body paints. The shadow is the dancer, Lostara Yil. Not you.

Years of discipline, of limb-stretching training that loosened every joint, that drew out the spine, that would allow the Caster to flow with seamless movement – and all for naught.

The world had been changing outside the temple's high walls. Events unknown to Lostara were systematically crushing their entire civilization. The Malazan Empire had invaded. Cities were falling. Foreign ships had blockaded Ehrlitan's harbour.

The cult of Rashan was spared the purges of the new, harsh masters of Seven Cities, for it was a recognized religion. Other temples did not fare as well. She recalled seeing smoke in the sky above Ehrlitan and wondering at its source, and she was awakened at night by terrible sounds of chaos in the streets.

Lostara was a middling Caster. Her shadow seemed to have a mind of its own and was a recalcitrant, halting partner in the training. She did not ask herself if she was happy or otherwise. Rashan's Empty Throne did not draw her faith as it did the other students'. She lived, but it was an unquestioning life. Neither circular nor linear, for in her mind there was no movement at all, and the notion of progress was measured only in terms of mastering the exercises forced upon her.

The cult's destruction was sudden, unexpected, and it came from within.

She recalled the night when it had all begun. Great excitement in the temple. A High Priest from another city was visiting. Come to speak with Master Bidithal on matters of vast importance. There would be a dance in the stranger's honour, for which Lostara and her fellow students would provide a background sequence of rhythms to complement the Shadow Dancers.

Lostara herself had been indifferent to the whole affair, and had been nowhere close to the best of the students in their minor role in the performance. But she remembered the stranger.

So unlike sour old Bidithal. Tall, thin, a laughing face, remarkably long-fingered, almost effeminate hands – hands the sight of which awakened in her new emotions.

Emotions that stuttered her mechanical dancing, that sent her shadow twisting into a rhythm that was counterpoint to that cast by not only her fellow students,

388

but the Shadow Dancers themselves – as if a third strain had slipped into the main chamber.

Too striking to remain unnoticed.

Bidithal himself, his face darkening, had half risen – but the stranger spoke first.

'Pray let the Dance continue,' he said, his eyes finding Lostara's own. 'The Song of the Reeds has never been performed in quite this manner before. No gentle breeze here, eh, Bidithal? Oh no, a veritable gale. The Dancers are virgins, yes?' His laugh was low yet full. 'Yet there is nothing virginal about this dance, now, is there? Oh, storm of desire!'

And those eyes held Lostara still, in fullest recognition of the desire that overwhelmed her – that gave shape to her shadow's wild cavort. Recognition, and a certain pleased, but cool . . . acknowledgement. As if flattered, but with no invitation offered in return.

The stranger had other tasks that night – and in the nights that followed – or so Lostara would come to realize much later. At the moment, however, her face burned with shame, and she had broken off her dance to flee the chamber.

Of course, Delat had not come to steal the heart of a Caster. He had come to destroy Rashan.

Delat, who, it proved, was both a High Priest and a Bridgeburner, and whatever the Emperor's reason for annihilating the cult, his was the hand that delivered the death-blow.

Although not alone. The night of the killings, at the bell of the third hour – two past midnight – after the Song of Reeds, there had been another, hidden in the black clothes of an assassin . . .

Lostara knew more of what had happened that night in the Rashan Temple of Ehrlitan than anyone else barring the players themselves, for Lostara had been the only resident to be spared. Or so she had believed for a long time, until the name of Bidithal rose once more, from Sha'ik's Apocalypse army.

Ah, I was more than spared that night, wasn't I?
Delat's lovely, long-fingered hands . . .

Setting foot onto the city's streets the following morning, after seven years' absence, she had been faced with the terrifying knowledge that she was alone, truly alone. Resurrecting an ancient memory of when she was awakened following the fifth birthday, and thrust into the hands of an old man hired to take her away, to leave her in a strange neighbourhood on the other side of the city. A memory that echoed with a child's cries for her mother.

The short time that followed her departure from the temple, before she joined the Red Blades – the newly formed company of Seven Cities natives who avowed loyalty to the Malazan Empire – held its own memories, ones she had long since repressed. Hunger, denigration, humiliation and what seemed a fatal, spiralling descent. But the recruiters had found her, or perhaps she found them. The Red Blades would be a statement to the Emperor, the marking of a new era in Seven Cities. There would be peace. None of this interested Lostara, however. Rather, it was the widely-held rumour that the Red Blades sought to become the deliverers of Malazan justice.

She had not forgotten those impassive eyes. The citizens who were indifferent to her pleas, who had watched the acolyte drag her past to an unknown fate. She had not forgotten her own parents.

Betrayal could be answered by but one thing, and one thing alone, and the once-captain Lostara Yil of the Red Blades had grown skilled in that answer's brutal delivery.

And now, am I being made into a betrayer?

She turned away from the wooden chest. She was a Red Blade no longer.

In a short while, Pearl would arrive, and they would set out to find the cold, cold trail of Tavore's hapless sister, Felisin. Along which they might find opportunity to drive a blade into the heart of the Talons. Yet were not the Talons of the empire? Dancer's own, his spies and killers, the deadly weapon of his will. Then what had turned them into traitors?

Betrayal was a mystery. Inexplicable to Lostara. She only knew that it delivered the deepest wounds of all.

And she had long since vowed that she would never again suffer such wounds.

She collected her sword-belt from the hook above the bed and drew the thick leather band about her hips, hooking it in place.

Then froze.

The small room before her was filled with dancing shadows.

And in their midst, a figure. A pale face of firm features, made handsome by smile lines at the corners of the eyes – and the eyes themselves, which, as he looked upon her, settled like depthless pools.

Into which she felt, in a sudden rush, she could plunge. Here, now, for ever.

The figure made a slight bow with his head, then spoke, 'Lostara Yil. You may doubt my words, but I remember you—'

She stepped back, her back pressing up against the wall, and shook her head. 'I do not know you,' she whispered.

'True. But there were three of us that night, so very long ago in Ehrlitan. I was witness to your . . . unexpected performance. Did you know Delat – or, rather, the man I would eventually learn was Delat – would have taken you for his own? Not just the one night. You would have joined him as a Bridgeburner, and that would well have pleased him. Or so I believe. No way to test it, alas, since it all went – outwardly – so thoroughly awry.'

'I remember,' she said.

The man shrugged. 'Delat, who had a different name for that mission and was my partner's responsibility besides – Delat let Bidithal go. I suppose it seemed a . . . a betrayal, yes? It certainly did to my partner. Certainly to this day Shadowthrone – who was not Shadowthrone then, simply a particularly adept and ambitious practitioner of Rashan's sister warren, Meanas – to this day, I was saying, Shadowthrone stokes eternal fires of vengeance. But Delat proved very capable of hiding . . . under our very noses. Like Kalam. Just another unremarked soldier in the ranks of the Bridgeburners.'

'I do not know who you are.'

The man smiled. 'Ah, yes, I am well ahead of myself . . .' His gaze fell to the shadows spread long before him, though his back was to an unlit, closed door, and his smile broadened as if he was reconsidering those words. 'I am Cotillion, Lostara Yil. Back then, I was Dancer, and yes, you can well guess the significance of that name, given what you were being trained to do. Of course, in Seven Cities, certain truths of the cult had been lost, in particular the true nature of Shadow Dancing. It was never meant for performance, Lostara. It was, in fact, an art most martial. Assassination.'

'I am no follower of Shadow – Rashan or your version—'

'That is not the loyalty I would call upon with you,' Cotillion replied.

She was silent, struggling to fit sense to her thoughts, to his words. Cotillion . . . was Dancer. Shadowthrone . . . *must have been Kellanved, the Emperor!* She scowled. 'My loyalty is to the Malazan Empire. The *Empire*—'

'Very good,' he replied. 'I am pleased.'

'And now you're going to try to convince me that the Empress Laseen should not be the empire's true ruler—'

'Not at all. She is welcome to it. But, alas, she is in some trouble right now, isn't she? She could do with some . . . help.'

'She supposedly assassinated you!' Lostara hissed. 'You and Kellanved both!' *She betrayed you.*

Cotillion simply shrugged again. 'Everyone had their . . . appointed tasks. Lostara, the game being played here is far larger than any mortal empire. But the empire in question – your empire – well, its success is crucial to what we seek.

And, were you to know the fullest extent of recent, distant events, you would need no convincing that the Empress sits on a tottering throne right now.'

'Yet even you betrayed the Emper— Shadowthrone. Did you not just tell me—'

'Sometimes, I see further than my dear companion. Indeed, he remains obsessed with desires to see Laseen suffer – I have other ideas, and while he may see them as party to his own, there is yet no pressing need to disabuse him of that notion. But I will not seek to deceive you into believing I am all-knowing. I admit to having made grave errors, indeed, to knowing the poison of suspicion. Quick Ben. Kalam. Whiskeyjack. Where did their loyalty truly reside? Well, I eventually got my answer, but I am not yet decided whether it pleases me or troubles me. There is one danger that plagues ascendants in particular, and that is the tendency to wait too long. Before acting, before stepping – if you will – from the shadows.' He smiled again. 'I would make amends for past, at times fatal, hesitation. And so here I stand before you, Lostara, to ask for your help.'

Her scowl deepened. 'Why should I not tell Pearl all about this . . . meeting?'

'No reason, but I'd rather you didn't. I am not yet ready for Pearl. For you, remaining silent will not constitute treason, for, if you do as I ask, you two will walk step in step. You will face no conflict, no matter what may occur, or what you may discover in your travels.'

'Where is this . . . Delat?'

His brows rose, as if he was caught off guard momentarily by the question, then he sighed and nodded. 'I have no hold over him these days, alas. Why? He is too powerful. Too mysterious. Too conniving. Too Hood-damned smart. Indeed, even Shadowthrone has turned his attentions elsewhere. I would love to arrange a reunion, but I am afraid I have not that power.' He hesitated, then added, 'Sometimes, one must simply trust in fate, Lostara. The future can ever promise but one thing and one thing only:

surprises. But know this, we would all save the Malazan Empire, in our own ways. Will you help me?'

'If I did, would that make me a Talon?'

Cotillion's smile broadened. 'But, my dear, the Talons no longer exist.'

'Oh, really, Cotillion, would you ask my help and then play me for a fool?'

The smile slowly faded. 'But I am telling you, the Talons no longer exist. Surly annihilated them. Is there knowledge you possess that would suggest otherwise?'

She was silent a moment, then turned away. 'No. I simply . . . assumed.'

'Indeed. Will you help me then?'

'Pearl is on his way,' Lostara said, facing the god once again.

'I am capable of brevity when need be.'

'What is it you want me to do?'

Half a bell later there was a light rap upon the door and Pearl entered.

And immediately halted. 'I smell sorcery.'

Seated on the bed, Lostara shrugged then rose to collect her kit bag. 'There are sequences in the Shadow Dance,' she said casually, 'that occasionally evoke Rashan.'

'Rashan! Yes.' He stepped close, his gaze searching. 'The Shadow Dance. You?'

'Once. Long ago. I hold to no gods, Pearl. Never have. But the Dance, I've found, serves me in my fighting. Keeps me flexible, and I need that the most when I am nervous or unhappy.' She slung the bag over a shoulder and waited.

Pearl's eyebrows rose. 'Nervous or unhappy?'

She answered him with a sour look, then walked to the doorway. 'You said you've stumbled on a lead . . .'

He joined her. 'I have at that. But a word of warning first. Those sequences that evoke Rashan – it would be best for us both if you avoided them in the future. That kind of activity risks drawing . . . attention.'

'Very well. Now, lead on.'

A lone guard slouched outside the estate's gate, beside a bound bundle of straw. Pale green eyes tracked Lostara and Pearl as they approached from across the street. The man's uniform and armour were dull with dust. A small human finger bone hung on a brass loop from one ear. His expression was sickly, and he drew a deep breath before saying, 'You the advance? Go back and tell her we're not ready.'

Lostara blinked and glanced over at Pearl.

Her companion was smiling. 'Do we look like messengers, soldier?'

The guard's eyes thinned. 'Didn't I see you dancing on a table down at Pugroot's Bar?'

Pearl's smile broadened. 'And have you a name, soldier?'

'Maybe.'

'Well, what is it?'

'I just told you. Maybe. Do you need me to spell it or something?'

'Can you?'

'No. I was just wondering if you was stupid, that's all. So, if you're not the Adjunct's advance, come to warn us about that surprise inspection, then what do you want?'

'A moment,' Pearl said, frowning. 'How can an inspection be a surprise if there's advance warning?'

'Hood's leathery feet, you are stupid after all. That's how it's done—'

'A warning, then.' He glanced at Lostara and winked as he added, 'Seems I'm offering those all day. Listen, Maybe, the Adjunct won't be warning you about her inspections – and don't expect your officers to do so either. She has her own rules, and you'd better get used to it.'

'You still ain't told me what you want.'

'I need to speak to a certain soldier of the 5th squad of the 9th Company, and I understand he is stationed in the temporary barracks here.'

'Well, I'm in the 6th, not the 5th.'

'Yes . . . so?'

'Well, it's obvious then, isn't it? You don't want to speak to me at all. Go on in, you're wasting my time. And hurry up, I'm not feeling too well.'

The guard opened the gate and watched them stride inside, his eyes falling to Lostara's swaying hips for a long moment before he slammed the reinforced gate shut.

Beside him, the bale of straw shimmered suddenly then reformed as an overweight young man seated cross-legged on the cobbles.

Maybe's head turned and he sighed. 'Don't do that again – not near me, Balgrid. Magic makes me want to puke.'

'I had no choice but to maintain the illusion,' Balgrid replied, drawing a sleeve across his sweat-beaded brow. 'That bastard was a Claw!'

'Really? I could have sworn I saw him wearing a woman's clothes and dancing at Pug—'

'Will you shut up with that! Pity the poor bastard he's looking for in the 5th!'

Maybe suddenly grinned. 'Hey, you just fooled a real live Claw with that damned illusion! Nice work!'

'You ain't the only one feeling sick,' Balgrid muttered.

Thirty paces took Lostara and Pearl across the compound to the stables.

'That was amusing,' said the man at her side.

'And what was the point?'

'Oh, just to see them sweat.'

'Them?'

'The man and the bale, of course. Well, here we are.' As she reached to draw back one of the broad doors, Pearl closed a hand on her wrist. 'In a moment. Now, there's actually more than one person within that we need to question. A couple of veterans – leave them to me. There's also a lad, was a guard at a mining camp. Work your charms on him while I'm talking with the other two.'

Lostara stared at him. 'My charms,' she said, deadpan.

Pearl grinned. 'Aye, and if you leave him smitten, well, consider it a future investment in case we need the lad later.'

'I see.'

She opened the door, stepping back to let Pearl precede her. The air within the stables was foul. Urine, sweat, honing oil and wet straw. Soldiers were everywhere, lying or sitting on beds or on items from a collection of ornate furniture that had come from the main house. There was little in the way of conversation, and even that fell away as heads turned towards the two strangers.

'Thank you,' Pearl drawled, 'for your attention. I would speak with Sergeant Gesler and Corporal Stormy . . .'

'I'm Gesler,' a solid-looking, bronze-skinned man said from where he sprawled on a plush couch. 'The one snoring under those silks is Stormy. And if you come from Oblat tell him we'll pay up . . . eventually.'

Smiling, Pearl gestured at Lostara to follow and strode up to the sergeant. 'I am not here to call in your debts. Rather, I would like to speak with you in private . . . concerning your recent adventures.'

'Is that right. And who in Fener's hoofprint are you?'

'This is an imperial matter,' Pearl said, his gaze falling to Stormy. 'Will you wake him or shall I? Further, my companion wishes to speak with the soldier named Pella.'

Gesler's grin was cool. 'You want to wake my corporal? Go right ahead. As for Pella, he's not here at the moment.'

Pearl sighed and stepped to the side of the bed. A moment's study of the heap of expensive silks burying the snoring corporal, then the Claw reached down and flung the coverings clear.

The hand that snapped to Pearl's right shin – halfway between knee and ankle – was large enough to almost close entirely around the limb. The surge that followed left Lostara gaping.

Up. Pearl yelling. Up, as Stormy reared from the bed like

a bear prodded from its hibernation, a roar rolling from his lungs.

Had the chamber contained a ceiling of normal height – rather than a few simple crossbeams spanning the space beneath the stable roof, none of which were, mercifully, directly overhead – Pearl would have struck it, and hard, as he was lifted into the air by that single hand clasped around his shin. Lifted, then thrown.

The Claw cavorted, arms flailing, his knees shooting up over his head, spinning, legs kicking free as Stormy's hand let go. He came down hard on one shoulder, the breath leaving his lungs in a grunting whoosh. He lay unmoving, drawing his legs up, in increments, into a curled position.

The corporal was standing now, shaggy-haired, his red beard in wild disarray, the oblivion of sleep vanishing from his eyes like pine needles in a fire – a fire that was quickly flaring into a rage. 'I said no-one wakes me!' he bellowed, huge hands held out to either side and clutching at the air, as if eager to close on offending throats. His bright blue eyes fixed suddenly on Pearl, who was only now moving onto his hands and knees, his head hanging low. 'Is this the bastard?' Stormy asked, taking a step closer.

Lostara blocked his path.

Grunting, Stormy halted.

'Leave them be, Corporal,' Gesler said from the couch. 'That fop you just tossed is a Claw. And a sharper look at that woman in front of you will tell you she's a Red Blade, or was, and can likely defend herself just fine. No need to get into a brawl over lost sleep.'

Pearl was climbing to his feet, massaging his shoulder, his breaths deep and shuddering.

Hand on the pommel of her sword, Lostara stared steadily into Stormy's eyes. 'We were wondering,' she said conversationally, 'which of you is the better story-teller. My companion here would like to hear a tale. Of course, there will be payment for the privilege. Perhaps your debts to this

on the western shore of Otataral Island. Did the
s occur as planned?'

ve so,' Truth replied after a moment. 'But we
art of that plan – we just happened to find our-
he same boat with Kulp, and it was Kulp who was
 collect them.'

The cadre mage from the Seventh?'

im. He'd been sent by Duiker—'

mperial historian?' *Gods, what twisted trail is this?*
 would he have any interest in saving Felisin?'

aid it was the injustice,' Truth answered. 'But you
ng – it wasn't Felisin that Duiker wanted to help.
boric.'

poke in a low voice quite unlike what she had
n him moments earlier. 'If Duiker is going to be
as some kind of traitor . . . well, lass, better think
is is Aren, after all. The city that watched. That
r delivering the refugees to safety. He was the last
gh the gate, they say.' The emotion riding his
 now raw. 'And Pormqual had him *arrested*!'

 rippled through Lostara. 'I know,' she said.
osed us Red Blades from the gaols. We were on
by the time Pormqual had his army out there
in. If Duiker was seeking to free Heboric, a fellow
ell, I have no complaint with that. The trail we
elisin's.'

odded at that. 'Tavore has sent you, hasn't she?
hat Claw inside, listening to Gesler and Stormy.'
 briefly closed her eyes. 'I am afraid I lack Pearl's
 his mission was meant to be . . . secret.'

ith me,' Pella said. 'And you, Truth?'

ll lad nodded. 'It doesn't really matter anyway.
dead. They all are. Heboric. Kulp. They all died.
s just telling that part.'

Jone the less, please say nothing to anyone else.
e pursuing our task, if only to gather her bones.
es, that is.'

Oblat can be . . . taken care of, as a show of our appreciation.'

Stormy scowled and glanced back at Gesler.

The sergeant slowly rose from the couch. 'Well, lass, the corporal here's better with the scary ones . . . since he tells them so bad they ain't so scary any more. Since you're being so kind with . . . uh, our recent push of the Lord at knuckles, me and the corporal will both weave you a tale, if that's what you're here for. We ain't shy, after all. Where should we start? I was born—'

'Not that early,' Lostara cut in. 'I will leave the rest to Pearl – though perhaps someone could get him something to drink to assist in his recovery. He can advise you on where to start. In the meantime, where is Pella?'

'He's out back,' Gesler said.

'Thank you.'

As she was making her way to the narrow, low door at the back of the stables, another sergeant emerged to move up alongside her. 'I'll escort you,' he said.

Another damned Falari veteran. And what's with the finger bones? 'Am I likely to get lost, Sergeant?' she asked as she swung open the door. Six paces beyond was the estate's back wall. Heaps of sun-dried horse manure were banked against it. Seated on one of them was a young soldier. At the foot of a nearby pile lay two dogs, both asleep, one huge and terribly scarred, the other tiny – a snarl of hair and a pug nose.

'Possibly,' the sergeant replied. He touched her arm as she made to approach Pella, and she faced him with an enquiring look. 'Are you with one of the other legions?' he asked.

'No.'

'Ah.' He glanced back at the stables. 'Newly assigned to handmaid the Claw.'

'Handmaid?'

'Aye. The man needs . . . learning. Seems he chose well in you, at least.'

'What is it you want, Sergeant?'

'Never mind. I'll leave you now.'

She watched him re-enter the stables. Then, with a shrug, she swung about and walked up to Pella.

Neither dog awoke at her approach.

Two large burlap sacks framed the soldier, the one on the soldier's right filled near to bursting, the other perhaps a third full. The lad himself was hunched over, holding a small copper awl which he was using to drill a hole into a finger bone.

The sacks, Lostara realized, contained hundreds of such bones.

'Pella.'

The young man looked up, blinked. 'Do I know you?'

'No. But we perhaps share an acquaintance.'

'Oh.' He resumed his work.

'You were a guard in the mines—'

'Not quite,' he replied without looking up. 'I was garrisoned at one of the settlements. Skullcup. But then the rebellion started. Fifteen of us survived the first night – no officers. We stayed off the road and eventually made our way to Dosin Pali. Took four nights, and we could see the city burning for the first three. Wasn't much left when we arrived. A Malazan trader ship showed up at about the same time as us, and took us, eventually, here to Aren.'

'Skullcup,' Lostara said. 'There was a prisoner there. A young girl—'

'Tavore's sister, you mean. Felisin.'

Her breath caught.

'I was wondering when somebody would find me about that. Am I under arrest, then?' He looked up.

'No. Why? Do you think you should be?'

He returned to his work. 'Probably. I helped them escape, after all. The night of the Uprising. Don't know if they ever made it, though. I left them supplies, such as I could find. They were planning on heading north then west ... across the desert. I'm pretty sure I wasn't the only one

aiding them, but I never found ou

Lostara slowly crouched down level. 'Not just Felisin, then. Wh

'Baudin – a damned frighten strangely loyal to Felisin, though . met her gaze. 'Well, she wasn't on know what I mean. Anyway. Bau

'Heboric? Who is that?'

'Was once a priest of Fener – a the Boar. Had no hands – they them three.'

'Across the desert,' Lostara r coast of the island has . . . nothin

'Well, they were expecting a b was planned, right? Anyway, tha tale. For the rest, ask my sergean

'Truth? Who is he?'

'He's the one who's just sho behind you . . . come to deliver r voice. 'No need to hesitate, T woman here has some questions

Another one with the strange s gangly youth who cautiously app bulging burlap sack from which dusty cloud. *Hood take me, a com vulnerability would get on my* straightened. 'I would know of some iron into her tone.

Sufficient to catch Pella's no sharp look.

Both dogs had awakened at T rose from where they lay – they lad.

Truth set down the bag attentiveness. Colour rose in his

My charms. It's not Pella who Pella who'll find someone to wor

'That would be a good thing,' Truth said with a sigh.

Lostara made to leave but Pella gestured to catch her attention. 'Here.' He held out to her the finger bone he had been drilling a hole through. 'Take this for yourself. Wear it in plain sight.'

'Why?'

Pella scowled. 'You've just asked a favour of us . . .'

'Very well.' She accepted the grisly object.

Pearl appeared in the doorway. 'Lostara,' he called. 'Are you done here?'

'I am.'

'Time to leave, then.'

She could see by his expression that he too had been told of Felisin's death. Though probably in greater detail than the little that Truth had said.

In silence, they retraced their route through the stables, out into the compound, then across to the gate. The door swung open as they arrived and the soldier named Maybe waved them out. Lostara's attention was drawn to the bale of straw, which seemed to be wavering, strangely melting where it squatted, but Pearl simply waved her on.

As they drew some distance from the estate, the Claw voiced a soft curse, then said, 'I need a healer.'

'Your limp is barely noticeable,' Lostara observed.

'Years of discipline, my dear. I'd much rather be screaming. The last time I suffered such strength used against me was with that Semk demon, that godling. The three of them – Gesler, Stormy and Truth – there's more that's strange about them than just their skin.'

'Any theories?'

'They went through a warren of fire – and somehow survived, though it seems that Felisin, Baudin and Heboric didn't. Though their actual fate remains unknown. Gesler simply assumes they died. But if something unusual happened to those coastal guards in that warren, then why not the same to the ones who were washed overboard?'

'I'm sorry. I was not told the details.'

'We must pay a visit to a certain impounded ship. I will explain on the way. Oh, and next time don't offer to pay off someone else's debt . . . until you find out how big it is.'

And next time, leave that pompous attitude at the stable doors. 'Very well.'

'And stop taking charge.'

She glanced over at him. 'You advised me to use my charm, Pearl. It's hardly my fault if I possess more of that quality than you.'

'Really? Let me tell you, that corporal was lucky you stepped between us.'

She wanted to laugh, but pushed it back. 'You clearly did not notice the weapon under the man's bed.'

'Weapon? I care—'

'It was a two-handed flint sword. The weapon of a T'lan Imass, Pearl. It probably weighs as much as I do.'

He said no more until they reached the *Silanda.*

The ship's berth was well guarded, yet clearly permission for Pearl and Lostara had been provided earlier, for the two were waved onto the old dromon's battered deck then left deliberately alone, the ship itself cleared of all others.

Lostara scanned the area amidships. Flame-scarred and mud-smeared. A strange pyramidal mound surrounded the main mast, draped in a tarpaulin. New sails and sheets had been fitted, clearly taken from a variety of other vessels.

Standing at her side, Pearl's gaze fell upon the covered mound, and he voiced a soft grunt. 'Do you recognize this ship?' he asked.

'I recognize it's a ship,' Lostara replied.

'I see. Well, it's a Quon dromon of the old, pre-imperial style. But much of the wood and the fittings are from Drift Avalii. Do you know anything of Drift Avalii?'

'It's a mythical island off the Quon Tali coast. A *drifting* island, peopled with demons and spectres.'

'Not mythical, and it does indeed drift, though the pattern seems to describe a kind of wobbly circle. As for demons and spectres . . . well . . .' he strode to the tarpaulin, 'hardly anything so frightening.' He drew the covering back.

Severed heads, neatly piled, all facing outward, eyes blinking and fixing on Pearl and Lostara. The glimmer of wet blood.

'If you say so,' Lostara croaked, stepping back.

Even Pearl seemed taken aback, as if what he had unveiled was not entirely what he had expected. After a long moment he reached down and touched a fingertip to the pooled blood. 'Still warm . . .'

'B-but that's impossible.'

'Any more impossible than the damned things being still conscious – or alive at the very least?' He straightened and faced her, then waved expansively. 'This ship is a lode-stone. There are layers upon layers of sorcery, soaked into the very wood, into the frame. It descends upon you with the weight of a thousand cloaks.'

'It does? I don't feel it.'

He looked at her blankly, then faced the mound of severed heads once more. 'Neither demons nor spectres, as you can see. Tiste Andii, most of them. A few Quon Talian sailors. Come, let us go and examine the captain's cabin – magic tumbles from that room in waves.'

'What kind of magic, Pearl?'

He had already begun walking towards the hatch. A dis-missive gesture. 'Kurald Galain, Tellann, Kurald Emurlahn, Rashan—' He paused suddenly and swung round. 'Rashan. Yet you feel nothing?'

She shrugged. 'Are there more . . . heads . . . in there, Pearl? If so, I think I'd rather not—'

'Follow me,' he snapped.

Inside, black wood, the air thick as if roiling with memories of violence. A grey-skinned, barbaric-looking corpse pinned to the captain's chair by a massive spear. Other bodies, sprawled here and there as if grabbed, broken then tossed aside.

A dull, sourceless glow permeated the low, cramped

room. Barring strange patches on the floor, smeared with, Lostara saw, otataral dust.

'Not Tiste Andii,' Pearl muttered. 'These must be Tiste Edur. Oh, there are plenty of mysteries here. Gesler told me about the crew manning the oars down below – headless bodies. Those poor Tiste Andii on the deck. Now, I wonder who killed these Edur . . .'

'How does all this lead us further onto Felisin's trail, Pearl?'

'She was here, wasn't she? Witness to all this. The captain here had a whistle, strung around his neck, which was used to direct the rowers. It's disappeared, alas.'

'And without that whistle, this ship just sits here.'

Pearl nodded. 'Too bad, isn't it? Imagine, a ship with a crew you never have to feed, that never needs rest, that never mutinies.'

'You can have it,' Lostara said, turning back to the door-way. 'I hate ships. Always have. And now I'm leaving this one.'

'I see no reason not to join you,' Pearl said. 'We have a journey ahead of us, after all.'

'We do? Where?'

'The *Silanda* travelled warrens between the place where it was found by Gesler, and where it reappeared in this realm. From what I can gather, that journey crossed the mainland, from the north Otataral Sea down to Aren Bay. If Felisin, Heboric and Baudin jumped off, they might well have reappeared on land somewhere on that route.'

'To find themselves in the midst of the rebellion.'

'Given what seems to have led up to it, they might well have considered that a far less horrendous option.'

'Until some band of raiders stumbled onto them.'

Captain Keneb's 9th Company was called to muster in three successive assemblies on the parade ground. There had been no advance warning, simply the arrival of an officer commanding the soldiers to proceed at double-time.

Squads 1, 2 and 3 went first. These were heavy infantry, thirty soldiers in all, loaded down in scale armour and chain vambraces and gauntlets, kite shields, weighted longswords, stabbing spears strapped to their backs, visored and cheek-guarded helms with lobster tails, dirks and pig-stickers at their belts.

The marines were next. Ranal's 4th, 5th and 6th squads. Following them were the bulk of the company's troops, medium infantry, the 7th to the 24th squads. Only slightly less armoured than the heavy infantry, there was, among them, the addition of soldiers skilled in the use of the short bow, the longbow, and the spear. Each company was intended to work as a discrete unit, self-reliant and mutually supportive.

As he stood in front of his squad, Strings studied the 9th. Their first assembly as a separate force. They awaited the Adjunct's arrival in mostly precise ranks, saying little, not one out of uniform or weaponless.

Dusk was fast approaching, the air growing mercifully cool.

Lieutenant Ranal had been walking the length of the three squads of marines for some time, back and forth, his steps slow, a sheen of sweat on his smooth-shaven cheeks. When he finally halted, it was directly before Strings.

'All right, Sergeant,' he hissed. 'It's your idea, isn't it?'

'Sir?'

'Those damned finger bones! They showed up in your squad first – as if I wouldn't have noticed that. And now I've heard from the captain that it's spreading through every legion. Graves are being robbed all over the city! And I'll tell you this—' He stepped very close and continued in a rough whisper. 'If the Adjunct asks who is responsible for this last spit in her face over what happened yesterday, I won't hesitate in directing her to you.'

'Spit in her face? Lieutenant, you are a raging idiot. Now, a clump of officers have just appeared at the main gate. I suggest you take your place, sir.'

Face dark with fury, Ranal wheeled and took position before the three squads.

The Adjunct led the way, her entourage trailing.

Captain Keneb awaited her. Strings remembered the man from the first, disastrous mustering. A Malazan. The word was out that he had been garrisoned inland, had seen his share of fighting when their company had been overrun. Then the flight southward, back to Aren. There was enough in that to lead Strings to wonder if the man hadn't taken the coward's route. Rather than dying with his soldiers, he'd been first in the rout. That's how many officers outlived their squads, after all. Officers weren't worth much, as far as the sergeant was concerned.

The Adjunct was speaking with the man now, then the captain stepped back and saluted, inviting Tavore to approach the troops. But instead she drew a step closer to the man, reached out and touched something looped about Keneb's neck.

Strings's eyes widened slightly. *That's a damned finger bone.*

More words between the man and the woman, then the Adjunct nodded and proceeded towards the squads.

Alone, her steps slow, her face expressionless.

Strings saw the flicker of recognition as she scanned the squads. Himself, then Cuttle. After a long moment, during which she entirely ignored the ramrod-straight Lieutenant Ranal, she finally turned to the man. 'Lieutenant.'

'Adjunct.'

'There seems to be a proliferation of non-standard accoutrements on your soldiers. More so here than among any of the other companies I have reviewed.'

'Yes, Adjunct. Against my orders, and I know the man responsible—'

'No doubt,' she replied. 'But I am not interested in that. I would suggest, however, that some uniformity be established for those . . . trinkets. Perhaps from the hip belt, opposite the scabbard. Furthermore, there have been complaints from Aren's citizenry. At the very least, the looted pits and tombs should be returned to their original state . . . as much as that is possible, of course.'

Ranal's confusion was obvious. 'Of course, Adjunct.'

'And you might note, as well,' the Adjunct added drily, 'that you are alone in wearing a . . . non-standard uniform of the Fourteenth Army, at this time. I suggest you correct that as soon as possible, Lieutenant. Now, you may dismiss your squads. And on your way out, convey my instruction to Captain Keneb that he can proceed with moving the company's medium infantry to the fore.'

'Y-yes, Adjunct. At once.' He saluted.

Strings watched her walk back to her entourage. *Oh, well done, lass.*

Gamet's chest was filled with aching as he studied the Adjunct striding back to where he and the others waited. A fiercely welling emotion. Whoever had come up with the idea deserved . . . well, a damned kiss, as Cuttle would have said. *They've turned the omen. Turned it!*

And he saw the rekindled fire in Tavore's eyes as she reached them. 'Fist Gamet.'

'Adjunct?'

'The Fourteenth Army requires a standard.'

'Aye, it does indeed.'

'We might take our inspiration from the soldiers themselves.'

'We might well do that, Adjunct.'

'You will see to it? In time for our departure tomorrow?'

'I will.'

From the gate a messenger arrived on horseback. He had been riding hard, and drew up sharply upon seeing the Adjunct.

Gamet watched the man dismount and approach. *Gods, not bad news . . . not now . . .*

'Report,' the Adjunct demanded.

'Three ships, Adjunct,' the messenger gasped. 'Just limped into harbour.'

'Go on.'

'Volunteers! Warriors! Horses and wardogs! It's chaos at the docks!'

'How many?' Gamet demanded.

'Three hundred, Fist.'

'Where in Hood's name are they from?'

The messenger's gaze snapped away from them – over to where Nil and Nether stood. 'Wickans.' He met Tavore's gaze once more. 'Adjunct! Clan of the Crow. *The Crow! Coltaine's own!*'

CHAPTER NINE

At night ghosts come
In rivers of grief,
To claw away the sand
Beneath a man's feet

G'danii saying

The twin long-knives were slung in a faded leather harness stitched in swirling Pardu patterns. They hung from a nail on one of the shop's corner posts, beneath an elaborate Kherahn shaman's feather headdress. The long table fronting the canopied stall was crowded with ornate obsidian objects looted from some tomb, each one newly blessed in the name of gods, spirits or demons. On the left side, behind the table and flanking the toothless proprietor who sat cross-legged on a high stool, was a tall screened cabinet.

The burly, dark-skinned customer stood examining the obsidian weapons for some time before a slight flip of his right hand signalled an interest to the hawker.

'The breath of demons!' the old man squealed, jabbing a gnarled finger at various stone blades in confusing succession. 'And these, kissed by Mael – see how the waters have smoothed them? I have more—'

'What lies in the cabinet?' the customer rumbled.

'Ah, you've a sharp eye! Are you a Reader, perchance? Could you smell the chaos, then? Decks, my wise friend! Decks! And oh, haven't they awakened! Yes, all

411

anew. All is in flux—'

'The Deck of Dragons is *always* in flux—'

'Ah, but a new House! Oh, I see your surprise at that, friend! A new House. Vast power, 'tis said. Tremors to the very roots of the world!'

The man facing him scowled. 'Another new House, is it? Some local impostor cult, no doubt—'

But the old man was shaking his head, eyes darting past his lone customer, suspiciously scanning the market crowd – paltry as it was. He then leaned forward. 'I do not deal in those, friend. Oh, I am as loyal to Dryjhna as the next, make no claims otherwise! But the Deck permits no bias, does it? Oh no, balanced wise eyes and mind is necessary. Indeed. Now, why does the new House ring with truth? Let me tell you, friend. First, a new Unaligned card, a card denoting that a Master now commands the Deck. An arbiter, yes? And then, spreading out like a runaway stubble fire, the new House. Sanctioned? Undecided. But not rejected out of hand, oh no, not rejected. And the Readers – the patterns! The House will be sanctioned – not one Reader doubts that!'

'And what is the name of this House?' the customer asked. 'What throne? Who claims to rule it?'

'The House of Chains, my friend. To your other questions, there is naught but confusion in answer. Ascendants vie. But I will tell you this: the Throne where the King shall sit – the Throne, my friend, is *cracked*.'

'You are saying this House belongs to the Chained One?'

'Aye. The Crippled God.'

'The others must be assailing it fiercely,' the man murmured, his expression thoughtful.

'You would think, but not so. Indeed, it is they who are assailed! Do you wish to see the new cards?'

'I may return later and do that very thing,' the man replied. 'But first, let me see those poor knives on that post.'

'Poor knives! Aaii! Not poor, oh no!' The old man spun on his seat, reached up and collected the brace of weapons.

He grinned, blue-veined tongue darting between red gums. 'Last owned by a Pardu ghost-slayer!' He drew one of the knives from its sheath. The blade was blackened, inlaid with a silver serpent pattern down its length.

'That is not Pardu,' the customer growled.

'Owned, I said. You've a sharp eye indeed. They are Wickan. Booty from the Chain of Dogs.'

'Let me see the other one.'

The old man unsheathed the second blade.

Kalam Mekhar's eyes involuntarily widened. Quickly regaining his composure, he glanced up at the proprietor – but the man had seen and was nodding.

'Aye, friend. Aye . . .'

The entire blade, also black, was feather-patterned, the inlay an amber-tinged silver – *that amber taint . . . . alloyed with otataral. Crow clan. But not a lowly warrior's weapon. No, this one belonged to someone important.*

The old man resheathed the Crow knife, tapped the other one with a finger. 'Invested, this one. How to challenge the otataral? Simple. Elder magic.'

'Elder. Wickan sorcery is not Elder—'

'Oh, but this now-dead Wickan warrior had a friend. See, here, take the knife in your hand. Squint at this mark, there, at the base – see, the serpent's tail coils around it—'

The long-knife was startlingly heavy in Kalam's hand. The finger ridges in the grip were overlarge, but the Wickan had compensated for this with thicker leather straps. The stamp impressed into the metal in the centre of the looped tail was intricate, almost beyond belief, given the size of the hand that must have inscribed it. *Fenn. Thelomen Toblakai. The Wickan had a friend indeed. And worse, I know that mark. I know precisely who invested this weapon. Gods below, what strange cycles am I striding into here?*

There was no point in bartering. Too much had been revealed. 'Name your price,' Kalam sighed.

The old man's grin broadened. 'As you can imagine, a cherished set – my most valuable prize.'

'At least until the dead Crow warrior's son comes to collect it – though I doubt he will be interested in paying you in gold. I will inherit that vengeful hunter, so rein in your greed and name the price.'

'Twelve hundred.'

The assassin set a small pouch on the table and watched the proprietor loosen the strings and peer inside.

'There is a darkness to these diamonds,' the old man said after a moment.

'It is that shadow that makes them so valuable and you know it.'

'Aye, I do indeed. Half of what is within will suffice.'

'An honest hawker.'

'A rarity, yes. These days, loyalty pays.'

Kalam watched the old man count out the diamonds. 'The loss of imperial trade has been painful, it seems.'

'Very. But the situation here in G'danisban is doubly so, friend.'

'And why is that?'

'Why, everyone is at B'ridys, of course. The siege.'

'B'ridys? The old mountain fortress? Who is holed up there?'

'Malazans. They retreated from their strongholds in Ehrlitan, here and Pan'potsun – were chased all the way into the hills. Oh, nothing so grand as the Chain of Dogs, but a few hundred made it.'

'And they're still holding out?'

'Aye. B'ridys is like that, alas. Still, not much longer, I wager. Now, I am done, friend. Hide that pouch well, and may the gods ever walk in your shadow.'

Kalam struggled to keep the grin from his face as he collected the weapons. 'And with you, sir.' *And so they will, friend. Far closer than you might want.*

He walked a short distance down the market street, then paused to adjust the clasps of the weapon harness. The previous owner had not Kalam's bulk. Then again, few did. When he was done he slipped into the harness, then drew his telaba's overcloak around once more. The heavier weapon jutted from under his left arm.

The assassin continued on through G'danisban's mostly empty streets. Two long-knives, both Wickan. The same owner? Unknown. They were complementary in one sense, true, yet the difference in weight would challenge anyone who sought to fight using both at the same time.

In a Fenn's hand, the heavier weapon would be little more than a dirk. The design was clearly Wickan, meaning the investment had been a favour, or in payment. *Can I think of a Wickan who might have earned that? Well, Coltaine – but he carried a single long-knife, unpatterned. Now, if only I knew more about that damned Thelomen Toblakai . . .*

Of course, the High Mage named Bellurdan Skullcrusher was dead.

Cycles indeed. And now this House of Chains. The damned Crippled God—

You damned fool, Cotillion. You were there at the last Chaining, weren't you? You should have stuck a knife in the bastard right there and then.

Now, I wonder, was Bellurdan there as well?

Oh, damn, I forgot to ask what happened to that Pardu ghost-slayer . . .

The road that wound southwest out of G'danisban had been worn down to the underlying cobbles. Clearly, the siege had gone on so long that the small city that fed it was growing gaunt. The besieged were probably faring worse. B'ridys had been carved into a cliffside, a long-standing tradition in the odhans surrounding the Holy Desert. There was no formal, constructed approach – not even steps, nor handholds, cut into the stone – and the tunnels behind the fortifications reached deep. Within those tunnels, springs supplied water. Kalam had only seen B'ridys from the out-side, long abandoned by its original inhabitants, suggesting that the springs had dried up. And while such strongholds contained vast storage chambers, there was little chance that the Malazans who'd fled to it had found those chambers supplied.

The poor bastards were probably starving.

Kalam walked the road in the gathering dusk. He saw no-one else on the track, and suspected that the supply trains would not set out from G'danisban until the fall of night, to spare their draught animals the heat. Already, the road had begun its climb, twisting onto the sides of the hills.

The assassin had left his horse with Cotillion in the Shadow Realm. For the tasks ahead, stealth, not speed, would prove his greatest challenge. Besides, Raraku was hard on horses. Most of the outlying sources of water would have been long since fouled, in anticipation of the Adjunct's army. He knew of a few secret ones, however, which would of necessity have been kept untainted.

This land, Kalam realized, was in itself a land under siege – and the enemy had yet to arrive. Sha'ik had drawn the Whirlwind close, a tactic that suggested to the assassin a certain element of fear. Unless, of course, Sha'ik was deliberately playing against expectations. Perhaps she simply sought to draw Tavore into a trap, into Raraku, where her power was strongest, where her forces knew the land whilst the enemy did not.

But there's at least one man in Tavore's army who knows Raraku. And he'd damn well better speak up when the time comes.

Night had arrived, stars glittering overhead. Kalam pressed on. Burdened beneath a pack heavy with food and waterskins, he continued to sweat as the air chilled. Reaching the summit of yet another hill, he discerned the glow of the besiegers' camp beneath the ragged horizon's silhouette. From the cliffside itself there was no light at all.

He continued on.

It was midmorning before he arrived at the camp. Tents, wagons, stone-ringed firepits, arrayed haphazardly in a

416

rough semicircle before the rearing cliff-face with its smoke-blackened fortress. Heaps of rubbish surrounded the area, latrine pits overflowing and reeking in the heat. As he made his way down the track, Kalam studied the situation. He judged that there were about five hundred besiegers, many of them – given their uniforms – originally part of Malazan garrisons, but of local blood. There had been no assault in some time. Makeshift wooden towers waited off to one side.

He had been spotted, but no challenge was raised, nor was much interest accorded him as he reached the camp's edge. Just another fighter come to kill Malazans. Carrying his own food, ensuring he would not burden anyone else, and therefore welcome.

As the hawker in G'danisban had suggested, the patience of the attackers had ended. Preparations were under way for a final push. Probably not this day, but the next. The scaffolds had been left untended for too long – ropes had dried out, wood had split. Work crews had begun the repairs, but without haste, moving slowly in the enervating heat. There was an air of dissolution to the camp that even anticipation could not hide.

The fires have cooled here. Now, they're only planning an assault so they can get this over with, so they can go home.

The assassin noted a small group of soldiers near the centre of the half-ring where it seemed the orders were coming from. One man in particular, accoutred in the armour of a Malazan lieutenant, stood with hands on hips and was busy haranguing a half-dozen sappers.

The workmen wandered off a moment before Kalam arrived, desultorily making for the towers.

The lieutenant noticed him. Dark eyes narrowed beneath the rim of the helm. There was a crest on that skullcap. Ashok Regiment.

Stationed in Genabaris a few years past. Then sent back to . . . Ehrlitan, I think. Hood rot the bastards, I'd have thought they would have stayed loyal.

'Come to see the last of them get their throats cut?' the lieutenant asked with a hard grin. 'Good. You've the look of an organized and experienced man, and Beru knows, I've far too few of them here in this mob. Your name?'

'Ulfas,' Kalam replied.

'Sounds Barghast.'

The assassin shrugged as he set down his pack. 'You're not the first to think that.'

'You will address me as *sir*. That's if you want to be part of this fight.'

'You're not the first to think that . . . sir.'

'I am Captain Irriz.'

Captain . . . in a lieutenant's uniform. Felt unappreciated in the regiment, did you? 'When does the assault begin, sir?'

'Eager? Good. Tomorrow at dawn. There's only a handful left up there. It shouldn't take long once we breach the balcony entrance.'

Kalam looked up at the fortress. The balcony was little more than a projecting ledge, the doorway beyond narrower than a man's shoulders. 'They only need a handful,' he muttered, then added, 'sir.'

Irriz scowled. 'You just walked in and you're already an expert?'

'Sorry, sir. Simply an observation.'

'Well, we've a mage just arrived. Says she can knock a hole where that door is. A big hole. Ah, here she comes now.'

The woman approaching was young, slight and pallid. And Malazan. Ten paces away, her steps faltered, then she halted, light brown eyes fixing now on Kalam. 'Keep that weapon sheathed when you're near me,' she drawled. 'Irriz, get that bastard to stand well away from us.'

'Sinn? What's wrong with him?'

'Wrong? Nothing, probably. But one of his knives is an otataral weapon.'

The sudden avarice in the captain's eyes as he studied Kalam sent a faint chill through the assassin. 'Indeed. And where did you come by that, Ulfas?'

'Took it from the Wickan I killed. On the Chain of Dogs.'

There was sudden silence. Faces turned to regard Kalam anew.

Doubt flickered onto Irriz's face. 'You were there?'

'Aye. What of it?'

There were hand gestures all round, whispered prayers. The chill within Kalam grew suddenly colder. *Gods, they're voicing blessings . . . but not on me. They're blessing the Chain of Dogs. What truly happened there, for this to have been born?*

'Why are you not with Sha'ik, then?' Irriz demanded. 'Why would Korbolo have let you leave?'

'Because,' Sinn snapped, 'Korbolo Dom is an idiot, and Kamist Reloe even worse. Personally, I am amazed he didn't lose half his army after the Fall. What true soldier would stomach what happened there? Ulfas, is it? You deserted Korbolo's Dogslayers, yes?'

Kalam simply shrugged. 'I went looking for a cleaner fight.'

Her laugh was shrill, and she spun in mocking pirouette in the dust. 'And you came *here*? Oh, you fool! That's so funny! It makes me want to scream, it's so funny!'

Her mind is broken. 'I see nothing amusing in killing,' he replied. 'Though I find it odd that you are here, seemingly so eager to kill fellow Malazans.'

Her face darkened. 'My reasons are my own, Ulfas. Irriz, I would speak with you in private. Come.'

Kalam held his expression impassive as the captain flinched at the imperious tone. Then the renegade officer nodded. 'I will join you in a moment, Sinn.' He turned back to the assassin. 'Ulfas. We want to take most of them alive, to give us sport. Punishment for being so stubborn. I especially want their commander. He is named Kindly—'

'Do you know him, sir?'

Irriz grinned. 'I was 3rd Company in the Ashok. Kindly leads the 2nd.' He gestured at the fortress. 'Or what's left of it. This is a personal argument for me, and that is why I intend to win. And it's why I want those bastards alive. Wounded and disarmed.'

Sinn was waiting impatiently. Now she spoke up, 'There's a thought. Ulfas, with his otataral knife – he can make their mage useless.'

Irriz grinned. 'First into the breach, then. Acceptable to you, Ulfas?'

First in, last out. 'It won't be my first time, sir.'

The captain then joined Sinn and the two strode off.

Kalam stared after them. *Captain Kindly. Never met you, sir, but for years you've been known as the meanest officer in the entire Malazan military. And, it now seems, the most stubborn, too.*

Excellent. I could use a man like that.

He found an empty tent to stow his gear – empty because a latrine pit had clawed away the near side of its sand-crusted wall and was now soaking the ground beneath the floor's single rug along the back. Kalam placed his bag beside the front flap then stretched out close to it, shutting his mind and senses away from the stench.

In moments he was asleep.

He awoke to darkness. The camp beyond was silent. Slipping out from his telaba, the assassin rose into a crouch and began winding straps around his loose-fitting clothes. When he was done, he drew on fingerless leather gloves, then wound a black cloth around his head until only his eyes remained uncovered. He edged outside.

A few smouldering firepits, two tents within sight still glowing with lamplight. Three guards sitting in a makeshift picket facing the fortress – about twenty paces distant.

Kalam set out, silently skirting the latrine pit and approaching the skeletal scaffolding of the siege towers. They had posted no guard there. *Irriz was probably a bad lieutenant, and now he's an even worse captain.* He moved closer.

The flicker of sorcery at the base of one of the towers froze him in place. After a long, breathless moment, a second muted flash, dancing around one of the support fittings.

Kalam slowly settled down to watch.

Sinn moved from fitting to fitting. When she finished with the closest tower, she proceeded to the next. There were three in all.

When she was working on the last fitting at the base of the second tower, Kalam rose and slipped forward. As he drew near her, he unsheathed the otataral blade.

He smiled at her soft curse. Then, as realization struck her, she whirled.

Kalam held up a staying hand, slowly raised his knife, then sheathed it once more. He padded to her side. 'Lass,' he whispered in Malazan, 'this is a nasty nest of snakes for you to play in.'

Her eyes went wide, gleaming like pools in the starlight. 'I wasn't sure of you,' she replied quietly. Her thin arms drew tight around herself. 'I'm still not. Who are you?'

'Just a man sneaking to the towers . . . to weaken all the supports. As you have done. All but one of them, that is. The third one is the best made – Malazan, in fact. I want to keep that one intact.'

'Then we are allies,' she said, still hugging herself.

She's very young. 'You showed fine acting abilities earlier on. And you've surprising skill as a mage, for one so . . .'

'Minor magicks only, I'm afraid. I was being schooled.'

'Who was your instructor?'

'Fayelle. Who's now with Korbolo Dom. Fayelle, who slid her knife across the throats of my father and mother. Who went hunting for me, too. But I slipped away, and even with her sorcery she could not find me.'

'And this is to be your revenge?'

Her grin was a silent snarl. 'I have only begun my revenge, Ulfas. I want her. But I need soldiers.'

'Captain Kindly and company. You mentioned a mage in that fortress. Have you been in touch with him?'

She shook her head. 'I have not that skill.'

'Then why do you believe that the captain will join you in your cause?'

'Because one of his sergeants is my brother – well, my half-brother. I don't know if he still lives, though . . .'

He settled a hand on her shoulder, ignoring the answering flinch. 'All right, lass. We will work together on this. You've your first ally.'

'Why?'

He smiled unseen behind the cloth. 'Fayelle is with Korbolo Dom, yes? Well, I have a meeting pending with Korbolo. And with Kamist Reloe. So, we'll work together in convincing Captain Kindly. Agreed?'

'Agreed.'

The relief in her voice sent a twinge through the assassin. She'd been alone for far too long in her deadly quest. In need of help . . . but with no-one around to whom she could turn. Just one more orphan in this Hood-cursed rebellion. He recalled his first sight of those thirteen hundred children he had unwittingly saved all those months back, his last time crossing this land. *And there, in those faces, was the true horror of war. Those children had been alive when the carrion birds came down for their eyes . . .* A shudder ran through him.

'What is wrong? You seemed far away.'

He met her eyes. 'No, lass, far closer than you think.'

'Well, I have already done most of my work this night. Irriz and his warriors won't be worth much come the morning.'

'Oh? And what did you have planned for me?'

'I wasn't sure. I was hoping that, with you up front, you'd get killed quick. Captain Kindly's mage wouldn't go near you – he'd leave it to the soldiers with their crossbows.'

'And what of this hole you were to blast into the cliff-face?'

'Illusion. I've been preparing for days. I think I can do it.'

Brave and desperate. 'Well, lass, your efforts seem to have far outstripped mine in ambition. I'd intended a little mayhem and not much more. You mentioned that Irriz and his men wouldn't be worth much. What did you mean by that?'

'I poisoned their water.'

Kalam blanched behind his mask. 'Poison? What kind?'

'Tralb.'

The assassin said nothing for a long moment. Then, 'How much?'

She shrugged. 'All that the healer had. Four vials. He once said he used it to stop tremors, such as afflicted old people.'

Aye. A drop. 'When?'

'Not long ago.'

'So, unlikely anyone's drunk it yet.'

'Except maybe a guard or two.'

'Wait here, lass.' Kalam set out, silent in the darkness, until he came within sight of the three warriors manning the picket. Earlier, they had been seated. That was no longer the case. But there was movement, low to the ground – he slipped closer.

The three figures were spasming, writhing, their limbs jerking. Foam caked their mouths and blood had started from their bulging eyes. They had fouled themselves. A waterskin lay nearby in a patch of wet sand that was quickly disappearing beneath a carpet of capemoths.

The assassin drew his pig-sticker. He would have to be careful, since to come into contact with blood, spit or any other fluid was to invite a similar fate. The warriors were doomed to suffer like this for what to them would be an eternity – they would still be spasming by dawn, and would continue to do so until either their hearts gave out or they died from dehydration. Horribly, with Tralb it was often the latter rather than the former.

He reached the nearest one. Saw recognition in the man's leaking eyes. Kalam raised his knife. Relief answered the gesture. The assassin drove the narrow-bladed weapon down into the guard's left eye, angled upward.

The body stiffened, then settled with a frothy sigh.

He quickly repeated the grisly task with the other two.

Then meticulously cleaned his knife in the sand.

Capemoths, wings rasping, were descending on the scene. Hunting rhizan quickly joined them. The air filled with the sound of crunching exoskeletons.

Kalam faced the camp. He would have to stove the casks. Enemies of the empire these warriors might be, but they deserved a more merciful death than this.

A faint skittering sound spun him around.

A rope had uncoiled down the cliff-face from the stone balcony. Figures began descending, silent and fast.

They had watchers.

The assassin waited.

Three in all, none armed with more than daggers. As they came forward one halted while still a dozen paces distant.

The lead man drew up before the assassin. 'And who in Hood's name are you?' he hissed, gold flashing from his teeth.

'A Malazan soldier,' was Kalam's whispered reply. 'Is that your mage hanging back over there? I need his help.'

'He says he can't—'

'I know. My otataral long-knife. But he need not get close – all he has to do is empty this camp's water casks.'

'What for? There's a spring not fifty paces downtrail – they'll just get more.'

'You've another ally here,' Kalam said. 'She fouled the water with Tralb – what do you think afflicted these poor bastards?'

The second man grunted. 'We was wondering. Not pleasant, what happened to them. Still, it's no less than they deserved. I say leave the water be.'

'Why not take the issue to Captain Kindly? He's the one making the decisions for you, right?'

The man scowled.

His companion spoke. 'That's not why we're down here.

We're here to retrieve you. And if there's another one, we'll take her, too.'

'To do what?' Kalam demanded. He was about to say *Starve? Die of thirst?* but then he realized that neither soldier before him looked particularly gaunt, nor parched. 'You want to stay holed up in there for ever?'

'It suits us fine,' the second soldier snapped. 'We could leave at any time. There's back routes. But the question is, then what? Where do we go? The whole land is out for Malazan blood.'

'What is the last news you've heard?' Kalam asked.

'We ain't heard any at all. Not since we quitted Ehrlitan. As far as we can see, Seven Cities ain't part of the Malazan Empire any more, and there won't be nobody coming to get us. If there was, they'd have come long since.'

The assassin regarded the two soldiers for a moment, then he sighed. 'All right, we need to talk. But not here. Let me get the lass – we'll go with you. On condition that your mage do me the favour I asked.'

'Not an even enough bargain,' the second soldier said. 'Grab for us Irriz. We want a little sit-down with that fly-blown corporal.'

'Corporal? Didn't you know, he's a captain now. You want him. Fine. Your mage destroys the water in those casks. I'll send the lass your way – be kind to her. All of you head back up. I may be a while.'

'We can live with that deal.'

Kalam nodded and made his way back to where he'd left Sinn.

She had not left her position, although instead of hiding she was dancing beneath one of the towers, spinning in the sand, arms floating, hands fluttering like capemoth wings.

The assassin hissed in warning as he drew near. She halted, saw him, and scurried over. 'You took too long! I thought you were dead!'

And so you danced? 'No, but those three guards are. I've made contact with the soldiers from the fortress. They've invited us inside – conditions seem amenable up there. I've agreed.'

'But what about the attack tomorrow?'

'It will fail. Listen, Sinn, they can leave at any time, unseen – we can be on our way into Raraku as soon as we can convince Kindly. Now, follow me – and quietly.'

They returned to where the three Malazan imperials waited.

Kalam scowled at the squad mage, but he grinned in return. 'It's done. Easy when you're not around.'

'Very well. This is Sinn – she's a mage as well. Go on, all of you.'

'Lady's luck to you,' one of the soldiers said to Kalam.

Without replying, the assassin turned about and slipped back into the camp. He returned to his own tent, entered and crouched down beside his kit bag. Rummaging inside it, he drew out the pouch of diamonds and selected one at random.

A moment's careful study, holding it close in the gloom. Murky shadows swam within the cut stone. *Beware of shadows bearing gifts.* He reached outside and dragged in one of the flat stones used to hold down the tent walls, and set the diamond onto its dusty surface.

The bone whistle Cotillion had given him was looped on a thong around his neck. He pulled it clear and set it to his lips. *'Blow hard and you'll awaken all of them. Blow soft and directly at one in particular, and you'll awaken that one alone.'* Kalam hoped the god knew what he was talking about. *Better if these weren't Shadowthrone's toys . . .* He leaned forward until the whistle was a mere hand's width from the diamond.

Then softly blew through it.

There was no sound. Frowning, Kalam pulled the whistle from his lips and examined it. He was interrupted by a soft tinkling sound.

The diamond had crumbled to glittering dust.

From which a swirling shadow rose.

As I'd feared. Azalan. From a territory in the Shadow Realm bordering that of the Aptorians. Rarely seen, and never more than one at a time. Silent, seemingly incapable of language – how Shadowthrone commanded them was a mystery.

Swirling, filling the tent, dropping to all six limbs, the spiny ridge of its massive, hunched back scraping against the fabric to either side of the ridge-pole. Blue, all-too-human eyes blinked out at Kalam from beneath a black-skinned, flaring, swept-back brow. Wide mouth, lower lip strangely protruding as if in eternal pout, twin slits for a nose. A mane of thin bluish-black hair hung in strands, tips brushing the tent floor. There was no indication of its gender. A complicated harness crisscrossed its huge torso, studded with a variety of weapons, not one of which seemed of practical use.

The azalan possessed no feet as such – each appendage ended in a wide, flat, short-fingered hand. The homeland of these demons was a forest, and these creatures commonly lived in the tangled canopy high overhead, venturing down to the gloomy forest floor only when summoned.

Summoned . . . only to then be imprisoned in diamonds. If it was me, I'd be pretty annoyed by now.

The demon suddenly smiled.

Kalam glanced away, considering how to frame his request. *Get Captain Irriz. Alive, but kept quiet. Join me at the rope.* There would need to be some explaining to do, and with a beast possessing no language—

The azalan turned suddenly, nostrils twitching. The broad, squat head dipped down on its long, thickly muscled neck. Down to the tent's back wall at the base.

Where urine from the latrine pit had soaked through.

A soft cluck, then the demon wheeled about and lifted a hind limb. Two penises dropped into view from a fold of flesh.

Twin streams reached down to the sodden carpet.

Kalam reeled back at the stench, back, out through the

flap and outside into the chill night air, where he remained, on hands and knees, gagging.

A moment later the demon emerged. Lifted its head to test the air, then surged into the shadows – and was gone.

In the direction of the captain's tent.

Kalam managed a lungful of cleansing air, slowly brought his shuddering under control. 'All right, pup,' he softly gasped, 'guess you read my mind.' After a moment he rose into a crouch, reached back with breath held into the tent to retrieve his pack, then staggered towards the cliff-face.

A glance back showed steam or smoke rising out from his tent's entrance, a whispering crackle slowly growing louder from within it.

Gods, who needs a vial of Tralb?

He padded swiftly to where the rope still dangled beneath the balcony.

A sputtering burst of flames erupted from where his tent had been.

Hardly an event to go unnoticed. Hissing a curse, Kalam sprinted for the rope.

Shouts rose from the camp. Then screams, then shrieks, each one ending in a strange mangled squeal.

The assassin skidded to a halt at the cliff-face, closed both hands on the rope, and began climbing. He was halfway up to the balcony when the limestone wall shook suddenly, puffing out dust. Pebbles rained down. And a hulking shape was now beside him, clinging to the raw, runnelled rock. Tucked under one arm was Irriz, unconscious and in his bedclothes. The azalan seemed to flow up the wall, hands gripping the rippled ribbons of shadow as if they were iron rungs. In moments the demon reached the balcony and swung itself over the lip and out of sight.

And the stone ledge groaned.

Cracks snaked down.

Kalam stared upward to see the entire balcony sagging, pulling away from the wall.

His moccasins slipped wildly as he tried to scrabble his

way to one side. Then he saw long, unhuman hands close on the lip of the stone ledge. The sagging ceased.

H-how in Hood's name—

The assassin resumed climbing. Moments later he reached the balcony and pulled himself over the edge.

The azalan was fully stretched over it. Two hands gripped the ledge. Three others held shadows on the cliffside above the small doorway. Shadows were unravelling from the demon like layers of skin, vaguely human shapes stretching out to hold the balcony to the wall – and being torn apart by the immense strain. As Kalam scrambled onto its surface, a grinding, crunching sound came from where the balcony joined the wall, and it dropped a hand's width along the seam.

The assassin launched himself towards the recessed doorway, where he saw a face in the gloom, twisted with terror – the squad mage.

'Back off!' Kalam hissed. 'It's a friend!'

The mage reached out and clasped Kalam's forearm.

The balcony dropped away beneath the assassin even as he was dragged into the corridor.

Both men tumbled back, over Irriz's prone body.

Everything shook as a tremendous thump sounded from below. The echoes were slow to fade.

The azalan swung in from under the lintel stone. Grinning.

A short distance down the corridor crouched a squad of soldiers. Sinn had an arm wrapped round one of them – her half-brother, Kalam assumed as he slowly regained his feet.

One of the soldiers the assassin had met earlier moved forward, edging past the assassin and – with more difficulty – the azalan, back out to the edge. After a moment he called back. 'All quiet down there, Sergeant. The camp's a mess, though. Can't see anyone about . . .'

The other soldier from before frowned. 'No-one, Bell?'

'No. Like they all ran away.'

Kalam offered nothing, though he had his suspicions.

429

There was something about all those shadows in the demon's possession . . .

The squad mage had disentangled himself from Irriz and now said to the assassin, 'That's a damned frightening friend you have there. And it ain't imperial. Shadow Realm?'

'A temporary ally,' Kalam replied with a shrug.

'How temporary?'

The assassin faced the sergeant. 'Irriz has been delivered – what do you plan on doing with him?'

'Haven't decided yet. The lass here says you're named Ulfas. Would that be right? A Genabackan Barghast name? Wasn't there a war chief by that name? Killed at Blackdog.'

'I wasn't about to tell Irriz my real name, Sergeant. I'm a Bridgeburner. Kalam Mekhar, rank of corporal.'

There was silence.

Then the mage sighed. 'Wasn't you outlawed?'

'A feint, one of the Empress's schemes. Dujek needed a free hand for a time.'

'All right,' the sergeant said. 'It don't matter if you're telling the truth or not. We've heard of you. I'm Sergeant Cord. The company mage here is Ebron. That's Bell, and Corporal Shard.'

The corporal was Sinn's half-brother, and the young man's face was blank, no doubt numbed by the shock of Sinn's sudden appearance.

'Where's Captain Kindly?'

Cord winced. 'The rest of the company – what's left, is down below. We lost the captain and the lieutenant a few days ago.'

'Lost? How?'

'They, uh, they fell down a well shaft. Drowned. Or so Ebron found out, once he climbed down and examined the situation more closely. It's fast-running, an underground river. They were swept away, the poor bastards.'

'And how do two people fall down a well shaft, Sergeant?'

The man bared his gold teeth. 'Exploring, I imagine. Now, Corporal, it seems I outrank you. In fact, I'm the only sergeant left. Now, if you aren't outlawed, then you're still a soldier of the empire. And as a soldier of the empire . . .'

'You have me there,' Kalam muttered.

'For now, you'll be attached to my old squad. You've got seniority over Corporal Shard, so you'll be in charge.'

'Very well, and what's the squad's complement?'

'Shard, Bell and Limp. You've met Bell. Limp's down below. He broke his leg in a rock-slide, but he's mending fast. There's fifty-one soldiers in all. Second Company, Ashok Regiment.'

'It seems your besiegers are gone,' Kalam observed. 'The world hasn't been entirely still while you've been shut up in here, Sergeant. I think I should tell you what I know. There are alternatives to waiting here – no matter how cosy it might be – until we all die of old age . . . or drowning accidents.'

'Aye, Corporal. You'll make your report. And if I want to ask for advice on what to do next, you'll be first in line. Now, enough with the opinions. Time to go below – and I suggest you find a leash for that damned demon. And tell it to stop smiling.'

'You'll have to tell it yourself, Sergeant,' Kalam drawled.

Ebron snapped, 'The Malazan Empire don't need allies from the Shadow Realm – get rid of it!'

The assassin glanced over at the mage. 'As I said earlier, changes have come, Mage. Sergeant Cord, you're entirely welcome to try throwing a collar round this azalan's neck. But I should tell you first – even though you're not asking for my advice – that even though those weird gourds, pans and knobby sticks strapped on to the beast's belts don't look like weapons, this azalan has just taken the lives of over five hundred rebel warriors. And how long did that take? Maybe fifty heartbeats. Does it do what I ask? Now that's a question worth pondering, don't you think?'

Cord studied Kalam for a long moment. 'Are you threatening me?'

'Having worked alone for some time, Sergeant,' the assassin replied in a low voice, 'my skin's grown thin. I'll take your squad. I'll even follow your orders, unless they happen to be idiotic. If you have a problem with all this, take it up with my own sergeant next time you see him. That'd be Whiskeyjack. Apart from the Empress herself, he's the only man I answer to. You want to make use of me? Fine. My services are available to you . . . for a time.'

'He's on some secret mission,' Ebron muttered. 'For the Empress, is my guess. He's probably back in the Claw – that's where he started, after all, isn't it?'

Cord looked thoughtful, then he shrugged and turned away. 'This is making my head ache. Let's get below.'

Kalam watched the sergeant push between the clump of soldiers crowding the corridor. *Something tells me I'm not going to enjoy this much.*

Sinn danced a step.

A blurred sword of dark iron rose along the horizon, a massive, bruised blade that flickered as it swelled ever larger. The wind had fallen off, and it seemed that the island in the path of the sword's tip grew no closer. Cutter moved up to the lone mast and began storm-rigging the luffing sail. 'I'm going to man the sweeps for a while,' he said. 'Will you take the tiller?'

With a shrug Apsalar moved to the stern.

The storm still lay behind the island of Drift Avalii, over which hung a seemingly permanent, immovable bank of heavy clouds. Apart from a steeply rising shoreline, there seemed to be no high ground; the forest of cedars, firs and redwoods looked impenetrable, their boles ever cloaked in gloom.

Cutter stared at the island for a moment longer, then gauged the pace of the approaching storm. He settled onto the bench behind the mast and collected the sweeps. 'We might make it,' he said, as he dropped the oar blades into the murky water and pulled.

'The island will shatter it,' Apsalar replied.

He narrowed his eyes on her. It was the first time in days that she had ventured a statement without considerable prodding on his part. 'Well, I may have crossed a damned ocean, but I still understand nothing of the sea. Why should an island without a single mountain break that storm?'

'A normal island wouldn't,' she answered.

'Ah, I see.' He fell silent. Her knowledge came from Cotillion's memories, appearing to add yet another layer to Apsalar's miseries. The god was with them once more, a haunting presence between them. Cutter had told her of the spectral visitation, of Cotillion's words. Her distress – and barely constrained fury – seemed to originate from the god's recruitment of Cutter himself.

His choosing of his new name had displeased her from the very first, and that he had now become, in effect, a minion of the patron god of assassins appeared to wound her deeply. He had been naïve, it now seemed in retrospect, to have believed that such a development would bring them closer.

Apsalar was not happy with her own path – a realization that had rocked the Daru. She drew no pleasure or satisfaction from her own cold, brutal efficiency as a killer. Cutter had once imagined that competency was a reward in itself, that skill bred its own justification, creating its own hunger and from that hunger a certain pleasure. A person was drawn to his or her own proficiency – back in Darujhistan, after all, his thieving habits had not been the product of necessity. He'd suffered no starvation on the city's streets, no depredation by its crueller realities. He had stolen purely for pleasure, and because he had been good at it. A future as a master thief had seemed a worthy goal, notoriety indistinguishable from respect.

But now, Apsalar was trying to tell him that competence was not justification. That necessity demanded its own path and there was no virtue to be found at its heart.

433

He'd found himself at subtle war with her, the weapons those of silence and veiled expressions.

He grunted at the sweeps. The seas were growing choppy. 'Well, I hope you're right,' he said. 'We could do with the shelter . . . though from what the Rope said, there will be trouble among the denizens of Drift Avalii.'

'Tiste Andii,' Apsalar said. 'Anomander Rake's own. He settled them there, to guard the Throne.'

'Do you recall Dancer – or Cotillion – speaking with them?'

Her dark eyes flicked to his for a moment, then she looked away. 'It was a short conversation. These Tiste Andii have known isolation for far too long. Their master left them there, and has never returned.'

'Never?'

'There are . . . complications. The shore ahead offers no welcome – see for yourself.'

He drew the oars back in and twisted round on the seat.

The shoreline was a dull grey sandstone, wave-worn into undulating layers and shelves. 'Well, we can draw up easily enough, but I see what you mean. No place to pull the runner up, and tethering it risks battering by the waves. Any suggestions?'

The storm – or the island – was drawing breath, tugging the sail. They were quickly closing on the rocky coast.

The sky's rumbles were nearer now, and Cutter could see the wavering treetops evincing the arrival of a high and fierce wind, stretching the clouds above the island into long, twisting tendrils.

'I have no suggestions,' Apsalar finally replied. 'There is another concern – currents.'

And he could see now. The island did indeed drift, unmoored to the sea bottom. Spinning vortices roiled around the sandstone. Water was pulled under, flung back out, seething all along the shoreline. 'Beru fend us,' Cutter muttered, 'this won't be easy.' He scrambled to the bow.

Apsalar swung the runner onto a course parallel to the

shore. 'Look for a shelf low to the water,' she called. 'We might be able to drag the boat onto it.'

Cutter said nothing to that. It would take four or more strong men to manage such a task . . . *but at least we'd get onto shore in one piece.* The currents tugged at the hull, throwing the craft side to side. A glance back showed Apsalar struggling to steady the tiller.

The dull grey sandstone revealed, in its countless shelves and modulations, a history of constantly shifting sea levels. Cutter had no idea how an island could float. If sorcery was responsible, then its power was vast, and yet, it seemed, far from perfect.

'There!' he shouted suddenly, pointing ahead where the coast's undulations dropped to a flat stretch barely a hand's width above the roiling water.

'Get ready,' Apsalar instructed, half rising from her seat.

Clambering up alongside the prow, a coil of rope in his left hand, Cutter prepared to leap onto the shelf. As they drew closer, he could see that the stone ledge was thin, deeply undercut.

They swiftly closed. Cutter jumped.

He landed square-footed, knees flexing into a crouch.

There was a sharp crack, then the stone was falling away beneath his moccasined feet. Cold water swept around his ankles. Unbalanced, the Daru pitched backward with a yelp. Behind him, the boat rushed inward on the wave that tumbled into the sinking shelf's wake. Cutter plunged into deep water, even as the encrusted hull rolled over him.

The currents yanked him downward into icy darkness. His left heel thumped against the island's rock, the impact softened by a thick skin of seaweed.

Down, a terrifyingly fast plummet into the deep.

Then the rock wall was gone, and he was pulled by the currents under the island.

A roar filled his head, the sound of rushing water. His last lungful of air was dwindling to nothing in his chest. Something hard hammered into his side – a piece of the runner's hull, wreckage being dragged by the currents – their boat had overturned. Either Apsalar was somewhere in the swirling water with him, or she had managed to leap onto solid sandstone. He hoped it was the latter, that they would not both drown – for drowning was all that was left to him.

Sorry, Cotillion. I hope you did not expect too much of me—

He struck stone once more, was rolled along it, then the current tugged him upward and suddenly spat him loose.

He flailed with his limbs, clawing the motionless water, his pulse pounding in his head. Disorientated, panic ripping through him like wildfire, he reached out one last time.

His right hand plunged into cold air.

A moment later his head broke the surface.

Icy, bitter air poured into his lungs, as sweet as honey. There was no light, and the sounds of his gasping returned no echoes, seeming to vanish in some unknown immensity.

Cutter called out to Apsalar, but there was no reply.

He was swiftly growing numb. Choosing a random direction, he set out.

And quickly struck a stone wall, thick with wet, slimy growth. He reached up, found only sheerness. He swam along it, his limbs weakening, a deadly lassitude stealing into him. He struggled on, feeling his will seep away.

Then his outstretched hand slapped down onto the flat surface of a ledge. Cutter threw both arms onto the stone. His legs, numbed by the cold, pulled at him. Moaning, he sought to drag himself out of the water, but his strength was failing. Fingers gouging tracks through the slime, he slowly sank backward.

A pair of hands closed, one on each shoulder, to gather the sodden fabric in a grip hard as iron. He felt himself lifted clear from the water, then dropped onto the ledge.

Weeping, Cutter lay unmoving. Shivers racked him.

Eventually, a faint crackling sound reached through,

seeming to come from all sides. The air grew warmer, a dull glow slowly rising.

The Daru rolled onto his side. He had expected to see Apsalar. Instead, standing above him was an old man, extraordinarily tall, his white hair long and dishevelled, white-bearded though his skin was black as ebony, with eyes a deep, glittering amber – the sole source, Cutter realized with a shock – of the light.

All around them, the seaweed was drying, shrivelling, as waves of heat radiated from the stranger.

The ledge was only a few paces wide, a single lip of slick stone flanked by vertical walls stretching out to the sides.

Sensation was returning to Cutter's legs, his clothes steaming now in the heat. He struggled into a sitting position. 'Thank you, sir,' he said in Malazan.

'Your craft has littered the pool,' the man replied. 'I suppose you will want some of the wreckage recovered.'

Cutter twisted to stare out on the water, but could see nothing. 'I had a companion—'

'You arrived alone. It is probable that your companion drowned. Only one current delivers victims here. The rest lead only to death. On the isle itself, there is but one landing, and you did not find it. Few corpses of late, of course, given our distance from occupied lands. And the end of trade.'

His words were halting, as if rarely used, and he stood awkwardly.

She drowned? More likely she made it onto shore. Not for Apsalar the ignoble end that almost took me. Then again . . . She was not yet immortal, as subject to the world's cruel indifference as anyone. He pushed the thought away for the moment.

'Are you recovered?'

Cutter glanced up. 'How did you find me?'

A shrug. 'It is my task. Now, if you can walk, it is time to leave.'

The Daru pushed himself to his feet. His clothing was

almost dry. 'You possess unusual gifts,' he observed. 'I am named . . . Cutter.'

'You may call me Darist. We must not delay. The very presence of life in this place risks his awakening.'

The ancient Tiste Andii turned to face the stone wall. At a gesture, a doorway appeared, beyond which were stone stairs leading upward. 'That which survived the wrecking of your craft awaits you above, Cutter. Come.'

The Daru set off after the man. 'Awakening? Who might awaken?'

Darist did not reply.

The steps were worn and slick, the ascent steep and seemingly interminable. The cold water had stolen Cutter's strength, and his pace grew ever slower. Again and again Darist paused to await him, saying nothing, his expression closed.

They eventually emerged onto a level hallway down which ran, along the walls, pillars of rough-skinned cedars. The air was musty and damp beneath the sharp scent of the wood. There was no-one else in sight. 'Darist,' Cutter asked as they walked down the aisle, 'are we still beneath ground level?'

'We are, but we shall proceed no higher for the time being. The island is assailed.'

'What? By whom? What of the Throne?'

Darist halted and swung round, the glow in his eyes somehow deepening. 'A question carelessly unasked. What has brought you, human, to Drift Avalii?'

Cutter hesitated. There was no love lost between the present rulers of Shadow and the Tiste Andii. Nor had Cotillion even remotely suggested actual contact be made with the Children of Darkness. They had been placed here, after all, to ensure that the true Throne of Shadow remain unoccupied. 'I was sent by a mage – a scholar, whose studies had led him to believe the island – and all it contained – was in danger. He seeks to discover the nature of that threat.'

438

Darist was silent for a moment, his lined face devoid of expression. Then he said, 'What is this scholar's name?'

'Uh, Baruk. Do you know him? He lives in Darujhistan—'

'What lies in the world beyond the island is of no concern to me,' the Tiste Andii replied.

And that, old man, is why you're in this mess. Cotillion was right. 'The Tiste Edur have returned, haven't they? To reclaim the Throne of Shadow. But it was Anomander Rake who left you here, entrusted with—'

'He lives still, does he? If Mother Dark's favoured son is displeased with how we have managed this task, then he must come and tell us so himself. It was not some human mage who sent you here, was it? Do you kneel before the Wielder of Dragnipur? Does he renew his claims to the blood of the Tiste Andii, then? Has he renounced his Draconian blood?'

'I wouldn't know—'

'Does he now appear as an old man – older by far than me? Ah, I see by your face the truth of it. He has not. Well, you may go back to him and tell him—'

'Wait! I do not serve Rake! Aye, I saw him in person, and not very long ago, and he looked young enough at the time. But I did not kneel to him – Hood knows, he was too busy at the time in any case! Too busy fighting a demon to converse with me! We but crossed paths. I don't know what you're talking about, Darist. Sorry. And I am most certainly not in any position to find him and tell him whatever it is you want me to say to him.'

The Tiste Andii studied Cutter for a moment longer, then he swung about and resumed the journey.

The Daru followed, his thoughts wild with confusion. It was one thing to accept the charge of a god, but the further he travelled on this dread path, the more insignificant he himself felt. Arguments between Anomander Rake and these Tiste Andii of Drift Avalii ... well, that was no proper business of his. The plan had been to sneak onto this island and remain unseen. To determine if indeed the Edur had found this place, though what Cotillion would do with such knowledge was anyone's guess.

But that's something I should think about, I suppose. Damn it, Cutter – Crokus would've had questions! Mowri knows, he would've hesitated a lot longer before accepting Cotillion's bargain. If he accepted at all! This new persona was imposing a certain sense of stricture – he'd thought it would bring him more freedom. But now it was beginning to appear that the truly free one had been Crokus.

Not that freedom ensured happiness. Indeed, to be free was to live in absence. Of responsibilities, of loyalties, of the pressures that expectation imposed. *Ah, misery has tainted my views. Misery, and the threat of true grieving, which draws nearer – but no, she must be alive. Somewhere up above. On an island assailed . . .*

'Darist, please, wait a moment.'

The tall figure stopped. 'I see no reason to answer your questions.'

'I am concerned . . . for my companion. If she's alive, she's somewhere above us, on the surface. You said you were under attack. I fear for her—'

'We sense the presence of strangers, Cutter. Above us, there are Tiste Edur. But no-one else. She is drowned, this companion of yours. There is no point in holding out hope.'

The Daru sat down suddenly. He felt sick, his heart stuttering with anguish. And despair.

'Death is not an unkind fate,' Darist said above him. 'If she was a friend, you will miss her company, and that is the true source of your grief – your sorrow is for yourself. My words may displease you, but I speak from experience. I have felt the deaths of many of my kin, and I mourn the spaces in my life where they once stood. But such losses serve only to ease my own impending demise.'

Cutter stared up at the Tiste Andii. 'Darist, forgive me. You may be old, but you are also a damned fool. And I begin to understand why Rake left you here then forgot about you. Now, kindly shut up.' He pushed himself upright, feeling hollowed out inside, but determined not to surrender to the despair that threatened to overwhelm him. *Because surrendering is what this Tiste Andii has done.*

'Your anger leaves me undamaged,' Darist said. He turned and gestured to the double doors directly ahead. 'Through here you will find a place to rest. Your salvage awaits there, as well.'

'Will you tell me nothing of the battle above?'

'What is there to tell you, Cutter? We have lost.'

'Lost! Who is left among you?'

'Here in the Hold, where stands the Throne, there is only me. Now, best rest. We shall have company soon enough.'

The howls of rage reverberated through Onrack's bones, though he knew his companion could hear nothing. These were cries of the spirits – two spirits, trapped within two of the towering, bestial statues rearing up on the plain before them.

The cloud cover overhead had broken apart, was fast vanishing in thinning threads. Three moons rode the heavens, and there were two suns. The light flowed with shifting hues as the moons swung on their invisible tethers. A strange, unsettling world, Onrack reflected.

The storm was spent. They had waited in the lee of a small hill while it thrashed around the gargantuan statues, the wind howling past from its wild race through the rubble-littered streets of the ruined city lying beyond. And now the air steamed.

'What do you see, T'lan Imass?' Trull asked from where he sat hunched, his back to the edifices.

Shrugging, the T'lan Imass turned away from his lengthy study of the statues. 'There are mysteries here . . . of which I suspect you know more than I.'

The Tiste Edur glanced up with a wry expression. 'That

441

seems unlikely. What do you know of the Hounds of Shadow?'

'Very little. The Logros crossed paths with them only once, long ago, in the time of the First Empire. Seven in number. Serving an unknown master, yet bent on destruction.'

Trull smiled oddly, then asked, 'The human First Empire, or yours?'

'I know little of the human empire of that name. We were drawn into its heart but once, Trull Sengar, in answer to the chaos of the Soletaken and D'ivers. The Hounds made no appearance during that slaughter.' Onrack looked back at the massive stone Hound before them. 'It is believed,' he said slowly, 'by the bonecasters, that to create an icon of a spirit or a god is to capture its essence within that icon. Even the laying of stones prescribes confinement. Just as a hut can measure out the limits of power for a mortal, so too are spirits and gods sealed into a chosen place of earth or stone or wood . . . or an object. In this way power is chained, and so becomes manageable. Tell me, do the Tiste Edur concur with that notion?'

Trull Sengar climbed to his feet. 'Do you think we raised these giant statues, Onrack? Do your bonecasters also believe that power begins as a thing devoid of shape, and thus beyond control? And that to carve out an icon – or make a circle of stones – actually forces order upon that power?'

Onrack cocked his head, was silent for a time. 'Then it must be that we make our own gods and spirits. That belief demands shape, and shaping brings life into being. Yet were not the Tiste Edur fashioned by Mother Dark? Did not your goddess *create* you?'

Trull's smile broadened. 'I was referring to these statues, Onrack. To answer you – I do not know if the hands that fashioned these were Tiste Edur. As for Mother Dark, it may be that in creating us, she but simply separated what was not separate before.'

442

'Are you then the shadows of Tiste Andii? Torn free by the mercy of your goddess mother?'

'But Onrack, we are all torn free.'

'Two of the Hounds are here, Trull Sengar. Their souls are trapped in the stone. And one more thing of note – these likenesses cast no shadows.'

'Nor do the Hounds themselves.'

'If they are but reflections, then there must be Hounds of Darkness, from which they were torn,' Onrack persisted. 'Yet there is no knowledge of such . . .' The T'lan Imass suddenly fell silent.

Trull laughed. 'It seems you know more of the human First Empire than you first indicated. What was that tyrant emperor's name? No matter. We should journey onward, to the gate—'

'Dessimbelackis,' Onrack whispered. 'The founder of the human First Empire. Long vanished by the time of the unleashing of the Beast Ritual. It was believed he had . . . veered.'

'D'ivers?'

'Aye.'

'And beasts numbered?'

'Seven.'

Trull stared up at the statues, then gestured. 'We didn't build these. No, I am not certain, but in my heart I feel . . . no empathy. They are ominous and brutal to my eyes, T'lan Imass. The Hounds of Shadow are not worthy of worship. They are indeed untethered, wild and deadly. To truly command them, one must sit in the Throne of Shadow – as master of the realm. But more than that. One must first draw together the disparate fragments. Making Kurald Emurlahn whole once more.'

'And this is what your kin seek,' Onrack rumbled. 'The possibility troubles me.'

The Tiste Edur studied the T'lan Imass, then shrugged. 'I did not share your distress at the prospect – not at first. And indeed, had it remained . . . pure, perhaps I would still be standing alongside my brothers. But another power acts behind the veil in all this – I know not who or what, but I would tear aside that veil.'

'Why?'

Trull seemed startled by the question, then he shivered. 'Because what it has made of my people is an abomination, Onrack.'

The T'lan Imass set out towards the gap between the two nearest statues.

After a moment, Trull Sengar followed. 'I imagine you know little of what it is like to see your kin fall into dissolution, to see the spirit of an entire people grow corrupt, to struggle endlessly to open their eyes – as yours have been opened by whatever clarity chance has gifted you.'

'True,' Onrack replied, his steps thumping the sodden ground.

'Nor is it mere naïveté,' the Tiste Edur went on, limping in Onrack's wake. 'Our denial is wilful, our studied in-difference conveniently self-serving to our basest desires. We are a long-lived people who now kneel before short-term interests—'

'If you find that unusual,' the T'lan Imass muttered, 'then it follows that the one behind the veil has need for you only in the short term – if indeed that hidden power is manipulating the Tiste Edur.'

'An interesting thought. You may well be right. The question then is, once that short-term objective is reached, what will happen to my people?'

'Things that outlive their usefulness are discarded,' Onrack replied.

'Abandoned. Yes—'

'Unless, of course,' the T'lan Imass went on, 'they would then pose a threat to one who had so exploited them. If so, then the answer would be to annihilate them once they are no longer useful.'

'There is the unpleasant ring of truth to your words, Onrack.'

'I am generally unpleasant, Trull Sengar.'

'So I am learning. You say the souls of two Hounds are imprisoned within these – which ones again?'

'We now walk between them.'

'What are they doing here, I wonder?'

'The stone has been shaped to encompass them, Trull Sengar. No-one asks the spirit or the god, when the icon is fashioned, if it wishes entrapment. Do they? The need to make such vessels is a mortal's need. That one can rest eyes on the thing one worships is an assertion of control at worst, or at best the illusion that one can negotiate over one's own fate.'

'And you find such notions suitably pathetic, Onrack?'

'I find most notions pathetic, Trull Sengar.'

'Are these beasts trapped for eternity, do you think? Is this where they go when they are destroyed?'

Onrack shrugged. 'I have no patience with these games. You possess your own knowledge and suspicions, yet would not speak them. Instead, you seek to discover what I know, and what I sense of these snared spirits. I care nothing for the fate either way of these Hounds of Shadow. Indeed, I find it unfortunate that – if these two were slain in some other realm and so have ended up here – there are but five remaining, for that diminishes my chances of killing one myself. And I think I would enjoy killing a Hound of Shadow.'

The Tiste Edur's laugh was harsh. 'Well, I won't deny that confidence counts for a lot. Even so, Onrack of the Logros, I do not think you would walk away from a violent encounter with a Hound.'

The T'lan Imass halted and swung towards Trull Sengar. 'There is stone, and there is stone.'

'I am afraid I do not understand—'

In answer, Onrack unsheathed his obsidian sword. He strode up to the nearer of the two statues. The creature's forepaw was itself taller than the T'lan Imass. He raised his weapon two-handed, then swung a blow against the dark, unweathered stone.

An ear-piercing crack ripped the air.

Onrack staggered, head tilting back as fissures shot up through the enormous edifice.

It seemed to shiver, then exploded into a towering cloud of dust.

Yelling, Trull Sengar leapt back, scrambling as the billowing dust rolled outward to engulf him.

The cloud hissed around Onrack. He righted himself, then dropped into a fighting stance as a darker shape appeared through the swirling grey haze.

A second concussion thundered – this time behind the T'lan Imass – as the other statue exploded. Darkness descended as the twin clouds blotted out the sky, closing the horizons to no more than a dozen paces on all sides.

The beast that emerged before Onrack was as tall at the shoulder as Trull Sengar's full height. Its hide was colourless, and its eyes burned black. A broad, flat head, small ears . . .

Faint through the grey gloom, something of the two suns' light, and that reflected from the moons, reached down – to cast beneath the Hound a score of shadows.

The beast bared fangs the size of tusks, lips peeling back in a silent snarl that revealed blood-red gums.

The Hound attacked.

Onrack's blade was a midnight blur, flashing to kiss the creature's thick, muscled neck – but the swing cut only dusty air. The T'lan Imass felt enormous jaws close about his chest. He was yanked from his feet. Bones splintered. A savage shake that ripped the sword from his hands, then he was sailing through the grainy gloom—

To be caught with a grinding snap by a second pair of jaws.

The bones of his left arm shattered into a score of pieces within its taut hide of withered skin, then it was torn entirely from his body.

Another crunching shake, then he was thrown into the air once more. To crash in a splintered heap

446

on the ground, where he rolled once, then was still.

There was thunder in Onrack's skull. He thought to fall to dust, but for the first time he possessed neither the will nor, it seemed, the capacity to do so.

The power was shorn from him – the Vow had been broken, ripped away from his body. He was now, he realized, as those of his fallen kin, the ones that had sustained so much physical destruction that they had ceased to be one with the T'lan Imass.

He lay unmoving, and felt the heavy tread of one of the Hounds as it padded up to stand over him. A dust- and shard-flecked muzzle nudged him, pushed at the broken ribs of his chest. Then lifted away. He listened to its breathing, the sound like waves riding a tide into caves, could feel its presence like a heaviness in the damp air.

After a long moment, Onrack realized that the beast was no longer looming over him. Nor could he hear the heavy footfalls through the wet earth. As if it and its companion had simply vanished.

Then the scrape of boots close by, a pair of hands dragging him over, onto his back.

Trull Sengar stared down at him. 'I do not know if you can still hear me,' he muttered. 'But if it is any consolation, Onrack of the Logros, those were not Hounds of Shadow. Oh, no, indeed. They were the real ones. The Hounds of Darkness, my friend. I dread to think what you have freed here . . .'

Onrack managed a reply, his words a soft rasp. 'So much for gratitude.'

Trull Sengar dragged the shattered T'lan Imass to a low wall at the city's edge, where he propped the warrior into a sitting position. 'I wish I knew what else I could do for you,' he said, stepping back.

'If my kin were present,' Onrack said, 'they would complete the necessary rites. They would sever my head from my body, and find for it a suitable place so that I might

447

look out upon eternity. They would dismember the headless corpse and scatter the limbs. They would take my weapon, to return it to the place of my birth.'

'Oh.'

'Of course, you cannot do such things. Thus, I am forced into continuation, despite my present condition.' With that, Onrack slowly clambered upright, broken bones grinding and crunching, splinters falling away.

Trull grunted, 'You could have done that before I dragged you.'

'I regret most the loss of an arm,' the T'lan Imass said, studying the torn muscles of his left shoulder. 'My sword is most effective when in the grip of two hands.' He staggered over to where the weapon lay in the mud. Part of his chest collapsed when he leaned down to retrieve it. Straightening, Onrack faced Trull Sengar. 'I am no longer able to sense the presence of gates.'

'They should be obvious enough,' the Tiste Edur replied. 'I expect near the centre of the city. We are quite a pair, aren't we?'

'I wonder why the Hounds did not kill you.'

'They seemed eager to leave.' Trull set off down the street directly opposite, Onrack following. 'I am not even certain they noticed me – the dust cloud was thick. Tell me, Onrack. If there were other T'lan Imass here, then they would have done all those things to you? Despite the fact that you remain . . . functional?'

'Like you, Trull Sengar, I am now shorn. From the Ritual. From my own kind. My existence is now without meaning. The final task left to me is to seek out the other hunters, to do what must be done.'

The street was layered in thick, wet silt. The low buildings to either side, torn away above the ground level, were similarly coated, smoothing every edge – as if the city was in the process of melting. There was no grand architecture, and the rubble in the streets revealed itself to be little more than fired bricks. There was no sign of life anywhere.

They continued on, their pace torturously slow. The street slowly broadened, forming a vast concourse flanked by pedestals that had once held statues. Brush and uprooted trees marred the vista, all a uniform grey that gradually assumed an unearthly hue beneath the now-dominant blue sun, which in turn painted a large moon the colour of magenta.

At the far end was a bridge, over what had once been a river but was now filled with silt. A tangled mass of detritus had ridden up on one side of the bridge, spilling flotsam onto the walkway. Among the garbage lay a small box.

Trull angled over towards it as they reached the bridge. He crouched down. 'It seems well sealed,' he said, reaching out to pry the clasp loose, then lifting the lid. 'That's odd. Looks like clay pots. Small ones . . .'

Onrack moved up alongside the Tiste Edur. 'They are Moranth munitions, Trull Sengar.'

The Tiste Edur glanced up. 'I have no knowledge of such things.'

'Weapons. Explosive when the clay breaks. They are generally thrown. As far as is possible. Have you heard of the Malazan Empire?'

'No.'

'Human. From my birth realm. These munitions belong to that empire.'

'Well, that is troubling indeed – for why are they here?'

'I do not know.'

Trull Sengar closed the lid and collected the box. 'While I would prefer a sword, these will have to do. I was not pleased at being unarmed for so long.'

'There is a structure beyond – an arch.'

Straightening, the Tiste Edur nodded. 'Aye. It is what we seek.'

They continued on.

The arch stood on pedestals in the centre of a cobbled square. Floodwaters had carried silt to its mouth where it had dried in strange, jagged ridges. As the two travellers came closer, they discovered that the clay was rock hard. Although the gate did not manifest itself in any discernible way, a pulsing heat rolled from the space beneath the arch.

The pillars of the structure were unadorned. Onrack studied the edifice. 'What can you sense of this?' the T'lan Imass asked after a moment.

Trull Sengar shook his head, then approached. He halted within arm's reach of the gate's threshold. 'I cannot believe this is passable – the heat pouring from it is scalding.'

'Possibly a ward,' Onrack suggested.

'Aye. And no means for us to shatter it.'

'Untrue.'

The Tiste Edur glanced back at Onrack, then looked down at the box tucked under his arm. 'I do not understand how a mundane explosive could destroy a ward.'

'Sorcery depends on patterns, Trull Sengar. Shatter the pattern and the magic fails.'

'Very well, let us attempt this thing.'

They retreated twenty paces from the gate. Trull unlatched the box and gingerly drew forth one of the clay spheres. He fixed his gaze on the gate, then threw the munition.

The explosion triggered a coruscating conflagration from the portal. White and gold fires raged beneath the arch, then the violence settled back to form a swirling golden wall.

'That is the warren itself,' Onrack said. 'The ward is broken. Still, I do not recognize it.'

'Nor I,' Trull muttered, closing the munitions box once more. Then his head snapped up. 'Something's coming.'

'Yes.' Onrack was silent then for a long moment. He suddenly lifted his sword. 'Flee, Trull Sengar – back across the bridge. *Flee!*'

The Tiste Edur spun and began running.

Onrack proceeded to back up a step at a time. He could feel the power of the ones on the other side of the gate, a power brutal and alien. The breaking of the ward had been noted, and the emotion reaching through the barrier was one of indignant outrage.

A quick look over his shoulder showed that Trull Sengar had crossed the bridge and was now nowhere in sight. Three more steps and Onrack would himself reach the bridge. And there, he would make his stand. He expected to be destroyed, but he intended to purchase time for his companion.

The gate shimmered, blindingly bright, then four riders cantered through. Riding white, long-limbed horses with wild manes the colour of rust. Ornately armoured in enamel, the warriors were a match for their mounts – pale-skinned and tall, their faces mostly hidden behind slitted visors, cheek and chin guards. Curved scimitars that appeared to have been carved from ivory were held in gauntleted fists. Long silver hair flowed from beneath the helms.

They rode directly towards Onrack. Canter to gallop. Gallop to charge.

The battered T'lan Imass widened his stance, lifted his obsidian sword and stood ready to meet them.

The riders could only come at him on the narrow bridge two at a time, and even then it was clear that they simply intended their horses to ride Onrack down. But the T'lan Imass had fought in the service of the Malazan Empire, in Falar and in Seven Cities – and he had faced horse warriors in many a battle. A moment before the front riders reached him, Onrack leapt forward. Between the two mounts. Ignoring the sword that whirled in from his left, the T'lan Imass slashed his blade into the other warrior's midsection.

Two ivory blades struck him simultaneously, the one on his left smashing through clavicle and cutting deep into his shoulder blade, then through in a spray of bone shards. The scimitar on his right chopped down through the side of his face, sheering it off from temple to the base of the jaw.

Onrack felt his own obsidian blade bite deep into the warrior's armour. The enamel shattered.

Then both attackers were past him, and the remaining two arrived.

The T'lan Imass dropped into a crouch and positioned his sword horizontally over his head. A pair of ivory blades hammered down on it, the impacts thundering through Onrack's battered frame.

They were all past him now, emerging out onto the concourse to wheel their horses round, visored heads turned to regard the lone warrior who had somehow survived their attacks.

Hoofs thudding the clay-limned cobbles, the four warriors reined in, weapons lowering. The one whose armour had been shattered by Onrack's obsidian sword was leaning forward, one arm pressed against his stomach. Spatters of blood speckled his horse's flank.

Onrack shook himself, and pieces of shattered bone fell away to patter on the ground. He then settled his own weapon, point to the ground, and waited while one of the riders walked his horse forward.

A gauntleted hand reached up to draw the visor upward, revealing features that were startlingly similar to Trull Sengar's, apart from the white, almost luminous skin. Eyes of cold silver fixed on the T'lan Imass with distaste. 'Do you speak, Lifeless One? Can you understand the Language of Purity?'

'It seems no purer than any other,' Onrack replied.

The warrior scowled. 'We do not forgive ignorance. You are a servant of Death. There is but one necessity when dealing with a creature such as you, and that is annihilation. Stand ready.'

'I serve no-one,' Onrack said, raising his sword once more. 'Come, then.'

But the wounded one held up a hand. 'Hold, Enias. This world is not ours – nor is this deathless savage one of the trespassers we seek. Indeed, as you yourself must sense, none of them are here. This portal has not been used in millennia. We must needs take our quest elsewhere. But first, I require healing.' The warrior gingerly dismounted, one arm still pressed against his midsection. 'Orenas, attend me.'

'Allow me to destroy this thing first, Seneschal—'

'No. We shall tolerate its existence. Perhaps it will have answers for us, to guide us further on our quest. Failing that, we can destroy it later.'

The one named Orenas slipped down from his horse and approached the seneschal.

Enias edged his horse closer to the T'lan Imass, as if still mindful of a fight. He bared his teeth. 'There is not much left of you, Lifeless One. Are those the scorings of fangs? Your chest has been in the jaws of some beast, I think. The same that stole your arm? By what sorcery do you hold on to existence?'

'You are of Tiste blood,' Onrack observed.

The man's face twisted into a sneer. 'Tiste blood? Only among the Liosan is the Tiste blood pure. You have crossed paths with our tainted cousins, then. They are little more than vermin. You have not answered my questions.'

'I know of the Tiste Andii, but I have yet to meet them. Born of Darkness, they were the first—'

'The first! Oh, indeed. And so tragically imperfect. Bereft of Father Light's purifying blood. They are a most sordid creation. We tolerate the Edur, for they contain something of the Father, but the Andii – death by our hands is the only mercy they deserve. But I grow weary of your rudeness, Lifeless One. I have asked you questions and you are yet to answer a single one.'

'Yes.'

'Yes? What does that mean?'

'I agree that I have not answered them. Nor do I feel compelled to do so. My kind has much experience with arrogant creatures. Although that experience is singular: in answer to their arrogance we proclaimed eternal war, until they ceased to exist. I have always believed the T'lan Imass should seek out a new enemy. There is, after all, no shortage to be noted among arrogant beings. Perhaps you Tiste Liosan are numerous enough in your own realm to amuse us for a time.'

The warrior stared, as if shocked speechless.

Behind him, one of his companions laughed. 'There is little value in conversing with lesser creatures, Enias. They will seek to confound you with falsehoods, to lead you away from the righteous path.'

'I see now,' Enias replied, 'the poison of which you have long warned me, Malachar.'

'There will be more to come, young brother, on the trail we must follow.' The warrior strode up to Onrack. 'You call yourself a T'lan Imass, yes?'

'I am Onrack, of the Logros T'lan Imass.'

'Are there others of your kind in this ruined realm, Onrack?'

'If I did not answer your brother's questions, why imagine I would answer yours?'

Malachar's face darkened. 'Play such games with young Enias, but not with me—'

'I am done with you, Liosan.' Onrack sheathed his sword and swung away.

'You are done with us! Seneschal Jorrude! If Orenas has completed his ministrations, I humbly request your attention. The Lifeless One seeks to flee.'

'I hear you, Malachar,' the seneschal rumbled, striding forward. 'Hold, Lifeless One! We have not yet released you. You will tell us what we wish to know, or you will be destroyed here and now.'

Onrack faced the Liosan once more. 'If that was a threat, the pathos of your ignorance proves an amusing distraction. But I weary of it, and of you.'

Four ivory scimitars lifted threateningly.

Onrack drew his sword once more.

And hesitated, his gaze drawn to something beyond them. Sensing a presence at their backs, the warriors turned.

Trull Sengar stood fifteen paces away, the box of munitions at his feet. There was something odd about his smile. 'This seems an uneven fight. Friend Onrack, do you require assistance? Well, you need not answer, for it has arrived. And for that, I am sorry.'

Dust swirled upward around the Tiste Edur. A moment later, four T'lan Imass stood on the muddy cobbles. Three held weapons ready. The fourth figure stood a pace behind and to Trull's right. This one was massively boned, its arms disproportionately long. The fur riding its shoulders was black, fading to silver as it rose up to surround the bonecaster's head in a mangled hood.

Onrack allowed his sword's point to rest on the muddy cobbles once more. With his link, born of the Ritual, now severed, he could only communicate with these T'lan Imass by speaking out loud. 'I, Onrack, greet you, Bonecaster, and recognize you as from the Logros, as I once was. You are Monok Ochem. One of many chosen to hunt the renegades, who, as did those of my own hunt, followed their trail into this realm. Alas, I alone of my hunt survived the flood.' His gaze shifted to the three warriors. The clan leader, its torso and limbs tightly wrapped in the outer skin of a dhenrabi and a denticulated grey flint sword in its hands, was Ibra Gholan. The remaining two, both armed with bone-hafted, double-bladed axes of chalcedony, were of Ibra's clan, but otherwise unknown to Onrack. 'I greet you as well, Ibra Gholan, and submit to your command.'

Bonecaster Monok Ochem strode forward with a heavy, shambling gait. 'You have failed the Ritual, Onrack,' it said with characteristic abruptness, 'and so must be destroyed.'

'That privilege will be contested,' Onrack replied. 'These horse warriors are Tiste Liosan and would view me as their prisoner, to do with as they please.'

Ibra Gholan gestured to his two warriors to join him and the three walked towards the Liosan.

The seneschal spoke. 'We release our prisoner, T'lan

Imass. He is yours. Our quarrel with you is at an end, and so we shall leave.'

The T'lan Imass halted, and Onrack could sense their disappointment.

The Liosan commander regarded Trull for a moment, then said, 'Edur – would you travel with us? We have need of a servant. A simple bow will answer the honour of our invitation.'

Trull Sengar shook his head. 'Well, that is a first for me. Alas, I will accompany the T'lan Imass. But I recognize the inconvenience this will cause you, and so I suggest that you alternate in the role as servant to the others. I am a proponent of lessons in humility, Tiste Liosan, and I sense that among you there is some need.'

The seneschal smiled coldly. 'I will remember you, Edur.' He whirled. 'On your horses, brothers. We now leave this realm.'

Monok Ochem spoke. 'You may find that more difficult than you imagine.'

'We have never before been troubled by such endeavours,' the seneschal replied. 'Are there hidden barriers in this place?'

'This warren is a shattered fragment of Kurald Emurlahn,' the bonecaster said. 'I believe your kind have remained isolated for far too long. You know nothing of the other realms, nothing of the Wounded Gates. Nothing of the Ascendants and their wars—'

'We serve but one Ascendant,' the seneschal snapped. 'The Son of Father Light. Our lord is Osric.'

Monok Ochem cocked its head. 'And when last has Osric walked among you?'

All four Liosan visibly flinched.

In his affectless tone, the bonecaster continued, 'Your lord, Osric, the Son of Father Light, numbers among the contestants in the other realms. He has not returned to you, Liosan, because he is unable to do so. Indeed, he is unable to do much of anything at the moment.'

The seneschal took a step forward. 'What afflicts our lord?'

Monok Ochem shrugged. 'A common enough fate. He is lost.'

'Lost?'

'I suggest we work together to weave a ritual,' the bonecaster said, 'and so fashion a gate. For this, we shall need Tellann, your own warren, Liosan, and the blood of this Tiste Edur. Onrack, we shall undertake your destruction once we have returned to our own realm.'

'That would seem expedient,' Onrack replied.

Trull's eyes had widened. He stared at the bonecaster. 'Did you say my blood?'

'Not all of it, Edur . . . if all goes as planned.'

CHAPTER TEN

> All that breaks
> must be discarded
> even as the thunder
> of faith returns
> ever fading
> echoes.
>
> *Prelude to Anomandaris*
>
> Fisher

The day the faces in the rock awakened was celebrated among the Teblor by a song. The memories of his people were, Karsa Orlong now knew, twisted things. Surrendered to oblivion when unpleasant, burgeoning to a raging fire of glory when heroic. Defeat had been spun into victory in the weaving of every tale.

He wished Bairoth still lived, that his sagacious companion did more than haunt his dreams, or stand before him as a thing of rough-carved stone in which some chance scarring of his chisel had cast a mocking, almost derisive expression.

Bairoth could have told him much of what he needed to know at this moment. While Karsa's familiarity with their homeland's sacred glade was far greater than either Bairoth's or Delum Thord's, and so ensured the likenesses possessed some accuracy, the warrior sensed that something essential was missing from the seven faces he had carved into the stone trees. Perhaps his lack of talent had betrayed him, though that did not seem the case with the carvings of Bairoth and Delum. The energy of their lives seemed to emanate from their statues, as if merged with the petrified wood's own memory. As with the entire forest, in which there was the sense that the trees but awaited the coming of spring, of rebirth beneath the wheel of the stars, it seemed that the two Teblor warriors were but awaiting the season's turn.

But Raraku defied every season. Raraku itself was eternal in its momentousness, perpetually awaiting rebirth. Patience in the stone, in the restless, ever-murmuring sands.

The Holy Desert seemed, to Karsa's mind, a perfect place for the Seven Gods of the Teblor. It was possible, he reflected as he slowly paced before the faces he had carved into the boles, that something of that sardonic sentiment had poisoned his hands. If so, the flaw was not visible to his eyes. There was little in the faces of the gods that could permit expression or demeanour – his recollection was of skin stretched over broad, robust bone, of brows that projected like ridges, casting the eyes in deep shadow. Broad, flat cheekbones, a heavy, chinless jaw . . . a bestiality so unlike the features of the Teblor . . .

He scowled, pausing to stand before Urugal which, as with the six others, he had carved level with his own eyes. Serpents slithered over his dusty, bared feet, his only company in the glade. The sun had begun its descent, though the heat remained fierce.

After a long moment of contemplation, Karsa spoke out loud. 'Bairoth Gild, look with me upon our god. Tell me what is wrong. Where have I erred? That was your greatest talent, wasn't it? Seeing so clearly my every wrong step. You might ask: what did I seek to achieve with these carvings? You would ask that, for it is the only question worth answering. But I have no answer for you – ah, yes, I can almost hear you laugh at my pathetic reply.' *I have no answer.* 'Perhaps, Bairoth, I imagined you wished their company. The great Teblor gods, who one day awakened.'

In the minds of the shamans. Awakened in their dreams. There, and there alone. Yet now I know the flavour of those dreams, and it is nothing like the song. Nothing at all.

He had found this glade seeking solitude, and it had been solitude that had inspired his artistic creations. Yet now that he was done, he no longer felt alone here. He had brought his own life to this place, the legacies of his deeds. It had ceased to be a refuge, and the need to visit was born now from the lure of his efforts, drawing him back again and again. To walk among the snakes that came to greet him, to listen to the hiss of sands skittering on the moaning desert wind, the sands that arrived in the glade to caress the trees and the faces of stone with their bloodless touch.

Raraku delivered the illusion that time stood motionless, the universe holding its breath. An insidious conceit. Beyond the Whirlwind's furious wall, the hourglasses were still turned. Armies assembled and began their march, the sound of their boots, shields and gear a deathly clatter and roar. And, on a distant continent, the Teblor were a people under siege.

Karsa continued staring at the stone face of Urugal. *You are not Teblor. Yet you claim to be our god. You awakened, there in the cliff, so long ago. But what of before that time? Where were you then, Urugal? You and your six terrible companions?*

A soft chuckle from across the clearing brought Karsa around.

'And which of your countless secrets is this one, friend?'

'Leoman,' Karsa rumbled, 'it has been a long time since you last left your pit.'

Edging forward, the desert warrior glanced down at the snakes. 'I was starved for company. Unlike you, I see.' He gestured at the carved boles. 'Are these yours? I see two Toblakai – they stand in those trees as if alive and but moments from striding forth. It disturbs me to be reminded that there are more of you. But what of these others?'

'My gods.' He noted Leoman's startled expression and elaborated, 'The Faces in the Rock. In my homeland, they adorn a cliffside, facing onto a glade little different from this one.'

'Toblakai—'

'They call upon me still,' Karsa continued, turning back to study Urugal's bestial visage once more. 'When I sleep. It is as Ghost Hands says – I am haunted.'

'By what, friend? What is it your . . . gods . . . demand of you?'

Karsa shot Leoman a glance, then he shrugged. 'Why have you sought me out?'

Leoman made to say one thing, then chose another. 'Because my patience is at an end. There has been news of events concerning the Malazans. Distant defeats. Sha'ik and her favoured few are much excited . . . yet achieve nothing. Here we await the Adjunct's legions. In one thing Korbolo Dom is right – the march of those legions should be contested. But not as he would have it. No pitched battles. Nothing so dramatic or precipitous. In any case, Toblakai, Mathok has given me leave to ride out with a company of warriors – and Sha'ik has condescended to permit us beyond the Whirlwind.'

Karsa smiled. 'Indeed. And you are free to harass the Adjunct? Ah, I thought as much. You are to scout, but no further than the hills beyond the Whirlwind. She will not permit you to journey south. But at least you will be doing something, and for that I am pleased for you, Leoman.'

The blue-eyed warrior stepped closer. 'Once beyond the Whirlwind, Toblakai—'

'She will know none the less,' Karsa replied.

'And so I will incur her displeasure.' Leoman sneered. 'There is nothing new in that. And what of you, friend? She calls you her bodyguard, yet when did she last permit you into her presence? In that damned tent of hers? She is reborn indeed, for she is not as she once was—'

'She is Malazan,' Toblakai said.

'What?'

'Before she became Sha'ik. You know this as well as I—'

'She was reborn! She became the will of the goddess, Toblakai. All that she was before that time is without meaning—'

'So it is said,' Karsa rumbled. 'Yet her memories remain. And it is those memories that chain her so. She is trapped by fear, and that fear is born of a secret which she will not share. The only other person who knows that secret is Ghost Hands.'

Leoman stared at Karsa for a long moment, then slowly settled into a crouch. The two men were surrounded by snakes, the sound of slithering on sand a muted undercurrent. Lowering one hand, Leoman watched as a flare-neck began entwining itself up his arm. 'Your words, Toblakai, whisper of defeat.'

Shrugging, Karsa strode to where his tool kit waited at the base of a tree. 'These years have served me well. Your company, Leoman. Sha'ik Elder. I once vowed that the Malazans were my enemies. Yet, from what I have seen of the world since that time, I now understand that they are no crueller than any other lowlander. Indeed, they alone seem to profess a sense of justice. The people of Seven Cities, who so despise them and wish them gone – they seek nothing more than the power that the Malazans took from them. Power that they used to terrorize their own people. Leoman, you and your kind make war against justice, and it is not my war.'

'Justice?' Leoman bared his teeth. 'You expect me to challenge your words, Toblakai? I will not. Sha'ik Reborn says there is no loyalty within me. Perhaps she is right. I have seen too much. Yet here I remain – have you ever wondered why?'

Karsa drew out a chisel and mallet. 'The light fades

– and that makes the shadows deeper. It is the light, I now realize. That is what is different about them.'

'The Apocalyptic, Toblakai. Disintegration. Annihilation. Everything. Every human . . . lowlander. With our twisted horrors – all that we commit upon each other. The depredations, the cruelties. For every gesture of kindness and compassion, there are ten thousand acts of brutality. Loyalty? Aye, I have none. Not for my kind, and the sooner we obliterate ourselves the better this world will be.'

'The light,' Karsa said, 'makes them look almost human.'

Distracted as he was, the Toblakai did not notice Leoman's narrowing eyes, nor the struggle to remain silent.

One does not step between a man and his gods.

The snake's head lifted in front of Leoman's face and hovered there, tongue flicking.

'The House of Chains,' Heboric muttered, his expression souring at the words.

Bidithal shivered, though it was hard to tell whether from fear or pleasure. 'Reaver. Consort. The Unbound – these are interesting, yes? For all the world like shattered—'

'From whence came these images?' Heboric demanded. Simply looking upon the wooden cards with their lacquered paintings – blurred as they were – was filling the ex-priest's throat with bile. *I sense . . . flaws. In each and every one. That is no accident, no failing of the hand that brushed them into being.*

'There is no doubting,' L'oric said in answer to his question, 'their veracity. The power emanating from them is a sorcerous stench. I have never before witnessed such a vigorous birth within the Deck. Not even Shadow felt—'

'Shadow!' Bidithal snapped. 'Those deceivers could never unveil that realm's true power! No, here, in this new House, the theme is pure. Imperfection is celebrated, the twist of chaotic chance mars one and all—'

'Silence!' Sha'ik hissed, her arms wrapped tight about

herself. 'We must think on this. No-one speak. Let me think!'

Heboric studied her for a moment, squinting to bring her into focus, even though she sat beside him. The cards from the new House had arrived the same day as the news of the Malazan defeats on Genabackis. And the time since then had been one of seething discord among Sha'ik's commanders, sufficient to dampen her pleasure at hearing of her brother Ganoes Paran's survival, and now leading her to uncharacteristic distraction.

The House of Chains was woven into their fates. An insidious intrusion, an infection against which they'd had no chance to prepare. But was it an enemy, or the potential source for renewed strength? It seemed Bidithal was busy convincing himself that it was the latter, no doubt drawn in that direction by his growing disaffection with Sha'ik Reborn. L'oric, on the other hand, seemed more inclined to share Heboric's own misgivings; whilst Febryl was unique in remaining silent on the entire matter.

The air within the tent was close, soured by human sweat. Heboric wanted nothing more than to leave, to escape all this, yet he sensed Sha'ik clinging to him, a spiritual grip as desperate as anything he'd felt from her before.

'Show once more the new Unaligned.'

Yes. For the thousandth time.

Scowling, Bidithal searched through the Deck, then drew out the card, which he laid down in the centre of the goat-hair mat. 'If any of the new arrivals is dubious,' the old man sneered, 'it is this one. Master of the Deck? Absurd. How can one control the uncontrollable?'

There was silence.

The uncontrollable? Such as the Whirlwind itself?

Sha'ik had clearly not caught the insinuation. 'Ghost Hands, I would you take this card, feel it, seek to sense what you can from it.'

'You make this request again and again, Chosen One,'

Heboric sighed. 'But I tell you, there is no link between the power of my hands and the Deck of Dragons. I am of no help to you—'

'Then listen closely and I shall describe it. Never mind your hands – I ask you now as a once-priest, as a scholar. Listen. The face is obscured, yet hints—'

'It is obscured,' Bidithal interrupted in a derisive tone, 'because the card is no more than the projection of someone's wishful thinking.'

'Cut me off again and you will regret it, Bidithal,' Sha'ik said. 'I have heard you enough on this subject. If your mouth opens again I will tear out your tongue. Ghost Hands, I will continue. The figure is slightly above average in height. There is the crimson streak of a scar – or blood perhaps – down one side of the face – a wounding, yes? He – yes, I am certain it's a man, not a woman – he stands on a bridge. Of stone, shot through with cracks. The horizon is filled with flames. It seems he and the bridge are surrounded, as if by followers, or servants—'

'Or guardians,' L'oric added. 'Your pardon, Chosen One.'

'Guardians. Yes, a good possibility. They have the look of soldiers, do they not?'

'On what,' Heboric asked, 'do these guardians stand? Can you see the ground they stand upon?'

'Bones – there is much fine detail there, Ghost Hands. How did you know?'

'Describe those bones, please.'

'Not human. Very large. Part of a skull is visible, long-snouted, terribly fanged. It bears the remnants of a helmet of some sort—'

'A helmet? On the skull?'

'Yes.'

Heboric fell silent. He began rocking yet was only remotely aware of the motion. There was a sourceless keening growing in his head, a cry of grief, of anguish.

'The Master,' Sha'ik said, her voice trembling, 'he stands strangely. Arms held out, bent at the elbows so that the hands depend, away from the body – it is the strangest posture—'

'Are his feet together?'

'Almost impossibly so.'

As if forming a point. Dull and remote to his own ears, Heboric asked, 'And what does he wear?'

'Tight silks, from the way they shimmer. Black.'

'Anything else?'

'There is a chain. It cuts across his torso, left shoulder down to right hip. It is a robust chain, black wrought iron. There are wooden discs on his shoulders – like epaulets, but large, a hand's span each—'

'How many in all?'

'Four. You know something now, Ghost Hands. Tell me!'

'Yes,' L'oric murmured, 'you have thoughts on this—'

'He lies,' Bidithal growled. 'He has been forgotten by everyone – even his god – and he now seeks to invent a new importance.'

Febryl spoke in a mocking rasp. 'Bidithal, you foolish man. He is a man who touches what we cannot feel, and sees what we are blind to. Speak on, Ghost Hands. Why does this Master stand so?'

'Because,' Heboric said, 'he is a sword.'

But not any sword. He is one sword, above all, and it cuts cold. That sword is as this man's own nature. He will cleave his own path. None shall lead him. He stands now in my mind. I see him. I see his face. Oh, Sha'ik . . .

'A Master of the Deck,' L'oric said, then sighed. 'A lodestone to order . . . in opposition to the House of Chains – yet he stands alone, guardians or no, while the servants of the House are many.'

Heboric smiled. 'Alone? He has always been thus.'

'Then why is your smile that of a broken man, Ghost Hands?'

I grieve for humanity. This family, so at war with itself. 'To that, L'oric, I shall not answer.'

466

'I shall now speak with Ghost Hands alone,' Sha'ik pronounced.

But Heboric shook his head. 'I am done speaking, for now, even with you, Chosen One. I will say this and nothing more: have faith in the Master of the Deck. He shall answer the House of Chains. He shall answer it.'

Feeling ancient beyond his years, Heboric climbed to his feet. There was a stir of motion beside him, then young Felisin's hand settled on his forearm. He let her guide him from the chamber.

Outside, dusk had arrived, marked by the cries of the goats as they were led into the enclosures. To the south, just beyond the city's outskirts, rumbled the thunder of horse hoofs. Kamist Reloe and Korbolo Dom had absented themselves from the meeting to oversee the exercises of the troops. Training conducted in the Malazan style, which Heboric had to admit was the renegade Fist's only expression of brilliance thus far. For the first time, a Malazan army would meet its match in all things, barring Moranth munitions. Tactics and disposition of forces would be identical, ensuring that numbers alone would decide the day. The threat of the munitions would be answered with sorcery, for the Army of the Whirlwind possessed a full cadre of High Mages, whilst Tavore had – as far as they knew – none. Spies in Aren had noted the presence of the two Wickan children, Nil and Nether, but both, it was claimed, had been thoroughly broken by Coltaine's death.

Yet why would she need mages? She carries an otataral sword, after all. Even so, its negating influence cannot be extended over her entire army. Dear Sha'ik, you may well defeat your sister after all.

'Where would you go, Ghost Hands?' Felisin asked.

'To my home, lass.'

'That is not what I meant.'

He cocked his head. 'I do not know—'

'If indeed you do not, then I have seen your path before

you have, and this I find hard to believe. You must leave here, Ghost Hands. You must retrace your path, else what haunts you will kill you—'

'And that matters? Lass—'

'Look beyond yourself for a moment, old man! Something is contained within you. Trapped within your mortal flesh. What will happen when your flesh fails?'

He was silent for a long moment, then he asked, 'How can you be so sure of this? My death might simply negate the risk of escape – it might shut the portal, as tightly sealed as it had been before—'

'Because there is no going back. It's here – the power behind those ghostly hands of yours – not the otataral, which is fading, ever fading—'

'*Fading?*'

'Yes, fading! Have not your dreams and visions worsened? Have you not realized why? Yes, my mother has told me – on the Otataral Isle, in the desert – that statue. Heboric, an entire island of otataral was created to contain that statue, to hold it prisoner. But you have given it a means to escape – there, through your hands. You must return!'

'Enough!' he snarled, flinging her hand away. 'Tell me, did she also tell you of herself on that journey?'

'That which she was before no longer matters—'

'Oh, but it does, lass! It does matter!'

'What do you mean?'

The temptation came close to overwhelming him. *Because she is Malazan! Because she is Tavore's sister! Because this war is no longer the Whirlwind's – it has been stolen away, twisted by something far more powerful, by the ties of blood that bind us all in the harshest, tightest chains! What chance a raging goddess against that?*

Instead, he said nothing.

'You must undertake the journey,' Felisin said in a low voice. 'But I know, it cannot be done alone. No. I will go with you—'

He staggered away at her words, shaking his head. It was a horrible idea, a terrifying idea. Yet brutally perfect, a nightmare of synchronicity.

'Listen! It need not be just you and I – I will find someone else. A warrior, a loyal protector—'

'Enough! No more of this!' *Yet it will take her away – away from Bidithal and his ghastly desires. It will take her away . . . from the storm that is coming.* 'With whom else have you spoken of this?' he demanded.

'No-one, but I thought . . . Leoman. He could choose for us someone from Mathok's people—'

'Not a word, lass. Not now. Not yet.'

Her hand gripped his forearm once more. 'We cannot wait too long, Ghost Hands.'

'Not yet, Felisin. Now, take me home, please.'

'Will you come with me, Toblakai?'

Karsa dragged his gaze from Urugal's stone face. The sun had set with its characteristic suddenness, and the stars overhead were bright. The snakes had begun dispersing, driven into the eerily silent forest in search of food. 'Would you I run beside you and your puny horses, Leoman? There are no Teblor mounts in this land. Nothing to match my size—'

'Teblor mounts? Actually, friend, you are wrong in that. Well, not here, true, as you say. But to the west, in the Jhag Odhan, there are wild horses that are a match to your stature. Wild now, in any case. They are Jhag horses – bred long ago by the Jaghut. It may well be that your Teblor mounts are of the same breed – there were Jaghut on Genabackis, after all.'

'Why have you not told me this before?'

Leoman lowered his right hand to the ground, watched as the flare-neck unwound down the length of his arm. 'In truth, this is the first time you have ever mentioned that you Teblor possessed horses. Toblakai, I know virtually nothing of your past. No-one here does. You are not a loquacious man. You and I, we have ever travelled on foot, haven't we?'

'The Jhag Odhan. That is beyond Raraku.'

'Aye. Strike west through the Whirlwind, and you will come to cliffs, the broken shoreline of the ancient sea that once filled this desert. Continue on until you come to a small city – Lato Revae. Immediately to the west lies the tip of the Thalas Mountains. Skirt their south edge, ever westward, until you come to River Ugarat. There is a ford south of Y'Ghatan. From the other side, strike west and south and west, for two weeks or more, and you will find yourself in the Jhag Odhan. Oh, there is some irony in this – there were once nomadic bands of Jaghut there. Hence the name. But these Jaghut were fallen. They had been predated on for so long they were little more than savages.'

'And are they still there?'

'No. The Logros T'lan Imass slaughtered them. Not so long ago.'

Karsa bared his teeth. 'T'lan Imass. A name from the Teblor past.'

'Closer than that,' Leoman muttered, then he straightened. 'Seek leave from Sha'ik to journey into the Jhag Odhan. You would make an impressive sight on the battlefield, astride a Jhag horse. Did your kind fight on horseback, or simply use them for transport?'

Karsa smiled in the darkness. 'I will do as you say, Leoman. But the journey will take long – do not wait for me. If you and your scouts are still beyond the Whirlwind upon my return, I will ride out to find you.'

'Agreed.'

'What of Felisin?'

Leoman was silent for a moment, then he replied, 'Ghost Hands has been awakened to the . . . threat.'

Karsa sneered. 'And what value will that be? I should kill Bidithal and be done with it.'

'Toblakai, it is more than you that troubles Ghost Hands. I do not believe he will remain in camp much longer.

And when he leaves, he will take the child with him.'

'And that is a better option? She will become no more than his nurse.'

'For a time, perhaps. I will send someone with them, of course. If Sha'ik did not need you – or at least believe she does – I would ask you.'

'Madness, Leoman. I have travelled once with Ghost Hands. I shall not do so again.'

'He holds truths for you, Toblakai. One day, you will need to seek him out. You might even need to ask for his help.'

'Help? I need no-one's help. You speak unpleasant words. I will hear them no more.'

Leoman's grin was visible in the gloom. 'You are as you always are, friend. When will you journey into the Jhag Odhan, then?'

'I shall leave tomorrow.'

'Then I had best get word to Sha'ik. Who knows, she might even condescend to see me in person, whereupon I might well succeed in ending her distraction with this House of Chains—'

'This what?'

Leoman waved a dismissive hand. 'The House of Chains. A new power in the Deck of Dragons. It is all they talk about these days.'

'Chains,' Karsa muttered, swinging round to stare at Urugal. 'I so dislike chains.'

'I will see you in the morning, Toblakai? Before you depart?'

'You shall.'

Karsa listened to the man stride away. His mind was a maelstrom. Chains. They haunted him, had haunted him ever since he and Bairoth and Delum rode out from the village. Perhaps even before then. Tribes fashioned their own chains, after all. As did kinship, and companions, and stories with their lessons in honour and sacrifice. *And chains as well between the Teblor and their seven gods. Between me and my gods. Chains again, there in my visions – the dead I have slain, the souls Ghost Hands says I drag behind me. I am – all that I am – has been shaped by such chains.*

This new House – is it mine?

The air in the clearing was suddenly cold, bitterly so. A final, thrashing rush as the last of the snakes fled the clearing. Karsa blinked his eyes into focus, and saw Urugal's indurated visage . . . *awakening.*

A presence, there in the dark holes of the face's eyes.

Karsa heard a howling wind, filling his mind. A thousand souls moaning, the snapping thunder of chains. Growling, he steeled himself before the onslaught, fixed his gaze on his god's writhing face.

'Karsa Orlong. We have waited long for this. Three years, the fashioning of this sacred place. You wasted so much time on the two strangers – your fallen friends, the ones who failed where you did not. This temple is not to be sanctified by sentimentality. Their presence offends us. Destroy them this night.'

The seven faces were all wakeful now, and Karsa could feel the weight of their regard, a deathly pressure behind which lurked something . . . avid, dark and filled with glee.

'By my hand,' Karsa said to Urugal, 'I have brought you to this place. By my hand, you have been freed from your prison of rock in the lands of the Teblor – yes, I am not the fool you believe me to be. You have guided me in this, and now you are come. Your first words are of chastisement? Careful, Urugal. Any carving here can be shattered by my hand, should I so choose.'

He felt their rage, buffeting him, seeking to make him wither beneath the onslaught, yet he stood before it unmoving, and unmoved. The Teblor warrior who would quail before his gods was no more.

'You have brought us closer,' Urugal eventually rasped. 'Close enough to sense the precise location of what we desire. And there you must now go, Karsa Orlong. You have delayed the journey for so long – your journey to ourselves, and on to the path we have set before you. You have hidden too long in the company of this petty spirit who does little more than spit sand.'

'This path, this journey – to what end? What is it you seek?'

'Like you, warrior, we seek freedom.'

Karsa was silent. *Avid indeed.* Then he spoke. 'I am to travel west. Into the Jhag Odhan.'

He sensed their shock and excitement, then the chorus of suspicion that poured out from the seven gods.

'West! Indeed, Karsa Orlong. But how do you know this?'

Because, at last, I am my father's son. 'I shall leave with the dawn, Urugal. And I will find for you what you desire.'

He could feel their presence fading, and knew instinctively that these gods were not as close to freedom as they wanted him to believe. Nor as powerful.

Urugal had called this clearing a temple, but it was a contested one, and now, as the Seven withdrew, and were suddenly gone, Karsa slowly turned from the faces of the gods, and looked upon those for whom this place had been in truth sanctified. By Karsa's own hands. In the name of those chains a mortal could wear with pride.

'My loyalty,' the Teblor warrior quietly said, 'was misplaced. I served only glory. Words, my friends. And words can wear false nobility. Disguising brutal truths. The words of the past, that so clothed the Teblor in a hero's garb – this is what I served. While the true glory was before me. Beside me. You, Delum Thord. And you, Bairoth Gild.'

From the stone statue of Bairoth emerged a distant, weary voice. 'Lead us, Warleader.'

Karsa flinched. *Do I dream this?* Then he straightened. 'I have drawn your spirits to this place. Did you travel in the wake of the Seven?'

'We have walked the empty lands,' Bairoth Gild replied. 'Empty, yet we were not alone. Strangers await us all, Karsa Orlong. This is the truth they would hide from you. We are summoned. We are here.'

'None,' came Delum Thord's voice from the other statue, 'can defeat you on this journey. You lead the enemy in circles, you defy every prediction, and so deliver the edge of your will. We sought to follow, but could not.'

'Who, Warleader,' Bairoth asked, his voice bolder, 'is our enemy, now?'

Karsa drew himself up before the two Uryd warriors. 'Witness my answer, my friends. Witness.'

Delum spoke, 'We failed you, Karsa Orlong. Yet you invite us to walk with you once again.'

Karsa fought back an urge to scream, to unleash a warcry – as if such a challenge might force back the approaching darkness. He could make no sense of his own impulses, the torrential emotions threatening to engulf him. He stared at the carved likeness of his tall friend, the awareness in those unmarred features – Delum Thord before the Forkassal – the Forkrul Assail named Calm – had, on a mountain trail on a distant continent, so casually destroyed him.

Bairoth Gild spoke. 'We failed you. Do you now ask that we walk with you?'

'Delum Thord. Bairoth Gild.' Karsa's voice was hoarse. 'It is I who failed you. I would be your warleader once more, if you would so permit me.'

A long moment of silence, then Bairoth replied, 'At last, something to look forward to.'

Karsa almost fell to his knees, then. Grief, finally unleashed. At an end, his time of solitude. His penance was done. The journey to begin again. *Dear Urugal, you shall witness. Oh, how you shall witness.*

The hearth was little more than a handful of dying coals. After Felisin Younger left, Heboric sat motionless in the gloom. A short time passed, then he collected an armload of dried dung and rebuilt the fire. The night had chilled him – even the hands he could not see felt cold, like heavy pieces of ice at the end of his wrists.

The only journey that lay ahead of him was a short one,

and he must walk it alone. He was blind, but in this no more blind than anyone else. Death's precipice, whether first glimpsed from afar or discovered with the next step, was ever a surprise. A promise of the sudden cessation of questions, yet there were no answers waiting beyond. Cessation would have to be enough. *And so it must be for every mortal. Even as we hunger for resolution. Or, even more delusional: redemption.*

Now, after all this time, he was able to realize that every path eventually, inevitably dwindled into a single line of footsteps. There, leading to the very edge. Then . . . gone. And so, he faced only what every mortal faced. The solitude of death, and oblivion's final gift that was indifference.

The gods were welcome to wrangle over his soul, to snipe and snap over the paltry feast. And if mortals grieved for him, it was only because by dying he had shaken them from the illusion of unity that comforted life's journey. One less on the path.

A scratch at the flap entrance, then the hide was drawn aside and someone entered.

'Would you make of your home a pyre, Ghost Hands?' The voice was L'oric's.

The High Mage's words startled Heboric into a sudden realization of the sweat running down his face, the gusts of fierce heat from the now raging hearth. Unthinking, he had fed the flames with piece after piece of dung.

'I saw the glow – difficult to miss, old man. Best leave it, now, let it die down.'

'What do you want, L'oric?'

'I acknowledge your reluctance to speak of what you know. There is no value, after all, in gifting Bidithal or Febryl with such details. And so I shall not demand that you explain what you've sensed regarding this Master of the Deck. Instead, I offer an exchange, and all that we say will remain between the two of us. No-one else.'

'Why should I trust you? You are hidden – even to

475

Sha'ik. You give no reason as to why you are here. In her cadre, in this war.'

'That alone should tell you I am not like the others,' L'oric replied.

Heboric sneered. 'That earns you less than you might think. There can be no exchange because there is nothing you can tell me that I would be interested in hearing. The schemes of Febryl? The man's a fool. Bidithal's perversions? One day a child will slip a knife between his ribs. Korbolo Dom and Kamist Reloe? They war against an empire that is far from dead. Nor will they be treated with honour when they are finally brought before the Empress. No, they are criminals, and for that their souls will burn for eternity. The Whirlwind? That goddess has my contempt, and that contempt does naught but grow. Thus, what could you possibly tell me, L'oric, that I would value?'

'Only the one thing that might interest you, Heboric Light Touch. Just as this Master of the Deck interests me. I would not cheat you with the exchange. No, I would tell you all that I know of the Hand of Jade, rising from the otataral sands – the Hand that you have touched, that now haunts your dreams.'

'How could you know these—' He fell silent. The sweat on his brow was now cold.

'And how,' L'oric retorted, 'can you sense so much from a mere description of the Master's card? Let us not question these things, else we trap ourselves in a conversation that will outlive Raraku itself. So, Heboric, shall I begin?'

'No. Not now. I am too weary for this. Tomorrow, L'oric.'

'Delay may prove ... disastrous.' After a moment, the High Mage sighed. 'Very well. I can see your exhaustion. Permit me, at least, to brew your tea for you.'

The gesture of kindness was unexpected, and Heboric lowered his head. 'L'oric, promise me this – that when the final day comes, you be a long way from here.'

'A difficult promise. Permit me to think on it. Now, where is the hen'bara?'

'Hanging from a bag above the pot.'

'Ah, of course.'

Heboric listened to the sounds of preparation, the rustle of flower-heads from the bag, the slosh of water as L'oric filled the pot. 'Did you know,' the High Mage murmured as he worked, 'that some of the oldest scholarly treatises on the warrens speak of a triumvirate. Rashan, Thyr and Meanas. As if the three were all closely related to one another. And then in turn seek to link them to corresponding Elder warrens.'

Heboric grunted, then nodded. 'All flavours of the same thing? I would agree. Tiste warrens. Kurald this and Kurald that. The human versions can't help but overlap, become confused. I am no expert, L'oric, and it seems you know more of it than I.'

'Well, there certainly appears to be a mutual insinuation of themes between Darkness and Shadow, and, presumably, Light. A confusion among the three, yes. Anomander Rake himself has asserted a proprietary claim on the Throne of Shadow, after all . . .'

The smell of the brewing tea tugged at Heboric's mind. 'He has?' he murmured, only remotely interested.

'Well, of a sort. He set kin to guard it, presumably from the Tiste Edur. It is very difficult for us mortals to make sense of Tiste histories, for they are such a long-lived people. As you well know, human history is ever marked by certain personalities, rising from some quality or notoriety to shatter the status quo. Fortunately for us, such men and women are few and far between, and they all eventually die or disappear. But among the Tiste . . . well, those personalities never go away, or so it seems. They act, and act yet again. They persist. Choose the worst tyrant you can from your knowledge of human history, Heboric, then imagine him or her as virtually undying. In your mind, bring that tyrant back again and again and again. How, having done so, would you imagine our history then?'

'Far more violent than that of the Tiste, L'oric. Humans

are not Tiste. Indeed, I have never heard of a Tiste tyrant . . .'

'Perhaps I used the wrong word. I meant only – in human context – a personality of devastating power, or potential. Look at this Malazan Empire, born from the mind of Kellanved, a single man. What if he had been eternal?'

Something in L'oric's musings had reawakened Heboric. 'Eternal?' He barked a laugh. 'Perhaps he is at that. There is one detail you might consider, perhaps more relevant than anything else that's been said here. And that is, the Tiste are no longer isolated in their scheming. There are humans now, in their games – humans, who've not the patience of the Tiste, nor their legendary remoteness. The warrens of Kurald Galain and Kurald Emurlahn are no longer pure, unsullied by human presence. Meanas and Rashan? Perhaps they are proving the doors into both Darkness and Shadow. Or perhaps the matter is more complex than even that – how can one truly hope to separate the themes of Darkness and Light from Shadow? They are as those scholars said, an interdependent triumvirate. Mother, father and child – a family ever squabbling . . . only now the in-laws and grandchildren are joining in.'

He waited for a reply from L'oric, curious as to how his comments had been received, but none was forthcoming. The ex-priest looked up, struggled to focus on the High Mage—

—who sat motionless, a cup in one hand, the ring of the brewing pot in the other. Motionless, and staring at Heboric.

'L'oric? Forgive me, I cannot discern your expression—'

'Well that you cannot,' the High Mage rasped. 'Here I sought to raise the warning of Tiste meddling in human affairs – to have you then voice a warning in the opposite direction. As if it is not us who must worry, but the Tiste themselves.'

Heboric said nothing. A strange, whispering suspicion

flitted through him for a moment, as if tickled into being by something in L'oric's voice. After a moment, he dismissed it. Too outrageous, too absurd to entertain.

L'oric poured the tea.

Heboric sighed. 'It seems I am to be ever denied the succour of that brew. Tell me, then, of the giant of Jade.'

'Ah, and in return you will speak of the Master of the Deck?'

'In some things I am forbidden to elaborate—'

'Because they relate to Sha'ik's own secret past?'

'Fener's tusk, L'oric! Who in this rat's nest might be listening in to our conversation right now? It is madness to speak—'

'No-one is listening, Heboric. I have made certain of that. I am not careless with secrets. I have known much of your recent history since the very beginning—'

'How?'

'We agreed to not discuss sources. My point is, no-one else is aware that you are Malazan, or that you are an escapee from the otataral mines. Except Sha'ik, of course. Since she escaped with you. Thus, I value privacy – with my knowledge and with my thoughts – and am ever vigilant. Oh, there have been probes, sorcerous questings – a whole menagerie of spells as various inhabitants seek to keep track of rivals. As occurs every night.'

'Then your absence will be detected—'

'I sleep restful in my tent, Heboric, as far as those questings are concerned. As do you in your tent. Each alone. Harmless.'

'You are more than a match for their sorceries, then. Which makes you more powerful than any of them.' He heard as much as saw L'oric's shrug, and after a moment the ex-priest sighed. 'If you wish details concerning Sha'ik and this new Master of the Deck, then it must be the three of us who meet. And for that to occur, you will have to reveal more of yourself to the Chosen One than you might wish.'

'Tell me this, at least. This new Master – he was created

in the wake of the Malazan disaster on Genabackis. Or do you deny that? That bridge on which he stands – he was of, or is somehow related to, the Bridgeburners. And those ghostly guardians are all that remains of the Bridgeburners, for they were destroyed in the Pannion Domin.'

'I cannot be certain of any of that,' Heboric replied, 'but what you suggest seems likely.'

'So, the Malazan influence ever grows – not just on our mundane world, but throughout the warrens, and now in the Deck of Dragons.'

'You make the mistake of so many of the empire's enemies, L'oric. You assume that all that is Malazan is perforce unified, in intent and in goal. Things are far more complicated than you imagine. I do not believe this Master of the Deck is some servant of the Empress. Indeed, he kneels before no-one.'

'Then why the Bridgeburner guardians?'

Heboric sensed that the question was a leading one, but decided he would play along. 'Some loyalties defy Hood himself—'

'Ah, meaning he was a soldier in that illustrious company. Well, things are beginning to make sense.'

'They are?'

'Tell me, have you heard of a Spiritwalker named Kimloc?'

'The name is vaguely familiar. But not from around here. Karakarang? Rutu Jelba?'

'Now resident of Ehrlitan. His history is not relevant here, but somehow he must have come into recent contact with a Bridgeburner. There is no other explanation for what he has done. He has given them a song, Heboric. A *Tanno* song, and, curiously, it begins here. In Raraku. Raraku, friend, is the birthplace of the Bridgeburners. Do you know the significance of such a song?'

Heboric turned away, faced the hearth and its dry heat, and said nothing.

'Of course,' L'oric went on after a moment, 'that

significance has now diminished somewhat, since the Bridgeburners are no more. There can be no sanctification . . .'

'No, I suppose not,' Heboric murmured.

'For the song to be sanctified, a Bridgeburner would have to return to Raraku, to the birthplace of the company. And that does not seem likely now, does it?'

'Why is it necessary a Bridgeburner return to Raraku?'

'Tanno sorcery is . . . elliptical. The song must be like a serpent eating its tail. Kimloc's Song of the Bridgeburners is at the moment without an end. But it has been sung, and so lives.' L'oric shrugged. 'It's like a spell that remains active, awaiting resolution.'

'Tell me of the giant of jade.'

The High Mage nodded. He poured out the tea and set the cup down in front of Heboric. 'The first one was found deep in the otataral mines—'

'The *first* one!'

'Aye. And the contact proved, for those miners who ventured too close, fatal. Or, rather, they disappeared. Leaving no trace. Sections of two others have been discovered – all three veins are now sealed. The giants are . . . intruders to our world. From some other realm.'

'Arriving,' Heboric muttered, 'only to be wrapped in chains of otataral.'

'Ah, you are not without your own knowledge, then. Indeed, it seems their arrival has, each time, been anticipated. Someone, or something, is ensuring that the threat these giants impose is negated—'

But Heboric shook his head at that and said, 'No, I think you are wrong, L'oric. It is the very passage – the portal through which each giant comes – that creates the otataral.'

'Are you certain?'

'Of course not. There are too many mysteries surrounding the nature of otataral to be certain of anything. There was a scholar – I forget her name – who once suggested that otataral is created by the annihilation of all that is necessary for sorcery to operate. Like slag with all the ore burned out. She called it the absolute draining of energy – the energy that rightfully exists in all things, whether animate or otherwise.'

'And had she a theory as to how that could occur?'

'Perhaps the magnitude of the sorcery unleashed – a spell that is all-devouring of the energy it feeds on.'

'But not even the gods could wield such magic.'

'True, but I think it is nevertheless possible . . . through ritual, such as a cadre – or army – of mortal sorcerers could achieve.'

'In the manner of the Ritual of Tellann,' L'oric nodded. 'Aye.'

'Or,' Heboric said softly as he reached for the cup, 'the calling down of the Crippled God . . .'

L'oric was motionless, staring fixedly at the tattooed ex-priest. He said nothing for a long time, whilst Heboric sipped the hen'bara tea. He finally spoke. 'Very well, there is one last piece of information I will tell you – I see now the need, the very great need to do so, though it shall . . . reveal much of myself.'

Heboric sat and listened, and as L'oric continued speaking, the confines of his squalid hut dimmed to insignificance, the heat of the hearth no longer reaching him, until the only sensation left came from his ghostly hands. Together, there at the ends of his wrists, they became the weight of the world.

The rising sun washed all tones from the sky to the east. Karsa checked his supplies one last time, the foodstuffs and waterskins, the additional items and accoutrements necessary for survival in a hot, arid land. A kit wholly unlike what he had carried for most of his life. Even the sword was different – ironwood was heavier than blood-wood, its edge rougher although almost – but not quite – as hard. It did not slice the air with the ease of his oiled bloodwood sword. Yet it had served him well enough. He glanced skyward; dawn's colours were almost entirely gone, now, the blue directly above vanishing behind suspended dust.

Here, in Raraku's heart, the Whirlwind Goddess had stolen the colour of the sun's own fire, leaving the landscape pallid and deathly. *Colourless, Karsa Orlong?* Bairoth Gild's ghostly voice was filled with wry humour. *Not so. Silver, my friend. And silver is the colour of oblivion. Of chaos. Silver is when the last of the blood is washed from the blade—*

'No more words,' Karsa growled.

Leoman spoke from nearby. 'Having just arrived, Toblakai, I am yet to even speak. Do you not wish my farewell?'

Karsa slowly straightened, slinging his pack over a shoulder. 'Words need not be spoken aloud, friend, to prove unwelcome. I but answered my own thoughts. That you are here pleases me. When I began my first journey, long ago, none came to witness.'

'I asked Sha'ik,' Leoman replied from where he stood ten paces away, having just passed through the trail's gap in the low, crumbled wall – the mud bricks, Karsa saw, were on their shaded side covered with rhizan, clinging with wings contracted, their mottled colourings making them almost identical to the ochre bricks. 'But she said she would not join me this morning. Even stranger, it seemed as if she already knew of your intentions, and was but awaiting my visit.'

Shrugging, Karsa faced Leoman. 'A witness of one suffices. We may now speak our parting words. Do not hide overlong in your pit, friend. And when you ride out with your warriors, hold to the Chosen One's commands – too many jabs from the small knife can awaken the bear no matter how deep it sleeps.'

'It is a young and weak bear, this time, Toblakai.'

Karsa shook his head. 'I have come to respect the

Malazans, and fear that you would awaken them to themselves.'

'I shall consider your words,' Leoman replied. 'And now ask that you consider mine. Beware your gods, friend. If you must kneel before a power, first look upon it with clear eyes. Tell me, what would your kin say to you in parting?'

' "May you slay a thousand children." '

Leoman blanched. 'Journey well, Toblakai.'

'I shall.'

Karsa knew that Leoman could neither see nor sense that he was flanked where he stood at the trail's gap in the wall. Delum Thord on the left, Bairoth Gild on the right. Teblor warriors, blood-oil smeared in crimson tones even the Whirlwind could not eradicate, and they stepped forward as the Teblor swung about to face the western trail.

Lead us. Lead your dead, Warleader.

Bairoth's mocking laugh clicked and cracked like the potsherds breaking beneath Karsa Orlong's moccasins. The Teblor grimaced. There would be, it seemed, a fierce price for the honour.

None the less, he realized after a moment, if there must be ghosts, it was better to lead them than to be chased by them.

If that is how you would see it, Karsa Orlong.

In the distance rose the swirling wall of the Whirlwind. It would be good, the Teblor reflected, to see the world beyond it again, after all these months. He set out, westward, as the day was born.

'He has left,' Kamist Reloe said as he settled onto the cushions.

Korbolo Dom eyed the mage, his blank expression betraying nothing of the contempt he felt for the man. Sorcerers did not belong in war. And he had shown the truth of that when destroying the Chain of Dogs. Even so, there were necessities to contemplate, and Reloe was the least of them. 'That leaves only Leoman,' he rumbled from where he lay on the pillows and cushions.

'Who departs with his rats in a few days.'

'Will Febryl now advance his plans?'

The mage shrugged. 'It is hard to say, but there is a distinct avidness in his gaze this morning.'

Avidness. Indeed. Another High Mage, another insane wielder of powers better left untapped. 'There is one who remains, who perhaps presents us with the greatest threat of them all, and that is Ghost Hands.'

Kamist Reloe sneered. 'A blind, doddering fool. Does he even know that hen'bara tea is itself the source of the thinning fabric between his world and all that he would flee from? Before long, his mind will vanish entirely within the nightmares, and we need concern ourselves with him no more.'

'She has secrets,' Korbolo Dom muttered, leaning forward to collect a bowl of figs. 'Far beyond those gifted her by the Whirlwind. Febryl proceeds headlong, unmindful of his own ignorance. When the battle with the Adjunct's army is finally joined, success or failure will be decided by the Dogslayers – by my army. Tavore's otataral will defeat the Whirlwind – I am certain of it. All that I ask of you and Febryl and Bidithal is that I am unobstructed in commanding the forces, in shaping that battle.'

'We are both aware,' Kamist growled, 'that this struggle goes far beyond the Whirlwind.'

'Aye, so it does. Beyond all of Seven Cities, Mage. Do not lose sight of our final goal, of the throne that will one day belong to us.'

Kamist Reloe shrugged. 'That is our secret, old friend. We need only proceed with caution, and all that opposes us will likely vanish before our very eyes. Febryl kills Sha'ik, Tavore kills Febryl, and we destroy Tavore and her army.'

'And then become Laseen's saviour – as we crush this rebellion utterly. Gods, I swear I will see this entire land empty of life if need be. A triumphant return to Unta, an audience with the Empress, then the driven knife. And who will stop us? The Talon are poised to cut down the Claws. Whiskeyjack and the Bridgeburners are no more, and Dujek remains a continent away. How fares the Jhistal priest?'

'Mallick travels without opposition, ever southward. He is a clever man, a wise man, and he will play out his role to perfection.'

Korbolo Dom made no reply to that. He despised Mallick Rel, but could not deny his usefulness. Still, the man was not one to be trusted ... to which High Fist Pormqual would attest, were the fool still alive. 'Send for Fayelle. I would a woman's company now. Leave me, Kamist Reloe.'

The High Mage hesitated, and Korbolo scowled.

'There is the matter,' Kamist whispered, 'of L'oric ...'

'Then deal with him!' Korbolo snapped. 'Begone!'

Bowing his head, the High Mage backed out of the tent. Sorcerers. Could he find a way to destroy magic, the Napan would not hesitate. The extinction of powers that could slaughter a thousand soldiers in an instant would return the fate of mortals to the mortals themselves, and this could not but be a good thing. The death of warrens, the dissolution of gods as memory of them and their meddling slowly vanished, the withering of all magic ... the world then would belong to men such as Korbolo himself. And the empire he would shape would permit no ambiguity, no ambivalence.

His will unopposed, the Napan could end, once and for all, the dissonant clangour that so plagued humanity – now and throughout its history.

I will bring order. And from that unity, we shall rid the world of every other race, every other people, we shall overpower and crush every discordant vision, for there can in the end be only one way, one way of living, of ruling this realm. And that way belongs to me.

A good soldier well knew that success was found in careful planning, in incremental steps.

Opposition had a way of stepping aside all on its own. *You are now at Hood's feet, Whiskeyjack. Where I have always wanted you. You and your damned company, feeding worms in a foreign land. None left to stop me, now . . .*

CHAPTER ELEVEN

This was a path she did not welcome.

The Sha'ik Rebellion
Tursabaal

The breaths of the horses plumed in the chill morning air. Dawn had but just arrived, the air hinting nothing of the heat the coming day would deliver. Wrapped in the furs of a bhederin, old sweat making the lining of his helm clammy as the touch of a corpse, Fist Gamet sat motionless on his Wickan mount, his gaze fixed on the Adjunct.

The hill just south of Erougimon where Coltaine had died had come to be known as the Fall. Countless humps on the summit and slopes indicated where bodies had been buried, the metal-strewn earth already cloaked in grasses and flowers.

Ants had colonized this entire hill, or so it seemed. The ground swarmed with them, their red and black bodies coated in dust yet glittering none the less as they set about their daily tasks.

Gamet, the Adjunct and Tene Baralta had ridden out from the city before dawn. Outside the gates to the west, the army had begun to stir. The march would begin this day. The journey north, to Raraku, to Sha'ik and the Whirlwind. To vengeance.

Perhaps it was the rumours that had drawn Tavore out here to the Fall, but already Gamet regretted her decision to bring him along. This place showed him nothing he wanted to see. Nor, he suspected, was the Adjunct well pleased with what they had found.

Red-stained braids, woven into chains, draped across the summit, and coiled around the twin stumps of the cross that had once stood there. Dog skulls crowded with indecipherable hieroglyphs looked out along the crest through empty sockets. Crow feathers dangled from upright-thrust broken arrow shafts. Ragged banners lay pinned to the ground on which were painted various representations of a broken Wickan long-knife. Icons, fetishes, a mass of detritus to mark the death of a single man.

And all of it was aswarm in ants. Like mindless keepers of this now hallowed ground.

The three riders sat in their saddles in silence.

Finally, after a long while, Tavore spoke. 'Tene Baralta.' Inflectionless.

'Aye, Adjunct?'

'Who – who is responsible for . . . for all of this? Malazans from Aren? Your Red Blades?'

Tene Baralta did not immediately reply. Instead, he dismounted and strode forward, his eyes on the ground. Near one of the dog skulls he halted and crouched down. 'Adjunct, these skulls – the runes on them are Khundryl.' He pointed towards the wooden stumps. 'The woven chains, Kherahn Dhobri.' A gesture to the slope. 'The banners . . . unknown, possibly Bhilard. Crow feathers? The beads at their stems are Semk.'

'Semk!' Gamet could not keep the disbelief from his voice. 'From the other side of Vathar River! Tene, you must be in error . . .'

The large warrior shrugged. He straightened and gestured towards the rumpled hills directly north of them. 'The pilgrims only come at night – unseen, which is how they will have it. They're hiding out there, even now. Waiting for night.'

Tavore cleared her throat. 'Semk. Bhilard – these tribes

fought against him. And now they come to worship. How is this? Explain, please, Tene Baralta.'

'I cannot, Adjunct.' He eyed her, then added, 'But, from what I understand, this is . . . modest, compared with what lines the Aren Way.'

There was silence once more, though Gamet did not need to hear her speak to know Tavore's thoughts.

This – this is the path we now take. We must walk, step by step, the legacy. We? No. Tavore. Alone. 'This is no longer Coltaine's war!' she said to Temul. But it seems it remains just that. And she now realizes, down in the depths of her soul, that she will stride that man's shadow . . . all the way to Raraku.

'You will both leave me now,' the Adjunct said. 'I shall rejoin you on the Aren Way.'

Gamet hesitated, then said, 'Adjunct, the Crow Clan still claim the right to ride at the forefront. They will not accept Temul as their commander.'

'I will see to their disposition,' she replied. 'For now, go.'

He watched Tene Baralta swing back onto his horse. They exchanged a glance, then both wheeled their mounts and set off at a canter along the track leading to the west gate.

Gamet scanned the rock-studded ground rolling past beneath his horse's hoofs. This was where the historian Duiker drove the refugees towards the city – this very sweep of empty ground. Where, at the last, that old man drew rein on his weary, loyal mare – the mare that Temul now rode – and watched as the last of his charge was helped through the gate.

Whereupon, it was said, he finally rode into the city.

Gamet wondered what had gone through the man's mind at that moment. Knowing that Coltaine and the remnants of the Seventh were still out there, fighting their desperate rearguard action. Knowing that they had achieved the impossible.

Duiker had delivered the refugees.

Only to end up staked to a tree. It was beyond him,

Gamet realized, to comprehend the depth of that betrayal.

A body never recovered. No bones laid to rest.

'There is so much,' Tene Baralta rumbled at Gamet's side.

'So much?'

'To give answer to, Gamet. Indeed, it takes words from the throat, yet the silence it leaves behind – that silence *screams.*'

Discomforted by Tene's admission, Gamet said nothing.

'Pray remind me,' the Red Blade went on, 'that Tavore is equal to this task.'

Is that even possible? 'She is.' *She must be. Else we are lost.*

'One day, Gamet, you shall have to tell me what she has done, to earn such loyalty as you display.'

Gods, what answer to make to that? Damn you, Tene, can you not see the truth before you? She has done . . . nothing. I beg you. Leave an old man to his faith.

'Wish whatever you like,' Gesler growled, 'but faith is for fools.'

Strings cleared the dust from his throat and spat onto the side of the track. Their pace was torturously slow, the three squads trailing the wagon loaded down with their supplies. 'What's your point?' he asked the sergeant beside him. 'A soldier knows but one truth, and that truth is, without faith, you are already as good as dead. Faith in the soldier at your side. But even more important – and no matter how delusional it is in truth – there is the faith that you cannot be killed. Those two and those two alone – they are the legs holding up every army.'

The amber-skinned man grunted, then waved at the nearest of the trees lining Aren Way. 'Look there and tell me what you see – no, not those Hood-damned fetishes – but what's still visible under all that mess. The spike holes, the dark stains of bile and blood. Ask the ghost of the soldier who was on that tree – ask that soldier about faith.'

'A faith betrayed does not destroy the notion of faith

itself,' Strings retorted. 'In fact, it does the very opposite—'

'Maybe for you, but there are some things you can't step around with words and lofty ideals, Fid. And that comes down to who is in that vanguard somewhere up ahead. The Adjunct. Who just lost an argument with that pack of hoary Wickans. You've been lucky – you had Whiskeyjack, and Dujek. Do you know who my last commander was – before I was sentenced to the coastal guard? Korbolo Dom. I'd swear that man had a shrine to Whiskeyjack in his tent – but not the Whiskeyjack you know. Korbolo saw him differently. Unfulfilled potential, that's what he saw.'

Strings glanced over at Gesler. Stormy and Tarr were walking in step behind the two sergeants, close enough to hear, though neither had ventured a comment or opinion. 'Unfulfilled potential? What in Beru's name are you talking about?'

'Not me. Korbolo Dom. "If only the bastard had been hard enough," he used to say, "he could've taken the damned throne. Should've." As far as Dom is concerned, Whiskeyjack betrayed him, betrayed us all – and that's something that renegade Napan won't forgive.'

'Too bad for him,' Strings growled, 'since there's a good chance the Empress will send the whole Genabackan army over in time for the final battle. Dom can take his complaints to Whiskeyjack himself.'

'A pleasant thought,' Gesler laughed. 'But my point was, you've had commanders worthy of the faith you put in them. Most of the rest of us didn't have that luxury. So we got a different feeling about it all. That's it, that's all I was trying to say.'

The Aren Way marched past on both sides. Transformed into a vast, open-air temple, each tree cluttered with fetishes, cloths braided into chains, figures painted on the rough bark to approximate the soldiers who had once writhed there on spikes driven in by Korbolo Dom's warriors. Most of the soldiers ahead and behind Strings walked in silence. Despite the vast, empty expanse of blue sky overhead, the road was oppressive.

There had been talk of cutting the trees down, but one of the Adjunct's first commands upon arriving in Aren had been to forbid it. Strings wondered if she now regretted her decision.

His gaze travelled up to one of the Fourteenth's new standards, barely visible through clouds of roiling dust up ahead. She had understood the whole thing with the finger bones well enough, understood the turning of the omen. The new standard well attested to that. A grimy, thin-limbed figure holding a bone aloft, the details in shades of dun colours that were barely visible on the yellow ochre field, the border a woven braid of the imperial magenta and dark grey. A defiant figure standing before a sandstorm. That the standard could as easily apply to Sha'ik's army of the Apocalypse was a curious coincidence. *As if Tavore and Sha'ik – the two armies, the forces in opposition – are in some way mirrored reflections of the other.*

There were many strange . . . occurrences in all this, nibbling and squirming beneath Strings's skin like bot-fly larvae, and it seemed indeed that he was feeling strangely fevered throughout the day. Strains of a barely heard song rose up from the depths of his mind on occasion, a haunting song that made his flesh prickle. And stranger still, the song was entirely unfamiliar.

Mirrored reflections. Perhaps not just Tavore and Sha'ik. What of Tavore and Coltaine? Here we are, reversing the path on that blood-soaked road. And it was that road that proved Coltaine to most of those he led. Will we see the same with our journey? How will we see Tavore the day we stand before the Whirlwind? And what of my own return? To Raraku, the desert that saw me destroyed only to rise once more, mysteriously renewed – a renewal that persists, since for an old man I neither look nor feel old. And so it remains for all of us Bridgeburners, as if Raraku stole something of our mortality, and replaced it with . . . with something else.

He glanced back to check on his squad. None were

lagging, which was a good sign. He doubted any of them were in the shape required for the journey they were now on. The early days would prove the most difficult, before marching in full armour and weapons became second nature – not that it would ever prove a comfortable second nature – this land was murderously hot and dry, and the handful of minor healers in each of the companies would recall this march as a seemingly endless nightmare of fending off heat prostration and dehydration.

There was no way yet to measure the worth of his squad. Koryk certainly had the look, the nature, of the mailed fist that every squad needed. And the stubborn set to Tarr's blockish features hinted at a will not easily turned aside. There was something about the lass, Smiles, that reminded Strings all too much of Sorry – the remorseless chill of her eyes belonged to those of a murderer, and he wondered at her past. Bottle had all the diffident bluster of a young mage, probably one versed in a handful of spells from some minor warren. The last soldier in his squad, of course, the sergeant had no worries about. He'd known men like Cuttle all his life. A burlier, more miserable version of Hedge. Having Cuttle there was like . . . coming home.

The testing would come, and it would probably be brutal, but it would temper those who survived.

They were emerging from the Aren Way, and Gesler gestured to the last tree on their left. 'That's where we found him,' he said in a low tone.

'Who?'

'Duiker. We didn't let on, since the lad – Truth – was so hopeful. Next time we came out, though, the historian's body was gone. Stolen. You've seen the markets in Aren – the withered pieces of flesh the hawkers claim belonged to Coltaine, or Bult, or Duiker. The broken long-knives, the scraps of feathered cape . . .'

Strings was thoughtful for a moment, then he sighed. 'I saw Duiker but once, and that at a distance. Just a soldier the Emperor decided was worth schooling.'

'A soldier indeed. He stood on the front line with all the others. A crusty old bastard with his short-sword and shield.'

'Clearly, something about him caught Coltaine's eye – after all, Duiker was the one Coltaine chose to lead the refugees.'

'I'd guess it wasn't Duiker's soldiering that decided Coltaine, Strings. It was that he was the Imperial Historian. He wanted the tale to be told, and told right.'

'Well, it's turned out that Coltaine told his own tale – he didn't need a historian, did he?'

Gesler shrugged. 'As you say. We weren't in their company long, just long enough to take on a shipload of wounded. I talked a bit with Duiker, and Captain Lull. And then Coltaine broke his hand punching me in the face—'

'He what?' Strings laughed. 'No doubt you deserved it—'

Stormy spoke behind them. 'Broke his hand, aye, Gesler. And your nose, too.'

'My nose has been broke so many times it does it on instinct,' the sergeant replied. 'It wasn't much of a punch.'

Stormy snorted. 'He dropped you to the ground like a sack of turnips! That punch rivalled Urko's, the time he—'

'Not even close,' Gesler drawled. 'I once saw Urko punch down the side of a mudbrick house. Three blows, no more than four, anyway, and the whole thing toppled in a cloud of dust. That Napan bastard could punch.'

'And that's important to you?' Strings asked.

Gesler's nod was serious. 'The only way any commander will ever earn my respect, Fid.'

'Planning on testing the Adjunct soon?'

'Maybe. Of course, I'll make allowances, she being nobleborn and all.'

Once beyond Aren Way's battered gate and the abandoned ruins of a small village, they could now see the Seti and Wickan outriders on their flanks – a comforting sight to Strings. The raiding and sniping could begin at any time, now that the army had left the walls of Aren behind. Most of the tribes had, if the rumours were true, conveniently forgotten the truces they had won from the Malazan Empire. The old ways did naught but sleep restless beneath the surface of such peoples.

The landscape ahead and to either side was sun-blasted and broken, a place where even wild goats grew lean and listless. The mounded, flat-topped heaps of rubble that marked long-dead cities were visible on every horizon. Ancient raised roads, now mostly dismantled, stitched the rugged hillsides and ridges.

Strings wiped sweat from his brow. 'Green as we are, it's about time she called—'

Horns sounded along the massive train's length. Motion ceased, and the shouts of the water crews rose into the dusty air as they scrambled for the barrels. Strings swung about and studied his squad – they were already on the ground, sitting or sprawled, their long-sleeved undershirts darkened with sweat.

Among Gesler's and Borduke's squads, the reaction to the rest-halt had been identical, and Borduke's mage, Balgrid – slightly overweight and clearly unused to the armour he was wearing – looked pale and shivering. That squad's healer, a quiet, small man named Lutes, was already moving towards him.

'A Seti summer,' Koryk said, offering Strings a carnivorous smile. 'When the grasslands are driven to dust by the herds, when the earth underfoot clicks like breaking metal.'

'Hood take you,' Smiles snapped. 'This land's full of dead things for a reason.'

'Aye,' the Seti half-blood replied, 'only the tough survive. There are tribes aplenty out there – they've left enough sign in passing.'

'You have seen that, have you?' Strings said. 'Good. You're now the squad's scout.'

Koryk's white grin broadened. 'If you insist, Sergeant.'

'Unless it's night,' Strings added. 'Then it'll be Smiles. And Bottle, assuming his warren is suitable.'

Bottle scowled, then nodded. 'Well enough, Sergeant.'

'So what's Cuttle's role, then?' Smiles demanded. 'Lying around like a beached porpoise?'

Beached porpoise? Grew up by the sea, did you? Strings glanced over at the veteran soldier. The man was asleep. *I used to do that, back in the days when nothing was expected of me, when I wasn't in charge of a damned thing. I miss those days.* 'Cuttle's task,' Strings replied, 'is keeping the rest of you alive when I'm not close by.'

'Then why isn't he the corporal?' Smiles wanted to know, a belligerent set to her petite features.

'Because he's a sapper, and you don't want a sapper for a corporal, lass.' *Of course, I'm a sapper, too. Best keep that to myself . . .*

Three soldiers from the company's infantry arrived with waterskins.

'Drink it down slow,' Strings instructed. Gesler caught his eye from a few paces away, near the wagon, and Strings headed over. Borduke joined them.

'Well, this is curious,' Gesler muttered. 'Borduke's sickly mage – his warren's Meanas. And my mage is Tavos Pond, and he's the same. Now, Strings, your lad, Bottle . . .'

'I'm not sure yet.'

'He's also Meanas,' Borduke growled, pulling at his beard in a habitual gesture Strings knew would come to irritate him. 'Balgrid's confirmed it. They're all Meanas.'

'Like I said.' Gesler sighed. 'Curious.'

'That could be put to use,' Strings said. 'Get all three of them working on rituals – illusions are damned useful, when done right. Quick Ben could pull a few – the key is in the details. We should drag them all together tonight—'

'Ah,' said a voice from beyond the wagon, and Lieutenant Ranal strode into view, 'all my sergeants together in one place. Convenient.'

'Come to eat dust with the rest of us?' Gesler asked. 'Damned generous of you.'

'Don't think I haven't heard about you,' Ranal sneered.

497

'Had it been my choice, you'd be one of the lads carrying those waterskins, Gesler—'

'You'd go thirsty if I was,' the sergeant replied.

Ranal's face darkened. 'Captain Keneb wants to know if there's any mages in your squads. The Adjunct needs a tally of what's available.'

'None—'

'Three,' Strings interrupted, ignoring Gesler's glare. 'All minor, as would be expected. Tell the captain we'll be good for covert actions.'

'Keep your opinions to yourself, Strings. Three, you said. Very well.' He wheeled about and marched off.

Gesler rounded on Strings. 'We could lose those mages—'

'We won't. Go easy on the lieutenant, Gesler, at least for now. The lad knows nothing of being an officer in the field. Imagine, telling sergeants to keep their opinions quiet. With Oponn's luck, Keneb will explain a few things to the lieutenant, eventually.'

'Assuming Keneb's any better,' Borduke muttered. He combed his beard. 'Rumour has it he was the only one of his company to survive. And you know what that likely means.'

'Let's wait and see,' Strings advised. 'It's a bit early to start honing the knives—'

'Honing the knives,' Gesler said, 'now you're talking a language I understand. I'm prepared to wait and see, as you suggest, Fid. For now. All right, let's gather the mages tonight, and if they can actually get along without killing each other, then we might find ourselves a step or two ahead.'

Horns sounded to announce the resumption of the march. Soldiers groaned and swore as they clambered upright once more.

The first day of travel was done, and to Gamet it seemed they had travelled a paltry, pathetic distance from Aren. To be expected, of course. The army was a long way from finding its feet.

As am I. Saddle sore and light-headed from the heat, the Fist watched from a slight rise alongside the line of march as the camp slowly took shape. Pockets of order amidst a chaotic sea of motion. Seti and Wickan horse warriors continued to range well beyond the outlying pickets, far too few in number, however, to give him much comfort. *And those Wickans – grandfathers and grandmothers one and all. Hood knows, I might well have crossed blades with some of those old warriors. Those ancient ones, they were never settled with the idea of being in the Empire*. They were here for another reason entirely. For the memory of Coltaine. And the children – well, they were being fed the singular poison of bitter old fighters filled with tales of past glory. *And so, ones who've never known the terror of war and ones who've forgotten. A dreadful pairing . . .*

He stretched to ease the kinks in his spine, then forced himself into motion. Down from the ridge, along the edge of the rubble-filled ditch, to where the Adjunct's command tent sat, its canvas pristine, Temul's Wickans standing guard around it.

Temul was not in sight. Gamet pitied the lad. He was already fighting a half-dozen skirmishes, without a blade drawn, and he was losing. *And there's not a damned thing any of us can do about it.*

He approached the tent's entrance, scratched at the flap and waited.

'Come in, Gamet,' the Adjunct's voice called from within.

She was kneeling in the fore-chamber before a long, stone box, and was just settling the lid into place when he stepped through the entrance. A momentary glimpse – her otataral sword – then the lid was in place. 'There is some softened wax – there in that pot over the brazier. Bring it over, Gamet.'

He did so, and watched as she brushed the inset join between lid and base, until the container was entirely sealed. Then she rose and swept the windblown sand from her knees. 'I am already weary of this pernicious sand,' she muttered.

She studied him for a moment, then said, 'There is watered wine behind you, Gamet. Pour yourself some.'

'Do I look in need, Adjunct?'

'You do. Ah, I well know, you sought out a quiet life when you joined our household. And here I have dragged you into a war.'

He felt himself bridling and stood straighter. 'I am equal to this, Adjunct.'

'I believe you. None the less, pour yourself some wine. We await news.'

He swung about in search of the clay jug, found it and strode over. 'News, Adjunct?'

She nodded, and he saw the concern on her plain features, a momentary revelation that he turned away from as he poured out a cup of wine. *Show me no seams, lass. I need to hold on to my certainty.*

'Come stand beside me,' she instructed, a sudden urgency in her tone.

He joined her. They faced the clear space in the centre of the chamber.

Where a portal flowered, spreading outward like liquid staining a sheet of gauze, murky grey, sighing out a breath of stale, dead air. A tall, green-clad figure emerged. Strange, angular features, skin the shade of coal-dust marble; the man's broad mouth had the look of displaying a perpetual half-smile, but he was not smiling now.

He paused to brush grey dust from his cloak and leggings, then lifted his head and met Tavore's gaze. 'Adjunct, greetings from the Empress. And myself, of course.'

'Topper. I sense your mission here will be an unpleasant one. Fist Gamet, will you kindly pour our guest some wine?'

'Of course.' *Gods below, the damned master of the Claw.* He glanced down at his own cup, then offered it to Topper. 'I have yet to sip. Here.'

500

The tall man tilted his head in thanks and accepted the cup.

Gamet went to where the jug waited.

'You have come directly from the Empress?' Tavore asked the Clawmaster.

'I have, and before that, from across the ocean . . . from Genabackis, where I spent a most glum evening in the company of High Mage Tayschrenn. Would it shock you to know that he and I got drunk that night?'

Gamet's head turned at that. It seemed such an unlikely image in his mind that he was indeed shocked.

The Adjunct looked equally startled, then she visibly steeled herself. 'What news have you to tell me?'

Topper swallowed down a large mouthful of wine, then scowled. 'Watered. Ah well. Losses, Adjunct. On Genabackis. Terrible losses . . .'

Lying motionless in a grassy depression thirty paces beyond the squad's fire, Bottle closed his eyes. He could hear his name being called. Strings – who was called Fid by Gesler – wanted him, but the mage was not ready. Not yet. He had a different conversation to listen to, and managing that – without being detected – was no easy task.

His grandmother back in Malaz City would have been proud. *'Never mind those damned warrens, child, the deep magic is far older. Remember, seek out the roots and tendrils, the roots and tendrils. The paths through the ground, the invisible web woven from creature to creature. Every creature – on the land, in the land, in the air, in the water – they are all linked. And it is within you, if you have been awakened, and spirits below, you've been awakened, child! Within you, then, to ride those tendrils . . .'*

And ride them he did, though he would not surrender his private fascination with warrens, with Meanas in particular. Illusions . . . playing with those tendrils, with those roots of being, twisting and tying them into deceptive knots that tricked the eye, the touch, that deceived every sense, now that was a game worth playing . . .

But for the moment, he had immersed himself in the old ways, the undetectable ways – if one were careful, that is. Riding the life-sparks of capemoths, of rhizan, of crickets and chigger fleas, of roving bloodflies. Mindless creatures dancing on the tent's wall, hearing but not comprehending the sound shivers of the words coming from the other side of that tent wall.

Comprehension was Bottle's task. And so he listened. As the newcomer spoke, interrupted by neither the Adjunct nor Fist Gamet. Listened, and comprehended.

Strings glared down at the two seated mages. 'You can't sense him?'

Balgrid's shrug was sheepish. 'He's out there, hiding in the dark somewhere.'

'And he's up to something,' Tavos Pond added. 'But we can't tell what.'

'It's strange,' Balgrid muttered.

Strings snorted and strode back to Gesler and Borduke. The other squad members were brewing tea at the small fire they had built to one side of the path. Cuttle's snores were loud from the tent beyond. 'The bastard's vanished,' Strings said.

Gesler grunted. 'Maybe he's deserted, and if that's the case the Wickans will hunt him down and come back with his head on a spear. There won't be—'

'He's here!'

They turned to see Bottle settling down by the fire. Strings stamped over. 'Where in Hood's name have you been?' he demanded.

Bottle looked up, his brows slowly lifting. 'Nobody else felt it?' He glanced over at Balgrid and Tavos Pond, who were both approaching. 'That portal? The one that opened in the Adjunct's tent?' He frowned at the blank expressions on the faces of the two other mages, then asked in a deadpan voice, 'Have you two mastered hiding pebbles yet? Making coins disappear?'

Strings lowered himself opposite Bottle. 'What was all that about a portal?'

'Bad news, Sergeant,' the young man replied. 'It all went foul on Genabackis. Dujek's army mostly wiped out. The Bridgeburners annihilated. Whiskeyjack's dead—'

'Dead!'

'Hood take us!'

'Whiskeyjack? Gods below!'

The curses grew more elaborate, along with postulations of disbelief, but Strings no longer heard them. His mind was numb, as if a wildfire had ripped through his inner landscape, scorching the ground barren. He felt a heavy hand settle on his shoulder and vaguely heard Gesler murmuring something, but after a moment he shook the man off, rose and walked into the darkness beyond the camp.

He did not know how long, or how far he walked. Each step was senseless, the world outside his body not reaching through to him, remaining beyond the withered oblivion of his mind. It was only when a sudden weakness took his legs that he sank down onto the wiry, colourless grasses.

The sound of weeping, coming from somewhere ahead, a sound of sheer despair that pierced through the fog and thrummed in his chest. He listened to the ragged cries, winced to hear how they seemed torn from a constricted throat, like a dam finally sundered by a flood of grief.

He shook himself, growing mindful once more of his surroundings. The ground beneath the thin skein of grasses was hard and warm beneath his knees. Insects buzzed and flitted through the dark. Only starlight illuminated the wastes stretching out to all sides. The encamped army was easily a thousand or more paces behind him.

Strings drew a deep breath, then rose. He walked slowly towards the sound of the weeping.

A lad, lean – no, damn near scrawny, crouched down with arms wrapped about his knees, head sunk low. A single crow feather hung from a plain leather headband. A few paces beyond stood a mare, bearing a Wickan saddle, a tattered vellum scroll hanging from the horn. The horse was placidly tugging at the grass, her reins dangling.

Strings recognized the youth, though for the moment he could not recall his name. But Tavore had placed him in command of the Wickans.

After a long moment, the sergeant moved forward, making no effort to stay quiet, and sat down on a boulder a half-dozen paces from the lad.

The Wickan's head snapped up. Tear-streaked warpaint made a twisted net of his narrow face. Venom flared in his dark eyes and he hissed, a hand unsheathing his long-knife as he staggered upright.

'Relax,' Strings muttered. 'I'm in grief's arms this night myself, though likely for an entirely different reason. Neither of us expected company, but here we are.'

The Wickan hesitated, then snapped the weapon back into its sheath and made to walk away.

'Hold a moment, Horsewarrior. There's no need to flee.'

The youth spun round, mouth twisting into a snarl.

'Face me. I will be your witness this night, and we alone will know of it. Give me your words of sorrow, Wickan, and I will listen. Hood knows, it would serve me well right now.'

'I flee no-one,' the warrior rasped.

'I know. I just wanted to get your attention.'

'Who are you?'

'Nobody. And that is how I will stay, if you like. Nor will I ask for your name—'

'I am Temul.'

'Ah, well. So your bravery puts me in my place. My name is Fiddler.'

'Tell me,' Temul's voice was suddenly harsh, and he wiped angrily at his face, 'did you think my grief a noble thing? Did I weep for Coltaine? For my fallen kin? I did not. My pity was for myself! And now you may go. Proclaim me

– I am done with commanding, for I cannot command myself—'

'Easy there, I've no intention of proclaiming anything, Temul. But I can guess at your reasons. Those wrinkled Wickans of the Crow, is my guess. Them and the survivors who walked off Gesler's ship of wounded. They won't accept you as their leader, will they? And so, like children, they blunt you at every turn. Defy you, displaying a mocking regard to your face then whispering behind your back. And where does that leave you? You can't challenge them all, after all—'

'Perhaps I can! I shall!'

'Well, that will please them no end. Numbers alone will defeat your martial prowess. So you will die, sooner or later, and they will win.'

'You tell me nothing I do not know, Fiddler.'

'I know. I'm just reminding you that you've good reason to rail at the injustice, at the stupidity of those you would lead. I had a commander once, Temul, who was faced with the same thing you're facing. He was in charge of a bunch of children. Nasty children at that.'

'And what did he do?'

'Not much, and ended up with a knife in his back.'

There was a moment of silence, then Temul barked a laugh.

Fiddler nodded. 'Aye, I'm not one for stories with lessons in life, Temul. My mind bends to more practical choices.'

'Such as?'

'Well, I would imagine that the Adjunct shares your frustration. She wants you to lead, and would help you do so – but not so you lose face. She's too clever for that. No, the key here is deflection. Tell me, where are their horses right now?'

Temul frowned. 'Their horses?'

'Aye. I would think the Seti outriders could do without the Crow Clan for a day, don't you think? I'm sure the Adjunct would agree – those Seti are young, by and large,

505

and untested. They need the room to find themselves. There's good reason, then, militarily, to keep the Wickans from their horses come tomorrow. Let them walk with the rest of us. Barring your loyal retinue, of course. And who knows, a day might not be enough. Could end up being three, or even four.'

Temul spoke softly, thoughtfully. 'To get to their horses, we would need to be quiet . . .'

'Another challenge for the Seti, or so I'm sure the Adjunct would note. If children your kin must be, then take away their favoured playthings – their horses. Hard to look tall and imperious when you're spitting dust behind a wagon. In any case, you'd best hurry, so as not to awaken the Adjunct—'

'She may already be asleep—'

'No, she isn't, Temul. I am certain of it. Now, before you leave, answer me a question, please. You've a scroll hanging from your mare's saddle. Why? What is written on it?'

'The horse belonged to Duiker,' Temul answered, turning to the animal. 'He was a man who knew how to read and write. I rode with him, Fiddler.' He spun back with a glare. 'I rode with him!'

'And the scroll?'

The young Wickan waved a hand. 'Men such as Duiker carried such things! Indeed, I believe it once belonged to him, was once in his very hands.'

'And the feather you wear . . . to honour Coltaine?'

'To honour Coltaine, yes. But that is because I must. Coltaine did what he was expected to do. He did nothing that was beyond his abilities. I honour him, yes, but Duiker . . . Duiker was different.' He scowled and shook his head. 'He was old, older than you. Yet he fought. When fighting was not even expected of him – I know this to be true, for I knew Coltaine and Bult and I heard them speak of it, of the historian. I was there when Coltaine drew the others together, all but Duiker. Lull, Bult, Chenned, Mincer. And all spoke true and with certainty. Duiker would lead the refugees. Coltaine even gave him the stone the traders brought—'

'The stone? What stone?'

'To wear about his neck, a saving stone, Nil called it. A soul trapper, delivered from afar. Duiker wore it, though he liked it not, for it was meant for Coltaine, so that he would not be lost. Of course, we Wickans knew he would not be lost. We knew the crows would come for his soul. The elders who have come, who hound me so, they speak of a child born to the tribe, a child once empty, then filled, for the crows came. They came.'

'Coltaine has been reborn?'

'He has been reborn.'

'And Duiker's body disappeared,' Strings muttered. 'From the tree.'

'Yes! And so I keep his horse for him, for when he returns. I rode with him, Fiddler!'

'And he looked to you and your handful of warriors to guard the refugees. To you, Temul – not just Nil and Nether.'

Temul's dark eyes hardened as he studied Strings, then he nodded. 'I go now to the Adjunct.'

'The Lady's pull on you, Commander.'

Temul hesitated, then said, 'This night . . . you saw . . .'

'I saw nothing,' Strings replied.

A sharp nod, then the lad was swinging onto the mare, the reins in one long-fingered, knife-scarred hand.

Strings watched him ride into the darkness. He sat motionless on the boulder for a time, then slowly lowered his head into his hands.

The three were seated now, in the lantern-glow of the tent's chamber. Topper's tale was done, and it seemed that all that remained was silence. Gamet stared down at his cup, saw that it was empty, and reached for the jug. Only to find that it too was empty.

Even as exhaustion tugged at him, Gamet knew he

would not leave, not yet. Tavore had been told of, first, her brother's heroism, then his death. *Not a single Bridgeburner left alive. Tayschrenn himself saw their bodies, witnessed their interment in Moon's Spawn. But lass, Ganoes redeemed himself – redeemed the family name. He did that much at least.* But that was where the knife probably dug deepest. She had made harrowing sacrifices, after all, to resurrect the family's honour. Yet all along, Ganoes was no renegade; nor had he been responsible for Lorn's death. Like Dujek, like Whiskeyjack, his outlawry was nothing but a deception. There had been no dishonour. Thus, the sacrifice of young Felisin might have, in the end, proved . . . *unnecessary.*

And there was more. Jarring revelations. It had, Topper explained, been the hope of the Empress to land Onearm's Host on the north coast, in time to deliver a double blow to the Army of the Apocalypse. Indeed, the expectation all along had been for Dujek to assume overall command. Gamet could understand Laseen's thinking – to place the fate of the imperial presence on Seven Cities in the hands of a new, young and untested Adjunct was far too long a reach of faith.

Though Tavore had believed the Empress had done just that. Now, to find this measure of confidence so lacking . . . gods, this had been a Hood-damned night indeed.

Dujek Onearm was still coming, with a scant three thousand remaining in his Host, but he would arrive late, and, by both Topper's and Tayschrenn's unforgiving assessments, the man's spirit was broken. By the death of his oldest friend. Gamet wondered what else had happened in that distant land, in that nightmarish empire called the Pannion.

Was it worth it, Empress? Was it worth the devastating loss?

Topper had said too much, Gamet decided. Details of Laseen's plans should have been filtered through a more circumspect, less emotionally damaged agent. If the truth was so important, after all, then it should have been laid out for the Adjunct long before now – when it actually mattered. To tell Tavore that the Empress had no confidence in her, then follow that with the brutal assertion that she was now the empire's last hope for Seven Cities . . . well, few were the men or women who would not be rocked to their knees by that.

The Adjunct's expression revealed nothing. She cleared her throat. 'Very well, Topper. Is there more?'

The Clawmaster's oddly shaped eyes widened momentarily, then he shook his head and rose. 'No. Do you wish me to convey a message to the Empress?'

Tavore frowned. 'A message? No, there is no message. We have begun our march to the Holy Desert. Nothing more need be said.'

Gamet saw Topper hesitate, then the Clawmaster said, 'There is one more thing, Adjunct. There are probably worshippers of Fener among your army. I do not think the truth of the god's . . . fall . . . can be hidden. It seems the Tiger of Summer is the lord of war, now. It does an army little good to mourn; indeed, grief is anathema to an army as we all well know. There may prove some period of difficult adjustment – it would be well to anticipate and prepare for desertions—'

'There will be no desertions,' Tavore said, the flat assertion silencing Topper. 'The portal is weakening, Clawmaster – even a box of basalt cannot entirely block the effects of my sword. If you would leave this night, I suggest you do so now.'

Topper stared down at her. 'We are badly hurt, Adjunct. And hurting. It is the hope of the Empress that you will exercise due caution, and make no precipitous actions. Suffer no distraction on your march to Raraku – there will be attempts to draw you from the trail, to wear you down with skirmishes and pursuits—'

'You are a Clawmaster,' Tavore said, sudden iron in her tone. 'Dujek's advice I will listen to, for he is a soldier, a commander. Until such time as he arrives, I shall follow my own instincts. If the Empress is dissatisfied, she is

509

welcome to replace me. Now, that is all. Goodbye, Topper.'

Scowling, the Clawmaster swung about and strode without ceremony into the Imperial Warren. The gate collapsed behind him, leaving only a sour smell of dust.

Gamet let out a long sigh, pushed himself gingerly from the rickety camp chair. 'You have my sorrow, Adjunct, on the loss of your brother.'

'Thank you, Gamet. Now, get some sleep. And stop by—'

'T'amber's tent, aye, Adjunct.'

She quirked an eyebrow. 'Is that disapproval I hear?'

'It is. I'm not the only one in need of sleep. Hood take us, we've not even eaten this night.'

'Until tomorrow, Fist.'

He nodded. 'Aye. Goodnight, Adjunct.'

There was but one figure seated at the ebbing fire when Strings returned.

'What are you doing up, Cuttle?'

'I've done my sleep. You'll be dragging your feet tomorrow, Sergeant.'

'I don't think rest will come to me this night,' Strings muttered, sitting down cross-legged opposite the burly sapper.

'It's all far away,' Cuttle rumbled, tossing a last scrap of dung onto the flames.

'But it feels close.'

'At least you're not walking in the footprints of your fallen companions, Fiddler. But even so, it's all far away.'

'Well, I'm not sure what you mean but I'll take your word for it.'

'Thanks for the munitions, by the way.'

Strings grunted. 'It's the damnedest thing, Cuttle. We always find more, and they're meant to be used, but instead we hoard them, tell no-one we have them – in case they order us to put them to use—'

'The bastards.'

'Aye, the bastards.'

'I'll use the ones you've given me,' Cuttle avowed. 'Once I've crawled under Korbolo Dom's feet. I don't mind going to Hood at the same time, either.'

'Something tells me that's what Hedge did, in his last moment. He always threw them too close – that man had so many pieces of clay in him you could've made a row of pots from his insides.' He slowly shook his head, eyes on the dying fire. 'I wish I could have been there. That's all. Whiskeyjack, Trotts, Mallet, Picker, Quick Ben—'

'Quick's not dead,' Cuttle said. 'There was more after you'd left – I heard from my tent. Tayschrenn's made your wizard a High Mage.'

'Well, that doesn't surprise me, actually. That he'd survive, somehow. I wonder if Paran was still the company's captain—'

'He was. Died with them.'

'The Adjunct's brother. I wonder if she grieves this night.'

'Wondering's a waste of time, Fiddler. We got lads and lasses that need taking care of, right here. Korbolo Dom's warriors know how to fight. My guess is, we'll get whipped and sent back with our tails between our legs – and it'll be another chain, as we stagger back to Aren, only this time we won't get even close.'

'Well, that's a cheering prediction, Cuttle.'

'It don't matter. So long as I kill that Napan traitor – and his mage, too, if possible.'

'And what if you can't get close?'

'Then I take as many of them with me as I can. I ain't walking back, Fid, not again.'

'I'll remember that if the moment arrives. But what about taking care of these recruits of ours, Cuttle?'

'Well, that's the walk, isn't it? This march. We deliver them to that battle, we do that much, if we can. Then we see what kind of iron they're holding.'

'Iron,' Strings smiled. 'It's been a long time since I last

heard that saying. Since we're looking for revenge, you'll want it hot, I expect.'

'You expect wrong. Look at Tavore – there won't be any heat from her. In that she's just like Coltaine. It's obvious, Fiddler. The iron needs to be cold. Cold. We get it cold enough, who knows, we might earn ourselves a name.'

Strings reached across the fire and tapped the finger bone hanging from Cuttle's belt. 'We've made a start, I think.'

'We might have at that, Sergeant. Them and the standards. A start. She knows what's in her, give her that. She knows what's in her.'

'And it's for us to bring it out into view.'

'Aye, Fid, it is at that. Now, go away. These are the hours I spend alone.'

Nodding, the sergeant climbed to his feet. 'Seems I might be able to sleep after all.'

'It's my scintillating conversation what's done you in.'

'So it was.'

As Strings made his way to his small tent, something of Cuttle's words came back to him. *Iron. Cold iron. Yes, it's in her. And now I'd better search and search hard . . . to find it in me.*

BOOK THREE

SOMETHING BREATHES

The art of Rashan is found in the tension that binds the games of light, yet its aspect is one of dissipation— the creation of shadow and of dark, although in this case the dark is not absolute, such as is the aspect of the ancient warren, Kurald Galain. No, this dark is particular, for it exists, not through an absence of light, but by virtue of being *seen*.

The Mysteries of Rashan – a madman's discourse
Untural of Lato Revae

CHAPTER TWELVE

Light, shadow and dark –
This is a war unending.

Fisher

Glistening silver, the armour lay over a t-shaped stand. Oil had dripped down from the ragged knee-length tassels to form a pool on the flagstoned floor beneath. The sleeves were not loose, but appeared intended to be worn almost skin-tight. It had seen much use, and where mended the rings appeared to be a darker, carbon-stained iron.

Beside it, on a free-standing iron frame with horizontal hooks, waited a two-handed sword, the scabbard parallel directly beneath it on another pair of hooks. The sword was extraordinarily thin, with a long, tapered tip, edges on both sides, twin-fluted. Its surface was a strangely mottled oily blue, magenta and silver. The grip was round instead of flat, banded in gut, the pommel a single, large oblong sphere of polished haematite. The scabbard was of black wood, banded at the point and at the mouth in silver but other-wise unadorned. The harness belt attached to it was of small, almost delicate, black chain links.

Chain gauntlets waited on a wooden shelf on the wall behind the armour. The dull iron helm beside them was little more than a skullcap within a cage of studded bars, the bars reaching down like a massive hand, the gnarled fingers curving down to bridge nose, cheeks and jaw lines.

A lobster tail of chain depended from the slightly flared neck rim.

Standing just within the entrance to the modest, low-ceilinged room, Cutter watched as Darist began preparations for donning his martial accoutrements. The Daru youth was finding it difficult to convince himself that such beautiful weapons and armour – which had clearly seen decades, if not centuries, of use – could belong to this silver-haired man, who carried himself like an absent-minded scholar, whose amber eyes seemed to hold a perpetual look of confused distraction beneath the glowing sheen. Who moved slowly as if protecting brittle bones—

Yet I have experienced the old Tiste Andii's strength. And there is a mindfulness to his every movement which I should recognize – for I last saw it on another Tiste Andii, an ocean away. A racial trait? Perhaps, but it whispers like a song of threat, sunk deep in the marrow of my bones.

Darist stood facing his suit of armour, as if frozen in some startled contemplation – as if he'd forgotten how to put it on.

'These Tiste Edur, Darist,' Cutter said. 'How many are there?'

'Will we survive the coming attack, is your question? Unlikely, is my answer. At least five ships survived the storm. Two have reached our shore and managed landing. There would have been more, but they were engaged by a Malazan fleet that happened upon them by chance. We witnessed the clash from the Cliffs of Purahl . . .' The Tiste Andii slowly glanced back at Cutter. 'Your human kin did well – far better than the Edur no doubt anticipated.'

'A sea battle between the Malazans and the Tiste Edur? When was this?'

'Perhaps a week ago. There were but three Malazan war dromons, yet each managed to find company before plunging to the deep. There was a skilled mage among the humans – the exchange of sorcery was impressive—'

'You and your kin *watched*? Why didn't you help?

You must have known the Edur were seeking this island!'

Darist stepped towards the armour, lifted it seemingly effortlessly from its frame. 'We no longer leave this island. For many decades now, we hold to our decision to remain isolated.'

'Why?'

The Tiste Andii gave no answer. He slipped the mail suit over his shoulders. The sound it made as it flowed down was like liquid. He then reached for the sword.

'That looks as if it would snap with the first block of a heavier weapon.'

'It will not. There are many names for this particular sword.' Darist lifted it free of the hooks. 'Its maker named it Vengeance. T'an Aros, in our language. But I call it K'orladis.'

'Which means?'

'Grief.'

A faint chill rippled through Cutter. 'Who was its maker?'

'My brother.' He sheathed the sword, slipped his arms through the chain harness. Then he reached for the gauntlets. 'Before he found one ... more suited to his nature.' Darist turned, his gaze travelling the length of Cutter, head to toe, then back again. 'Do you have skill with those knives hidden about your person?'

'Some, though I draw no pleasure from spilling blood.'

'What else are they for?' the Tiste Andii asked as he donned the helm.

Cutter shrugged, wishing he had an answer to that question.

'Do you intend to fight the Edur?'

'Since they are seeking the throne, yes.'

Darist slowly cocked his head. 'Yet this is not your battle. Why would you choose to borrow this cause?'

'On Genabackis – my homeland – Anomander Rake and his followers chose to fight against the Malazan Empire. It wasn't their battle, but they have now made it so.'

He was surprised to see a wry smile twist the Tiste Andii's weathered features beneath the crooked iron fingers of the guards.

'That is interesting. Very well, Cutter, join me – though I tell you now it will prove your final fight.'

'I hope not.'

Darist led him from the room, out into the broad hallway once more, then through a narrow, black-wood-framed archway. The passage within appeared to be a tunnel through a single piece of wood, like the hollowed core of a massive, toppled tree trunk. It stretched on into the gloom, inclining slightly upward.

Cutter walked behind the Tiste Andii, the sound of the man's armour soft as the hiss of rain on a beach. The tunnel ended abruptly with an upward turn, the ceiling opening to reveal a vertical shaft. A rough ladder of roots climbed towards a small, pale disc of light.

Darist's ascent was slow and measured, Cutter impatient on the rungs directly beneath until the thought that he might soon die struck him, at which point a dull lassitude settled into his muscles, and it became a struggle to keep up with the ancient Tiste Andii.

They eventually emerged onto a leaf-cluttered floor of flagstones. Sunlight speared shafts of dust from slitted windows and gaps in the roof overhead – the storm seemed to have missed this place entirely. One wall had mostly collapsed and it was towards this that Darist strode.

Cutter followed. 'Some sort of upkeep might well have made this defensible,' he muttered.

'These surface structures are not Andii – they are Edur, and were in ruin when we first arrived.'

'How close are they?'

'They range through the forest, working inland. Cautious. They know they are not alone.'

'How many can you sense?'

'This first party numbers perhaps a score. We shall meet them in the courtyard, permitting us sufficient room for

518

swordplay yet allowing us a wall to which we can set our backs in the last few moments.'

'Hood's breath, Darist, if we drive them back you'll likely die of shock.'

The Tiste Andii glanced back at the Daru, then gestured. 'Follow me.'

A half-dozen similarly ruined chambers were traversed before they came to the courtyard. The vine-latticed walls were twice the height of a human, ragged-topped. Faded frescoes were hinted at beneath the overgrowth. Opposite the inner entrance through which they strode was an arched gateway, beyond which a trail of pine needles, snaking roots and moss-covered boulders wound into the shadows of enormous trees.

Cutter judged the yard to be twenty paces wide, twenty-five deep. 'There's too much room here, Darist,' he said. 'We'll get flanked—'

'I will command the centre. You remain behind, for those who might indeed try to get past me.'

Cutter recalled Anomander Rake's battle with the demon on the Darujhistan street. The two-handed fighting style the Son of Darkness had employed demanded plenty of room, and it now appeared that Darist would fight in a similar manner – but the sword's blade was, to Cutter's mind, far too thin for such fierce, wheeling swings. 'Is there sorcery invested in that blade of yours?' he asked.

'Not as investment is commonly known,' the Tiste Andii replied, drawing the weapon and wrapping both hands about the grip, one high under the hilt, the other just above the pommel. 'The power of Grief lies in the focused intent in its creation. The sword demands a singular will in its wielder. With such a will, it cannot be defeated.'

'And have you that singular will?'

Darist slowly lowered the tip to the ground. 'Had I, human, this would not be your last day this side of Hood's gate. Now, I suggest you draw your weapons. The Edur have discovered the path and now approach.'

Cutter found his hands were trembling as he drew out his leading knives. He possessed four others, two under each arm, sheathed in leather and peace-looped by thongs – which he now pulled clear. These four were weighted for throwing. Once done, he adjusted his grip on the knives in his hands, then had to dry his palms and repeat the task.

A soft whisper of sound made him look up, to see that Darist had slipped into a fighting stance, though the tip of the sword still rested on the flagstones.

And Cutter saw something else. The leaf clutter and detritus on the flagstones was in motion, crawling as if pushed by an unseen wind, gathering towards the gate's end of the courtyard, and out to heap against the walls to either side.

'Keep your eyes slitted,' Darist said in a low tone.

Slitted?

There was movement in the gloom beyond the gateway, furtive, then three figures stepped into view beneath the arch.

As tall as Darist, their skin a dusky pallor. Long brown hair, knotted and snarled with fetishes. Necklaces of claws and canines competed with the barbarity of their roughly tanned leather armour that was stitched with articulating strips of bronze. Their helms, also bronze, were shaped like bear or wolf skulls.

Among them, there was nothing of the natural majesty evident in Darist – or in Anomander Rake. A far more brutal cast, these Edur. Tip-heavy black-bladed scimitars were in their hands, sealskin-covered round shields on their forearms.

They hesitated before Darist, then the one in the centre snarled something in a language Cutter could not understand.

The silver-haired Tiste Andii shrugged, said nothing.

The Edur shouted something that was clearly a demand. Then they readied their weapons and swung their shields around.

520

Cutter could see more of the savage warriors gathered on the trail beyond the gate.

The three stepped from the archway, spread out to form a slight pincer position – the centre Edur a step further away than his companions on either side.

'They don't know how you will do this,' Cutter murmured. 'They've never fought against—'

The flankers moved forward in perfect unison.

Darist's sword snapped upward, and with that motion, a fierce gust of wind lifted in the courtyard, and the air around the three Edur was suddenly filled with skirling leaves and dust.

Cutter watched as the Tiste Andii attacked. The blade tipped horizontal, point threatening the Edur on the right, but the actual attack was with the pommel, against the warrior on the left. A blurring sideways dip to close, then the pommel struck the swiftly upraised shield, splitting it clean in half. Darist's left hand slipped off the pommel and slapped the warrior's sword away even as the Tiste Andii dropped into a squat, drawing the edge of Grief down his opponent's front.

It seemed there was no contact at all, yet blood gushed from a rent that began above the Edur's left collar bone and descended in a straight line down to his crotch.

The squat became a backward springing motion that landed Darist two paces back, his blade already hissing to fend off the other two warriors, both of whom leapt away in alarm.

The wounded Edur crumpled in a pool of his own blood, and as he fell Cutter saw that Grief had cut through the collar bone and every rib in the cage down the left side.

The warriors beyond the archway screamed battlecries and surged into the wind-whipped courtyard.

Their only chance of success lay in closing on Darist, inside the man's reach, closing and fouling that whispering blade, and the Edur lacked nothing in courage.

Cutter saw another cut down, then a third took the

pommel on the side of his helm, and the bronze collapsed inward far too deep – the warrior's limbs flailed in strange jerking motions as he fell to the flagstones.

Both leading knives were in the Daru's left hand, and his right reached to a throwing knife. He sent the weapon darting out with a back-handed throw, saw it sink to the hilt in an Edur's eye socket – and knew the tip had snapped against the inside of the man's skull at the back. He threw the second one and swore as a shield lifted to take it.

In the storm of spinning leaves Darist's sword seemed to be everywhere at once, blocking attack after attack, then an Edur flung himself forward to grapple, and managed to wrap both arms around the Tiste Andii's legs.

A scimitar lashed in. There was a spray of blood from Darist's right shoulder. Grief's pommel dented the helm of the grappling warrior, and the Edur sagged. Another swing chopped into the Tiste Andii's hip, the blade bouncing back out from the bone. Darist staggered.

Cutter rushed forward as the remaining Edur closed. Through spinning, clattering leaves, into the calmed air at the centre. The Daru had already learned that direct, head-on confrontation was not an ideal tactic when fighting with knives. He chose an Edur whose attention was fixed solely on Darist and was therefore turned slightly away – the warrior caught sight of him peripherally, and was quick to react.

A back-handed slash of the scimitar, followed by the shield swinging round.

Cutter punched his left knife at the blade, to intercept a third of the way down from the tip. Simultaneously, he stop-hit the swing with his other knife, midway along the man's forearm – the point of his weapon punching through leather and stabbing between the bones with both edges on. The hilt of his other weapon then contacted the scimitar – and knocked the weapon from a numbed hand.

The Edur's grunt was loud, and he swore as, yanking on the knife, Cutter moved past him. The blade was reluctant to pull free and dragged the impaled arm after it. The warrior's legs tangled and he fell to one knee.

Even as he lifted his shield, Cutter's free knife darted in over it, spearing him through the throat.

The shield's rim cracked hard against the Daru's out-thrust wrist, nearly springing the knife loose, but he managed to retain his grip.

Another tug and the other knife tore free of the Edur's forearm.

A shield struck him a body blow from his left, lifting Cutter upward, his moccasins leaving the flagstones. He twisted and slashed out at the attacker, and missed. The shield's impact had turned his left side into a mass of thrumming pain. He hit the ground and folded into a roll.

Something thumped in pursuit, bounced once, then twice, and as the Daru regained his feet an Edur's de-capitated head cracked hard against his right shin.

The agony of this last blow – absurdly to his mind – over-whelmed all else thus far. He screamed a curse, hopped backward one-legged.

An Edur was rushing him.

A fouler word grated out from Cutter. He flung the knife from his left hand. Shield surged up to meet it, the warrior ducking from view.

Grimacing, Cutter lunged after the weapon – while the Edur remained blind – and stabbed overhand above the shield. The knife sank down behind the man's left collar-bone, sprouting a geyser of blood as he pulled it back out.

There were shouts now in the courtyard – and suddenly it seemed the fighting was everywhere, on all sides. Cutter reeled back a step to see that other Tiste Andii had arrived – and, in their midst, Apsalar.

Three Edur were on the ground in her wake, all writhing amidst blood and bile.

The rest, barring their kin who had fallen to Apsalar, Cutter and Darist, were retreating, back through the archway.

Apsalar and her Tiste Andii companions pursued only so far as the gate.

Slowly, the spinning wind dwindled, the leaf fragments drifting down like ash.

Cutter glanced over to see Darist still standing, though he leaned against a side wall, his long, lean frame sheathed in blood, helm gone, his hair matted and hanging down over his face, dripping. The sword Grief remained in his two hands, point once more on the flagstones.

One of the new Tiste Andii moved to the three noisily dying Edur and unceremoniously slit their throats. When finished, she raised her gaze to study Apsalar for a long moment.

Cutter realized that all of Darist's kin were white-haired, though none were as old – indeed, they appeared very young, in appearance no older than the Daru himself. They were haphazardly armed and armoured, and none held their weapons with anything like familiarity. Quick, nervous glances were thrown at the gateway – then over to Darist.

Sheathing her Kethra knives, Apsalar strode up to Cutter. 'I am sorry we were late.'

He blinked, then shrugged. 'I thought you'd drowned.'

'No, I made shore easily enough – though everything else went with you. There was sorcerous questing, then, but I evaded that.' She nodded to the youths. 'I found these camped a fair distance inland. They were . . . hiding.'

'Hiding. But Darist said—'

'Ah, so that is Darist. Andarist, to be more precise.' She turned a thoughtful gaze on the ancient Tiste Andii. 'It was by his command. He didn't want them here . . . because I imagine he expected they would die.'

'And so they shall,' Darist growled, finally lifting his head to meet her eyes. 'You have condemned them all, for the Edur will now hunt them down in earnest – the old hatreds, rekindled once more.'

She seemed unaffected by his words. 'The throne must be protected.'

Darist bared red-stained teeth, his eyes glittering in the half-shadows. 'If he truly wants it protected, then he can come here and do it himself.'

Apsalar frowned. 'Who?'

Cutter answered, 'His brother, of course. Anomander Rake.'

It had been a guess, but Darist's expression was all the affirmation needed. Anomander Rake's *younger* brother. In his veins, nothing of the Son of Darkness's Draconian blood. And in his hands, a sword that its maker had judged insufficient, when compared to Dragnipur. But this knowledge alone was barely a whisper – the twisted, dark storm of all that existed between the two siblings was an epic neither man was ever likely to orate, or so Cutter suspected.

And the skein of bitter grievances proved even more knotted than the Daru had first imagined, for it was then revealed that the youths were, one and all, close kin to Anomander – grandchildren. Their parents had one and all succumbed to their sire's flaw, the hunger for wandering, for vanishing into the mists, for shaping private worlds in forgotten, isolated places. *'The search for loyalty and honour'*, Darist had said, with a sneer, whilst Phaed – the young woman who had shown mercy to Apsalar's victims – bound his wounds.

A task not done quickly. Darist – *Andarist* – had been slashed at least a dozen times, each time the heavy scimitar parting chain then flesh down to the bone, in various places on his body. How he had managed to stand upright, much less continue fighting, belied his earlier claim that his will was not of sufficient purity to match the sword, Grief. Now that the skirmish had been suspended, however, the force that had fired the old warrior fast dissipated. His right arm was incapacitated; the wound on his hip dragged him onto the flagstones – and he could not rise again without help.

There were nine dead Tiste Edur. Their retreat had probably been triggered by a desire to regroup rather than being hard-pressed.

Worse, they were but an advance party. The two ships just off the shore were massive: each could easily hold two hundred warriors. Or so Apsalar judged, having scouted the inlet where they were moored.

'There is plenty of wreckage in the water,' she added, 'and both Edur ships have the look of having been in a fight—'

'Three Malazan war dromons,' Cutter said. 'A chance encounter. Darist says the Malazans gave a good account of themselves.'

They were seated on some tumbled rubble a dozen paces from the Tiste Andii, watching the youths hover and fuss over Darist. Cutter's left side ached, and though he did not look beneath his clothes he knew that bruises were spreading. He struggled to ignore the discomfort and continued eyeing the Tiste Andii.

'They are not what I expected,' he said quietly. 'Not even schooled in the art of fighting—'

'True. Darist's desire to protect them could prove a fatal one.'

'Now that the Edur know they exist. Not a part of Darist's plan.'

Apsalar shrugged. 'They were given a task.'

He fell silent, pondering that brusque statement. He'd always believed that a singular capacity to inflict death engendered a certain wisdom – of the fragility of the spirit, of its mortality – as he had known, and experienced first-hand, with Rallick Nom in Darujhistan. But Apsalar revealed nothing of such wisdom; her words were hard with judgement, often flatly dismissive. She had taken focus and made of it a weapon . . . *or a means of self-defence.*

She had not intended any of the three Edur she had taken down to die swiftly. Yet it seemed she drew no pleasure, as a sadist might. *It is more as if she was trained to do so . . . trained as a torturer. Yet Cotillion – Dancer – was no torturer. He was an assassin. So where does the vicious streak come from? Does it belong to her own nature?* An unpleasant, disturbing thought.

He lifted his left arm, gingerly, wincing. Their next fight would likely be a short one, even with Apsalar at their side.

'You are in no condition to fight,' she observed.

'Nor is Darist,' Cutter retorted.

'The sword will carry him. But you will prove a liability. I would not be distracted by protecting you.'

'What do you suggest? I kill myself now so I'm not in your way?'

She shook her head – as if the suggestion had been, on its face, entirely reasonable, just not what she had in mind – and spoke in a low voice. 'There are others on this island. Hiding well, but not well enough to escape my notice. I want you to go to them. I want you to enlist their help.'

'Who are these others?'

'You yourself identified them, Cutter. Malazans. Survivors, I would assume, from the three war dromons. There is one of power among them.'

Cutter glanced over at Darist. The youths had moved the old man so that he sat with his back against the wall beside the inside doorway, opposite the gate. His head was lowered, bearded chin to chest, and only the faint rise and fall of his chest indicated that he still lived. 'All right. Where will I find them?'

The forest was filled with ruins. Crumbled, moss-covered, often little more than overgrown heaps, but it was evident to Cutter as he padded along the narrow, faint trail Apsalar had described for him that this forest had risen from the heart of a dead city – a huge city, dominated by massive buildings. Pieces of statuary lay scattered here and there, figures of enormous stature, constructed in sections and fixed together with a glassy substance he did not recognize. Although mostly covered in moss, he suspected the figures were Edur.

An oppressive gloom suffused all that lay beneath the forest canopy. A number of living trees showed torn bark, and while the bark was black, the smooth, wet wood underneath was blood red. Fallen companions revealed that the fierce crimson turned black with death. The wounded upright trees reminded Cutter of Darist – of the Tiste Andii's black skin and the deep red cuts slashing through it.

He found he was shivering in the damp air as he padded along. His left arm was now entirely useless, and though he had retrieved his knives – including the broken-tipped one – he doubted that he would be able to put up much of a fight should the need arise.

He could make out his destination directly ahead. A mound of rubble, pyramidal and particularly large, its summit sunbathed. There were trees on its flanks, but most were dead in the strangling grip of vines. A gaping hole of impenetrable darkness yawned from the side nearest Cutter.

He slowed, then, twenty paces from the cave, halted. What he was about to do ran against every instinct. 'Malazans!' he called out, then winced at his own loudness. *But the Edur are closing on the Throne – no-one nearby to hear me. I hope.* 'I know you are within! I would speak with you!'

Figures appeared at the flanking edges of the cave, two on each side, crossbows cocked and trained on Cutter. Then, from the centre, emerged three more, two women and a man. The woman on the left gestured and said, 'Come closer, hands out to your sides.'

Cutter hesitated, then stretched out his right hand. 'My left arm won't lift, I'm afraid.'

'Come ahead.'

He approached.

The speaker was tall, muscular. Her hair was long, stained red. She wore tanned leathers. A longsword was scabbarded at her hip. Her skin was a deep bronze in hue. Cutter judged she was ten or more years older than him, and he felt a shiver run through him when he lifted his gaze and met her tilted, gold-hued eyes.

The other woman was unarmed, older, and her entire right side, head, face, torso and leg, was horrifically burned – the flesh fused with wisps of clothing, mangled and melted by the ravages of a sorcerous attack. It was a wonder that she was standing – or even alive.

Hanging back a step from these two was the man. Cutter guessed that he was Dal Honese, dusky-skinned, grey-shot black curled hair on his head cut short – though his eyes were, incongruously, a deep blue. His features were even enough, though crisscrossed with scars. He wore a battered hauberk, a plain longsword at his belt, and an expression so closed he could be Apsalar's brother.

The flanking marines were in full armour, helmed and visored.

'Are you the only survivors?' Cutter asked.

The first woman scowled.

'I have little time,' the Daru went on. 'We need your help. The Edur are assailing us—'

'Edur?'

Cutter blinked, then nodded. 'The seafarers you fought. Tiste Edur. They are seeking something on this island, something of vast power – and we'd rather it not fall into their hands. And why should you help? Because if it *does* fall into their hands, the Malazan Empire is likely finished. In fact, so is all of humanity—'

The burned woman cackled, then broke into a fit of coughing that frothed her mouth with red bubbles. After a long moment, the woman recovered. 'Oh, to be young again! All of humanity, is it? Why not the whole world?'

'The Throne of Shadow is on this island,' Cutter said.

At this, the Dal Honese man started slightly.

The burned woman was nodding. 'Yes yes yes, true words. The sense of things arrives – in a flood! Tiste Edur, Tiste Edur, a fleet set out on a search, a fleet from far away, and now they've found it. Ammanas and Cotillion are about to be usurped, and what of it? The Throne of Shadow

529

– we fought the Edur for *that*! Oh, what a waste – our ships, the marines – my own life, for the *Throne of Shadow?*' She spasmed into coughing once more.

'Not our battle,' the other woman growled. 'We weren't even looking for a fight, but the fools weren't interested in actually talking, in exchanging emissaries – Hood knows, this is not our island, not within the Malazan Empire. Look elsewhere—'

'No,' the Dal Honese rumbled.

The woman turned in surprise. 'We were clear enough, Traveller, in our gratitude to you for saving our lives. But that hardly permits you to assume command—'

'The Throne must not be claimed by the Edur,' the man named Traveller said. 'I have no desire to challenge your command, Captain, but the lad speaks without exaggeration when he describes the risks . . . to the empire and to all of humanity. Like it or not, the Warren of Shadow is now human-aspected . . .' he smiled crookedly, 'and it well suits our natures.' The smile vanished. 'This battle is ours – we face it now or we face it later.'

'You claim this fight in the name of the Malazan Empire?' the captain asked.

'More than you know,' Traveller replied.

The captain gestured to one of her marines. 'Gentur, get the others out here, but leave Mudslinger with the wounded. Then have the squads count quarrels – I want to know what we have.'

The marine named Gentur uncocked his crossbow then slipped back into the cave. A few moments later more soldiers emerged, sixteen in all when counting those who had originally come out.

Cutter walked up to the captain. 'There is one of power among you,' he murmured, casting a glance at the burned woman – who was leaning over and spitting out murky blood. 'Is she a sorceress?'

The captain followed his gaze and frowned. 'She is, but she is dying. The power you—'

The air reverberated to a distant concussion and Cutter wheeled. 'They've attacked again! With magic this time – follow me!' Without a backward look, the Daru set off down the trail. He heard a faint curse behind him, then the captain began shouting orders.

The path led directly to the courtyard, and from the thundering detonations pounding again and again, Cutter judged the troop would have no difficulty in finding the place of battle – he would not wait for them. Apsalar was there, and Darist, and a handful of untrained Tiste Andii youths – they would have little defence against sorcery.

But Cutter believed he did.

He sprinted on through the gloom, his right hand closed about his aching left arm, seeking to hold it in place, though each jostling stride lanced pain into his chest.

The nearest wall of the courtyard came into view. Colours were playing wildly in the air, thrashing the trees to all sides, deep reds and magenta and blues, a swirling chaos. The waves of concussions were increasing in frequency, pounding within the courtyard.

There were no Edur outside the archway – an ominous sign.

Cutter raced for the opening. Movement to his right caught his attention, and he saw another company of Edur, coming up from a coast trail but still sixty paces distant. *The Malazans will have to deal with those . . . Queen of Dreams help them.* The gate was before him, and he caught first sight of what was happening in the courtyard.

Four Edur stood in a line in the centre, their backs to him. A dozen or more Edur warriors waited on each flank, scimitars held ready. Waves of magic rolled out from the four, pulsing, growing ever stronger – and each one flowed over the flagstones in a tumbling storm of colours, to hammer into Darist.

Who stood alone, at his feet a dead or unconscious Apsalar. Behind him, the scattered bodies of Anomander Rake's grandchildren. Somehow, Darist still held his sword upright – though he was a shredded mass of blood, bones visible through the wreckage of his chest. He stood before the crashing waves, yet would not take a single step back, even as they tore him apart. The sword Grief was white hot, the metal singing a terrible, keening note that grew louder and more piercing with every moment that passed.

'Blind,' Cutter hissed as he closed, 'I need you *now*!'

Shadows blossomed around him, then four heavy paws thumped onto the flagstones, and the Hound's looming presence was suddenly at his side.

One of the Edur spun round. Unhuman eyes widened on seeing Blind, then the sorcerer snapped out something in a harsh, commanding tone.

Blind's forward rush halted in a skid of claws.

And the Hound cowered.

'Beru fend!' Cutter swore, scrabbling to draw a knife—

The courtyard was suddenly filled with shadows, a strange crackling sound ripping through the air—

And a fifth figure was among the four Edur sorcerers now, grey-clad, gloved, face hidden in a rough hood. In its hands, a rope, that seemed to writhe with a life of its own. Cutter saw it snap out to strike a sorcerer in one eye, and when the rope whipped back out, a stream of blood and minced brains followed. The sorcerer's magic winked out and the Edur toppled.

The rope was too fast to follow, as its wielder moved among the three remaining mages, but in its twisting wake a head tumbled from shoulders, intestines spilled out from a gaping rip, and whatever felled the last sorcerer happened in a blur that left no obvious result, except that the Edur was dead before he hit the ground.

There were shouts from the Edur warriors, and they converged from both sides.

It was then that the screams began. The rope lashed out from Cotillion's right hand; a long-knife was in his left, seeming to do little but lick and touch everyone it came close to – but the result was devastating. The air was a mist

532

of suspended blood around the patron god of assassins, and before Cutter drew his fourth breath since the battle began, it was over, and around Cotillion there was naught but corpses.

A final snap of the rope whipped blood across a wall, then the god threw back his hood and wheeled to face Blind. He opened his mouth to say something, then shut it once more. An angry gesture, and shadows swept out to engulf the trembling Hound. When they dissipated a moment later Blind was gone.

There was the sound of fighting beyond the courtyard and Cutter turned. 'The Malazans need help!' he shouted to Cotillion.

'No they don't,' the god growled.

Both spun at a loud clatter, to see Darist lying motionless beside Apsalar, the sword lying nearby, its heat igniting the leaves it lay on.

Cotillion's face fell, as if with a sudden, deep sorrow. 'When he's done out there,' he said to Cutter, 'guide him to this sword. Tell him its names.'

'He?'

A moment later, with a final survey of the mayhem surrounding him, Cotillion vanished.

Cutter rushed over to Apsalar. He knelt down beside her.

Her clothes were crisped, smoke rising in tendrils in the now still air. Fire had swept through her hair, but only momentarily, it seemed, for she had plenty left; nor was her face burned, although a long red welt, already blistering, was visible in a diagonal slash down her neck. Faint jerks of her limbs – the after-effects of the sorcerous attack – showed him she still lived.

He tried to wake her, failed. A moment later he looked up, listened. The sounds of fighting had ceased and now a single set of boots slowly approached, crunching on scorched ground.

Cutter slowly rose and faced the archway.

Traveller stepped into view. A sword broken three-quarters

of the way up the blade was in one gauntleted hand. Though spattered with blood, he seemed unwounded. He paused to study the scene in the courtyard.

Somehow, Cutter knew without asking that he was the last left alive. Yet he moved none the less to look out through the archway. The Malazans were all down, motionless. Surrounding them in a ring were the corpses of half a hundred or more Tiste Edur. Quarrel-studded others lay on the trail approaching the clearing.

I called those Malazans to their deaths. That captain – with the beautiful eyes . . . He returned to where Traveller walked among the fallen Tiste Andii. And the question he asked came from a constricted throat. 'Did you speak true, Traveller?'

The man glanced over.

'This battle,' Cutter elaborated. 'Was it truly a Malazan battle?'

Traveller's answering shrug chilled the Daru. 'Some of these are still alive,' he said, gesturing at the Tiste Andii.

'And there are wounded in the cave,' Cutter pointed out.

He watched as the man walked over to where lay Apsalar and Darist. 'She is a friend,' Cutter said.

Traveller grunted, then he flung his broken sword aside and stepped over Darist. He reached down for the sword.

'Careful—'

But the man closed his gauntleted hand on the grip and lifted the weapon.

Cutter sighed, closed his eyes for a long moment, then opened them and said, 'It is named Vengeance . . . or Grief. You can choose which best suits you.'

Traveller turned, met Cutter's eyes. 'Do you not wish it for yourself?'

The Daru shook his head. 'It demands its wielder possess a singular will. I am not for that sword, nor, I think, will I ever be.'

Traveller studied the blade in his hand. 'Vengeance,' he

murmured, then nodded and crouched down to retrieve the scabbard from Darist's body. 'This old man, who was he?'

Cutter shrugged. 'A guardian. He was named Andarist. And now he's gone, and so the Throne is without a protector—'

Traveller straightened. 'I will abide here a time. As you said, there are wounded to tend to . . . and corpses to bury.'

'I'll help—'

'No need. The god who·strode through this place has visited the Edur ships – there are small craft aboard, and supplies. Take your woman and leave this island. If more Edur chance upon this location, your presence will only impede me.'

'How long will you plan on staying here, in Andarist's role?'

'Long enough to do him honour.'

A groan came from Apsalar, drawing Cutter to her. She began thrashing, as if fevered.

'Carry her from this place,' Traveller said. 'The sorcery's effects linger.'

He looked up, met those eyes – and saw sorrow there, the first emotion yet to be revealed from the man. 'I would help you bury—'

'I need no help. It will not be the first time I have buried companions. Go. Take her.'

He lifted her in his arms. Her thrashing stilled and she sighed as if sinking into deep, peaceful sleep. Then he stood studying Traveller for a moment.

The man turned away. 'Thank your god, mortal,' he growled, his back still to Cutter, 'for the sword . . .'

An elongated mass of the stone floor had fallen away, down to the black rushing water of the subterranean river. Athwart the gaping hole lay a bundle of spears, around which was tied a rope that reached down into the water, snaking about as the current tugged at it. The air of the rough-hewn chamber was chill and damp.

Kalam crouched at the edge and studied the swirling water below for a long moment.

'The well,' Sergeant Cord said from where he stood beside the assassin.

Kalam grunted, then asked, 'What in Hood's name inspired the captain and lieutenant to climb down there?'

'If you look long enough, with the torches gone from this room, you'll see a glow. There's something lying on the bottom, maybe twice a man's height in depth.'

'Something?'

'Looks like a man . . . all in armour. Lying spread-eagled.'

'So take the torches out. I want to see this.'

'Did you say something, *Corporal*? Your demon friend has disappeared, remember – vanished.'

Kalam sighed. 'Demons will do that, and in this case you should be thankful for that. Right now, Sergeant, I am of the opinion that you've all been cooped up in this mountain for far too long. I'm thinking maybe you've lost your minds. And I have also reconsidered your words about my position in your company, and I've reached a decision and it's this.' He turned his head and fixed his gaze on Cord's eyes. 'I'm not *in* your company, Cord. I'm a Bridgeburner. You're Ashok Regiment. And if that's not enough for you, I am resurrecting my old status . . . as a Claw, a Leader of a Hand. And as such, I'm only outranked in the field by Clawmaster Topper, the Adjunct, and the Empress herself. Now, take the damned torches out of here!'

Cord suddenly smiled. 'You want to take command of this company? Fine, you can have it. Though we want to deal with Irriz ourselves.' He reached up to collect the first of the sputtering torches on the wall behind him.

The sudden alteration of attitude from Cord startled Kalam, then filled him with suspicion. *Until I sleep, that is. Gods below, I was far better off on my own. Where did that damned demon go, anyway?* 'And when you've done that, Sergeant, head back up to the others and begin preparations – we're leaving this place.'

'What about the captain and the lieutenant?'

'What about them? They were swept away and they either drowned or were sprung loose in some watering hole. Either way, they're not with us now, and I doubt they're coming back—'

'You don't know that—'

'They've been gone too long, Cord. If they didn't drown they would have had to reach the surface somewhere close. You can hold your breath only so long. Now, enough with this discussion – get going.'

'Aye . . . sir.'

A torch in each hand, Cord headed up the stairs.

Darkness swiftly engulfed the chamber.

Kalam waited for his eyes to adjust, listening to the sergeant's bootsteps growing ever fainter.

And there, finally, far below, the glowing figure, indistinct, rippling beneath the rushing water.

The assassin retrieved the rope and coiled it to one side. About twenty arm-lengths had been played out, but the bundle of spears held a lot more. Then he pried a large chunk of stone from the ragged edge and tied the sodden, icy-cold end of the rope to it.

With Oponn's luck, the rock was sufficiently heavy to sink more or less straight down. He checked the knots once more, then pushed it from the ledge.

It plummeted, dragging the coiled rope down with it. The spears clacked tight, and Kalam peered down. The stone was suspended the full length of the rope – a distance that Kalam, and, no doubt, the captain and the lieutenant, had judged sufficient to make contact with the figure. But it hadn't, though it looked close. *Meaning he's a big bastard. All right . . . let's see how big.* He grasped the spears and began lifting and rolling the bundle, playing out ever greater lengths.

A pause to study the stone's progress, then more playing out of rope.

It finally reached the figure – given the sudden bowing of

the line as the current took the slack. Kalam looked down once more. 'Hood's breath!' The rock lay on the figure's chest . . . and the distance made that stone look small.

The armoured figure was enormous, three times a man's height at least. The captain and the lieutenant had been deceived by the scale. Probably fatally so.

He squinted down at it, wondering at the strange glow, then grasped the rope to retrieve the stone—

And, far below, a massive hand flashed up and closed on it – and pulled.

Kalam shouted as he was pulled down into the torrent. As he plunged into the icy water, he reached up in an attempt to grasp the bundle of spears.

There was a fierce tug, and the spears snapped with an explosive splintering sound directly overhead.

The assassin still held on to the rope, even as the current swept him along. He felt himself being pulled down.

The cold was numbing. His ears popped.

Then he was drawn close by a pair of massive chain-clad fists – close, and face to face with the broad grille of the creature's helm. In the swirling darkness beneath that grille, the glimmer of a rotted, bestial visage, most of the flesh in current-fluttering strips. Teeth devoid of lips—

And the creature spoke in Kalam's mind. *The other two eluded me . . . but you I will have. I am so hungry—*

Hungry? Kalam answered. *Try this.*

He drove both long-knives into the creature's chest.

A thundering bellow, and the fists shot upward, pushing Kalam away – harder and faster than he had thought possible. Both weapons yanked – almost breaking the grip of his hands, but he held on. The current had no time to grasp him as he was thrown upward, shooting back through the hole in an exploding geyser of water. The ledge caught one of his feet and tore the boot off. He struck the chamber's low stone ceiling, driving the last of his breath from his lungs, then dropped.

He landed half on the pit's ledge, and was nearly swept

back into the river, but he managed to splay himself, clawing to regain the floor, moving clear of the hole. Then he lay motionless, numbed, his boot lying beside him, until he was able to draw in a ragged lungful of bitter cold air.

He heard feet on the stairs, then Cord burst into the chamber and skidded to a halt directly above Kalam. The sergeant's sword was in one hand, a torch flaring in the other. He stared down at the assassin. 'What was that noise? What happened? Where are the damned spears—'

Kalam rolled onto his side, looked down over the ledge.

The frothing torrent was impenetrable – opaqued red with blood. 'Stop,' the assassin gasped.

'Stop what? Look at that water! *Stop what?*'

'Stop . . . drawing . . . from this well . . .'

It was a long time before the shivers left his body, to be replaced with countless aches from his collision with the chamber's ceiling. Cord had left then returned with others from his company, as well as Sinn, carrying blankets and more torches.

There was some difficulty in prying the long-knives from Kalam's hands. The separation revealed that the grips had somehow scorched the assassin's palms and fingerpads.

'Cold,' Ebron muttered, 'that's what did that. Burned by cold. What did you say that thing looked like?'

Kalam, huddled in blankets, looked up. 'Like something that should have been dead a long time ago, Mage. Tell me, how much do you know of B'ridys – this fortress?'

'Probably less than you,' Ebron replied. 'I was born in Karakarang. It was a monastery, wasn't it?'

'Aye. One of the oldest cults, long extinct.' A squad healer crouched beside him and began applying a numbing salve to the assassin's hands. Kalam leaned his head against the wall and sighed. 'Have you heard of the Nameless Ones?'

Ebron snorted. 'I said Karakarang, didn't I? The Tanno cult claims a direct descent from the cult of the Nameless

539

Ones. The Spiritwalkers say their powers, of song and the like, arose from the original patterns that the Nameless Ones fashioned in their rituals – those patterns supposedly crisscross this entire subcontinent, and their power remains to this day. Are you saying this monastery belonged to the Nameless Ones? Yes, of course you are. But they weren't demons, were they—'

'No, but they were in the habit of chaining them. The one in the pool is probably displeased with its last encounter, but not as displeased as you might think.'

Ebron frowned, then paled. 'The blood – if anyone drinks water tainted with that . . .'

Kalam nodded. 'The demon takes that person's soul . . . and makes the *exchange*. Freedom.'

'Not just people, either!' Ebron hissed. 'Animals, birds – insects! Anything!'

'No, I think it will have to be big – bigger than a bird or insect. And when it does escape—'

'It'll come looking for you,' the mage whispered. He suddenly wheeled to Cord. 'We have to get out of here. Now! Better still—'

'Aye,' Kalam growled, 'get as far away from me as you can. Listen – the Empress has sent her new Adjunct, with an army – there will be a battle, in Raraku. The Adjunct has little more than recruits. She could do with your company, even as beaten up as it is—'

'They march from Aren?'

Kalam nodded. 'And have likely already started. That gives you maybe a month . . . of staying alive and out of trouble—'

'We can manage,' Cord grated.

Kalam glanced over at Sinn. 'Be careful, lass.'

'I will. I think I'll miss you, Kalam.'

The assassin spoke to Cord. 'Leave me my supplies. I will rest here a while longer. So we don't cross paths, I will be heading due west from here, skirting the north edge of the Whirlwind . . . for a time. Eventually, I will try to breach it, and make my way into Raraku itself.'

'Lady's luck to you,' Cord replied, then he gestured. 'Everyone else, let's go.' At the stairway, the sergeant glanced back at the assassin. 'That demon . . . did it get the captain and the lieutenant, do you think?'

'No. It said otherwise.'

'It spoke to you?'

'In my mind, aye. But it was a short conversation.'

Cord grinned. 'Something tells me, with you, they're all short.'

A moment later and Kalam was alone, still racked with waves of uncontrollable shivering. Thankfully, the soldiers had left a couple of torches. It was too bad, he reflected, that the azalan demon had vanished. *Seriously too bad.*

It was dusk when the assassin emerged from the narrow fissure in the rock, opposite the cliff, that was the monastery's secret escape route. The timing was anything but pleasant. The demon might already be free, might already be hunting him – in whatever form fate had gifted it. The night ahead did not promise to be agreeable.

The signs of the company's egress were evident on the dusty ground in front of the fissure, and Kalam noted that they had set off southward, preceding him by four or more hours. Satisfied, he shouldered his pack and, skirting the outcropping that was the fortress, headed west.

Wild bhok'arala kept pace with him for a time, scampering along the rocks and voicing their strangely mournful hooting calls as night gathered. Stars appeared overhead through a blurry film of dust, dulling the desert's ambient silver glow to something more like smudged iron. Kalam made his way slowly, avoiding rises where he would be visible along a skyline.

He froze at a distant scream to the north. An enkar'al. Rare, but mundane enough. *Unless the damned thing recently landed to drink from a pool of bloody water.* The bhok'arala had scattered at that cry, and were nowhere to be seen.

There was no wind that Kalam could detect, but he knew that sound carried far on nights like these, and, worse, the huge winged reptiles could detect motion from high above . . . and the assassin would make a good meal.

Cursing to himself, Kalam faced south, to where the Whirlwind's solid wall of whirling sand rose, three and a half, maybe four thousand paces distant. He tightened the straps of his pack, then gingerly reached for his knives. The effects of the salve were fading, twin throbbing pulses of pain slowly rising. He had donned his fingerless gloves and gauntlets – risking the danger of infection – but even these barriers did little to lessen the searing pain as he closed his hands on the weapons and tugged them loose.

Then he set off down the slope, moving as quickly as he dared. A hundred heartbeats later he reached the blistered pan of Raraku's basin. The Whirlwind was a muted roar ahead, steadily drawing a flow of cool air towards it. He fixed his gaze on that distant, murky wall, then began jogging.

Five hundred paces. The pack's straps were abrading the telaba on his shoulders, wearing through to the lightweight chain beneath. His supplies were slowing him down, but without them, he knew, he was as good as dead here in Raraku. He listened to his breathing grow harsher.

A thousand paces. Blisters had broken on his palms, soaking the insides of his gauntlets, making the grips of the long-knives slippery, uncertain. He was drawing in great lungfuls of night air now, a burning sensation settling into his thighs and calves.

Two thousand paces left, in so far as he could judge. The roar was fierce, and sheets of sand whipped around him from behind. He could feel the rage of the goddess in the air.

Fifteen hundred remaining—

A sudden hush – as if he'd entered a cave – then he was cartwheeling through the air, the contents of his pack loose and spinning away from the shredded remains on his back.

Filling his ears, the echoes of a sound – a bone-jarring impact – that he had not even heard. Then he struck the ground and rolled, knives flying from his hands. His back and shoulders were sodden, covered in warm blood, his chain armour shredded by the enkar'al's talons.

A mocking blow, for all the damage inflicted. The creature could more easily have ripped his head off.

And now a familiar voice entered his skull, '*Aye, I could have killed you outright, but this pleases me more. Run, mortal, to that saving wall of sand.*'

'I freed you,' Kalam growled, spitting out blood and grit. 'And this is your gratitude?'

'*You delivered pain. Unacceptable. I am not one to feel pain. I only deliver it.*'

'Well,' the assassin grated as he slowly rose to his hands and knees, 'it comforts me to know in these, my last moments, that you'll not live long in this new world with that attitude. I'll wait for you other side of Hood's gate, Demon.'

Enormous talons snapped around him, their tips punching through chain – one in his lower back, three others in his abdomen – and he was lifted from the ground.

Then flung through the air once more. This time he descended from a distance of at least three times his own height, and when he struck blackness exploded in his mind.

Consciousness returned, and he found himself lying sprawled on the cracked pan, the ground directly beneath him muddy with his own blood. The stars were swimming wildly overhead, and he was unable to move. A deep thrumming reverberation rang in the back of his skull, coming up from his spine.

'*Ah, awake once more. Good. Shall we resume this game?*'

'As you like, Demon. Alas, I'm no longer much of a plaything. You broke my back.'

'*Your error was in landing head first, mortal.*'

'My apologies.' But the numbness was fading – he could

feel a tingling sensation, spreading out through his limbs. 'Come down and finish it, Demon.'

He felt the ground shake as the enkar'al settled on the ground somewhere to his left. Heavy thumping steps as the creature approached. *Tell me your name, mortal. It is the least I can do, to know the name of my first kill after so many thousands of years.*

'Kalam Mekhar.'

'And what kind of creature are you? You resemble Imass . . .'

'Ah, so you were imprisoned long before the Nameless Ones, then.'

'I know nothing of Nameless Ones, Kalam Mekhar.'

He could sense the enkar'al at his side now, a massive, looming presence, though the assassin kept his eyes shut. Then he felt its carnivore's breath gust down on him, and knew the reptile's jaws were opening wide.

Kalam rolled over and drove his right fist down into the creature's throat.

Then released the handful of blood-soaked sand, gravel and rocks it had held.

And drove the dagger in his other hand deep between its breast bones.

The huge head jerked back, and the assassin rolled in the opposite direction, then regained his feet. The motion took all feeling from his legs and he toppled to the ground once more – but in the interval he had seen one of his long-knives, lying point embedded in the ground about fifteen paces distant.

The enkar'al was thrashing about now, choking, talons ripping into the bleached earth in its frenzied panic.

Sensation ebbed back into his legs, and Kalam began dragging himself across the parched ground. Towards the long-knife. *The serpent blade, I think. How appropriate.*

Everything shuddered and the assassin twisted around to see that the creature had leapt, landing splay-legged directly behind him – where he had been a moment ago. Blood was weeping from its cold eyes, which flashed in recognition – before panic overwhelmed them once more. Blood and gritty froth shot out from between its serrated jaws.

He resumed dragging himself forward, and was finally able to draw his legs up and manage a crawl.

Then the knife was in his right hand. Kalam slowly turned about, his head swimming, and began crawling back. 'I have something for you,' he gasped. 'An old friend, come to say hello.'

The enkar'al heaved and landed heavily on its side, snapping the bones of one of its wings in the process. Tail lashing, legs kicking, talons spasming open and shut, head thumping repeatedly against the ground.

'Remember my name, Demon,' Kalam continued, crawling up to the beast's head. He drew his knees under him, then raised the knife in both hands. The point hovered over the writhing neck, rose and fell until in time with its motion. 'Kalam Mekhar ... the one who stuck in your throat.' He drove the knife down, punching through the thick pebbled skin, and the blood of a severed jugular sprayed outward.

Kalam reeled back, barely in time to avoid the deadly fount, and dropped into another roll.

Three times over, to end finally on his back once more. Paralysis stealing through him once again.

He stared upward at the spinning stars ... until the darkness devoured them.

In the ancient fortress that had once functioned as a monastery for the Nameless Ones, but had been old even then – its makers long forgotten – there was only darkness. On its lowermost level there was a single chamber, its floor rifted above a rushing underground river.

In the icy depths, chained by Elder sorcery to the bedrock, lay a massive, armoured warrior. Thelomen Toblakai, pure of blood, that had known the curse of demonic possession, a possession that had devoured its own sense of self – the noble warrior had ceased to exist long, long ago.

Yet now, the body writhed in its magical chains. The demon was gone, fled with the outpouring of blood – blood that should never have existed, given the decayed state of the creature, yet existed it had, and the river had swept it to freedom. To a distant waterhole, where a bull enkar'al – a beast in its prime – had been crouching to drink.

The enkar'al had been alone for some time – not even the spoor of others of its kind could be found anywhere nearby. Though it had not sensed the passage of time, decades had in fact passed since it last encountered its own kind. Indeed, it had been fated – given a normal course of life – to never again mate. With its death, the extinction of the enkar'al anywhere east of the Jhag Odhan would have been complete.

But now its soul raged in a strange, gelid body – no wings, no thundering hearts, no prey-laden scent to draw from the desert's night air. Something held it down, and imprisonment was proving a swift path to mindless madness.

Far above, the fortress was silent and dark. The air was motionless once more, barring the faint sighs from draughts that flowed in from the outer chambers.

Rage and terror. Unanswered, except by the promise of eternity.

Or so it would have remained.

Had the Beast Thrones stayed unoccupied.

Had not the reawakened wolf gods known an urgent need . . . for a champion.

Their presence reached into the creature's soul, calmed it with visions of a world where there were enkar'al in the muddy skies, where bull males locked jaws in the fierce heat of the breeding season, the females banking in circles far above. Visions that brought peace to the ensnared soul – though with it came a deep sorrow, for the body that now clothed it was . . . *wrong*.

546

A time of service, then. The reward – to rejoin its kin in the skies of another realm.

Beasts were not strangers to hope, nor unmindful of such things as rewards.

Besides, this champion would taste blood . . . and soon.

For the moment, however, there was a skein of sorcerous bindings to unravel . . .

Limbs stiff as death. But the heart laboured on.

A shadow slipping over Kalam's face awakened him. He opened his eyes.

The wrinkled visage of an old man hovered above him, swimming behind waves of heat. Dal Honese, hairless, jutting ears, his expression twisted into a scowl. 'I was looking for you!' he accused, in Malazan. 'Where have you been? What are you doing lying out here? Don't you know it's *hot*?'

Kalam closed his eyes again. 'Looking for me?' He shook his head. 'No-one's looking for me,' he continued, forcing his eyes open once more despite the glare lancing up from the ground around the two men. 'Well, not any more, that is—'

'Idiot. Heat-addled fool. Stupid – but maybe I should be crooning, encouraging even? Will that deceive him? Likely. A change in tactics, yes. You! Did you kill this enkar'al? Impressive! Wondrous! But it stinks. Nothing worse than a rotting enkar'al, except for the fact that you've fouled yourself. Lucky for you your urinating friend found me, then led me here. Oh, and it's marked the enkar'al, too – what a stench! Sizzling hide! Anyway, it'll carry you. Yes, back to my haunted abode—'

'Who in Hood's name are you?' Kalam demanded, struggling to rise. Though the paralysis was gone, he was crusted in dried blood, the puncture wounds burning like coals, his every bone feeling brittle.

'Me? You do not know? You do not recognize the very famosity exuding from me? Famosity? There must be such a word. I used it! The act of being famous. Of course. Most devoted servant of Shadow! Highest Archpriest Iskaral Pust! God to the bhok'arala, bane of spiders, Master Deceiver of all the world's Soletaken and D'ivers! And now, your saviour! Provided you have something for me, that is, something to deliver. A bone whistle? A small bag, perchance? Given to you in a shadowy realm, by an even shadowier god? A bag, you fool, filled with dusky diamonds?'

'You're the one, are you?' Kalam groaned. 'The gods help us. Aye, I have the diamonds—' He tried to sit up, reaching for the pouch tucked under his belt – and caught a momentary glimpse of the azalan demon, flowing amidst shadows behind the priest, until oblivion found him.

When he awoke once more he was lying on a raised stone platform that suspiciously resembled an altar. Oil lamps flickered from ledges on the walls. The room was small, the air acrid.

Healing salves had been applied – and likely sorcery as well – leaving him feeling refreshed, though his joints remained stiff, as if he had not moved for some time. His clothing had been removed, a thin blanket stiff with grime laid over him. His throat ached with a raging thirst.

The assassin slowly sat up, looking down at the purple weals where the enkar'al's talons had plunged, then almost jumped at a scurrying sound across the floor – a bhok'aral, casting a single, absurdly guilty, glance over a knobby shoulder a moment before darting out through the doorway.

A dusty jug of water and a clay cup lay on a reed mat on the stone floor. Flinging the blanket aside, Kalam moved towards it.

A bloom of shadows in one corner of the chamber caught his attention as he poured a cup, so he was not surprised to see Iskaral Pust standing there when the shadows faded.

The priest was hunched down, looking nervously at the doorway, then tiptoeing up to the assassin. 'All better now, yes?'

'Is there need to whisper?' Kalam asked.

The man flinched. 'Quiet! My wife!'

'Is she sleeping?'

Iskaral Pust's small face was so like a bhok'aral's that the assassin was wondering at the man's bloodlines – *no, Kalam, don't be ridiculous* – 'Sleeping?' the priest sputtered. 'She *never* sleeps! No, you fool, she *hunts*!'

'Hunts? What does she hunt?'

'Not what. Who. She hunts for me, of course.' His eyes glittered as he stared at Kalam. 'But has she found me? No! We've not seen each other for months! Hee hee!' He jutted his head closer. 'It's a perfect marriage. I've never been happier. You should try it.'

Kalam poured himself another cup. 'I need to eat—'

But Iskaral Pust was gone.

He looked around, bemused.

Sandalled feet approached from the corridor without, then a wild-haired old woman leapt in through the doorway. Dal Honese – not surprisingly. She was covered in cobwebs. She glared about. 'Where is he? He was here, wasn't he? I can smell him! The bastard was here!'

Kalam shrugged. 'Look, I'm hungry—'

'Do I look appetising?' she snapped. A quick, appraising glance at Kalam. 'Mind you, you do!' She began searching the small room, sniffing at corners, crouching to peer into the jug. 'I know every room, every hiding place,' she muttered, shaking her head. 'And why not? When veered, I was everywhere—'

'You're a Soletaken? Ah, spiders . . .'

'Oh, aren't you a clever and long one!'

'Why not veer again? Then you could search—'

'If I veered, *I'd* be the one hunted! Oh no, old Mogora's not stupid, she won't fall for that! I'll find him! You watch!'

She scurried from the room.

Kalam sighed. With luck, his stay with these two would be a short one.

Iskaral Pust's voice whispered in his ear. 'That was close!'

Cheekbone and orbital ridge were both shattered, the pieces that remained held in place by strips of withered tendon and muscle. Had Onrack possessed anything more than a shrunken, mummified nugget for an eye, it would have been torn away by the Tiste Liosan's ivory scimitar.

There was, of course, no effect on his vision, for his senses existed in the ghostly fire of the Tellann Ritual – the unseen aura hovering around his mangled body, burning with memories of completeness, of vigour. Even so, the severing of his left arm created a strange, queasy sense of conflict, as if the wound bled in both the world of the ritual ghost-shape and in the physical world. A seeping away of power, of self, leaving the T'lan Imass warrior with vaguely confused thoughts, a malaise of ephemeral . . . *thinness*.

He stood motionless, watching his kin prepare for the ritual. He was outside them, now, no longer able to conjoin his spirit with theirs. From this jarring fact there was emerging, in Onrack's mind, a strange shifting of perspective. He saw only their physicality now – the ghost-shapes were invisible to his sight.

Withered corpses. Ghastly. Devoid of majesty, a mockery of all that was once noble. Duty and courage had been made animate, and this was all the T'lan Imass were, and had been for hundreds of thousands of years. Yet, without choice, such virtues as duty and courage were transformed into empty, worthless words. Without mortality, hovering like an unseen sword overhead, meaning was without relevance, no matter the nature – or even the motivation behind – an act. Any act.

Onrack believed he was finally seeing, when fixing his gaze upon his once-kin, what all those who were not T'lan Imass saw, when looking upon these horrific, undead warriors.

An extinct past refusing to fall to dust. Brutal reminders of rectitude and intransigence, of a vow elevated into insanity.

And this is how I have been seen. Perhaps how I am still seen. By Trull Sengar. By these Tiste Liosan. Thus. How, then, shall I feel? What am I supposed to feel? And when last did feelings even matter?

Trull Sengar spoke beside him. 'Were you anyone else, I would hazard to read you as being thoughtful, Onrack.' He was seated on a low wall, the box of Moranth munitions at his feet.

The Tiste Liosan had pitched a camp nearby, a picket line paced out and bulwarks of rubble constructed, three paces between each single-person tent, horses within a staked-out rope corral – in all, the precision and diligence verging on the obsessive.

'Conversely,' Trull continued after a moment, his eyes on the Liosan, 'perhaps your kind are indeed great thinkers. Solvers of every vast mystery. Possessors of all the right answers ... if only I could pose the right questions. Thankful as I am for your companionship, Onrack, I admit to finding you immensely frustrating.'

'Frustrating. Yes. We are.'

'And your companions intend to dismantle what's left of you once we return to our home realm. If I was in your place, I'd be running for the horizon right now.'

'Flee?' Onrack considered the notion, then nodded. 'Yes, this is what the renegades – those we hunt – did. And yes, now I understand them.'

'They did more than simply flee,' Trull said. 'They found someone or something else to serve, to avow allegiance to ... while at the moment, at least, that option is not available to you. Unless, of course, you choose those Liosan.'

'Or you.'

Trull shot him a startled look, then grinned. 'Amusing.'

'Of course,' Onrack added, 'Monok Ochem would view

551

such a thing as a crime, no different from that which has been committed by the renegades.'

The T'lan Imass had nearly completed their preparations. The bonecaster had inscribed a circle, twenty paces across, in the dried mud with a sharpened bhederin rib, then had scattered seeds and dust-clouds of spores within the ring. Ibra Gholan and his two warriors had raised the equivalent of a sighting stone – an elongated chunk of mortared fired bricks from a collapsed building wall – a dozen paces outside the circle, and were making constant adjustments beneath the confusing play of light from the two suns, under Monok Ochem's directions.

'That won't be easy,' Trull observed, watching the T'lan Imass shifting the upright stone, 'so I suppose I can expect to keep my blood for a while longer.'

Onrack slowly swung his misshapen head to study the Tiste Edur. 'It is you who should be fleeing, Trull Sengar.'

'Your bonecaster explained that they needed only a drop or two.'

My bonecaster . . . no longer. 'True, if all goes well.'

'Why shouldn't it?'

'The Tiste Liosan. Kurald Thyrllan – this is the name they give their warren. Seneschal Jorrude is not a sorcerer. He is a warrior-priest.'

Trull frowned. 'It is the same for the Tiste Edur, for my people, Onrack—'

'And as such, the seneschal must kneel before his power. Whereas a sorcerer commands power. Your approach is fraught, Trull Sengar. You assume that a benign spirit gifts you that power. If that spirit is usurped, you may not even know it. And then, you become a victim, a tool, manipulated to serve unknown purposes.'

Onrack fell silent, and watched the Tiste Edur . . . as a deathly pallor stole the life from Trull's eyes, as the expression became one of horrified revelation. *And so I give answer to a question you were yet to ask. Alas, this does not make me all-knowing.* 'The spirit that grants the seneschal his power may be corrupted. There is no way to know . . . until it is unleashed. And even then, malign spirits are highly skilled at hiding. The one named Osseric is . . . lost. Osric, as humans know him. No, I do not know the source of Monok Ochem's knowledge in this matter. Thus, the hand behind the seneschal's power is probably *not* Osseric, but some other entity, hidden behind the guise and the name of Osseric. Yet these Tiste Liosan proceed unawares.'

It was clear that Trull Sengar was, for the moment, unable to offer comment, or pose questions, so Onrack simply continued – wondering at the sudden extinction of his own reticence – 'The seneschal spoke of their own hunt. In pursuit of trespassers who crossed through their fiery warren. But these trespassers are not the renegades we hunt. Kurald Thyrllan is not a sealed warren. Indeed, it lies close to our own Tellann – for Tellann draws from it. Fire is life and life is fire. Fire is the war against the cold, the slayer of ice. It is our salvation. Bonecasters have made use of Kurald Thyrllan. Probably, others have as well. That such incursions should prove cause for enmity among the Liosan was never considered. For it seemed there *were no Tiste Liosan.*

'Monok Ochem considers this, now. He cannot help but consider this. Where are these Liosan from? How distant – how remote – their home? Why are they now awakened to resentment? What does the one hidden behind the guise of Osseric now seek? Where—'

'Stop! Please, Onrack, stop! I need to think – I need—' Trull rose suddenly, flinging a dismissive gesture at the T'lan Imass, then strode off.

'I think,' Onrack said quietly to himself as he watched the Tiste Edur storm away, 'that I will revert to reticence.'

A small chunk of mortared brick had now been positioned in the centre of the ring; its top was being inscribed with slashes and grooves by the bonecaster, and Onrack realized that Monok Ochem had already discerned the celestial patterns of the two suns and the numerous moons that wheeled overhead.

Colours played constantly over this landscape in sullen blood hues, occasionally overwhelmed by deep blues that limned everything in a cold, almost metallic sheen. At the moment, magenta dominated, a lurid tone as of reflected conflagration. Yet the air remained still and damp, eternally pensive.

A world aswarm in shadows. The hounds that Onrack had inadvertently freed from their stone prisons had cast scores of them. The battered warrior wondered where the two beasts had gone. He was fairly certain that they were no longer in this realm, in this place known as the Nascent.

Shadow and spirit reunited ... the beasts had possessed something ... unusual. As if each was shaped of two distinct powers, two aspects chained together. Onrack had unleashed those hounds, yet, on second consideration, perhaps not freed them. *Shadow from Dark. That which is cast ... from that which has cast it.* The warrior lowered his gaze to study his own multiple shadows. Was there tension between him and them? Clearly, there was a binding. But he was the master and they his slaves.

Or so it seemed ... *Silent kin of mine. You precede. You follow. You strive on my flanks. Huddle beneath me. Your world finds its shape from my bone and flesh. Yet your breadth and length belong to Light. You are the bridge between worlds, yet you cannot be walked.* No substance, then. Only perception.

'Onrack, you are closed to us.'

He lifted his gaze. Monok Ochem stood before him. 'Yes, Bonecaster. I am closed to you. Do you doubt me?'

'I would know your thoughts.'

'They are ... insubstantial.'

Monok Ochem cocked his head. 'None the less.'

Onrack was silent for a long moment. 'Bonecaster. I remain bound to your path.'

'Yet you are severed.'

'The renegade kin must be found. They are our ... shadows. I now stand between you and them, and so I can guide you. I now know where to look, the signs to seek.

Destroy me and you shall lose an advantage in your hunt.'

'You bargain for . . . persistence?'

'I do, Bonecaster.'

'Tell us, then, the path the renegades have taken.'

'I shall . . . when it becomes relevant.'

'Now.'

'No.'

Monok Ochem stared down at the warrior, then swung away and returned to the circle.

Tellann commanded that place now. Tundra flowers had erupted from the mud, along with lichen and mosses. Blackflies swarmed at ankle height. A dozen paces beyond stood the four Tiste Liosan, their enamel armour glowing in the strange magenta light.

Trull Sengar watched from a position fifteen paces to Onrack's left, his arms tightly crossed about himself, a haunted expression on his lean face.

Monok Ochem approached the seneschal. 'We are ready, Liosan.'

Jorrude nodded. 'Then I shall begin my prayers, Undead Priest. And there shall be proof that our Master, Osric, is far from lost to us. You shall know his power.'

The bonecaster said nothing.

'And when,' Trull asked, 'shall I start spraying blood around? Which one of you has the pleasure of wounding me?'

'The choice is yours,' Monok Ochem replied.

'Good. I choose Onrack – he's the only one here I'm prepared to trust. Apologies to those of you who might take offence at that.'

'That task should be mine,' Seneschal Jorrude said. 'Blood lies at the heart of Osric's power—'

Onrack was alone noting the slight start from the bonecaster at that, and the warrior nodded to himself. Much answered with those words.

'—and indeed,' Jorrude continued, 'I shall have to spill some of my own as well.'

But Trull Sengar shook his head. 'No. Onrack . . . or no-one.' And he then uncrossed his arms, revealing a clay ball in each hand.

There was a snort from Jorrude, and the Liosan named Enias growled, 'Grant me leave to kill him, Seneschal. I shall ensure that there is no shortage of Edur blood.'

'Do so, and I guarantee the same lack of shortage,' Trull responded, 'concerning Liosan blood. Bonecaster, do you recognize these munitions?'

'They are known by the Malazans as cussers,' answered Ibra Gholan, the clan leader. 'One will suffice, given our collective proximities.'

Trull grinned over at the T'lan Imass warrior. 'Even that dhenrabi skin on your shoulders won't help much, will it?'

'True,' Ibra Gholan replied. 'While armour is not entirely ineffectual, such value invariably proves wanting.'

Monok Ochem turned to the seneschal. 'Agree to the stipulation,' he said. 'Begin your prayers, Liosan.'

'Such commands are not for you to utter,' Jorrude snarled. He glared at Trull. 'You, Edur, have much to learn. We shall create this gate, and then there will come a reckoning.'

Trull Sengar shrugged. 'As you like.'

Adjusting his bloodstained cloak, the seneschal strode into the centre of the circle. Then he lowered himself onto his knees, chin settling onto his chest, closing his gleaming, silver eyes.

Blackflies formed a humming cloud around him.

Whatever link existed between Jorrude and his god proved both strong and swift. Gold fire flickered into life here and there beyond the circumference of the circle. The remaining three Tiste Liosan returned to their own camp and began packing.

Monok Ochem strode into the circle, followed by the two clansmen Haran Epal and Olar Shayn. The clan leader faced Onrack and said, 'Guard your companion close, if you would he survive. Cleave to that singular concern, Onrack. No matter what you might witness.'

'I shall,' Onrack replied. In many essential matters, the warrior realized, he had no need for a binding of souls with his kin . . . to know their minds. He strode to Trull Sengar. 'Follow me,' he instructed. 'We must now enter the circle.'

The Tiste Edur scowled, then nodded. 'Take the box of munitions, then. My hands are full.'

Trull had fixed straps to the box. Onrack collected it then led his companion into the circle.

The three Liosan had completed breaking their camp and were now saddling their white horses.

The fires continued flickering in and out of existence around the periphery, none large enough to pose a threat. But Onrack could sense the approach of the Liosan god. Or at least the outermost layers of its disguise. Cautious, mistrustful – not of the seneschal, of course – but for this to work, the hidden spirit would have to come to this realm's very edge.

And when Jorrude offered up his own blood, the bridge of power between him and his god would be complete.

The thud of horse hoofs announced the arrival of the other three Liosan, the four mounts in tow.

Onrack drew forth from beneath rotted furs a small crescent-shaped obsidian knife, single-edged on the inward-curving line, and held it out to Trull. 'When I so instruct you, Trull Sengar, cut yourself. A few drops will suffice.'

The Tiste Edur frowned. 'I thought you were—'

'I would not be distracted, in the moment of crossing.'

'Distracted?'

'Say nothing. Attend to yourself.'

His frown deepening, Trull crouched to return the two cussers to the box, affixed the lid once more and slung the contrivance over a shoulder, then straightened and accepted the stone blade.

The flames were now growing, unbroken immediately beyond the inscribed ring. Kurald Thyrllan, but the ascendant shaping it remained unseen. Onrack wondered at its nature. If these Liosan were any indication, it found sustenance from purity, as if such a thing was even possible. Intransigence. *Simplicity.*

The simplicity of blood, a detail whispering of antiquity, of primeval origins. A spirit, then, before whom a handful of savages once bowed. There had been many such entities, once, born of that primitive assertion of meaning to object, meaning shaped by symbols and portents, scratchings on rock-faces and in the depths of caves.

No shortage . . . but tribes died out, were winnowed out, were devoured by more powerful neighbours. The secret language of the scratchings, the caves with their painted images that came alive to the pounding of drums – those most mysterious cathedrals of thunder . . . all lost, forgotten. And with that fading away of secrets, so too the spirits themselves dwindled, usually into oblivion.

That some lingered was not surprising to Onrack. Even unto usurping the faith of a new tribe. What was new to the warrior, rising like a tightness into his desiccated throat, was the sense of . . . pathos.

In the name of purity, the Liosan worship their god. In the name of . . . of nostalgia, the god worships what was and shall never again return.

The spilling of blood was the deadliest of games.

As is about to be seen.

A harsh cry from the seneschal, and the flames rose into a wall on all sides, raging with unbridled power. Jorrude had laid open his left palm. Within the circle, a swirling wind rose, laden with the smells of a thaw – of spring in some northern clime.

Onrack turned to Trull. 'Now.'

The Tiste Edur slashed the obsidian blade across the edge of his left hand, then stared down disbelieving at the gash – clear, the flesh neatly parted, frighteningly deep.

The blood emerged a moment later, welling forth, red roots racing and branching down his grey-skinned forearm.

The gate seemed to tear itself open, surrounding the group within the circle. Spiralling tunnels reached outward from it, each seeming to lead on into eternity. A roar of chaos on the flanks, miasmic grey fire in the spaces between the portals. Onrack reached out to catch a reeling Trull Sengar. The blood was spraying out from his left hand, as if the Edur's entire body was being squeezed by some unseen, but unrelenting pressure.

Onrack glanced over – to see Monok Ochem standing alone, head tilted back as the winds of Tellann whipped the silver-tipped fur around his unhelmed head. Beyond the bonecaster, a momentary glimpse of Ibra Gholan, Olar Shayn and Haran Epal vanishing down a tunnel of fire.

The seneschal's companions were now running towards their master's prone, unconscious body.

Satisfied that the others were occupied – temporarily unmindful – Onrack dragged Trull close until their bodies made contact, the T'lan Imass managing a one-armed embrace. 'Hold on to me,' he rasped. 'Trull Sengar, hold on to me – but free your left hand.'

Fingers clutched at Onrack's ragged cloak, began dragging with growing weight. The T'lan Imass relinquished his one-armed hug and snapped out his hand – to close on Trull's. The blood bit like acid into flesh that had forgotten pain. Onrack almost tore his grip free in the sudden, overwhelming agony, but then he tightened his hold and leaned close to the Tiste Edur. 'Listen! I, Onrack, once of the Logros but now stranger to the Ritual, avow service to Trull Sengar of the Tiste Edur. I pledge to defend your life. This vow cannot be sundered. Now, lead us from here!'

Their hands still locked together, sealed for the moment by a slowing flow of blood, Onrack pulled Trull around until they faced one of the spiralling tunnels. Then they plunged forward.

Onrack saw the bonecaster wheel to face them. But the distance was too great, and the ritual had already begun tearing itself apart.

Then Monok Ochem veered into his Soletaken form. A blur, then a massive, hulking beast was thundering in pursuit.

Onrack sought to tear his grip from Trull to reach for his sword, to block the Soletaken and so ensure Trull's escape – but the Edur had turned, had seen, and would not let go. Instead, he pulled, hard. Onrack stumbled back.

Knuckles pounded on the ground – the ape that Monok Ochem had become was, despite being gaunt with death, enormous. Patched grey and black skin, tufts of silver-tipped black hair on the broad shoulders and the nape of the neck, a sunken-eyed, withered face, jaws stretching wide to reveal canines – voicing a deep, grating roar.

Then Monok Ochem simply vanished. Swallowed by a surge of chaos.

Onrack stumbled over something, crashed down onto hard-packed ground, gravel skidding under him. Beside him, on his knees, was Trull Sengar.

The fall had broken their grip, and the Tiste Edur was staring down at his left hand – where only a thin, white scar remained.

A single sun blazed down on them, and Onrack knew they had returned to his native realm.

The T'lan Imass slowly climbed to his feet. 'We must leave this place, Trull Sengar. My kin shall pursue. Perhaps only Monok Ochem remains, but he will not relent.'

Trull raised his head. 'Remains? What do you mean? Where did the others go?'

Onrack looked down on the Tiste Edur. 'The Liosan were too late to realize. The turning of Tellann succeeded in driving all awareness from the seneschal. They were entirely unprepared. Ibra Gholan, Olar Shayn and Haran Epal walked into the warren of Kurald Thyrllan.'

'Walked into? Why?'

Onrack managed a one-sided shrug. 'They went, Trull Sengar, to kill the Liosan god.'

* * *

Little more than bones and scraps of armour, what had once been an army lay in the thick grey ash, encircling a steeply sloped pit of some kind. There was no way to tell whether the army had faced outward – defending some sort of subterranean entrance – or inward, seeking to prevent an escape.

Lostara Yil stood ankle-deep in the trail's ashes. Watching Pearl walk gingerly among the bones, reaching down every now and then to drag some item free for a closer look. Her throat was raw, her hatred of the Imperial Warren deepening with every passing moment.

'The scenery is unchanging,' Pearl had noted, 'yet never the same. I have walked this path before – this very path. There were no ruins, then. And no heap of bones or hole in the ground.'

And no winds to shift the ashes.

But bones and other larger objects had a way of rising to the surface, eventually. Or so it was true in the sands – why should ashes be any different? None the less, some of those ruins were massive. Vast expanses of flagstones, unstained, devoid even of dust. Tall, leaning towers – like the rotted stubs of fangs. A bridge spanning nothing, its stones so precisely set that a knife-tip could not be slipped between them.

Slapping the dust from his gloved hands, Pearl strode up. 'Curious indeed.'

Lostara coughed, hacked out grey sputum. 'Just find us a gate and get us out of here,' she rasped.

'Ah, well, as to that, my dear, the gods are smiling down upon us. I have found a gate, and a lively one it is.'

She scowled at him, knowing he sought the inevitable question from her, but she was in no mood to ask it.

'Alas, I know your thoughts,' Pearl continued after a moment, with a quick wry grin. He pointed back towards the pit. 'Down there . . . unfortunately. Thus, we are left with a dire choice. Continue on – and risk you spitting out your lungs – in search of a more easily approachable gate. Or take the plunge, as it were.'

'You're leaving the choice to me?'

'Why not? Now, I'm waiting. Which shall it be?'

She drew the scarf over her mouth and nose once more, tightened the straps on her pack, then marched off . . . towards the pit.

Pearl fell in step. 'Courage and foolishness, the distinction so often proves problematic—'

'Except in hindsight.' Lostara kicked herself free of a rib cage that had fouled her stride, then swore at the resultant clouds of ash and dust. 'Who were these damned soldiers? Do you know?'

'I may possess extraordinary powers of observation and unfathomable depths of intelligence, lass, but I cannot read when there is nothing to be seen. Corpses. Human, in so far as I can tell. The only detail I can offer is that they fought this battle knee-deep in this ash . . . meaning—'

'That whatever crisped this realm had already happened,' Lostara cut in. 'Meaning, they either survived the event, or were interlopers . . . like us.'

'Very possibly emerging from the very gate we now approach.'

'To cross blades with whom?'

Pearl shrugged. 'I have no idea. But I have a few theories.'

'Of course you do,' she snapped. 'Like all men – you hate to say you don't know and leave it at that. You have an answer to every question, and if you don't you make one up.'

'An outrageous accusation, my dear. It is not a matter of making up answers, it is rather an exercise in conjecture. There is a difference—'

'That's what you say, not what I have to listen to. All the time. Endless words. Does a man even exist who believes there can be too many words?'

'I don't know,' Pearl replied.

After a moment she shot him a glare, but he was studiously staring ahead.

They came to the edge of the slope and halted, looking down.

The descent would be treacherous, jumbled bones, swords jagged with decay, and an unknown depth of ash and dust. The hole at the base was perhaps ten paces across, yawning black.

'There are spiders in the desert,' Lostara muttered, 'that build such traps.'

'Slightly smaller, surely.'

She reached down and collected a thigh bone, momentarily surprised at its weight, then tossed it down the slope.

A thud.

Then the packed ash beneath their boots vanished.

And down they went, amidst explosions of dust, ashes and splinters of bone. A hissing rush – blind, choking – then they were falling through a dry downpour. To land heavily on yet another slope that tumbled them down a roaring, echoing avalanche.

It was a descent through splintered bones and bits of iron, and it seemed unending.

Lostara was unable to draw breath – they were drowning in thick dust, sliding and rolling, sinking then bursting free once more. Down, down through absolute darkness. A sudden, jarring collision with something – possibly wood – then a withered, rumpled surface that seemed tiled, and down once more.

Another thump and tumble.

Then she was rolling across flagstones, pushed on by a wave of ash and detritus, finally coming to a crunching halt, flat on her back, a flow of frigid air rising up on her left side – where she reached out, groping, then down, to where the floor should have been. Nothing. She was lying on an edge, and something told her that, had she taken this last descent, Hood alone would greet her at its conclusion.

Coughing from slightly further up the slope on her right. A faint nudge as the heaped bones and ashes on that side shifted.

Another such nudge, and she would be pushed over the edge. Lostara rolled her head to the left and spat, then tried to speak. The word came out thin and hoarse. 'Don't.'

Another cough, then, 'Don't what?'

'Move.'

'Oh. That doesn't sound good. It's not good, is it?'

'Not good. Another ledge. Another drop . . . this one I think for ever.'

'Judicious use of my warren seems appropriate at this point, don't you think?'

'Yes.'

'A moment, then . . .'

A dull sphere of light emerged, suspended above them, its illumination struggling in the swirling clouds of dust.

It edged closer – grew larger. Brightened.

Revealing all that was above them.

Lostara said nothing. Her chest had contracted as if unwilling to take another breath. Her heart thundered. Wood. An X-shaped cross, tilting over them, as tall as a four-storey building. The glint of enormous, pitted spikes.

And nailed to the cruciform—

—a dragon.

Wings spread, pinned wide. Hind limbs impaled. Chains wrapped about its neck, holding its massive wedge-shaped head up, as if staring skyward—

—to a sea of stars marked here and there with swirls of glowing mist.

'It's not here . . .' Pearl whispered.

'What? It's right above—'

'No. Well, yes. But . . . look carefully. It's enclosed in a sphere. A pocket warren, a realm unto itself—'

'Or the entranceway,' she suggested. 'Sealing—'

'A gate. Queen of Dreams, I think you're right. Even so, its power doesn't reach us . . . thank the spirits and gods and demons and ascendants and—'

'Why, Pearl?'

'Because, lass – that dragon is aspected.'

'I thought they all were.'

'Aye. You keep interrupting me, Lostara Yil. Aspected, I was saying. But not to a warren. Gods! I cannot fathom—'

'Damn you, Pearl!'

'Otataral.'

'What?'

'Otataral. Her aspect is otataral, woman! *This is an otataral dragon.*'

Neither spoke for a time. Lostara began edging herself away from the ledge, shifting weight incrementally, freezing at every increase in the stream of dust slipping away beneath her.

Turning her head, she could make out Pearl. He had unveiled enough of his warren to draw himself upward, hovering slightly above the slope. His gaze remained fixed on the crucified dragon.

'Some help down here . . .' Lostara growled.

He started, then looked down at her. 'Right. My deepest apologies, lass. Here, I shall extend my warren . . .'

She felt herself lifted into the air.

'Make no struggle, lass. Relax, and you'll float up beside me, then pivot upright.'

She forced herself to grow still, but the result was one of rigid immobility.

Pearl chuckled. 'Lacks grace, but it will do.'

A half-dozen heart-beats later she was beside him, hovering upright.

'Try to relax again, Lostara.'

She glared at him, but he was staring upward once more. Reluctantly, she followed his gaze.

'It's still alive, you know,' Pearl whispered.

'Who could have done this?'

'Whoever it was, we have a lot for which to thank him, her . . . or them. This thing devours magic. Consumes warrens.'

'All the old legends of dragons begin with the statement that they are the essence of sorcery. How, then, could this thing even exist?'

'Nature always seeks a balance. Forces strive for symmetry. This dragon answers every other dragon that ever existed, or ever will.'

Lostara coughed and spat once more, then she shivered. 'The Imperial Warren, Pearl. What was it before it was . . . turned to ash?'

He glanced over at her, eyes narrowing. He shrugged and began brushing dust from his clothes. 'I see no value in lingering in this horrendous place—'

'You said there was a gate down here – not *that* one, surely—'

'No. Beyond that ledge. I suspect the last time it was used was by whoever or whatever nailed this dragon onto the cross. Surprisingly, they didn't seal the gate behind them.'

'Careless.'

'More like supremely confident, I would think. We'll make our descent a little more orderly this time, agreed? You need not move – leave this to me.'

'I despise that suggestion in principle, Pearl, but what I hate more is that I see no choice.'

'Haven't you had your fill of bared bones yet, lass? A simple sweet smile would have sufficed.'

She fixed him with a look of steel.

Pearl sighed. 'A good try, lass. We'll work on it.'

As they floated out over the ledge, Lostara looked up one last time, but not at the dragon, rather at the starscape beyond. 'What do you make of that night sky, Pearl? I do not recognize the constellations . . . nor have I ever before seen those glowing swirls in any night sky I've looked at.'

He grunted. 'That's a foreign sky – as foreign as can be. A hole leading into alien realms, countless strange worlds filled with creatures unimaginable—'

'You really don't know, do you?'

'Of course I don't!' he snapped.

'Then why didn't you just say so?'

'It was more fun conjecturing creatively, of course. How can a man be the object of a woman's interest if he's always confessing his ignorance?'

'You want me to be interested in you? Why didn't you say so? Now I will hang on your every word, of course. Shall I gaze adoringly into your eyes as well?'

He swung on her a glum look. 'Men really have no chance, do they?'

'Typical conceit to have thought otherwise, Pearl.'

They were falling gently through darkness. The sorcerous globe of light followed, but at some distance, smudged and faint behind the suspended dust.

Lostara looked downward, then snapped her head up and closed her eyes, fighting vertigo. Through gritted teeth she asked, 'How much farther do we sink, do you think?'

'I don't know.'

'You could've given a better answer than that!' When he made no reply she glanced over at him through slitted eyes.

He looked positively despondent.

'Well?' she demanded.

'If these are the depths of despair, lass, we're almost there.'

As it turned out, another hundred heartbeats passed before they reached the dust-laden floor. The sphere of light arrived a short while later, illuminating the surrounding area.

The floor was solid rock, uneven and littered with still more bones. No walls were in sight.

The magic that had slowly lowered them dissipated. Pearl took two strides then gestured, and, as if he had flung aside an invisible current, the glimmering outlines of a gate appeared before them. The Claw grunted.

'Now what?' Lostara asked.

'Thyr. Or, to be more precise, the Elder Warren from which Thyr derived. I can't recall its name. Kurald something. Tiste. Not Edur, not Andii, but the other one. And . . .' he added in a low voice, 'the last things to use it left tracks.'

Lostara stared down at the threshold. Somewhat obscured, but discernible none the less. *Dragons.* 'I can make out at least three sets,' she said after a moment.

'More like six, maybe more. Those two sets' – he pointed – 'were the last to leave. Big bastards. Well, that answers the question of who, or what, was capable of subduing the Otataral Dragon. Other dragons, of course. Even so, it could not have been easy.'

'Thyr, you said. Can we use it?'

'Oh, I imagine so.'

'Well, what are we waiting for?'

He shrugged. 'Follow me, then.'

Staying close, she fell in step behind him.

They strode through the gate.

And stumbled into a realm of gold fire.

Wild storms on all horizons, a raging, blinding sky.

They stood on a scorched patch of glittering crystals, the past passage of immense heat having burnished the sharp-edged stones with myriad colours. Other such patches were visible here and there.

Immediately before them rose a pillar, shaped like an elongated pyramid, withered and baked, with only the surface facing them dressed smooth. Words in an unknown language had been carved on it.

The air was searing in Lostara's lungs, and she was sodden with sweat.

But it was, for the moment, survivable.

Pearl walked up to the pillar.

'We have to get out of here!' Lostara shouted.

The firestorms were deafening, but she was certain he heard her, and chose to ignore it.

Lostara rarely tolerated being ignored. She strode after him. 'Listen to me!'

'Names!' He spun to her. 'The names! The ones

who imprisoned the Otataral Dragon! They're all here!'

A growing roar caught her attention, and she turned to face right – to see a wall of flame rolling towards them. 'Pearl!'

He looked, visibly blanched. Stepped back – and his foot skidded out from beneath him, dropping him hard onto his backside. Blankly, he reached down under him, and when he brought his gloved hand back up, it was slick with blood.

'Did you—'

'No!' He clambered upright – and now they both saw the blood-trail, cutting crossways over the patch, vanishing into the flames on the other side.

'Something's in trouble!' Pearl said.

'So are we if we don't get moving!'

The firestorm now filled half the sky – the heat—

He grasped her arm and they plunged around the pillar—

—into a glittering cavern. Where blood had sprayed, gouted out to paint walls and ceiling, and where the shattered pieces of a desiccated warrior lay almost at their feet.

A T'lan Imass.

Lostara stared down at it. Rotted wolf fur the colour of the desert, a broken bone-hafted double-bladed axe of reddish-brown flint almost entirely obscured beneath a pool of blood. Whatever it had attacked had struck back. The warrior's chest was crushed flat. Both arms had been torn off at the shoulders. And the T'lan Imass had been decapitated. A moment's search found the head, lying off to one side.

'Pearl – let's get out of here.'

He nodded. Then hesitated.

'Now what?'

'Your favourite question,' he muttered. Then he scrambled over to collect the severed head. Faced her once more. 'All right. Let's go.'

The strange cave blurred, then vanished.

And they were standing on a sun-bleached rock shelf,

overlooking a stony basin that had once known a stream.

Pearl grinned over at her. 'Home.' He held up the ghastly head before him and spoke to it. 'I know you can hear me, T'lan Imass. I'll find for you the crotch of a tree for your final resting place, provided I get some answers.'

The warrior's reply was strangely echoing, the voice thick and halting. 'What is it you wish to know?'

Pearl smiled. 'That's better. First off, your name.'

'Olar Shayn, of the Logros T'lan Imass. Of Ibra Gholan's clan. Born in the Year of the Two-Headed Snake—'

'Olar Shayn. What in Hood's name were you doing in that warren? Who were you trying to kill?'

'We did not try; we succeeded. The wounds delivered were mortal. It will die, and my kin pursue to witness.'

'It? What, precisely?'

'A false god. I know no more than that. I was commanded to kill it. Now, find for me a worthy place of rest, mortal.'

'I will. As soon as I find a tree.'

Lostara wiped sweat from her brow, then went over to sit on a boulder. 'It doesn't need a tree, Pearl,' she said, sighing. 'This ledge should do.'

The Claw swung the severed head so that it faced the basin and the vista beyond. 'Is this pleasing enough, Olar Shayn?'

'It is. Tell me your name, and you shall know my eternal gratitude.'

'Eternal? I suppose that's not an exaggeration either, is it? Well, I am Pearl, and my redoubtable companion is Lostara Yil. Now, let's find a secure place for you, shall we?'

'Your kindness is unexpected, Pearl.'

'Always is and always will be,' he replied, scanning the ledge.

Lostara stared at her companion, surprised at how thoroughly her sentiments matched those of the T'lan Imass. 'Pearl, do you know precisely where we are?'

He shrugged. 'First things first, lass. I'd appreciate it if you allowed me to savour my merciful moment. Ah! Here's the spot, Olar Shayn!'

Lostara closed her eyes. From ashes and dust . . . to sand. At least it was home. Now, all that remained was finding the trail of a Malazan lass who vanished months ago. 'Nothing to it,' she whispered.

'Did you say something, lass?'

She opened her eyes and studied him where he crouched anchoring stones around the undead warrior's severed head. 'You don't know where we are, do you?'

He smiled. 'Is this a time, do you think, for some creative conjecture?'

Thoughts of murder flashed through her, not for the first time.

CHAPTER THIRTEEN

It is not unusual to see the warrens of Meanas and
Rashan as the closest of kin. Yet are not the games of
illusion and shadow games of light? At some point,
therefore, the notion of distinctions between these
warrens ceases to have meaning. Meanas, Rashan and
Thyr. Only the most fanatic of practitioners among
these warrens would object to this. The aspect all three
share is ambivalence; their games the games of
ambiguity. All is deceit, all is deception. Among them,
nothing – nothing at all – is as it seems.

A Preliminary Analysis of the Warrens
Konoralandas

Fifteen hundred desert warriors had assembled at the
southern edge of the ruined city, their white horses
ghostly through the clouds of amber dust, the glint of
chain vests and scaled hauberks flashing dully every now
and then from beneath golden telabas. Five hundred spare
mounts accompanied the raiders.

Korbolo Dom stood near Sha'ik and Ghost Hands atop a
weathered platform that had once been the foundation of
a temple or public building of some sort, allowing them a
clear view of the assembling warriors.

The Napan renegade watched, expressionless, as
Leoman of the Flails rode up for a last word with the
Chosen One. He himself would not bother with any false
blessings, for he would much prefer that Leoman never

return. And if he must, then not in triumph in any case. And though his scarred face revealed nothing, he well knew that Leoman entertained no delusions about Korbolo's feelings for him.

They were allies only in so far as they both served Sha'ik. And even that was far less certain than it might have outwardly seemed. Nor did the Malazan believe that the Chosen One was deluded as to the spite and enmity that existed between her generals. Her ignorance existed solely in the plans that were slowly, incrementally settling into place to achieve her own demise. Of that Korbolo was certain.

Else she would have acted long before now.

Leoman reined in before the platform. 'Chosen One! We set out now, and when we return we shall bring you word of the Malazan army. Their disposition. Their rate of march—'

'But not,' Sha'ik cut in sternly, 'their mettle. No engagements, Leoman. The first blooding of her army will be here. By my hand.'

Mouth pressing into a thin line, Leoman nodded, then he said, 'Tribes will have conducted raids on them, Chosen One. Likely beginning a league beyond the walls of Aren. They will have already been blooded—'

'I cannot see such minor exchanges as making a difference either way,' Sha'ik replied. 'Those tribes are sending their warriors here – they arrive daily. Your forces would be the largest she would have to face – and I will not have that. Do not argue this point again, Leoman, else I forbid you to leave Raraku!'

'As you say, Chosen One,' Leoman grated. His startling blue eyes fixed on Ghost Hands. 'If you require anything, old man, seek out Mathok.'

Korbolo's brows rose.

'An odd thing to say,' Sha'ik commented. 'Ghost Hands is under *my* protection, after all.'

'Minor requirements only, of course,' Leoman said, 'such

as might prove distracting, Chosen One. You have an army to ready, after all—'

'A task,' Korbolo cut in, 'which the Chosen One has entrusted in me, Leoman.'

The desert warrior simply smiled. Then he collected his reins. 'May the Whirlwind guard you, Chosen One.'

'And you, Leoman.'

The man rode back to his waiting horse warriors.

May your bones grow white and light as feathers, Leoman of the Flails. Korbolo swung to Sha'ik. 'He will disobey you, Chosen One.'

'Of course he will.'

The Napan blinked, then his gaze narrowed. 'Then it would be madness to yield the wall of sand to him.'

She faced him, her eyes questioning. 'Do you fear the Adjunct's army, then? Have you not said to me again and again how superior you have made our forces? In discipline, in ferocity? This is not Onearm's Host you will be facing. It is a shaky mass of recruits, and even should they have known hardening in a minor engagment or two, what chance have they against your Dogslayers? As for the Adjunct . . . leave her to me. Thus, what Leoman does with his fifteen hundred desert wolves is, in truth, without relevance. Or are you now revising all your opinions, Korbolo Dom?'

'Of course not, Chosen One. But a wolf like Leoman should remain leashed.'

'Leashed? The word you'd rather have used is *killed*. Not a wolf, but a mad dog. Well, he shall not be killed, and if indeed he is a mad dog then where better to send him than against the Adjunct?'

'You are wiser in these ways than I, Chosen One.'

Ghost Hands snorted at that, and even Sha'ik smiled. The blood was suddenly hot in Korbolo's face.

'Febryl awaits you in your tent,' Sha'ik said. 'He grows impatient with your lateness, Korbolo Dom. You need not remain here any longer.'

From heat to ice. The Malazan did not trust himself to speak, and at the Chosen One's dismissive wave he almost flinched. After a moment, he managed to find his voice, 'I had best find out what he wants, then,' he said.

'No doubt he views it as important,' Sha'ik murmured. 'It is a flaw among ageing men, I think, that brittle self-importance. I advise you to calm him, Korbolo Dom, and so slow his pounding heart.'

'Sound advice, Chosen One.' With a final salute, Korbolo strode to the platform's steps.

Heboric sighed as the Napan's bootsteps faded behind them. 'The poor bastard's been left reeling. Would you panic them into acting, then? With Leoman now gone? And Toblakai as well? Who is there left to trust, lass?'

'Trust? Do you imagine I trust anyone but myself, Heboric? Oh, perhaps Sha'ik Elder knew trust ... in Leoman and Toblakai. But when they look upon me, they see an impostor – I can see that well enough, so do not attempt to argue otherwise.'

'And what about me?' Heboric asked.

'Ah, Ghost Hands, now we come to it, don't we? Very well, I shall speak plain. Do not leave. Do not leave me, Heboric. Not now. That which haunts you can await the conclusion of the battle to come. When that is done, I shall extend the power of the Whirlwind – back to the very edge of the Otataral Isle. Within that warren, your journey will be virtually effortless. Otherwise, wilful as you are, I fear you will not survive the long, long walk.'

He looked at her, though the effort earned him little more than a blur where she stood, enfolded in her white telaba. 'Is there anything you do not know about, lass?'

'Alas, far too much, I suspect. L'oric, for example. A true mystery, there. He seems able to fend off even the Whirlwind's Elder magic, evading my every effort to discern his soul. And yet he has revealed much to you, I think.'

'In confidence, Chosen One. I am sorry. All I can offer you is this: L'oric is not your enemy.'

'Well, that means more to me than you perhaps realize. Not my enemy. Does that make him my ally, then?'

Heboric said nothing.

After a moment, Sha'ik sighed. 'Very well. He remains a mystery, then, in the most important of details. What can you tell me of Bidithal's explorations of his old warren? Rashan.'

He cocked his head. 'Well, the answer to that, Chosen One, depends in part on your own knowledge. Of the goddess's warren – your *Elder* warren fragment that is the Whirlwind.'

'Kurald Emurlahn.'

He nodded. 'Indeed. And what do you know of the events that saw it torn apart?'

'Little, except that its true rulers had ceased to exist, thus leaving it vulnerable. The relevant fact is this, however: the Whirlwind is the largest fragment in this realm. And its power is growing. Bidithal would see himself as its first – and its penultimate – High Priest. What he does not understand is that there is no such role to be taken. I am the High Priestess. I am the Chosen One. I am the single mortal manifestation of the Whirlwind Goddess. Bidithal would enfold Rashan into the Whirlwind, or, conversely, use the Whirlwind to cleanse the Shadow Realm of its false rulers.' She paused, and Heboric sensed her shrug. 'Those false rulers once commanded the Malazan Empire. Thus. We are all here, preparing for a singular confrontation. Yet what each of us seeks from that battle is at odds. The challenge, then, is to cajole all those disparate motives into one, mutually triumphant effect.'

'That,' Heboric breathed, 'is quite a challenge, lass.'

'And so I need you, Ghost Hands. I need the secret you possess—'

'Of L'oric I can say nothing—'

'Not *that* secret, old man. No, the secret I seek lies in your *hands*.'

He started. 'My hands?'

'That giant of jade you touched – it is defeating the otataral. Destroying it. I need to discover how. I need an answer to otataral, Heboric.'

'But Kurald Emurlahn is Elder, Sha'ik – the Adjunct's sword—'

'Will annihilate the advantage I possess in my High Mages. Think! She knows she can't negate the Whirlwind with her sword . . . so she will not even try! No, instead she will challenge my High Mages. Remove them from the field. She will seek to isolate me—'

'But if she cannot defeat the Whirlwind, what does that matter?'

'Because the Whirlwind, in turn, cannot defeat her!'

Heboric was silent. He had not heard this before, but after a moment's thought, it began to make sense. Kurald Emurlahn might be Elder, but it was also in pieces. Weakened, riven through with Rashan – a warren that was indeed vulnerable to the effects of otataral. The power of the Adjunct's sword and that of Sha'ik's Whirlwind Goddess would effectively cancel each other out.

Leaving the outcome in the hands of the armies themselves. And there, the otataral would cut through the sorcery of the High Mages. *In turn leaving it all to Korbolo Dom. And Korbolo knows it, and he has his own ambitions. Gods, lass, what a mess.* 'Alas, Chosen One,' he muttered, 'I cannot help you, for I do not know why the otataral in me is failing. I have, however, a warning. The power of the jade giant is not one to be manipulated. Not by me, nor by you. If the Whirlwind Goddess seeks to usurp it, she will do more than suffer in the attempt – she will likely get obliterated.'

'Then we must win knowledge without yielding an opportunity.'

'And how in Hood's name do you propose achieving that?'

'I would you give me the answer to that, Heboric.'

Me? 'Then we are lost. I have no control over that alien power. I have no understanding of it at all!'

'Perhaps not yet,' she replied, with a chilling confidence in her voice. 'But you grow ever closer, Heboric. Every time you partake of hen'bara tea.'

The tea? That which you gave me so that I might escape my nightmares? Calling upon Sha'ik Elder's knowledge of the desert, you said. A gift of compassion, I thought. A gift . . . He felt something crumbling inside him. *A fortress in the desert of my heart, I should have known it would be a fortress of sand.*

He swung away, made insensate by layer upon layer of blindness. Numbed to the outside world, to whatever Sha'ik was now saying, to the brutal heat of the sun overhead.

Stay?

He felt no longer able to leave.

Chains. She has made for me a house of chains . . .

Felisin Younger came to the edge of the pit and looked down. The sun had left the floor, leaving naught but darkness below. There was no glimmer of hearthlight, confirming that no-one had come to take up residence in Leoman's abode.

A scraping sound nearby made her turn. Toblakai's once-slavemaster had crawled into view around a wall foundation. His sun-blistered skin was caked in dust and excrement, the stumps at the ends of his arms and legs weeping a yellow, opaque liquid. The first signs of leprosy marred his joints at elbow and knee. Red-rimmed eyes fixed on Felisin and the man offered a blackened smile. 'Ah, child. See me your humble servant. Mathok's warrior—'

'What do you know of that?' she demanded.

The smile broadened. 'I bring word. See me your humble servant. Everyone's humble servant. I have lost my name, did you know that? I knew it once, but it has fled me. My mind. But I do what I am told. I bring word. Mathok's warrior. He cannot meet you here. He would not be seen.

You understand? There, across the plaza, in the sunken ruin. He awaits.'

Well, she considered, the secrecy made sense. Their escape from the camp demanded it, although Heboric Ghost Hands was by far the one most likely to be under surveillance. And he had gone into his tent days ago and refused all visitors. Even so, she appreciated Mathok's caution.

Though she had not known that Toblakai's slavemaster was a part of their conspiracy. 'The sunken temple?'

'Yes, there. See me your humble servant. Go. He awaits.'

She set out across the flagstoned plaza. Hundreds of the camp's destitute had settled here, beneath palm-frond shelters, making no efforts at organization – the expanse reeked of piss and faeces, streams of the foul mess flowing across the stones. Hacking coughs, mumbled entreaties and blessings followed her as she made her way towards the ruin.

The temple's foundation walls were hip high; within, a steep set of stone stairs led down to the subterranean floor. The sun's angle had dipped sufficiently to render the area below in darkness.

Felisin halted at the top of the stairs and peered down, seeking to penetrate the gloom. 'Are you there?' she called.

A faint sound from the far end. The hint of movement.

She descended.

The sandy floor was still warm. Groping, she edged forward.

Less than ten paces from the back wall and she could finally make him out. He was seated with his back to the stone. The gleam of a helm, scale armour on his chest.

'We should wait for night,' Felisin said, approaching. 'Then make our way to Ghost Hands's tent. The time has come – he can hide no longer. What is your name?'

There was no reply.

Something black and smothering rose up to clamp over her mouth, and she was lifted from the ground. The blackness flowed like serpents around her, pinning her arms and binding her thrashing legs. A moment later she hung motionless, suspended slightly above the sandy floor.

A gnarled fingertip brushed her cheek and her eyes widened as a voice whispered in her ear. 'Sweetest child. Mathok's fierce warrior felt Rashan's caress a short while ago, alas. Now, there is only me. Only humble Bidithal, here to welcome you. Here to drink all pleasure from your precious body, leaving naught but bitterness, naught but dead places within. It is necessary, you understand.' His wrinkled hands were stroking, plucking, pinching, pawing her. 'I take no unsavoury pleasure in what I must do. The children of the Whirlwind must be riven barren, child, to make of them perfect reflections of the goddess herself – oh, you did not know that, did you? The goddess cannot create. Only destroy. The source of her fury, no doubt. So it must be with her children. My duty. My task. There is naught for you to do now but surrender.'

Surrender. It had been a long time since she had last been made to surrender, to give away all that was within her. A long time since she'd let darkness devour all that she was. Years ago, she had not known the magnitude of the loss, for there had been nothing to offer a contrast to misery, hunger and abuse.

But all that had changed. She had discovered, under Sha'ik's protective wing, the notion of inviolacy.

And it was that notion that Bidithal now proceeded to destroy.

Lying on the landing at the top of the stairs, the creature that had once been a slavemaster on Genabackis smiled at Bidithal's words, then the smile grew wider at her muffled cries.

Karsa Orlong's favoured child was in the hands of that sick old man. And all that would be done to her could not be undone.

The sick old man had been kindly with his offers of gifts.

580

Not just the impending return of his hands and feet, but the promise of vengeance against the Teblor. He would find his name once more. He knew he would. And with it, the confusion would go away, the hours of blind terror would no longer plague him, and the beatings at the hands of the others in this plaza would cease. It would have to, for he would be their master.

They would pay for what they did. Everyone would pay. As soon as he found his name.

There was weeping now. Despair's own laughter, those racking heaves.

That lass would no longer look upon him with disgust. How could she? She was now like him. It was a good lesson. Viciously delivered – even the slavemaster could see that, could imagine it at least, and wince at the images he conjured in his head. But still, a good lesson.

Time to leave – footsteps approached from below. He slithered back into the daylight, and the sound he made over the gravel, potsherds and sand was strangely reminiscent of chains. Chains dragging in his wake.

Though there had been none to witness it, a strange glow had suffused L'oric's tent shortly after noon. Momentary, then all was normal once more.

Now, as dusk finally approached, a second flare of light burgeoned briefly then died away, again unnoticed.

The High Mage staggered through the warren's impromptu, momentary gate. He was drenched in blood. He stumbled with his burden across the hide-covered floor, then sank to his knees, dragging the misshapen beast into his arms, a single red hand pulling free to stroke its thick, matted hair.

Its whimpers of pain had ceased. Mercifully, for each soft cry had broken anew L'oric's heart.

The High Mage slowly lowered his head, finally stricken with the grief he had been forced to hold back during his desperate, ineffectual efforts to save the ancient demon. He was filled with self-loathing, and he cursed his own complacency. Too long separated, too long proceeding as if the other realms held no danger to them.

And now his familiar was dead, and the mirrored deadness inside him seemed vast. And growing, devouring his soul as sickness does healthy flesh. He was without strength, for the rage had abated.

He stroked the beast's blood-caked face, wondering anew at how its ugliness – now so still and free of pain – could nevertheless trigger depthless wellsprings of love from him. 'Ah, my friend, we were more of a kind than either of us knew. No . . . you knew, didn't you? Thus the eternal sorrow in your eyes, which I saw but chose to ignore, each time I visited. I was so certain of the deceit, you see. So confident that we could go on, undetected, maintaining the illusion that our father was still with us. I was . . .' He crumpled then and could speak no further for a time.

The failure had been his, and his alone. He was here, ensnaring himself in these paltry games, when he should have been guarding his familiar's back – as it had done for him for century upon century.

Oh, it had been close in any case – one less T'lan Imass, and the outcome might have proved different – *no, now you lie to yourself, L'oric. That first axe-blow had done the damage, had delivered the fatal wound. All that transpired thereafter was born of dying rage. Oh, my beloved was no weakling, and the wielder of that stone axe paid for his ambush. And know this, my friend, I left the second one scattered through the fires. Only the clan leader escaped me. But I will hunt him down. This I swear.*

But not yet. He forced clarity into his thoughts, as the weight of the familiar where it lay against his thighs slowly diminished, its very substance ebbing away. Kurald Thyrllan was undefended, now. How the T'lan Imass had managed to penetrate the warren remained a mystery, but they had done so, completing the task they had set out to do with their legendary brutality.

Would the Liosan have sensed the death? Perhaps only the seneschals, at first. Would they speak of it to the others? *Not if they pause, for even a moment, and think about it.* Of course, they had been the victims of the deceit all along. Osric had vanished – their god was gone – and Kurald Thyrllan was ripe for usurpation. And, eventually, those seneschals would realize that, had it truly been Osric behind the power that answered their prayers, then three T'lan Imass warriors would not have been enough – not nearly enough. *My father is many things, but weak does not count among them.*

The withered, bird-sized thing that had been his familiar slipped down to the tent floor. L'oric stared at it, then slowly wrapped himself in his own arms. *I need . . . I need help. Father's companions. Which one? Anomander Rake? No. A companion, yes, on occasion, but never Osric's friend. Lady Envy? Gods, no! Caladan Brood . . . but he carries his own burdens, these days. Thus, but one left . . .*

L'oric closed his eyes, and called upon the Queen of Dreams. 'By your true name, T'riss, I would speak with you. In Osric my father's name, hear my prayer . . .'

A scene slowly formed in his mind, a place unfamiliar to him. A formal garden, high-walled, with a circular pool in the centre. Marble benches waited beneath the shadows of the surrounding growth. The flagstones around the pool were rippled with fine, white sand.

He found himself approaching the pool, staring down into the mirrored surface.

Where swam stars in inky blackness.

'The resemblance is there.'

He turned at the liquid voice, to see a woman now seated on the pool's edge. She looked to be no more than twenty, her hair copper-gold and long. A heart-shaped face, pale, the eyes a light grey. She was not looking at him, her languid gaze on the pool's unmarred surface instead. 'Although,' she added, with a faint smile, 'you have done well to hide your Liosan traits.'

'We are skilled in such things, Queen of Dreams.'

She nodded, still not meeting his eyes. 'As are all the Tiste. Anomander once spent almost two centuries in the guise of a royal bodyguard . . . human, in the manner you have achieved.'

'Mistress,' L'oric said, 'my father—'

'Sleeps. We all long ago made our choices, L'oric. Behind us, our paths stretch, long and worn deep. There is bitter pathos in the prospect of retracing them. Yet, for those of us who remain . . . awake, it seems we do nothing but just that. An endless retracing of paths, yet each step we take is forward, for the path has proved itself to be a circle. Yet – and here is the true pathos – the knowledge never slows our steps.'

'"Wide-eyed stupid", the Malazans say.'

'Somewhat rough-edged, but accurate enough,' she replied. She reached a long-fingered hand down to the water.

L'oric watched it vanish beneath the surface, but it was the scene around them that seemed to waken, a faint turbulence, the hint of ripples. 'Queen of Dreams, Kurald Thyrllan has lost its protector.'

'Yes. Tellann and Thyr were ever close, and now more than ever.'

A strange statement . . . that he would have to think on later. 'I cannot do it alone—'

'No, you cannot. Your own path is about to become fraught, L'oric. And so you have come to me, in the hopes that I will find a suitable . . . protector.'

'Yes.'

'Your desperation urges you to trust . . . where no trust has been earned—'

'You were my father's friend!'

'Friend? L'oric, we were too powerful to know friendship. Our endeavours far too fierce. Our war was with chaos itself, and, at times, with each other. We battled to shape all that would follow. And some of us lost that battle. Do not misapprehend, I held no deep enmity for your father. Rather, he was as unfathomable as the rest of us – a bemusement we all shared, perhaps the only thing we shared.'

'You will not help?'

'I did not say that.'

He waited.

She continued holding her hand beneath the pool's placid surface, had yet to lift her head and meet his eyes. 'This will take some time,' she murmured. 'The present . . . vulnerability . . . will exist in the interval. I have someone in mind, but the shaping towards the opportunity remains distant. Nor do I think my choice will please you. In the meantime . . .'

'Yes?'

She shrugged. 'We had best hope that potentially interested entities remain suitably distracted.'

He saw her expression suddenly change, and when she spoke again the tone was urgent. 'Return to your realm, L'oric! Another circle has been closed – terribly closed.' She drew her hand from the pool.

L'oric gasped.

It was covered in blood.

His eyes snapped open, and he was kneeling in his tent once more. Night had arrived, and the sounds outside were muted, peaceful, a city settling down to its evening meal. Yet, he knew, something horrible had happened. He went still, questing outward. His powers – so weakened, so tremulous – 'Gods below!' A swirl of violence, knotted upon itself, radiating waves of agony – a figure, small, twisted inward, in shredded clothes soaked through with blood, crawling through darkness.

L'oric lurched to his feet, head spinning with anguish.

Then he was outside, and suddenly running.

He found her trail, a smeared track through sand and dust, out beyond the ruins, into the petrified forest. Towards, he knew instinctively, the sacred glade that had been fashioned by Toblakai.

But there would be no succour for her there. Another abode of false gods. And Toblakai was gone, off to cross blades with his own fate.

But she was without clear thought. She was only pain, lancing out to fire instincts of flight. She crawled as would any dying creature.

He saw her at the edge of the glade, small, bedraggled, pulling herself forward in torturous increments.

L'oric reached her side, a hand reaching to settle at the back of her head, onto sweat-snarled hair. She flinched away with a squeal, fingers clawing against his arm. 'Felisin! He's gone! It is L'oric. You are safe with me. Safe, now—'

But still she sought to escape.

'I shall call upon Sha'ik—'

'No!' she shrieked, curling tight on the sand. 'No! She needs him! She needs him still!' Her words were blunted by broken lips but understandable none the less.

L'oric sank back, struck mute by the horror. Not simply a wounded creature, then. A mind clear enough to weigh, to calculate, to put itself aside . . . 'She will know, lass – she can't help but know.'

'No! Not if you help me. Help me, L'oric. Just you – not even Heboric! He would seek to kill Bidithal, and that cannot be.'

'Heboric? *I* want to kill Bidithal!'

'You mustn't. You can't. He has power—'

He saw the shudder run through her at that.

L'oric hesitated, then said, 'I have healing salves, elixirs . . . but you will need to stay hidden for a time.'

'Here, in Toblakai's temple. Here, L'oric.'

'I will bring water. A tent.'

'Yes!'

The rage that burned in him had contracted down to a white-hot core. He struggled to control it, his resolve sporadically weakened by doubts that he was doing the right thing. This was . . . monstrous. There would be an answer to it. There would have to be an answer to it.

Even more monstrous, he realized with a chill, they had all known the risk. *We knew he wanted her. Yet we did nothing.*

Heboric lay motionless in the darkness. He had a faint sense of being hungry, thirsty, but it remained remote. Hen'bara tea, in sufficient amounts, pushed the needs of the outer world away. Or so he had discovered.

His mind was floating on a swirling sea, and it seemed eternal. He was waiting, still waiting. Sha'ik wanted truths. She would get them. And then he was done, done with her.

And probably done with life, as well.

So be it. He had grown older than he had ever expected to, and these extra weeks and months had proved anything but worth the effort. He had sentenced his own god to death, and now Fener would not be there to greet him when he finally stepped free of his flesh and bones. Nor would Hood, come to that.

It did not seem he would awaken from this – he had drunk far more of the tea than he ever had before, and he had drunk it scalding hot, when it was most potent. And now he floated on a dark sea, an invisible liquid warm on his skin, barely holding him up, flowing over his limbs and chest, around his face.

The giant of jade was welcome to him. To his soul, and to whatever was left of his days as a mortal man. The old gifts of preternatural vision had long vanished, the visions of secrets hidden from most eyes – secrets of antiquity, of history – were long gone. He was old. He was blind.

The waters slipped over his face.

And he felt himself sliding down – amidst a sea of stars that swirled in the blackness yet were sharp with sudden clarity. In what seemed a vast distance, duller spheres swam, clustering about the fiery stars, and realization struck him a hammer blow. *The stars, they are as the sun. Each star. Every star. And those spheres – they are worlds, realms, each one different yet the same.*

The Abyss was not as empty as he'd believed it to be. *But . . . where dwell the gods? These worlds – are they warrens? Or are the warrens simply passageways connecting them?*

A new object, growing in his vision as it drifted nearer. A glimmer of murky green, stiff-limbed, yet strangely contorted, torso twisted as if caught in the act of turning. Naked, spinning end over end, starlight playing across its jade surface like beads of rain.

And behind it, another, this one broken – a leg and an arm snapped clean off yet accompanying the rest in its silent, almost peaceful sailing through the void.

Then another.

The first giant cartwheeled past Heboric, and he felt he could simply extend a hand to brush its supple surface as it passed, but he knew it was in truth far too distant for that. Its face came into view. Too perfect for human, the eyes open, an expression too ambiguous to read, though Heboric thought he detected resignation within it.

There were scores now, all emerging from what seemed a single point in the inky depths. Each one displaying a unique posture; some so battered as to be little more than a host of fragments and shards, others entirely unmarred. Sailing out of the blackness. An army.

Yet unarmed. Naked, seemingly sexless. There was a perfection to them – their proportions, their flawless surfaces – that suggested to the ex-priest that the giants could never have been alive. They were constructs, statues in truth, though no two were alike in posture or expression.

Bemused, he watched them spin past. It occurred to him that he could turn, to see if they simply dwindled down to another point far behind him, as if he but lay alongside an eternal river of green stone.

His own motion was effortless.

As he swung round, he saw—

—and cried out.

A cry that made no sound.

A vast – impossibly vast – red-limned wound cut

across the blackness, suppurating flames along its ragged edges. Grey storms of chaos spiralled out in lancing tendrils.

And the giants descended into its maw. One after another. To vanish. Revelation filled his mind.

Thus, the Crippled God was brought down to our world. Through this . . . this terrible puncture. And these giants . . . follow. Like an army behind its commander.

Or an army in pursuit.

Were all of the jade giants appearing somewhere in his own realm? That seemed impossible. They would be present in countless locations, if that was the case. Present, and inescapably visible. No, the wound was enormous, the giants diminishing into specks before reaching its waiting oblivion. A wound such as that could swallow thousands of worlds. Tens, hundreds of thousands.

Perhaps all he witnessed here was but hallucination, the creation of a hen'bara-induced fever.

Yet the clarity was almost painful, the vision so brutally . . . *strange* . . . that he believed it to be true, or at the very least the product of what his mind could comprehend, could give shape to – statues and wounds, storms and bleeding, an eternal sea of stars and worlds . . .

A moment's concentration and he was turning about once more. To face that endless progression.

And then he was moving towards the nearest giant.

It was naught but torso and head, its limbs shorn off and spinning in its wake.

The mass burgeoned swiftly before him, too fast, too huge. Sudden panic gripped Heboric. He could see *into* that body, as if the world within the jade was scaled to his own. The evidence of that was terrible – and horrifying.

Figures. Bodies like his own. Humans, thousands upon thousands, all trapped within the statue. Trapped . . . and screaming, their faces twisted in terror.

A multitude of those faces suddenly swung to him. Mouths opened in silent cries – of warning, or hunger, or fear – there was no way to tell. If they screamed, no sound reached him.

Heboric added his own silent shriek and desperately willed himself to one side, out of the statue's path. For he thought he understood, now – they were prisoners, ensnared within the stone flesh, trapped in some unknown torment.

Then he was past, flung about in the turbulent wake of the broken body's passage. Spinning end over end, he caught a flash of more jade, directly in front of him.

A hand.

A finger, plunging down as if to crush him.

He screamed as it struck.

He felt no contact, but the blackness simply vanished, and the sea was emerald green, cold as death.

And Heboric found himself amidst a crowd of writhing, howling figures.

The sound was deafening. There was no room to move – his limbs were trapped against him. He could not breathe.

A prisoner.

There were voices roaring through his skull. Too many, in languages he could not recognize, much less comprehend. Like storm-waves crashing on a shore, the sound hammered through him, surging and falling, the rhythm quickening as a faint reddish gleam began to stain the green. He could not turn, but did not need to, to know that the wound was moments from swallowing them all.

Then a string of words reached through the tumult, close as if whispered in his ear, and he understood them.

'You came from there. What shall we find, Handless One? What lies beyond the gash?'

Then another voice spoke, louder, more imperious: 'What god now owns your hands, old man? Tell me! Even their ghosts are not here – who is holding on to you? Tell me!'

'There are no gods,' a third voice cut in, this one female.

'So *you* say!' came yet another, filled with spite. 'In your empty, barren, miserable world!'

'Gods are born of belief, and belief is dead. We murdered it, with our vast intelligence. You were too primitive—'

'Killing gods is not hard. The easiest murder of all. Nor is it a measure of intelligence. Not even of civilization. Indeed, the indifference with which such death-blows are delivered is its own form of ignorance.'

'More like forgetfulness. After all, it's not the *gods* that are important, it is the stepping outside of oneself that gifts a mortal with virtue—'

'Kneel before Order? You blind fool—'

'Order? I was speaking of compassion—'

'Fine, then go ahead! Step outside yourself, Leandris! No, better yet. Step *outside*.'

'Only the new one can do that, Cassa. And he'd better be quick about it.'

Twisting, Heboric managed to look down, to catch a glimpse of his left forearm, the wrist, the hand – that was not there. *A god. A god has taken them. I was blind to that – the jade's ghost hands made me blind to that—*

He tilted his head back, as the screams and shrieks suddenly rose higher, deafening, mind-numbing. The world turned red, the red of blood—

Something tugged on his arms. Hard. Once. Twice.

Darkness.

Heboric opened his eyes. Saw above him the colourless canvas of his tent. The air was cold.

A barely human sound escaped him, and he rolled onto his side beneath the blankets, curling tight into a ball. Shivers thrummed through him.

A god. A god has found me.

But which god?

It was night, perhaps only a bell from dawn. The camp outside was silent, barring the distant, sorrow-filled howls of desert wolves.

After a while, Heboric stirred once more. The dung fire was out. No lanterns had been lit. He drew aside the blankets and slowly sat up.

Then stared down at his hands, disbelieving.

They remained ghostly, but the otataral was gone. The power of the jade remained, pulsing dully. Yet now there were slashes of black through it. Lurid – almost liquid – barbs banded the backs of his hands, then tracked upward, shifting angle as they continued up his forearms.

His tattoos had been transformed.

And, in this deepest darkness, he could see. Unhumanly sharp, every detail crisp as if it was day outside.

His head snapped round at a sound and a motion – but it was simply a rhizan, alighting light as a leaf on the tent roof.

A rhizan? On the tent roof?

Heboric's stomach rumbled in sudden hunger.

He looked down at his tattoos once more. *I have found a new god. Not that I was seeking one. And I know who. What.*

Bitterness filled him. 'In need of a Destriant, Treach? So you simply . . . took one. Stole from him his own life. Granted, not much of a life, but still, I owned it. Is this how you recruit followers? Servants? By the Abyss, Treach, you have a lot to learn about mortals.'

The anger faded. There had been gifts, after all. An exchange of sorts. He was no longer blind. Even more extraordinary, he could actually *hear* the sounds of neighbours sleeping in their tents and yurts.

And there, faint on the near-motionless air . . . the smell of . . . violence. But it was distant. The blood had been spilled some time earlier in the night. Some domestic dispute, probably. He would have to teach himself to filter out much of what his newly enlivened senses told him.

Heboric grunted under his breath, then scowled. 'All right, Treach. It seems we both have some learning to do. But first . . . something to eat. And drink.'

When he rose from his sleeping mat, the motion was startlingly fluid, though it was some time before Heboric finally noted the absence of aches, twinges, and the dull throb of his joints.

He was far too busy filling his belly.

Forgotten, the mysteries of the jade giants, the innumerable imprisoned souls within them, the ragged wound in the Abyss.

Forgotten, as well, that faint blood-scented tremor of distant violence . . .

The burgeoning of some senses perforce took away from others. Leaving him blissfully unaware of his newfound singlemindedness. Two truths he had long known did not, for some time, emerge to trouble him.

No gifts were truly clean in the giving.

And nature ever strives for balance. But balance was not a simple notion. Redress was not simply found in the physical world. A far grimmer equilibrium had occurred . . . between the past and the present.

Felisin Younger's eyes fluttered open. She had slept, but upon awakening discovered that the pain had not gone away, and the horror of what he had done to her remained as well, though it had grown strangely cold in her mind.

Into her limited range of vision, close to the sand, a serpent slipped into view directly in front of her face. Then she realized what had awoken her – there were more snakes, slithering over her body. Scores of them.

Toblakai's glade. She remembered now. She had crawled here. And L'oric had found her, only to set off once again. To bring medicine, water, bedding, a tent. He had not yet returned.

Apart from the whispering slither of the snakes, the glade was silent. In this forest, the branches did not move. There were no leaves to flutter in the cool, faint wind. Dried blood in folds of skin stung as she slowly sat up. Sharp pains flared beneath her belly, and the raw wound where he had cut flesh away – there, between her legs – burned fiercely.

'I shall bring this ritual to our people, child, when I am the Whirlwind's High Priest. All girls shall know this, in my newly

shaped world. The pain shall pass. All sensation shall pass. You are to feel nothing, for pleasure does not belong in the mortal realm. Pleasure is the darkest path, for it leads to the loss of control. And we mustn't have that. Not among our women. Now, you shall join the rest, those I have already corrected . . .'

Two such girls had arrived, then, bearing the cutting instruments. They had murmured encouragement to her, and words of welcome. Again and again, in pious tones, they had spoken of the virtues that came of the wounding. Propriety. Loyalty. A leavening of appetites, the withering of desire. All good things, they said to her. Passions were the curse of the world. Indeed, had it not been passions that had enticed her own mother away, that were responsible for her own abandonment? The lure of pleasure had stolen Felisin's mother . . . away from the duties of motherhood . . .

Felisin leaned over and spat into the sand. But the taste of their words would not go away. It was not surprising that men could think such things, could do such things. But that women could as well . . . that was indeed a bitter thing to countenance.

But they were wrong. Walking the wrong trail. Oh, my mother abandoned me, but not for the embrace of some lover. No, it was Hood who embraced her.

Bidithal would be High Priest, would he? The fool. Sha'ik would find a place for him in her temple – or at least a place for his skull. A cup of bone to piss in, perhaps. And that time was not long in coming.

Still . . . too long. Bidithal takes girls into his arms every night. He makes an army, a legion of the wounded, the bereft. And they will be eager to share out their loss of pleasure. They are human, after all, and it is human nature to transform loss into a virtue. So that it might be lived with, so that it might be justified.

A glimmer of dull light distracted her, and she looked up. The carved faces in the trees around her were glowing. Bleeding grey, sorcerous light. Behind each there was . . . a presence.

Toblakai's gods.

'Welcome, broken one.' The voice was the sound of limestone boulders grinding together. 'I am named Ber'ok. Vengeance swarms about you, with such power as to awaken us. We are not displeased with the summons, child.'

'You are Toblakai's god,' she muttered. 'You have nothing to do with me. Nor do I want you. Go away, Ber'ok. You and the rest – go away.'

'We would ease your pain. I shall make of you my special . . . responsibility. You seek vengeance? Then you shall have it. The one who has damaged you would take the power of the desert goddess for himself. He would usurp the entire fragment of warren, and twist it into his own nightmare. Oh, child, though you might believe otherwise – now – the wounding is of no matter. The danger lies in Bidithal's ambition. A knife must be driven into his heart. Would it please you to be that knife?'

She said nothing. There was no way to tell which of the carved faces belonged to Ber'ok, so she could only look from one to the next. A glance to the two fully rendered Toblakai warriors revealed that they possessed no emanation, were grey and lifeless in the pre-dawn darkness.

'Serve us,' Ber'ok murmured, 'and we in turn shall serve you. Give us your answer quickly – someone comes.'

She noted the wavering lantern light on the trail. L'oric. 'How?' she asked the gods. 'How will you serve me?'

'We shall ensure that Bidithal's death is in a manner to match his crimes, and that it shall be . . . timely.'

'And how am I to be the knife?'

'Child,' the god calmly replied, 'you already are.'

CHAPTER FOURTEEN

> The Teblor have long earned their reputation as slayers
> of children, butcherers of the helpless, as mortal
> demons delivered unto the Nathii in a curse altogether
> undeserved. The sooner the Teblor are obliterated from
> their mountain fastnesses the sooner the memory of
> them will finally begin to fade. Until Teblor is no more
> than a name used to frighten children, we see our
> cause as clear and singular.
>
> *The Crusade of 1147*
> Ayed Kourbourn

The wolves loped through the almost luminescent fog, their eyes flashing when they swung their massive heads in his direction. As if he was an elk, struggling through deep snow, the huge beasts kept pace on either side, ghostly, with the implacable patience of the predators they were.

Though it was unlikely these mountain beasts had ever before hunted a Teblor warrior. Karsa had not expected to find snow, particularly since his route took him alongside the north shoulder of the jagged range – it was fortunate that he would not have to climb through any passes. On his right, less than two leagues distant, he could still see the ochre sands of the desert basin, and well knew that down there, the sun blazed hot – the same sun that looked down upon him now, a blurred orb of cold fire.

The snow was shin-deep, slowing his steady jog.

596

Somehow, the wolves managed to run across its wind-hardened, crusty surface, only occasionally plunging a paw through. The fog enshrouding hunters and prey was in fact snow crystals, glittering with bright, blinding light.

Somewhere to the west, Karsa had been told, the range of mountains would end. There would be sea on his right, a narrow rumpled passage of hills ahead and on his left. Across those hills, then southward, there would be a city. Lato Revae. The Teblor had no interest in visiting it, though he would have to skirt it. The sooner he left civilized lands behind, the better. But that was two river crossings distant, with weeks of travel between now and then.

Though he ran alone along the slope, he could feel the presence of his two companions. Ghost spirits at the most, but perhaps nothing more than fractured selves of his own mind. Sceptical Bairoth Gild. Stolid Delum Thord. Facets of his own soul, so that he might persist in this dialogue of self-doubt. Perhaps, then, nothing more than an indulgence.

Or so it would seem, if not for the countless, blood-scoring edges of Bairoth Gild's commentary. At times, Karsa felt as if he was a slave once more, hunched beneath endless flagellation. The notion that he was delivering this to himself was beyond contemplating.

'Not entirely beyond, Warleader, if you'd spare yourself but a moment to regard your own thoughts.'

'Not now, Bairoth Gild,' Karsa replied. 'I am running short on breath as it is.'

'Altitude, Karsa Orlong,' came Delum Thord's voice. 'Though you do not feel it, with each step westward you are descending. Soon you will leave the snow behind. Raraku may have once been an inland sea, but it was a sea couched in the lap of high mountains. Your entire journey thus far, Warleader, has been a descent.'

Karsa could spare that thought only a grunt. He had *felt* no particular descent, but horizons played deceptive games in this land. The desert and mountains ever lied, he had long since discovered.

'When the snow is gone,' Bairoth Gild murmured, 'the wolves will attack.'

'I know. Now be quiet – I see bare rock ahead.'

As did his hunters. They numbered at least a dozen, taller at the shoulder than those of Karsa's homeland, and furred in tones of dun, grey and speckled white. The Teblor watched as four of the beasts sprinted ahead, two on each side, making for the exposed rock.

Growling, Karsa unslung his wooden sword. The bitter cold air had left his hands slightly numb. Had the western end of the Holy Desert held any sources of water, he would not have climbed to these heights, but there was little point in second-guessing that decision now.

The panting breaths of the wolves were audible on either side and behind him.

'They want the sure footing, Warleader. Then again, so do you. Beware the three in your wake – they will strike first, likely a pace or two before you reach the rock.'

Karsa bared his teeth at Bairoth's unnecessary advice. He well knew what these beasts would do, and when.

A sudden thumping of paws, flurries of snow springing into the air, and all the wolves raced past a surprised Karsa. Claws clattered on the bared rock, water spraying from the sun's melt, and the beasts wheeled to form a half-circle before the Teblor.

He slowed his steps, readying his weapon. For once, even Bairoth Gild was silenced – no doubt as uncertain as he himself was.

A rasping, panting stranger's voice hissed through Karsa's mind: 'We enjoyed that, Toblakai. You have run without pause for three nights and almost four days. That we are impressed would be a tragic understatement. We have never before seen the like. See our heaving flanks? You have exhausted us. And look at you – you breathe deep and there is red around your eyes, yet you stand ready, with not a waver in your legs, or from *the strange sword in your hands. Will you now do us harm, warrior?'*

Karsa shook his head. The language was Malazan. 'You are like a Soletaken, then. But many, not one. This would be . . . D'ivers? I have killed Soletaken – this fur on my shoulders is proof enough of that, if you doubt me. Attack me if you will, and when I have killed all of you, I will have a cloak even the gods will envy.'

'We are no longer interested in killing you, warrior. Indeed, we accost you now to deliver a warning.'

'What kind of warning?'

'You are on someone's trail.'

Karsa shrugged. 'Two men, both heavy, though one is taller. They walk side by side.'

'Side by side, yes. And what does that tell you?'

'Neither leads, neither follows.'

'Danger rides your shoulders, Toblakai. About you is an air of threat – another reason why we will not cross you. Powers vie for your soul. Too many. Too deadly. But heed our warning: should you cross one of those travellers . . . the world will come to regret it. The world, warrior.'

Karsa shrugged a second time. 'I am not interested in fighting anyone at the moment, D'ivers. Although, if I am in turn crossed, then I am not the one to answer for whatever regret the world then experiences. Now, I am done with words. Move from my path, or I will kill you all.'

The wolves hesitated. *'Tell them that Ryllandaras sought to dissuade you. Before you make your last living act one that sees this world destroyed.'*

He watched them wheel and make their way down the slope.

Bairoth Gild's laugh was a faint thunder in his mind. Karsa nodded. 'None would accept the blame for what has not yet occurred,' he rumbled. 'That, by itself, constitutes a curiously potent warning.'

'You do indeed grow into yourself, Karsa Orlong. What will you do?'

Karsa bared his teeth as he reslung his sword over a fur-clad shoulder. 'Do, Bairoth Gild? Why, I would meet these dire travellers, of course.'

This time, Bairoth Gild did not laugh.

Strains of meltwater flowed over the brittle rock beneath Karsa's moccasins. Ahead, the descent continued into a crowded maze of sandstone mesas, their level tops capped with ice and snow. Despite the bright, mid-afternoon sun in the cloudless sky, the narrow, twisting channels between the mesas remained in deep shadow.

But the snow underfoot had vanished, and already he could feel a new warmth in the air. There seemed but one way down, and it was as much a stream as a trail. Given the lack of signs, the Teblor could only assume that the two strangers ahead of him had taken the same route.

He moved slower now, his legs heavy with fatigue. The truth of his exhaustion had not been something he would reveal to the D'ivers wolves, but that threat was behind him now. He was close to collapse – hardly ideal if he was about to cross blades with a world-destroying demon.

Still his legs carried him forward, as if of their own accord. As if fated.

'And fate, Karsa Orlong, carries its own momentum.'

'Returned at last to hound me once more, Bairoth Gild? At the very least, you should speak words of advice. This Ryllandaras, this D'ivers – portentous words, yes?'

'Absurdly so, Warleader. There are no powers in this world – or any other – that pose such absolute threat. Spoken through the frenzied currents of fear. Likely personal in nature – whoever walks ahead has had dealings with the one named Ryllandaras, and it was the D'ivers who suffered with the meeting.'

'You are probably right, Bairoth Gild. Delum Thord, you have been silent a long while. What are your thoughts?'

'I am troubled, Warleader. The D'ivers was a powerful demon, after all. To take so many shapes, yet remain one. To speak in your mind as would a god . . .'

Karsa grimaced. 'A god . . . or a pair of ghosts. Not a demon, Delum Thord. We Teblor are too careless with that word. Forkrul Assail. Soletaken. D'ivers. None are demons in truth, for none were summoned to this world, none belong to any other realm but this one. They are in truth no different from us Teblor, or the lowlanders. No different from rhizan and capemoths, from horses and dogs. They are all of this world, Delum Thord.'

'As you say, Warleader. But we Teblor were never simplistic in our use of the word. Demon also refers to behaviour, and in this manner all things can be demonic. The one named Ryllandaras hunted us, and had you not driven it into exhaustion, it would have attacked, despite your words to the contrary.'

Karsa considered, then nodded. 'True enough, Delum Thord. You advise caution. This was always your way, so I am not surprised. I will not ignore your words for that, however.'

'Of course you will, Karsa Orlong.'

A last stretch of sunlight, then the Teblor was in shadow. The run-off swept around his ankles as the track narrowed, the footing growing treacherous. Once more he could see his breath.

A short climb to his left ran a broad ledge of some kind, out of the shadow and looking bone dry. Karsa swung from the trail and clambered up the gully's eroded bank until he was able to pull himself onto it. He straightened. Not a natural ledge after all. A road, running parallel to the gorge as it girdled the first mesa on his left. The wall of the mesa itself seemed to have been smoothed once, long ago, to a height twice Karsa's own. Faint pictographic images were visible on it, pitted and made colourless by passing centuries. A procession of figures, each scaled to that of a lowlander, bareheaded and wearing naught but a loincloth. They held their hands high overhead, fingers stretched out as if clutching at empty air.

The road itself was latticed in cracks, battered by

incessant rocks tumbling down from the mesa. Despite this, it seemed as if the road was made of a single piece of stone, though of course that was impossible. Heaved and rumpled, it wound along the curve of the mesa wall then shifted away onto a ramp of sorts, hazy in the distance, that presumably led down to the plain. The horizon directly ahead and to Karsa's right was cut short by towers of stone, though he knew that, beyond them, stretched the waters of the Longshan Sea.

Weariness forced the Teblor to slowly settle on the road, removing his pack and sitting against the mesa's rock wall. The journey had been long, but he knew his path ahead was still longer. And, it seemed, he would ever walk it alone. *For these ghosts remain just that. Perhaps, in truth, no more than my mind's own conjuring.* A displeasing thought.

He leaned his head back on the rough, sun-warmed stone.

His eyes blinked open – to darkness.

'Awake once more, Warleader? We were wondering if your sleep would prove eternal. There are sounds ahead – can you hear them? Oh, they've travelled far, but that is the way with this land, isn't it? Still . . . stones are being moved, I think. Tossed. Too slow, too regular to be a rockfall. The two strangers, one might conclude.'

Karsa slowly stood, stretching to ease his sore, chilled muscles. He could hear the steady clack of stones striking stone, but Bairoth Gild was right – they were distant. The warrior crouched down beside his pack and removed food-stuffs and a bladder of meltwater.

It was near dawn. Whoever it was working somewhere ahead had begun early.

Karsa took his time breaking his fast, and when he was finally done and ready to resume his journey, the sky was pink to the east. A final examination of the condition of his sword and the fittings on his armour, then he was on the move once again.

The steady clangour of the stones continued through

half the morning. The road skirted the mesa for a distance that was longer than he had originally judged, revealing the ramp ahead to be massive, its sides sheer, the plain beneath a third of a league or more below. Just before the road departed the mesa, it opened out into a shelf-like expanse, and here, set into the mesa wall, was the face of a city. Rockslides had buried fully half of it, and the spreading ridges of secondary slides lay atop the main one.

Before one of these lesser slides sat a pair of tents.

Three hundred paces away from them, Karsa halted.

There was a figure at the secondary slide, clearing rocks with a steady, almost obsessive rhythm, tossing huge chunks of sandstone out behind him to bounce and roll on the flat concourse. Nearby, seated on a boulder, was another figure, and where the first one was tall – taller than a lowlander by far – this one was impressively wide at the shoulders, dark-skinned, heavy-maned. A large leather sack was beside him, and he was gnawing on a smoke-blackened hind leg – the rest of the small mountain goat was still spitted on a huge skewer over a stone-lined hearth near the tents.

Karsa studied the scene for a time, then, shrugging, made his way towards the two figures.

He was less than twenty paces away before the huge, barbaric man seated on the boulder swung his head around.

And gestured with the haunch in his hand. 'Help yourself. The thing damn near brained me, falling from the cliffside, so I feel obliged to eat it. Funny, that. You always see them, scampering and clambering way up there, and so you naturally believe they never make a misstep. Well, another delusion shattered.'

He was speaking a desert dialect, a lowlander tongue, yet he was no lowlander. Large, thick canines, hair on shoulders like a boar's bristles, a heavy-boned face wide and flat. Eyes the hue of the sandstone cliffs around them.

At his words, the stranger's companion ceased throwing

rocks and straightened, and was now regarding Karsa curiously.

The Teblor was equally frank as he returned the stare. Almost as tall as he was, though leaner. Greyish, green-tinged skin. Lower canines large enough to be tusks. A longbow leaned nearby, along with a quiver, and a leather-strap harness to which a scabbarded sword was attached. The first weapons Karsa had seen – for the other one appeared to be entirely unarmed, barring the thick hunting knife at his belt.

The mutual examination continued for a moment longer, then the tusked warrior resumed his excavation, disappearing from sight as he strode into the cavity he had cleared in the rockfall.

Karsa glanced back at the other man.

Who gestured again with the goat leg.

The Teblor approached. He set down his pack near the hearth and drew a knife, then cut away a slab of meat and returned to where the other sat. 'You speak the language of the tribes,' Karsa said, 'yet I have never before seen your kind. Nor that of your companion.'

'And you are an equally rare sight, Thelomen Toblakai. I am named Mappo, of the people known as Trell, who hail from west of the Jhag Odhan. My single-minded companion is Icarium, a Jhag—'

'Icarium? Is that a common name, Mappo? There is a figure in my tribe's own legends who is so named.'

The Trell's ochre eyes narrowed momentarily. 'Common? Not in the way you ask. The name certainly appears in the tales and legends of countless people.'

Karsa frowned at the odd pedantry, if that was what it was. Then he crouched down opposite Mappo and tore off a mouthful of the tender meat.

'It occurs to me, of a sudden,' Mappo said, a hint of a grin flickering across his bestial features, 'that this chance encounter is unique . . . in ways too numerous to list. A Trell, a Jhag, and a Thelomen Toblakai . . . and we each are likely the only one of our respective kinds in all of Seven Cities. Even more extraordinary, I believe I know of you – by reputation only, of course. Sha'ik has a bodyguard . . . a Thelomen Toblakai, with an armoured vest made of petrified shells, and a wooden sword . . .'

Karsa nodded, swallowing down the last of the meat in his mouth before replying, 'Aye, I am in the service of Sha'ik. Does this fact make you my enemy?'

'Not unless you choose to be,' Mappo answered, 'and I would advise against that.'

'So does everyone,' Karsa muttered, returning to his meal.

'Ah, so you are not as ignorant of us as you first said.'

'A score of wolves spoke to me,' Karsa explained. 'Little was said, barring the warning itself. I do not know what makes you two so dangerous, nor do I much care. Impede me in my journey and I will kill you. It is as simple as that.'

Mappo slowly nodded. 'And have we cause to impede you?'

'Not unless you choose to have,' Karsa responded.

The Trell smiled. 'Thus, it is best we learn nothing of each other, then.'

'Aye, that would be best.'

'Alas,' Mappo sighed, 'Icarium already knows all he needs to of you, and as to what he intends, while already decided, he alone knows.'

'If he believes he knows me,' Karsa growled, 'he deceives himself.'

'Well, let us consider the matter. On your shoulders is the fur of a Soletaken. One we both happen to know – you killed a formidable beast, there. Luckily, he was no friend of ours, but the measure of your martial prowess has been taken. Next, you are haunted by ghosts – not just the two kinsmen who even now hover behind you. But the ghosts of those you have slain in your short, but clearly terrible life. They are appallingly numerous, and their hatred for you is a palpable hunger. But who carries their dead in such a manner? Only one who has been cursed, I think. And I speak from long experience; curses are horrible things. Tell me, has Sha'ik ever spoken to you of convergence?'

'No.'

'When curses collide, you might say. Flaws and virtues, the many faces of fateful obsession, of singular purpose. Powers and wills are drawn together, as if one must by nature seek the annihilation of the other. Thus, you and Icarium are now here, and we are moments from a dreadful convergence, and it is my fate to witness. Helpless unto desperate madness. Fortunately for my own sake, I have known this feeling before.'

Karsa had been eating throughout Mappo's words. Now he examined the bone in his hands, then tossed it aside, wiped his palms on the white bear fur of his cloak, and straightened. 'What else have you and Icarium discovered about me, Mappo?'

'A few more things. Ryllandaras gauged you, and concluded that he had no wish to add his skins to your collection. He is ever wise, is Ryllandaras. A score of wolves, you said? His power has grown, then, a mystery both ominous and curious, given the chaos in his heart. What else? Well, the rest I choose not to reveal.'

Karsa grunted. He untied the bear cloak and let it fall to the ground, then unslung his sword and turned to face the rockslide.

A boulder sailed out from the cavity, of a size and weight that would strain even Bairoth Gild. The ground shook when it struck and bounced and rolled to a dusty halt.

'Will he now make me wait?' Karsa growled.

As if in answer Icarium emerged from the cave, slapping the dust from his long-fingered hands. 'You are not Fenn,' he said. 'Indeed, I believe you are Teblor, a son of the fallen tribes in Laederon. You have travelled far, warrior, to meet your end.'

'If you are so eager,' Karsa growled, 'cease your words.'

The Jhag's expression grew troubled. 'Eager? No. I am

never eager. This is a moment of pathos, I believe. The first time I have felt such a thing, which is strange.' He turned to his companion. 'Have we known such moments as this one before, Mappo Runt?'

'Aye, my friend. We have.'

'Ah, well, then the burden of recollection is yours alone.'

'As it ever was, Icarium.'

'I grieve for you, friend.'

Mappo nodded. 'I know you do. Now, best unsheathe your sword, Icarium. This Teblor evinces frustration and impatience.'

The Jhag went to his weapon. 'What will come of this, Mappo?'

The Trell shook his head. 'I do not know, but I am filled with dread.'

'I shall endeavour to be efficient, then, so as to diminish the duration of your discomfort.'

'Clearly impossible,' Karsa muttered, 'given your love of words.' He readied his sword. 'Be on with it, then, I have a horse to find.'

Icarium's brows rose fractionally, then he drew out his sword. An unusual weapon, single-edged and looking ancient. He approached.

The Jhag's attack was a flicker of motion, faster than anything Karsa had seen before, yet his sword flashed to meet it.

Blades collided.

There was a peculiar *snick* and Karsa found himself holding nothing more than a handle.

Outrage exploded within him and he stepped forward, his huge fist hammering into Icarium's face. The Jhag was thrown backward, leaving his feet, his sword cartwheeling away to clatter on the slope of the rockfall. Icarium landed with a heavy thump, and did not move.

'Bastard broke my sword—' Karsa began, turning towards Mappo.

White light detonated in his skull.

And he knew no more.

Mappo stared down at the motionless Thelomen Toblakai, noting the slow rise and fall of the giant's chest. Hefting his mace, he glanced over to where Icarium lay, saw a hand slowly lift from the ground, twitch, then settle once more.

The Trell sighed. 'Better than I could have hoped for, I think.'

He walked back and returned his weapon to the large leather sack, then set out to strike the camp.

Pounding pain behind his eyes, a sound of roaring, as of a river raging through a narrow channel. Karsa groaned.

Some time passed before he finally pushed himself onto his hands and knees.

It was dawn . . . again.

'Say nothing, Bairoth Gild,' he muttered. 'Nor you, Delum Thord. I can well guess what happened. That bastard Trell struck me from behind. Aye, he didn't kill me, but one day he will wish he had.'

A slow, cautious look around confirmed that he was alone. His broken sword had been positioned beside him, handle and blade side by side, with a small bound bundle of desert flowers lying atop them.

The blow to his head left him nauseous, and he found he was shaking once he'd managed to climb to his feet. He unstrapped his dented helm and tossed it aside. Dried blood matted his hair and covered the back of his neck.

'At least you are now well rested, Karsa Orlong.'

'You are less amused than you would have me think, Bairoth Gild. The one named Icarium. He is the one from our legends, isn't he?'

'And you alone among the living Teblor have crossed blades with him.'

'He broke my sword.'

There was no reply to that. Karsa set about preparing to resume his journey, once more donning the bear cloak,

608

then shouldering the pack. He left the wooden sword pieces and their bouquet, and made to set off down the descending road. Then he paused, turning his attention instead to the cavity that Icarium had excavated into the rockslide.

The Jhag's efforts had partially uncovered a statue, broken here and there, with what remained fissured with cracks, but recognizable none the less. A grotesque construct, as tall as Karsa, made of a black, grainy stone.

A seven-headed hound.

It had been completely buried by the fall, and so would have revealed no sign that it existed beneath the rubble. Yet Icarium had found it, though his reasons for uncovering the monstrosity were still unfathomable. 'He has lived too long, I think,' Karsa murmured.

He strode back out from the cavity, then swung onto the road.

Six days later, the city of Lato Revae far behind him, the Teblor lay prone in the shadows of a guldindha tree at the edge of a grove, watching a pair of drovers switching their herd of goats towards a dusty corral. A small village lay beyond, its low buildings roofed in palm fronds, the air above it hazy with dung smoke and dust.

The sun would be down soon, and he could resume his journey. He had waited out the day, unseen. These lands between Lato Revae and the Mersin River were relatively crowded, compared to all that he had seen thus far, reminding him that his travels, since his landing at Ehrlitan, had been mostly through unbroken wilderness. The Pan'potsun Odhan – the Holy Desert itself – was a world virtually abandoned by civilization.

But here, irrigation ditches ribboned the plain. Wells and groves and villages abounded, and there were more roads than he had ever seen before, even in the lands of the Nathii. Most were dusty, winding tracks at ground level, usually situated between ditches. Thus far, the only exceptions were the imperial tracks, raised and straight and substantial enough to permit two wagons to pass each other with room to spare. These Malazan roads had suffered in the last year – despite their obvious value, foundation boulders had been dug out, league-markers uprooted. But the ditches alongside them were deep and wide, and Karsa had used those ditches to remain hidden from sight as he made his way southwestward.

The village ahead crouched on a crossroads of Malazan tracks, and a squat, square tower rose above the low roofs near the centre. Its limestone walls were stained black, streaks flaring up from arrow-slits and windows. When the sun finally settled beyond the horizon, no lights showed from the tower.

Though it was likely that there were rebel soldiers of the Apocalypse stationed in the village, given its strategic placement on the crossroads, Karsa had no interest in initiating contact. His was a private journey, if for no reason but that he chose to have it so. In any case, it seemed the rebellion was not quite as fierce here; either that or the unbridled bloodthirst had long since abated. There had been no widespread destruction of farms and fields, no slaughter in the village and town streets. Karsa wondered if there had been as many Malazan traders and landowners this far west, or if the garrisons had all been recalled into the major cities, such as Kayhum, Sarpachiya and Ugarat – their fellow noncombatants accompanying them. If so, then it had not helped them.

He disliked being weaponless, barring the Malazan short-sword he used as a knife, sheathed at his hip. But there was no suitable wood in this region. There were said to be iron-wood trees in the Jhag Odhan, and he would wait until then.

The swift descent into night was done. The Teblor warrior stirred, collecting his pack, then set out along the edge of the guldindha grove. One of the imperial roads led off in the direction he sought, likely the main artery connecting Lato Revae with the Holy City Ugarat. If any bridges across the Mersin River had survived the uprising, it would be the Malazan-built one on that road.

He skirted the village on its north side, through knee-high grains, the soil soft from the previous night's irrigating. Karsa assumed the water came from the river somewhere ahead, though he could not imagine how the flow was regulated. The notion of a life spent tilling fields was repellent to the Teblor warrior. The rewards seemed to be exclusive to the highborn landowners, whilst the labourers themselves had only a minimal existence, prematurely aged and worn down by the ceaseless toil. And the distinction between high and low status was born from farming itself – or so it appeared to Karsa. Wealth was measured in control over other people, and the grip of that control could never be permitted to loosen. Odd, then, that this rebellion had had nothing to do with such inequities, that in truth it had been little more than a struggle between those who would be in charge.

Yet the majority of the suffering had descended upon the lowborn, upon the common folk. What matter the colour of the collar around a man's neck, if the chains linked to them were identical?

Better to struggle against helplessness, as far as he was concerned. This blood-soaked Apocalypse was pointless, a misdirected explosion of fury that, when it passed, left the world unchanged.

He bounded across a ditch, crossed through a narrow fringe of overgrown brush, and found himself at the edge of a shallow pit. Twenty paces across and at least thirty paces wide. The town's refuse was piled here, not entirely successful at covering the mass of lowlander bones.

Here, then, were the Malazans. As tamed and broken as the earth itself. The wealth of flesh, flung back into the ground. Karsa had no doubt that it was their rivals in status who were loudest in exhorting their deaths.

'And so, once again, Karsa Orlong, we are given the truths

of the lowlanders.' Bairoth Gild's ghostly voice was palpably bitter. *'For every virtue they espouse, a thousand self-serving evils belie their piety. Know them, Warleader, for one day they will be your enemy.'*

'I am no fool, Bairoth Gild. Nor am I blind.'

Delum Thord spoke. *'A place of haunting lies ahead, Karsa Orlong. As ancient as our own blood. Those who live here avoid it, and have always avoided it.'*

'Not entirely,' Bairoth interjected. *'Fear has inspired them on occasion. The place is damaged. None the less, the Elder power lingers. The path beckons – will you walk it, Warleader?'*

Karsa made his way around the pit. He could see something ahead, earthworks rising to break the flatness of the surrounding plain. Elongated barrows, the slabs of stone that formed them visible in places although they were mostly covered in thorny brush and tufts of yellow grasses. The mounds formed an irregular ring around a larger, circular hill that was flat-topped, though slightly canted as if one side had settled over time. Rising at angles from the summit were standing stones, a score or more.

Rocks from clearing the nearby fields had been discarded in this once-holy site, around the barrows, heaped against the slope of the central hill, along with other detritus: the withered wooden skeletons of ox ploughs, palm fronds from roofs, piles of potsherds and the bones of butchered livestock.

Karsa slipped between two barrows and made his way up the central slope. The nearest standing stone reached barely to his waist. Black symbols crowded it, the spit and charcoal paint relatively recent. The Teblor recognized various signs, such as had been employed as a secret, native language during the Malazan occupation. 'Hardly a place of fear,' he muttered. Fully half of the stones were either shattered or toppled, and from the latter Karsa noted that they were, in fact, taller than he was, so deeply had they been anchored in the artificial hill. The summit itself was pitted and uneven.

'Oh, these are the signs of fear, Karsa Orlong, do not doubt that. This desecration. Were this a place without power, the answer would have been indifference.'

Karsa grunted, stepping carefully on the treacherous ground as he approached the nominal centre of the stone ring. Four smaller slabs had been tilted together there, the wiry grasses stopping a pace away on all sides, leaving only bare earth flecked with bits of charcoal.

And fragments, Karsa noted as he crouched, of bone. He picked one up and studied it in the starlight. From a skull, lowlander in scale though somewhat more robust, the outer edge of an eye socket. Thick . . . *like that of my gods . . .* 'Bairoth Gild. Delum Thord. Do either of you sense the presence of a spirit or a god here?'

'No,' Delum Thord replied.

Bairoth spoke. 'A shaman was buried here, Warleader. His head was severed and left fixed in the apex of the four cardinal stones. Whoever shattered it did so long afterwards. Centuries. Perhaps millennia. So that it would no longer see. No longer watch.'

'Then why is this place of value to me?'

'For the way through it offers, Warleader.'

'The way through what, Bairoth Gild?'

'Passage westward, into the Jhag Odhan. A trail in the dreamworld. A journey of months will become one of mere days, should you choose to walk it. It lives still, for it was used not long ago. By an army.'

'And how can I walk this trail?'

Delum Thord replied, 'We can lead you, Karsa Orlong. For, like the one once buried here, we are neither dead nor alive. The lord Hood cannot find our spirits, for they are here with you. Our presence adds to the god of death's hatred of you, Warleader.'

'Hatred?'

'For what you have taken and would not give to him. Will not. Would you become your own Keeper of Souls? So he must now fear. When last did Hood know a rival?'

Karsa scowled and spat onto the ground. 'I have no interest in being his rival. I would break these chains. I would free even you and Bairoth Gild.'

'*We would rather you did not, Warleader.*'

'You and Bairoth Gild are perhaps alone in that sentiment, Delum Thord.'

'*What of it?*' Bairoth snapped.

Karsa said nothing, for he had begun to understand the choice that lay ahead, sometime in the future. *To cast off my enemies . . . I must also cast off my friends. And so Hood follows, and waits. For the day that must come.*

'*You hide your thoughts now, Karsa Orlong. This new talent does not please us.*'

'I am warleader,' Karsa growled. 'It is not my task to please you. Do you now regret that you follow?'

'*No, Karsa Orlong. Not yet.*'

'Take me into this trail in the dreamworld, Delum Thord.'

The air grew suddenly colder, the smell reminding Karsa of the sloped clearings on high mountain sides when spring arrived, the smell of enlivened, softened lichen and moss. And before him, where there had been night-softened farmland a moment ago, there was now tundra, beneath a heavily overcast sky.

A broad path lay before him, stretching across the rolling land, where the lichen had been crushed, the mosses kicked aside and trampled. As Bairoth Gild had said, an army had passed this way, although by the signs it seemed their journey had been but a moment ago – he half expected to see the tail end of that solemn column on the distant horizon, but there was nothing. Simply an empty, treeless expanse, stretching out on all sides.

He moved forward, in the army's wake.

This world seemed timeless, the sky unchanging. On occasion, herds appeared, too distant to make out the kind of beasts, rolling across hillsides then slipping from view as they streamed down into valleys. Birds flew in arrowhead formation, a strange long-necked breed high overhead, all of them consistently flying back the way Karsa had come. Apart from the whine of the insects swarming about the Teblor, a strange, unreal silence emanated from the landscape.

A dream world, then, such as the elders of his tribe were wont to visit, seeking portents and omens. The scene not unlike what Karsa had glimpsed when, in delirium, he had found himself before his god, Urugal.

He continued on.

Eventually, the air grew colder, and frost glittered amidst the lichen and moss to either side of the wide trail. The smell of rotting ice filled Karsa's nose. Another thousand paces brought him to the first dirt-studded sweep of snow, filling a shallow valley on his right. Then shattered chunks of ice, half buried in the ground as if they had fallen from the sky, many of them larger than a lowlander wagon. The land itself was more broken here, the gentle roll giving way to sharp-walled drainage gullies and channels, to upthrust hillsides revealing banded sandstone beneath the frozen, thick skin of peat. Fissures in the stone gleamed with greenish ice.

Bairoth Gild spoke. *'We are now at the border of a new warren, Warleader. A warren inimical to the army that arrived here. And so, a war was waged.'*

'How far have I travelled, Bairoth Gild? In my world, am I approaching Ugarat? Sarpachiya?'

The ghost's laughter was like a boulder rolled over gravel. *'They are behind you now, Karsa Orlong. You approach the land known as the Jhag Odhan.'*

It had seemed no more than a half-day's worth of travel in this dream world.

Signs of the army's passage grew less distinct, the ground underfoot frozen rock hard and now consisting mostly of rounded stones. Ahead, a plain studded with huge flat slabs of black rock.

Moments later, Karsa was moving among them.

There were bodies beneath the stones. Pinned down.

'Will you free these, Karsa Orlong?'

'No, Delum Thord, I shall not. I shall pass through this place, disturbing nothing.'

'Yet these are not Forkrul Assail. Many are dead, for they had not the power their kind once possessed. While others remain alive, and will not die for a long time. Hundreds, perhaps thousands of years. Karsa Orlong, do you no longer believe in mercy?'

'My beliefs are my own, Delum Thord. I shall not undo what I do not understand, and that is all.'

He travelled on, and soon left the terrible plain behind.

Before him now stretched a field of ice, crack-riven, with pools of water reflecting the silver sky. Bones were scattered on it, from hundreds, perhaps thousands of figures. Bones of a type he had seen before. Some still sheathed in withered skin and muscle. Shards of stone weapons lay among them, along with fragments of fur, antlered helms and torn, rotting hides.

The fallen warriors formed a vast semicircle around a low, square-walled tower. Its battered stones were limned in runnelled ice, its doorway gaping, the interior dark.

Karsa picked his way across the field, his moccasins crunching through the ice and snow.

The tower's doorway was tall enough to permit the Teblor to stride through without ducking. A single room lay within. Broken furniture and the pieces of more fallen warriors cluttered the stone floor. A spiral staircase that seemed made entirely of iron rose from the centre.

From what he could determine from the wreckage, the furniture was of a scale to suit a Teblor, rather than a lowlander.

Karsa made his way up the ice-sheathed staircase.

There was a single level above, a high-ceilinged chamber that had once held wooden shelves on all four walls. Torn scrolls, bound books ripped apart, vials and clay jars containing various pungent mixes crushed underfoot, a large table split in half and pushed up against one wall, and on a cleared space on the floor . . .

Karsa stepped off the landing and looked down.

'Thelomen Toblakai, welcome to my humble abode.'

Karsa scowled. 'I crossed blades with one much like you. He was named Icarium. Like you, yet less so.'

'Because he is a half-blood, of course. Whilst I am not. Jaghut, not Jhag.'

She lay spread-eagled within a ring of fist-sized stones. A larger stone rested on her chest, from which heat rose in waves. The air in the chamber was a swirling mix of steam and suspended frost.

'You are trapped within sorcery. The army was seeking you, yet they did not kill you.'

'*Could* not would be more accurate. Not immediately, in any case. But eventually, this Tellann Ritual will destroy this core of Omtose Phellack, which will in turn lead to the death of the Jhag Odhan – even now, the north forest creeps onto the plains, whilst from the south the desert claims ever more of the odhan that was my home.'

'Your refuge.'

She bared her tusks in something like a smile. 'Among the Jaghut, they are now one and the same, Thelomen Toblakai.'

Karsa looked around, studying the wreckage. He saw no weapons; nor was the woman wearing armour. 'When this core of Omtose Phellack dies, so will you, yes? Yet you spoke only of the Jhag Odhan. As if your own death was of less importance than that of this land.'

'It *is* less important. On the Jhag Odhan, the past lives still. Not just in my fallen kin, the Jhag – the few that managed to escape the Logros T'lan Imass. There are ancient beasts that walk the treeless lands beside the sheets of ice. Beasts that have died out everywhere else, mostly on the spears of the T'lan Imass. But there were no Imass in the Jhag Odhan. As you said, a refuge.'

'Beasts. Including Jhag horses?'

He watched her strange eyes narrow. The pupils were vertical, surrounded in pearlescent grey. 'The horses we once bred to ride. Yes, they have gone feral in the odhan. Though few remain, for the Trell come from the west to hunt them. Every year. They drive them off cliffs. As they do to many of the other beasts.'

'Why did you not seek to stop them?'

'Because, dear warrior, I was *hiding*.'

'A tactic that failed.'

'A scouting party of T'lan Imass discovered me. I destroyed most of them, but one escaped. From that moment, I knew their army would come, eventually. Granted, they took their time about it, but time is what they have aplenty.'

'A scouting party? How many did you destroy?'

'Seven.'

'And are their remains among those surrounding this tower?'

She smiled again. 'I would think not, Thelomen Toblakai. To the T'lan Imass, destruction is failure. Failure must be punished. Their methods are . . . elaborate.'

'Yet what of the warriors lying below, and those around the tower?'

'Fallen, but not in failure. Here I lie, after all.'

'Enemies should be killed,' the Teblor growled, 'not imprisoned.'

'I would not argue that sentiment,' the Jaghut replied.

'I sense nothing evil from you.'

'It has been a long time since I heard that word. In the wars with the T'lan Imass, even, that word had no place.'

'I must answer injustice,' he rumbled.

'As you will.'

'The need overwhelms all caution. Delum Thord would smile.'

'Who is Delum Thord?'

Not answering, Karsa unslung his pack then threw off his bear cloak and stepped towards the ring of stones.

'Stay back, warrior!' the Jaghut hissed. 'This is High Tellann—'

'And I am Karsa Orlong, of the Teblor,' the warrior growled. He kicked at the nearest stones.

Searing flame swept up to engulf Karsa. He snarled and pushed his way through it, reaching down both hands to take the slab of stone, grunting as he lifted it from the woman's chest. The flames swarmed him, seeking to rend his flesh from his bones, but his growl simply deepened. Pivoting, flinging the huge slab to one side. Where it struck a wall, and shattered.

The flames died.

Karsa shook himself, then looked down once more.

The ring was now broken. The Jaghut's eyes were wide as she stared up at him, movement stirring her limbs.

'Never before,' she sighed, then shook her head as if in disbelief. 'Ignorance, honed into a weapon. Extraordinary, Thelomen Toblakai.'

Karsa crouched down beside his pack. 'Are you hungry? Thirsty?'

She was slow in sitting up. The T'lan Imass had stripped her, leaving her naked, but she seemed unaffected by the bitter cold air now filling the chamber. Though she appeared young, he suspected she was anything but. He felt her eyes watching him as he prepared the meal.

'You crossed swords with Icarium. There had ever been but a single conclusion to such an ill-fated thing, but that you are here is proof that you somehow managed to avoid it.'

Karsa shrugged. 'No doubt we will resume our disagreement the next time we meet.'

'How did you come to be here, Karsa Orlong?'

'I am seeking a horse, Jaghut. The journey was long, and I was led to understand that this dream world would make it shorter.'

'Ah, the ghost-warriors hovering behind you. Even so, you take a grave risk travelling the Tellann Warren. I owe you my life, Karsa Orlong.' She cautiously climbed to her feet. 'How can I repay you?'

He straightened to face her, and was surprised – and pleased – to see that she almost matched him in height. Her hair was long, murky brown, tied at the back. He studied her for a moment, then said, 'Find for me a horse.'

Her thin eyebrows rose fractionally. 'That is all, Karsa Orlong?'

'Perhaps one more thing – what is your name?'

'That is what you would ask?'

'No.'

'Aramala.'

He nodded and turned once more to readying the meal. 'I would know all you can tell me, Aramala, of the seven who first found you.'

'Very well. If I may ask something in turn. You passed through a place on your way here, where Jhag had been . . . imprisoned. I shall of course free those who have survived.'

'Of course.'

'They are half-bloods.'

'Aye, so I am told.'

'Do you not wonder at what the other half is?'

He glanced up, then slowly frowned.

She smiled. 'There is much, I think, that I must tell you.'

Some time later, Karsa Orlong strode from the tower. He moved on, resuming the trail of the army where it began once again beyond the frozen ground of Omtose Phellack.

When he finally emerged from the warren, into the heat of late afternoon on the world of his birth, he found himself on the edge of a ridge of battered hills. Pausing, he glanced behind him, and could make out, at the very rim of the horizon, a city – probably Sarpachiya – and the glimmer of a vast river.

The hills ahead formed a spine, a feature on the land that he suspected showed up only on local maps. There were no farms on the lowlands before it, no herds on its broken slopes.

The T'lan Imass had reappeared in this place before him, though their passage onwards, into those hills, left no sign, for decades had passed in this world since that time. He was on the edge of the Jhag Odhan.

Dusk had arrived by the time he reached the foothills and began making his way up the weathered slope. The exposed rock here had a diseased look, as if afflicted by some kind of unnatural decay. Pieces of it collapsed under his feet as he climbed.

The summit was little more than a ridge, less than three paces across, crusted with rotten stone and dead grasses. Beyond, the land fell away sharply, forming a broad valley marked by sunken, banded sandstone mesas rising from its base. The valley's opposite side, five thousand or more paces distant, was a sheer cliff of rust-coloured rock.

Karsa could not imagine the natural forces that could have created such a landscape. The mesas below were born of erosion, as if floods had run the length of the valley, or perhaps fierce winds roared down the channels – less dramatic and demanding much greater lengths of time. Or the entire valley could have once stood level with the surrounding hills, only to suffer some subterranean slump. The decayed outcroppings suggested some kind of leaching process afflicting the region.

He made his way down the steep slope.

And quickly discovered that it was honeycombed with caves and pits. Mines, if the scree of calcreted rubble fanning out from them was any indication. But not tin or copper. Flint. Vast veins of the glassy brown material lay exposed like raw wounds in the hillside.

Karsa's eyes narrowed on the mesas ahead. The bands in the sandstone were all sharply tilted, and not all at the same angle. Their caps displayed nothing of the flat plateau formation that one would expect; instead, they were jagged and broken. The valley floor itself – for as far as he could see amidst the squat mesas – seemed to be sharp-edged gravel. Shatter flakes from the mining.

In this single valley, an entire army could have fashioned its weapons of stone . . .

And the flint in this place was far from exhausted.

Bairoth Gild's voice filled his head. *'Karsa Orlong, you circle the truths as a lone wolf circles a bull elk.'*

Karsa grunted, his only reply. He could see, on the cliff on the other side, more caves, these ones carved into the sheer wall. Reaching the shadowed valley floor, he set out for them. The gravel underfoot was thick, shifting treacherously, the sharp edges slicing into the hide soles of his moccasins. The air smelled of limestone dust.

He approached a large cave mouth situated a third of the way up the cliff. A broad slope of scree led up to within reach of it, though it shifted ominously under the Teblor as he scrambled upward. He finally managed to clamber onto the uneven floor.

With the cliff wall facing northeast, and the sun already riding the horizon, there was no ambient light in the cave. The Teblor set down his pack and drew out a small lantern.

The walls were calcined limestone, blackened by generation upon generation of woodsmoke, the ceiling high and roughly domed. Ten paces further in, the passage swiftly diminished as ceiling, walls and floor converged. Crouching, Karsa slipped through the choke point.

Beyond was a vast cavern. Dimly seen on the wall opposite was a monolithic projection of solid, pure flint, reaching almost up to the ceiling. Deeply recessed niches had been bored into the flanking walls. A fissure above the centre of the hewn chamber bled grey light from the dusk outside. Directly beneath it was a heap of sand, and growing from that mound was a knotted, twisted tree – a guldindha, no higher than the Teblor's knee, its leaves a deeper hue of green than was usual.

That daylight could reach down two-thirds of this cliff was itself a miracle . . . *but this tree . . .*

Karsa walked over to one of the niches and extended the lantern into it. Another cavern lay beyond. And it was filled with flint weapons. Some were broken but most were whole. Swords, double-bladed axes with bone shafts, hundreds upon hundreds covering the floor. The next niche contained the same, as did the one after that. Twenty-two side-chambers in all. *The weapons of the dead. The weapons of the failed.* In every cave on this cliff, he knew, he would find the same.

But none of the others were important to him. He set the lantern down near the pillar of flint, then straightened. 'Urugal the Woven. Beroke Soft Voice, Kahlb the Silent Hunter, Thenik the Shattered, 'Siballe the Unfound, Halad the Giant, Imroth the Cruel. Faces in the Rock, gods of the Teblor, I, Karsa Orlong of the Uryd Tribe of the Teblor, have delivered you to this place. You were broken. Severed. Weaponless. I have done as you commanded me to do. I have brought you to this place.'

Urugal's broken rasp replied, 'You have found that which was taken from us, Karsa Orlong. You have *freed* your gods.'

The Teblor watched the ghost of Urugal slowly take shape before him. A squat, heavy-boned warrior, shorter than a lowlander but much broader. The bones of his limbs were split – where Karsa could see between the taut straps of leather and hide that bound them, that *held him together*. More straps crossed his chest.

'Karsa Orlong, you have found our weapons.'

The warrior shrugged. 'If indeed they are among the thousands in the chambers beyond.'

'They are. *They* did not fail us.'

'But the Ritual did.'

Urugal cocked his head. His six kin were taking shape around him. 'You understand, then.'

'I do.'

'Our physical forms approach, Karsa Orlong. They have journeyed far, bereft of spirit, held only by our wills—'

'And the one you now serve,' the Teblor growled.

'Yes. The one we now serve. We have guided you in turn, Warleader. And now shall come your reward, for what you have given us.'

'Siballe the Unfound now spoke. 'We have gathered an army, Karsa Orlong. All the children sacrificed before the Faces in the Rock. They are alive, Warleader. They have been prepared. For you. An army. Your people are assailed. The lowlanders must be driven back, their armies annihilated. You shall sweep down with your legions, down into their lands, and reap destruction upon the lowlanders.'

'I shall.'

'The Seven Gods of the Teblor,' Urugal said, 'must now become Eight.'

The one named Halad – the largest of the seven by far, hulking, bestial – stepped forward. 'You must now fashion a sword, Karsa Orlong. Of stone. The mines outside await you – we shall guide you in the knowledge—'

'There is no need,' Karsa said. 'I have learned the many hearts of stone. The knowledge is mine, and so too shall the sword be mine. Those you fashion are well enough for your own kind. But I am Teblor. I am Thelomen Toblakai.' With that he swung about and walked towards the monolithic pillar of flint.

'That spar will defeat you,' Halad said behind him. 'To draw a long enough blade for a sword, you must strike from above. Examine this vein carefully, and you will see that, pure as it is, the flow of the stone is unforgiving. None of our kind has ever managed to draw forth a flake longer than our own height. The spar before you can no longer be worked; thus its abandonment. Strike and it shall shatter. And that failure shall stain your next efforts, and so weaken the sorcery of the making.'

Karsa stood before the brown, almost black, flint pillar.

'You must fashion a fire at its base,' Halad said. 'Left to burn without cessation for a number of days and nights. There is little wood in the valley below, but in the Jhag Odhan beyond, the bhederin herds have travelled in their multitudes. Fire, Karsa Orlong, then cold water—'

'No. All control is lost with that method, T'lan Imass. Your kind are not unique in knowing the truths of stone. This task is mine and mine alone. Now, enough words.'

'The name you have given us,' Urugal rasped, 'how did you come by such knowledge?'

Karsa turned, face twisting into a sneer. 'Foolish Teblor. Or so you believed. So you would have us. Fallen Thelomen Toblakai, but he who has fallen can rise once again, Urugal. Thus, you were once T'lan Imass. But now, you are the Unbound.' The sneer became a snarl. 'From wandering to hold. From hold to *house*.'

The warrior climbed the spar of flint. Perched on its top, he drew out his Malazan short-sword. A moment's examination of the stone's surface, then he leaned over to study the almost vertical sweep of flawless flint reaching down to the cave's floor. Reversing the sword, Karsa began scraping the top of the pillar, a hand's width in from the sharp edge. He could see the tracks of old blows – the T'lan Imass had tried, despite Halad's words, but had failed.

Karsa continued roughing the surface where he would strike. In his mind, he spoke. *Bairoth Gild. Delum Thord. Hear me, when none other can. One day, I shall break my chains, I shall free the souls that now hound me. You would not be among them, or so you said. Nor would I wish Hood's embrace upon you. I have considered your desires in this. And have fashioned an alternative . . .*

'*Warleader, Delum Thord and I understand your intent. Your genius never fails to astonish me, Karsa Orlong. Only with our consent will you succeed. And so you give us words and lo, we find our path forced. Hood's embrace . . . or what you seek.*'

Karsa shook his head. *Not just me, Bairoth Gild. But you yourself. Do you deny it?*

'*No, Warleader. We do not. Thus, we accept what you offer.*'

Karsa knew that he alone could see the ghosts of his friends at this moment, as they seemed to dissolve, reduced to pure will, that then flowed down into the flint. Flowed, to find a shape, a form of cohesion . . .

Awaiting . . . He swept dust and grit from the roughened surface, then closed both hands about the short-sword's stubby grip. He lifted the weapon high, fixing his gaze upon the battered striking platform, then drove the pommel down.

A strange snapping sound—

Then Karsa was leaping forward, short-sword flung aside, down through the air, spinning as he dropped. His knees flexed to absorb the impact, even as he raised his hands to intersect the toppling spear of flint.

A spear almost as tall as the Teblor himself.

It fell away from the pillar, a flattened shard, and settled into his hands. A warm lick on his palms, and suddenly blood was running down his forearms. Karsa quickly backed up, lowering the blade to the floor. When he drew his hands away he saw that they had been cut down to the bone. *Clever Bairoth, to drink my blood to seal the bargain.*

'You . . . surpass us,' Halad whispered.

Karsa went to his pack and drew out a bundle of field dressings and a sewing kit. There would be no infection, of course, and he would heal swiftly. Still, he would need to close the cuts before he could hope to begin work on the huge blade's edges, and hack out a grip of sorts.

'We shall invest the weapon,' Urugal announced behind him. 'So that it cannot be broken.'

Karsa nodded.

'We shall make you the Eighth God of the Teblor.'

'No,' he replied as he began working on his left hand. 'I am not as you, Urugal. I am not Unbound. You yourself closed the chains about me. By your own hands, you saw to it that the souls of those I have slain will pursue me eternally. You have shaped my haunting, Urugal. Beneath such a curse, I can never be *unbound*.'

'There is place for you none the less,' Urugal said, 'in the House of Chains.'

'Aye. Knight of Chains, champion of the Crippled God.'

'You have learned much, Karsa Orlong.'

He stared down at his bloodied hands. 'I have, T'lan Imass. As you shall witness.'

CHAPTER FIFTEEN

How many times, dear traveller, will you walk
the same path?

Kayessan

To the north, the dust of the imperial army obscured the forest-mantled hills of Vathar. It was late afternoon, the hottest part of the day, when the wind died and the rocks radiated like flatstones on a hearth. Sergeant Strings remained motionless beneath his ochre rain cloak, lying flat as he studied the lands to the southwest. Sweat streamed down his face to prickle in his iron-shot red beard.

After a long moment studying the mass of horse warriors that had emerged out of the dusty odhan in their wake, Strings lifted a gloved hand and gestured.

The others of his squad rose from their places of concealment and edged back from the crest. The sergeant watched them until they reached cover once more, then slid around and followed.

Endless skirmishes with raiders these last weeks, beginning just outside Dojal, with more heated clashes with Kherahn Dhobri tribes at Tathimon and Sanimon . . . but nothing like the army now trailing them. Three thousand warriors, at the very least, of a tribe they'd not seen before. Countless barbaric standards rose above the host, tall spears topped with ragged streamers, antlers, horns and skulls. The glitter of bronze scale armour was visible beneath the black telabas and furs, as well as – more prolific – a strange greyish armour that was too supple to be anything but hide. The helms, from what Strings could make out with the distance, looked to be elaborate, many of them crow-winged, of leather and bronze.

Strings slid down to where his squad waited. They'd yet to engage in hand-to-hand combat, their sum experience of fighting little more than firing crossbows and occasionally holding a line. *So far . . . so good.* The sergeant faced Smiles. 'All right, it's settled – climb on that miserable horse down below, lass, and ride to the lieutenant. Looks like we've got a fight coming.'

Sweat had tracked runnels through the dust sheathing her face. She nodded, then scrambled off.

'Bottle, go to Gesler's position, and have him pass word to Borduke. I want a meeting. Quick, before their scouts get here.'

'Aye, Sergeant.'

After a moment, Strings drew out his waterskin and passed it to Corporal Tarr, then he tapped Cuttle on the shoulder and the two of them made their way back to the ridge.

They settled down side by side to resume studying the army below.

'These ones could maul us,' the sergeant muttered. 'Then again, they're riding so tight it makes me wonder . . .'

Cuttle grunted, eyes thinned to slits. 'Something's gnawing my knuckles here, Fid. They know we're close, but they ain't arrayed for battle. They should've held back until night, then hit all along our line. And where are their scouts, anyway?'

'Well, those outriders—'

'Way too close. Local tribes here know better—'

A sudden scattering of stones and Strings and Cuttle twisted round – to see riders cresting the ridge on either side of them, and others cantering into view on the back-slope, closing on his squad.

629

'Hood take us! Where did—'

Yipping warcries sounded, weapons waving in the air, yet the horse warriors then drew rein, rising in their stirrups as they surrounded the squad.

Frowning, Strings clambered to his feet. A glance back at the army below showed a vanguard climbing the slope at a canter. The sergeant met Cuttle's eyes and shrugged.

The sapper grimaced in reply.

Escorted by the riders on the ridge, the two soldiers made their way down to where Tarr and Koryk stood. Both had their crossbows loaded, though no longer trained on the tribesmen wheeling their mounts in a prancing circle around them. Further down the ridge Strings saw Gesler and his squad appear, along with Bottle; and their own company of horse warriors.

'Cuttle,' the sergeant muttered, 'did you clash with these anywhere north of the River Vathar?'

'No. But I think I know who they are.'

None of these scouts wore bronze armour. The grey hide beneath their desert-coloured cloaks and furs looked strangely reptilian. Crow wings had been affixed to their forearms, like swept-back fins. Their faces were pale by local standards, unusual in being bearded and long-moustached. Tattoos of black tears ran down the lengths of their weathered cheeks.

Apart from lances, fur-covered wooden scabbards were slung across their backs, holding heavy-bladed tulwars. All had crow-feet earrings dangling from under their helms.

The tribe's vanguard reached the crest above them and drew to a halt, as, on the opposite side, there appeared a company of Wickans, Seti and Malazan officers.

Beru fend, the Adjunct herself's with them. Also Fist Gamet, Nil, Nether and Temul, as well as Captain Keneb and Lieutenant Ranal.

The two mounted forces faced one another on either side of the shallow gully, and Strings could see Temul visibly start, then lean over to speak to the Adjunct.

A moment later, Tavore, Gamet and Temul rode forward.

From the tribe's vanguard a single rider began the descent on the back-slope. A chieftain, Strings surmised. The man was huge; two tulwars were strapped to a harness crossing his chest, one of them broken just above the hilt. The black tears tattooed down his broad cheeks looked to have been gouged into the flesh. He rode down fairly close to where Strings and Cuttle stood and paused beside them.

He nodded towards the approaching group and asked in rough Malazan, 'This is the Plain Woman who leads you?'

Strings winced, then nodded. 'Adjunct Tavore, aye.'

'We have met the Kherahn Dhobri,' the chieftain said, then smiled. 'They will harass you no more, Malazan.'

Tavore and her officers arrived, halting five paces away. The Adjunct spoke. 'I welcome you, Warchief of the Khundryl. I am Adjunct Tavore Paran, commander of the Fourteenth Army of the Malazan Empire.'

'I am Gall, and we are the Burned Tears of the Khundryl.'

'The Burned Tears?'

The man made a gesture of grief. 'Blackwing, leader of the Wickans. I spoke with him. My warriors sought to challenge, to see who were the greatest warriors of all. We fought hard, but we were humbled. Blackwing is dead, his clan destroyed, and Korbolo Dom's Dogslayers dance on his name. That must be answered, and so we have come. Three thousand – all that fought for Blackwing the first time. We are changed, Adjunct. We are other than we once were. We grieve the loss of ourselves, and so we shall remain lost, for all time.'

'Your words sadden me, Gall,' Tavore replied, her voice shaky.

Careful now, lass . . .

'We would join you,' the Khundryl warchief rasped, 'for we have nowhere else to go. The walls of our yurts look strange to our eyes. The faces of our wives, husbands, children – all those we once loved and who once loved us – strangers, now. Like Blackwing himself, we are as ghosts in this world, in this land that was once our home.'

'You would join us – to fight under my command, Gall?'

'We would.'

'Seeking vengeance against Korbolo Dom.'

He shook his head. 'That will come, yes. But we seek to make amends.'

She frowned beneath her helm. 'Amends? By Temul's account you fought bravely, and well. Without your intercession, the Chain of Dogs would have fallen at Sanimon. The refugees would have been slaughtered—'

'Yet we then rode away – back to our lands, Adjunct. We thought only to lick our wounds. While the Chain marched on. To more battles. To its final battle.' He was weeping in truth now, and an eerie keening sound rose from the other horse warriors present. 'We should have been there. That is all.'

The Adjunct said nothing for a long moment.

Strings removed his helm and wiped the sweat from his brow. He glanced back up the slope, and saw a solid line of Khundryl on the ridge. Silent. Waiting.

Tavore cleared her throat. 'Gall, Warchief of the Burned Tears . . . the Fourteenth Army welcomes you.'

The answering roar shook the ground underfoot. Strings turned and met Cuttle's eyes. *Three thousand veterans of this Hood-damned desert. Queen of Dreams, we have a chance. Finally, it looks like we have a chance.* He did not need to speak aloud to know that Cuttle understood, for the man slowly nodded.

But Gall was not finished. Whether he realized the full measure of his next gesture – no, Strings would conclude eventually, he could not have – even so . . . The Warchief gathered his reins and rode forward, past the Adjunct. He halted his horse before Temul, then dismounted.

Three strides forward. Under the eyes of over three hundred Wickans, and five hundred Seti, the burly Khundryl – his grey eyes fixed on Temul – halted. Then he unslung his broken tulwar and held it out to the Wickan youth.

Temul was pale as he reached down to accept it.

Gall stepped back and slowly lowered himself to one knee. 'We are not Wickans,' the warchief grated, 'but this I swear – we shall *strive* to be.' He lowered his head.

Temul sat unmoving, visibly struggling beneath a siege of emotions, and Strings suddenly realized that the lad did not know how to answer, did not know what to do.

The sergeant took a step, then swung his helm upward, as if to put it back on. Temul caught the flash of movement, even as he looked about to dismount, and he froze as he met Strings's eyes.

A slight shake of the head. *Stay in that saddle, Temul!* The sergeant reached up and touched his own mouth. *Talk. Answer with words, lad!*

The commander slowly settled back into his saddle, then straightened. 'Gall of the Burned Tears,' he said, barely a tremble to his voice, 'Blackwing sees through the eyes of every Wickan here. Sees, and answers. Rise. In Blackwing's name, I, Temul of the Crow Clan, accept you … the Burned Tears … of the Crow Clan, of the Wickans.' He then took the loop of leather to which the broken tulwar was tied, and lowered it over his shoulder.

With the sound of a wave rolling up a league-long strand of beach, weapons were unsheathed along the ridge, a salute voiced by iron alone.

A shiver rippled through Strings.

'Hood's breath,' Cuttle muttered under his breath. 'That is a lot more frightening than their warcries were.'

Aye, as ominous as Hood's smile. He looked back to Temul and saw the Wickan watching him. The sergeant lowered the helm onto his head once more, then grinned and nodded. *Perfect, lad. Couldn't have done better myself.*

And now, Temul wasn't alone any more, surrounded by sniping arthritic wolves who still wouldn't accept his command. Now, the lad had Gall and three thousand blooded warriors to back his word. *And that's the last of that. Gall, if I was a religious man, I'd burn a crow-wing in your name tonight. Hood take me, I might do it anyway.*

'Gall of the Burned Tears,' the Adjunct announced. 'Please join us at our command quarters. We can discuss the disposition of your forces over a meal – a modest meal, alas—'

The Khundryl finally straightened. He faced the Adjunct. 'Modest? No. We have brought our own food, and this night there shall be a feast – not a single soldier shall go without at least a mouthful of bhederin or boar!' He swung about and scanned his retinue until he spied the one he sought. 'Imrahl! Drag your carcass back to the wagons and bring them forward! And find the two hundred cooks and see if they've sobered up yet! And if they haven't, I will have their heads!'

The warrior named Imrahl, an ancient, scrawny figure who seemed to be swimming beneath archaic bronze armour, answered with a broad, ghastly smile, then spun his horse round and kicked it into a canter back up the slope.

Gall swung about and raised both hands skyward, the crow-wings attached to the forearms seeming to snap open beneath them. 'Let the Dogslayers cower!' he roared. 'The Burned Tears have begun the hunt!'

Cuttle leaned close to Strings. 'That's one problem solved – the Wickan lad's finally on solid ground. One wound sewn shut, only to see another pried open.'

'Another?' *Oh. Yes, true enough. That Wickan Fist's ghost keeps rearing up, again and again. Poor lass.*

'As if Coltaine's legacy wasn't already dogging her heels . . . if you'll excuse the pun,' the sapper went on. 'Still, she's putting a brave face on it . . .'

No choice. Strings faced his squad. 'Collect your gear, soldiers. We've got pickets to raise . . . before we eat.' At their groans he scowled. 'And consider yourselves lucky – missing those scouts don't bode well for our capabilities, now, does it?'

He watched them assemble their gear. Gesler and Borduke were approaching with their own squads. Cuttle grunted at the sergeant's side. 'In case it's slipped your mind, Fid,' he said, low, '*we* didn't see the bastards, either.'

'You're right,' Strings replied, 'it's slipped my mind completely. Huh, there it goes again. Gone.'

Cuttle scratched the bristle on his heavy jaw. 'Strange, what were we talking about?'

'Bhederin and boar, I think. Fresh meat.'

'Right. My mouth's watering at the thought.'

Gamet paused outside the command tent. The revelry continued unabated, as the Khundryl roved through the camp, roaring their barbaric songs. Jugs of fermented milk had been broached and the Fist was grimly certain that more than one bellyful of half-charred, half-raw meat had returned to the earth prematurely out beyond the fires, or would in the short time that remained before dawn.

Next day's march had been halved, by the Adjunct's command, although even five bells' walking was likely to make most of the soldiers regret this night's excesses.

Or maybe not.

He watched a marine from his own legion stumble past, a Khundryl woman riding him, legs wrapped around his waist, arms around his neck. She was naked, the marine nearly so. Weaving, the pair vanished into the gloom.

Gamet sighed, drawing his cloak tighter about himself, then turned and approached the two Wickans standing guard outside the Adjunct's tent.

They were from the Crow, grey-haired and looking miserable. Recognizing the Fist they stepped to either side of the entrance. He passed between them, ducking to slip between the flaps.

All of the other officers had left, leaving only the Adjunct and Gall, the latter sprawled on a massive, ancient-looking wooden chair that had come on the Khundryl wagons. The warchief had removed his helm, revealing a mass of curly hair, long and black and shimmering with grease. The midnight hue was dye, Gamet suspected, for the man had seen at least fifty summers. The tips of his moustache rested on his chest and he looked half asleep, a jug gripped by the clay handle in one huge hand. The Adjunct stood nearby, eyes lowered onto a brazier, as if lost in thought.

Were I an artist, I would paint this scene. This precise moment, and leave the viewer to wonder. He strode over to the map table, where another jug of wine waited. 'Our army is drunk, Adjunct,' he murmured as he poured a cup full.

'Like us,' Gall rumbled. 'Your army is lost.'

Gamet glanced over at Tavore, but there was no reaction for him to gauge. He drew a breath, then faced the Khundryl. 'We are yet to fight a major battle, Warchief. Thus, we do not yet know ourselves. That is all. We are not lost—'

'Just not yet found,' Gall finished, baring his teeth. He took a long swallow from his jug.

'Do you regret your decision to join us, then?' Gamet asked.

'Not at all, Fist. My shamans have read the sands. They have learned much of your future. The Fourteenth Army shall know a long life, but it shall be a restless life. You are doomed to search, destined to ever *hunt* . . . for what even you do not know, nor, perhaps, shall you ever know. Like the sands themselves, wandering for eternity.'

Gamet was scowling. 'I do not wish to offend, Warchief, but I hold little faith in divination. No mortal – no *god* – can say we are doomed, or destined. The future remains unknown, the one thing we cannot force a pattern upon.'

The Khundryl grunted. 'Patterns, the lifeblood of the shamans. But not them alone, yes? The Deck of Dragons – are they not used for divination?'

Gamet shrugged. 'There are some who hold much store in the Deck, but I am not one of them.'

'Do you not see patterns in history, Fist? Are you blind to the cycles we all suffer through? Look upon this desert, this wasteland you cross. Yours is not the first empire that would

636

claim it. And what of the tribes? Before the Khundryl, before the Kherahn Dhobri and the Tregyn, there were the Sanid, and the Oruth, and before them there were others whose names have vanished. Look upon the ruined cities, the old roads. The past is all patterns, and those patterns remain beneath our feet, even as the stars above reveal their own patterns – for the stars we gaze upon each night are naught but an illusion from the past.' He raised the jug again and studied it for a moment. 'Thus, the past lies beneath and above the present, Fist. This is the truth my shamans embrace, the bones upon which the future clings like muscle.'

The Adjunct slowly turned to study the warchief. 'We shall reach Vathar Crossing tomorrow, Gall. What will we find?'

The Khundryl's eyes glittered. 'That is for you to decide, Tavore Paran. It is a place of death, and it shall speak its words to you – words the rest of us will not hear.'

'Have you been there?' she asked.

He nodded, but added nothing more.

Gamet drank down a mouthful of wine. There was a strangeness to this night, to this moment here in the Adjunct's tent, that left his skin crawling. He felt out of place, like a simpleton who'd just stumbled into the company of scholars. The revelry in the camp beyond was dying down, and come the dawn, he knew, there would be silence. Drunken oblivion was, each time, a small, temporary death. Hood walked where the self once stood, and the wake of the god's passage sickened mortal flesh afterwards.

He set his cup down on the map table. 'If you'll forgive me,' he muttered, 'the air in here is too . . . close.'

Neither replied as he walked back to the flap.

Outside, in the street beyond the two motionless Wickan guards, Gamet paused and looked up. *Ancient light, is it? If so, then the patterns I see . . . may have died long ago. No, that does not bear thinking about. It is one of those truths that have no value, for it offers nothing but dislocation.*

And he needed no fuel for that cold fire. He was too old for this war. *Hood knows, I didn't enjoy it much the first time round.* Vengeance belonged to the young, after all. The time when emotions burned hottest, when life was sharp enough to cut, fierce enough to sear the soul.

He was startled by the passing of a large cattle dog. Head low, muscles rippling beneath a mottled hide literally seamed with countless scars, the silent beast padded down the aisle between the tent rows. A moment later and it disappeared into the gloom.

'I've taken to following it,' a voice said behind him.

Gamet turned. 'Captain Keneb. I am surprised to find you still awake.'

The soldier shrugged. 'That boar's not sitting too well in my gut, sir.'

'More likely that fermented milk the Khundryl brought – what is it called again?'

'Urtathan. But no, I have experienced that brew before, and so chose to avoid it. Come the morning, I suspect three-quarters of the army will realize a similar wisdom.'

'And the remaining quarter?'

'Dead.' He smiled at Gamet's expression. 'Sorry, sir, I wasn't entirely serious.'

The Fist gestured for the captain to accompany him, and they began walking. 'Why do you follow that dog, Keneb?'

'Because I know its tale, sir. It survived the Chain of Dogs. From Hissar to the Fall outside Aren. I watched it fall almost at Coltaine's feet. Impaled by spears. It should not have survived that.'

'Then how did it?'

'Gesler.'

Gamet frowned. 'The sergeant in our legion's marines?'

'Aye, sir. He found it, as well as another dog. What happened then I have no idea. But both beasts recovered from what should have been mortal wounds.'

'Perhaps a healer . . .'

Keneb nodded. 'Perhaps, but none among Blistig's guard – I made enquiries. No, there's a mystery yet to be solved. Not just the dogs, but Gesler himself, and his corporal, Stormy, and a third soldier – have you not noted their strangely hued skin? They're Falari, yet Falari are pale-skinned, and a desert tan doesn't look like that at all. Curious, too, it was Gesler who delivered the *Silanda*.'

'Do you believe they have made a pact with a god, Captain? Such cults are forbidden in the imperial army.'

'I cannot answer that, sir. Nor have I evidence sufficient to make such a charge against them. Thus far, I have kept Gesler's squad, and a few others, as the column's rearguard.'

The Fist grunted. 'This news is disturbing, Captain. You do not trust your own soldiers. And this is the first time you've told me of any of this. Have you considered confronting the sergeant directly?'

They had reached the edge of the camp. Before them stretched a broken line of hills; to their right, the dark forest of Vathar.

To Gamet's questions, Keneb sighed and nodded. 'They in turn do not trust me, Fist. There is a rumour in my company . . . that I abandoned my last soldiers, at the time of the uprising.'

And did you, Keneb? Gamet said nothing.

But it seemed that the captain heard the silent question none the less. 'I didn't, although I will not deny that some of the decisions I made back then could give cause to question my loyalty to the empire.'

'You had better explain that,' Gamet said quietly.

'I had family with me. I sought to save them, and for a time nothing else mattered. Sir, whole companies went over to the rebels. You did not know who to trust. And as it turned out, my commander—'

'Say no more of that, Captain. I've changed my mind. I don't want to know. Your family? Did you manage to save them?'

'Aye, sir. With some timely help from an outlawed Bridgeburner—'

'A *what*? Who, in Hood's name?'

'Corporal Kalam, sir.'

'He's here? In Seven Cities?'

'He was. On his way, I think, to the Empress. From what I gathered, he had some issues he wanted to, uh, raise with her. In person.'

'Who else knows all this?'

'No-one, sir. I've heard the tale, that the Bridgeburners were wiped out. But I can tell you, Kalam was not among them. He was here, sir. And as to where he is now, perhaps the Empress alone knows.'

There was a smudge of motion in the grasses, about twenty paces distant. *That dog. Hood knows what it's up to.* 'All right, Captain. Keep Gesler in the rearguard for now. But at some point, before the battle, we'll have to test him – I need to know if he's reliable.'

'Aye, sir.'

'Your beast is wandering out there.'

'I know. Every night. As if looking for something. I think it might be ... Coltaine. Looking for Coltaine. And it breaks my heart, sir.'

'Well, if it's true, Captain, that the dog's looking for Coltaine, I admit to being surprised.'

'What do you mean, sir?'

'Because the bastard's here. You'd have to be blind, dumb and deaf to miss him, Captain. Goodnight to you.' He turned and strode off, feeling the need to spit, but he knew the bitter taste in his mouth would not so easily leave him.

The fire was long dead. Wrapped in his cloak, Strings sat before it, looking at but not seeing the layered bricks of ash that were all that remained of the pieces of dung. Beside him lay the scrawny Hengese lapdog that Truth said was named Roach. The bone the creature gnawed on was bigger than it, and had that bone teeth and appetite it would be the one doing the eating right now.

Contented company, then, to mock this miserable night. The blanketed forms of his squad lay motionless on all sides. They'd been too exhausted to get drunk, after raising the pickets then sitting first watch, and full bellies had quickly dragged them into sleep. Well enough, he mused, they'd be among the few spared the ravages of hangover in a few bells' time. Even Cuttle had yet to awaken, as was his custom – or perhaps his eyes were open where he lay with his back to the hearth.

It did not matter. The loneliness Strings suffered could not be alleviated by company, not such as he might find here, in any case. Nor were his thoughts the kind he would willingly share.

They'd been spitting dust almost since the march began. Not the place for marines, unless a massive pursuit threatened the rear of the column, which was not the case. No. Keneb was punishing them, and Strings had no idea why. Even the lieutenant, who had somehow managed to avoid actually being present to command the squads, was uncertain as to the captain's motivations. *Though not displeased, of course. Then again, how can Ranal hope to acquire his stellar reputation with his soldiers coughing the entire Fourteenth's dust?*

And do I even give a damn, any more?

The night air stank of bile, as if Poliel herself stalked the camp. The sudden acquisition of three thousand veterans had done much to lift the Fourteenth's spirits – Strings hoped there was no omen in the aftermath.

All right then, let's consider the matter at hand. This army has its chance, now. It doesn't need bastards like me. Why would I want to go back to Raraku anyway? I hated it the first time. I'm not that young, mouthy fool – not what I once was. Did I really think I could recapture something in that holy desert? What, exactly? Lost years? That charging momentum that belongs to the young? To soldiers like Smiles and Koryk and Bottle and Tarr. I joined for revenge, but it's not filling my belly like it used to – Hood knows, nothing does any more. Not revenge. Not loyalty. Not even friendship. Damn you, Kalam, you should've talked me out of it. Right there in Malaz City. You should've called me a fool to my face.

Gesler's cattle dog padded into view.

Roach growled, and the bigger beast paused, nose testing the air, then settled down a few paces away. The lapdog returned to its gnawing.

'Come ahead, then, Gesler,' Strings muttered.

The sergeant appeared, a jug in one hand. He sat down opposite, studied the jug for a moment, then made a disgusted sound and tossed it away. 'Can't get drunk any more,' he said. 'Not me, not Stormy or Truth. We're cursed.'

'I can think of worse curses,' Strings muttered.

'Well, so can I, but still. What's really bad is I can't sleep. None of us can. We was at Vathar Crossing – that's where we drew the *Silanda* in to wait for the Chain of Dogs. Where I got punched good and hard, too. Damn, but that surprised me. Anyway, I'm not looking forward to seeing it again. Not after what happened there.'

'So long as the bridge hasn't been swept away,' Strings replied.

Gesler grunted.

Neither spoke for a time, then: 'You're thinking of running, aren't you, Fid?'

He scowled.

Gesler slowly nodded. 'It's bad when you lose 'em. Friends, I mean. Makes you wonder why you're still here, why the damned sack of blood and muscle and bones keeps on going. So you run. Then what? Nothing. You're not here, but wherever you are, you're still there.'

Strings grimaced. 'I'm supposed to make sense of that? Listen, it's not just what happened to the Bridgeburners. It's about being a soldier. About doing this all over again. I've realized that I didn't even like it much the first time round. There's got to come a point, Gesler, when it's no longer the right place to be, or the right thing to do.'

'Maybe, but I ain't seen it yet. It comes down to what you're good at. Nothing else, Fid. You don't want to be a soldier no more. Fine, but what are you going to do instead?'

'I was apprenticed as a mason, once—'

'And apprentices are ten years old, Fiddler. They ain't crabby creakbones like you. Look, there's only one thing for a soldier to do, and that's soldiering. You want it to end? Well, there's a battle coming. Should give you plenty of opportunity. Throw yourself on a sword and you're done.' Gesler paused and jabbed a finger at Strings. 'But that's not the problem, is it? It's because now you've got a squad, and you're responsible for 'em. *That's* what you don't like, and that's what's got you thinking of running.'

Strings rose. 'Go pet your dog, Gesler.' He walked off into the darkness.

The grass was wet underfoot as he made his way through the pickets. Muted challenges sounded, to which he replied, and then he was out beyond the camp. Overhead, the stars had begun to withdraw as the sky lightened. Capemoths were winging in swirling clouds towards the forested hills of Vathar, the occasional rhizan diving through them, upon which they exploded outward, only to reform once the danger was past.

On the ridge three hundred paces ahead of the sergeant stood a half-dozen desert wolves. They'd done their howling for the night, and now lingered out of curiosity, or perhaps simply awaiting the army's departure, so they could descend into the basin and pick at the leavings.

Strings paused at a faint singing, low and mournful and jarring, that seemed to emanate from a depression just this side of the ridge. He'd heard it other nights, always beyond the encampment, but had not been inclined to investigate. There was nothing inviting to that thin, atonal music.

But now it called to him. With familiar voices. Heart suddenly aching, he walked closer.

The depression was thick with yellowed grasses, but a circle had been flattened in the centre. The two Wickan children, Nil and Nether, were seated there, facing one another, with the space between them occupied by a broad, bronze bowl.

Whatever filled it was drawing butterflies, a score at present, but more were gathering.

Strings hesitated, then made to leave.

'Come closer,' Nil called out in his reedy voice. 'Quickly, the sun rises!'

Frowning, the sergeant approached. As he reached the edge of the depression, he halted in sudden alarm. Butterflies swarmed around him, a pale yellow frenzy filling his eyes – brushing air against his skin like a thousand breaths. He spun in place, but could see nothing beyond the mass of fluttering wings.

'Closer! He wants you here!' Nether's high, piping voice.

But Strings could not take another step. He was enveloped, and within that yellow shroud, there was a . . . *presence*.

And it spoke. '*Bridgeburner. Raraku waits for you. Do not turn back now.*'

'Who are you?' Strings demanded. 'Who speaks?'

'*I am of this land, now. What I was before does not matter. I am awakened. We are awakened. Go to join your kin. In Raraku – where he will find you. Together, you must slay the goddess. You must free Raraku of the stain that lies upon it.*'

'My kin? Who will I find there?'

'*The song wanders, Bridgeburner. It seeks a home. Do not turn back.*'

All at once the presence vanished. The butterflies rose skyward, spinning and swirling into the sunlight. Higher, ever higher . . .

Small hands clutched at him, and he looked down. Nether stared up at him, her face filled with panic. Two paces behind her stood Nil, his arms wrapped about himself, his eyes filling with tears.

Nether was screaming. 'Why you? We have called and called! *Why you!?*'

Shaking his head, Strings pushed her away. 'I – I don't know!'

'What did he say? Tell us! He had a message for us, yes? What did he say?'

'For you? Nothing, lass – why, who in Hood's name do you think that was?'

'Sormo E'nath!'

'The warlock? But he—' Strings staggered another step back. '*Stop that damned singing!*'

The Wickans stared.

And Strings realized that neither was singing – neither could have been – for it continued, filling his head.

Nether asked, 'What singing, soldier?'

He shook his head again, then turned and made his way back towards camp. Sormo had no words for them. Nor did he. Nor did he want to see their faces – their helpless desperation, their yearning for a ghost that was gone – gone for ever. *That was not Sormo E'nath. That was something else – Hood knows what. 'We are awakened.' What does that mean? And who's waiting for me in Raraku? My kin – I've none, barring the Bridgeburners – gods below! Quick Ben? Kalam? One, or both?* He wanted to scream, if only to silence the song that whispered through his head, the dreadful, painfully incomplete music that gnawed at his sanity.

Raraku, it seemed, was not yet done with him. Strings silently railed. *Damn all of this!*

To the north, through the smoky wreaths of the encampment, the mantled hills of Vathar seemed to unfurl the sun's golden light. On the ridge behind him, the wolves began howling.

Gamet settled back in the saddle as his horse began the descent towards the river. It had not been long enough for the land to entirely swallow the victims of the slaughter that had occurred here. Bleached bones gleamed in the sandy mud of the shoreline. Fragments of cloth, pieces of leather and iron. And the ford itself was barely recognizable. Remnants of a floating bridge were heaped on it on the upstream side, and on this barrier more detritus had piled. Sunken, waterlogged wagons, trees, grasses and reeds, now anchored by silts, a hulking, bowed mass that had formed a kind of bridge. To the Fist's eye, it seemed the whole thing was moments from breaking loose.

Scouts had crossed it on foot. Gamet could see a score of mud-smeared Seti on the opposite side, making their way up the steep slope.

The forests on both sides of the river were a mass of colour, their branches festooned with strips of cloth, with braids and painted human bones that twisted in the wind. *Mesh'arn tho'ledann. The Day of Pure Blood.* Upstream, on either bank for as far as he could see, long poles had been thrust into the mud at angles so that they hung over the swirling water. The carcasses of sheep and goats hung from them. From some the blood still drained, whilst others were well along in their rot, seething with flies, capemoths and carrion birds. Small white flecks rained down from the sacrificed animals, to which fish swarmed, and it was a moment before Gamet realized what those flecks were – maggots, falling into the river.

Captain Keneb drew his horse alongside Gamet's own as they approached the bank. 'That's not mud binding that flotsam, is it? Oh, a little silt and sand, but mostly—'

'Blood, aye,' Gamet muttered.

They were trailing the Adjunct, who was flanked by Nil and Nether. The three reached the water's edge and halted their mounts. Behind Gamet and Keneb, the front companies of the 10th Legion were on the slope, within sight of the river and its ragged bridge.

'Those sacrifices, do you think they were done to welcome us, Fist? I can't imagine such slaughter to be ongoing – the herds would be wiped out in no time.'

'Some have been here a while,' Gamet observed. 'But you must be right, Captain.'

'So we would cross a river of blood. If these damned tribes consider that gesture an honourable one, then the Queen has stolen their sanity. This notion of seeing the world metaphorically has ever driven me to distraction. The Seven Cities native sees everything differently. To them, the landscape is animate – not just the old notion of spirits, but in some other, far more complicated way.'

Gamet glanced at the man. 'Is it worth making a study of it, Captain?'

Keneb started, then half smiled, adding a strangely despondent shrug. 'That particular dialogue spoke of the rebellion and only the rebellion – for months and months before it finally happened. Had we bothered to read those signs, Fist, we could have been better prepared.'

They had drawn up behind the Adjunct and the two Wickans. At Keneb's words, Tavore turned her horse round and faced the captain. 'Sometimes,' she said, 'knowledge is not enough.'

'Your pardon, Adjunct,' Keneb said.

Tavore fixed her flat gaze on Gamet. 'Bring forward the marines, Fist. We will require sappers and munitions. We shall cross a ford, not a bridge of detritus held in place by blood.'

'Aye, Adjunct. Captain, if you will join me . . .'

They pulled their horses round and made their way back up the slope. Glancing over at Keneb, Gamet saw that the man was grinning. 'What amuses you, Captain?'

'Munitions, sir. The sappers will weep.'

'So long as they don't destroy the ford itself, I will be glad to give them comforting hugs.'

'I wouldn't let them hear a promise like that, sir.'

'No, I suppose you're right.'

They reached the front ranks of the 10th Legion and Gamet waved a messenger over. As the rider approached,

Fist Tene Baralta joined the woman and the two arrived together.

'Sappers?' the Red Blade asked.

Gamet nodded. 'Aye.'

Tene Baralta nodded and said to the messenger, 'Take word to the marine lieutenants. The Adjunct requires some demolition. Immediately.'

'Aye, sir,' she replied, wheeling her horse round.

They watched her canter back along the line, then the Red Blade faced Gamet. 'They will see it as an insult. This bridge of blood is intended as a blessing.'

'She knows that, Tene Baralta,' Gamet replied. 'But the footing is far too treacherous. That should be obvious, even to our hidden observers.'

The large man shrugged, armour clanking with the motion. 'Perhaps a quiet word to Gall of the Khundryl, a rider sent out to find those observers, to ensure that no misunderstanding occurs.'

'A good suggestion,' Gamet replied.

'I shall see to it, then.'

The Red Blade rode off.

'Forgive me if I am too forward, Fist,' Keneb murmured, 'but what just occurred strikes me as the very thing that the Adjunct would dislike most.'

'Do you believe she dislikes initiative among her officers, Captain?'

'I wouldn't presume—'

'You just did.'

'Ah, well, I see your point. My apologies, Fist.'

'Never apologize when you're right, Keneb. Wait here for the squads.' He set off down to where the Adjunct still sat astride her horse at the shoreline.

Nil and Nether had dismounted and were now kneeling, heads bowed, in the muddy water.

Gamet could see, upon arriving, Tavore's tightly bridled anger. *Aye, they cling still to the chains, and it seems letting go is the last thing they would do . . . given the choice. Well, I was the one who mentioned initiative*. 'I see the children are playing in the mud, Adjunct.'

Her head snapped round and her eyes narrowed.

Gamet went on, 'I advise we assign a minder for them, lest they injure themselves in their exuberance. After all, Adjunct, I doubt the Empress intended you to *mother* them, did she?'

'Well, no,' she drawled after a moment. 'They were to be my mages.'

'Aye, so I wonder, have you instructed them to commune with the ghosts? Do they seek to appease the river spirits?'

'No, again, Fist. In truth, I have no idea what they're doing.'

'I am of the opinion that you are proving far too permissive a mother, Adjunct.'

'Indeed. Then I give you leave to act in my stead, Fist.'

There was no way Nil and Nether were uncognizant of the conversation behind them, but neither altered their position. With a loud sigh, Gamet dismounted and walked to the muddy waterline.

Then reached down and closed a hand on their hide shirts, just behind their necks, and yanked the two Wickans upright.

Loud squeals, then hissing fury as the Fist shook them both for a moment, then turned them round until they faced the Adjunct. 'This is what a Wickan grandmother would have done. I know, somewhat harsher than is the Malazan style of parenting. Then again, these two children are not Malazan, are they?' He set them down.

'Perhaps it's too late, Fist,' Tavore said, 'but I would remind you that these two children are also warlocks.'

'I've seen no sign of it yet, Adjunct. But if they want to curse me, then so be it.'

For the moment, however, neither seemed inclined to do so. Rage had given way to something very much resembling a sulk.

Tavore cleared her throat. 'Nil, Nether, I believe there

will be need for representatives of our army to seek out the local tribes in this forest, to assure them we are aware of the meaning behind their gesture. None the less, we must ensure safe passage across this ford.'

'Adjunct, Fist Tene Baralta has suggested something similar, but using the Khundryl.'

'Perhaps representatives from both, then.' To the Wickans: 'Report to Fist Tene Baralta.'

Gamet watched the siblings exchange a glance, then Nil said to the Adjunct, 'As you wish.'

Nether cast a parting look of venom at Gamet as they headed off.

'Pray you won't have to pay for that,' Tavore said when they were out of earshot.

Gamet shrugged.

'And next time, have Tene Baralta bring his suggestions to me personally.'

'Aye, Adjunct.'

Cuttle and Strings scrambled back from the shoreline. Soaked and sheathed in blood-crusted mud, they none the less could not keep grins from their faces. A doubling of pleasure in that the munitions had come from the Fourteenth's stores, not their own. Twelve crackers that would drive the explosions horizontally, three cussers placed shallow in the detritus to loosen the wreckage.

And a bare handful of heartbeats before it all went up.

The rest of the army had pulled back to the top of the slope on this side; the Seti scouts on the opposite side were nowhere to be seen. Leaving only the two sappers—

—running like madmen.

A thundering *whump* sent both men flying. Sand, mud, water, followed by a rain of debris.

Hands over their heads, they lay motionless for a long moment, with the only sound to reach them the rush of water sweeping over the cleared ford. Then Strings looked across at Cuttle, to find him looking back.

Maybe two cussers would have done.

They exchanged nods, then clambered to their feet.

The ford was indeed clear. The water beyond seethed with flotsam, now making its way down to the Dojal Hading Sea.

Strings wiped mud from his face. 'Think we made any holes, Cuttle?'

'Nothing that'll drown anyone, I'd wager. Good thing you didn't run,' Cuttle added in a murmur, as riders made their way down the slope behind them.

Strings shot the man a glance. 'What *don't* you hear?'

'Not a question I can answer, is it, Fid?'

The first rider arrived – their fellow sapper, Maybe, from the 6th squad. 'Flat and clean,' he said, 'but you left it too close – what's the point of making a big explosion when you've got your face in the dirt when it goes off?'

'Any other bright comments to make, Maybe?' Cuttle growled, brushing himself down – a gesture that clearly had no chance of any kind of measurable success. 'If not, then kindly ride out there and check for holes.'

'Slowly,' Strings added. 'Let your horse find its own pace.'

Maybe's brows rose. 'Really?' Then he nudged his mount forward.

Strings stared after the soldier. 'I hate satirical bastards like him.'

'The Wickans will skin him alive if he breaks that horse's legs.'

'That has the sound of a feud in the making.'

Cuttle paused in his fruitless efforts to clean himself, then frowned. 'What?'

'Never mind.'

Ranal and Keneb rode up. 'Nicely done,' the captain said. 'I think.'

'Should be all right,' Strings replied. 'So long as nobody starts firing arrows at us.'

'Taken care of, Sergeant. Well, to your squad, the privilege of first crossing.'

'Aye, sir.'

There should have been pleasure, in a task well done, but Strings felt nothing beyond the initial rush that had immediately followed the detonation. The broken song whispered on in his mind, a dirge lying beneath his every thought.

'The way ahead seems clear,' Cuttle muttered.

Aye. Doesn't mean I have to like it.

The land rose steeply on the north side of the Vathar River, with a treeless butte towering over the trail to the west. The army's crossing continued as the Adjunct and Gamet climbed the goat trail towards the butte's summit. The sun was low in the sky – their second full day at the ford – and the river was made molten by the lurid streams of light off to their left, although this side of the rock prominence was in deep shadow.

The mud covering Gamet's leather-clad legs was drying to a stiff, crack-latticed skin that shed dust as he clambered in Tavore's wake. He was breathing hard, his under-garments soaked with sweat.

They reached the summit, emerging once more into sunlight. A brisk, hot wind swept the barren, flat rock. A ring of stones on a lower shelf, on what passed for the lee side, marked where a hearth or watch-fire had once been constructed, possibly at the time of the Chain of Dogs.

The Adjunct wiped dust from her gloves, then strode to the north edge. After a moment, Gamet followed.

The city of Ubaryd was visible, dun-coloured and sheathed in smoke, to the northeast. Beyond it glittered the Dojal Hading Sea. The city's harbour was crowded with ships.

'Admiral Nok,' the Adjunct said.

'He's retaken Ubaryd, then.'

'Where we will resupply, yes.' Then she pointed northward. 'There, Gamet. Do you see it?'

He squinted, wondering what he was supposed to look at

652

across the vast wasteland that was the Ubaryd Odhan. Then the breath hissed between his teeth.

A fiery wall of red on the horizon, as if a second sun was setting.

'The Whirlwind,' Tavore said.

Suddenly, the wind was much colder, pushing hard against Gamet where he stood.

'Beyond it,' the Adjunct continued, 'waits our enemy. Tell me, do you think Sha'ik will contest our approach?'

'She would be a fool not to,' he replied.

'Are you certain of that? Would she rather not face unblooded recruits?'

'It is a huge gamble, Adjunct. The march alone will have hardened the Fourteenth. Were I her, I would prefer to face a battle-weary, bruised enemy. An enemy burdened with wounded, with a shortage of arrows, horses and whatnot. And by that time of final meeting, I would also have learned something of you, Adjunct. Your tactics. As it is, Sha'ik has no way to take your measure.'

'Yes. Curious, isn't it? Either she is indifferent to me, or she feels she has already taken my measure – which of course is impossible. Even assuming she has spies in our army, thus far I have done little more than ensure that we march in an organized fashion.'

Spies? Gods below, I hadn't even considered that!

Neither spoke for a time, each lost in their own thoughts as they stared northward.

The sun was vanishing on their left.

But the Whirlwind held its own fire.

CHAPTER SIXTEEN

Power has voice, and that voice is the Song of the Tanno
Spiritwalker.

Kimloc

He awoke to a faint, damp nuzzling against his side.
His eyes slowly opened, head tilted downward, to see a
bhok'aral pup, patchy with some sort of skin
infection, curled against his stomach.

Kalam sat up, suppressing the urge to grab the creature
by the neck and fling it against a wall. Compassion was not
the consideration, of course. Rather, it was the fact that
this subterranean temple was home to hundreds, perhaps
even thousands of bhok'arala, and the creatures possessed a
complex social structure – harm this pup and Kalam might
find himself beneath a swarm of bull males. And small as
the beasts were, they had canines to rival a bear's. Even so,
he fought to contain his revulsion as he gently pushed the
mottled pup away.

It mewled pathetically and looked up at him with huge,
liquid eyes.

'Don't even try,' the assassin muttered, slipping free of
the furs and rising. Flecks of mouldy skin covered his
midriff, and the thin woollen shirt was sodden from the
pup's runny nose. Kalam removed the shirt and flung it into
a corner of the small chamber.

He'd not seen Iskaral Pust in over a week. Apart from
occasional tingling sensations at the tips of his fingers and

toes, he was more or less recovered from the enkar'al demon's attack. Kalam had delivered the diamonds and was now chafing to leave.

Faint singing echoed from the hallway. The assassin shook his head. *Maybe one day Mogora will get it right, but in the meantime . . . gods below, it grates!* He strode to his tattered backpack and rummaged inside until he found a spare shirt.

Sudden thumping sounded outside his door, and he turned in time to see it flung open. Mogora stood framed in the doorway, a wooden bucket in one hand, a mop in the other. 'Was he here? Just now? Was he here? Tell me!'

'I haven't seen him in days,' Kalam replied.

'He has to clean the kitchen!'

'Is this all you do, Mogora? Chase after Iskaral Pust's shadow?'

'*All!*' The word was a shriek. She stormed up to him, mop thrust forward like a weapon. 'Am *I* the only one using the kitchen! No!'

Kalam stepped back, wiping spittle from his face, but the Dal Honese woman advanced.

'And *you*! Do you think your suppers arrive all by themselves? Do you think the shadow gods simply conjure them out of thin air? Did I invite you here? Are you my guest? Am I your serving wench?'

'Gods forbid—'

'Be quiet! I'm talking, not you!' She thrust the mop and bucket into Kalam's hands, then, spying the bhok'aral pup curled up on the cot, dropped into a predatory crouch and edged closer, fingers hooked. 'There you are,' she murmured. 'Leave your skin everywhere, will you? Not for much longer!'

Kalam stepped into her path. 'Enough, Mogora. Get out of here.'

'Not without my pet.'

'Pet? You're intending to wring its neck, Mogora!'

'So?'

He set the mop and bucket down. *I can't believe this. I'm defending a mangy bhok'aral . . . from a D'ivers witch.*

There was movement in the doorway. Kalam gestured. 'Look behind you, Mogora. Harm this pup and you'll have to face *them*.'

She spun, then hissed. 'Scum! Iskaral's beget – always spying! That's how he hides – using them!'

With a ululating scream she charged into the doorway. The bhok'arala massed there shrieked in answer and scattered, although Kalam saw one dart between her legs and leap onto the cot. It scooped the pup up under one arm then bolted for the corridor.

Mogora's wailing cries dwindled as she continued her pursuit.

'Hee hee.'

Kalam turned.

Iskaral Pust emerged from the shadows in the far corner. He was covered in dust, a sack draped over one bony shoulder.

The assassin scowled. 'I've waited long enough in this madhouse, Priest.'

'Indeed you have.' He cocked his head, tugging at one of the few wisps of hair that remained on his pate. 'I'm done and he can go, yes? I should be kindly, open, scattering gold dust to mark his path out into the waiting world. He'll suspect nothing. He'll believe he leaves of his own free will. Precisely as it should be.' Iskaral Pust suddenly smiled, then held out the sack. 'Here, a few diamonds for you. Spend them here and there, spend them everywhere! But remember, you must breach the Whirlwind – into the heart of Raraku, yes?'

'That is my intent,' Kalam growled, accepting the sack and stuffing it into his own backpack. 'We do not proceed at cross-purposes, Priest, although I realize you'd rather we did, given your perverse mind. Even so . . . breach the Whirlwind . . . without being detected. How will I manage that?'

'With the help of Shadowthrone's chosen mortal. Iskaral Pust, High Priest and Master of Rashan and Meanas and Thyr! The Whirlwind is a goddess, and her eyes cannot be everywhere. Now, quickly collect your belongings. We must leave! She's coming back, and I've made another mess in the kitchen! Hurry!'

They emerged from the warren of shadow beneath a large outcropping, in daylight, less than a hundred paces from the raging wall of the Whirlwind. After three strides forward Kalam reached out and grabbed the priest by the arm and spun him round.

'That singing? Where in Hood's name is that singing coming from, Iskaral? I'd heard it in the monastery and thought it was Mogora—'

'Mogora can't sing, you fool! I hear nothing, nothing but the wild winds and the hiss of sands! You are mad! Is he mad? Yes, possibly. No, likely. The sun broiled his brain in that thick skull. A gradual dissolution – but of course not, of course not. It's the Tanno song, that's what it is. Even so, he's probably still mad. Two entirely separate issues. The song. And his madness. Distinct, unrelated, both equally confounding of all that my masters plan. Or potentially so. Potentially. There is no certainty, not in this damned land, especially not here. Restless Raraku. Restless!'

With a snarl, Kalam pushed the man away, began walking towards the wall of the Whirlwind. After a moment, Iskaral Pust followed.

'Tell me how we're going to manage this, Priest.'

'It's simple, really. She'll know the breach. Like a knife stab. That cannot be avoided. Thus, misdirection! And there is none better at misdirection than Iskaral Pust!'

They arrived to within twenty paces of the seething wall of sand. Swirling clouds of dust engulfed them. Iskaral Pust moved close, revealing a grin filled with grit. 'Hold tight, Kalam Mekhar!' Then he vanished.

A massive shape loomed over the assassin, and he was suddenly gathered up in a swarm of arms.

The azalan.

Running, now, flowing faster than any horse along the edge of the Whirlwind Wall. The demon tucked Kalam close under its torso – then plunged through.

A thundering roar filled the assassin's ears, sand flailing against his skin. He squeezed shut his eyes.

Multiple thuds, and the azalan was racing across packed sand. Ahead lay the ruins of a city.

Fire flared beneath the demon, a path of flames raging in its wake.

The raised tel of the dead city rose before them. The azalan did not even slow, swarming up the ragged wall. A fissure loomed, not large enough for the demon – but sufficient for Kalam.

He was flung into the crack as the azalan flowed over it. Landing heavily amidst rubble and potsherds. Deep in the fissure's shadow.

Sudden thunder overhead, shaking the rock. Then again and again, seeming to stitch a path back towards the wall of sand. The detonations then ceased, and only the roar of the Whirlwind remained.

I think he made it back out. Fast bastard.

The assassin remained motionless for a time, wondering if the ruse had succeeded. Either way, he would wait for night before venturing out.

He could no longer hear the song. *Something to be grateful for.*

The walls of the fissure revealed layer upon layer of potsherds on one side, a sunken and heaved section of cobblestone street on another, and the flank of a building's interior wall – the plaster chipped and scarred – on the last. The rubble beneath him was loose and felt deep.

Checking his weapons, Kalam settled down to wait.

Apsalar in his arms, Cutter emerged from the gateway. The

woman's weight sent waves of pain through his bruised shoulder, and he did not think he would be able to carry her for long.

Thirty paces ahead, at the edge of the clearing where the two trails converged, lay scores of corpses. And in their midst stood Cotillion.

Cutter walked over to the shadow god. The Tiste Edur lay heaped in a ring around a clear spot off to the left, but Cotillion's attention seemed to be on one body in particular, lying at his feet. As the Daru approached, the god slowly settled down into a crouch, reaching out to brush hair back from the corpse's face.

It was the old witch, Cutter saw, the one who had been burned. *The one I thought was the source of power in the Malazan party. But it wasn't her. It was Traveller.* He halted a few paces away, brought up short by Cotillion's expression, the ravaged look that made him suddenly appear twenty years older. The gloved hand that had swept the hair back now caressed the dead woman's scorched face.

'You knew her?' Cutter asked.

'Hawl,' he replied after a moment. 'I'd thought Surly had taken them all out. None of the Talon's command left. I thought she was dead.'

'She is.' Then he snapped his mouth shut. *A damned miserable thing to say—*

'I made them good at hiding,' Cotillion went on, eyes still on the woman lying in the bloody, trampled grass. 'Good enough to hide even from me, it seems.'

'What do you think she was doing here?'

Cotillion flinched slightly. 'The wrong question, Cutter. Rather, why was she with Traveller? What is the Talon up to? And Traveller . . . gods, did he know who she was? Of course he did – oh, she's aged and not well, but even so . . .'

'You could just ask him,' Cutter murmured, grunting as he shifted Apsalar's weight in his arms. 'He's in the courtyard behind us, after all.'

Cotillion reached down to the woman's neck and lifted

into view something strung on a thong. A yellow-stained talon of some sort. He pulled it loose, studied it for a moment, then twisted round and flung it towards Cutter.

It struck his chest, then fell to lie in Apsalar's lap.

The Daru stared down at it for a moment, then looked up and met the god's eyes.

'Go to the Edur ship, Cutter. I am sending you two to another . . . agent of ours.'

'To do what?'

'To wait. In case you are needed.'

'For what?'

'To assist others in taking down the Master of the Talon.'

'Do you know where he or she is?'

He lifted Hawl into his arms and straightened. 'I have a suspicion. Now, finally, a suspicion about all of this.' He turned, the frail figure held lightly in his arms, and studied Cutter for a moment. A momentary, wan smile. 'Look at the two of us,' he said, then he swung away and began walking towards the forest trail.

Cutter stared after him.

Then shouted: 'It's not the same! It's not! *We're not*—'

The forest shadows swallowed the god.

Cutter hissed a curse, then he turned to the trail that led down to the shoreline.

The god Cotillion walked on until he reached a small glade off to one side of the path. He carried his burden into its centre, and gently set her down.

A host of shadows spun into being opposite, until the vague, insubstantial form of Shadowthrone slowly resolved itself. For a change, the god said nothing for a long time.

Cotillion knelt beside Hawl's body. 'Traveller is here, Ammanas. In the Edur ruins.'

Ammanas grunted softly, then shrugged. 'He'll have no interest in answering our questions. He never did. Stubborn as any Dal Honese.'

'You're Dal Honese,' Cotillion observed.

'Precisely.' Ammanas slipped noiselessly forward until he was on the other side of the corpse. 'It's her, isn't it.'

'It is.'

'How many times do our followers have to die, Cotillion?' the god asked, then sighed. 'Then again, she clearly ceased being a follower some time ago.'

'She thought we were gone, Ammanas. The Emperor and Dancer. Gone. Dead.'

'And in a way, she was right.'

'In a way, aye. But not in the most important way.'

'Which is?'

Cotillion glanced up, then grimaced. 'She was a friend.'

'Ah, that most important way.' Ammanas was silent for a moment, then he asked, 'Will you pursue this?'

'I see little choice. The Talon is up to something. We need to stop them—'

'No, friend. We need to ensure that they *fail*. Have you found a . . . trail?'

'More than that. I've realized who is masterminding the whole thing.'

Shadowthrone's hooded head cocked slightly. 'And that is where Cutter and Apsalar are going now?'

'Yes.'

'Are they sufficient?'

Cotillion shook his head. 'I have other agents available. But I would Apsalar be relatively close, in case something goes wrong.'

Ammanas nodded. 'So, where?'

'Raraku.'

Though he could not see it, Cotillion knew that his companion's face was splitting into a broad grin. 'Ah, dear Rope, time's come, I think, that I should tell you more of my own endeavours . . .'

'The diamonds I gave Kalam? I'd wondered about those.'

Ammanas gestured at Hawl's corpse. 'Let us take her home – our home, that is. And then we must speak . . . at length.'

Cotillion nodded.

'Besides,' Shadowthrone added as he straightened, 'Traveller being so close by makes me nervous.'

A moment later, the glade was empty, barring a few sourceless shadows that swiftly dwindled into nothing.

Cutter reached the sandstone shoreline. Four runners had been pulled up on the flat, grainy shelf of rock. Anchored in the bay beyond were two large dromons, both badly damaged.

Around the runners gear lay scattered, and two huge trees had been felled and dragged close – probably intended to replace the snapped masts. Barrels containing salted fish had been broached, while other casks stood in a row nearby, refilled with fresh water.

Cutter set Apsalar down, then approached one of the runners. They were about fifteen paces from bow to stern, broad of beam with an unstepped mast and side-mounted steering oar. There were two oarlocks to a side. The gunnels were crowded with riotous carvings.

A sudden coughing fit from Apsalar swung him round.

She bolted upright, spat to clear her throat, then wrapped her arms about herself as shivering racked through her.

Cutter quickly returned to her side.

'D-Darist?'

'Dead. But so are all the Edur. There was one among the Malazans . . .'

'The one of power. I felt him. Such . . . *anger!*'

Cutter went over to the nearest water cask, found a ladle. He dipped it full and walked back. 'He called himself Traveller.'

'I know him,' she whispered, then shuddered. 'Not my memories. Dancer's. Dancer knew him. Knew him well. They were . . . three. It was never just the two of them – did you know that? Never just Dancer and Kellanved. No, *he* was there. Almost from the very beginning. Before Tayschrenn, before Dujek, before even Surly.'

'Well, it makes no difference now, Apsalar,' Cutter said. 'We need to leave this damned island – Traveller can have it, as far as I'm concerned. Are you recovered enough to help me get one of these runners into the water? We've a bounty in supplies, too—'

'Where are we going?'

He hesitated.

Her dark eyes flattened. 'Cotillion.'

'Another task for us, aye.'

'Do not walk this path, Crokus.'

He scowled. 'I thought you'd appreciate the company.' He offered her the ladle.

She studied him for a long moment, then slowly accepted it.

'Pan'potsun Hills.'

'I know,' Lostara drawled.

Pearl smiled. 'Of course you would. And now, at last, you discover the reason I asked you along—'

'Wait a minute. You couldn't have known where this trail would lead—'

'Well, true, but I have faith in blind nature's penchant for cycles. In any case, is there a buried city nearby?'

'Nearby? You mean, apart from the one we're standing on?' She was pleased to see his jaw drop. 'What did you think all these flat-topped hills were, Claw?'

He loosened his cloak. 'Then again, this place will suit just fine.'

'For what?'

He cast her a sardonic glance. 'Well, dear, a ritual. We need to find a trail, a sorcerous one, and it's old. Did you imagine we would just wander directionless through this wasteland in the hopes of finding something?'

'Odd, I thought that was what we've been doing for days.'

'Just getting some distance between us and that damned Imass head,' he replied, walking over to a flat stretch of stone, where he began kicking it clear of rubble. 'I could feel its unhuman eyes on us all the way across that valley.'

'Him and the vultures, aye.' She tilted her head back and studied the cloudless sky. 'Still with us, in fact. Those damned birds. Not surprising. We're almost out of water, with even less food. In a day or two we'll be in serious trouble.'

'I will leave such mundane worries with you, Lostara.'

'Meaning, if all else fails, you can always kill and eat me, right? But what if I decide to kill you first? Obsessed as I am with mundane worries.'

The Claw settled down into a crosslegged position. 'It's become much cooler here, don't you think? A localized phenomenon, I suspect. Although I would imagine that some measure of success in the ritual I am about to enact should warm things up somewhat.'

'If only the excitement of disbelief,' Lostara muttered, walking over to the edge of the tel and looking south-westward to where the red wall of the Whirlwind cut a curving slash across the desert. Behind her, she heard muted words, spoken in some language unknown to her. *Probably gibberish. I've seen enough mages at work to know they don't need words . . . not unless they're performing.* Pearl was probably doing just that. He was one for poses, even while affecting indifference to his audience of one. *A man seeking his name in tomes of history. Some crucial role upon which the fate of the empire pivots.*

She turned as he slapped dust from hands, and saw him rising, a troubled frown on his all-too-handsome face.

'That didn't take long,' she said.

'No.' Even he sounded surprised. 'I was fortunate indeed. A local earth spirit was killed . . . close by. By a confluence of dire fates, an incidental casualty. Its ghost lingers, like a child seeking lost parents, and so would speak to any and every stranger who happens by, provided that stranger is prepared to listen.'

Lostara grunted. 'All right, and what did it have to say?'

'A terrible incident – well, *the* terrible incident, the one that killed the spirit – the details of which lead me to conclude there is some connec—'

'Good,' she interrupted. 'Lead on, we're wasting time.'

He fell silent, giving her a wounded look that might well have been sincere. *I asked the question, I should at least let him answer it.*

A gesture, and he was making his way down the tel's steep, stepped side.

She shouldered her pack and followed.

Reaching the base, the Claw led her around its flank and directly southward across a stony flat. The sunlight bounced from its bleached surface with a fierce, blinding glare. Barring a few ants scurrying underfoot, there was no sign of life on this withered stretch of ground. Small stones lay in elongated clusters here and there, as if describing the shorelines of a dying lake, a lake that had dwindled into a scatter of pools, leaving nothing but crusted salt.

They walked on through the afternoon, until a ridge of hills became visible to the southwest, with another massive mesa rising to its left. The flat began to form a discernible basin that seemed to continue on between the two formations. With dusk only moments away, they reached the even base of that descent, the mesa looming on their left, the broken hill ahead and to their right.

Towards the centre of this flat lay the wreckage of a trader's wagon, surrounded by scorched ground where white ashes spun in small vortices that seemed incapable of going anywhere.

Pearl leading, they strode into the strange burned circle.

The ashes were filled with tiny bones, burned white and grey by some intense heat, crunching underfoot. Bemused, Lostara crouched down to study them. 'Birds?' she wondered aloud.

Pearl's gaze was on the wagon or, perhaps, something just beyond it. At her question he shook his head. 'No, lass. Rats.'

She saw a tiny skull lying at her feet, confirming his words. 'There are rats of a sort, in the rocky areas—'

He glanced over at her. 'These are – were – D'ivers. A particularly unpleasant individual named Gryllen.'

'He was slain here?'

'I don't think so. Badly hurt, perhaps.' Pearl walked over to a larger heap of ash, and squatted to sweep it away.

Lostara approached.

He was uncovering a corpse, nothing but bones – and those bones were all terribly gnawed.

'Poor bastard.'

Pearl said nothing. He reached down into the collapsed skeleton and lifted into view a small chunk of metal. 'Melted,' he muttered after a moment, 'but I'd say it's a Malazan sigil. Mage cadre.'

There were four additional heaps similar to that which had hidden the chewed bones. Lostara walked to the nearest one and began kicking the ash away.

'This one's whole!' she hissed, seeing fire-blackened flesh.

Pearl came over. Together, they brushed the corpse clear from the hips upward. Its clothing had been mostly burned off, and fire had raced across the skin but had seemed incapable of doing much more than scorch the surface.

As the Claw swept the last of the ash from the corpse's face, its eyes opened.

Cursing, Lostara leapt back, one hand sweeping her sword free of its scabbard.

'It's all right,' Pearl said, 'this thing isn't going anywhere, lass.'

Behind the corpse's wrinkled, collapsed lids, there were only gaping pits. Its lips had peeled back with desiccation, leaving it with a ghastly, blackened grin.

'What remains?' Pearl asked it. 'Can you still speak?'

Faint sounds rasped from it, forcing Pearl to lean closer.

'What did it say?' Lostara demanded.

The Claw glanced back at her. 'He said, "I am named Clam, and I died a terrible death."'

'No argument there—'

'And then he became an undead porter.'

'For Gryllen?'

'Aye.'

She sheathed her tulwar. 'That seems a singularly unpleasant profession following death.'

Pearl's brows rose, then he smiled. 'Alas, we won't get much more from dear old Clam. Nor the others. The sorcery holding them animate fades. Meaning Gryllen is either dead or a long way away. In any case, recall the warren of fire – it was unleashed here, in a strange manner. And it left us a trail.'

'It's too dark, Pearl. We should camp.'

'Here?'

She reconsidered, then scowled in the gloom. 'Perhaps not, but none the less I am weary, and if we're looking for signs, we'll need daylight in any case.'

Pearl strode from the circle of ash. A gesture and a sphere of light slowly formed in the air above him. 'The trail does not lead far, I believe. One last task, Lostara. Then we can find somewhere to camp.'

'Oh, very well. Lead on, Pearl.'

Whatever signs he followed, they were not visible to Lostara. Even stranger, it seemed to be a weaving, wandering one, a detail that had the Claw frowning, his steps hesitant, cautious. Before too long, he was barely moving at all, edging forward by the smallest increments. And she saw that his face was beaded with sweat.

She bit back on her questions, but slowly drew her sword once more.

Then, finally, they came to another corpse.

The breath whooshed from Pearl, and he sank down to his knees in front of the large, burned body.

She waited until his breathing slowed, then cleared her throat and said, 'What just happened, Pearl?'

'Hood was here,' he whispered.

'Aye, I can well see that—'

'No, you don't understand.' He reached out to the corpse, his hand closing into a fist above its broad chest, then punched down.

The body was simply a shell. It collapsed with a dusty crunch beneath the blow.

He glared back at her. 'Hood was *here*. The god himself, Lostara. Came to take this man – not just his soul, but also the flesh – all that had been infected by the warren of fire – the warren of light, to be more precise. Gods, what I would do for a Deck of Dragons right now. There's been a change in Hood's . . . household.'

'And what is the significance of all this?' she asked. 'I thought we were looking for Felisin.'

'You're not thinking, lass. Remember Stormy's tale. And Truth's. Felisin, Heboric, Kulp and Baudin. We found what was left of Kulp back at Gryllen's wagon. And this' – his gesture was fierce – 'is Baudin. The damned Talon – though the proof's not around his neck, alas. Remember their strange skin? Gesler, Stormy, Truth? The same thing happened to Baudin, here.'

'You called it an infection.'

'Well, I don't know what it is. That warren *changed* them. There's no telling in what way.'

'So, we're left with Felisin and Heboric Light Touch.'

He nodded.

'Then I feel I should tell you something,' Lostara continued. 'It may not be relevant . . .'

'Go on, lass.'

She turned to face the hills to the southwest. 'When we trailed that agent of Sha'ik's . . . into those hills—'

'Kalam Mekhar.'

'Aye. And we ambushed Sha'ik up at the old temple at the summit – on the trail leading into Raraku—'

'As you have described.'

She ignored his impatience. 'We would have seen all this. Thus, the events we've just stumbled upon here occurred after our ambush.'

'Well, yes.'

She sighed and crossed her arms. 'Felisin and Heboric are with the army of the Apocalpyse, Pearl. In Raraku.'

'What makes you so certain?'

She shrugged. 'Where else would they be? Think, man. Felisin's hatred of the Malazan Empire must be all-consuming. Nor would Heboric hold much love for the empire that imprisoned and condemned him. They were desperate, after Gryllen's attack. After Baudin and Kulp died. Desperate, and probably hurting.'

He slowly nodded, straightened from his crouch beside the corpse. 'One thing you've never explained to me, Lostara. Why did your ambush fail?'

'It didn't. We killed Sha'ik – I would swear to it. A quarrel in the forehead. We could not recover the body because of her guards, who proved too much for our company. We killed her, Pearl.'

'Then who in Hood's name is commanding the Apocalypse?'

'I don't know.'

'Can you show me this place of ambush?'

'In the morning, aye. I can take you right there.'

He simply stared at her, even as the sphere of light above them began to waver, then finally vanished with a faint sigh.

His memories had awakened. What had lain within the T'lan Imass, layered, indurated by the countless centuries, was a landscape Onrack could read once more. And so, what he saw before him now . . . gone were the mesas on the horizon, the wind-sculpted towers of sandstone, the sweeps of windblown sand and white ribbons of ground coral. Gone the gorges, arroyos and dead riverbeds, the planted fields and irrigation ditches. Even the city to the north, on the horizon's very edge, clinging like a tumour to the vast winding river, became insubstantial, ephemeral to his mind's eye.

And all that he now saw was as it had been . . . so very long ago.

The inland sea's cloudy waves, rolling like the promise of eternity, along a shoreline of gravel that stretched north, unbroken all the way to the mountains that would one day be called the Thalas, and south, down to encompass the remnant now known as the Clatar Sea. Coral reefs revealed their sharkskin spines a sixth of a league beyond the beach, over which wheeled seagulls and long-beaked birds long since extinct.

There were figures walking along the strand. Renig Obar's clan, come to trade whale ivory and dhenrabi oil from their tundra homelands, and it seemed they had brought the chill winds with them . . . or perhaps the unseemly weather that had come to these warm climes hinted of something darker. A Jaghut, hidden in some fasthold, stirring the cauldron of Omtose Phellack. Much more of this and the reefs would die, and with them all the creatures that depended on them.

A breath of unease fluttered through the Onrack who was flesh and blood. But he had stepped aside. No longer a bonecaster for his clan – Absin Tholai was far superior in the hidden arts, after all, and more inclined to the hungry ambition necessary among those who followed the Path of Tellann. All too often, Onrack had found his mind drawn to other things.

To raw beauty, such as he saw before him now. He was not one for fighting, for rituals of destruction. He was always reluctant to dance in the deeper recesses of the caves, where the drums pounded and the echoes rolled through flesh and bone as if one was lying in the path of a stampeding herd of ranag – a herd such as the one Onrack had blown onto the cave walls around them. His mouth bitter with spit, charcoal and ochre, the backs of his hands stained where they had blocked the spray from his lips, defining the shapes on the stone. Art was done in solitude, images fashioned without light, on unseen walls, when the rest of the clan slept in the outer caverns. And it was a simple truth, that Onrack had grown skilled in the sorcery of paint out of that desire to be apart, to be alone.

Among a people where solitude was as close to a crime as possible. Where to separate was to weaken. Where the very breaking of vision into its components – from seeing to observing, from resurrecting memory and reshaping it beyond the eye's reach, onto walls of stone – demanded a fine-edged, potentially deadly propensity.

A poor bonecaster. Onrack, you were never what you were meant to be. And when you broke the unwritten covenant and painted a truthful image of a mortal Imass, when you trapped that lovely, dark woman in time, there in the cavern no-one was meant to find . . . ah, then you fell to the wrath of kin. Of Logros himself, and the First Sword.

But he remembered the expression on the young face of Onos T'oolan, when he had first looked upon the painting of his sister. Wonder and awe, and a resurgence of an abiding love – Onrack was certain that he had seen such in the First Sword's face, was certain that others had, as well, though of course none spoke of it. The law had been broken, and would be answered with severity.

He never knew if Kilava had herself gone to see the painting; had never known if she had been angered, or had seen sufficient to understand the blood of his own heart that had gone into that image.

But that is the last memory I now come to.

'Your silences,' Trull Sengar muttered, 'always send shivers through me, T'lan Imass.'

'The night before the Ritual,' Onrack replied. 'Not far from this place where we now stand. I was to have been banished from my tribe. I had committed a crime to which there was no other answer. Instead, events eclipsed the clans. Four Jaghut tyrants had risen and had formed a compact. They sought to destroy this land – as indeed they have.'

The Tiste Edur said nothing, perhaps wondering what,

precisely, had been destroyed. Along the river there were irrigation ditches, and strips of rich green crops awaiting the season's turn. Roads and farmsteads, the occasional temple, and only to the southwest, along that horizon, did the broken ridge of treeless bluffs mar the scene.

'I was in the cavern – in the place of my crime,' Onrack continued after a moment. 'In darkness, of course. My last night, I'd thought, among my own kind. Though in truth I was already alone, driven from the camp to this final place of solitude. And then someone came. A touch. A body, warm. Soft beyond belief – no, not my wife, she had been among the first to shun me, for what I had done, for the betrayal it had meant. No, a woman unknown to me in the darkness . . .'

Was it her? I will never know. She was gone in the morning, gone from all of us, even as the Ritual was proclaimed and the clans gathered. She defied the call – no, more horrible yet, she had killed her own kin, all but Onos himself. He had managed to drive her off – the truest measure of his extraordinary martial prowess.

Was it her? Was there blood unseen on her hands? That dried, crumbled powder I found on my own skin – which I'd thought had come from the overturned bowl of paint. Fled from Onos . . . to me, in my shameful cave.

And who did I hear in the passage beyond? In the midst of our lovemaking, did someone come upon us and see what I myself could not?

'You need say no more, Onrack,' Trull said softly.

True. And were I mortal flesh, you would see me weep, and thus say what you have just said. Thus, my grief is not lost to your eyes, Trull Sengar. And yet still you ask why I proclaimed my vow . . .

'The trail of the renegades is . . . fresh,' Onrack said after a moment.

Trull half smiled. 'And you enjoy killing.'

'Artistry finds new forms, Edur. It defies being silenced.' The T'lan Imass slowly turned to face him. 'Of course, changes have come to us. I am no longer free to pursue this hunt . . . unless you wish the same.'

Trull grimaced, scanned the lands to the southwest. 'Well, it's not as inviting a prospect as it once was, I'll grant you. But, Onrack, these renegades are agents in the betrayal of my people, and I mean to discover as much as I can of their role. Thus, we must find them.'

'And speak with them.'

'Speak with them first, aye, and then you can kill them.'

'I no longer believe I am capable of that, Trull Sengar. I am too badly damaged. Even so, Monok Ochem and Ibra Gholan are pursuing us. They will suffice.'

The Tiste Edur's head had turned at this. 'Just the two of them? You are certain?'

'My powers are diminished, but yes, I believe so.'

'How close?'

'It does not matter. They withhold their desire for vengeance against me . . . so that I might lead them to those they have hunted from the very beginning.'

'They suspect you will join the renegades, don't they?'

'Broken kin. Aye, they do.'

'And will you?'

Onrack studied the Tiste Edur for a moment. 'Only if you do, Trull Sengar.'

They were at the very edge of cultivated land, and so it was relatively easy to avoid contact with any of the local residents. The lone road they crossed was empty of life in both directions for as far as they could see. Beyond the irrigated fields, the rugged natural landscape reasserted itself. Tufts of grasses, sprawls of water-smoothed gravel tracking down dry gulches and ravines, the occasional guldindha tree.

The hills ahead were saw-toothed, the facing side clawed into near cliffs.

Those hills were where the T'lan Imass had broken the

ice sheets, the first place of defiance. To protect the holy sites, the hidden caves, the flint quarries. Where, now, the weapons of the fallen were placed.

Weapons these renegades would reclaim. There was no provenance to the sorcery investing those stone blades, at least with respect to Tellann. They would feed the ones who held them, provided they were kin to the makers – or indeed made by those very hands long ago. Imass, then, since the art among the mortal peoples was long lost. Also, finding those weapons would give the renegades their final freedom, severing the power of Tellann from their bodies.

'You spoke of betraying your clan,' Trull Sengar said as they approached the hills. 'These seem to be old memories, Onrack.'

'Perhaps we are destined to repeat our crimes, Trull Sengar. Memories have returned to me – all that I had thought lost. I do not know why.'

'The severing of the Ritual?'

'Possibly.'

'What was your crime?'

'I trapped a woman in time. Or so it seemed. I painted her likeness in a sacred cave. It is now my belief that, in so doing, I was responsible for the terrible murders that followed, for her leaving the clan. She could not join in the Ritual that made us immortal, for by my hand she had already become so. Did she know this? Was this the reason for her defying Logros and the First Sword? There are no answers to that. What madness stole her mind, so that she would kill her closest kin, so that, indeed, she would seek to kill the First Sword himself, her own brother?'

'A woman not your mate, then.'

'No. She was a bonecaster. A Soletaken.'

'Yet you loved her.'

A lopsided shrug. 'Obsession is its own poison, Trull Sengar.'

A narrow goat trail led up into the range, steep and winding in its ascent. They began climbing.

'I would object,' the Tiste Edur said, 'to this notion of being doomed to repeat our mistakes, Onrack. Are no lessons learned? Does not experience lead to wisdom?'

'Trull Sengar. I have just betrayed Monok Ochem and Ibra Gholan. I have betrayed the T'lan Imass, for I chose not to accept my fate. Thus, the same crime as the one I committed long ago. I have always hungered for solitude from my kind. In the realm of the Nascent, I was content. As I was in the sacred caves that lie ahead.'

'Content? And now, at this moment?'

Onrack was silent for a time. 'When memories have returned, Trull Sengar, solitude is an illusion, for every silence is filled by a clamorous search for meaning.'

'You're sounding more . . . mortal with every day that passes, friend.'

'Flawed, you mean.'

The Tiste Edur grunted. 'Even so. Yet look at what you are doing right now, Onrack.'

'What do you mean?'

Trull Sengar paused on the trail and looked at the T'lan Imass. His smile was sad. 'You're returning home.'

A short distance away were camped the Tiste Liosan. Battered, but alive. Which was, Malachar reflected, at least something.

Strange stars gleamed overhead, their light wavering, as if brimming with tears. The landscape stretching out beneath them seemed a lifeless wasteland of weathered rock and sand.

The fire they had built in the lee of a humped mesa had drawn strange moths the size of small birds, as well as a host of other flying creatures, including winged lizards. A swarm of flies had descended on them earlier, biting viciously before vanishing as quickly as they had come. And now, those bites seemed to *crawl*, as if the insects had left something behind.

There was, to Malachar's mind, an air of . . . unwelcome to this realm. He scratched at one of the lumps on his arm, hissed as he felt something squirm beneath the hot skin. Turning back to the fire, he studied his seneschal.

Jorrude knelt beside the hearth, head lowered – a position that had not changed in some time – and Malachar's disquiet deepened. Enias squatted close by the seneschal, ready to move if yet another fit of anguish over-whelmed his master, but those disturbing sessions were arriving ever less frequently. Orenas remained guarding the horses, and Malachar knew he stood with sword drawn in the darkness beyond the fire's light.

There would be an accounting one day, he knew, with the T'lan Imass. The Tiste Liosan had proceeded with the ritual in good faith. They had been too open. *Never trust a corpse.* Malachar did not know if such a warning was found in the sacred text of Osric's Visions. If not, he would see that it was added to the collected wisdom of the Tiste Liosan. *When we return. If we return.*

Jorrude slowly straightened. His face was ravaged with grief. 'The Guardian is dead,' he announced. 'Our realm is assailed, but our brothers and sisters have been warned and even now ride out to the gates. The Tiste Liosan will hold. Until Osric's return, we shall hold.' He slowly swung to face each of them in turn, including Orenas who silently appeared out of the gloom. 'For us, another task. The one we were assigned to complete. On this realm, somewhere, we will find the trespassers. The thieves of the Fire. I have quested, and they have never been closer to my senses. They are in this world, and we shall find them.'

Malachar waited, for he knew there was more.

Jorrude then smiled. 'My brothers. We know nothing of this place. But that is a disadvantage that will prove temporary, for I have also sensed the presence of an old friend to the Tiste Liosan. Not far away. We shall seek him out – our first task – and ask him to acquaint us with the rigours of this land.'

'Who is this old friend, Seneschal?' Enias asked.

'The Maker of Time, Brother Enias.'

Malachar slowly nodded. *A friend of the Tiste Liosan indeed. Slayer of the Ten Thousand. Icarium.*

'Orenas,' Jorrude said, 'prepare our horses.'

CHAPTER SEVENTEEN

Seven faces in the rock
Six faces turned to the Teblor
One remains Unfound
Mother to the tribe of ghosts –
the Teblor children
we were told
to turn away

Mother's Prayer of Giving
among the Teblor

Karsa orlong was no stranger to stone. Raw copper gouged from outcroppings, tin and their mating that was bronze, such materials had their place. But wood and stone were the words of the hands, the sacred shaping of will.

Parallel flakes, long and thin, translucent slivers punched away from the blade, leaving ripples reaching across, from edge to wavy spine. Smaller flakes removed from the twin edges, first one side, then flipping the blade over between blows, back and forth, all the way up the length.

To fight with such a weapon would demand changes to the style with which Karsa was most familiar. Wood flexed, slid with ease over shield rims, skipped effortlessly along out-thrust sword-blades. This flint sword's serrated edges would behave differently, and he would have to adjust, especially given its massive weight and length.

The handle proved the most challenging. Flint did not welcome roundness, and the less angular the handle became, the less stable the striking platforms. For the pommel he worked the stone into a step-fractured, oversized diamond shape – the nearly right-angled step-fractures would normally be viewed as dangerous flaws, inviting a focus for shattering energies, but the gods had promised to make the weapon unbreakable, so Karsa dismissed his instinctive worry. He would wait until he found suitable materials for a cross-hilt.

He had no idea how much time passed during his making of the sword. All other considerations vanished for him – he felt no hunger, no thirst, and did not notice as the walls of the cavern grew slick with condensation, as the temperature ever rose, until both he and the stone were sheathed in sweat. He was also unmindful of the fire in the boulder-lined hearth that burned ceaselessly, unfuelled, the flames flickering with strange colours.

The sword commanded all. The feel of his companion ghosts resonated from the blade into his fingertips, then along every bone and muscle in his body. Bairoth Gild, whose cutting irony seemed to have somehow infused the weapon, as had Delum Thord's fierce loyalty – these were unexpected gifts, a mysterious contortion of themes, of aspects, that imbued a personality to the sword.

Among the legends there were songs celebrating cherished weapons and the Teblor heroes who wielded them. Karsa had always held that the notion of weapons possessing wills of their own was little more than a poet's conceit. And those heroes who had betrayed their blades and so suffered tragic ends, well, in each tale, Karsa had no difficulty in citing other, more obvious flaws in their actions, sufficient to explain the hero's demise.

The Teblor never passed down weapons to heirs – all possessions accompanied the one who had died, for what worth a ghost bereft of all it had acquired in its mortal life?

The flint sword that found shape in Karsa's hands was

therefore unlike anything he had known – or heard of – before. It rested on the ground before him, strangely naked despite the leather he had wrapped around the grip. No hilt, no scabbard. Massive and brutal, yet beautiful in its symmetry, despite the streaks of blood left by his lacerated hands.

He became aware of the searing heat in the cavern, and slowly looked up.

The seven gods stood facing him in a flattened crescent, the hearth's flames flickering across their battered, broken bodies. They held weapons to match the one now lying before him, though scaled down to suit their squat forms.

'You have come in truth,' Karsa observed.

The one he knew as Urugal replied, 'We have. We are now free of the Ritual's bindings. The chains, Karsa Orlong, are broken.'

Another spoke in a low, rasping voice. 'The Warren of Tellann has found your sword, Karsa Orlong.' The god's neck was mangled, broken, the head fallen onto a shoulder and barely held in place by muscle and tendons. 'It shall never shatter.'

Karsa grunted. 'There are broken weapons in the caverns beyond.'

'Elder sorcery,' Urugal answered. 'Inimical warrens. Our people have fought many wars.'

'You T'lan Imass have indeed,' the Teblor warrior said. 'I walked upon stairs made of your kin. I have seen your kind, fallen in such numbers as to defy comprehension.' He scanned the seven creatures standing before him. 'What battle took you?'

Urugal shrugged. 'It is of no significance, Karsa Orlong. A struggle of long ago, an enemy now dust, a failure best forgotten. We have known wars beyond counting, and what have they achieved? The Jaghut were doomed to extinction – we but hastened the inevitable. Other enemies announced themselves and stood in our path. We were indifferent to their causes, none of which was sufficient to turn us aside. And so we slaughtered them. Again and again. Wars without meaning, wars that changed virtually nothing. To live is to suffer. To exist – even as we do – is to *resist*.'

'This is all that was learned, Karsa Orlong,' said the T'lan Imass woman known as 'Siballe. 'In its totality. Stone, sea, forest, city – and every creature that ever lived – all share the same struggle. Being resists unbeing. Order wars against the chaos of dissolution, of disorder. Karsa Orlong, this is the only worthy truth, the greatest of all truths. What do the gods themselves worship, but perfection? The unattainable victory over nature, over nature's uncertainty. There are many words for this struggle. Order against chaos, structure against dissolution, light against dark, life against death. But they all mean the same thing.'

The broken-necked T'lan Imass spoke in a whisper, his words a droning chant. 'The ranag has fallen lame. Is distanced from the herd. Yet walks on in its wake. Seeking the herd's protection. Time will heal. Or weaken. Two possibilities. But the lame ranag knows naught but stubborn hope. For that is its nature. The ay have seen it and now close. The prey is still strong. But alone. The ay know weakness. Like a scent on the cold wind. They run with the stumbling ranag. And drive it away from the herd. Still, it is stubborn hope. It makes its stand. Head lowered, horns ready to crush ribs, send the enemy flying. But the ay are clever. Circle and attack, then spring away. Again and again. Hunger wars with stubborn hope. Until the ranag is exhausted. Bleeding. Staggering. Then the ay all attack at once. Nape of neck. Legs. Throat. Until the ranag is dragged down. And stubborn hope gives way, Karsa Orlong. It gives way, as it always must, to mute inevitability.'

The Teblor bared his teeth. 'Yet your new master would harbour that lame beast. Would offer it a haven.'

'You cross the bridge before we have built it, Karsa Orlong,' Urugal said. 'It seems Bairoth Gild taught you how to think, before he himself failed and so died. You are indeed worthy of the name Warleader.'

'Perfection is an illusion,' 'Siballe said. 'Thus, mortal and immortal alike are striving for what cannot be achieved. Our new master seeks to alter the paradigm, Karsa Orlong. A third force, to change for ever the eternal war between order and dissolution.'

'A master demanding the worship of imperfection,' the Teblor growled.

'Siballe's head creaked in a nod. 'Yes.'

Karsa realized he was thirsty and walked over to his pack, retrieving a waterskin. He drank deep, then returned to his sword. He closed both hands about the grip and lifted it before him, studying its rippled length.

'An extraordinary creation,' Urugal said. 'If Imass weapons could have a god . . .'

Karsa smiled at the T'lan Imass he had once knelt before, in a distant glade, in a time of youth – when the world he saw was both simple and . . . perfect. 'You are not gods.'

'We are,' Urugal replied. 'To be a god is to possess worshippers.'

'To guide them,' 'Siballe added.

'You are wrong, both of you,' Karsa said. 'To be a god is to know the burden of believers. Did you protect? You did not. Did you offer comfort, solace? Were you possessed of compassion? Even pity? To the Teblor, T'lan Imass, you were slavemasters, eager and hungry, making harsh demands, and expecting cruel sacrifices – all to feed your own desires. You were the Teblor's unseen chains.' His eyes settled on 'Siballe. 'And you, woman, 'Siballe the Unfound, you were the taker of children.'

'Imperfect children, Karsa Orlong, who would otherwise have died. And they do not regret my gifts.'

'No, I would imagine not. The regret remains with the mothers and fathers who surrendered them. No matter how brief a child's life, the love of the parents is a power that should not be denied. And know this, 'Siballe, it is immune

682

to imperfection.' His voice was harsh to his own ears, grating out from a constricted throat. '*Worship imperfection*, you said. A metaphor you made real by demanding that those children be sacrificed. Yet you were – and remain – unmindful of the most crucial gift that comes from worship. You have no understanding of what it is to *ease* the burdens of those who would worship you. But even that is not your worst crime. No. You then gave us your own burdens.' He shifted his gaze. 'Tell me, Urugal, what have the Teblor done to deserve that?'

'Your own people have forgotten—'

'Tell me.'

Urugal shrugged. 'You failed.'

Karsa stared at the battered god, unable to speak. The sword trembled in his hands. He had held it up for all this time, and now, finally, its weight threatened to drag his arms down. He fixed his eyes on the weapon, then slowly lowered the tip to rest on the stone floor.

'We too failed, once, long ago,' 'Siballe said. 'Such things cannot be undone. Thus, you may surrender to it, and so suffer beneath its eternal torment. Or you can choose to free yourself of the burden. Karsa Orlong, our answer to you is simple: to fail is to reveal a flaw. Face that revelation, do not turn your back on it, do not make empty vows to never repeat your mistakes. It is done. *Celebrate it!* That is our answer, and indeed is the answer shown us by the Crippled God.'

The tension drained from Karsa's shoulders. He drew a deep breath, released it slowly. 'Very well. To you, and to the Crippled God, I now give my answer.'

Rippled stone made no silent passage through the air. Instead, it roared, like pine needles exploding into flame. Up, over Karsa's head, wheeling in a sliding circle that then swept down and across.

The edge taking 'Siballe between left shoulder and neck. Bones snapping as the massive blade ploughed through, diagonally, across the chest, severing the spine, down and through the ribcage, sweeping clear just above her right hip.

She had lifted her own sword to intercept at some point, and it had shattered, flinging shards and slivers into the air – Karsa had not even felt the impact.

He whipped the huge blade in a curving arc in his follow-through, lifting it to poise, suddenly motionless, over his head.

The ruined form that was 'Siballe collapsed in clattering pieces onto the stone floor. The T'lan Imass had been cut in half.

The remaining six had raised their own weapons, but none moved to attack.

Karsa snarled. 'Come ahead, then.'

'Will you now destroy the rest of us?' Urugal asked.

'Her army of foundlings will follow me,' the Teblor growled, sneering down at 'Siballe. Then he glared up once more. 'You will leave my people – leave the glade. You are done with us, T'lan Imass. I have delivered you here. I have freed you. If you ever appear before me again, I will destroy you. Walk the dreams of the tribal elders, and I will come hunting you. And I shall not relent. I, Karsa Orlong, of the Uryd, of the Teblor *Thelomen Toblakai*, so avow.' He took a step closer, and the six T'lan Imass flinched. 'You used us. You used *me*. And, for my reward, what did you just offer?'

'We sought—'

'You offered a *new set of chains*. Now, leave this place. You have all you desired. Get out.'

The six T'lan Imass walked towards the cave mouth. A momentary occluding of the sunlight spilling into the front cavern, then they were gone.

Karsa lowered his sword. He looked down at 'Siballe.

'Unexpected,' she said.

The warrior grunted. 'I'd heard you T'lan Imass were hard to kill.'

'Impossible, Karsa Orlong. We . . . persist. Will you leave me here?'

'There is to be no oblivion for you?'

'Once, long ago, a sea surrounded these hills. Such a sea would free me to the oblivion you speak of. You return me to a fate – and a punishment – that I have spent millennia seeking to escape. I suppose that is apt enough.'

'What of your new master, this Crippled God?'

'He has abandoned me. It would appear that there are acceptable levels of imperfection – and unacceptable levels of imperfection. I have lost my usefulness.'

'Another god that understands nothing of what it is to be a god,' Karsa rumbled, walking over to his pack.

'What will you do now, Karsa Orlong?'

'I go in search of a horse.'

'Ah, a Jhag horse. Yes, they can be found to the southwest of here, on the odhan. Rare. You may be searching for a long time.'

The Teblor shrugged. He loosened the strings that closed the mouth of the pack and walked over to the shambles that was 'Siballe. He lifted the part of her containing the head and right shoulder and arm.

'What are you doing?'

'Do you need the rest?'

'No. What—'

Karsa pushed her head, shoulder and arm into his pack, then drew the strings once more. He would need a harness and a scabbard for the sword, but that would have to wait. He shrugged into the pack's straps, then straightened and leaned the sword over his right shoulder.

A final glance around.

The hearth still raged with a sorcerous fire, though it had begun flickering more rapidly now, as if using up the last of its unseen fuel. He thought about kicking gravel over it to douse it, then shrugged and turned to the cave mouth.

As he came to the entrance, two figures suddenly rose before him, blocking the light.

Karsa's sword whipped across his path, the flat of the

blade thundering against both figures, sending them flying off the ledge.

'Get out of my way,' the warrior growled, stepping out into the sunlight.

He spared neither intruder another glance as he set off along the trail, where it angled southwest.

Trull Sengar groaned, then opened his eyes. He lifted his head, wincing at the countless sharp pains pressing into his back. That flint sword had thrown him down a scree of stone chips . . . although it had been hapless Onrack who had taken the brunt of the blow. Even so, his chest ached, and he feared his ribs were bruised, if not cracked.

The T'lan Imass was awkwardly regaining its feet a dozen paces away.

Trull spat and said, 'Had I known the door was barred, I would have knocked first. That was a damned Thelomen Toblakai.'

The Tiste Edur saw Onrack's head snap round to stare back up at the cave.

'What is it?' Trull demanded. 'He's coming down to finish us?'

'No,' the T'lan Imass replied. 'In that cave . . . the Warren of Tellann lingers . . .'

'What of it?'

Onrack began climbing the rock slide toward the cavern's mouth.

Hissing his frustration, Trull clambered upward and followed, slowly, pausing every few steps until he was able to find his breath once more.

When he entered the cave he gave a shout of alarm. Onrack was standing inside a fire, the rainbow-coloured flames engulfing him. And the T'lan Imass held, in its right hand, the shattered remains of another of its kind.

Trull stepped forward, then his feet skidded out from under him and he fell hard onto a bed of sharp flint chips. Pain thundered from his ribs, and it was some time before he could breathe once more. Cursing, he rolled onto his side – gingerly – then carefully climbed upright. The air was hot as a forge.

Then the cavern was suddenly dark – the strange fire had gone out.

A pair of hands closed on Trull's shoulders.

'The renegades have fled,' said Onrack. 'But they are close. Come.'

'Right, lead on, friend.'

A moment before they emerged into the sunlight, sudden shock raced through Trull Sengar.

A pair of hands.

Karsa skirted the valley side, making his way along what passed for a trail. Countless rockslides had buried it every ten paces or so, forcing him to scramble across uncertain, shifting gravel, raising clouds of dust in his wake.

On second consideration, he realized that one of the two strangers who had blocked his exit from the cave had been a T'lan Imass. Not surprising, since the entire valley, with all its quarries, mines and tombs, was a site holy to them . . . assuming anything could be holy to creatures that were undead. And the other – *not human at all. But familiar none the less. Ah, like the ones on the ship. The grey-skinned ones I killed.*

Perhaps he should retrace his route. His sword had yet to drink real blood, after all. Barring his own, of course.

Ahead, the trail cut sharply upward, out of the valley. Thoughts of having to repeat this dust-fouled, treacherous route decided him. He would save the blooding of his sword for more worthy enemies. He made his way upward.

It was clear the six T'lan Imass had not taken this route. Fortunate for them. He had lost his patience with their endless words, especially when the deeds they had done shouted louder, loud enough to overwhelm their pathetic justifications. He reached the crest and pulled himself onto level ground. The vista stretching to the southwest was as untamed as any place Karsa had yet to see in Seven Cities. No signs of civilization were apparent – no evidence at all that this land had ever been broken. Tall prairie grasses waved in the hot wind, cloaking low, rolling hills that continued on to the horizon. Clumps of low, bushy trees filled the basins, flickering dusty green and grey as the wind shook their leaves.

The Jhag Odhan. He knew, suddenly, that this land would capture his heart with its primal siren call. Its scale . . . matched his own, in ways he could not define. *Thelomen Toblakai have known this place, have walked it before me.* A truth, though he was unable to explain how he knew it to be so.

He lifted his sword. 'Bairoth Delum – so I name you. Witness. The Jhag Odhan. So unlike our mountain fastnesses. To this wind I give your name – see how it races out to brush the grasses, to roll against the hill and through the trees. I give this land your name, Bairoth Delum.'

That warm wind sang against the sword's rippled blade with moaning cadence.

A flash of movement in the grasses, a thousand paces distant. Wolves, fur the colour of honey, long-limbed, taller than any he had ever before seen. Karsa smiled.

He set forth.

The grasses reached to just beneath his chest, the ground underfoot hardpacked between the knotted roots. Small creatures rustled continually from his path, and he startled the occasional deer – a small breed, reaching no higher than his knees, that hissed like an arrow between the stalks as it fled.

One proved not quite fast enough to avoid his scything blade, and Karsa would eat well this night. Thus, his sword's virgin thirst was born of necessity, not the rage of battle. He wondered if the ghosts had known displeasure at such an ignoble beginning. They had surrendered their ability to communicate with him upon entering the stone, though Karsa's imagination had no difficulty in finding

Bairoth's sarcastic commentary, should he seek it. Delum's measured wisdom was more difficult, yet valued all the more for that.

The sun swept its even arc across the cloudless sky as he marched on. Towards dusk he saw bhederin herds to the west, and, two thousand paces ahead, a herd of striped antelope crested a hilltop to watch him for a time, before wheeling as one and vanishing from sight.

The western horizon was a fiery conflagration when he reached the place where they had stood.

Where a figure awaited him.

The grasses had been flattened in a modest circle. A three-legged brazier squatted in its centre, filled with orange-glowing pieces of bhederin dung that cast forth no smoke. Seated behind it was a Jaghut. Bent and gaunt to the point of emaciation, wearing ragged skins and hides, long grey hair hanging in strands over a blotched, wrinkled brow, eyes the colour of the surrounding grass.

The Jaghut glanced up as Karsa approached, offering the Teblor something between a grimace and a smile, his yellowed tusks gleaming. 'You have made a mess of that deer skin, Toblakai. I will take it none the less, in exchange for this cookfire.'

'Agreed,' Karsa replied, dropping the carcass beside the brazier.

'Aramala contacted me, and so I have come to meet you. You have done her a noble service, Toblakai.'

Karsa set down his pack and squatted before the brazier. 'I hold no loyalty to the T'lan Imass.'

The Jaghut reached across and collected the deer. A small knife flashed in his hand and he began cutting just above the animal's small hoofs. 'An expression of their gratitude, after she fought alongside them against the Tyrants. As did I, although I was fortunate enough to escape with little more than a broken spine. Tomorrow, I will lead you to one far less fortunate than either Aramala or myself.'

Karsa grunted. 'I seek a Jhag horse, not an introduction to your friends.'

The ancient Jaghut cackled. 'Blunt words. Thelomen Toblakai indeed. I had forgotten, and so lost my appreciation. The one I will take you to shall call out to the wild horses – and they will come.'

'A singular skill.'

'Aye, and hers alone, for it was, by and large, by her hand and her will that the horses came into being.'

'A breeder, then.'

'Of sorts,' the Jaghut nodded amicably. He began peeling the hide from the deer. 'The few of my fallen kin still alive will greatly appreciate this skin, despite the damage wrought by your ghastly stone sword. The aras deer are fleet, and clever. They never use the same trail – ha, they do not even *make* trails! And so one cannot lie in wait. Nor are snares of any use. And when pursued, where do they go? Why, into the bhederin herds, under the very beasts themselves. Clever, I said. Very clever.'

'I am Karsa Orlong, of the Uryd—'

'Yes, yes, I know. From distant Genabackis. Little different from my fallen kin, the Jhag. Ignorant of your great and noble history—'

'Less ignorant than I once was.'

'Good. I am named Cynnigig, and now you are even less ignorant.'

Karsa shrugged. 'The name means nothing to me.'

'Of course not, it's mine. Was I infamous? No, though once I aspired to be. Well, for a moment or two. But then I changed my mind. You, Karsa Orlong, you are destined for infamy. Perhaps indeed you have already achieved it, back in your homeland.'

'I think not. No doubt I am believed dead, and nothing of what I did is known to my family or my tribe.'

Cynnigig cut off a haunch and threw it on the flames. A cloud of smoke rose from the hissing, spitting fire. 'So you might think, but I would hazard otherwise. Word travels, no matter what the barriers. The day you return, you will see.'

'I care not for fame,' Karsa said. 'I did once . . .'

'And then?'

'I changed my mind.'

Cynnigig laughed once again, louder this time. 'I have brought wine, my young friend. In yonder chest, yes, there.'

Karsa straightened and walked over. The chest was massive, iron-bounded and thick-planked, robust enough to challenge even Karsa, should he choose to lift it. 'This should have wheels and a train of oxen,' the Teblor muttered as he crouched before it. 'How did you bring it with you?'

'I didn't. It brought me.'

Games with words. Scowling, Karsa lifted the lid.

A single carafe of crystal stood in its centre, flanked by a pair of chipped clay beakers. The wine's deep red colour gleamed through the transparent crystal, bathing the otherwise empty interior of the chest with a warm, sunset hue. Karsa stared down into it for a moment, then grunted. 'Aye, I can see that it would fit you, provided you curled up. You and the wine and the brazier—'

'The brazier! That would be a hot journey!'

The Teblor's scowl deepened. 'Unlit, of course.'

'Ah, yes, of course. Cease your gawking, then, and pour us some wine. I'm about to turn the meat here.'

Karsa reached down, then snatched his hand back. 'It's *cold* in there!'

'I prefer my wine chilled, even the red. I prefer everything chilled, in fact.'

Grimacing, the Teblor picked up the carafe and the two beakers. 'Then someone must have carried you here.'

'Only if you believe all that I tell you. And all that you see, Karsa Orlong. A T'lan Imass army marched by here, not so long ago. Did they find me? No. Why? I was hidden in my chest, of course. Did they find the chest? No, because it was a rock. Did they note the rock? Perhaps. But then, it was only a rock. Now, I know what you're thinking, and you would be precisely correct. The sorcery I speak of is not Omtose Phellack. But why would I seek to employ Omtose Phellack, when that is the very scent the T'lan Imass hunted? Oh no. Is there some cosmic law that Jaghut can only use Omtose Phellack? I've read a hundred thousand night skies and have yet to see it written there – oh, plenty of other laws, but nothing approaching that one, neither in detail nor intent. Thus saving us the bloody recourse of finding a Forkrul Assail to adjudicate, and believe me, such adjudication is invariably bloody. Rarely indeed is anyone satisfied. Rarer still that anyone is left alive. Is there justice in such a thing, I ask you? Oh yes, perhaps the purest justice of all. On any given day, the aggrieved and the aggriever could stand in each other's clothes. Never a question of right and wrong, in truth, simply one of deciding who is least wrong. Do you grasp—'

'What I grasp,' Karsa cut in, 'is the smell of burning meat.'

'Ah, yes. Rare are my moments of discourse—'

'I had no idea.'

'—which cannot be said for this meat. Of course you wouldn't, since we have just met. But I assure you, I have little opportunity to talk—'

'There in your chest.'

Cynnigig grinned. 'Precisely. You have the gist of it. Precisely. Thelomen Toblakai indeed.'

Karsa handed the Jaghut a beaker filled with wine. 'Alas, my hand has warmed it some.'

'I'll suffer the degradation, thank you. Here, help yourself to the deer. Charcoal is good for you, did you know that? Cleanses the digestive tract, confounds the worms, turns your excrement black. Black as a forest bear's. Recommended if you are being pursued, for it will fool most, barring those who have made a study of excrement, of course.'

'And do such people exist?'

'I have no idea. I rarely get out. What preening empires have risen only to then fall beyond the Jhag Odhan? Pomposity choking on dust, these are cycles unending among short-lived creatures. I do not grieve for my own ignorance. Why should I? Not knowing what I have missed means I do not miss what I do not know. How could I? Do you see? Aramala was ever questing for such pointless knowledge, and look where it got her. Same for Phyrlis, whom you will meet tomorrow. She can never see beyond the leaves in front of her face, though she ceaselessly strives to do so, as if the vast panorama offers something other than time's insectile crawl. Empires, thrones, tyrants and liberators, a hundred thousand tomes filled with versions of the same questions, asked over and over again. Will answers deliver their promised solace? I think not. Here, cook some more, Karsa Orlong, and drink more wine – you see the carafe never empties. Clever, isn't it? Now, where was I?'

'You rarely get out.'

'Indeed. What preening empires have risen only to then fall beyond the Jhag Odhan? Pomposity choking . . .'

Karsa's eyes narrowed on the Jhag Odhan, then he reached for the wine.

A lone tree stood on ground that was the summit of a hill that in turn abutted a larger hill. Sheltered from the prevailing winds, it had grown vast, its bark thin and peeling as if it was skin unable to contain the muscular breadth underneath. Branches as thick around as Karsa's thigh reached out from the massive, knotted trunk. Its top third was thickly leaved, forming broad, flattened canopies of dusty green.

'Looks old, doesn't it?' Cynnigig said as they climbed towards it, the Jaghut walking with a hooked, sideways gait. 'You have no idea how old, my young friend. No idea. I dare not reveal to you the truth of its antiquity. Have you seen its like before? I think not. Perhaps reminiscent of the guldindha, such as can be found here and there across the odhan. Reminiscent, as a ranag is reminiscent of a goat. More than simply a question of stature. No, it is in truth a question of antiquity. An Elder species, this tree. A sapling when an inland sea hissed salty sighs over this land. Tens of thousands of years, you wonder? No. Hundreds of thousands. Once, Karsa Orlong, these were the dominant trees across most of the world. All things know their time, and when that time is past, they vanish—'

'But this one hasn't.'

'No sharper an observance could be made. And why, you ask?'

'I do not bother, for I know you will tell me in any case.'

'Of course I shall, for I am of a helpful sort, a natural proclivity. The reason, my young friend, shall soon be made evident.'

They clambered over the last of the rise and came to the flat ground, eternally shadowed beneath the canopy and so free of grasses. The tree and all its branches, Karsa now saw, were wrapped in spiders' webs that somehow remained entirely translucent no matter how thickly woven, revealed only by a faint flickering reflection. And beneath that glittering shroud, the face of a Jaghut stared back at him.

'Phyrlis,' Cynnigig said, 'this is the one Aramala spoke of, the one seeking a worthy horse.'

The Jaghut woman's body remained visible here and there, revealing that the tree had indeed grown around her. Yet a single shaft of wood emerged from just behind her right collarbone, rejoining the main trunk along the side of her head.

'Shall I tell him your story, Phyrlis? Of course, I must, if only for its remarkability.'

Her voice did not come from her mouth, but sounded, fluid and soft, inside Karsa's head. *'Of course you must, Cynnigig. It is your nature to leave no word unsaid.'*

Karsa smiled, for there was too much affection in the tone to lend the words any edge.

'My Thelomen Toblakai friend, a most extraordinary tale, for which true explanations remain beyond us all,' Cynnigig began, settling down cross-legged on the stony ground. 'Dear Phyrlis was a child – no, a babe, still suckling from her mother's breast – when a band of T'lan Imass ran them down. The usual fate ensued. The mother was slain, and Phyrlis was dealt with also in the usual fashion – spitted on a spear, the spear anchored into the earth. None could have predicted what then followed, neither Jaghut nor T'lan Imass, for it was unprecedented. That spear, wrought of native wood, took what it could of Phyrlis's life-spirit and so was reborn. Roots reached down to grip the bedrock, branches and leaves sprang anew, and in return the wood's own lifespirit rewarded the child. Together, then, they grew, escaping their relative fates. Phyrlis renews the tree, the tree renews Phyrlis.'

Karsa set his sword's point down and leaned on it. 'Yet she was the maker of the Jhag horses.'

'A small role, Karsa Orlong. From my blood came their longevity. The Jhag horses breed infrequently, insufficient to increase, or even maintain, their numbers, were they not so long-lived.'

'I know, for the Teblor – my own people, who dwell in the mountains of north Genabackis – maintain herds of what must be Jhag horses.'

'If so, then I am pleased. They are being hunted to extinction here on the Jhag Odhan.'

'Hunted? By whom?'

'By distant kin of yours, Thelomen Toblakai: Trell.'

Karsa was silent for a moment, then he scowled. 'Such as the one known as Mappo?'

'Yes indeed. Mappo Runt, who travels with Icarium. Icarium, who carries arrows made from my branches. Who, each time he visits me, remembers naught of the previous encounter. Who asks, again and again, for my heartwood, so that he may fashion from it a mechanism to measure time, for my heartwood alone can outlive all other constructs.'

'And do you oblige him?' Karsa asked.

'*No, for it would kill me. Instead, I bargain. A strong shaft for a bow. Branches for arrows.*'

'Have you no means to defend yourself, then?'

'*Against Icarium, no-one has, Karsa Orlong.*'

The Teblor warrior grunted. 'I had an argument with Icarium, which neither of us won.' He tapped his stone sword. 'My weapon was of wood, but now I wield this one. The next time we meet, even Mappo Trell's treachery shall not save Icarium.'

Both Jaghut were silent for a long moment, and Karsa realized that Phyrlis was speaking to Cynnigig, for he saw his expression twist with alarm. Ochre eyes flicked momentarily up to the Teblor, then away again.

Finally, Cynnigig loosed a long sigh and said, 'Karsa Orlong, she now calls upon the nearest herd – the lone herd she knows has come close to this area in answer to her first summons. She had hoped for more – evidence, perhaps, of how few Jhag horses remain.'

'How many head in this herd?'

'*I cannot say, Karsa Orlong. They usually number no more than a dozen. Those that now approach are perhaps the last left in the Jhag Odhan.*'

Karsa lifted his gaze suddenly as the noise of hoofs sounded, rumbling through the ground underfoot. 'More than a dozen, I think,' he murmured.

Cynnigig clambered upright, wincing with the effort.

Movement in the valley below. Karsa swung around.

The ground was shaking, the roar of thunder on all sides now. The tree behind him shook as if struck by a sudden gale. In his mind, the Teblor heard Phyrlis cry out.

The horses came in their hundreds. Grey as iron, larger even than those Karsa's tribe had bred. Streaming, tossing manes of black. Stallions, flinging their heads back and bucking to clear a space around them. Broad-backed mares, foals racing at their flanks.

Hundreds into thousands.

The air filled with dust, lifting on the wind and corkscrewing skyward as if to challenge the Whirlwind itself.

More of the wild horses topped the hill above them, and the thunder suddenly fell away as every beast halted, forming a vast iron ring facing inward. Silence, the dust cloud rolling, tumbling away on the wind.

Karsa faced the tree once more. 'It seems you need not worry that they near extinction, Phyrlis. I have never seen so many foals and yearlings in a herd. Nor have I ever before seen a herd of this size. There must ten, fifteen thousand head – and we cannot even see all of them.'

Phyrlis seemed incapable of replying. The tree's branches still shook, the branches rattling in the hot air.

'You speak true, Karsa Orlong,' Cynnigig rasped, his gaze eerily intent on the Thelomen Toblakai. 'The herds have come together – and some have come far indeed in answer to the summons. But not that of Phyrlis. No, not in answer to her call. But in answer to yours, Karsa Orlong. And to this, we have no answer. But now, you must choose.'

Nodding, he turned to study the horses.

'Karsa Orlong, you spoke earlier of a wooden weapon. What kind of wood?'

'Ironwood, the only choice remaining to me. In my homeland, we use bloodwood.'

'And blood-oil?'

'Yes.'

'Rubbed into the wood. Blood-oil, staining your hands. They can smell it, Karsa Orlong—'

'But I have none.'

'Not on you. In you. It courses in your veins, Karsa Orlong. Bloodwood has not existed in the Jhag Odhan for tens of thousands of years. Yet these horses remember. Now, you must choose.'

'Bloodwood and blood-oil,' Cynnigig said. 'This is an insufficient explanation, Phyrlis.'

'Yes, it is. But it is all I have.'

Karsa left them to their argument and, leaving his sword thrust upright in the ground, walked down to the waiting horses. Stallions tossed their heads at his approach and the Teblor smiled – careful not to show his teeth, knowing that they saw him as predator, and themselves as his prey. *Though they could easily kill me. Among such numbers I would have no chance.* He saw one stallion that was clearly dominant among all others, given the wide space around it and its stamping, challenging demeanour, and walked past it, murmuring, 'Not you, proud one. The herd needs you more than I do.' He spied another stallion, this one just entering adulthood, and made his way towards it. Slowly, approaching at an angle so that the horse could see him.

A mane and tail of white, not black. Long-limbed, muscles rippling beneath its sleek hide. Grey eyes.

Karsa halted a single pace away. He slowly reached out his right hand, until his fingertips settled on the beast's trembling bridge. He began applying pressure. The stallion resisted, backing up a step. He pushed the head further down, testing the flexibility of the neck. Still further, the neck bowing, until the horse's chin almost rested in the space between its breast bones.

Then he withdrew the pressure, maintaining contact as the stallion slowly straightened its neck.

'I name you Havok,' he whispered.

He moved his hand down until his fingertips rested, palm upward, beneath its chin, then slowly walked backward, leading the stallion out from the herd.

The dominant stallion screamed then, and the herd exploded into motion once more. Outward, dispersing into smaller groups, thundering through the high grasses. Wheeling around the twin hills, west and south, out once more into the heartland of the Jhag Odhan.

Havok's trembling had vanished. The beast walked at Karsa's pace as he backed up the hillside.

As he neared the summit, Cynnigig spoke behind him. 'Not even a Jaghut could so calm a Jhag horse, Karsa

Orlong, as you have done. Thelomen Toblakai, yes, you Teblor are that indeed, yet you are also unique among your kind. Thelomen Toblakai horse warriors. I had not thought such a thing possible. Karsa Orlong, why have the Teblor not conquered all of Genabackis?'

Karsa glanced back at the Jaghut. 'One day, Cynnigig, we shall.'

'And are you the one who will lead them?'

'I am.'

'We have witnessed, then, the birth of infamy.'

Karsa moved alongside Havok, his hand running the length of its taut neck. *Witness? Yes, you are witness. Even so, what I, Karsa Orlong, shall shape, you cannot imagine.*

No-one can.

Cynnigig sat in the shade of the tree that contained Phyrlis, humming softly. It was approaching dusk. The Thelomen Toblakai was gone, with his chosen horse. He had vaulted onto its back and ridden off without need for saddle or even reins. The herds had vanished, leaving the vista as empty as it had been before.

The bent-backed Jaghut removed a wrapped piece of the aras deer cooked the night before and began cutting it into small slices. 'A gift for you, dear sister.'

'I see,' she replied. *'Slain by the stone sword?'*

'Aye.'

'A bounty, then, to feed my spirit.'

Cynnigig nodded. He paused to gesture carelessly with the knife. 'You've done well, disguising the remains.'

'The foundations survive, of course. The House's walls. The anchor-stones in the yard's corners – all beneath my cloak of soil.'

'Foolish, unmindful T'lan Imass, to drive a spear into the grounds of an Azath House.'

'What did they know of houses, Cynnigig? Creatures of caves and hide tents. Besides, it was already dying and had been for years. Fatally wounded. Oh, Icarium was on his knees by the

time he finally delivered the mortal blow, raving with madness. And had not his Toblakai companion taken that opportunity to strike him unconscious . . .'

'He would have freed his father.' Cynnigig nodded around a mouthful of meat. He rose and walked to the tree. 'Here, sister,' he said, offering her a slice.

'It's burnt.'

'I doubt you could have managed better.'

'True. Go on, push it down – I won't bite.'

'You *can't* bite, my dear. I do appreciate the irony, by the way – Icarium's father had no desire to be saved. And so the House died, weakening the fabric . . .'

'Sufficiently for the warren to be torn apart. More, please – you're eating more of it than I am.'

'Greedy bitch. So, Karsa Orlong . . . surprised us.'

'I doubt we are the first victims of misapprehension regarding that young warrior, brother.'

'Granted. Nor, I suspect, will we be the last to suffer such shock.'

'Did you sense the six T'lan Imass spirits, Cynnigig? Hovering there, beyond the hidden walls of the yard?'

'Oh yes. Servants of the Crippled God, now, the poor things. They would tell him something, I think—'

'Tell who? The Crippled God?'

'No. Karsa Orlong. They possess knowledge, with which they seek to guide the Thelomen Toblakai – but they dared not approach. The presence of the House, I suspect, had them fearful.'

'No, it is dead – all that survived of its lifespirit moved into the spear. Not the House, brother, but Karsa Orlong himself – that was who they feared.'

'Ah.' Cynnigig smiled as he slipped another sliver of meat into Phyrlis's wooden mouth, where it slid from view, falling down into the hollow cavity within. There to rot, to gift the tree with its nutrients. 'Then those Imass are not so foolish after all.'

BOOK FOUR

HOUSE OF CHAINS

You have barred the doors
caged the windows
every portal sealed
to the outside world,
and now you find
what you feared most –
there are killers,
and they are in the House.

House
Talanbal

CHAPTER EIGHTEEN

The rage of the Whirlwind Goddess
was an inferno, beaten on the forge
of Holy Raraku.

The legions that marched in the dust
of blood burned by the eye of the sun
were cold iron.

There, on the dry harbour of the dead city
where the armies joined to battle
Hood walked the fated ground

where he walked many times before.

The Divided Heart
Fisher

S he had wormed her way alongside the carefully stacked cut
stones, to the edge of the trench – knowing her mother
would be furious at seeing how she had ruined her new
clothes – and finally came within sight of her sister.

Tavore had claimed her brother's bone and antler toy soldiers,
and in the rubble of the torn-up estate wall, where repairs had
been undertaken by the grounds workers, she had arranged a
miniature battle.

Only later would Felisin learn that her nine-year-old sister
had been, in fact, recreating a set battle, culled from historical
accounts of a century-old clash between a Royal Untan army

and the rebelling House of K'azz D'Avore. A battle that had seen the annihilation of the renegade noble family's forces and the subjugation of the D'Avore household. And that, taking on the role of Duke Kenussen D'Avore, she was working through every possible sequence of tactics towards achieving a victory. Trapped by a series of unfortunate circumstances in a steep-sided valley, and hopelessly outnumbered, the unanimous consensus among military scholars was that such victory was impossible.

Felisin never learned if her sister had succeeded where Kenussen D'Avore – reputedly a military genius – had failed. Her spying had become a habit, her fascination with the hard, remote Tavore an obsession. It seemed, to Felisin, that her sister had never been a child, had never known a playful moment. She had stepped into their brother's shadow and sought only to remain there, and when Ganoes had been sent off for schooling, Tavore underwent a subtle transformation. No longer in Ganoes's shadow, it was as if she had become his shadow, severed and haunting.

None of these thoughts were present in Felisin's mind all those years ago. The obsession with Tavore existed, but its sources were formless, as only a child's could be.

The stigma of meaning ever comes later, like a brushing away of dust to reveal shapes in stone.

At the very edge of the ruined city on its south side, the land fell away quickly in what had once been clastic slumps of silty clay, fanning out onto the old bed of the harbour. Centuries of blistering sun had hardened these sweeps, transforming them into broad, solid ramps.

Sha'ik stood at the head of the largest of these ancient fans born of a dying sea millennia past, trying to see the flat basin before her as a place of battle. Four thousand paces away, opposite, rose the saw-toothed remnants of coral islands, over which roared the Whirlwind. That sorcerous storm had stripped from those islands the formidable mantle of sand that had once covered them. What remained offered little in the way of a secure ridge on which to assemble and prepare legions. Footing would be treacherous, formations impossible. The islands swept in a vast arc across the south approach. To the east was an escarpment, a fault-line that saw the land falling sharply away eighty or more arm-lengths onto a salt flat – what had once been the inland sea's deepest bed. The fault was a slash that widened in its southwestward reach, just the other side of the reef islands, forming the seemingly endless basin that was Raraku's southlands. To the west lay dunes, the sand deep and soft, wind-sculpted and rife with sink-pits.

She would assemble her forces on this very edge, positioned to hold the seven major ramps. Mathok's horse archers on the wings, Korbolo Dom's new heavy infantry – the elite core of his Dogslayers – at the head of each of the ramps. Mounted lancers and horse warriors held back as screens for when the Malazans reeled back from the steep approaches and the order was given to advance.

Or so Korbolo Dom had explained – she was not entirely sure of the sequence. But it seemed that the Napan sought an initial defensive stance, despite their superior numbers. He was eager to prove his heavy infantry and shock troops against the Malazan equivalent. Since Tavore was marching to meet them, it was expedient to extend the invitation to its bitter close on these ramps. The advantage was entirely with the Army of the Apocalypse.

Tavore was, once again, Duke Kenussen D'Avore in Ibilar Gorge.

Sha'ik drew her sheep-hide cloak about her, suddenly chilled despite the heat. She glanced over to where Mathok and the dozen bodyguards waited, discreetly distanced yet close enough to reach her side within two or three heartbeats. She had no idea why the taciturn warchief so feared that she might be assassinated, but there was no danger in humouring the warrior. With Toblakai gone and Leoman somewhere to the south, Mathok had assumed the role of protector of her person. Well enough, although she did not think it likely that Tavore would attempt to send killers – the Whirlwind Goddess could not be breached undetected. Even a Hand of the Claw could not pass unnoticed through her multi-layered barriers, no matter what warren they sought to employ.

Because the barrier itself defines a warren. The warren that lies like an unseen skin over the Holy Desert. This usurped fragment is a fragment no longer, but whole unto itself. And its power grows. Until one day, soon, it will demand its own place in the Deck of Dragons. As with the House of Chains. A new House, of the Whirlwind.

Fed by the spilled blood of a slain army.

And when she kneels before me . . . what then? Dear sister, broken and bowed, smeared in dust and far darker streaks, her legions a ruin behind her, feast for the capemoths and vultures – shall I then remove my warhelm? Reveal to her, at that moment, my face?

We have taken this war. Away from the rebels, away from the Empress and the Malazan Empire. Away, even, from the Whirlwind Goddess herself. We have supplanted, you and I, Tavore, Dryjhna and the Book of the Apocalypse – for our own, private apocalypse. The family's own blood, and nothing more. And the world, then, Tavore – when I show myself to you and see the recognition in your eyes – the world, your world, will shift beneath you.

And at that moment, dear sister, you will understand. What has happened. What I have done. And why I have done it.

And then? She did not know. A simple execution was too easy, indeed, a cheat. Punishment belonged to the living, after all. The sentence was to survive, staggering beneath the chains of knowledge. A sentence not just of living, but of living *with*; that was the only answer to . . . everything.

She heard boots crunching on potsherds behind her and turned. No welcoming smile for this one – not this time. 'L'oric. I am delighted you deigned to acknowledge my request – you seemed to have grown out of the habit of late.' *Oh, how he hides from me, the secrets now stalking him, see how he will not meet my gaze – I sense struggles within him. Things he would tell me. Yet he will say nothing. With all the goddess's powers at my behest, and still I cannot trap this elusive man, cannot force from him his truths. This alone warns me – he is not as he seems. Not simply a mortal man . . .*

'I have been unwell, Chosen One. Even this short journey from the camp has left me exhausted.'

'I grieve for your sacrifice, L'oric. And so I shall come to my point without further delay. Heboric has barred his place of residence – he has neither emerged nor will he permit visitors, and it has been weeks.'

There was nothing false in his wince. 'Barred to us all, mistress.'

She cocked her head. 'Yet, you were the last to speak with him. At length, the two of you in his tent.'

'I was? That was the last time?'

Not the reaction she had anticipated. *Very well, then whatever secret he possesses has nothing to do with Ghost Hands.* 'It was. Was he distressed during your conversation?'

'Mistress, Heboric has long been distressed.'

'Why?'

His eyes flicked momentarily to hers, wider than usual, then away again. 'He . . . grieves for your sacrifice, Chosen One.'

She blinked. 'L'oric, I had no idea my sarcasm could so wound you.'

'Unlike you,' he replied gravely, 'I was not being facetious, mistress. Heboric grieves—'

'For my sacrifices. Well, that is odd indeed, since he did not think much of me before my . . . rebirth. Which particular loss does he mark?'

'I could not say – you will have to ask him that, I'm afraid.'

'Your friendship had not progressed to the point of an exchange of confessions, then.'

He said nothing to that. *Well, no, he couldn't. For that would acknowledge he has something to confess.*

She swung her gaze from him and turned once more to regard the potential field of battle. *I can envision the armies arrayed, yes. But then what? How are they moved? What is possible and what is impossible? Goddess, you have no answer to such questions. They are beneath you. Your power is your will, and that alone. But, dear Goddess, sometimes will is not enough.* 'Korbolo Dom is pleased with this pending . . . arena.'

'I am not surprised, mistress.'

She glanced back at him. 'Why?'

He shrugged, and she watched him search for an alternative to what he had been about to say. 'Korbolo Dom would have Tavore do precisely what he wants her to do. To array her forces here, or there, and nowhere else. To make this particular approach. To contest where he would have her contest. He expects the Malazan army to march up to be slaughtered, as if by will alone he can make Tavore foolish, or stupid.' L'oric nodded towards the vast basin. 'He wants her to fight there. Expects her to. But, why would she?'

She shivered beneath the cloak as her chill deepened. *Yes, why would she? Korbolo's certainty . . . is it naught but bluster? Does he too demand something to be simply because that is how he must have it? But then, were any of the others any different? Kamist Reloe and his tail-sniffing pups, Fayelle and Henaras? And Febryl and Bidithal? Leoman . . . who sat with that irritating half-smile, through all of Korbolo's descriptions of the battle to come. As if he knew something . . . as if he alone is indeed different. But then, that half-smile . . . the fool is sunk in the pit of durhang, after all. I should expect nothing of him, especially not military genius. Besides, Korbolo Dom has something to prove . . .*

'There is danger,' L'oric murmured, 'in trusting to a commander who wars with the aim of slaughter.'

'Rather than what?'

His brows rose fractionally. 'Why, victory.'

'Does not slaughter of the enemy achieve victory, L'oric?'

'But therein lies the flaw in Korbolo's thinking, Chosen One. As Leoman once pointed out, months ago, the flaw is one of sequence. Mistress, victory *precedes* slaughter. Not the other way round.'

She stared at him. 'Why, then, have neither you nor Leoman voiced this criticism when we discussed Korbolo Dom's tactics?'

'Discussed?' L'oric smiled. 'There was no discussion, Chosen One. Korbolo Dom is not a man who welcomes discussions.'

'Nor is Tavore,' she snapped.

'That is not relevant,' L'oric replied.

'What do you mean?'

'Malazan military doctrine – something Coltaine well understood, but also something that High Fist Pormqual had clearly lost sight of. Tactics are consensual. Dassem Ultor's original doctrine, when he was finally made First Sword of the Malazan Empire. "Strategy belongs to the commander, but tactics are the first field of battle, and it is fought in the command tent." Dassem's own words. Of course, such a system relied heavily upon capable officers. Incompetent officers – such as those that subseqently infiltrated the chain of—'

'Nobleborn officers, you mean.'

'Bluntly, yes. The purchasing of commissions – Dassem would never have permitted that, and from what I gather, nor does the Empress. Not any more, in any case. There was a cull—'

'Yes, I know, L'oric. By your argument, then, Tavore's personality has no relevance—'

'Not entirely, mistress. It has, for tactics are the child of strategy. And the truth of Tavore's nature will shape that strategy. Veteran soldiers speak of hot iron and cold iron. Coltaine was cold iron. Dujek Onearm is cold iron, too, although not always – he's a rare one in being able to shift as necessity demands. But Tavore? Unknown.'

'Explain this "cold iron", L'oric.'

'Mistress, this subject is not my expertise—'

'You have certainly fooled me. Explain. Now.'

'Very well, such as I understand it—'

'Cease equivocating.'

He cleared his throat, then turned and called out, 'Mathok. Would you join us, please.'

Sha'ik scowled at the presumption behind that invitation, but then inwardly relented. *This is important, after all. I feel it. The heart of all that will follow.* 'Join us, Mathok,' she said.

He dismounted and strode over.

L'oric addressed him. 'I have been asked to explain "cold iron", Warchief, and for this I need help.'

The desert warrior bared his teeth. 'Cold iron. Coltaine. Dassem Ultor – if the legends speak true. Dujek Onearm. Admiral Nok. K'azz D'Avore of the Crimson Guard. Inish Garn, who once led the Gral. Cold iron, Chosen One. Hard. Sharp. It is held before you, and so you reach.' He crossed his arms.

'You reach,' L'oric nodded. 'Yes, that's it. You reach. And are stuck fast.'

'Cold iron,' Mathok growled. 'The warchief's soul – it either rages with the fire of life, or is cold with death. Chosen One, Korbolo Dom is hot iron, as am I. As are you. We are as the sun's fires, as the desert's heat, as the breath of the Whirlwind Goddess herself.'

'The Army of the Apocalypse is hot iron.'

'Aye, Chosen One. And thus, we must pray that the forge of Tavore's heart blazes with vengeance.'

'That she too is hot iron? Why?'

'For then, we shall not lose.'

Sha'ik's knees suddenly weakened and she almost staggered. L'oric moved close to support her, alarm on his face.

'Mistress?'

'I am . . . I am all right. A moment . . .' She fixed her gaze on Mathok once more, saw the brief gauging regard in his eyes that then quickly slipped once again behind his impassive mien. 'Warchief, what if Tavore is cold iron?'

'The deadliest clash of all, Chosen One. Which shall shatter first?'

L'oric said, 'Military histories reveal, mistress, that cold iron defeats hot iron more often than not. By a count of three or four to one.'

'Yet Coltaine! Did he not fall to Korbolo Dom?'

She noted L'oric's eyes meet Mathok's momentarily.

'Well?' she demanded.

'Chosen One,' Mathok rumbled, 'Korbolo Dom and Coltaine fought nine major engagements – nine battles – on the Chain of Dogs. Of these, Korbolo was clear victor in one, and one only. At the Fall. Outside the walls of Aren. And for that he needed Kamist Reloe, and the power of Mael, as channelled through the jhistal priest, Mallick Rel.'

Her head was spinning, panic ripping through her, and she knew L'oric could feel her trembling.

'Sha'ik,' he whispered, close by her ear, 'you know Tavore, don't you? You know her, and she is *cold iron*, isn't she?'

Mute, she nodded. She did not know how she knew, for neither Mathok nor L'oric seemed able to give a concrete definition, suggesting to her that the notion derived from a gut level, a place of primal instinct. And so, *she knew*.

L'oric had lifted his head. 'Mathok.'

'High Mage?'

'Who, among us, is cold iron? Is there anyone?'

'There are two, High Mage. And one of these is capable of both: Toblakai.'

'And the other?'

'Leoman of the Flails.'

Corabb Bhilan Thenu'alas lay beneath a sheath of sand. The sweat had soaked through his telaba beneath him, packing down his body's moulded imprint, and had cooled, so that he now shivered unceasingly. The sixth son of a deposed chief among the Pardu, he had been a wanderer of the wastelands for most of his adult life. A wanderer, trader, and worse. When Leoman had found him, three Gral warriors had been dragging him behind their horses for most of a morning.

The purchase price had been pathetically small, since his skin had been flayed away by the burning sands, leaving only a bloodied mass of raw flesh. But Leoman had taken him to a healer, an old woman from some tribe he'd never heard of before, or since, and she in turn had taken him to a rockspring pool, where he'd lain immersed, raving with fever, for an unknown time, whilst she'd worked a ritual of mending and called upon the water's ancient spirits. And so he had recovered.

Corabb had never learned the reason behind Leoman's mercy, and, now that he knew him well – as well as any who'd sworn fealty to the man – he knew better than to ask. It was one with his contrary nature, his unknowable qualities that could be unveiled but once in an entire lifetime. But Corabb knew one thing: for Leoman of the Flails, he would give his life.

They had lain side by side, silent and motionless, through the course of the day, and now, late in the afternoon, they saw the first of the outriders appear in the distance, cautiously ranging out as they ventured onto the pan of cracked salts and clay.

Corabb finally stirred. 'Wickans,' he hissed.

'And Seti,' Leoman rumbled in reply.

'Those grey-armoured ones look . . . different.'

The man beside him grunted, then swore. 'Khundryl, from south of the Vathar River. I had hoped . . . Still, that arcane armour looks heavy. The Seven know what ancestral tombs they looted for those. The Khundryl came late to the horse, and it's no wonder with that armour, is it?'

Corabb squinted at the vast dust cloud behind the outriders. 'The vanguard rides close to the scouts.'

'Aye. We'll have to do something about that.'

Without another word the two warriors edged back from the crest, beyond the sight of the outriders, pausing briefly to reach back and brush sand over where their bodies had lain, then made their way back to the gully where they'd left their horses.

'Tonight,' Leoman said, collecting his mount's reins and swinging up into the saddle.

Corabb did the same and then nodded. Sha'ik would know, of course, that she had been defied. For the Whirlwind Goddess had her eyes on all her children. But this was their land, wasn't it? The invaders could not be left to walk it uncontested. No, the sands would drink their blood, giving voice on this night to the Shrouded Reaper's dark promise.

L'oric stood near the trail that led to Toblakai's glade. A casual look around, then the faintest of gestures from one hand marked a careful unveiling of sorcery – that vanished almost as soon as it arrived. Satisfied, he set off down the trail.

She might be distracted, but her goddess was not. Increasingly, he sensed questing attention directed towards him, sorcerous tendrils reaching out in an effort to find him, or track his movements. And it was becoming more difficult to elude such probes, particularly since they were coming from more than a single source.

Febryl was growing more nervous, as was Kamist Reloe. Whilst Bidithal's paranoia needed no fuel – *and nor should it.* Sufficient, then, all these signs of increased restlessness, to convince L'oric that whatever plans existed were soon to seek resolution. One way or another.

He had not expected to discover Sha'ik so ... unprepared. True, she had conveyed a none too subtle hint that she was preternaturally aware of all that went on in the camp, including an alarming ability to defeat his own disguising wards intended to mask his travels. Even so, there was knowledge that, had she possessed it – or even suspected – would have long since triggered a deadly response. *Some places must remain closed to her. I had expected her to ask far more dangerous questions of me today. Where is Felisin? Then again, maybe she didn't ask that because she already knew.* A chilling thought, not just for evincing the breadth of her awareness, but for what it suggested about Sha'ik herself. *That she knows what Bidithal did to Felisin . . . and she does not care.*

Dusk ever seemed eager to arrive in the forest of stone trees. The tracks he left in the dusty path revealed, to his relief, that he was still alone in walking the trail these days.

Not that the goddess needed trails. But there was a strangeness to Toblakai's glade, hinting at some kind of investment, as if the clearing had undergone a sanctification of some sort. And if that had indeed occurred, then it might exist as a blind spot in the eye of the Whirlwind Goddess.

But none of this explained why Sha'ik did not ask about Felisin. *Ah, L'oric, you are the blind one. Sha'ik's obsession is Tavore. With each day that leaves us, bringing the two armies ever closer, her obsession grows. As does her doubt and, perhaps, her fear. She is Malazan, after all – I was right in that. And within that waits another secret, this one buried deepest of all. She knows Tavore.*

And that knowledge had guided her every action since the Rebirth. Her recalling the Army of the Apocalpyse when virtually within sight of the Holy City's walls. Retreating into the heart of Raraku . . . *gods, was all that a flight of terror?*

A notion that did not bear thinking about.

The glade appeared before him, the ring of trees with their cold, unhuman eyes gazing down upon the small, bedraggled tent – and the young woman huddled before the stone-lined hearth a few paces from it.

She did not look up as he came near. 'L'oric, I was wondering, how can one tell Bidithal's cult of murderers from Korbolo Dom's? It's a crowded camp these days – I am glad I am hiding here, and in turn I find myself pitying you. Did you finally speak with her today?'

Sighing, he settled down opposite her, removing his shoulder pack and drawing food from it. 'I did.'

'And?'

'Her concerns for the impending clash are . . . overwhelming her—'

'My mother did not ask after me,' Felisin cut in, with a slight smile.

L'oric looked away. 'No,' he conceded in a whisper.

'She knows, then. And has judged as I have – Bidithal is close to exposing the plotters. They need him, after all, either to join the conspiracy, or stand aside. This is a truth that has not changed. And the night is drawing nearer, the night of betrayal. And so, Mother needs him to play out his role.'

'I am not sure of that, Felisin,' L'oric began, then shut up.

But she had understood, and her terrible smile broadened. 'Then the Whirlwind Goddess has stolen the love from her soul. Ah, well, she has been under siege for a long time, after all. In any case, she was not my mother in truth – that was a title she assumed because it amused her to do so—'

'Not true, Felisin. Sha'ik saw your plight—'

'I was the first one to see her, when she returned, reborn. A chance occurrence, that I should be out gathering hen'bara on that day. Before that day, Sha'ik had never noticed me – why would she? I was one among a thousand orphans, after all. But then she was . . . reborn.'

'Returned to the living as well, perhaps—'

Felisin laughed. 'Oh, L'oric, you ever strive, don't you? I knew then, as you must know by now – Sha'ik Reborn is not the same woman as Sha'ik Elder.'

'That hardly matters, lass. The Whirlwind Goddess chose her—'

'Because Sha'ik Elder died, or was killed. You did not see the truth as I did, in the faces of Leoman and Toblakai. I saw their uncertainty – they did not know if their ruse would succeed. And that it did, more or less, was as much to me as to any of them. The Whirlwind Goddess chose her out of necessity, L'oric.'

'As I said, Felisin, it does not matter.'

'Not to you, perhaps. No, you don't understand. I saw Sha'ik Elder up close, once. Her glance swept past me, and that glance saw no-one, and at that moment, child though I was, I knew the truth of her. Of her, and of her goddess.'

L'oric unstoppered the jug that had followed the food and raised it to wet a mouth that had suddenly gone dry. 'And what truth was that?' he whispered, unable to meet her eyes. Instead, he drank down a deep draught of the unwatered wine.

'Oh, that we are, one and all, nothing but slaves. We are the tools she will use to achieve her desires. Beyond that, our lives mean nothing to the goddess. But with Sha'ik Reborn, I thought I saw . . . something different.'

His peripheral vision caught her shrug.

'But,' she continued, 'the goddess is too strong. Her will too absolute. The poison that is indifference . . . and I well know that taste, L'oric. Ask any orphan, no matter how old they are now, and they will tell you the same. We all sucked at that same bitter tit.'

He knew his tears had broken from his eyes, were running down his cheeks, yet could do nothing to stem them.

'And now, L'oric,' she went on after a moment, 'we are all revealed. Every one of us here. We are all orphans. Think on it. Bidithal, who lost his temple, his entire cult. The same for Heboric. Korbolo Dom, who once stood as an equal in rank with great soldiers, like Whiskeyjack, and Coltaine. Febryl – did you know he murdered his own father and mother? Toblakai, who has lost his own people. And all the rest of us here, L'oric – we were children of the

Malazan Empire, once. And what have we done? We cast off the Empress, in exchange for an insane goddess who dreams only of destruction, who seeks to feed on a sea of blood . . .'

'And,' he asked softly, 'am I too an orphan?'

She had no need to answer, for they both heard the truth in his own pained words.

Osric . . .

'Leaving only . . . Leoman of the Flails.' Felisin took the wine from his hands. 'Ah, Leoman. Our flawed diamond. I wonder, can he save us all? Will he get the chance? Among us, only he remains . . . unchained. No doubt the goddess claims him, but it is an empty claim – you do see that, don't you?'

He nodded, wiping at his eyes. 'And I believe I have led Sha'ik to that realization, as well.'

'She knows, then, that Leoman is our last hope?'

His sigh was ragged. 'I think so . . .'

They were silent for a time. Night had arrived, and the fire had died down to ashes, leaving only starlight to illuminate the glade.

It seemed, then, that eyes of stone had slowly assumed life, a crescent row fixed now upon the two of them. A regard avid, gleaming with hunger. L'oric's head snapped up. He stared out at the ghostly faces, then at the two Toblakai figures, then settled once more, shivering.

Felisin laughed softly. 'Yes, they do haunt one, don't they?'

L'oric grunted. 'A mystery here, in Toblakai's creations. Those faces – they are T'lan Imass. Yet . . .'

'He thought them his gods, yes. So Leoman told me, once, beneath the fumes of durhang. Then he warned me to say nothing to Toblakai.' She laughed again, louder this time. 'As if I would. A fool indeed, to step between Toblakai and his gods.'

'There is nothing simple about that simple warrior,' L'oric murmured.

'Just as you are not simply a High Mage,' she said. 'You must act soon, you know. You have choices to make. Hesitate too long and they will be made for you, to your regret.'

'I could well say the same to you in return.'

'Well then, it seems we still have more to discuss this night. But first, let us eat – before the wine makes us drunk.'

Sha'ik recoiled, staggered back a step. The breath hissed from her in a gust of alarm – and pain. A host of wards swirled around Heboric's abode, still flickering with the agitation her collision had triggered.

She bit down on her outrage, pitched her voice low as she said, 'You know who it is who has come, Heboric. Let me pass. Defy me, and I will bring the wrath of the goddess down, here and now.'

A moment's silence, then, 'Enter.'

She stepped forward. There was a moment's pressure, then she stumbled through, brought up short against the crumbled foundation wall. A sudden ... *absence*. Terrifying, bursting like the clearest light where all had been, but a moment earlier, impenetrable gloom. Bereft ... *yet free. Gods, free – the light –* 'Ghost Hands!' she gasped. 'What have you done?'

'The goddess within you, Sha'ik,' came Heboric's words, 'is not welcome in my temple.'

Temple? Roaring chaos was building within her, the vast places in her mind where the Whirlwind Goddess had been now suddenly vacant, filling with the dark, rushing return of ... *of all that I was.* Bitter fury grew like a wildfire as memories rose with demonic ferocity to assail her. *Beneth. You bastard. You closed your hands around a child, but what you shaped was anything but a woman. A plaything. A slave to you and your twisted, brutal world.*

I used to watch that knife in your hands, the flickering games that were your idle habits. And that's what you taught me, isn't it? Cutting for fun and blood. And oh, how I cut. Baudin. Kulp. Heboric—

A physical presence beside her now, the solid feel of hands – jade green, black-barred – a figure, squat and wide and seemingly beneath the shadow of fronds – no, tattoos. *Heboric* . . .

'Inside, lass. I have made you . . . bereft. An unanticipated consequence of forcing the goddess from your soul. Come.'

And then he was guiding her into the tent's confines. The air chill and damp, a single small oil lamp struggling against the gloom – a flame that suddenly moved as he lifted the lamp and brought it over to a brazier, where he used its burning oil to light the bricks of dung. And, as he worked, he spoke. 'Not much need for light . . . the passage of time . . . before tasked with sanctioning a makeshift temple . . . what do I know of Treach, anyway?'

She was sitting on cushions, her trembling hands held before the brazier's growing flames, furs wrapped about her. At the name 'Treach' she started, looked up.

To see Heboric squatting before her. *As he had squatted that day, so long ago now, in Judgement's Round. When Hood's sprites had come to him . . . to foretell of Fener's casting down. The flies would not touch his spiral tattoos. I remember that. Everywhere else, they swarmed like madness.* Now, those tattoos had undergone a transformation. 'Treach.'

His eyes narrowed on hers – *a cat's eyes, now – he can see!* 'Ascended into godhood, Sha'ik—'

'Don't call me that. I am Felisin Paran of House Paran.' She hugged herself suddenly. 'Sha'ik waits for me . . . out there, beyond this tent's confines – beyond your wards.'

'And would you return to that embrace, lass?'

She studied the brazier's fire, whispered, 'No choice, Heboric.'

'No, I suppose not.'

A thunderous shock bolted her upright. 'Felisin!'

'What?'

'Felisin Younger! I have not . . . not seen her! Days? Weeks? What – where is she!'

Heboric's motion was feline as he straightened, fluid and precise. 'The goddess must know, lass—'

'If she does, she's not told *me*!'

'But why would . . .'

She saw a sudden knowledge in his eyes, and felt her own answering stab of fear. 'Heboric, what do you—'

Then he was guiding her to the tent flap, speaking as he drove her back step by step. 'We spoke, you and I, and all is well. Nothing to concern yourself over. The Adjunct and her legions are coming and there is much to do. As well, there are the secret plans of Febryl to keep an eye on, and for that you must rely upon Bidithal—'

'Heboric!' She struggled against him, but he would not relent. They reached the flap and he pushed her outside. 'What are you—' A hard shove and she stumbled back.

Through a flare of wards.

Sha'ik slowly righted herself. She must have stumbled. *Oh yes, a conversation with Ghost Hands. All is well. I'm relieved by that, for it allows me to think on more important things. My nest of betrayers, for example. Must have words with Bidithal again tonight. Yes . . .*

She turned from the ex-priest's tent and made her way back to the palace.

Overhead, the stars of the desert sky were shimmering, as they often did when the goddess had come close . . . Sha'ik wondered what had drawn her this time. Perhaps no more than casting a protective eye on her Chosen One . . .

She was unmindful – as was her goddess – of the barely visible shape that slipped out from the entrance to Heboric's tent, flowing in a blur into the nearest shadows. Unmindful, also, of the scent that barbed shape now followed.

Westward, to the city's edge, and then onto the trail, padding between the stone trees, towards a distant glade.

Bidithal sat in the seething shadows, alone once more, although the smile remained fixed on his withered face.

Febryl had his games, but so did the once High Priest of the Shadow cult. Even betrayers could be betrayed, after all, a sudden turning of the knife in the hand.

And the sands would fold one more time, the way they did when the air breathed hard, in, out, back, forth, stirring and shifting the grains as would waves against a beach, to lay one layer over another in thin seams of colour. There were no limits to the number of layers, and this Febryl and his fellow conspirators would soon discover, to their grief.

They sought the warren for themselves. It had taken Bidithal a long time to unveil that truth, that deep-buried motivation, for it had remained in the silence between every spoken word. This was not a simple, mundane struggle for power. No. This was usurpation. Expropriation – a detail that itself whispered of yet deeper secrets. They wanted the warren . . . but why? A question yet to be answered, but find an answer he would, and soon.

In this, he knew, the Chosen One relied upon him, and he would not fail her. *In so far as what she expects from me, yes, I will deliver. Of course, there are other issues that extend far beyond Sha'ik, this goddess and the Whirlwind Warren she would rule. The shape of the pantheon itself is at stake . . . my long-overdue vengeance against those foreign pretenders to the Throne of Shadow.*

Even now, if he listened very – *very* – carefully, he could hear them. And they were coming. Closer, ever closer.

A tremble of fear took his limbs, and shadows scurried away from him momentarily, only returning when he had settled once more. *Rashan . . . and Meanas. Meanas and Thyr. Thyr and Rashan. The three children of the Elder Warrens. Galain, Emurlahn and Thyrllan. Should it be so surprising that they war once more? For do not we ever inherit the spites of our fathers and mothers?*

But a ghost of that fear remained. He had not called them, after all. Had not understood the truth of what lay *beneath* the Whirlwind Warren, the reason why the warren was held in this single place and nowhere else. Had not *comprehended* how the old battles never died, but simply slept, every bone in the sand restless with memory.

Bidithal raised his hands and the army of shadows crowded within his temple gathered closer.

'My children,' he whispered, beginning the Closing Chant.

'Father.'

'Do you remember?'

'We remember.'

'Do you remember the dark?'

'We remember the dark. Father—'

'Ask it and close this moment, children.'

'Do you remember the dark?'

The priest's smile broadened. A simple question, one that could be asked of anyone, anyone at all. And perhaps they would understand. But probably not. *Yet I understand it.*

Do you remember the dark?

'I remember.'

As, with sighs, the shadows dispersed, Bidithal stiffened once more to that almost inaudible call. He shivered again. They were getting close indeed.

And he wondered what they would do, when they finally arrived.

There were eleven in all. His chosen.

Korbolo Dom leaned back on his cushions, eyes veiled as he studied the silent, shrouded line of figures standing before him. The Napan held a goblet carved from crystal in his right hand, in which swirled a rare wine from the Grisian valleys on Quon Tali. The woman who had kept him amused earlier this night was asleep, her head resting on his right thigh. He had plied her with enough durhang to ensure oblivion for the next dozen bells, though it was the expedience of security rather than any insipid desire on his part that necessitated such measures.

Drawn from his Dogslayers, the eleven killers were

appallingly skilled. Five of them had been personal assassins to Holy Falah'dan in the days before the Empire, rewarded with gifts of alchemy and sorcery to maintain their youthful appearance and vigour.

Three of the remaining six were Malazan – Korbolo Dom's own, created long ago, when he realized he had cause to worry about the Claw. *Cause . . . now that's a simplification almost quaint in its coyness. A multitude of realizations, of sudden discoveries, of knowledge I had never expected to gain – of things I had believed long dead and gone.* There had been ten such bodyguards, once. Evidence of the need for them stood before him now. Three left, the result of a brutal process of elimination, leaving only those with the greatest skill and the most fortuitous alliance of Oponn's luck – two qualities that fed each other well.

The remaining three assassins were from various tribes, each of whom had proved his worth during the Chain of Dogs. The arrow from one had slain Sormo E'nath, from a distance of seventy paces, on the Day of Pure Blood. There had been other arrows striking true, but it had been the one through the warlock's neck – the assassin's – that had filled the lad's lungs with blood, that had drowned his very breath, so that he could not call upon his damned spirits for healing . . .

Korbolo sipped wine, slowly licked his lips. 'Kamist Reloe has chosen among you,' he rumbled after a moment, 'for the singular task that will trigger all that subsequently follows. And I am content with his choices. But do not think this diminishes the rest of you. There will be tasks – essential tasks – on that night. Here in this very camp. I assure you, you will get no sleep that night, so prepare yourselves. Also, two of you will remain with me at all times, for I can guarantee that my death will be sought before that fateful dawn arrives.'

I expect you to die in my place. Of course. It is what you are sworn to do, should the need arise.

'Leave me now,' he said, waving his free hand.

The eleven assassins bowed in unison, then filed silently out of the tent.

Korbolo lifted the woman's head from his thigh, by the hair – noting how she remained insensate to the rough handling – and rose from the cushions, letting her head thump back down. He paused to drink a mouthful of the wine, then stepped from the modest dais and approached the side chamber that had been partitioned off by silk hangings.

Within the private room, Kamist Reloe was pacing. Hands wringing, shoulders drawn up, neck taut.

Korbolo leaned against a support post, his mouth twisting into a slight sneer at seeing the High Mage's fretting. 'Which of your many fears plagues you now, Kamist? Oh, do not answer. I admit I've ceased caring.'

'Foolish complacency on your part, then,' the High Mage snapped. 'Do you think we are the only clever people?'

'In the world? No. Here, in Raraku, well, that's another matter. Who should we fear, Kamist Reloe? Sha'ik? Her goddess devours her acuity – day by day, the lass grows less and less aware of what goes on around her. And that goddess barely takes note of us – oh, there are suspicions, perhaps, but that is all. Thus. Who else? L'oric? I've known many a man like him – creating mystery around themselves – and I have found that what it usually hides is an empty vessel. He is all pose and nothing more.'

'You are wrong in that, I fear, but no, I do not worry about L'oric.'

'Who else? Ghost Hands? The man's vanished into his own pit of hen'bara. Leoman? He's not here and I've plans for his return. Toblakai? I think we've seen the last of him. Who is left? Why, none other than Bidithal. But Febryl swears he almost has him in our fold – it's simply a question of discovering what the bastard truly desires. Something squalid and disgusting, no doubt. He is slave to his vices, is Bidithal. Offer him ten thousand orphaned girls and the smile will never leave his ugly face.'

Kamist Reloe wrapped his arms about himself as he continued pacing. 'It's not who we know to be among us that is the source of my concerns, Korbolo Dom, it's who is among us that we do not know.'

The Napan scowled. 'And how many hundreds of spies do we have in this camp? And what of the Whirlwind Goddess herself – do you imagine she will permit the infiltration of strangers?'

'Your flaw, Korbolo Dom, is that you think in a strictly linear fashion. Ask that question again, only this time ask it in the context of the goddess having *suspicions* about us.'

The High Mage was too distracted to notice the Napan's half-step forward, one hand lifting. But Korbolo Dom's blow died at that very moment, as the import of Kamist Reloe's challenge reached him. His eyes slowly widened. Then he shook his head. 'No, that would be too great a risk to take. A Claw let loose in this camp would endanger *everyone* – there would be no way to predict their targets—'

'Would there be a need to?'

'What do you mean?'

'We are the *Dogslayers*, Korbolo Dom. The murderers of Coltaine, the Seventh, and the legions at Aren. More, we also possess the mage cadre for the Army of the Apocalypse. Finally, who will be commanding that army on the day of battle? How many reasons do the Claw need to strike at us, and at us specifically? What chance would Sha'ik have if we were all dead? Why kill Sha'ik at all? We can fight this war without her and her damned goddess – we've done it before. And we're about to—'

'Enough of that, Kamist Reloe. I see your point. So, you fear that the goddess will permit a Claw to infiltrate . . . in order to deal with us. With you, Febryl and myself. An interesting possibility, but I still think it remote. The goddess is too heavy-handed, too ensnared by emotion, to think with such devious, insidious clarity.'

'She does not have to initiate the scheme, Korbolo Dom.

She need only comprehend the *offer*, and then decide either to acquiesce or not. It is not *her* clarity that is relevant, but that of Laseen's Claw. And do you doubt the cleverness of Topper?'

Growling under his breath, Korbolo Dom looked away for a moment. 'No,' he finally admitted. 'But I do rely on the goddess being in no mind to accept communication from the Empress, from Topper, or anyone else who refuses to kneel to her will. You have thought yourself into a nightmare, Kamist Reloe, and now you invite me to join you. I decline the offer, High Mage. We are well protected, and too far advanced in our efforts for all of this fretting.'

'I have survived this long, Korbolo Dom, because of my talent in anticipating what my enemies would attempt. Soldiers say no plan of battle survives contact with the enemy. But the game of subterfuge is the very opposite. Plans derive from *persistent* contact with the enemy. Thus, you proceed on your terms, and I will proceed on mine.'

'As you like. Now, leave me. It is late, and I would sleep.'

The High Mage stopped pacing to fix the Napan with an unreadable look for a moment, then he swung about and left the chamber.

Korbolo listened until he heard the flap in the outer room swish open, then close. He listened on, and was satisfied to hear the draws being tightened by one of his bodyguards positioned just outside the entrance.

Draining the last of the wine – *damned expensive but tastes no different from the dockside swill I choked down on the Isle* – he flung the goblet down and strode to the mass of cushions at the far end. *Beds in every room. I wonder what that signifies of my personality? Then again, those other ones are not for sleeping in, are they. No, only this one . . .*

In the front room on the other side of the silk partitions, the woman lay unmoving on her own heap of cushions, where Korbolo had left her some time back.

Continuous, overwhelming imbibing of durhang – like

any other intoxicant – created a process of diminishment of its effects. Until, while a layer of insensate numbness still persisted – a useful barrier against such things as having her head yanked up by her hair then dropped back down – cool awareness remained beneath it.

Advantageous, as well, the rituals her master had inflicted upon her, rituals that eliminated the weakness of pleasure. There could be no loss of control, not any more, for her mind no longer warred with feelings, for of feelings she had none. An easy surrender, she had found to her delight, for there had been little in her life before her initiation to seed warm remembrances of childhood.

And so she was well suited to this task. Uttering the right sounds of pleasure to disguise her indifference to all of Korbolo Dom's peculiar preferences. And lying motionless, unmindful even of a throat slowly filling with phlegm from the near-liquid smoke of the durhang, for as much time as was needed, before the subtle, tasteless drops she had added to his wine took effect.

When she could hear his deep, slow breaths that told her he would not easily awaken, she rolled onto her side in a fit of coughing. When it had passed she paused again, just to be certain that the Napan still slept. Satisfied, she clambered to her feet and tottered to the tent flap.

Fumbled with the ties until a gruff voice from just beyond said, 'Scillara, off to the latrines again?'

And another voice softly laughed and added, 'It's a wonder there's any meat on her at all, the way she heaves night after night.'

'It's the rust-leaf and the bitter berries crushed in with the durhang,' the other replied, as his hands took over the task of loosening the draws, and the flap was drawn aside.

Scillara staggered out, bumping her way between the two guards.

The hands that reached out to steady invariably found unusual places to rest, and squeeze.

She would have enjoyed that, once, in a slightly

offended, irritated way that none the less tickled with pleasure. But now, it was nothing but clumsy lust to be endured.

As everything else in this world had to be endured, while she waited for her final reward, the blissful new world beyond death. '*The left hand of life, holding all misery. And the right hand – yes, the one with the glittering blade, dear – the right hand of death, holding, as it does, the reward you would offer to others, and then take upon yourself. At your chosen moment.*'

Her master's words made sense, as they always did. Balance was the heart of all things, after all. And life – that time of pain and grief – was but one side of that balance. '*The harder, the more miserable, the more terrible and disgusting your life, child, the greater the reward beyond death . . .*' Thus, as she knew, it all made sense.

No need, then, to struggle. Acceptance was the only path to walk.

Barring this one. She weaved her way between the tent rows. The Dogslayers' encampment was precise and ordered, in the Malazan fashion – a detail she knew well from her days as a child when her mother followed the train of the Ashok Regiment. Before that regiment went overseas, leaving hundreds destitute – lovers and their get, servants and scroungers. Her mother had then sickened and died. She had a father, of course, one of the soldiers. Who might be alive, or dead, but either way was thoroughly indifferent to the child he had left behind.

Balance.

Difficult with a head full of durhang, even inured to it as she had become.

But there were the latrines, down this slope, and onto the wooden walkways spanning the trench. Smudge-pots smouldering to cover some of the stench and keep the flies away. Buckets beside the holed seats, filled with hand-sized bundles of grass. Larger open-topped casks with water, positioned out over the trench and fixed to the walkways.

Hands held out to either side, Scillara navigated carefully across one of the narrow bridges.

Long-term camp trenches such as this one held more than just human wastes. Garbage was regularly dumped in by soldiers and others – or what had passed for garbage with them. But for the orphans of this squalid city, some of that refuse was seen as treasure. To be cleaned, repaired and sold.

And so, figures swarmed in the darkness below.

She reached the other side, her bare feet sinking into the mud made by splashes that had reached the ridge. 'I remember the dark!' she sang out, voice throaty from years of durhang smoke.

There was a scrabbling from the trench, and a small girl, sheathed in excrement, clambered up to her, teeth flashing white. 'Me too, sister.'

Scillara drew out a small bag of coins from her sash. Their master frowned on such gestures, and indeed, they ran contrary to his teachings, but she could not help herself. She pressed it into the girl's hands. 'For food.'

'He will be displeased, sister—'

'And of the two of us, I alone will suffer a moment of torment. So be it. Now, I have words from this night, to be brought to our master . . .'

He had always walked with a pitching gait, low to the ground, sufficient to have earned him a host of unflattering nicknames. Toad, crab-legs . . . the names children gave each other, some of which were known to persist into adulthood. But Heboric had worked hard as a youth – long before his first, fateful visit into a temple of Fener – to excoriate those appellations, to eventually earn *Light Touch*, in response to certain skills he had acquired on the streets. But now, his sidling walk had undergone a transformation, yielding to an instinctive desire to drop even lower, even to using his hands to propel him along.

Had he considered it, he would have concluded, sourly,

that he moved less like a cat than an ape, such as those found in the jungles of Dal Hon. Unpleasant to the eye, perhaps, but efficacious none the less.

He slowed on the trail as he approached Toblakai's glade. A faint smell of smoke, the dull gleam of a fast-cooling fire, the murmur of voices.

Heboric slipped to one side, among the stone trees, then sank down within sight of the two seated at the hearth.

Too long his self-obsession, the seemingly endless efforts to create his temple – that now struck him as a strange kind of neurotic nesting; he had ignored the world beyond the walls for too long. There had been, he realized with a surge of bitter anger, a host of subtle alterations to his personality, concomitant with the physical gifts he had received.

He had ceased being mindful.

And that, he realized as he studied the two figures in the glade, had permitted a terrible crime.

She's healed well . . . but not well enough to disguise the truth of what has happened. Should I reveal myself? No. Neither of them has made a move to expose Bidithal, else they would not be hiding here. That means they would try to talk me out of what must be done.

But I warned Bidithal. I warned him, and he was . . . amused. Well, I think that amusement is about to end.

He slowly backed away.

Then, deep in the shadows, Heboric hesitated. There was no clash between his new and old instincts on this matter. Both demanded blood. And this night. Immediately. But something of the old Heboric was reasserting itself. He was new to this role as Destriant. More than that, Treach himself was a newly arrived god. And while Heboric did not believe Bidithal held any position – not any more – within the realm of Shadow, his temple was sanctified to *someone*.

An attack would draw in their respective sources of power, and there was no telling how swiftly, and how uncontrollably, that clash could escalate.

Better had I just remained old Heboric. With hands of otataral entwined with an unknown being's immeasurable power . . . Then I could have torn him limb from limb.

He realized that, instead, he could do nothing. Not this night, in any case. He would have to wait, seeking an opportunity, a moment of distraction. But to achieve that, he would have to remain hidden, unseen – Bidithal could not discover his sudden elevation. Could not learn that he had become Destriant to Treach, the new god of war.

The rage suddenly returned, and he struggled to push it away.

After a moment his breathing slowed. He turned round and edged back onto the trail. This would require more thought. Measured thought. *Damn you, Treach. You knew the guise of a tiger. Gift me some of your cunning ways, a hunter's ways, a killer's . . .*

He approached the head of the trail, and halted at a faint sound. Singing. Muted, a child's, coming from the ruins of what had once been a modest building of some sort. Indifferent to the darkness, his eyes caught movement and fixed hard on that spot, until a shape resolved itself.

A girl in rags, carrying a stick that she held in both hands. A dozen or so dead rhizan hung by their tails from her belt. As he watched, he saw her leap up and swing the stick. It struck something and she scrambled in pursuit, jumping about to trap a tiny shape writhing on the ground. A moment later and she lifted the rhizan into view. A quick twist of the neck, then another tiny body was tied to her belt. She bent down and retrieved her stick. And began singing once more.

Heboric paused. He would have difficulty passing by her unnoticed. *But not impossible.*

Probably an unnecessary caution. Even so. He held to the shadows as he edged forward, moving only when her back was turned, his eyes never leaving her form for a moment.

A short while later and he was past.

Dawn was approaching, and the camp was moments from stirring awake. Heboric increased his pace, and eventually reached his tent, slipping inside.

Apart from the girl, he'd seen no-one.

And when she judged that he was finally gone, the girl slowly turned about, her singing falling away as she peered out into the gloom. 'Funny man,' she whispered, 'do you remember the dark?'

A sixth of a bell before dawn, Leoman and two hundred of his desert warriors struck the Malazan encampment. The infantry stationed at the pickets were at the end of their watch, gathered in weary groups to await the sun's rise – a lapse in discipline that presented easy targets for the archers who had, on foot, closed to within thirty paces of the line. A whispery flit of arrows, all loosed at the same time, and the Malazan soldiers were down.

At least half of the thirty or so soldiers had not been killed outright, and their screams of pain and fear broke the stillness of the night. The archers had already set their bows down and were darting forward with their kethra knives to finish the wounded sentries, but they had not gone ten paces before Leoman and his horse warriors thundered around them, striking hard through the breach.

And into the camp.

Corabb Bhilan Thenu'alas rode at his commander's side, a long-hafted weapon that was half sword, half axe, in his right hand. Leoman was the centre of a curved sweep of attackers, protecting a knot of additional horse warriors from which a steady whirring sound rose. Corabb knew what that sound signified – his commander had invented his own answer to Moranth munitions, employing a pair of clay balls filled with oil and connected by a thin chain. Lit like lamps, they were swung and thrown in the manner of bolas.

The desert warriors were among the huge supply wagons now, and Corabb heard the first of those bolas whip outward, the sound followed by a whooshing roar of fire. The darkness vanished in a red glare.

And then Corabb saw a figure running from his horse's path. He swung his long-bladed axe. The impact, as it struck the back of the fleeing Malazan's helmed head, nearly dislocated Corabb's shoulder. A spray of blood spattered hard against his forearm as he dragged the weapon free – it was suddenly heavier, and he glanced down at it, to see that the blade had taken the helm with it, having cut fully half through. Brains and bits of bone and scalp were spilling from the bronze bowl.

Swearing, he slowed his mount's wild charge and tried to shake the axe clear. There was fighting on all sides, now, as well as raging flames engulfing at least a dozen wagons – and squad-tents. And soldiers appearing, more and more of them. He could hear barked orders in the Malazan tongue, and crossbow quarrels had begun flitting through the air towards the horse warriors.

A horn sounded, high and wavering. His curses growing fiercer, Corabb wheeled his horse round. He had already lost contact with Leoman, although a few of his comrades were in sight. All of them responding to the call to withdraw. As he must, as well.

The axe dragged at his aching shoulder, still burdened with that damned helm. He drove his horse back up the broad track between the mess-tents. Smoke tumbled, obscuring the view before him, stinging his eyes and harsh in his lungs.

Sudden burning agony slashed across his cheek, snapping his head around. A quarrel clattered against the ground fifteen paces ahead and to one side. Corabb ducked low, twisting in search of where it had come from.

And saw a squad of Malazans, all with crossbows – all but one cocked and trained on the desert warrior, with a sergeant berating the soldier who had fired too early. A scene taken in, in its entirety, between heartbeats. The bastards were less then ten paces distant.

Corabb flung his axe away. With a scream, he pitched his horse sideways, directly into the wall of one of the mess-tents. Ropes tautened and snapped heavy stakes skyward, poles splintering. Amidst this stumbling chaos, the warrior heard the crossbows loose – but his horse was going down, onto its side – and Corabb was already leaping clear of the saddle, his moccasined feet slipping out from the stirrups as he dived.

Into the collapsing tent wall, a moment before his horse, rolling with a scream, followed.

The pressure of that waxed fabric vanished suddenly and Corabb tumbled into a somersault, once, twice, then skidded onto his feet, spinning round—

—in time to see his horse roll back upright.

Corabb leapt alongside his mount and vaulted up into the saddle – and they were off.

And in the desert warrior's mind: numb disbelief.

On the opposite side of the avenue, seven Malazan marines stood or crouched with spent crossbows, staring as the rider thundered off into the smoke.

'Did you see that?' one asked.

Another frozen moment, shattered at last when the soldier named Lutes flung his weapon down in disgust.

'Pick that up,' Sergeant Borduke growled.

'If Maybe hadn't fired early—'

'I wasn't sure!' Maybe replied.

'Load up, idiots – there might be a few left.'

'Hey, Sergeant, maybe that horse killed the cook.'

Borduke spat. 'The gods smiling down on us this night, Hubb?'

'Well . . .'

'Right. The truth remains, then. We'll have to kill him ourselves. Before he kills us. But never mind that for now. Let's move . . .'

The sun had just begun to rise when Leoman drew rein and

734

halted his raiders. Corabb was late in arriving – among the last, in fact – and that earned a pleased nod from his commander. As if he'd assumed that Corabb had been taking up the rear out of a sense of duty. He did not notice that his lieutenant had lost his main weapon.

Behind them, they could see the columns of smoke rising into sunlit sky, and the distant sound of shouts reached them, followed moments later by the thunder of horse hoofs.

Leoman bared his teeth. 'And now comes the real objective of our attack. Well done thus far, my soldiers. Hear those horses? Seti, Wickans and Khundryl – and that will be the precise order of the pursuit. The Khundryl, whom we must be wary of, will be burdened by their armour. The Wickans will range cautiously. But the Seti, once they sight us, will be headlong in their pursuit.' He then raised the flail in his right hand, and all could see the bloody, matted hair on the spike ball. 'And where shall we lead them?'

'To *death!*' came the roaring reply.

The rising sun had turned the distant wall of spinning, whirling sand gold, a pleasing colour to Febryl's old, watery eyes. He sat facing east, cross-legged atop what had once been a gate tower but was now a shapeless heap of rubble softened by windblown sand.

The city reborn lay to his back, slow to awaken on this day for reasons of which only a scant few were aware, and Febryl was one of those. The goddess *devoured*. Consuming life's forces, absorbing the ferocious will to survive from her hapless, misguided mortal servants.

The effect was gradual, yet, day after day, moment by moment, it *deadened*. Unless one was cognizant of that hunger, of course. And was able to take preventative measures to evade her incessant demands.

Long ago, Sha'ik Reborn had claimed to know him, to have plumbed his every secret, to have discerned the hue of his soul. And indeed, she had shown an alarming ability to speak in his mind – almost as if she was always present, and only spoke to occasionally remind him of that terrifying truth. But such moments had diminished in frequency – perhaps as a result of his renewed efforts to mask himself – until, now, he was certain that she could no longer breach his defences.

Perhaps, however, the truth was far less flattering to his own proficiencies. Perhaps the influence of the goddess had lured Sha'ik Reborn into . . . indifference. *Aye, it may be that I am already dead and am yet to know it. That all I have planned is known to the woman and goddess both. Am I alone in having spies? No. Korbolo has hinted of his own agents, and indeed, nothing of what I seek will come to pass without the efforts of the Napan's hidden cadre of killers.*

It was, he reflected with bitter humour, the nature of everyone in this game to hide as much of themselves from others as they could, from allies as well as enemies, since such appellations were in the habit of reversing without warning.

None the less, Febryl had faith in Kamist Reloe. The High Mage had every reason to remain loyal to the broader scheme – the scheme that was betrayal most prodigious – since the path it offered was the only one that ensured Reloe's survival in what was to come. And as for the more subtle nuances concerning Febryl himself, well, those were not Kamist Reloe's business. Were they?

Even if their fruition should prove fatal . . . to everyone but me.

They all thought themselves too clever, and that was a flaw inviting exploitation.

And what of me? Eh, dear Febryl? Do you think yourself clever? He smiled at the distant wall of sand. Cleverness was not essential, provided one insisted on keeping things simple. Complexity beckoned error, like a whore a soldier on leave. The lure of visceral rewards that proved never quite as straightforward as one would have imagined from

736

the start. *But I will avoid that trap. I will not suffer deadly lapses, such as has happened to Bidithal, since they lead to complications – although his failings will lead him into my hands, so I suppose I should not complain too much.*

'The sun's light folds over darkness.'

He started, twisted around. 'Chosen One!'

'Deep breaths, old man, will ease your hammering heart. I can wait a moment, for I am patient.'

She stood almost at his side – of course he had seen no shadow, for the sun was before him. But how had she come with such silence? How long had she been standing there? 'Chosen One, have you come to join me in greeting the dawn?'

'Is that what you do, when you come here at the beginning of each day? I'd wondered.'

'I am a man of humble habits, mistress.'

'Indeed. A certain bluntness that affects a quality of simplicity. As if by adhering to simple habits in the flesh and bone, your mind will in turn strive towards the same perfection.'

He said nothing, though his heart had anything but slowed its thundering pace.

Sha'ik then sighed. 'Did I say perfection? Perhaps I should tell you something, then, to aid you in your quest.'

'Please,' he gasped softly.

'The Whirlwind Wall is virtually opaque, barring that diffuse sunlight. And so I am afraid I must correct you, Febryl. You are facing northeast, alas.' She pointed. 'The sun is actually over there, High Mage. Do not fret so – you have at least been consistent. Oh, and there is another matter that I believe must be clarified. Few would argue that my goddess is consumed by anger, and so consumes in turn. But what you might see as the loss of many to feed a singular hunger is in truth worthy of an entirely different analogy.'

'Oh?'

'Yes. She does not strictly *feed* on the energies of her

737

followers, so much as provide for them a certain *focus*. Little different, in fact, from that Whirlwind Wall out there, which, while seeming to diffuse the light of the sun, in fact acts to trap it. Have you ever sought to pass through that wall, Febryl? Particularly at dusk, when the day's heat has most fully been absorbed? It would burn you down to bone, High Mage, in an instant. So, you see how something that appears one way is in truth the very opposite way? Burnt crisp – a horrible image, isn't it? One would need to be desert-born, or possess powerful sorcery to defy that. Or very deep shadows . . .'

Living simply, Febryl belatedly considered, should not be made synonymous with *seeing* simply, since the former was both noble and laudable, whilst the latter was a flaw most deadly. A careless error, and, alas, he had made it.

And now, he concluded, it was too late.

And as for altering the plans, oh, it was too late for that as well.

Somehow, the newly arriving day had lost its glamour.

CHAPTER NINETEEN

It was said the captain's adopted child – who at that time
was known by the unfortunate name of Grub – refused
the wagon on the march. That he walked the entire way,
even as, in the first week beneath the year's hottest sun,
fit and hale soldiers stumbled and fell.

This is perhaps invention, for by all accounts he was
at that time no more than five years of age. And the captain
himself, from whose journals much of that journey and
the clash in which it culminated is related in detail, writes
very little of Grub, more concerned as he was with the
rigours of command. As a result, of the future First
Sword of the Late Empire period, scant details, beyond
the legendary and probably fictitious, are known.

Lives of the Three
Moragalle

The sound of flies and wasps was a solid, buzzing hum
in the hot air of the gorge, and already the stench
had grown overpowering. Fist Gamet loosened the
clasp on the buckle and lifted the battered iron helmet
from his head. The felt liner was sodden with sweat, itch-
ing against his scalp, but, as the flies swarmed him, he did
not remove it.

He continued watching from the slight rise at the south
end of the gorge as the Adjunct walked her horse through
the carnage below.

Three hundred Seti and over a hundred horses lay dead,

mostly from arrows, in the steep-sided ravine they had been led into. It could not have taken long, even including rounding up and leading off the surviving mounts. There had been less than a bell between the advance Seti riders and the Khundryl, and had Temul not ordered his Wickans back to cover the main army . . . *well, we would have lost them as well.*

As it was, those Wickans had prevented another raid on the supply train, their presence alone sufficient to trigger a sudden withdrawal by the enemy – with not a single drop of blood spilled. The warleader commanding the desert horse warriors had been too cagey to see his force ensnared in an out-and-out battle.

Far better to rely upon . . . errors in judgement. The Seti not assigned as flanking riders to the vanguard had defied orders, and had died as a result. *And all the bastard needs from us is more stupid mistakes.*

Something in the scene below was raising the hairs on his neck. The Adjunct rode alone through the slaughter, her back straight, unmindful of her horse's skittish progress.

It's never the flies that are the trouble, it's the wasps. One sting and that well-bred beast will lose its mind. Could rear and throw her off, break her neck. Or could bolt, straight down the gorge, and then try to take one of the steep sides . . . like some of those Seti horses tried to do . . .

Instead, the horse simply continued picking its way over the bodies, and the clouds of wasps did little more than rise and then wheel from its path, alighting once more upon their feast as soon as mount and rider had passed.

An old soldier at the Fist's side coughed and spat, then, at Gamet's glance, mumbled an apology.

'No need . . . Captain. It's a grisly sight, and we're all too close . . .'

'Not that, sir. Only . . .' he paused, then slowly shook his head. 'Never mind, sir. Just an old memory, that's all.'

Gamet nodded. 'I've a few of those myself. So, Fist Tene Baralta wants to know if he needs to send his healers forward. The answer you may bring him lies before you.'

'Aye, sir.'

He watched the grizzled old soldier back his horse clear then swing it round and ride off. Then Gamet fixed his attention once more upon the Adjunct.

She had reached the far end, where most of the bodies lay, heaped up against blood-splashed stone walls, and, after a long moment, during which she scanned the scene on all sides, she gathered the reins and began retracing her path.

Gamet set the helm on his head once more and closed the clasp.

She reached the slope and rode up to halt alongside him.

He had never before seen her expression so severe. *A woman with few of a woman's charms, as they say of her,* in tones approaching pity. 'Adjunct.'

'He left many of them wounded,' she said. 'Anticipating, perhaps, that we'd reach them in time. Wounded Malazans are better than dead ones, after all.'

'Assuming that warleader seeks to delay us, aye.'

'He does. Even with the Khundryl supply lines, our resources are strained as it is. The loss of the wagons last night will be felt by everyone.'

'Then why didn't Sha'ik send this warleader against us as soon as we crossed the Vathar River? We're a week or less away from the Whirlwind Wall. She could have purchased another month or more, and we'd be in far worse shape when we finally arrived.'

'You are correct, Fist. And I have no answer for you. Temul has gauged this raiding party's strength at just under two thousand – he was fairly certain that the midday contact on the flank revealed the enemy's full force, since he sighted supply horses as well as those taken from the Seti. Thus, a rather large raiding army.'

Gamet ruminated on this for a time, then he grunted. 'It's almost as if we're facing a confused opposition, one at odds with itself.'

'The same thought had occurred to me. For the moment,

however, we must concern ourselves with this warleader, else he bleed us to death.'

Gamet swung his horse around. 'More words with Gall, then,' he said, grimacing. 'If we can get them out of their great-grandfathers' armour, they might actually manage a ride up a hill without leaving their horses blown.'

'I want the marines out tonight, Fist.'

His eyes narrowed. 'The marines, Adjunct? On foot? You wish the pickets bolstered?'

She drew a deep breath. 'In the year 1147, Dassem Ultor was faced with a similar situation, with a much smaller army and three entire tribal nations mauling him virtually every night.'

After a moment Gamet nodded. 'I know the scenario, Adjunct, and I recall his answer. The marines will be sent out tonight.'

'Be sure they understand what is expected of them, Fist Gamet.'

'There's some veterans among them,' he replied. 'And in any case, I plan to command the operation myself.'

'That will not be—'

'Yes, it will, Adjunct. My apologies. But . . . yes, it will.'

'So be it.'

It was one thing to doubt his commander's measure, but another entirely to doubt his own.

There were three types of scorpion common in the odhan, none of which displayed any toleration for either of the others. Early in the second week Strings had drawn his two fellow sergeants aside to unveil his scheme. Both Gesler and Borduke had proved agreeable, particularly at the offer of splitting the profits three ways. Borduke was first to draw the odd-coloured stone and was quick to choose the Red-backed Bastard – outwardly the meanest of the three scorpion types. Gesler had followed, choosing the amber In Out – so named for its transparent exoskeleton through which, if one was inclined to look carefully,

742

various poisons could be seen racing beneath its carapace.

The two sergeants had then looked with pity upon their hapless companion. The Lord's luck that the man with the idea in the first place should be left with the Birdshit scorpion – puny and flat and black and looking like its namesake. Of course, when it came to the three-way split of the main profits, none of that really mattered. Only in the private wagers between the three sergeants would Strings come out wanting.

But Strings had affected only mild disappointment at being left with the Birdshit, answering with naught but a slight shrug as he collected the handful of pebbles they had used in choosing the order of selection. And neither Gesler nor Borduke caught the old sapper's twitch of a smile as he turned away, nor his seemingly casual glance to where Cuttle sat in the shade of a boulder – a glance answered with the slightest of nods.

The squads were then set to the task of finding their respective champions whilst on the march, and, when that failed, at dusk when the horrid little creatures were wont to scuttle out from their hiding places in search of something to kill.

Word quickly spread, and soon the wagers started pouring in. Borduke's soldier, Maybe, was chosen for the task of bet-holder, given his extraordinary ability to retain facts. And one Holder was selected from each squad, who then in turn selected a Trainer.

The afternoon following the raid and the slaughter of the Seti, Strings slowed his pace during the march, until he fell in step with Bottle and Tarr. Despite his casual expression, the truth was, the bile roiled sour in his stomach. The Fourteenth had found its own scorpion, out there in the wastes beyond, and it had just delivered its first sting. The mood of the soldiers was low, and uncertainty gnawed at their confidence. None had believed, it was clear, that the first blood they tasted would be their own. *Got to get their minds off it.*

'How's little Joyful, Bottle?'

The mage shrugged. 'As hungry and nasty as ever, Sergeant.'

Strings nodded. 'And how's the training coming along, Corporal?'

Tarr frowned beneath the rim of his helm. 'All right, I suppose. As soon as I figure out what kind of training it needs, I'll get right on it.'

'Good, the situation sounds ideal. Spread the word. First battle's tonight, one bell after we set camp.'

Both soldiers swung their heads round at this.

'Tonight?' Bottle asked. 'After what just—'

'You heard me. Gesler and Borduke are getting their beauties primed, same as us. We're ready, lads.'

'It's going to draw quite a crowd,' Corporal Tarr said, shaking his head. 'The lieutenant won't help but wonder—'

'Not just the lieutenant, I'd imagine,' Strings replied. 'But there won't be much of a crowd. We'll use the old word-line system. Run the commentary back through the whole camp.'

'Joyful's going to get skewered,' Bottle muttered, his expression growing sorrowful. 'And here I been feeding her, every night. Big juicy capemoths . . . she'd just pounce real pretty, then start eating until there wasn't nothing left but a couple wings and a crunched-up ball. Then she'd spend half the night cleaning her pincers and licking her lips—'

'Lips?' Smiles asked from behind the three men. 'What lips? Scorpions don't have lips—'

'What do you know?' Bottle shot back. 'You won't even get close—'

'When I get close to a scorpion I kill it. Which is what any sane person would do.'

'Sane?' the mage retorted. 'You pick them up and start pulling things off! Tail, pincers, legs – I ain't seen nothing so cruel in my life!'

'Well, ain't that close enough to see if it's got lips?'

'Where's it all go, I wonder?' Tarr muttered.

Bottle nodded. 'I know, it's amazing. She's so tiny . . .'

'That's our secret,' Strings said quietly.

'What is?'

'The reason why I picked a Birdshit, soldiers.'

'You didn't pick . . .'

At the suspicious silence that followed, Strings simply smiled. Then he shrugged. 'Hunting's one thing. An easy thing. Birdshits don't need to get . . . elaborate, killing a maimed capemoth. It's when they have to fight. Protecting territory, or their young. That's when the surprise comes. You think Joyful's going to lose tonight, Bottle? Think your heart's going to get broken? Relax, lad, old Strings here has always got your tender feelings in mind . . .'

'You can drop that "Strings" bit, Sergeant,' Bottle said after a moment. 'We all know who you are. We all know your real name.'

'Well, that's damned unfortunate. If it gets out to the command—'

'Oh, it won't, Fiddler.'

'Maybe not on purpose, but in the heat of battle?'

'Who's going to listen to our screams of panic in a battle, Sergeant?'

Fiddler shot the young man a look, gauging, then he grinned. 'Good point. Still, be careful what you say and when you say it.'

'Aye, Sergeant. Now, could you explain that surprise you were talking about?'

'No. Wait and see.'

Strings fell silent then, noting a small party of riders approaching down the line of march. 'Straighten up, soldiers. Officers coming.'

Fist Gamet, the sergeant saw, was looking old, worn out. Getting dragged out of retirement was never a good thing, he knew, since the first thing that an old soldier put away was his nerve, and that was hard, if not impossible, to get back. That stepping away, of course, marked a particular kind of retirement – and one a cautious soldier usually avoided. Abandoning the lifestyle was one thing, but surrendering the deadly edge was another. Studying the Fist as the man rode up, Fiddler felt a tremor of unease.

Accompanying Gamet were Captain Keneb and the lieutenant, the latter so grim-faced as to be near comical. *His officer mask, with which he tries to look older and thus more professional. Instead, it's the scowl of a constipated man. Someone should tell him . . .*

The threesome reined in to walk their horses alongside Fiddler's own squad – somewhat unnerving to the sergeant, though he offered them a nod. Keneb's eyes, he noted, were on Cuttle.

But it was Ranal who spoke first. 'Sergeant Strings.'

'Aye, sir?'

'You and Cuttle, please, off to one side for a private conversation.' Then he raised his voice to the squad marching ahead. 'Sergeant Gesler and Corporal Stormy, back with us on the double.'

'Four should be enough,' the Fist rumbled, 'to see the instructions properly delivered to the other squads.'

'Yes, sir,' said Ranal, who had been about to call over Borduke.

When the four marines were assembled, Fist Gamet cleared his throat, then began, 'It's clear you are all veterans. And Captain Keneb informs me that you have marched in these lands before – no, I need no more details of that. My reliance depends on that very experience, however. The Adjunct wishes the marines to answer the desert raiders tonight.'

He fell silent then.

And no-one spoke for a time, as the significance of the Fist's words slowly settled in the minds of the four marines.

Finally, Captain Keneb said, 'Aye, Dassem's answer, all those years ago. It's fortunate, then, that you'd planned on using the word-line this evening. Simple enough to keep it going once the three-way fight's finished.' He leaned over slightly in his saddle and said to Fiddler, 'You've the

Birdshit, Sergeant? What are the odds running at right now?'

'Maybe says it's about forty to one,' Fiddler replied, keeping his face straight.

'Even better than I'd hoped,' Keneb replied, leaning back. 'But I should add, Sergeant, that I've convinced the Fist to back your Birdshit as well.'

'Ten jakatas,' Gamet said, 'and in this I rely upon the captain's . . . experience. And yours, Sergeant . . . Strings.'

'Uh, we'll do our best, sir.'

Gesler turned to Stormy. 'Smell something, Corporal?'

The huge Falari with the flint sword on his back scowled. 'Ain't no scorpions on the coasts, dammit. Aye, Sergeant, I'm smelling something all right.'

'Get used to it,' Cuttle advised.

Ranal was looking confused, but wisely said nothing . . . for now.

'Use the word-line,' Keneb said, resuming his instructions, 'and remember, make sure the toughest squads are the ones showing their smiles.'

'Aye, Captain,' Fiddler replied, wondering if he should reassess his opinion of Keneb.

'One last thing,' the man added. 'Fist Gamet will be commanding the operation tonight. Accordingly, I want your two squads and Borduke's to double your duties tonight.'

Oh, Hood's balls under a big rock. 'Understood, Captain.'

The soldiers of the Fourteenth Army were strangely arrayed throughout the encampment once the tents had been raised and the cookfires started, seemingly casually seated in a manner that, if seen from on high, would have resembled a vast, knotted rope. And following the meal, activities seemed to cease entirely, barring the reluctant marching out of the soldiers on first picket duty.

In one particular place, centred on the marines of the 9th Company of the 8th Legion, a somewhat different assembly of soldiers was apparent – a smallish, exclusive ring, surrounding a still smaller ring of daggers thrust into the ground, edge inward, at a spacing of two finger-widths. For the moment, that inner ring was empty, the sand smoothed flat and free of pebbles.

Maybe was the last soldier to join the others waiting impatiently around the modest arena, saying nothing though his lips moved in a silent recitation of numbers and names. Seeing the eyes of the others on him, he gave a single nod.

Fiddler swung to Bottle. 'Bring out Joyful Union, lad.'

Borduke and Gesler issued similar instructions for their respective combatants. The Red-backed Bastard had been named Mangonel by Borduke's squad, while Gesler and company had named their amber In Out scorpion Clawmaster.

The three boxes were brought forward and Fiddler said to his fellow sergeants, 'All right, here and now we're to look upon our beauties, and so swear that no alterations have been made to them, either by sorcery or alchemy or any other means. They are natural as the day we first found them. Unchanged. Each of us will examine each of the three scorpions – as closely as we might choose, including the assistance of a mage if desired, and then swear out loud, by whatever gods we normally swear by, as precise a statement of what we see as we can. Here, I'll start.'

He gestured and the three boxes were set down just outside the knife ring. The first wooden container – Borduke's – had its lid removed and Fiddler leaned close. He was silent for a long time, then he nodded. 'I, Sergeant Strings of the 4th squad in the 9th Company of the 8th Legion, swear by the ghosts of the Deadhouse and every other nasty nightmare that haunts me that the creature before me is a natural, unaltered Red-backed Bastard scorpion.'

The sergeant then moved on to Gesler's champion, and after a long examination he sighed and nodded, repeating his sworn vow on behalf of the In Out scorpion scuttling about in the small wooden box.

He then concluded with his own Joyful Union.

Gesler followed the procedure, seeking the added opinions of both Tavos Pond and Sands during his protracted examination of Joyful Union, whilst Fiddler leaned back with a slight smile on his bearded face, waiting patiently until, with a snarl, Gesler swore his vow. 'I, Sergeant Gesler of the 5th squad in the 9th Company of the 8th Legion, swear by the two Lords of Summer, Fener and Treach, that the creature before me is a natural, unaltered Birdshit scorpion – even though I know there's something about it I'm not seeing and I'm about to lose my life's savings on the Sergeants' Wager.'

Fiddler's smile broadened momentarily.

Borduke crawled up to Joyful Union and came as close as was possible without being stung, his face almost inside the small box. Since that draped the motionless creature in shadow he cursed and leaned back slightly. 'I should know about scorpions, shouldn't I? But all I ever do is stamp on them – like any sane man would do. Sure, I knew a whore once who kept one on a thong about her neck, as golden as the skin of her breasts – tender nipples, you see, and she didn't like them manhandled—'

'Get on with it,' Gesler snapped.

'Don't rush me. I don't like being rushed.'

'All right, I won't rush you. Just swear your damned vow before my heart flies out to fill my breeches.'

'I, Borduke of the 6th squad in the 9th Company of the 8th Legion, swear on the downy belly of the Queen of Dreams that the creature before me is a natural, unaltered Birdshit scorpion, and may my father's ghost remain in its tomb, since the inheritance was mine to lose anyway, right? Dead means you don't care any more, right? It had better, because if it doesn't, then I'm doomed to paternal haunting for the rest of my days.'

'The worst kind,' Lutes muttered.

'Another word from you, soldier,' Borduke growled, moving back into the circle, 'and I'll make you the only one smiling later tonight.'

'Besides,' Balgrid said, 'it ain't the worst kind. Maternal haunting – now that's a killer. How long can a man stand being seven years old?'

'Will you two be quiet!' Borduke snarled, his large-knuckled fingers clutching as if squeezing invisible throats.

'We ready?' Fiddler quietly asked.

'She'll hide, won't she?' Gesler demanded. 'Wait till the other two have chopped and stabbed each other up before pouncing on the mangled survivor! That's it, isn't it? Her jelly brains are purer than theirs, purer and smarter, aren't they?'

Fiddler shrugged. 'Wouldn't know about that, Gesler. Are you done?'

The bronzed-hued marine settled back, the muscles of his jaw bunching.

'How's the word-line, Cuttle?'

'Been repeating every word since we first settled, Fid,' the sapper replied.

'And so legends were born,' Koryk rumbled with facetious portent.

'Into the arena, then,' Fiddler instructed.

The boxes were gingerly lifted and held over the arena.

'Equidistant? Good. Tip 'em, lads.'

Mangonel was the first to land, tail arched and pincers out as it scuttled close to the knife-edge barrier, upon which, a hair's breadth from the iron blades, it halted and then backed away, its carapace flushing red with its characteristic mindless rage. Clawmaster was next, seeming to leap down ready for war, fluids racing beneath its amber-tinted shell.

Joyful Union came last, slow and measured, so low on the sand as to seem belly-down. Pincers tucked away, tail curled to port and quiescent. Dwarfed by the other two scorpions, its black shell somewhere between glossy and flat. Its multiple legs scuttled it forward slightly, then it froze.

Gesler hissed. 'If she plucks a couple knives from the ring and uses 'em, I'm going to kill you, Fid.'

'No need,' Fiddler replied, his attention divided between what was going on in the arena and Ibb's running commentary, the man's voice harsh with tension as he waxed creative in describing what had, up to now, been essentially nothing worth comment.

That suddenly changed as three things occurred almost simultaneously. Joyful Union sauntered into the middle of the arena. Mangonel's assortment of natural weapons all cocked in unison, even as the creature began backing up, its shell turning fiery red. Clawmaster suddenly wheeled and darted straight at the nearest wall of blades, halting a moment before impact, pincers waving wildly.

'He wants mommy, looks like, Hubb,' Koryk drily observed.

Clawmaster's Holder softly whimpered in answer.

Then, after a frozen moment from all three scorpions, Joyful Union finally lifted its tail.

Upon which, all but Fiddler stared in utter disbelief, as Joyful Union seemed to . . . *split*. Horizontally. Into two identical, but *thinner, flatter* scorpions. That then raced outward, one to Mangonel, the other to Clawmaster – each like a village mongrel charging a bull bhederin, so extreme their comparative sizes.

Red-backed Bastard and In Out both did their best, but were no match in speed, nor ferocity, as tiny pincers snipped – audibly – through legs, through tail, through arm-joints, then, with the larger creature immobile and helpless, a casual, almost delicate stab of stinger.

With In Out's translucent shell, the horrid bright green of that poison was visible – and thus described in ghastly detail by Ibb – as it spread out from the puncture until Clawmaster's once beautiful amber was gone, replaced by a sickly green that deepened before their eyes to a murky black.

'Dead as dung,' Hubb moaned. 'Clawmaster . . .'

Mangonel suffered an identical fate.

With its enemies vanquished, the two Birdshit scorpions

rushed back into each other's arms – and, in the blink of an eye, were as one once more.

'Cheat!' Stormy bellowed, rearing to his feet and fumbling to draw his flint sword.

Gesler leapt up and, along with Truth, struggled to restrain their raging comrade. 'We *looked*, Stormy!' Gesler yelled. 'We looked for anything – then we swore! I swore! By Fener and Treach, damn you! How could any of us have known "Joyful Union" wasn't just a cute name?'

Glancing up, Fiddler met Cuttle's steady gaze. The sapper mouthed the words *We're rich, you bastard*.

The sergeant, with a final glance at Gesler and Truth – who were dragging a foaming Stormy away – then moved to crouch down beside Ibb. 'All right, lad, what follows is for the marines only, and especially the sergeants. We're about to become our own Joyful Union to big, bad Mangonel tonight. I'll explain what the Adjunct has ordered – repeat what I say, Ibb, word for word – got it?'

Three bells had passed since the sunset. Dust from the Whirlwind Wall obscured the stars, making the darkness beyond the hearth-fires almost impenetrable. Squads from the infantry trooped out to relieve those stationed at the pickets. In the Khundryl camp, the warriors removed their heavy armour and prepared to settle in for the night. Along the army encampment's outermost trenches, Wickan and Seti horse warriors patrolled.

At the 4th squad's fire, Fiddler returned from the company's wagons with his kit bag. He set it down and untied the draws.

Nearby sprawled Cuttle, his eyes glittering reflected flames, watching as the sergeant began withdrawing variously sized, hide-wrapped objects. Moments later he had assembled a dozen such items, which he then began unwrapping, revealing the glint of polished wood and blackened iron.

The others in the squad were busy checking over their

weapons and armour one last time, saying nothing as the tension slowly built among the small group of soldiers.

'Been some time since I last saw one of those,' Cuttle muttered as Fiddler laid out the objects. 'I've seen imitations, some of them almost as good as the originals.'

Fiddler grunted. 'There's a few out there. It's the knock-back where the biggest danger lies, since if it's too hard the whole damn thing explodes upon release. Me and Hedge worked out this design ourselves, then we found a Mare jeweller in Malaz City – what she was doing there I've no idea—'

'A jeweller? Not a weaponsmith?'

'Aye.' He began assembling the crossbow. 'And a wood-carver for the stops and plugs – those need replacing after twenty or so shots—'

'When they're pulped.'

'Or splitting, aye. It's the ribs, when they spring back – that's what sends the shockwave forward. Unlike a regular crossbow, where the quarrel's fast enough out of the slot to escape that vibration. Here, the quarrel's a pig, heavy and weighted on the head end – it never leaves the slot as fast as you'd like, so you need something to absorb that knock-back, before it gets to the quarrel shaft.'

'And the clay ball attached to it. Clever solution, Fid.'

'It's worked so far.'

'And if it does fail . . .'

Fiddler looked up and grinned. 'I won't be the one with breath to complain.' The last fitting clicked into place, and the sergeant set the bulky weapon down, turning his attention to the individually wrapped quarrels.

Cuttle slowly straightened. 'Those ain't got sharpers on them.'

'Hood no, I can *throw* sharpers.'

'And that crossbow can lob cussers far enough? Hard to believe.'

'Well, the idea is to aim and shoot, then bite a mouthful of dirt.'

'I can see the wisdom in that, Fid. Now, you let us all know when you're firing, right?'

'Nice and loud, aye.'

'And what word should we listen for?'

Fiddler noticed that the rest of his squad had ceased their preparations and were now waiting for his answer. He shrugged. 'Duck. Or sometimes what Hedge used to use.'

'Which was?'

'A scream of terror.' He climbed to his feet. 'All right, soldiers, it's time.'

When the last grains trickled down, the Adjunct turned from the hourglass and nodded to Gamet. 'When will you join your companies, Fist?'

'In a few moments, Adjunct. Although, because I intend to remain in my saddle, I will not ride out to them until the fighting starts.'

He saw her frown at that, but she made no comment, focusing instead on the two Wickan youths standing near the tent's entrance. 'Have you completed your rituals?'

The lad, Nil, shrugged. 'We have spoken with the spirits, as you ordered.'

'Spoken? That is all?'

'Once, perhaps, we could have . . . compelled. But as we warned you long ago in Aren, our power is not as it once was.'

Nether added, 'This land's spirits are agitated at the moment, easily distracted. Something else is happening. We have done all we could, Adjunct. At the very least, if the desert raiders have a shaman among them, there will be little chance of the secret's unveiling.'

'Something else is happening, you said. What, specifically?'

Before she could answer, Gamet said, 'Your pardon, Adjunct. I will take my leave now.'

'Of course.'

The Fist left them to resume their conversation. A fog

had settled on his mind, the moments before an engagement when uncertainty engendered unease and confusion. He had heard of this affliction claiming other commanders, but had not thought it would befall him. The rush of his own blood had created a wall of sound, muting the world beyond. And it seemed his other senses had dulled as well.

As he made his way towards his horse – held ready by a soldier – he shook his head, seeking to clear it. If the soldier said something to him when he took the reins and swung up into the saddle, he did not hear it.

The Adjunct had been displeased by his decision to ride into the battle. But the added mobility was, to Gamet's mind, worth the risk. He set out through the camp at a slow canter. Fires had been allowed to die, the scenes surrounding him strangely ethereal. He passed figures hunched down around coals and envied them their freedom. Life had been simpler as a plain soldier. Gamet had begun to doubt his ability to command.

Age is no instant purchase of wisdom. But it's more than that, isn't it? She may have made me a Fist and given me a legion. And soldiers might well salute when they pass – though of course not here, in enemy territory, thank Hood. No, all these trappings are no assurance of my competence.

This night shall be my first test. Gods, I should have stayed retired. I should have refused her insistence – dammit, her assumption – that I would simply accept her wishes.

There was, he had come to believe, a weakness within him. A fool might call it a virtue, such ... pliable equanimity. But he knew better.

He rode on, the fog of his mind growing ever thicker.

Eight hundred warriors crouched motionless, ghostly, amidst the boulders on the plain. Wearing dulled armour and telabas the colour of the terrain around them, they were virtually invisible, and Corabb Bhilan Thenu'alas felt a surge of dark pride, even as another part of his mind wondered at Leoman's protracted ... hesitation.

Their warchief lay flat on the slope's rise ten paces ahead. He had not moved in some time. Despite the chill, sweat trickled beneath Corabb's armour, and he shifted his grip once more on the unfamiliar tulwar in his right hand. He'd always preferred axe-like weapons – something with a haft he could, if need be, grip with his other hand. He disliked the blade edge that reached down all the way to the hilt and wished he'd had time to file it blunt for the first half of its length.

I am a warrior who cannot tolerate sharp edges close to his body. Which spirits thought to make of me such an embodiment of confused irony? I curse them all.

He could wait no longer, and slowly crawled up alongside Leoman of the Flails.

Beyond the crest sprawled another basin, this one hummocked and thick with thorny brush. It flanked the encamped Malazan army on this side, and was between sixty and seventy paces in breadth.

'Foolish,' Corabb muttered, 'to have chosen to stop here. I think we need have nothing to fear from this Adjunct.'

The breath slowly hissed between Leoman's teeth. 'Aye, plenty of cover for our approach.'

'Then why do we wait, Warchief?'

'I am wondering, Corabb.'

'Wondering?'

'About the Empress. She was once Mistress of the Claw. Its fierce potency was given shape by her, and we have all learned to fear those mage-assassins. Ominous origins, yes? And then, as Empress, there were the great leaders of her imperial military. Dujek Onearm. Admiral Nok. Coltaine. Greymane.'

'But here, this night, Warchief, we face none of those.'

'True. We face the Adjunct Tavore, who was personally chosen by the Empress. To act as the fist of her vengeance.'

Corabb frowned, then he shrugged. 'Did the Empress not also choose High Fist Pormqual? Korbolo Dom? Did she not demote Whiskeyjack – the fiercest Malazan our tribes ever faced? And, if the tales are true, she was also responsible for the assassination of Dassem Ultor.'

'Your words are sharp, Corabb. She is not immune to grave . . . errors in judgement. Well then, let us make her pay for them.' He twisted round and gestured his warriors forward.

Corabb Bhilan Thenu'alas grinned. Perhaps the spirits would smile on him this night. *Pray that I find a worthy axe or mace among the countless dead Malazan soldiers.*

Borduke's squad had found a small hill for their position, swearing and cursing as they clawed their way to its modest summit, then began digging holes and repositioning rocks.

Their hill was likely some old round barrow – the hummocks in this basin were far too regular to be natural. Twenty paces away, Fiddler listened to the 6th squad marines muttering and shuffling about on their strongpoint, their efforts punctuated every now and then by Borduke's impatient growl. Fifty paces to the west another squad was digging in on another hill, and the sergeant began to wonder if they'd held off too long. Barrows tended to be big heaps of rocks beneath the cloak of sandy soil, after all, and burrowing into them was never easy. He could hear rocks being pried loose, iron shovels grating on heavy granite, and a few tumbling wildly down the hillsides through the thick, brittle bushes.

Hood's breath, how clumsy do you idiots have to get?

As Corabb was about to move on to the next cover, Leoman's gloved hand reached out and snagged his shoulder. The warrior froze.

And now he could hear it. There were soldiers in the basin.

Leoman moved up alongside him. 'Outlying pickets,' he muttered under his breath. 'On those barrows. It seems she's sent us a gift after all,' the Warchief added with a grin. 'Listen to them stumble about – they waited too long, and now the darkness confounds them.'

There was no difficulty in locating the enemy positions – they'd selected the barrows one and all, and were making loud work of digging in. And, Corabb realized, they were spaced too far apart for mutual support. Each position could be easily isolated, surrounded, and every last soldier slaughtered. Long before any relief could arrive from the main camp.

Likely, Corabb reflected as he slipped through the darkness towards the nearest enemy position, the Malazans had been anticipating a pre-dawn raid, identical to the first one. And so the Adjunct had ordered the emplacements as a pre-emptive measure. But, as Leoman had once explained to him, every element of an army in the field needed to follow the rules of mutual support – even the pickets where first contact would occur. Clearly, the Adjunct had failed to apply this most basic tenet.

Added to her inability to control her Seti horse warriors, this was further proof, in Corabb's eyes, of Tavore's incompetence.

He adjusted his grip on the tulwar, halting fifteen paces from the nearest strong-point. He could actually see the helms of at least two of the Malazan soldiers, poking up over the holes they had dug. Corabb concentrated on slowing his breathing, and waited for the signal.

Gamet reined in at the edge of the now unoccupied marine camp. The quiet call would have gone out through the rest of the army, awakening the cutters and healers. Precautionary, of course, since there was no way to predict whether the raiders would attack from the approach the Adjunct had arranged. Given that all the other angles held either natural obstacles or easily defensible positions, the desert warleader might well balk at such an obvious invitation. As he waited, the Fist began to think that nothing would come of this gambit, at least on this night. And what were the chances that a day's march would bring the army to yet another ideal combination of terrain and timing?

He settled back in the saddle, the strange, cloying lassitude in his mind deepening. The night had, if anything, grown even darker, the stars struggling to pierce the veil of suspended dust.

A capemoth flitted in front of his face, triggering an involuntary flinch. *An omen?* He shook himself and straightened once more. Three bells remained before dawn. But there could be no recall and so the marines would take shifts on the wagons come the morrow's march. *And I had better do the same, if we're to repeat this—*

A wavering wolf howl broke the stillness of the night. Although Corabb had been waiting for it, he was still startled into a momentary immobility. To either side, warriors rose from their cover and sprinted for the barrow. Arrows whispered, struck the visible helms with solid crunching sounds. He saw one of those bronze helms spin away through the air – realized that it had not been covering a soldier's head.

A flash of unease—

Warcries filled the air. The glint of heavily armoured figures rising up on the barrows, crossbows lowering. Smaller objects flew out, one of them striking the ground five paces to Corabb's right.

A detonation that stabbed at his ears. The blast threw him to one side, and he stumbled, then fell over a thorn bush.

Multiple explosions – flames shot up to light the scene—

At the wolf's howl, Fiddler flattened himself still further beneath his cloak of sand and brush – not a moment too soon as a moccasined foot thumped down on his back as a raider ran over him.

The barrows had done their job – drawing the attackers in to what, by all outward appearances, seemed isolated positions. One squad in three had shown face to the enemy; the remaining two had preceded them by a bell or more to take cover between the barrows.

And now the trap was sprung.

The sergeant lifted his head, and saw a dozen backs between him and Borduke's strong-point. Their charge slowed as three of their number suddenly pitched down to the ground, quarrels buried deep.

'*Up, dammit!*' Fiddler hissed.

His soldiers rose around him, shedding dusty sand and branches.

Crouching low, cusser-fitted crossbow cradled in his arms, the sergeant set out, away from Borduke's position. Gesler's marines were easily sufficient to support the squad at the barrow. Fiddler had seen a mass of raiders moving along the ridge beyond the basin – easily two hundred in all – and suspected they were moving to flank the ambush. The narrowest of corridors awaited them, but if they overran the infantry picket stationed there, they could then strike into the heart of the supply camp.

He grinned at the snapping *crack* of sharpers detonating behind him, along with the deadly whoosh of burners filling the basin with red, flaring light. The raid had been stopped in its tracks, and confusion had snared the attackers. Fiddler and the five marines trailing in his wake were low enough to keep their silhouettes from being backlit by the flames as they reached the base of the slope.

They had ascended halfway to the ridge when Fiddler held up a fisted hand.

Cuttle scrambled up beside him. 'We won't even have to duck on this one,' he growled.

The sergeant raised his crossbow, sighting well above the crest line and settling the metal stock against his shoulder. He drew a breath, held it, and slowly pressed the release.

The iron ribs thunked, and the cusser quarrel leapt away, describing a graceful arc up and over the ridge. It sank out of sight.

Bodies were thrown skyward at the explosion, and screams filled the air.

'Crossbows to bear,' Cuttle snapped, 'in case they come rolling over the—'

On the crest above them, the skyline was suddenly crowded with warriors.

'Fall back!' Fiddler shouted as he continued to reload. *'Fall back!'*

After sprawling into the thorn bush, Corabb dragged himself clear, spitting curses, and scrambled to his feet. The bodies of his comrades lay on all sides, struck down by heavy crossbow bolts or those terrible Moranth munitions. There had been more marines, hidden between the barrows, and now he could hear horses behind them, sweeping on to take the ridge – Khundryl – the bastards were in light armour only, and they had been ready and waiting.

He looked for Leoman, but could not see him among those warriors made visible by the sheets of flames left by the Malazan fire-grenados – and of those, few were still on their feet. Time had come, he decided, to withdraw.

He collected the tulwar from where it had fallen, then spun about and ran for the ridge.

And plunged headlong into a squad of marines.

Sudden shouts.

A huge soldier wearing the trappings of a Seti slammed a hide-wrapped shield into Corabb's face. The desert warrior reeled back, blood gushing from his nose and mouth, and took a wild swing. The tulwar's heavy blade cracked hard against something – and snapped clean just above the hilt.

Corabb landed hard on the ground.

A soldier passed close and left something on his lap.

Somewhere just up on the ridge another explosion ripped through the night – this one louder by far than any he had yet heard.

Stunned, blinking tears, Corabb sat up, and saw a small round clay ball roll down to land in front of his crotch.

Smoke rose from it – sputtering, foaming acid, just a drop, eating its way through.

Whimpering, Corabb rolled to one side – and came up against a discarded helm. He grabbed it and lunged back at the sharper, slamming the bronze cap over it.

Then he closed his eyes.

As the squad continued its retreat – the slope behind it a mass of blasted bodies from Fiddler's second cusser, with Khundryl Burned Tears now crashing into the flank of the remaining attackers – Cuttle grabbed the sergeant's shoulder and spun him around.

'The bastard Koryk knocked down is about to be surprised, Fid.'

Fiddler fixed his gaze on the figure just now sitting up.

'Left a smoking sharper in his lap,' Cuttle added.

Both sappers halted to watch.

'Four . . .'

The warrior made his horrific discovery and plunged to one side.

'Three . . .'

Then rolled back directly onto the sharper.

'Two . . .'

Thumping a helm down over it.

'One.'

The detonation lifted the hapless man into the air on a man-high column of fire.

Yet he had managed to hold on to the helm, even as it lifted him still higher, up and over. Feet scything wildly in the air, he plummeted back down, landing to kick up a cloud of dust and smoke.

'Now that—'

But Cuttle got no further, and both sappers simply stared in disbelief as the warrior scrambled upright, looked around, collected a discarded lance, then raced off back up the slope.

* * *

Gamet drove heels into his horse's flanks. The mount pounded down into the basin from the west side, opposite where the Khundryl had come from.

Three knots of desert warriors had managed to weather the cross-bow fire and munitions to assault one of the strong-points. They had driven the two hidden squads back onto the barrow as well, and the Fist saw his marines dragging wounded comrades into the trenchworks. Fewer than ten soldiers among the three squads were still fighting, desperately holding back the screaming raiders.

Gamet pulled his sword free as he urged his horse directly towards the beleaguered position. As he approached, he saw two marines go down before an onrush from one of the attacking groups – and the barrow was suddenly overrun.

The fugue gripping his senses seemed to redouble, and he began sawing the reins, confused, bewildered by the roar of sounds surrounding him.

'Fist!'

He lifted his sword, as his horse cantered, as if of its own will, towards the barrow.

'Fist Gamet! Pull out of there!'

Too many voices. Screams of the dying. The flames – they're falling away. Darkness closing in. My soldiers are dying. Everywhere. It's failed – the whole plan has failed—

A dozen raiders were rushing at him – and more movement, there, to his right – another squad of marines, fast closing, as if they'd been on their way to relieve the overrun strong-point, but now they were sprinting in his direction.

I don't understand. Not here – the other way. Go there, go to my soldiers—

He saw something large fly from one of the marines' hands, down into the midst of the warriors attacking him.

'Fist!'

Two lances whipped out, seeking him.

Then the night exploded.

He felt his horse lifted beneath him, pushing him down

over the back of the saddle. The animal's head snapped upward, impossibly so, as it continued arching back – to thump down between Gamet's thighs a moment before he tumbled, boots leaving the stirrups, over the horse's rump.

Down into a mist of blood and grit.

He blinked his eyes open, found himself lying in sodden mud, amidst bodies and parts of bodies, at the base of a crater. His helmet was gone. No sword in his hand.

I was . . . I was on a horse . . .

Someone slid down to slam against his side. He attempted to clamber away, but was dragged back down.

'Fist Gamet, sir! I'm Sergeant Gesler – Captain Keneb's 9th Company – can you hear me?'

'Y-yes – I thought you were—'

'Aye, Fist. But we dropped 'em, and now the rest of my squad and Borduke's are relieving 3rd Company's marines. We need to get you to a healer, sir.'

'No, that's all right.' He struggled to sit up, but something was wrong with his legs – they were indifferent to his commands. 'Tend to those on the barrow, Sergeant—'

'We are, sir. Pella! Down here, help me with the Fist.'

Another marine arrived, this one much younger – *oh, no, too young for this. I will ask the Adjunct to send him home. To his mother and father, yes. He should not have to die* – 'You should not have to die.'

'Sir?'

'Only his horse between him and a cusser blast,' Gesler said. 'He's addled, Pella. Now, take his arms . . .'

Addled? No, my mind is clear. Perfectly clear, now. Finally. They're all too young for this. It's Laseen's war – let her fight it. Tavore – she was a child, once. But then the Empress murdered that child. Murdered her. I must tell the Adjunct . . .

Fiddler settled wearily beside the now dead hearth. He set his crossbow down and wiped the sweat and grime from his eyes. Cuttle eased down beside him. 'Koryk's head still aches,' the sapper muttered, 'but it don't look like anything's broken that wasn't already broken.'

'Except his helm,' Fiddler replied.

'Aye, except that. The only real scrap of the night for our squad, barring a few dozen quarrels loosed. And we didn't even kill the bastard.'

'You got too cute, Cuttle.'

The man sighed. 'Aye, I did. Must be getting old.'

'That's what I concluded. Next time, just stab a pig-sticker in the bastard.'

'Amazed he survived it in any case.'

The pursuit by the Khundryl had taken the Burned Tears far beyond the ridge, and what had begun as a raid against a Malazan army was now a tribal war. Two bells remained before dawn. Infantry had moved out into the basin to collect wounded, retrieve quarrels, and strip down the Malazan corpses – leaving nothing for the enemy to use. The grim, ugly conclusion to every battle, the only mercy the cover of darkness.

Sergeant Gesler appeared out of the gloom and joined them at the lifeless hearth. He drew off his gauntlets and dropped them into the dust, then rubbed at his face.

Cuttle spoke. 'Heard a position was overrun.'

'Aye. We'd had it in hand, at least to start. Closing in fast. Most of the poor bastards could have walked away from that barrow. As it is, only four did.'

Fiddler looked up. 'Out of three squads?'

Gesler nodded, then spat into the ashes.

Silence.

Then Cuttle grunted. 'Something always goes wrong.'

Gesler sighed, collected his gauntlets and rose. 'Could have been worse.'

Fiddler and Cuttle watched the man wander off.

'What happened, do you think?'

Fiddler shrugged. 'I suppose we'll find out soon enough. Now, find Corporal Tarr and get him to gather the rest. I need to explain all the things we did wrong tonight.'

'Starting with you leading us up the slope?'

Fiddler grimaced. 'Starting with that, aye.'

'Mind you, if you hadn't,' Cuttle mused, 'more of those raiders could have followed down to the overrun barrow through the breach. Your lobbed cusser did its work – distracted them. Long enough for the Khundryl to arrive and keep them busy.'

'Even so,' the sergeant conceded. 'But if we'd been alongside Gesler, maybe we could have saved a few more marines.'

'Or messed it up worse, Fid. You know better than to think like that.'

'I guess you're right. Now, gather them up.'

'Aye.'

Gamet looked up as the Adjunct entered the cutters' tent. She was pale – from lack of sleep, no doubt – and had removed her helm, revealing her short-cropped, mouse-coloured hair.

'I will not complain,' Gamet said, as the healer finally moved away.

'Regarding what?' the Adjunct asked, head turning to scan the other cots on which wounded soldiers lay.

'The removal of my command,' he replied.

Her gaze fixed on him once more. 'You were careless, Fist, in placing yourself at such risk. Hardly cause to strip you of your rank.'

'My presence diverted marines rushing to the aid of their comrades, Adjunct. My presence resulted in lives lost.'

She said nothing for a moment, then stepped closer. 'Every engagement takes lives, Gamet. This is the burden of command. Did you think this war would be won without the spilling of blood?'

He looked away, grimacing against the waves of dull pain that came from forced healing. The cutters had removed a dozen shards of clay from his legs. Muscles had been shredded. Even so, he knew that the Lady's luck had been with him this night. The same could not be said for his hapless horse. 'I was a soldier once, Adjunct,' he rasped. 'I am one no longer. This is what I discovered tonight. As for being a Fist, well, commanding house guards was a fair representation of my level of competence. An entire legion? No. I am sorry, Adjunct . . .'

She studied him, then nodded. 'It will be some time before you are fully recovered from your wounds. Which of your captains would you recommend for a temporary field promotion?'

Yes, the way it should be done. Good. 'Captain Keneb, Adjunct.'

'I concur. And now I must leave you. The Khundryl are returning.'

'With trophies, I hope.'

She nodded.

Gamet managed a smile. 'That is well.'

The sun was climbing near zenith when Corabb Bhilan Thenu'alas reined in his lathered horse alongside Leoman. Other warriors were straggling in all the time, but it might be days before the scattered elements of the company were finally reassembled. In light armour, the Khundryl had been able to maintain persistent contact with the Raraku horse warriors, and had proved themselves fierce and capable fighters.

The ambush had been reversed, the message delivered with succinct precision. They had underestimated the Adjunct.

'Your first suspicions were right,' Corabb growled as he settled down in his saddle, the horse trembling beneath him. 'The Empress chose wisely.'

Leoman's right cheek had been grazed by a crossbow quarrel, leaving a crusted brown line that glistened in places through the layer of dust. At Corabb's observation he grimaced, leaned to one side and spat.

'Hood curse those damned marines,' Corabb continued.

'If not for their grenados and those assault crossbows, we would have taken them all down. Would that I had found one of those crossbows – the loading mechanism must be—'

'Be quiet, Corabb,' Leoman muttered. 'I have orders for you. Select a worthy messenger and have him take three spare horses and ride back to Sha'ik as fast as he can. He is to tell her I will be continuing with my raids, seeking the pattern to this Adjunct's responses, and will rejoin the Chosen One three days before the Malazan army arrives. Also, that I no longer hold any faith in Korbolo Dom's strategy for the day of battle, nor his tactics – aye, Corabb, she will not listen to such words, but they must be said, before witnesses. Do you understand?'

'I do, Leoman of the Flails, and I shall choose the finest rider among us.'

'Go, then.'

CHAPTER TWENTY

Shadow is ever besieged, for that is its nature. Whilst
darkness devours, and light steals. And so one sees
shadow ever retreat to hidden places, only to return
in the wake of the war between dark and light.

Observations of the Warrens
Insallan Enura

The rope had visited the edur ships. corpses lay everywhere, already rotting on the deck beneath
squabbling, shrieking gulls and crows. Cutter stood
near the prow and watched in silence as Apsalar walked
among the bodies, pausing every now and then to examine
some detail or other, her measured calm leaving the Daru
chilled.

They had drawn the sleek runner up alongside, and
Cutter could hear its steady bumping against the hull as the
morning breeze continued to freshen. Despite the enliven-
ing weather, lassitude gripped them both. They were to sail
away, but precisely where had not been specified by the
patron god of assassins. Another servant of Shadow awaited
them . . . somewhere.

He tested his left arm once more, lifting it out to the
side. The shoulder throbbed, but not as badly as yesterday.
Fighting with knives was all very well, until one had to face
an armoured sword-wielder, then the drawbacks to short-
bladed, close-in stickers became all too apparent.

He needed, he concluded, to learn the use of the bow.

And then, once he'd acquired some competence, perhaps a long-knife – a Seven Cities weapon that combined the advantages of a knife with the reach of a three-quarter-length longsword. For some reason, the thought of using a true longsword did not appeal to him. Perhaps because it was a soldier's weapon, best used in conjunction with a shield or buckler. A waste of his left hand, given his skills. Sighing, Cutter looked down at the deck and, fighting revulsion, scanned the corpses beneath the jostling birds.

And saw a bow. Its string had been cut through, and the arrows lay scattered out from a quiver still strapped to an Edur's hip. Cutter stepped over and crouched down. The bow was heavier than it looked, sharply recurved and braced with horn. Its length was somewhere between a longbow and a horse warrior's bow – probably a simple short bow for these Edur. Unstrung, it stood at a height matching Cutter's shoulders.

He began collecting the arrows, then, waving to drive back the gulls and crows, he dragged the archer's corpse clear and removed the belted quiver. He found a small leather pouch tied near it containing a half-dozen waxed strings, spare fletching, a few nuggets of hard pine sap, a thin iron blade and three spare barbed arrowheads.

Selecting one of the strings, Cutter straightened. He slipped one of the cord-bound ends into the notch at the bow's base end, then anchored the weapon against the outside of his right foot and pushed down on the upper rib.

Harder than he'd expected. The bow shook as he struggled to slip the loop into the notch. Finally succeeding, Cutter lifted the bow for a more gauging regard, then drew it back. The breath hissed between his teeth as he sought to hold the weapon taut. This would, he realized as he finally relaxed the string, prove something of a challenge.

Sensing eyes on him, he turned.

Apsalar stood near the main mast. Flecks and globules of dried blood covered her forearms.

'What have you been doing?' he asked.

She shrugged. 'Looking around.'

Inside someone's chest? 'We should go.'

'Have you decided where yet?'

'I'm sure that will be answered soon enough,' he said, bending down to collect the arrows and the belt holding the quiver and kit pouch.

'The sorcery here is . . . strange.'

His head snapped up. 'What do you mean?'

'I am not sure. My familiarity with warrens is somewhat vicarious.'

I know.

'But,' she continued, 'if this is Kurald Emurlahn, then it is tainted in some way. Necromantically. Life and death magicks, carved directly into the wood of this ship. As if warlocks and shoulder-women had done the consecrating.'

Cutter frowned. 'Consecrating. You make it sound as if this ship was a temple.'

'It was. Is. The spilling of blood has done nothing to desecrate it, which is precisely my point. Perhaps even warrens can sink into barbarity.'

'Meaning the wielders of a warren can affect its nature. My late uncle would have found the notion fascinating. Not desecration, then, but *denigration*.'

She slowly glanced around. 'Rashan. Meanas. Thyr.'

He comprehended the thought. 'You think all warrens accessible to humans are in fact denigrations of Elder Warrens.'

She raised her hands then. 'Even blood decays.'

Cutter's frown deepened. He was not sure what she meant by that, and found himself disinclined to ask. Easier, safer, to simply grunt and make his way to the gunnel. 'We should make use of this breeze. Assuming you're done here.'

In answer she walked to the ship's side and clambered over the rail.

Cutter watched her climb down to the runner, taking her

place at the tiller. He paused for a final look around. And stiffened.

On the distant strand of Drift Avalii, there stood a lone figure, leaning on a two-handed sword.

Traveller.

And Cutter now saw that there were others, squatting or seated around him. A half-dozen Malazan soldiers. In the trees behind them stood Tiste Andii, silver-haired and ghostly. The image seemed to burn in his mind, as of a touch so cold as to feel like fire. He shivered, pulling his gaze away with an effort, and quickly joined Apsalar in the runner, taking the mooring line with him.

He set the oars in their locks and pushed the craft away from the ship's black hull.

'I believe they intend to commandeer this Edur dromon,' Apsalar said.

'What about protecting the Throne?'

'There are demons from Shadow on the island now. Your patron god has clearly decided to take a more active role in defending the secret.'

'*Your patron god.*' *Thank you for that, Apsalar. And who was it who held your soul cupped in his two hands? A killer's hands.* 'Why not just take it back to the Shadow Realm?'

'No doubt if he could, he would,' she replied. 'But when Anomander Rake placed his kin here to guard it, he also wrought sorcery around the Throne. It will not be moved.'

Cutter shipped the oars and began preparing the sail. 'Then Shadowthrone need only come here and plant his scrawny arse on it, right?'

He disliked her answering smile. 'Thus ensuring that no-one else could claim its power, or the position of King of High House Shadow. Unless, of course, they killed Shadowthrone first. A god of courage and unassailable power might well plant his scrawny arse on that throne to end the argument once and for all. But Shadowthrone did just that, once before, as Emperor Kellanved.'

'He did?'

'He claimed the First Throne. The throne of the T'lan Imass.'

Oh.

'Fortunately,' Apsalar continued, 'as Shadowthrone, he has shown little interest in making use of his role as Emperor of the T'lan Imass.'

'Well, why bother? This way, he negates the chance of anyone else finding and taking that throne, while his avoidance of using it himself ensures that no-one takes notice he has it in the first place – gods, I'm starting to sound like Kruppe! In any case, that seems clever, not cowardly.'

She studied him for a long moment. 'I had not thought of that. You are right, of course. Unveiling power invites convergence, after all. It seems Shadowthrone has absorbed well his early residence in the Deadhouse. More so, perhaps, than Cotillion has.'

'Aye, it's an Azath tactic, isn't it? Negation serves to *disarm*. Given the chance, he'd probably plant himself in every throne in sight, then, with all the power accrued to him, he would do nothing with it. Nothing at all.'

Her eyes slowly widened.

He frowned at her expression. Then his heart started pounding hard. *No. I was only kidding. That's not just ambitious, it's insane. He could never pull it off . . . but what if he did?* 'All the games of the gods . . .'

'Would be seriously . . . curtailed. Crokus, have you stumbled onto the truth? Have you just articulated Shadowthrone's vast scheme? His prodigious gambit to achieve absolute domination?'

'Only if he is truly mad, Apsalar,' the Daru replied, shaking his head. 'It's impossible. He would never succeed. He would not even get close.'

Apsalar settled back on the tiller as the sails filled and the runner leapt forward. 'For two years,' she said, 'Dancer and the Emperor vanished. Left the empire for Surly to rule. My stolen memories are vague of that time, but I do know that both men were changed, irrevocably, by all that happened to them during those two years. Not just the play for the Shadow Realm, which no doubt was central to their desires. Other things occurred ... truths revealed, mysteries uncovered. One thing I know for certain, Crokus, is that, for most of those two years, Dancer and Kellanved were *not in this realm*.'

'Then where in Hood's name were they?'

She shook her head. 'I cannot answer that question. But I sense that they were following a trail, one that wound through all the warrens, and to realms where even the known warrens do not reach.'

'What kind of trail? Whose?'

'Suspicions ... the trail had something to do with, well, with the Houses of the Azath.'

Mysteries uncovered indeed. The Azath – the deepest mystery of them all.

'You should know, Crokus,' Apsalar continued, 'that they knew that Surly was waiting for them. They knew what she had planned. Yet they returned none the less.'

'But that makes no sense.'

'Unless she proceeded to do precisely what they wanted her to do. After all, we both know that the assassinations failed – failed in killing either of them. The question then becomes: what did that entire mess achieve?'

'A rhetorical question?'

She cocked her head. 'No.' Surprised.

Cutter rubbed at the bristle on his jaw, then shrugged. 'All right. It left Surly on the Malazan throne. Empress Laseen was born. It stripped from Kellanved his secular seat of power. Hmm. Let's ask it another way. What if Kellanved and Dancer had returned and successfully reclaimed the imperial throne? But, at the same time, they had taken over the Shadow Realm. Thus, there would be an empire spanning two warrens, an empire of Shadow.' He paused, then slowly nodded. 'They wouldn't have stood for that – the gods, that is. Ascendants of all kinds would have converged on the Malazan Empire. They would have pounded the empire and the two men ruling it into dust.'

'Probably. And neither Kellanved nor Dancer was in any position to mount a successful resistance to such a protracted assault. They'd yet to consolidate their claim on the Shadow Realm.'

'Right, so they orchestrated their own deaths, and kept their identity as the new rulers of Shadow a secret for as long as they could, whilst laying out the groundwork for a resumption of their grand schemes. Well, that's all very cosy, if more than a little diabolical. But does it help us answer the question of what they're up to right now? If anything, I'm more confused than ever.'

'Why should you be? Cotillion recruited you to see to the true Throne of Shadow on Drift Avalii, the outcome of which could not have proved more advantageous to him and Shadowthrone. Darist dead, the sword Vengeance removed and in the hands of a darkly fated wanderer. The Edur expedition wiped out, the secret thus resurrected and likely to remain unviolated for some time to come. True, it ended up demanding Cotillion's direct, most personal intervention, which he would have liked to have avoided, no doubt.'

'Well, I doubt he would have bothered had not the Hound balked.'

'What?'

'I called upon Blind – you were already down. And one of the Edur mages made the Hound cower with a single word.'

'Ah. Then Cotillion has learned yet another vital fact – he cannot rely upon the Hounds when dealing with the Tiste Edur, for the Hounds remember their original masters.'

'I suppose so. No wonder he was disgusted with Blind.'

They would have continued, Cutter taking full advantage of Apsalar's lapse in taciturnity, had not the sky suddenly darkened, shadows rising on all sides, closing and swallowing them—

A thunderous crash—

The huge tortoise was the only object to break the flat plain, lumbering with the infinite patience of the truly mindless across the ancient seabed. Twin shadows grew to flank it.

'Too bad there's not two of them,' Trull Sengar said, 'then we could ride in style.'

'I would think,' Onrack replied, as they slowed their pace to match that of the tortoise, 'that it feels the same.'

'Hence this grand journey . . . indeed, a noble quest, in which I find a certain sympathy.'

'You miss your kin, then, do you, Trull Sengar?'

'Too general a statement.'

'Ah, the needs of procreation.'

'Hardly. My needs have nothing to do with engendering whelps with my hairline, nor, gods forbid, my ears.' He reached down and tapped the tortoise's dusty shell. 'Like this fellow here, there's no time to think of eggs it won't even lay. Singular intent, disconnected from time – from those messy consequences that inevitably follow, if only to afflict whatever lass tortoise our dogged friend here happens to pounce upon.'

'They are not wont to pounce, Trull Sengar. Indeed, the act is a far more clumsy endeavour—'

'Aren't they all?'

'My own memories—'

'Enough of that, Onrack. Do you think I want to hear of your supple prowess? I will have you know that I have yet to lie with a woman. Thus, I am left with naught but my sparsely seeded imagination. Inflict no luscious details upon me, I beg you.'

The T'lan Imass slowly turned its head. 'It is your people's custom to withhold such activities until marriage?'

'It is. It wasn't among the Imass?'

'Well, yes, it was. But the custom was flouted at every opportunity. In any case, as I explained earlier, I had a mate.'

'Whom you gave up because you fell in love with another woman.'

'Gave up, Trull Sengar? No. Whom I *lost*. Nor was that loss solitary. They never are. From all you have said, I assume then that you are rather young.'

The Tiste Edur shrugged. 'I suppose I am, especially in my present company.'

'Then let us leave this creature's side, so as to spare you the reminder.'

Trull Sengar shot the T'lan Imass a look, then grinned. 'Good idea.'

They increased their pace, and within a few strides had left the tortoise behind. Glancing back, Trull Sengar gave a shout.

Onrack halted and swung round.

The tortoise was turning back, stumpy legs taking it in a wide circle.

'What is it doing?'

'It has finally seen us,' Onrack replied, 'and so it runs away.'

'Ah, no fun and games tonight, then. Poor beast.'

'In time it will judge it safe to resume its journey, Trull Sengar. We have presented but a momentary obstacle.'

'A humbling reminder, then.'

'As you wish.'

The day was cloudless, heat rising from the old seabed in shimmering waves. The odhan's grassy steppes resumed a few thousand paces ahead. The salt-crusted ground resisted signs of passages, though Onrack could detect the subtle indications left behind by the six renegade T'lan Imass, a scrape here, a scuff there. One of the six dragged a leg as it walked, whilst another placed more weight on one side than the other. They were all no doubt severely damaged. The Ritual, despite the cessation of the Vow itself, had left residual powers, but there was something else as well, a vague hint of chaos, of unknown warrens – or perhaps familiar ones twisted beyond recognition. There was, Onrack suspected, a bonecaster among those six.

Olar Ethil, Kilava Onas, Monok Ochem, Hentos Ilm, Tem Benasto, Ulpan Nodost, Tenag Ilbaie, Ay Estos, Absin Tholai . . . the bonecasters of the Logros T'lan Imass. Who among them are lost? Kilava, of course, but that is as it has always been. Hentos Ilm and Monok Ochem have both in their turn partaken of the hunt. Olar Ethil seeks the other armies of the T'lan Imass – for the summons was heard by all. Benasto and Ulpan remain with Logros. Ay Estos was lost here on the Jhag Odhan in the last war. I know naught of the fate of Absin Tholai. Leaving Tenag Ilbaie, whom Logros sent to the Kron, to aid in the L'aederon Wars. Thus. Absin Tholai, Tenag Ilbaie or Ay Estos.

Of course, there was no reason to assume that the renegades were from the Logros, although their presence here on this continent suggested so, since the caves and the weapons caches were not the only ones to exist; similar secret places could be found on every other continent. Yet these renegades had come to Seven Cities, to the very birthplace of the First Empire, in order to recover their weapons. And it was Logros who was tasked with the holding of the homeland.

'Trull Sengar?'

'Yes?'

'What do you know of the cult of the Nameless Ones?'

'Only that they're very successful.'

The T'lan Imass cocked its head. 'What do you mean?'

'Well, their existence has remained hidden from me. I've never heard of them.'

Ah. 'Logros commanded that the First Throne be removed from this land, because the Nameless Ones were drawing ever closer to discovering its location. They had come to realize that its power could be claimed, that the

T'lan Imass could be made to bow in service to the first mortal to seat him or herself upon it.'

'And Logros didn't want one of these Nameless Ones to be that mortal. Why? What terrible purpose drives them? And before you answer, Onrack, I should tell you that as far as I am concerned, "terrible purpose" has rather dire measure, given both your kind and my own.'

'I understand, Trull Sengar, and it is a valid point you make. The Nameless Ones serve the Houses of the Azath. Logros believed that, had a priest of that cult taken the First Throne, the first and only command given to the T'lan Imass would be to voluntarily accept eternal imprisonment. We would have been removed from this world.'

'So the throne was moved.'

'Yes, to a continent south of Seven Cities. Where it was found by a mage – Kellanved, the Emperor of the Malazan Empire.'

'Who now commands all the T'lan Imass? No wonder the Malazan Empire is as powerful as it seems to be – then again, by now, it should have conquered the whole world, since he could have called upon all the T'lan Imass to fight his wars.'

'The Emperor's exploitation of our abilities was . . . modest. Surprisingly constrained. He was then assassinated. The new Empress does not command us.'

'Why didn't she just sit on the First Throne herself?'

'She would, could she find it.'

'Ah, so you are free once more.'

'So it seems,' Onrack replied after a moment. 'There are other . . . concerns, Trull Sengar. Kellanved was resident in a House of the Azath for a time . . .'

They reached the slope beyond the salt flat, began making their way upward. 'These are matters of which I know very little,' the Tiste Edur said. 'You fear that the Emperor was either one of these Nameless Ones, or had contact with them. If so, then why didn't he issue that one command you so dreaded?'

'We do not know.'

'How did he manage to find the First Throne in the first place?'

'We do not know.'

'All right. Now, what has all this to do with what we are up to right now?'

'A suspicion, Trull Sengar, regarding where these six renegade T'lan Imass are heading.'

'Well, southward, it seems. Oh, I see.'

'If there are among them kin of Logros, then they know where the First Throne will be found.'

'Well, is there any reason to believe that you are unique among the T'lan Imass? Do you not think others of your kind may have arrived at the same suspicion?'

'I am not sure of that. I share something with the renegades that they do not, Trull Sengar. Like them, I am unburdened. Freed from the Ritual's Vow. This has resulted in a certain . . . liberation of thought. Monok Ochem and Ibra Gholan pursue a quarry, and the mind of a hunter is ever consumed by that quarry.'

They reached the first rise and halted. Onrack drew out his sword and jammed it point first into the ground, so deep that it remained standing upright when he walked away from it. He took ten paces before stopping once more.

'What are you doing?'

'If you do not object, Trull Sengar, I would await Monok Ochem and Ibra Gholan. They, and Logros in turn, must be informed of my suspicion.'

'And you assume that Monok will spare us the time to talk? Our last moments together were less than pleasant, as I recall. I'd feel better if you weren't standing so far away from your sword.' The Tiste Edur found a nearby boulder to sit on, and regarded Onrack for a long moment before continuing, 'And what about what you did in the cave, where that Tellann Ritual was active?' He gestured at Onrack's new left arm and the melded additions to the other places where damage had occurred. 'It's . . . obvious. That arm's shorter than your own, you know. Noticeably. Something tells me you weren't supposed to do . . . what you did.'

'You are right . . . or would be, were I still bound by the Vow.'

'I see. And will Monok Ochem display similar equanimity when he sees what you have done?'

'I do not expect so.'

'Didn't you proclaim a vow to serve me, Onrack?'

The T'lan Imass lifted its head. 'I did.'

'And what if I don't want to see you put yourself – and me, I might add – at such risk?'

'You make a valid point, Trull Sengar, which I had not considered. However, let me ask you this. These renegades serve the same master as do your kin. Should they lead one of your mortal kin to take the First Throne, thus acquiring mastery over all the T'lan Imass, do you imagine they will be as circumspect in using those armies as was Emperor Kellanved?'

The Tiste Edur said nothing for a time, then he sighed. 'All right. But you lead me to wonder, if the First Throne is so vulnerable, why have you not set someone of your own choosing upon it?'

'To command the First Throne, one must be mortal. Which mortal can we trust to such a responsibility? We did not even choose Kellanved – his exploitation was opportunistic. Furthermore, the issue may soon become irrelevant. The T'lan Imass have been summoned – and all hear it, whether bound to the Vow or freed from it. A new, mortal bonecaster has arisen in a distant land.'

'And you want that bonecaster to take the First Throne.'

'No. We want the summoner to free us all.'

'From the Vow?'

'No. From existence, Trull Sengar.' Onrack shrugged heavily. 'Or so, I expect, the Bound will ask, or, perhaps, have already asked. Oddly enough, I find that I do not share that sentiment any more.'

'Nor would any others who'd escaped the Vow. I would

think, then, that this new mortal bonecaster is in grave danger.'

'And so protected accordingly.'

'Are you able to resist that bonecaster's summons?'

'I am . . . free to choose.'

The Tiste Edur cocked his head. 'It would seem, Onrack, that you are already free. Maybe not in the way that this bonecaster might offer you, but even so . . .'

'Yes. But the alternative I represent is not available to those still bound by the Vow.'

'Let's hope Monok Ochem is not too resentful.'

Onrack slowly turned. 'We shall see.'

Dust swirled upward from the grasses at the edge of the crest, twin columns that resolved into the bonecaster Monok Ochem and the clan leader, Ibra Gholan. The latter lifted its sword and strode directly towards Onrack.

Trull Sengar stepped into the warrior's path. 'Hold, Ibra Gholan. Onrack has information you will want to hear. Bonecaster Monok Ochem – you especially, so call off the clan leader. Listen first, then decide whether Onrack has earned a reprieve.'

Ibra Gholan halted, then took a single step back, lowering its sword.

Onrack studied Monok Ochem. Though the spiritual chains that had once linked them had since snapped, the bonecaster's enmity – Monok's fury – was palpable. Onrack knew his list of crimes, of outrages, had grown long, and this last theft of the body parts of another T'lan Imass was the greatest abomination, the most dire twisting of the powers of Tellann thus far. 'Monok Ochem. The renegades would lead their new master to the First Throne. They travel the paths of chaos. It is their intent, I believe, to place a mortal Tiste Edur upon that throne. Such a new ruler of the T'lan Imass would, in turn, command the new mortal bonecaster – the one who has voiced the summons.'

Ibra Gholan slowly turned to face Monok Ochem, and Onrack could sense their consternation.

Onrack then continued, 'Inform Logros that I, Onrack, and the one to whom I am now bound – the Tiste Edur Trull Sengar – share your dismay. We would work in concert with you.'

'Logros hears you,' Monok Ochem rasped, 'and accepts.'

The swiftness of that surprised Onrack and he cocked his head. A moment's thought, then, 'How many guardians protect the First Throne?'

'None.'

Trull Sengar straightened. '*None?*'

'Do any T'lan Imass remain on the continent of Quon Tali?' Onrack asked.

'No, Onrack the Broken,' Monok Ochem replied. 'This intention you describe was . . . unanticipated. Logros's army is massed here in Seven Cities.'

Onrack had never before experienced such agitation, rattling through him, and he identified the emotion, belatedly, as shock. 'Monok Ochem, why has Logros not marched in answer to the summons?'

'Representatives were sent,' the bonecaster replied. 'Logros holds his army here in anticipation of imminent need.'

Need? 'And none can be spared?'

'No, Onrack the Broken. None can be spared. In any case, we are closest to the renegades.'

'There are, I believe, six renegades,' Onrack said. 'And one among them is a bonecaster. Monok Ochem, while we may well succeed in intercepting them, we are too few . . .'

'At least let me find a worthy weapon,' Trull Sengar muttered. 'I may end up facing my own kin, after all.'

Ibra Gholan spoke. 'Tiste Edur, what is your weapon of choice?'

'Spear. I am fair with a bow as well, but for combat . . . spear.'

'I will acquire one for you,' the clan leader said. 'And a bow as well. Yet I am curious – there were spears to be found among the cache you but recently departed. Why

783

did you not avail yourself of a weapon at that time?'

Trull Sengar's reply was low and cool. 'I am not a thief.'

The clan leader faced Onrack, then said, 'You chose well, Onrack the Broken.'

I know. 'Monok Ochem, has Logros a thought as to who the renegade bonecaster might be?'

'Tenag Ilbaie,' Monok Ochem immediately replied. 'It is likely he has chosen a new name.'

'And Logros is certain?'

'All others are accounted for, barring Kilava Onas.'

Who remains in her mortal flesh and so cannot be among the renegades. 'Born of Ban Raile's clan, a tenag Soletaken. Before he was chosen as the clan's bonecaster, he was known as Haran 'Alle, birthed as he was in the Summer of the Great Death among the Caribou. He was a loyal bonecaster—'

'Until he failed against the Forkrul Assail in the L'aederon Wars,' Monok Ochem cut in.

'As we in turn fail,' Onrack rasped.

'What do you mean?' Monok Ochem demanded. 'In what way have we failed?'

'We chose to see failure as disloyalty, Bonecaster. Yet in our harsh judgement of fallen kin, we committed our own act of disloyalty. Tenag Ilbaie strove to succeed in his task. His defeat was not by choice. Tell me, when have we *ever* triumphed in a clash with Forkrul Assail? Thus, Tenag Ilbaie was doomed from the very beginning. Yet he accepted what was commanded of him. Knowing full well he would be destroyed and so condemned. I have learned this, Monok Ochem, and through you shall say to Logros and all the T'lan Imass: these renegades are of our own making.'

'Then it falls to us to deal with them,' Ibra Gholan growled.

'And what if we should fail?' Onrack asked.

To that, neither T'lan Imass gave answer.

Trull Sengar sighed. 'If we are to indeed intercept these renegades, we should get moving.'

'We shall travel by the Warren of Tellann,' Monok Ochem said. 'Logros has given leave that you may accompany us on that path.'

'Generous of him,' Trull Sengar muttered.

As Monok Ochem prepared to open the warren, the bonecaster paused and looked back at Onrack once more. 'When you . . . repaired yourself, Onrack the Broken . . . where was the rest of the body?'

'I do not know. It had been . . . taken away.'

'And who destroyed it in the first place?'

Indeed, a troubling question. 'I do not know, Monok Ochem. There is another detail that left me uneasy.'

'And that is?'

'The renegade was cut in half by a single blow.'

The winding track that led up the boulder-strewn hillside was all too familiar, and Lostara Yil could feel the scowl settling into her face. Pearl remained a few paces behind her, muttering every time her boots dislodged a stone that tumbled downward. She heard him curse as one such rock cracked against a shin, and felt the scowl shift into a savage smile.

The bastard's smooth surface was wearing off, revealing unsightly patches that she found cause both for derision and a strange, insipid attraction. Too old to dream of perfection, perhaps, she had instead discovered a certain delicious appeal in flaws. And Pearl had plenty of those.

He resented most the relinquishing of the lead, but this terrain belonged to Lostara, to her memories. The ancient, exposed temple floor lay directly ahead, the place where she had driven a bolt into Sha'ik's forehead. And, if not for those two bodyguards – that Toblakai in particular – that day would have ended in even greater triumph, as the Red Blades returned to G'danisban with Sha'ik's head riding a lance. Thus ending the rebellion before it began.

So many lives saved, had that occurred, had reality played out as seamlessly as the scene in her mind. On such things, the fate of an entire subcontinent had irrevocably tumbled headlong into this moment's sordid, blood-soaked situation.

That damned Toblakai. With that damned wooden sword. If not for him, what would this day be like? We'd likely not be here, for one thing. Felisin Paran would not have needed to cross all of Seven Cities seeking to avoid murder at the hands of frenzied rebels. Coltaine would be alive, closing the imperial fist around every smouldering ember before it rose in conflagration. And High Fist Pormqual would have been sent to the Empress to give an accounting of his incompetence and corruption. All, but for that one obnoxious Toblakai . . .

She passed by the large boulders they had hidden behind, then the one she had used to draw close enough to ensure the lethality of her shot. And there, ten paces from the temple floor, the scattered remains of the last Red Blade to fall during the retreat.

Lostara stepped onto the flagstoned floor and halted.

Pearl arrived at her side, looking around curiously.

Lostara pointed. 'She was seated there.'

'Those bodyguards didn't bother burying the Red Blades,' he commented.

'No, why would they?'

'Nor,' the Claw continued, 'it seems, did they bother with Sha'ik.' He walked over to a shadowed spot between the two pillars of an old arched gate.

Lostara followed, her heart suddenly pounding in her chest.

The form was tiny, wrapped in wind-frayed tent cloth. The black hair had grown, and grown, long after death, and the effect – after Pearl crouched and tugged the canvas away to reveal the desiccated face and scalp – was horrific. The hole the quarrel had punched into her forehead revealed a skull filled with windblown sand. More of the fine grains had pooled in the corpse's eye sockets, nose and gaping mouth.

'Raraku reclaims its own,' Pearl muttered after a

moment. 'And you're certain this was Sha'ik, lass?'

She nodded. 'The Book of Dryjhna was being delivered, as I explained. Directly into her hands. From which, it was prophesied, a rebirth would occur, and that in turn would trigger the Whirlwind, the Apocalypse . . . the rebellion.'

'Describe for me again these bodyguards.'

'A Toblakai and the one known as Leoman of the Flails. Sha'ik's most *personal* bodyguards.'

'Yet, it would appear that the rebellion had no need for Sha'ik, or the Whirlwind. It was well under way by the time Felisin arrived at this place. So, what occurred in that time? Are you suggesting that the bodyguards simply . . . waited? Here? Waited for what?'

Lostara shrugged. 'For the rebirth, perhaps. The beauty of prophecies is that they are so conveniently open to countless reinterpretations, as the demand presents itself. The fools waited, and waited . . .'

Frowning, Pearl straightened and looked around. 'But the rebirth *did* occur. The Whirlwind rose, to give focus – to provide a raging heart – for the rebellion. It all happened, just as it had been prophesied. I wonder . . .'

Lostara watched him from beneath half-closed lids. A certain grace to his movements, she conceded. An elegance that would have been feminine in a man less deadly. He was like a flare-neck snake, calm and self-contained . . . until provoked. 'But look at her,' she said. 'There was no rebirth. We're wasting time here, Pearl. So, maybe Felisin stumbled here, onto all this, before continuing onward.'

'You are being deliberately obtuse, dear,' Pearl murmured, disappointing her that he had not risen to the bait.

'Am I?'

Her irritation deepened at the smile he flashed her.

'You are quite right, Lostara, in observing that nothing whatsoever could have been reborn from this corpse. Thus, only one conclusion follows. The Sha'ik alive and well in the heart of Raraku is not the same Sha'ik. Those bodyguards found a . . . replacement. An impostor, someone they could fit neatly into the role – the flexibility of prophecies you noted a moment ago would have served them well. Reborn. Very well, *younger* in appearance, yes? An old woman cannot lead an army into a new war, after all. And further, an old woman would find it hard to convince anyone that she'd been reborn.'

'Pearl.'

'What?'

'I refuse the possibility – yes, I know what you are thinking. But it's impossible.'

'Why? Nothing else fits—'

'I don't care how well it fits! Is that all we mortals are? The victims of tortured irony to amuse an insane murder of gods?'

'A murder of crows, a murder of gods – I like that, lass. As for tortured irony, more like exquisite irony. You don't think Felisin would leap at the chance to become such a direct instrument of vengeance against her sister? Against the empire that sent her to a prison mine? Fate may well present itself, but the opportunity still must be embraced, wilfully, eagerly. There was less chance or coincidence in all this – more like a timely convergence of desires and necessities.'

'We must return to the Adjunct,' Lostara pronounced.

'Alas, the Whirlwind stands between us. I can use no warrens to hasten our journey within that sphere of power. And it would take us far too long to go around it. Fear not, we shall endeavour to reach Tavore in time, with our ghastly revelation. But we shall have to pass through the Whirlwind, through Raraku itself, and quietly, carefully. Discovery would prove fatal.'

'You are delighted with this, aren't you?'

His eyes widened – a look of his of which she had grown far too fond, she realized with a surge of irritation. 'Unfair, my dear Lostara Yil. I am satisfied that the mystery has been solved, that our task of ascertaining Felisin's fate has been concluded. As far as we can take it at the moment, that is.'

'And what of your hunt for the leader of the Talons?'

'Oh, I think I will find satisfaction in that area soon, as well. All things are converging nicely, in fact.'

'See, I knew you were pleased!'

He spread his hands. 'Would you rather I lacerate my flesh in flagellation?' At her cocked eyebrow his gaze narrowed suspiciously for a brief moment, then he drew a breath and resumed, 'We are nearly done, lass, with this mission. And soon we will be able to sit ourselves down in a cool tent, goblets of chilled wine in our hands, and ruminate at leisure over the countless discoveries we have made.'

'I can't wait,' she remarked drily, crossing her arms.

He swung about and faced the Whirlwind. The roaring, shrieking maelstrom commanded the sky, spinning out an endless rain of dust. 'Of course, first we will have to breach the goddess's defences, undetected. You are of Pardu blood, so she will take no heed of you. I, on the other hand, am one-fourth Tiste Andii—'

She started, breath catching. 'You are?'

He looked back, surprised. 'You didn't know? My mother was from Drift Avalii, a half-blood white-haired beauty – or so I'm told, as I have no direct recollection, since she left me with my father as soon as I'd been weaned.'

Lostara's imagination conjured up an image of Pearl suckling at his mother's breast, and found the scene alarming. 'So you were a live birth?'

And smiled at his offended silence.

They made their way down the trail towards the basin, where the Whirlwind's fierce storm raged ceaselessly, rising to tower over them the closer they approached. It was nearing dusk. They were short on food, though they had plenty of water, replenished from the spring near the ruined temple. Lostara's boots were falling apart around her feet, and Pearl's moccasins were now mostly wrapped rags. The seams of their clothing had frayed and grown brittle beneath the unrelenting sun. Leather had cracked and iron had become pitted and layered in patination and rust-stains from their harrowing passage through the Thyrllan Warren.

She felt worn out and weathered; in appearance, she knew, looking ten years older than she was in truth. All the more reason for her alternating fury and dismay at seeing Pearl's hale, unlined face and his oddly shaped eyes so clear and bright. The lightness of his step made her want to brain him with the flat of her sword.

'How do you intend to evade the Whirlwind's notice, Pearl?' she asked as they drew closer.

He shrugged. 'I have a plan. Which may or may not work.'

'Sounds like most of your plans. Tell me, then, what precarious role do you have in mind for me?'

'Rashan, Thyr and Meanas,' he replied. 'The perpetual war. This fragment of warren before us is not fully comprehended by the goddess herself. Not surprising, since she was likely little more than a zephyr spirit to begin with. I, however, do comprehend . . . well, better than her, anyway.'

'Are you even capable of answering succinctly? "Do your feet hurt?" "Oh, the warrens of Mockra and Rashan and Omtose Phellack, from which arise all aches below the knee—"'

'All right. Fine. I intend to hide in your shadow.'

'Well, I'm already used to that, Pearl. But I should point out, that Whirlwind Wall is obscuring the sunset rather thoroughly.'

'True, yet it exists none the less. I will just have to step carefully. Provided, of course, you make no sudden, unexpected moves.'

'In your company, Pearl, the thought has yet to occur to me.'

'Ah, that's good. I in turn feel I should point out, however, that you persist in fomenting a certain tension

790

between us. One that is anything but, uh, professional. Oddly enough, it seems to increase with every insult you throw my way. A peculiar flirtation—'

'Flirtation? You damned fool. I'd be much happier seeing you fall flat on your face and get beaten helpless by that damned goddess, if only for the satisfaction I'd receive—'

'Precisely as I was saying, dear.'

'Really? So if I was to pour boiling oil all over you, you'd be telling me – in between screams – to get my head out from between your—' She shut her mouth with an audible snap.

Wisely, Pearl made no comment.

Flat of the sword? No, the edge. 'I want to kill you, Pearl.'

'I know.'

'But for the moment, I'll settle with having you in my shadow.'

'Thank you. Now, just walk on ahead, a nice even pace. Straight into that wall of sand. And mind you squint your eyes right down – wouldn't want those glorious windows of fire damaged . . .'

She'd expected to meet resistance, but the journey proved effortless. Six steps within a dull, ochre world, then out onto the blasted plain of Raraku, blinking in the dusk's hazy light. Four more steps, out onto scoured bedrock, then she spun round.

Smiling, Pearl raised both hands, palms upward. Standing a pace behind her.

She closed the distance, one gloved hand reaching up to the back of his head, the other reaching much lower as she closed her mouth on his.

Moments later they were tearing at each other's clothes.

No resistance at all.

Less than four leagues to the southwest, as darkness descended, Kalam Mekhar woke suddenly, sheathed in sweat. The torment of his dreams still echoed, even as their substance eluded him. *That song again . . . I think. Rising to a roar that seemed to grip the throat of the world . . .* He slowly sat up, wincing at the various aches from his muscles and joints. Being jammed into a narrow, shadowed fissure was not conducive to restorative sleep.

And the voices within the song . . . strange, yet familiar. Like friends . . . who never sang a word in their lives. Nothing to quell the spirit – no, these voices give music to war . . .

He collected his waterskin and drank deep to wash the taste of dust from his mouth, then spent a few moments checking his weapons and gear. By the time he was done his heart had slowed and the trembling was gone from his hands.

He did not think it likely that the Whirlwind Goddess would detect his presence, so long as he travelled through shadows at every opportunity. And, in a sense, he well knew, night itself was naught but a shadow. Provided he hid well during the day, he expected to be able to reach Sha'ik's encampment undiscovered.

Shouldering his pack, he set off. The stars overhead were barely visible through the suspended dust. Raraku, for all its wild, blasted appearance, was crisscrossed with countless trails. Many led to false or poisoned springs; others to an equally certain death in the wastes of sand. And beneath the skein of footpaths and old tribal cairns, the remnants of coastal roads wound atop the ridges, linking what would have been islands in a vast, shallow bay long ago.

Kalam made his way in a steady jog across a stone-littered depression where a half-dozen ships – the wood petrified and looking like grey bones in the gloom – had scattered their remnants in the hard-packed clay. The Whirlwind had lifted the mantle of sands to reveal Raraku's prehistory, the long-lost civilizations that had known only darkness for millennia. The scene was vaguely disturbing, as if whispering back to the nightmares that had plagued his sleep.

And that damned song.

The bones of sea-creatures crunched underfoot as the assassin continued on. There was no wind, the air almost preternatural in its stillness. Two hundred paces ahead, the land rose once more, climbing to an ancient, crumbled causeway. A glance up to the ridge froze Kalam in his tracks. He dropped low, hands closing on the grips of his long-knives.

A column of soldiers was walking along the causeway. Helmed heads lowered, burdened with wounded comrades, pikes wavering and glinting in the grainy darkness.

Kalam judged their numbers as close to six hundred. A third of the way along the column rose a standard. Affixed to the top of the pole was a human ribcage, the ribs bound together by leather strips, in which two skulls had been placed. Antlers rode the shaft all the way down to the bearer's pallid hands.

The soldiers marched in silence.

Hood's breath. They're ghosts.

The assassin slowly straightened. Strode forward. He ascended the slope until he stood, like someone driven to the roadside by the army's passage, whilst the soldiers shambled past – those on his side close enough to reach out and touch, were they flesh and blood.

'He walks up from the sea.'

Kalam started. An unknown language, yet he understood it. A glance back – and the depression he had just crossed was filled with shimmering water. Five ships rode low in the waters a hundred sweeps of the oar offshore, three of them in flames, shedding ashes and wreckage as they drifted. Of the remaining two, one was fast sinking, whilst the last seemed lifeless, bodies visible on its deck and in the rigging.

'A soldier.'

'A killer.'

'Too many spectres on this road, friends. Are we not haunted enough?'

'Aye, Dessimbelackis throws endless legions at us, and no

matter how many we slaughter, the First Emperor finds more.'

'Not true, Kullsan. Five of the Seven Protectors are no more. Does that mean nothing? And the sixth will not recover, now that we have banished the black beast itself.'

'I wonder, did we indeed drive it from this realm?'

'If the Nameless Ones speak true, then yes—'

'Your question, Kullsan, confuses me. Are we not marching from the city? Were we not just victorious?'

The conversation had begun to fade as the soldiers who had been speaking marched onward, but Kalam heard the doubting Kullsan's reply: *'Then why is our road lined with ghosts, Erethal?'*

More importantly, Kalam added to himself, *why is mine?*

He waited as the last of the soldiers marched past, then stepped forward to cross the ancient road.

And saw, on the opposite side, a tall, gaunt figure in faded orange robes. Black pits for eyes. One fleshless hand gripping an ivory staff carved spirally, on which the apparition leaned as if it was the only thing holding it up.

'Listen to them now, spirit from the future,' it rasped, cocking its head.

And now Kalam heard it. The ghost soldiers had begun singing.

Sweat sprang out on the assassin's midnight skin. *I've heard that song before . . . or no, something just like it. A variation . . .* 'What in the Abyss . . . You, Tanno Spiritwalker, explain this—'

'Spiritwalker? Is that the name I will acquire? Is it an honorific? Or the acknowledgement of a curse?'

'What do you mean, priest?'

'I am no priest. I am Tanno, the Eleventh and last Seneschal of Yaraghatan, banished by the First Emperor for my treasonous alliance with the Nameless Ones. Did you know what he would do? Would any of us have guessed? Seven Protectors indeed, but far more than that, oh yes, far more . . .' Steps halting, the spectre walked onto the road and began dragging itself along in the wake of the column. 'I gave them a song, to mark their last battle,' it rasped. 'I gave them that at least . . .'

Kalam watched as the figures disappeared into the darkness. He swung about. The sea was gone, the basin's bones revealed once more. He shivered. *Why am I witness to these things? I'm reasonably certain I'm not dead . . . although I soon might be, I suppose. Are these death-visions?* He had heard of such things, but held little stock in them. Hood's embrace was far too random to be knotted into the skein of fate . . . until it had already occurred – or so the assassin's experience told him.

He shook his head and crossed the road, slipping down the crumbling verge to the boulder-strewn flat beyond. This stretch had once been naught but dunes, before the Whirlwind's rise. Its elevation was higher – perhaps twice the height of a man – than the ancient seabed he had just traversed, and here, beyond the tumbled stones, lay the gridwork foundations of a city. Deep canals cut through it, and he could make out where bridges had once spanned them here and there. Few of the wall foundations rose higher than the assassin's shins, but some of the buildings looked to have been large – a match to anything found in Unta, or Malaz City. Deep pits marked where cisterns had been built, where the seawater from the other side of the causeway could, stripped of salt by the intervening sands, collect. The remnants of terraces indicated a proliferation of public gardens.

He set out, and soon found himself walking down what had once been a main thoroughfare, aligned north–south. The ground underfoot was a thick, solid carpet of potsherds, scoured and bleached by sand and salt. *And now I am like a ghost, the last to walk these thoroughfares, with every wall transparent, every secret revealed.*

It was then that he heard horses.

Kalam sprinted to the nearest cover, a set of sunken stairs that once led to the subterranean level of a large building.

The thump of horse hoofs drew closer, approaching from one of the side avenues on the opposite side of the main street. The assassin ducked lower as the first rider appeared.

Pardu.

Drawing rein, cautious, weapons out. Then a gesture. Four more desert warriors appeared, followed by a fifth Pardu, this last one a shaman, Kalam concluded, given the man's wild hair, fetishes and ratty goat-hide cape. Glaring about, eyes glinting as if raging with some internal fire, the shaman drew out a long bone and began waving it in circles overhead. Then he lifted his head and loudly sniffed the air.

Kalam slowly eased his long-knives from their scabbards.

The shaman growled a few words, then pivoted on the high Pardu saddle and slipped to the ground. He landed badly, twisting an ankle, and spent the next few moments hobbling about, cursing and spitting. His warriors swung down from their horses in a more graceful fashion, and Kalam caught the flash of a quickly hidden grin from one of them.

The shaman began stamping around, muttering under his breath, reaching up with his free hand to tug at his tangled hair every now and then. And in his movements Kalam saw the beginnings of a ritual.

Something told the assassin that these Pardu did not belong to Sha'ik's Army of the Apocalypse. They were too furtive by far. He slowly sheathed his otataral long-knife and settled back in the deep shadow of the recess, to wait, and watch.

The shaman's muttering had fallen into a rhythmic cadence, and he reached into a bag of sewn hides at his belt, collecting a handful of small objects which he began scattering about as he walked his endless circle. Black and glittering, the objects crackled and popped on the ground as if they had been just plucked from a hearth. An acrid stench wafted out from the ritual circle.

Kalam never discovered if what occurred next had been intended; without doubt its conclusion was not. The darkness lying heavy on the street seemed to convulsively explode – and then screams tore the air. Two massive beasts had arrived, immediately attacking the Pardu warriors. As if darkness itself had taken form, only the shimmer of their sleek hides betrayed their presence, and they moved with blurring speed, amidst spraying blood and snapping bones. The shaman shrieked as one of the enormous beasts closed. Huge black head swung to one side, jaws opening wide, and the shaman's head vanished within the maw. A wet crunch as the jaws ground shut.

The hound – for that, Kalam realized, was what it was – then stepped away, as the shaman's headless body staggered back, then sat down with a thump.

The other hound had begun feeding on the corpses of the Pardu warriors, and the sickening sound of breaking bones continued.

These, Kalam could well see, were not Hounds of Shadow. If anything, they were larger, bulkier, massing more like a bear than a dog. Yet, as they now filled their bellies with raw human flesh, they moved with savage grace, primal and deadly. Devoid of fear and supremely confident, as if this strange place they had come to was as familiar to them as their own hunting grounds.

The sight of them made the assassin's skin crawl. Motionless, he had slowed his own breathing, then the pace of his heart. There were no other alternatives available to him, at least until the hounds left.

But they seemed to be in no hurry, both settling down to split the last long bones and gnaw at joints.

Hungry, these bastards. Wonder where they came from . . . and what they're going to do now.

Then one lifted its head, and stiffened. With a deep grunt it rose. The other continued crunching through a human knee, seemingly indifferent to its companion's sudden tension.

Even when the beast turned to stare at the place where Kalam crouched.

It came at him fast.

Kalam leapt up the worn stairs, one hand reaching into the folds of his telaba. He pivoted hard and sprinted, even as he flung his last handful of smoky diamonds – his own cache, not Iskaral Pust's – into his wake.

A skittering of claws immediately behind him, and he flung himself to one side, rolling over a shoulder as the hound flashed through the place where he had been a moment earlier. The assassin continued rolling until he was on his feet once more, tugging desperately at the whistle looped around his neck.

The hound skidded across dusty flagstones, legs cycling wildly beneath it as it twisted around.

A glance showed the other hound entirely unmindful, still gnawing away in the street beyond.

Then Kalam clamped the whistle between his teeth. He scrambled in a half-circle to bring the scatter of diamonds between himself and the attacking hound.

And blew through the bone tube as hard as he could.

Five azalan demons rose from the ancient stone floor. There seemed to be no moment of disorientation among them, for three of the five closed instantly on the nearer hound, whilst the remaining two flanked Kalam as they clambered, in a blur of limbs, towards the hound in the street. Which finally looked up.

Curious as he might have been to witness the clash of behemoths, Kalam wasted no time in lingering. He ran, angling southward as he leapt over wall foundations, skirted around black-bottomed pits, and set his gaze fixedly on the higher ground fifteen hundred paces distant.

Snaps and snarls and the crash and grind of tumbling stones evinced an ongoing battle in the main street behind him. *My apologies, Shadowthrone . . . but at least one of your demons should survive long enough to escape. In which case, you will be informed of a new menace unleashed on this world. And consider this – if there's two of them, there's probably more.*

He ran onward through the night, until all sounds behind him vanished.

An evening of surprises. In a jewelmonger's kiosk in G'danisban. At a sumptuous, indolent dinner shared by a Kaleffa merchant and one of his prized client's equally prized wives. And in Ehrlitan, among a fell gathering of flesh-traders and murderers plotting the betrayal of a Malazan collaborator who had issued a secret invitation to Admiral Nok's avenging fleet – which even now was rounding the Otataral Sea on its way to an ominous rendez-vous with eleven transports approaching from Genabackis – a collaborator who, it would turn out, would awaken the next morning not only hale, but no longer facing imminent assassination. And on the coastal caravan trail twenty leagues west of Ehrlitan, the quietude of the night would be broken by horrified screams – loud and lingering, sufficient to awaken a maul-fisted old man living alone in a tower overlooking the Otataral Sea, if only momentarily, before he rolled over and fell once more into dreamless, restful sleep.

At the distant, virtually inaudible whistle, countless smoky diamonds that had originated from a trader in G'danisban's market round crumbled into dust – whether placed for safe-keeping in locked chests, worn as rings or pendants, or residing in a merchant's hoard. And from the dust rose azalan demons, awakened long before their intended moment. But that suited them just fine.

They had, one and all, appointed tasks that demanded a certain solitude, at least initially. Making it necessary to quickly silence every witness, which the azalan were pleased to do. Proficiently and succinctly.

For those that had appeared in the ruins of a city in Raraku, however, to find two creatures whose existence was very nearly lost to the demons' racial memory, the moments immediately following their arrival proved somewhat more problematic. For it became quickly apparent that the hounds were not inclined to relinquish their territory, such as it was.

The fight was fierce and protracted, concluding unsatisfactorily for the five azalan, who were eventually driven off, battered and bleeding and eager to seek deep shadows in which to hide from the coming day. To hide, and lick their wounds.

And in the realm known as Shadow, a certain god sat motionless on his insubstantial throne. Already recovered from his shock, his mind was racing.

Racing.

Grinding, splintering wood, mast snapping overhead to drag cordage down, a heavy concussion that shivered through the entire craft, then only the sound of water dripping onto a stone floor.

With a muted groan, Cutter dragged himself upright. 'Apsalar?'

'I'm here.'

Their voices echoed. Walls and ceiling were close – the runner had landed in a chamber.

'So much for subtle,' the Daru muttered, searching for his pack amidst the wreckage. 'I've a lantern. Give me a moment.'

'I am not going anywhere,' she replied from somewhere near the stern.

Her words chilled him, so forlorn did they sound. His groping hands closed on his pack and he dragged it close. He rummaged inside until his hand closed on and retrieved first the small lantern and then the tinder box.

The fire-making kit was from Darujhistan, and consisted of flint and iron bar, wick-sticks, igniting powder, the fibrous inner lining from tree bark, and a long-burning gel the city's alchemists rendered from the gas-filled caverns beneath the city. Sparks flashed three times before the powder caught with a hiss and flare of flame. The bark lining followed, then, dipping a wick-stick into the gel,

Cutter set it alight. He then transferred the flame to the lantern.

A sphere of light burgeoned in the chamber, revealing the crushed wreckage of the runner, rough-hewn stone walls and vaulted ceiling. Apsalar was still seated near the splintered shaft of the tiller, barely illumined by the lantern's light. More like an apparition than a flesh and blood person.

'I see a doorway beyond,' she said.

He swung about, lifting the lantern. 'All right, at least we're not in a tomb, then. More like some kind of storage room.'

'I smell dust . . . and sand.'

He slowly nodded, then scowled in sudden suspicion. 'Let's do some exploring,' he grated as he began collecting his gear, including the bow. He froze at a chittering sound from the doorway, looked up to see a score of eyes, gleaming with the lantern's reflected light. Close-set but framing the doorway on all sides, including the arch where, Cutter suspected, they were hanging upside down.

'Bhok'arala,' Apsalar said. 'We've returned to Seven Cities.'

'I know,' the Daru replied, wanting to spit. 'We spent most of last year trudging across that damned wasteland, and now we're back where we started.'

'So it would seem. So, Crokus, are you enjoying being the plaything of a god?'

He saw little value in replying to that question, and chose instead to clamber down to the puddled floor and approach the doorway.

The bhok'arala scampered with tiny shrieks, vanishing into the darkness of the hallway beyond. Cutter paused at the threshold and glanced back. 'Coming?'

Apsalar shrugged in the gloom, then made her way forward.

The corridor ran straight and level for twenty paces, then twisted to the right, the floor forming an uneven, runnelled ramp that led upward to the next level. There were no side chambers or passages until they reached a circular room, where sealed doorways lining the circumference hinted at entrances to tombs. In one curved wall, between two such doorways, there was an alcove in which stairs were visible.

And crouched at the base of those stairs was a familiar figure, teeth gleaming in a wide smile.

'Iskaral Pust!'

'Missed me, didn't you, lad?' He edged forward like a crab, then cocked his head. 'I should soothe him now – both of them, yes. Welcoming words, a wide embrace, old friends, yes, reunited in a great cause once more. Never mind the extremity of what will be demanded of us in the days and nights to come. As if I need help – Iskaral Pust requires the assistance of no-one. Oh, she might be useful, but she hardly looks inclined, does she? Miserable with knowledge, is my dear lass.' He straightened, managing something between an upright stance and a crouch. His smile suddenly broadened. '*Welcome! My friends!*'

Cutter advanced on him. 'I've no time for any of this, you damned weasel—'

'No time? Of course you have, lad! There's much to be done, and much time in which to do it! Doesn't that make for a change? Rush about? Not us. No, we can *dawdle*! Isn't that wonderful?'

'What does Cotillion want of us?' Cutter demanded, forcing his fists to unclench.

'You are asking me what Cotillion wants of you? How should I know?' He ducked down. 'Does he believe me?'

'No.'

'No what? Have you lost your mind, lad? You won't find it here! Although my wife might – she's ever cleaning and clearing up – at least, I think she is. Though she refuses to touch the offerings – my little bhok'arala children leave them everywhere I go, of course. I've become used to the smell. Now, where was I? Oh yes, dearest Apsalar – should you and I flirt? Won't that make the witch spit and hiss! Hee hee!'

'I'd rather flirt with a bhok'aral,' she replied.

'That too – I'm not the jealous type, you'll be relieved to hear, lass. Plenty of 'em about for you to choose from, in any case. Now, are you hungry? Thirsty? Hope you brought your own supplies. Just head on up these stairs, and when she asks, you haven't seen me.'

Iskaral Pust stepped back and vanished.

Apsalar sighed. 'Perhaps his . . . wife will prove a more reasonable host.'

Cutter glanced back at her. *Somehow I doubt it.*

CHAPTER TWENTY-ONE

'There is no death in light.'

Anarmann,
High Priest of Osserc

'Mezla one and all,' Febryl muttered as he hobbled along the worn, dusty path, his breath growing harsher. There was little in this world that much pleased him any more. Malazans. His failing body. The blind insanity of power so brutally evinced in the Whirlwind Goddess. In his mind, the world was plunging into chaos, and all that it had been – all that he had been – was trapped in the past.

But the past was not dead. It merely slept. The perfect, measured resurrection of old patterns could achieve a rebirth. Not a rebirth such as had taken Sha'ik – that had been nothing more than the discarding of one, badly worn vessel for a new one not nearly so battered. No, the rebirth Febryl imagined was far more profound.

He had once served the Holy Falah'd Enqura. The Holy City of Ugarat and its host of tributary cities had been in the midst of a renaissance. Eleven great schools of learning were thriving in Ugarat. Knowledge long lost was being rediscovered. The flower of a great civilization had turned to face the sun, had begun to open.

The Mezla and their implacable legions had destroyed ... everything. Ugarat had fallen to Dassem Ultor. The schools were assailed by soldiers, only to discover, to their fury, that their many riches and texts had, along with philosophers and academics, vanished. Enqura had well understood the Mezla thirst for knowledge, the Emperor's lust for foreign secrets, and the city's Holy Protector would give them nothing. Instead, he had commanded Febryl, a week before the arrival of the Malazan armies, to shut down the schools, to confiscate the hundred thousand scrolls and bound volumes, the ancient relics of the First Empire, and the teachers and scholars themselves. By the Protector's decree, Ugarat's coliseum became the site of a vast conflagration, as everything was burned, destroyed. The scholars were crucified – those that did not fling themselves on the pyre in a fit of madness and grief – and their bodies dumped into the pits containing the smashed relics just outside the city wall.

Febryl had done as he had been commanded. His last gesture of loyalty, of pure, unsullied courage. The terrible act was necessary. Enqura's denial was perhaps the greatest defiance in the entire war. One for which the Holy Protector paid with his life, when the horror that was said to have struck Dassem Ultor upon hearing of the deed transformed into rage.

Febryl's loss of faith had come in the interval, and it had left him a broken man. In following Enqura's commands, he had so outraged his mother and father – both learned nobles in their own right – that they had disowned him to his face. And Febryl had lost his mind that night, recovering his sanity with dawn staining the horizon, to find that he had murdered his parents. And their servants. That he had unleashed sorcery to flay the flesh from the guards. That such power had poured through him as to leave him old beyond his years, wrinkled and withered, his bones brittle and bent.

The old man hobbling out through the city gate that day was beneath notice. Enqura searched for him, but Febryl succeeded in evading the Holy Protector, in leaving the man to his fate.

Unforgivable.

A hard word, a truth harder than stone. But Febryl was never able to decide to which crime it applied. Three betrayals, or two? Was the destruction of all that knowledge – the slaying of all those scholars and teachers – was it, as the Mezla and other Falad'han later pronounced – the foulest deed of all? Fouler even than the T'lan Imass rising to slaughter the citizens of Aren? So much so that Enqura's name has become a curse for Mezla and natives of Seven Cities alike? *Three, not two?*

And the bitch knew. She knew his every secret. It had not been enough to change his name; not enough that he had the appearance of an old man, when the High Mage Iltara, most trusted servant to Enqura, had been young, tall and lusted after by both men and women? No, she had obliterated, seemingly effortlessly, his every barricade, and plundered the pits of his soul.

Unforgivable.

No possessor of his secrets could be permitted to live. He refused to be so ... vulnerable. To anyone. Even Sha'ik. Especially Sha'ik.

And so she must be removed. Even if it means dealing with Mezla. He had no illusions about Korbolo Dom. The Napan's ambitions – no matter what claims he made at present – went far beyond this rebellion. No, his ambitions were imperial. Somewhere to the south, Mallick Rel, the Jhistal priest of Elder Mael, was trekking towards Aren, there to surrender himself. He would, in turn, be brought before the Empress herself.

And then what? That snake of a priest would announce an extraordinary reversal of fortunes in Seven Cities. Korbolo Dom had been working in her interests all along. Or some such nonsense. Febryl was certain of his suspicions. Korbolo Dom wanted a triumphant return into the imperial fold. Probably the title of High Fist of Seven Cities as well. Mallick Rel would have twisted his part in the events at the Fall and immediately afterwards. The dead man, Pormqual, would be made the singular focus for the debacle of Coltaine's death and the slaying of the High Fist's army. The Jhistal would slip through, somehow, or, if all went awry, he would somehow manage to escape. Korbolo Dom, Febryl believed, had agents in the palace in Unta – what was being played out here in Raraku was but a tremble on a much vaster web.

But I shall defeat it in the end. Even if I must appear to acquiesce right now. He has accepted my conditions, after all – a lie, of course – and I in turn accept his – another lie, naturally.

He had walked through the outskirts of the city and now found himself in the wilder region of the oasis. The trail had the appearance of long disuse, covered in crackling, dried palm fronds and gourd husks, and Febryl knew his careless passage was destroying that illusion, but he was indifferent to that. Korbolo's killers would repair the mess, after all. It fed their self-deceptions well enough.

He rounded a bend in the path and entered a clearing ringed in low stones. There had once been a well here, but the sands had long since filled it. Kamist Reloe stood near the centre, hooded and vulpine, with four of Korbolo's assassins positioned in a half-circle behind him.

'You're late,' Kamist Reloe hissed.

Febryl shrugged. 'Do I look like a prancing foal? Now, have you begun the preparations?'

'The knowledge here is yours, Febryl, not mine.'

Febryl hissed, then waved one claw-like hand. 'No matter. There's still time. Your words only remind me that I must suffer fools—'

'You're not alone in that,' Kamist Reloe drawled.

Febryl hobbled forward. 'The path your ... servants would take is a long one. It has not been trod by mortals since the First Empire. It has likely grown treacherous—'

'Enough warnings, Febryl,' Kamist Reloe snapped, his fear showing through. 'You need only open the path. That is all we ask of you – all we have ever asked.'

'You need more than that, Kamist Reloe,' Febryl said

with a smile. 'Would you have these fools stride in blind? The goddess was a spirit, once—'

'That is no secret.'

'Perhaps, but what kind of spirit? One that rides the desert winds, you might think. But you are wrong. A spirit of stone? Sand? No, none of these.' He waved one hand. 'Look about you. Raraku holds the bones of countless civilizations, leading back to the First Empire, the empire of Dessimbelackis. And still further – aye, the signs of that are mostly obliterated, yet some remain, if one has the eyes to see . . . and understand.' He limped over to one of the low stones ringing the clearing, struggling to hide the wince of pain from his overworked bones. 'Were you to dig down through this sand, Kamist Reloe, you would discover that these boulders are in fact menhirs, stones standing taller than any of us here. And their flanks are pitted and grooved in strange patterns . . .'

Kamist swung in a slow circle, studying the protruding rocks with narrowed eyes. 'T'lan Imass?'

Febryl nodded. 'The First Empire of Dessimbelackis, Kamist Reloe, was not the first. That belonged to the T'lan Imass. There was little, it is true, that you or I might recognize as being . . . imperial. No cities. No breaking of the ground to plant crops or irrigate. And its armies were undead. There was a throne, of course, upon which was meant to sit a mortal – the progeny race of the T'lan Imass. A human. Alas, humans viewed empire . . . differently. And their vision did not include T'lan Imass. Thus, betrayal. Then war. An unequal contest, but the T'lan Imass were reluctant to annihilate their mortal children. And so they left—'

'Only to return with the shattering of the warren,' Kamist Reloe muttered, nodding. 'When the chaos erupted with the ritual of Soletaken and D'ivers.' He faced Febryl once more. 'The goddess spirit is . . . was . . . T'lan Imass?'

Febryl shrugged. 'There were once texts – inscribed on fired clay – from a cult of the First Empire, copies of which survived until the fall of Ugarat. The few T'lan Imass the humans managed to destroy when they rebelled were each buried in sacred sites. Sites such as this one, Kamist Reloe.'

But the other mage shook his head. 'She is a creature of rage. Such fury does not belong to T'lan Imass—'

'Unless she had reason. Memories of a betrayal, perhaps, from her mortal life. A wound too deep to be eradicated by the Ritual of Tellann.' Febryl shrugged. 'It does not matter. The spirit is T'lan Imass.'

'It is rather late in the day for you to be revealing this to us,' Kamist Reloe growled, turning his head to spit. 'Does the Ritual of Tellann still bind her?'

'No. She broke those chains long ago and has reclaimed her soul – Raraku's secret gifts are those of life and death, as primal as existence itself. It returned to her all that she had lost – perhaps even the rebirth of her rage. Raraku, Kamist Reloe, remains the deepest mystery of all, for it holds its own memories . . . of the sea, of life's very own waters. And memories are power.'

Kamist Reloe drew his cloak tighter about his gaunt form. 'Open the path.'

And when I have done this for you and your Mezla friends, High Mage, you will be indebted to me, and my desires. Seven Cities shall be liberated. The Malazan Empire will withdraw all interests, and our civilization shall flower once more . . .

He stepped to the centre of the ring of stones and raised his hands.

Something was coming. Bestial and wild with power. And with each passing moment, as it drew ever nearer, L'oric's fear grew. *Ancient wars . . . such is the feel of this, as of enmity reborn, a hatred that defies millennia.* And though he sensed that no-one mortal in the oasis city was the subject of that wrath, the truth remained that . . . *we are all in the way.*

He needed to learn more. But he was at a loss as to which path he should take. Seven Cities was a land groaning beneath unseen burdens. Its skin was thick with layers, weathered hard. Their secrets were not easily prised loose, especially in Raraku.

He sat cross-legged on the floor of his tent, head lowered, thoughts racing. The Whirlwind's rage had never before been so fierce, leading him to suspect that the Malazan army was drawing close, that the final clash of wills was fast approaching. This was, in truth, a convergence, and the currents had trapped other powers, pulling them along with relentless force.

And behind it all, the whispers of a song . . .

He should flee this place. Take Felisin – and possibly Heboric as well – with him. And soon. Yet curiosity held him here, at least for the present. Those layers were splitting, and there would be truths revealed, and he would know them. *I came to Raraku because I sensed my father's presence . . . somewhere close.* Perhaps here no longer, but he had been, not long ago. The chance of finding his trail . . .

The Queen of Dreams had said Osric was lost. What did that mean? How? Why? He hungered for answers to such questions.

Kurald Thyrllan had been born of violence, the shattering of Darkness. The Elder Warren had since branched off in many directions, reaching to within the grasp of mortal humans as Thyr. And, before that, in the guise of life-giving fire, Tellann.

Tellann was a powerful presence here in Seven Cities, obscure and buried deep perhaps, but pervasive none the less. Whereas Kurald Thyrllan had been twisted and left fraught by the shattering of its sister warren. There were no easy passages into Thyrllan, as he well knew.

Very well, then. I shall try Tellann.

He sighed, then slowly climbed to his feet. There were plenty of risks, of course. Collecting his bleached telaba in the crook of one arm, he moved to the chest beside his cot. He crouched, passing a hand over it to temporarily dispel its wards, then lifted back the lid.

Liosan armour, the white enamel gouged and scarred. A

visored helm of the same material, the leather underlining webbed over eyes and cheeks by black iron mail. A light, narrow-bladed longsword, its point long and tapering, scabbarded in pale wood.

He drew the armour on, including the helm, then pulled his telaba over it, raising the hood as well. Leather gauntlets and sword and belt followed.

Then he paused.

He despised fighting. Unlike his Liosan kin, he was averse to harsh judgement, to the assertion of a brutally delineated world-view that permitted no ambiguity. He did not believe order could be shaped by a sword's edge. Finality, yes, but finality stained with failure.

Necessity was a most bitter flavour, but he saw no choice and so would have to suffer the taste.

Once more he would have to venture forth, through the encampment, drawing ever so carefully on his powers to remain unseen by mortals yet beneath the notice of the goddess. The ferocity of her anger was his greatest ally, and he would have to trust in that.

He set out.

The sun was a crimson glare behind the veil of suspended sand, still a bell from setting, when L'oric reached the Toblakai's glade. He found Felisin sleeping beneath the shade they had rigged between three poles on the side opposite the carved trees, and decided he would leave her to her rest. Instead, sparing a single bemused glance at the two Teblor statues, he strode over to stand before the seven stone faces.

Their spirits were long gone, if they had ever been present. These mysterious T'lan Imass who were Toblakai's gods. And the sanctification had been wrested from them, leaving this place sacred to something else. But a fissure remained, the trail, perhaps, from a brief visitation. Sufficient, he hoped, for him to breach a way into the Warren of Tellann.

He unveiled power, forcing his will into the fissure, widening it until he was able to step through—

Onto a muddy beach at the edge of a vast lake. His boots sank to the ankles. Clouds of insects flitted up from the shoreline to swarm around him. L'oric paused, stared upward at an overcast sky. The air was sultry with late spring.

I am in the wrong place . . . or the wrong time. This is Raraku's most ancient memory.

He faced inland. A marshy flat extended for another twenty paces, the reeds waving in the mild wind, then the terrain rose gently onto savanna. A low ridge of darker hills marked the horizon. A few majestic trees rose from the grasslands, filled with raucous white-winged birds.

A flash of movement in the reeds caught his attention, and his hand reached for the hilt of his sword as a bestial head appeared, followed by humped shoulders. A hyena, such as could be found west of Aren and, more rarely, in Karashimesh, but this one was as large as a bear. It lifted its wide, stubby head, nose testing the air, eyes seeming to squint.

The hyena took a step forward.

L'oric slid the sword from the scabbard.

At the blade's hiss the beast reared up, lunging to its left, and bolted into the reeds.

He could mark its flight by the waving stalks, then it appeared once more, sprinting up the slope.

L'oric resheathed his weapon. He strode from the muddy bank, intending to take the trail the hyena had broken through the reeds, and, four paces in, came upon the gnawed remains of a corpse. Far along in its decay, limbs scattered by the scavenger's feeding, it was a moment before the High Mage could comprehend its form. Humanoid, he concluded. As tall as a normal man, yet what remained of its skin revealed a pelt of fine dark hair. The waters had bloated the flesh, suggesting the creature had drowned. A moment's search and he found the head.

812

He crouched down over it and was motionless for some time.

Sloped forehead, solid chinless jaw, a brow ridge so heavy it formed a contiguous shelf over the deep-set eye sockets. The hair still clinging to fragments of scalp was little longer than what had covered the body, dark brown and wavy.

More ape-like than a T'lan Imass . . . the skull behind the face is smaller, as well. Yet it stood taller by far, more human in proportion. What manner of man was this?

There was no evidence of clothing, or any other sort of adornment. The creature – a male – had died naked.

L'oric straightened. He could see the hyena's route through the reeds, and he set out along it.

The overcast was burning away and the air growing hotter and, if anything, thicker. He reached the sward and stepped onto dry ground for the first time. The hyena was nowhere to be seen, and L'oric wondered if it was still running. An odd reaction, he mused, for which he could fashion no satisfactory explanation.

He had no destination in mind; nor was he even certain that what he sought would be found here. This was not, after all, Tellann. If anything, he had come to what lay beneath Tellann, as if the Imass, in choosing their sacred sites, had been in turn responding to a sensitivity to a still older power. He understood now that Toblakai's glade was not a place freshly sanctified by the giant warrior; nor even by the T'lan Imass he had worshipped as his gods. It had, at the very beginning, belonged to Raraku, to whatever natural power the land possessed. And so he had pushed through to a place of beginnings. *But did I push, or was I pulled?*

A herd of huge beasts crested a distant rise on his right, the ground trembling as they picked up speed, stampeding in wild panic.

L'oric hesitated. They were not running towards him, but he well knew that such stampedes could veer at any time. Instead, they swung suddenly the other way, wheeling as a single mass. Close enough for him to make out their shapes. Similar to wild cattle, although larger and bearing stubby horns or antlers. Their hides were mottled white and tan, their long manes black.

He wondered what had panicked them and swung his gaze back to the place where the herd had first appeared.

L'oric dropped into a crouch, his heart pounding hard in his chest.

Seven hounds, black as midnight, of a size to challenge the wild antlered cattle. Moving with casual arrogance along the ridge. And flanking them, like jackals flanking a pride of lions, a score or more of the half-human creatures such as the one he had discovered at the lakeshore. They were clearly subservient, in the role of scavengers to predators. No doubt there was some mutual benefit to the partnership, though L'oric could imagine no real threat in this world to those dark hounds.

And, there was no doubt in his mind, those hounds did not belong here.

Intruders. Strangers to this realm, against which nothing in this world can challenge. They are the dominators . . . and they know it.

And now he saw that other observers were tracking the terrible beasts. K'Chain Che'Malle, three of them, the heavy blades at the end of their arms revealing that they were K'ell Hunters, were padding along a parallel course a few hundred paces distant from the hounds. Their heads were turned, fixed on the intruders – who in turn ignored them.

Not of this world either, if my father's thoughts on the matter are accurate. He was Rake's guest for months in Moon's Spawn, delving its mysteries. But the K'Chain Che'Malle cities lie on distant continents. Perhaps they but recently arrived here, seeking new sites for their colonies . . . only to find their dominance challenged.

If the hounds saw L'oric, they made no sign of it. Nor did the half-humans.

The High Mage watched them continue on, until they finally dipped into a basin and disappeared from sight.

The K'ell Hunters all halted, then spread out cautiously and slowly closed to where the hounds had vanished.

A fatal error.

Blurs of darkness, launching up from the basin. The K'ell Hunters, suddenly surrounded, swung their massive swords. Yet, fast as they were, in the span of a single heartbeat two of the three were down, throats and bellies torn open. The third one had leapt high, sailing twenty paces to land in a thumping run.

The hounds did not pursue, gathering to sniff at the K'Chain Che'Malle corpses whilst the half-humans arrived with hoots and barks, a few males clambering onto the dead creatures and jumping up and down, arms waving.

L'oric thought he now understood why the K'Chain Che'Malle had never established colonies on this continent.

He watched the hounds and the half-humans mill about the kill site for a while longer, then the High Mage began a cautious retreat, back to the lake. He was nearing the edge of the slope down to the reeds when his last parting glance over one shoulder revealed the seven beasts all facing in his direction, heads raised.

Then two began a slow lope towards him. A moment later the remaining five fanned out and followed.

Oh . . .

Sudden calm descended upon him. He knew he was as good as already dead. There would be no time to open the warren to return to his own world – nor would he, in any case, since to do so would give the hounds a path to follow – *and I'll not have their arrival in the oasis a crime staining my soul. Better to die here and now. Duly punished for my obsessive curiosity.*

The hounds showed nothing of the speed they had unveiled against the K'ell Hunters, as if they sensed L'oric's comparative weakness.

He heard water rushing behind him and spun round.

A dragon filled his vision, low over the water – so fast as to lift a thrashing wave in its wake – and the talons spread wide, the huge clawed hands reaching down.

He threw his arms over his face and head as the enormous scaled fingers closed like a cage around him, then snatched him skyward.

A brief, disjointed glimpse of the hounds scattering from the dragon's shadow – the distant sound of half-human yelps and shrieks – then naught before his eyes but the glistening white belly of the dragon, seen between two curled talons.

He was carried far, out onto a sea, then towards an island where stood a squat tower, its flat roof broad and solid enough for the dragon, wings spreading to thunder against the air, to settle.

The claws opened, tumbling L'oric onto the gouged and scraped stones. He rolled up against the platform's low wall, then slowly sat up.

And stared at the enormous gold and white dragon, its lambent eyes fixed upon him with, L'oric knew instinctively, reproach. The High Mage managed a shrug.

'Father,' he said, 'I've been looking for you.'

Osric was not one for furnishings and decor. The chamber beneath the platform was barren, its floor littered with the detritus left by nesting swallows, the air pungent with guano.

L'oric leaned against a wall, arms crossed, watching his father pace.

He was pure Liosan in appearance, tall and pale as snow, his long, wavy hair silver and streaked with gold. His eyes seemed to rage with an inner fire, its tones a match to his hair, silver licked by gold. He was wearing plain grey leathers, the sword at his belt virtually identical to the one L'oric carried.

'Father. The Queen of Dreams believes you lost,' he said after a long moment.

'I am. Or, rather, I was. Further, I would remain so.'

'You do not trust her?'

He paused, studied his son briefly, then said, 'Of course I trust her. And my trust is made purer by her ignorance. What are you doing here?'

Sometimes longing is to be preferred to reality. L'oric sighed. 'I am not even sure where here is. I was . . . questing for truths.'

Osric grunted and began pacing once more. 'You said earlier you were looking for me. How did you discover my trail?'

'I didn't. My searching for you was more of a, ah, generalized sort of thing. This present excursion was an altogether different hunt.'

'That was about to see you killed.'

L'oric nodded. He looked around the chamber. 'You live here?'

His father grimaced. 'An observation point. The K'Chain Che'Malle skykeeps invariably approach from the north, over water.'

'Skykeeps . . . such as Moon's Spawn?'

A veiled glance, then a nod. 'Yes.'

'And it was in Rake's floating fortress that you first embarked on the trail that took you here. What did you discover that the Tiste Andii Lord of Darkness didn't?'

Osric snorted. 'Only that which was at his very feet. Moon's Spawn bore signs of damage, of breaching. Then slaughter. None the less, a few survived, at least long enough to begin it on its journey home. North, out over the icefields. Of course, it never made it past those icefields. Did you know that the glacier that held Moon's Spawn had travelled a thousand leagues with its prize? A thousand leagues, L'oric, before Rake and I stumbled upon it north of Laederon Plateau.'

'You are saying Moon's Spawn was originally one of these skykeeps that arrived here?'

'It was. Three have come in the time that I have been here. None survived the Deragoth.'

'The what?'

Osric halted and faced his son once more. 'The Hounds of Darkness. The seven beasts that Dessimbelackis made pact with – and oh, weren't the Nameless Ones shaken by that unholy alliance? The seven beasts, L'oric, that gave the name to Seven Cities, although no memory survives of that particular truth. The Seven Holy Cities of our time are not the original ones, of course. Only the number has survived.'

L'oric closed his eyes and leaned his head back against the damp stone wall. 'Deragoth. What happened to them? Why are they here and not there?'

'I don't know. Probably it had something to do with the violent collapse of the First Empire.'

'What warren is this?'

'Not a warren at all, L'oric. A memory. Soon to end, I believe, since it is . . . shrinking. Fly northward and by day's end you will see before you a wall of nothingness, of oblivion.'

'A memory. Whose memory?'

Osric shrugged. 'Raraku's.'

'You make that desert sound as if it is alive, as if it is an entity.'

'Isn't it?'

'You're saying it is?'

'No, I'm not saying that. I was asking you – have you not just come from there?'

L'oric opened his eyes and regarded his father. *You are a frustrating man. No wonder Anomander Rake lost his temper.* 'What of those half-humans that ran with these Deragoth?'

'A quaint reversal, wouldn't you say? The Deragoth's only act of domestication. Most scholars, in their species-bound arrogance, believe that humans domesticated dogs, but it may well have been the other way round, at least to start. Who ran with whom?'

'But those creatures aren't humans. They're not even Imass.'

'No, but they will be, one day. I've seen others, scampering on the edges of wolf packs. Standing upright gives them better vision, a valuable asset to complement the wolves' superior hearing and sense of smell. A formidable combination, but the wolves are the ones in charge. That will eventually change ... but not for those serving the Deragoth, I suspect.'

'Why?'

'Because something is about to happen. Here, in this trapped memory. I only hope that I will be privileged to witness it before the world fades entirely.'

'You called the Deragoth "Hounds of Darkness". Are they children of Mother Dark, then?'

'They are no-one's children,' Osric growled, then he shook his head. 'They have that stench about them, but in truth I have no idea. It just seemed an appropriate name. "Deragoth" in the Tiste Andii tongue.'

'Well,' L'oric muttered, 'actually, it would be Dera'tin'jeragoth.'

Osric studied his son. 'So like your mother,' he sighed. 'And is it any wonder we could not stand each other's company? The third day, always by the third day. We could make a lifetime of those three days. Exaltation, then comfort, then mutual contempt. One, two, three.'

L'oric looked away. 'And for your only son?'

Osric grunted. 'More like three bells.'

Climbing to his feet, L'oric brushed dust from his hands. 'Very well. I may require your help in opening the path back to Raraku. But you might wish to know something of the Liosan and Kurald Thyrllan. Your people and their realm have lost their protector. They pray for your return, Father.'

'What of your familiar?'

'Slain. By T'lan Imass.'

'So,' Osric said, 'find yourself another.'

819

L'oric flinched, then scowled. 'It's not as easy as that! In any case, do you hold no sense of responsibility for the Liosan? They worship you, dammit!'

'The Liosan worship themselves, L'oric. I happen to be a convenient figurehead. Kurald Thyrllan may appear vulnerable, but it isn't.'

'And what if these Deragoth are servants of Darkness in truth? Do you still make the same claim, Father?'

He was silent, then strode towards the gaping entrance-way. 'It's all her fault,' he muttered as he passed.

L'oric followed his father outside. 'This . . . observation tower. Is it Jaghut?'

'Yes.'

'So, where are they?'

'West. South. East. But not here – I've seen none.'

'You don't know where they are, do you?'

'They are not in this memory, L'oric. That is that. Now, stay back.'

The High Mage remained near the tower, watching his father veer into his draconic form. The air suddenly redolent with a sweet, spicy aroma, a blurring of shape before L'oric's eyes. Like Anomander Rake, Osric was more dragon than anything else. They were kin in blood, if not in personality. *I wish I could understand this man, this father of mine. Queen take me, I wish I could even like him.* He strode forward.

The dragon lifted one forelimb, talons opening.

L'oric frowned. 'I would rather ride your shoulders, Father—'

But the reptilian hand reached out and closed about him.

He resolved to suffer the indignity in silence.

Osric flew westward, following the coastline. Before too long forest appeared, and the land reached around north-ward. The air whipping between the dragon's scaled fingers grew cold, then icy. The ground far below began climbing, the forests flanking mountain sides shifting into conifers. Then L'oric saw snow, reaching like frozen rivers in crevasses and chasms.

He could recall no mountains from the future to match this ancient scene. *Perhaps this memory, like so many others, is flawed.*

Osric began to descend – and L'oric suddenly saw a vast white emptiness, as if the mountain rearing before them had been cut neatly in half. They were approaching that edge.

A vaguely level, snow-crusted stretch was the dragon's destination. Its southern side was marked by a sheer cliff. To the north . . . opaque oblivion.

Wings pounding, raising clouds of powdery white, Osric hovered for a moment, then released L'oric.

The High Mage landed in waist-deep snow. Cursing, he kicked his way onto firmer footing, as the enormous dragon settled with a shuddering crunch off to one side.

Osric quickly sembled into Liosan form, the wind whipping at his hair, and strode over.

There were . . . things near the faded edge of the memory. Some of them moving about feebly. Osric stomped through the deep snow towards them, speaking as he went. 'Creatures stumble out. You will find such all along the verge. Most of them quickly die, but some linger.'

'What are they?'

'Demons, mostly.'

Osric changed direction slightly, closing on one such creature, from which steam was rising. Its four limbs were moving, claws scraping through the slush surrounding it.

Father and son halted before it.

Dog-sized and reptilian, with four hands, similar to an ape's. A wide, flat head with a broad mouth, two slits for nostrils, and four liquid, slightly protruding eyes in a diamond pattern, the pupils vertical and, in the harsh glare of the snow and sky, surprisingly open.

'This one might suit Kurald Thyrllan,' Osric said.

'What kind of demon is it?' L'oric asked, staring down at the creature.

'I have no idea,' Osric replied. 'Reach out to it. See if it is amenable.'

'Assuming it has any mind at all,' L'oric muttered, crouching down.

Can you hear me? Can you comprehend?

The four eyes blinked up at him. And it replied. '*Sorcerer. Declaration. Recognition. We were told you'd come, but so soon? Rhetorical.*'

I am not from this place, L'oric explained. *You are dying, I think.*

'*Is that what this is? Bemused.*'

I would offer you an alternative. Have you a name?

'*A name? You require that. Observation. Of course. Comprehension. A partnership, a binding of spirits. Power from you, power from me. In exchange for my life. Uneven bargain. Position devoid of clout.*'

No, I will save you none the less. We will return to my world . . . to a warmer place.

'*Warmth? Thinking. Ah, air that does not steal my strength. Considering. Save me, Sorcerer, and then we will talk more of this alliance.*'

L'oric nodded. 'Very well.'

'It's done?' Osric asked.

His son straightened. 'No, but it comes with us.'

'Without the binding, you will have no control over the demon, L'oric. It could well turn on you as soon as you return to Raraku. Best we resume our search, find a creature more tractable.'

'No. I will risk this one.'

Osric shrugged. 'As you like, then. We must proceed now to the lake, where you first appeared.'

L'oric watched his father walk away, then halt and veer once more into his dragon form.

'*Eleint!*' the demon cried in the High Mage's mind. '*Wonder. You have an Eleint for a companion!*'

My father.

'Your father! Excited delight! Eager. I am named Greyfrog, born of Mirepool's Clutch in the Twentieth Season of Darkness. Proudly. I have fathered thirty-one clutches of my own—'

And how, Greyfrog, did you come here?

'Sudden moroseness. One hop too far.'

The dragon approached.

Greyfrog dragged itself onto the warm sand. L'oric turned about, but the gate was already closing. So, he had found his father, and the parting had been as blunt as the meeting. Not precisely indifference. More like . . . distraction. Osric's interest was with Osric. His own pursuits.

Only now did a thousand more questions rise in L'oric's thoughts, questions he should have asked.

'Regret?'

L'oric glanced down at the demon. 'Recovering, Greyfrog? I am named L'oric. Shall we now discuss our partnership?'

'I smell raw meat. I am hungry. Eat. Then talk. Firm.'

'As you wish. As for raw meat . . . I will find you something that is appropriate. There are rules, regarding what you can and cannot kill.'

'Explain them to me. Cautious. Not wishing to offend. But hungry.'

'I shall . . .'

Vengeance had been her lifeblood for so long, and now, within days, she would come face to face with her sister, to play out the game's end run. A vicious game, but a game none the less. Sha'ik knew that virtually every conceivable advantage lay with her. Tavore's legions were green, the territory was Sha'ik's own, her Army of the Apocalypse were veterans of the rebellion and numerically superior. The Whirlwind Goddess drew power from an Elder Warren – she now realized – perhaps not pure but either immune or resistant to the effects of otataral. Tavore's mages amounted to two Wickan warlocks both broken of spirit, whilst Sha'ik's cadre included four High Mages and a score of shamans, witches and sorcerers, including Fayelle and Henaras. In all, defeat seemed impossible.

And yet Sha'ik was terrified.

She sat alone in the central chamber of the vast, multi-roomed tent that was her palace. The braziers near the throne were slowly dimming, shadows encroaching on all sides. She wanted to run. The game was too hard, too fraught. Its final promise was cold – colder than she had ever imagined. *Vengeance is a wasted emotion, yet I have let it consume me. I gave it like a gift to the goddess.*

Fragments of clarity – they were diminishing, withering like flowers in winter – as the hold of the Whirlwind Goddess tightened on her soul. *My sister traded me for the faith of the Empress, to convince Laseen of Tavore's own loyalty. All to serve her ambition. And her reward was the position of Adjunct. Such are the facts, the cold truths. And I, in turn, have traded my freedom for the power of the Whirlwind Goddess, so that I can deliver just vengeance against my sister.*

Are we, then, so different?

Fragments of clarity, but they led nowhere. She could ask questions, yet seemed incapable of seeking answers. She could make statements, but they seemed strangely hollow, devoid of significance. She was being kept from thinking.

Why?

Another question she knew she would not answer, would not, even, make an effort to answer. *The goddess doesn't want me to think.* Well, at least that was a recognition of sorts.

She sensed the approach of someone, and issued a silent command to her guards – Mathok's chosen warriors – to permit the visitor to pass within. The curtains covering the entrance to the chamber parted.

'A late night for an ancient one such as you, Bidithal,' Sha'ik said. 'You should be resting, in preparation for the battle.'

'There are many battles, Chosen One, and some have already begun.' He leaned heavily on his staff, looking around with a slight smile on his wrinkled lips. 'The coals are fading,' he murmured.

'I would have thought the growing shadows would please you.'

His smile tightened, then he shrugged. 'They are not mine, Chosen One.'

'Aren't they?'

The smile grew more strained still. 'I was never a priest of Meanas.'

'No, here it was Rashan, ghost-child of Kurald Galain . . . yet the warren it claimed was, none the less, Shadow. We are both well aware that the distinctions diminish the closer one delves into the mysteries of the most ancient triumvirate. Shadow, after all, was born of the clash between Light and Dark. And Meanas is, in essence, drawn from the warrens of Thyrllan and Galain, Thyr and Rashan. It is, if you will, a hybrid discipline.'

'Most sorcerous arts available to mortal humans are, Chosen One. I do not, I am afraid, comprehend the point you wish to make.'

She shrugged. 'Only that you send your shadow servants here to spy on me, Bidithal. What is it you hope to witness? I am as you see me.'

He spread his hands, staff resting against one shoulder. 'Perhaps not spies, then, but protectors.'

'And I am in such dire need of protection, Bidithal? Are your fears . . . specific? Is this what you have come to tell me?'

'I am close to discovering the precise nature of that threat, Chosen One. Soon, I will be able to deliver my revelations. My present concerns, however, are with High Mage L'oric and, perhaps, Ghost Hands.'

'Surely you do not suspect either of them of being part of the conspiracy.'

'No, but I am coming to believe that other forces are at

play here. We are at the heart of a convergence, Chosen One, and not just between us and the Malazans.'

'Indeed.'

'Ghost Hands is not as he once was. He is a priest once more.'

Sha'ik's brows lifted in frank disbelief. 'Fener is gone, Bidithal—'

'Not Fener. But consider this. The god of war has been dethroned. And another has risen in its place, as necessity demanded. The Tiger of Summer, who was once the First Hero, Treach. A Soletaken of the First Empire . . . now a god. His need will be great, Chosen One, for mortal champions and avatars, to aid him in establishing the role he would assume. A Mortal Sword, a Shield Anvil, a Destriant – all of the ancient titles . . . and the powers the god invests in them.'

'Ghost Hands would never accept a god other than Fener,' Sha'ik asserted. 'Nor, I imagine, would a god be foolish enough to embrace him in turn. You know little of his past, Bidithal. He is not a pious man. He has committed . . . crimes—'

'None the less, Chosen One. The Tiger of Summer has made his choice.'

'As what?'

Bidithal shrugged. 'What else could he be but Destriant.'

'What proof have you of this extraordinary transformation?'

'He hides well . . . but not well enough, Chosen One.'

Sha'ik was silent for a long moment, then she replied with a shrug of her own. 'Destriant to the new god of war. Why wouldn't he be here? We are at war, after all. I will think of this . . . development, Bidithal. At the moment, however, I cannot – assuming it is true – see its relevance.'

'Perhaps, Chosen One, the most significant relevance is also the simplest one: Ghost Hands is not the broken, useless man he once was. And, given his . . . ambivalence to our cause, he presents us with a potential threat—'

'I think not,' Sha'ik said. 'But, as I said, I will give it some thought. Now, your vast web of suspicions has snared L'oric as well? Why?'

'He has been more elusive of late than is usual, Chosen One. His efforts to disguise his comings and goings have become somewhat extreme.'

'Perhaps he grows weary of your incessant spying, Bidithal.'

'Perhaps, though I am certain he remains unaware that the one ever seeking to maintain an eye on his activities is indeed me. Febryl and the Napan have their own spies, after all. I am not alone in my interests. They fear L'oric, for he has rebuffed their every approach—'

'It pleases me to hear that, Bidithal. Call off your shadows, regarding L'oric. And that is a command. You better serve the Whirlwind's interests in concentrating on Febryl, Korbolo Dom and Kamist Reloe.'

He bowed slightly. 'Very well, Chosen One.'

Sha'ik studied the old man. 'Be careful, Bidithal.'

She saw him pale slightly, then he nodded. 'I am ever that, Chosen One.'

A slight wave of her hand dismissed him.

Bidithal bowed once more, then, gripping his walking stick, he hobbled from the chamber. Out through the intervening chambers, past a dozen of Mathok's silent desert warriors, then out, finally into the cool night air.

Call off my shadows, Chosen One? Command or no, I am not so foolish as to do that.

Shadows gathered around him as he strode down the narrow alleyways between tents and huts. *Do you remember the dark?*

Bidithal smiled to himself. Soon, this fragment of shattered warren would become a realm unto itself. And the Whirlwind Goddess would see the need for a priesthood, a structure of power in the mortal world. And in such an organization, there would be no place for Sha'ik, except perhaps a minor shrine honouring her memory.

For now, of course, the Malazan Empire must be dealt with, summarily, and for that Sha'ik, as a vessel of the Whirlwind's power, would be needed. This particular path of shadows was narrow indeed. Bidithal suspected that Febryl's alliance with the Napan and Kamist Reloe was but temporary. The mad old bastard had no love for Malazans. Probably, his plans held a hidden, final betrayal, one concluding in the mutual annihilation of every interest but his own.

And I cannot pierce to the truth of that, a failure on my part that forces my hand. I must be . . . pre-emptive. I must side with Sha'ik, for it will be her hand that crushes the conspirators.

A hiss of spectral voices and Bidithal halted, startled from his dark musings.

To find Febryl standing before him.

'Was your audience with the Chosen One fruitful, Bidithal?'

'As always, Febryl,' Bidithal smiled, wondering at how the ancient High Mage managed to get so close before being detected by his secret guardians. 'What do you wish of me? It's late.'

'The time has come,' Febryl said in a low, rasping tone. 'You must choose. Join us, or stand aside.'

Bidithal raised his brows. 'Is there not a third option?'

'If you mean you would fight us, the answer is, regrettably, no. I suggest, however, we withhold on that discussion for the moment. Instead, hear our reward for you – granted whether you join us or simply remove yourself from our path.'

'Reward? I am listening, Febryl.'

'She will be gone, as will the Malazan Empire. Seven Cities will be free as it once was. Yet the Whirlwind Warren will remain, returned to the Dryjhna – to the cult of the Apocalypse which is and always has been at the heart of the rebellion. Such a cult needs a master, a High Priest, ensconced in a vast, rich temple, duly honoured by all. How would you shape such a cult?' Febryl smiled. 'It seems you have already begun, Bidithal. Oh yes, we know all about your . . . special children. Imagine, then, all of Seven Cities at your disposal. All of Seven Cities, honoured to deliver to you their unwanted daughters.'

Bidithal licked his lips, eyes shifting away. 'I must think on this—'

'There's no more time for that. Join us, or stand aside.'

'When do you begin?'

'Why, Bidithal, we already have. The Adjunct and her legions are but days away. We have already moved our agents, they are all in place, ready to complete their appointed tasks. The time for indecision is past. Decide. Now.'

'Very well. Your path is clear, Febryl. I accept your offer. But my cult must remain my own, to shape as I choose. No interference—'

'None. That is a promise—'

'Whose?'

'Mine.'

'And what of Korbolo Dom and Kamist Reloe?'

Febryl's smile broadened. 'What worth their vows, Bidithal? The Empress had Korbolo Dom's once. Sha'ik did as well . . .'

As she had yours, too, Febryl. 'Then we – you and I – understand each other.'

'We do indeed.'

Bidithal watched the High Mage stride away. *He knew my shadow spirits surrounded me, yet was dismissive of them. There was no third option. Had I voiced defiance, I would now be dead. I know it. I can feel Hood's cold breath, here in this alley. My powers are . . . compromised. How?* He needed to discover the source of Febryl's confidence. Before he could do anything, before he could make a single move. *And which move will that be? Febryl's offer . . . appeals.*

Yet Febryl had promised no interference, even as he had revealed an arrogant indifference to the power Bidithal had already fashioned. An indifference that bespoke of intimate knowledge. *You do not dismiss what you know nothing of, after all. Not at this stage.*

Bidithal resumed his journey back to his temple. He felt . . . vulnerable. An unfamiliar sensation, and it brought a tremble to his limbs.

A faint stinging bite, then numbness spreading out from her lungs. Scillara leaned her head back, reluctant to exhale, believing for the briefest of moments that her need for air had vanished. Then she exploded into coughing.

'Be quiet,' Korbolo Dom snarled, rolling a stoppered bottle across the blankets towards her. 'Drink, woman. Then open those screens – I can barely see with all the water wrung from my eyes.'

She listened to his boots on the rushes, moving off into one of the back chambers. The coughing was past. Her chest felt full of thick, cloying liquid. Her head was swimming, and she struggled to recall what had happened a few moments earlier. Febryl had arrived. Excited, she believed. Something about her master, Bidithal. The culmination of a long-awaited triumph. They had both gone to the inner rooms.

There had been a time, once, she was fairly certain, when her thoughts had been clear – though, she suspected, most of them had been unpleasant ones. And so there was little reason to miss those days. Except for the clarity itself – its acuity that made recollection effortless. She so wanted to serve her master, and serve him well. With distinction, sufficient to earn her new responsibilities, to assume new roles – ones that did not, perhaps, involve surrendering her body to men. One day, Bidithal would not be able to attend to all the new girls as he did now – there would be too many, even for him. She was certain she could manage the scarring, the cutting away of pleasure.

They would not appreciate the freeing, of course. Not at first. But she could help them in that. Kind words and plenty of durhang to blunt the physical pain . . . and the outrage.

Had she felt outrage? Where had that word come from, to arrive so sudden and unexpected in her thoughts?

She sat up, stumbled away from the cushions to the heavy screens blocking the outside night air. She was naked, but unmindful of the cold. A slight discomfort in the heaviness of her unbound breasts. She had twice been pregnant, but Bidithal had taken care of that, giving her bitter teas that broke the seed's roots and flushed it from her body. There had been that same heaviness at those times, and she wondered if yet another of the Napan's seeds had taken within her.

Scillara fumbled at the ties until one of the screens folded down, and she looked out onto the dark street.

The guards were both visible, near the entrance which was situated a few paces to her left. They glanced over, faces hidden by helms and the hoods of their telabas. And, it seemed, continued staring, though offering no greeting, no comment.

There was a strange dullness to the night air, as if the smoke filling the tent chamber had settled a permanent layer over her eyes, obscuring all that she looked at. She stood for a moment longer, weaving, then walked over to the entrance.

Febryl had left the flaps untied. She pushed them aside and stepped out between the two guards.

'Had his fill of you this night, Scillara?' one asked.

'I want to walk. It's hard to breathe. I think I'm drowning.'

'Drowning in the desert, aye,' the other grunted, then laughed.

She staggered past, choosing a direction at random.

Heavy. Filled up. Drowning in the desert.

'Not this night, lass.'

She stumbled as she turned about, threw both arms out for balance, and squinted at the guard who had followed. 'What?'

'Febryl has wearied of your spying. He wants Bidithal

blind and deaf in this camp. It grieves me, Scillara. It does. Truly.' He took her by the arm, gauntleted fingers closing tight. 'It's a mercy, I think, and I will make it as painless as possible. For I liked you, once. Always smiling, you were, though of course that was mostly the durhang.' He was leading her away as he spoke, down from the main avenue into the rubbish-cluttered aisles between tent-walls. 'I'm tempted to take my pleasure of you first. Better a son of the desert than a bow-legged Napan for your last memory of love, yes?'

'You mean to kill me?' She was having trouble with the thought, with thinking at all.

'I'm afraid I must, lass. I cannot defy my master, especially in this. Still, you should be relieved that it is me and not some stranger. For I will not be cruel, as I have said. Here, into these ruins, Scillara – the floor has been swept clean – not the first time it's seen use, but if all signs are removed immediately there is no evidence to be found, is there? There's an old well in the garden for the bodies.'

'You mean to throw me down the well?'

'Not you, just your body. Your soul will be through Hood's gate by then, lass. I will make certain of that. Now, lie yourself down, here, on my cloak. I have looked upon your lovely body unable to touch for long enough. I have dreamt of kissing those lips, too.'

She was lying on the cloak, staring up at dim, blurry stars, as the guard unhitched his sword-belt then began removing his armour. She saw him draw a knife, the blade gleaming black, and set it to one side on the flagstoned floor.

Then his hands were pushing her thighs apart.

There is no pleasure. It is gone. He is a handsome man. A woman's husband. He prefers pleasure before business, as I once did. I think. But now, I know nothing of pleasure.

Leaving naught but business.

The cloak was bunching beneath her as his grunts filled her ears. She calmly reached out to one side and closed her hand around the hilt of the knife. Raised it, the other hand joining it over and above the guard.

Then she drove the knife down into his lower back, the blade's edge gouging between two vertebrae, severing the cord, the point continuing on in a stuttering motion as it pierced membranes and tore deep into the guard's middle and lower intestines.

He spilled into her at the moment of death, his shudders becoming twitches, the breath hissing from a suddenly slack mouth as his forehead struck the stone floor beside her right ear.

She left the knife buried halfway to its hilt – as deep as her strength had taken it – in his back, and pushed at his limp body until it rolled to one side.

A desert woman for your last memory of love.

Scillara sat up, wanting to cough but swallowing until the urge passed. Heavy, and heavier still.

I am a vessel ever filled, yet there's always room for more. More durhang. More men and their seeds. My master found my place of pleasure and removed it. Ever filled, yet never filled up. There is no base to this vessel. This is what he has done.

To all of us.

She tottered upright. Stared down at the guard's corpse, at the wet stains spreading out beneath him.

A sound behind her. Scillara turned.

'You murdering bitch.'

She frowned at the second guard as he advanced, drawing a dagger.

'The fool wanted you alone for a time. This is what he gets for ignoring Febryl's commands – I warned him—'

She was staring at the hand gripping the dagger, so was caught unawares as the other hand flashed, knuckles cracking hard against her jaw.

Her eyes blinked open to jostling, sickening motion. She was being dragged through rubbish by one arm. From somewhere ahead flowed the stench of the latrine trench, thick as fog, a breath of warm, poisoned air. Her lips were broken and her mouth tasted of blood. The shoulder of the arm the guard gripped was throbbing.

The man was muttering. '. . . pretty thing indeed. Hardly. When she's drowning in filth. The fool, and now he's dead. It was a simple task, after all. There's no shortage of whores in this damned camp. What – who—'

He had stopped.

Head lolling, Scillara caught a blurred glimpse of a squat figure emerging from darkness.

The guard released her wrist and her arm fell with a thump onto damp, foul mud. She saw him reaching for his sword.

Then his head snapped up with a sound of cracked teeth, followed by a hot spray that spattered across Scillara's thighs. Blood.

She thought she saw a strange emerald glow trailing from one hand of the guard's killer – a hand taloned like a huge cat's.

The figure stepped over the crumpled form of the guard, who had ceased moving, and slowly crouched down beside Scillara.

'I've been looking for you,' the man growled. 'Or so I've just realized. Extraordinary, how single lives just fold into the whole mess, over and over again, all caught up in the greater swirl. Spinning round and round, and ever downward, it seems. Ever downward. Fools, all of us, to think we can swim clear of that current.'

The shadows were strange on him. As if he stood beneath palms and tall grasses – but no, there was only the night sky above the squat, broad-shouldered man. He was tattooed, she realized, in the barbs of a tiger.

'Plenty of killing going on lately,' he muttered, staring down at her with amber eyes. 'All those loose threads being knotted, I expect.'

She watched him reach down with that glowing, taloned hand. It settled, palm-downward, warm between her breasts. The tips of the claws pricked her skin and a tremble ran through her.

That spread, coursing hot through her veins. That heat grew suddenly fierce, along her throat, in her lungs, between her legs.

The man grunted. 'I thought it was consumption, that rattling breath. But no, it's just too much durhang. As for the rest, well, it's an odd thing about pleasure. Something Bidithal would have you never know. Its enemy is not pain. No, pain is simply the path taken to indifference. And indifference destroys the soul. Of course, Bidithal likes destroyed souls – to mirror his own.'

If he continued speaking beyond that, she did not hear, as sensations long lost flooded into her, only slightly blunted by the lingering, satisfying haze of the durhang. She felt badly used between her legs, but knew that feeling would pass.

'Outrage.'

He was gathering her into his arms, but paused. 'You spoke?'

Outrage. Yes. That. 'Where are you taking me?' The question came out between coughs, and she pushed his arms aside to bend over and spit out phlegm while he answered.

'To my temple. Fear not, it's safe. Neither Febryl nor Bidithal will find you there. You've been force-healed, lass, and will need to sleep.'

'What do you want with me?'

'I'm not sure yet. I think I will need your help, and soon. But the choice is yours. Nor will you have to surrender . . . anything you don't want to. And, if you choose to simply walk away, that is fine as well. I will give you money and supplies – and maybe even find you a horse. We can discuss that tomorrow. What is your name?'

He reached down once more and lifted her effortlessly.

'Scillara.'

'I am Heboric, Destriant to Treach, the Tiger of Summer and the God of War.'

She stared up at him as he began carrying her along the path. 'I am afraid I am going to disappoint you, Heboric. I think I have had my fill of priests.'

She felt his shrug, then he smiled wearily down at her. 'That's all right. Me too.'

Felisin awoke shortly after L'oric returned with a freshly slaughtered lamb for his demon familiar, Greyfrog. Probably, the High Mage reflected when she first stirred beneath the tarpaulin, she had been roused to wakefulness by the sound of crunching bones.

The demon's appetite was voracious, and L'oric admired its singlemindedness, if not its rather untidy approach to eating.

Felisin emerged, wrapped in her blankets, and walked to L'oric's side. She was silent, her hair in disarray around her young, tanned face, and watched the demon consuming the last of the lamb with loud, violent gulps.

'Greyfrog,' L'oric murmured. 'My new familiar.'

'Your familiar? You are certain it's not the other way round? That thing could eat both of us.'

'*Observant. She is right, companion L'oric. Maudlin. I would waddle. Alas. Torpid vulnerability. Distraught. All alone.*'

'All right.' L'oric smiled. 'An alliance is a better word for our partnership.'

'There is mud on your boots, and snagged pieces of reed and grass.'

'I have travelled this night, Felisin.'

'Seeking allies?'

'Not intentionally. No, my search was for answers.'

'And did you find any?'

He hesitated, then sighed. 'Some. Fewer than I would have hoped. But I return knowing one thing for certain. And that is, you must leave. As soon as possible.'

Her glance was searching. 'And what of you?'

'I will follow, as soon as I can.'

'I'm to go alone?'

'No. You will have Greyfrog with you. And one other . . . I hope.'

She nodded. 'I am ready. I have had enough of this place. I no longer dream of vengeance against Bidithal. I just want to be gone. Is that cowardly of me?'

L'oric slowly shook his head. 'Bidithal will be taken care of, lass, in a manner befitting his crimes.'

'If you are intending to murder him, then I would advise against sending Greyfrog with me. Bidithal is powerful – perhaps more so than you realize. I can travel alone – no-one will be hunting me, after all.'

'No. Much as I would like to kill Bidithal myself, it will not be by my hand.'

'There is something ominous in what you are saying, or, perhaps, in what you're not saying, L'oric.'

'There will be a convergence, Felisin. With some . . . unexpected guests. And I do not think anyone here will survive their company for long. There will be . . . vast slaughter.'

'Then why are you staying?'

'To witness, lass. For as long as I can.'

'Why?'

He grimaced. 'As I said, I am still seeking answers.'

'And are they important enough to risk your own life?'

'They are. And now, I will leave you here in Greyfrog's trust for a time. You are safe, and when I return it will be with the necessary supplies and mounts.'

She glanced over at the scaled, ape-like creature with its four eyes. 'Safe, you said. At least until it gets hungry.'

'*Appreciative. I will protect this one. But do not be gone too long. Ha ha.*'

Dawn was breathing light into the eastern sky as Heboric stepped outside to await his visitor. The Destriant remained in as much darkness as he could manage, not to hide from L'oric – whom he now watched stride into view and approach – but against any other watchers. They might well discern a figure, crouched there in the tent's doorway, but little more than that. He had drawn a heavy cloak about himself, hood drawn up over his head, and he kept his hands beneath the folds.

L'oric's steps slowed as he drew near. There would be no hiding the truth from this man, and Heboric smiled as he saw the High Mage's eyes widen.

'Aye,' Heboric muttered, 'I was reluctant. But it is done, and I have made peace with that.'

'And what is Treach's interest here?' L'oric asked after a long, uneasy moment.

'There will be a battle,' Heboric replied, shrugging. 'Beyond that . . . well, I'm not sure. We'll see, I expect.'

L'oric looked weary. 'I was hoping to convince you to leave. To take Felisin away from here.'

'When?'

'Tonight.'

'Move her camp a league, out beyond the northeast edge of the oasis. Three saddled horses, three more pack horses. Food and water sufficient for three, to take us as far as G'danisban.'

'Three?'

Heboric smiled. 'You are not aware of it, but there is a certain . . . poetry to there being three of us.'

'Very well. And how long should she expect to wait?'

'As long as she deems acceptable, L'oric. Like you, I intend to remain here for a few days yet.'

His eyes grew veiled. 'The convergence.'

Heboric nodded.

L'oric sighed. 'We are fools, you and I.'

'Probably.'

'I had once hoped, Ghost Hands, for an alliance between us.'

'It exists, more or less, L'oric. Sufficient to ensure Felisin's safety. Not that we have managed well in that responsibility thus far. I could have helped,' Heboric growled.

'I am surprised, if you know what Bidithal did to her, that you have not sought vengeance.'

'Vengeance? What is the point in that? No, L'oric, I have a better answer to Bidithal's butchery. Leave Bidithal to his fate . . .'

The High Mage started, then smiled. 'Odd, only a short time ago I voiced similar words to Felisin.'

Heboric watched the man walk away. After a moment, the Destriant turned and re-entered his temple.

'There is something . . . inexorable about them . . .'

They were in the path of the distant legions, seeing the glimmer of iron wavering like molten metal beneath a pillar of dust that, from this angle, seemed to rise straight up, spreading out in a hazy stain in the high desert winds. At Leoman's words, Corabb Bhilan Thenu'alas shivered. Dust was sifting down the folds of his ragged telaba; the air this close to the Whirlwind Wall was thick with suspended sand, filling his mouth with grit.

Leoman twisted in his saddle to study his warriors.

Anchoring his splintered lance into the stirrup cup, Corabb settled back in the saddle. He was exhausted. Virtually every night, they had attempted raids, and even when his own company had not been directly involved in the fighting there had been retreats to cover, counter-attacks to blunt, then flight. Always flight. Had Sha'ik given Leoman five thousand warriors, the Adjunct and her army would be the ones retreating. All the way back to Aren, mauled and limping.

Leoman had done what he could with what he had, how-ever, and they had purchased – with blood – a handful of precious days. Moreover, they had gauged the Adjunct's tactics, and the mettle of the soldiers. More than once, concerted pressure on the regular infantry had buckled them, and had Leoman the numbers, he could have pressed home and routed them. Instead, Gall's Burned Tears would arrive, or Wickans, or those damned marines, and the desert warriors would be the ones fleeing. Out into the night, pursued by horse warriors as skilled and tenacious as Leoman's own.

Seven hundred or so remained – they'd had to leave so many wounded behind, found and butchered by the Khundryl Burned Tears, with various body parts collected as trophies.

Leoman faced forward on his saddle once more. 'We are done.'

Corabb nodded. The Malazan army would reach the Whirlwind Wall by dusk. 'Perhaps her otataral will fail,' he offered. 'Perhaps the goddess will destroy them all this very night.'

The lines bracketing Leoman's blue eyes deepened as he narrowed his gaze on the advancing legions. 'I think not. There is nothing pure in the Whirlwind's sorcery, Corabb. No, there will be a battle, at the very edge of the oasis. Korbolo Dom will command the Army of the Apocalypse. And you and I, and likely Mathok, shall find ourselves a suitable vantage point . . . to watch.'

Corabb leaned to one side and spat.

'Our war is done,' Leoman finished, collecting his reins.

'Korbolo Dom will need us,' Corabb asserted.

'If he does, then we have lost.'

They urged their weary horses into motion, and rode through the Whirlwind Wall.

He could ride at a canter for half a day, dropping the Jhag horse into a head-dipping, loping gait for the span of a bell, then resume the canter until dusk. Havok was a beast unlike any other he had known, including his namesake. He had ridden close enough to the north side of Ugarat to see watchers on the wall, and indeed they had sent out a score of horse warriors to contest his crossing the broad stone bridge spanning the river – riders who should have reached it long before he did.

But Havok had understood what was needed, and canter

stretched out into gallop, neck reaching forward, and they arrived fifty strides ahead of the pursuing warriors. Foot traffic on the bridge scattered from their path, and its span was wide enough to permit easy passage around the carts and wagons. Broad as the Ugarat River was, they reached the other side within a dozen heartbeats, the thunder of Havok's hoofs changing in timbre from stone to hard-packed earth as they rode out into the Ugarat Odhan.

Distance seemed to lose relevance to Karsa Orlong. Havok carried him effortlessly. There was no need for a saddle, and the single rein looped around the stallion's neck was all he needed to guide the beast. Nor did the Teblor hobble the horse for the night, instead leaving him free to graze on the vast sweeps of grass stretching out on all sides.

The northern part of the Ugarat Odhan had narrowed between the inward curl of the two major rivers – the Ugarat and the other Karsa recalled as being named either Mersin or Thalas. A spine of hills had run north–south, dividing the two rivers, their summits and slopes hard-packed by the seasonal migration of bhederin over thousands of years. Those herds were gone, though their bones remained where predators and hunters had felled them, and the land was used now as occasional pasture, sparsely populated and that only in the wet season.

In the week it took to cross those hills, Karsa saw naught but signs of shepherd camps and boundary cairns, and the only grazing creatures were antelope and a species of large deer that fed only at night, spending days bedded down in low areas thick with tall, yellow grasses. Easily flushed then run down to provide Karsa with an occasional feast.

The Mersin River was shallow, almost dried up this late in the dry season. Fording it, he had then ridden northeast, coming along the trails skirting the south flanks of the Thalas Mountains, then eastward, to the city of Lato Revae, on the very edge of the Holy Desert.

He traversed the road south of the city's wall at night,

avoiding all contact, and reached the pass that led into Raraku at dawn the following day.

A pervasive urgency was driving him on. He was unable to explain the desire in his own mind, yet did not question it. He had been gone a long time, and though he did not believe the battle in Raraku had occurred, he sensed it was imminent.

And Karsa wanted to be there. Not to kill Malazans, but to guard Leoman's back. But there was a darker truth, he well knew. The battle would be a day of chaos, and Karsa Orlong meant to add to it. *Sha'ik or no Sha'ik, there are those in her camp who deserve only death. And I shall deliver it.* He did not bother conjuring a list of reasons, of insults delivered, contempt unveiled, crimes committed. He had been indifferent for long enough, indifferent to so many things. He had reined in his spirit's greatest strengths, among them his need to make judgements, and act decisively upon them in true Teblor fashion.

I have tolerated the deceitful and the malicious for long enough. My sword shall now answer them.

The Toblakai warrior was even less interested in creating a list of names, since names invited vows, and he had had enough of vows. No, he would kill as the mood took him.

He looked forward to his homecoming.

Provided he arrived in time.

Descending the slopes leading down into the Holy Desert, he was relieved to see, far to the north and east, the red crest of fury that was the Whirlwind Wall. Only days away, now.

He smiled at that distant anger, for he understood it. Constrained – chained – for so long, the goddess would soon unleash her wrath. He sensed her hunger, as palpable as that of the twin souls within his sword. The blood of deer was too thin.

He reined in Havok at an old camp near the edge of a salt flat. The slopes behind him would provide the last forage and water for the horse until just this side of the Whirlwind Wall, so he would spend time here bundling grasses for the journey, as well as refilling the waterskins from the spring ten paces from the camp.

He built a fire using the last of the bhederin dung from the Jhag Odhan – something he did only rarely – and, following a meal, opened the pack containing the ruined T'lan Imass and dragged the remnants out for the first time.

'You are impatient to get rid of me?' 'Siballe asked in a dry, rasping voice.

He grunted, staring down at the creature. 'We've travelled far, Unfound. It has been a long time since I last looked upon you.'

'Then why do you choose to look upon me now, Karsa Orlong?'

'I do not know. I regret it already.'

'I have seen the sun's light through the weave of the fabric. Preferable to darkness.'

'Why should what you prefer interest me?'

'Because, Karsa Orlong, we are within the same House. The House of Chains. Our master—'

'I have no master,' the Teblor growled.

'As he would have it,' 'Siballe replied. 'The Crippled God does not expect you to kneel. He issues no commands to his Mortal Sword, his Knight of Chains – for that is what you are, the role for which you have been shaped from the very beginning.'

'I am not in this House of Chains, T'lan Imass. Nor will I accept another false god.'

'He is not false, Karsa Orlong.'

'As false as you,' the warrior said, baring his teeth. 'Let him rise before me and my sword will speak for me. You say I have been shaped. Then there is much to which he must give answer.'

'The gods chained him.'

'What do you mean?'

'They chained him, Karsa Orlong, to dead ground. He is

broken. In eternal pain. He has been twisted by captivity and now knows only suffering.'

'Then I shall break his chains—'

'I am pleased—'

'And then kill him.'

Karsa grabbed the shattered T'lan Imass by its lone arm and stuffed it back into the pack. Then rose.

Great tasks lay ahead. The notion was satisfying.

A House is just another prison. And I have had enough of prisons. Raise walls around me, and I will knock them down.

Doubt my words, Crippled God, to your regret . . .

CHAPTER TWENTY-TWO

Otataral, I believe, was born of sorcery. If we hold that
magic feeds on hidden energies, then it follows that
there are limits to those energies. Sufficient unveiling
of power that subsequently cascades out of control could
well drain those life-forces dry.

Further, it is said that the Elder warrens resist the
deadening effect of otataral, suggesting that the world's
levels of energy are profoundly multilayered. One need
only contemplate the life energy of corporeal flesh,
compared to the undeniable energy within an inanimate
object, such as rock. Careless examination might
suggest that the former is alive, whilst the latter is not.
In this manner, perhaps otataral is not quite as negating
as it would first appear . . .

Musings on the Physical Properties of the World
Tryrssan of Mott

The 9th, 11th and 12th squads, medium infantry, had
been attached to the marines of the 9th Company.
There were rumours, as well, that the 1st, 2nd and
3rd squads – the heavy infantry with their oversized
muscles and sloping brows – would soon join them to form
a discrete fighting unit.

None from the newly arrived squads were entirely
strangers to Strings. He had made a point of learning names
and memorizing faces throughout the 9th Company.

Footsore and weary from interrupted nights, the sergeant

and his squad were sprawled around a cookfire, lulled by the incessant roar of the Whirlwind Wall a thousand paces north of the encamped army. Even rage could numb, it seemed.

Sergeant Balm of the 9th squad strode over after directing his soldiers into their new camp. Tall and wide-shouldered, the Dal Honese had impressed Strings with his cool indifference to pressure. Balm's squad had already done its share of fighting, and the names of Corporal Deadsmell, Throatslitter, Widdershins, Galt and Lobe were already among the tales travelling through the legion. The same was true of some from the other two squads. Moak, Burnt and Stacker. Thom Tissy, Tulip, Ramp and Able.

The heavy infantry were yet to wet their swords, but Strings had been impressed with their discipline – *easier with slope-brows, of course. Tell 'em to stand firm and they take root down to the bedrock.* A few of them were wandering in, he noted. Flashwit, Bowl, Shortnose and Uru Hela. Mean-looking one and all.

Sergeant Balm squatted down. 'You're the one named Strings, aren't you? Heard it's not your real name.'

Strings raised his brows. 'And "Balm" is?'

The dark-skinned young man frowned, his heavy eye-brows meeting as he did so. 'Why, yes, it is.'

Strings glanced over at another soldier from the 9th squad, a man standing nearby looking as if he wanted to kill something. 'And what about him? What's his name again, Throatslitter? Did his ma decide on that for her little one, do you think?'

'Can't say,' Balm replied. 'Give a toddler a knife and who knows what'll happen.'

Strings studied the man for a moment, then grunted. 'You wanted to see me about something?'

Balm shrugged. 'Not really. Sort of. What do you think of the captain's new units? Seems a little late to make changes like this . . .'

'It's not that new, actually. Greymane's legions are

sometimes set up in the same manner. In any case, our new Fist has approved it.'

'Keneb. Not sure about him.'

'And you are about our fresh-faced captain?'

'Aye, I am. He's nobleborn, is Ranal. Enough said.'

'Meaning?'

Balm looked away, started tracking a distant bird in flight. 'Oh, only that he's likely to get us all killed.'

Ah. 'Speak louder, not everyone heard that opinion.'

'Don't need to, Strings. They share it.'

'Sharing it ain't the same as saying it.'

Gesler, Borduke and the sergeants from the 11th and 12th squads came over and muttered introductions went round the group. Moak, of the 11th, was Falari, copper-haired and bearded like Strings. He'd taken a lance down his back, from shoulder to tailbone, and, despite the healer's efforts, was clearly struggling with badly knitted muscles. The 12th's sergeant, Thom Tissy, was squat, with a face that might be handsome to a female toad, his cheeks pocked and the backs of his hands covered in warts. He was, the others saw when he removed his helm, virtually hairless.

Moak squinted at Strings for a long moment, as if seeking to conjure recognition, then he drew out a fish spine from his belt pouch and began picking his teeth. 'Anybody else hear about that killer soldier? Heavy infantry, not sure what company, not even sure what legion. Named Neffarias Bredd. I heard he killed eighteen raiders all in one night.'

Strings lifted his gaze to meet Gesler's, but neither man's expression changed.

'I heard it was eighteen one night, thirteen the next,' Thom Tissy said. 'We'll have to ask the slope-brows when they show.'

'Well,' Strings pointed out, 'there's one over there.' He raised his voice. 'Flashwit! Come join us for a moment, if you please.'

The ground seemed to tremble with the woman's

847

approach. She was Napan and Strings wondered if she knew she was female. The muscles of her arms were larger than his thighs. She had cut all her hair off, her round face devoid of ornament barring a bronze nose-ring. Yet her eyes were startlingly beautiful, emerald green.

'Have you heard of another heavy, Flashwit? Neffarias Bredd?'

Those extraordinary eyes widened. 'Killed fifty raiders, they say.'

'Which legion?' Moak asked.

She shrugged. 'Don't know.'

'Not ours, though.'

'Not sure.'

'Well,' Moak snapped, 'what *do* you know?'

'He killed fifty raiders. Can I go now? I have to pee.'

They watched her walk away.

'Standing up, do you think?' Thom Tissy asked the others in general.

Moak snorted. 'Why don't you go ask her.'

'Ain't that eager to get killed. Why don't you, Moak?'

'Here come the heavy's sergeants,' Balm observed.

Mosel, Sobelone and Tugg could have been siblings. They all hailed from Malaz City, typical of the mixed breed prevalent on the island, and the air of threat around them had less to do with size than attitude. Sobelone was the oldest of the three, a severe-looking woman with streaks of grey in her shoulder-length black hair, her eyes the colour of the sky. Mosel was lean, the epicanthic folds of his eyes marking Kanese blood somewhere in his family line. His hair was braided and cut finger-length in the fashion of Jakatakan pirates. Tugg was the biggest of the three, armed with a short single-bladed axe. The shield strapped on his back was enormous, hardwood, sheathed in tin and rimmed in bronze.

'Which one of you is Strings?' Mosel asked.

'Me. Why?'

The man shrugged. 'Nothing. I was just wondering. And

you' – he nodded at Gesler – 'you're that coastal guard, Gesler.'

'So I am. What of it?'

'Nothing.'

There was a moment of awkward silence, then Tugg spoke, his voice thin, emerging from, Strings suspected, a damaged larynx. 'We heard the Adjunct was going to the wall tomorrow. With that sword. Then what? She stabs it? It's a storm of sand, there's nothing to stab. And aren't we already in Raraku? The Holy Desert? It don't feel any different, don't look any different, neither. Why didn't we just wait for 'em? Or let 'em stay and rot here in this damned wasteland? Sha'ik wants an empire of sand, let her have it.'

That fractured voice was excruciating to listen to, and it seemed to Strings that Tugg would never stop. 'Plenty of questions there,' he said as soon as the man paused to draw a wheezing breath. 'This empire of sand can't be left here, Tugg, because it's a rot, and it will spread – we'd lose Seven Cities, and far too much blood was spilled conquering it in the first place to just let it go. And, while we're in Raraku, we're on its very edge. It may be a Holy Desert, but it looks like any other. If it possesses a power, then that lies in what it does to you, after a while. Maybe not what it does, but what it gives. Not an easy thing to explain.' He then shrugged, and coughed.

Gesler cleared his throat. 'The Whirlwind Wall is sorcery, Tugg. The Adjunct's sword is otataral. There will be a clash between the two. If the Adjunct's sword fails, then we all go home . . . or back to Aren—'

'Not what I heard,' Moak said, pausing to spit before continuing. 'We swing east then north if we can't breach the wall. To G'danisban, or maybe Ehrlitan. To wait for Dujek Onearm and High Mage Tayschrenn. I've even heard that Greymane might be recalled from the Korelri campaign.'

Strings stared at the man. 'Whose shadow have you been standing in, Moak?'

'Well, it makes sense, don't it?'

Sighing, Strings straightened. 'It's all a waste of breath, soldiers. Sooner or later, we're all marching in wide-eyed stupid.' He strode over to where his squad had set up the tents.

His soldiers, Cuttle included, were gathered around Bottle, who sat cross-legged and seemed to be playing with twigs and sticks.

Strings halted in his tracks, an uncanny chill creeping through him. *Gods below, for a moment there I thought I was seeing Quick Ben, with Whiskeyjack's squad crowding round some damned risky ritual . . .* He could hear faint singing from somewhere in the desert beyond the camp, singing that sliced like a sword's edge through the roar of the Whirlwind Wall. The sergeant shook his head and approached.

'What are you doing, Bottle?'

The young man looked up guiltily. 'Uh, not much, Sergeant—'

'Trying a divination,' Cuttle growled, 'and as far as I can tell, getting nowhere.'

Strings slowly crouched down in the circle, opposite Bottle. 'Interesting style there, lad. Sticks and twigs. Where did you pick that up?'

'Grandmother,' he muttered.

'She was a witch?'

'More or less. So was my mother.'

'And your father? What was he?'

'Don't know. There were rumours . . .' He ducked his head, clearly uncomfortable.

'Never mind,' Strings said. 'That's earth-aspected, the pattern you have there. You need more than just what anchors the power . . .'

All the others were staring at Strings now.

Bottle nodded, then drew out a small doll made of woven grasses, a dark, purple-bladed variety. Strips of black cloth were wrapped about it.

The sergeant's eyes widened. 'Who in Hood's name is *that* supposed to be?'

'Well, the hand of death, sort of, or so I wanted it to be. You know, where it's going. But it's not co-operating.'

'You drawing from Hood's warren?'

'A little . . .'

Well, there's more to this lad than I'd first thought. 'Never mind Hood. He may hover, but won't stride forward until after the fact, and even then, he's an indiscriminate bastard. For that figure you've made, try the Patron of Assassins.'

Bottle flinched. 'The Rope? That's too, uh, close . . .'

'What do you mean by that?' Smiles demanded. 'You said you knew Meanas. And now it turns out you know Hood, too. And witchery. I'm starting to think you're just making it all up.'

The mage scowled. 'Fine, then. Now stop flapping your lips. I've got to concentrate.'

The squad settled down once more. Strings fixed his gaze on the various sticks and twigs that had been thrust into the sand before Bottle. After a long moment, the mage slowly set the doll down in their midst, pushing the legs into the sand until the doll stood on its own, then carefully withdrew his hand.

The pattern of sticks on one side ran in a row. Strings assumed that was the Whirlwind Wall, since those sticks began waving, like reeds in the wind.

Bottle was mumbling under his breath, with a growing note of urgency, then frustration. After a moment the breath gusted from him and he sat back, eyes blinking open. 'It's no use—'

The sticks had ceased moving.

'Is it safe to reach in there?' Strings asked.

'Aye, Sergeant.'

Strings reached out and picked up the doll. Then he set it back down . . . on the other side of the Whirlwind Wall. 'Try it now.'

Bottle stared across at him for a moment, then leaned forward and closed his eyes once more.

The Whirlwind Wall began wavering again. Then a number of the sticks along that row toppled.

A gasp from the circle, but Bottle's scowl deepened. 'It's not moving. The doll. I can feel the Rope . . . close, way too close. There's power, pouring into or maybe out of that doll, only it's not moving—'

'You're right,' Strings said, a grin slowly spreading across his features. 'It's not moving. But its shadow is . . .'

Cuttle grunted. 'Queen take me, he's right. That's a damn strange thing – I've seen enough.' He rose suddenly, looking nervous and shaken. 'Magic's creepy. I'm going to bed.'

The divination ended abruptly. Bottle opened his eyes and looked around at the others, his face glistening with sweat. 'Why didn't he move? Why only his shadow?'

Strings stood. 'Because, lad, he isn't ready yet.'

Smiles glared up at the sergeant. 'So, who is he? The Rope himself?'

'No,' Bottle answered. 'No, I'm sure of that.'

Saying nothing, Strings strode from the circle. *No, not the Rope. Someone even better, as far as I am concerned. As far as every Malazan is concerned, for that matter. He's here. And he's on the other side of the Whirlwind Wall. And I know precisely who he's sharpened his knives for.*

Now, if only that damned singing would stop . . .

He stood in the darkness, under siege. Voices assaulted him from all sides, pounding at his skull. It wasn't enough that he had been responsible for the death of soldiers; now they would not leave him alone. Now their spirits screamed at him, ghostly hands reaching out through Hood's Gate, fingers clawing through his brain.

Gamet wanted to die. He had been worse than useless. He had been a liability, joined now to the multitude of incompetent commanders who had left a river of blood in their wake, another name in that sullied, degrading history that fuelled the worst fears of the common soldier.

And it had driven him mad. He understood that now. The voices, the paralysing uncertainty, the way he was always cold, shivering, no matter how hot the daytime sun or how highly banked the nightly hearths. And the weakness, stealing through his limbs, thinning the blood in his veins, until it felt as if his heart was pumping muddy water. *I have been broken. I failed the Adjunct with my very first test of mettle.*

Keneb would be all right. Keneb was a good choice as the legion's new Fist. He was not too old, and he had a family – people to fight for, to return to, people that mattered in his life. Those were important things. A necessary pressure, fire for the blood. None of which existed in Gamet's life.

She has certainly never needed me, has she? The family tore itself apart, and there was nothing I could do about it. I was only a castellan, a glorified house guard. Taking orders. Even when a word from me could have changed Felisin's fate, I just saluted and said, 'Yes, mistress.'

But he had always known his own weakness of spirit. And there had been no shortage of opportunities in which he could demonstrate his flaws, his failures. No shortage at all, even if she saw those moments as ones displaying loyalty, as disciplined acceptance of orders no matter how horrendous their outcome.

'Loud.'

A new voice. Blinking, he looked around, then down, to see Keneb's adopted whelp, Grub. Half naked, sundarkened skin smeared with dirt, his hair a wild tangle, his eyes glittering in the starlight.

'Loud.'

'Yes, they are.' The child was feral. It was late, maybe even nearing dawn. What was he doing up? What was he doing out here, beyond the camp's pickets, inviting butchery by a desert raider?

'Not they. It.'

Gamet frowned down at him. 'What are you talking about? What's loud?' *All I hear is voices – you can't hear them. Of course you can't.*

'The sandstorm. Roars. Very . . . very . . . very very very LOUD!'

The storm? Gamet wiped grit from his eyes and looked around – to find himself not fifty paces from the Whirlwind Wall. And the sound of sand, racing between rocks on the ground, hissing skyward in wild, cavorting loops, the pebbles clattering here and there, the wind itself whirling through sculpted folds in the limestone – the sound was like . . . *like voices. Screaming, angry voices.* 'I am not mad.'

'Me neither. I'm happy. Father has a new shiny ring. Around his arm. It's all carved. He's supposed to give more orders, but he gives less. But I'm still happy. It's very shiny. Do you like shiny things? I do, even though they hurt my eyes. Maybe it's *because* they hurt my eyes. What do you think?'

'I don't think much of anything any more, lad.'

'I think you do too much.'

'Oh, really?'

'Father thinks the same. You think about things there's no point in thinking about. It makes no difference. But I know why you do.'

'You do?'

The lad nodded. 'The same reason I like shiny things. Father's looking for you. I'm going to go tell him I found you.'

Grub ambled away, quickly vanishing in the darkness.

Gamet turned and stared up at the Whirlwind Wall. Its rage buffeted him. The whirling sand tore at his eyes, snatched at his breath. It was hungry, had always been hungry, but something new had arrived, altering its shrill timbre. *What is it?* An urgency, a tone fraught with . . . something.

What am I doing here?

Now he remembered. He had come looking for death. A

raider's blade across his throat. Quick and sudden, if not entirely random.

An end to thinking all those thoughts . . . that so hurt my eyes.

The growing thunder of horse hoofs roused him once more, and he turned to see two riders emerge from the gloom, leading a third horse.

'We've been searching half the night,' Fist Keneb said as they reined in. 'Temul has a third of his Wickans out – all looking for you, sir.'

Sir? That's inappropriate. 'Your child had no difficulty in finding me.'

Keneb frowned beneath the rim of his helm. 'Grub? He came here?'

'He said he was off to tell you he'd found me.'

The man snorted. 'Unlikely. He's yet to say a word to me. Not even in Aren. I've heard he talks to others, when the mood takes him, and that's rare enough. But not me. And no, I don't know why. In any case, we've brought your horse. The Adjunct is ready.'

'Ready for what?'

'To unsheathe her sword, sir. To breach the Whirlwind Wall.'

'She need not wait for me, Fist.'

'True, but she chooses to none the less.'

I don't want to.

'She has commanded it, sir.'

Gamet sighed, walked over to the horse. He was so weak, he had trouble pulling himself onto the saddle. The others waited with maddening patience. Face burning with both effort and shame, Gamet finally clambered onto the horse, spent a moment searching for the stirrups, then took the reins from Temul. 'Lead on,' he growled to Keneb.

They rode parallel to the wall of roaring sand, eastward, maintaining a respectable distance. Two hundred paces along they rode up to a party of five sitting motionless on their horses. The Adjunct, Tene Baralta, Blistig, Nil and Nether.

Sudden fear gripped Gamet. 'Adjunct! A thousand warriors could be waiting on the other side! We need the army drawn up. We need heavy infantry on the flanks. Outriders – archers – marines—'

'That will be enough, Gamet. We ride forward now – the sun already lights the wall. Besides, can you not hear it? Its shriek is filled with fear. A new sound. A pleasing sound.'

He stared up at the swirling barrier of sand. *Yes, that is what I could sense earlier.* 'Then it knows its barrier shall fail.'

'The goddess knows,' Nether agreed.

Gamet glanced at the two Wickans. They looked miserable, a state that seemed more or less permanent with them these days. 'What will happen when the Whirlwind falls?'

The young woman shook her head, but it was her brother who answered, 'The Whirlwind Wall encloses a warren. Destroy the wall, and the warren is breached. Making the goddess vulnerable – had we a battalion of Claw and a half-dozen High Mages, we could hunt her down and kill her. But we can achieve no such thing.' He threw up his hands in an odd gesture. 'The Army of the Apocalypse will remain strengthened by her power. Those soldiers will never break, will fight on to the bitter end. Especially given the likelihood that that end will be ours, not theirs.'

'Your predictions of disaster are unhelpful, Nil,' the Adjunct murmured. 'Accompany me, all of you, until I say otherwise.'

They rode closer to the Whirlwind Wall, leaning in the face of the fierce, battering wind and sand. Fifteen paces from its edge, the Adjunct raised a hand. Then she dismounted, one gloved hand closing on the grip of her sword as she strode forward.

The rust-hued otataral blade was halfway out of its scabbard when a sudden silence descended, and before them the Whirlwind Wall's stentorian violence died, in tumbling clouds of sand and dust. The hiss of sifting rose into the storm's mute wake. A whisper. Burgeoning light. And, then, silence.

The Adjunct wheeled, shock writ on her features.

'She withdrew!' Nil shouted, stumbling forward. 'Our path is clear!'

Tavore threw up a hand to halt the Wickan. 'In answer to my sword, Warlock? Or is this some strategic ploy?'

'Both, I think. She would not willingly take such a wounding, I think. Now, she will rely upon her mortal army.'

The dust was falling like rain, in waves lit gold by the rising sun. And the Holy Desert's heartland was gradually becoming visible through gaps in the dying storm. There was no waiting horde, Gamet saw with a flood of relief. Naught but more wastes, with something like an escarpment on the northeast horizon, falling away as it proceeded west, where strangely broken hills ran in a natural barrier.

The Adjunct climbed back onto her horse. 'Temul. I want scouts out far ahead. I do not believe there will be any more raids. Now, they wait for us, at a place of their own choosing. It falls to us to find it.'

And then will come the battle. The death of hundreds, perhaps thousands of soldiers. The Adjunct, as the fist of the Empress. And Sha'ik, Chosen servant of the goddess. A clash of wills, nothing more. Yet it will decide the fate of hundreds of thousands.

I want nothing to do with this.

Tene Baralta had drawn his horse alongside Gamet. 'We need you now more than ever,' the Red Blade murmured as the Adjunct, with renewed energy, continued conveying orders to the officers now riding up from the main camp.

'You do not need me at all,' Gamet replied.

'You are wrong. She needs a cautious voice—'

'A coward's voice, is the truth of it, and no, she does not need that.'

'There is a fog that comes in battle—'

'I know. I was a soldier, once. And I did well enough at that. Taking orders, commanding no-one but myself. Occasionally a handful, but not thousands. I was at my level of competence, all those years ago.'

'Very well then, Gamet. Become a soldier once more. One who just happens to be attached to the Adjunct's retinue. Give her the perspective of the common soldier. Whatever weakness you feel is not unique – realize that it is shared, by hundreds or even thousands, there in our legions.'

Blistig had come up on the other side, and he now added, 'She remains too remote from us, Gamet. She is without our advice because we have no chance to give it. Worse, we don't know her strategy—'

'Assuming she has one,' Tene Baralta muttered.

'Nor her tactics for this upcoming battle,' Blistig continued. 'It's dangerous, against Malazan military doctrine. She's made this war personal, Gamet.'

Gamet studied the Adjunct, who had now ridden ahead, flanked by Nil and Nether, and seemed to be studying the broken hills beyond which, they all knew, waited Sha'ik and her Army of the Apocalypse. *Personal? Yes, she would do that. Because it is what she has always done.* 'It is how she is. The Empress would not have been ignorant of her character.'

'We will be walking into a carefully constructed trap,' Tene Baralta growled. 'Korbolo Dom will see to that. He'll hold every piece of high ground, he'll command every approach. He might as well paint a big red spot on the ground where he wants us to stand while he kills us.'

'She is not unaware of those possibilities,' Gamet said. *Leave me alone, Tene Baralta. You as well, Blistig. We are not three any more. We are two and one. Talk to Keneb, not me. He can shoulder your expectations. I cannot.* 'We must march to meet them. What else would you have her do?'

'Listen to us, that's what,' Blistig answered. 'We need to

find another approach. Come up from the south, perhaps—'

'And spend more weeks on this march? Don't you think Korbolo would have thought the same? Every waterhole and spring will be fouled. We would wander until Raraku killed us all, with not a single sword raised against us.'

He caught the momentary locking of gazes between Blistig and Tene Baralta. Gamet scowled. 'Conversations like this one will not mend what is broken, sirs. Save your breaths. I have no doubt the Adjunct will call a council of war at the appropriate time.'

'She'd better,' Tene Baralta snapped, gathering his reins and wheeling his horse round.

As he cantered off, Blistig leaned forward and spat. 'Gamet, when that council is called, be there.'

'And if I'm not?'

'We have enough baggage on this train, with all those nobleborn officers and their endless lists of grievances. Soldiers up from the ranks are rare enough in this army – too rare to see even one throw himself away. Granted, I didn't think much of you at first. You were the Adjunct's pet. But you managed your legion well enough—'

'Until the first night we fought the enemy.'

'Where a cusser killed your horse and nearly took your head off.'

'I was addled before then, Blistig.'

'Only because you rode into the skirmish. A Fist should not do that. You stay back, surrounded by messengers and guards. You may find yourself not issuing a single order, but you are the core position none the less, the immovable core. Just being there is enough. They can get word to you, you can get word to them. You can shore up, relieve units, and respond to developments. It's what an officer of high rank does. If you find yourself in the midst of a fight, you are useless, a liability to the soldiers around you, because they're obliged to save your skin. Even worse, you can see nothing, your messengers can't find you. You've lost perspective. If the core wavers or vanishes, the legion falls.'

Gamet considered Blistig's words for a long moment, then he sighed and shrugged. 'None of that matters any more. I am no longer a Fist. Keneb is, and he knows what to do—'

'He's *acting* Fist. The Adjunct made that clear. It's temporary. And it now falls to you to resume your title, and your command.'

'I will not.'

'You have to, you stubborn bastard. Keneb's a damned good captain. Now, there's a nobleborn in that role, replacing him. The man's a damned fool. So long as he was under Keneb's heel he wasn't a problem. You need to return things to their proper order, Gamet. And you need to do it today.'

'How do you know about this new captain? It's not even your legion.'

'Keneb told me. He would rather have promoted one of the sergeants – there's a few with more experience than anyone else in the entire army. They're lying low, but it shows anyway. But the officer corps the Adjunct had to draw from was filled with nobleborn – the whole system was its own private enterprise, exclusionary and corrupt. Despite the Cull, it persists, right here in this army.'

'Besides,' Gamet nodded, 'those sergeants are most useful right where they are.'

'Aye. So cease your selfish sulking, old man, and step back in line.'

The back of Gamet's gloved hand struck Blistig's face hard enough to break his nose and send him pitching backward off the rump of his horse.

He heard another horse reining in nearby and turned to see the Adjunct, a cloud of dust rolling out from under her mount's stamping hoofs. She was staring at him.

Spitting blood, Blistig slowly climbed to his feet.

Grimacing, Gamet walked his horse over to where the Adjunct waited. 'I am ready,' he said, 'to return to duty, Adjunct.'

One brow arched slightly. 'Very good. I feel the need to advise you, however, to give vent to your disagreements with your fellow Fists in more private locations in the future.'

Gamet glanced back. Blistig was busy dusting himself off, but there was a grim smile on his bloodied face.

The bastard. Even so, I owe him a free shot at me, don't I?

'Inform Keneb,' the Adjunct said.

Gamet nodded. 'With your leave, Adjunct, I'd like another word with Fist Blistig.'

'Less dramatic than the last one, I would hope, Fist Gamet.'

'We'll see, Adjunct.'

'Oh?'

'Depends on how patient he is, I suppose.'

'Be on your way then, Fist.'

'Aye, Adjunct.'

Strings and a few other sergeants had climbed up onto a hill – everyone else being busy with breaking camp and preparing for the march – for a clearer view of the collapsed Whirlwind Wall. Sheets of dust were still cascading down, though the freshening wind was quickly tearing through them.

'Not even a whimper,' Gesler sighed behind him.

'The goddess withdrew, is my guess,' Strings said. 'I would bet the Adjunct didn't even draw her sword.'

'Then why raise the wall in the first place?' Borduke wondered.

Strings shrugged. 'Who can say? There are other things going on here in Raraku, things we know nothing about. The world didn't sit still during the months we spent marching here.'

'It was there to keep the Claw out,' Gesler pronounced. 'Both Sha'ik and her goddess want this battle. They want it clean. Soldier against soldier, mage against mage, commander against commander.'

'Too bad for them,' Strings muttered.

'So you've been hinting at. Out with it, Fid.'

'Just a hunch, Gesler. I get those sometimes. They've been infiltrated. That's what I saw from Bottle's divination. The night before the battle, that oasis will get hairy. Wish I could be there to see it. Damn, wish I could be there to help.'

'We'll have our turn being busy, I think,' Gesler muttered.

The last sergeant who had accompanied them sighed, then said in a rasp, 'Moak thinks we won't be busy. Unless the new captain does something stupid. The Adjunct's going to do something unexpected. We may not get a fight at all.'

Strings coughed. 'Where does Moak get all this, Tugg?'

'Squatting over the latrine, is my guess,' Borduke grunted, then spat.

The heavy infantry sergeant shrugged. 'Moak knows things, that's all.'

'And how many times does he get it wrong?' Gesler asked, clearing his throat.

'Hard to say. He says so many things I can't remember them all. He's been right plenty of times, I think. I'm sure of it, in fact. Almost sure.' Tugg faced Strings. 'He says you were in Onearm's Host. And the Empress wants your head on a spike, because you've been outlawed.' The man then turned to Gesler. 'And he says you and your corporal, Stormy, are Old Guard. Underage marines serving Dassem Ultor, or maybe Cartheron Crust or his brother Urko. That you were the ones who brought that old Quon dromon into Aren Harbour with all the wounded from the Chain of Dogs. And you, Borduke, you once threw a nobleborn officer off a cliff, near Karashimesh, only they couldn't prove it, of course.'

The three other men stared at Tugg, saying nothing.

Tugg rubbed his neck. 'Well, that's what he says, anyway.'

'Amazing how wrong he got it all,' Gesler said drily.

'And I take it he's been spreading these tales around?' Strings asked.

'Oh no. Just me and Sobelone. He told us to keep our mouths shut.' Tugg blinked, then added, 'But not with you, obviously, since you already know. I was just making conversation. Just being friendly. Amazing how that Whirlwind Wall just collapsed like that, isn't it?'

Horns sounded in the distance.

'Time to march,' Gesler muttered, 'praise Hood and all . . .'

Keneb rode up alongside Gamet. Their legion had been positioned as rearguard for this day of travel and the dust was thick in the hot air.

'I'm starting to doubt the Whirlwind Wall ever vanished,' Keneb said.

'Aye, there's less we're kicking up than is still coming down,' Gamet replied. He hesitated, then said, 'My apologies, Captain—'

'No need, sir. I am in fact relieved – if you'll excuse the pun. Not just from the pressure of being a Fist, but also because Ranal's promotion was rescinded. It was a pleasure informing him of that. Were you aware he had restructured the units? Using Greymane's arrangements? Of course, Greymane was fighting a protracted war over a huge territory with no defined front. He needed self-contained fighting units, ready for any contingency. Even more irritating, he neglected to inform anyone else.'

'Are you returning the squads to their original placement, Captain?'

'Not yet, sir. Waiting for your word.'

Gamet thought about it for a time. 'I will inform the Adjunct of our legion's new structure.'

'Sir?'

'It might prove useful. We are to hold the rear at the battle, on a broken landscape. Ranal's decision, no doubt made in ignorance, is none the less suitable.'

Keneb sighed, but said nothing, and Gamet well understood. *I may have returned as Fist with the Adjunct's confirmation, but her decision on our positioning has made it clear she's lost confidence in me.*

They rode on in silence, but it was not a comfortable one.

CHAPTER TWENTY-THREE

Who among the pantheon would the Fallen One
despise and fear the most? Consider the last chaining,
in which Hood, Fener, the Queen of Dreams, Osserc
and Oponn all participated, in addition to Anomander
Rake, Caladan Brood and a host of other ascendants.
It is not so surprising, then, that the Crippled God
could not have anticipated that his deadliest enemy
was not found among those mentioned . . .

The Chainings
Istan Hela

'Just because I'm a woman – *all* woman – it doesn't
mean I can cook.'

Cutter glanced across at Apsalar, then said, 'No,
no, it's very good, really—'

But Mogora wasn't finished, waving a grass-snarled
wooden ladle about as she stomped back and forth. 'There's
no larder, nothing at all! And guests! Endless guests! And
is he around to go find us some food? Never! I think he's
dead—'

'He's not dead,' Apsalar cut in, holding her spoon
motionless above the bowl. 'We saw him only a short while
ago.'

'So *you* say, with your shiny hair and pouty lips – and
those breasts – just wait till you start dropping whelps,
they'll be at your ankles one day, big as they are – not the
whelps, the breasts. The whelps will be in your hair – no,

not that shiny hair on your head, well, yes, that hair, but only as a manner of speech. What was I talking about? Yes, I have to go out every day, climbing up and down that rope ladder, scrounging food – yes, that grass is edible, just chew it down. Chew and chew. Every day, armfuls of grasses, tubers, rhizan, cockroaches and bloodflies—'

Both Cutter and Apsalar put down their spoons.

'—and me tripping over my tits. And then!' She waved the ladle, flinging wet grass against a wall. 'Those damned bhok'arala get into my hoard and steal all the yummy bits – every single cockroach and bloodfly! Haven't you noticed? There's no vermin in this ruin anywhere! Not a mouse, not a bug – what's a thousand spiders to do?'

Cautiously, the two guests resumed eating, their sips preceded by close examination of the murky liquid in their spoons.

'And how long do you plan to stay here? What is this, a hostel? How do you expect my husband and me to return to domestic normality? If it's not you it's gods and demons and assassins messing up the bedrooms! Will I ever get peace?' With that she stomped from the room.

After a moment, Cutter blinked and sat straighter. 'Assassins?'

'Kalam Mekhar,' Apsalar replied. 'He left marks, an old Bridgeburner habit.'

'He's back? What happened?'

She shrugged. 'Shadowthrone and Cotillion have, it seems, found use for us all. If I were to guess, Kalam plans on killing as many of Sha'ik's officers as he can.'

'Well, Mogora did raise an interesting question. Cotillion wanted us here, but why? Now what?'

'I have no answers for you, Crokus. It would seem Cotillion's interests lie more with you than with me. Which is not surprising.'

'It isn't? It is to me. Why would you say otherwise?'

She studied him for a moment, then her eyes shifted away. 'Because I am not interested in becoming his servant.

I possess too many of his memories, including his mortal life as Dancer, to be entirely trustworthy.'

'That's not an encouraging statement, Apsalar—'

A new voice hissed from the shadows, 'Encouragement is needed? Simple, easy, unworthy of concern – why can't I think of a solution! Something stupid to say, that should be effortless for me. Shouldn't it?' After a moment, Iskaral Pust edged out from the gloom, sniffing the air. 'She's been . . . *cooking*!' His eyes then lit on the bowls on the table. 'And you've been *eating* it! Are you mad? Why do you think I've been hiding all these months? Why do you think I have my bhok'arala sift through her hoard for the edible stuff? Gods, you fools! Oh yes, fine food . . . if you're an antelope!'

'We're managing,' Cutter said. 'Is there something you want with us? If not, I'm with Mogora on one thing – the less I see of you the better—'

'She wants to see me, you Daru idiot! Why do you think she's always trying to hunt me down?'

'Yes, it's a good act, isn't it? But let's be realistic, Pust, she's happier without you constantly in her face. You're not wanted. Not necessary. In fact, Pust, you are completely useless.'

The High Priest's eyes widened, then he snarled and bolted back into the corner of the room, vanishing into its shadows.

Cutter smiled and leaned back in his chair. 'That worked better than I could have hoped.'

'You have stepped between husband and wife, Crokus. Not a wise decision.'

He narrowed his gaze on her. 'Where do you want to go from here, Apsalar?'

She would not meet his eyes. 'I have not yet made up my mind.'

And Cutter knew that she had.

The spear was a heavy wood, yet surprisingly flexible for its solid feel. Upright, its fluted chalcedony point reached to Trull Sengar's palm when he stood with one arm stretched upward. 'Rather short for my fighting style, but I will make do. I thank you, Ibra Gholan.'

The T'lan Imass swung round and strode to where Monok Ochem waited.

Onrack watched Trull Sengar blow on his hands, then rub them on his tattered buckskin leggings. He flexed the spear shaft once more, then leaned it on one shoulder and faced Onrack. 'I am ready. Although I could do with some furs – this warren is cold, and the wind stinks of ice – we'll have snow by nightfall.'

'We shall be travelling south,' Onrack said. 'Before long, we shall reach the tree line, and the snow will turn to rain.'

'That sounds even more miserable.'

'Our journey, Trull Sengar, shall be less than a handful of days and nights. And in that time we shall travel from tundra to savanna and jungle.'

'Do you believe we will reach the First Throne before the renegades?'

Onrack shrugged. 'It is likely. The path of Tellann will present to us no obstacles, whilst that of chaos shall slow our enemies, for its path is never straight.'

'Never straight, aye. That notion makes me nervous.'

Ah. That is what I am feeling. 'A cause for unease, granted, Trull Sengar. None the less, we are faced with a more dire concern, for when we reach the First Throne we must then defend it.'

Ibra Gholan led the way, Monok Ochem waiting until Onrack and the Tiste Edur passed by before falling in step.

'We are not trusted,' Trull Sengar muttered.

'That is true,' Onrack agreed. 'None the less, we are needed.'

'The least satisfying of alliances.'

'Yet perhaps the surest, until such time as the need passes. We must remain mindful, Trull Sengar.'

The Tiste Edur grunted in acknowledgement.

They fell silent then, as each stride took them further south.

As with so many tracts within Tellann, the scars of Omtose Phellack remained both visible and palpable to Onrack's senses. Rivers of ice had gouged this landscape, tracing the history of advance and, finally, retreat, leaving behind fluvial spans of silts, rocks and boulders in screes, fans and slides, and broad valleys with basins worn down to smooth-humped bedrock. Eventually, permafrost gave way to sodden peat and marshland, wherein stunted black spruce rose in knotted stands on islands formed by the rotted remains of ancestral trees. Pools of black water surrounded these islands, layered with mists and bubbling with the gases of decay.

Insects swarmed the air, finding nothing to their liking among the T'lan Imass and the lone mortal, though they circled in thick, buzzing clouds none the less. Before long, the marshes gave way to upthrust domes of bedrock, the low ground between them steep-sided and tangled with brush and dead pines. The domes then merged, creating a winding bridge of high ground along which the four travelled with greater ease than before.

It began to rain, a steady drizzle that blackened the basaltic bedrock and made it slick.

Onrack could hear Trull Sengar's harsh breathing and sensed his companion's weariness. But no entreaties to rest came from the Tiste Edur, even as he increasingly used his spear as a staff as they trudged onward.

Forest soon replaced the exposed bedrock, slowly shifting from coniferous to deciduous, the hills giving way to flatter ground. The trees then thinned, and suddenly, beyond a line of tangled deadfall, plains stretched before them, and the rain was gone. Onrack raised a hand. 'We shall halt here.'

Ibra Gholan, ten paces ahead, stopped and swung round. 'Why?'

'Food and rest, Ibra Gholan. You may have forgotten

869

that these number among the needs of mortals.'

'I have not forgotten, Onrack the Broken.'

Trull Sengar settled onto the grasses, a wry smile on his lips as he said, 'It's called indifference, Onrack. I am, after all, the least valuable member of this war party.'

'The renegades will not pause in their march,' Ibra Gholan said. 'Nor should we.'

'Then journey ahead,' Onrack suggested.

'No,' Monok Ochem commanded. 'We walk together. Ibra Gholan, a short period of rest will not prove a great inconvenience. Indeed, I would the Tiste Edur speak to us.'

'About what, Bonecaster?'

'Your people, Trull Sengar. What has made them kneel before the Chained One?'

'No easy answer to that question, Monok Ochem.'

Ibra Gholan strode back to the others. 'I shall hunt game,' the warrior said, then vanished in a swirl of dust.

The Tiste Edur studied the fluted spearhead of his new weapon for a moment, then, setting the spear down, he sighed. 'It is a long tale, alas. And indeed, I am no longer the best choice to weave it in a manner you might find useful—'

'Why?'

'Because, Monok Ochem, I am Shorn. I no longer exist. To my brothers, and my people, I *never* existed.'

'Such assertions are meaningless in the face of truth,' Onrack said. 'You are here before us. You exist. As do your memories.'

'There have been Imass who have suffered exile,' Monok Ochem rasped. 'Yet still we speak of them. We must speak of them, to give warning to others. What value a tale if it is not instructive?'

'A very enlightened view, Bonecaster. But mine are not an enlightened people. We care nothing for instruction. Nor, indeed, for truth. Our tales exist to give grandeur to the mundane. Or to give moments of great drama and significance an air of inevitability. Perhaps one might call that "instruction" but that is not their purpose. Every defeat justifies future victory. Every victory is propitious. The Tiste Edur make no misstep, for our dance is one of destiny.'

'And you are no longer in that dance.'

'Precisely, Onrack. Indeed, I never was.'

'Your exile forces you to lie even to yourself, then,' Onrack observed.

'In a manner of speaking, that is true. I am therefore forced to reshape the tale, and that is a difficult thing. There was much of that time that I did not understand at first – certainly not when it occurred. Much of my knowledge did not come to me until much later—'

'Following your Shorning.'

Trull Sengar's almond-shaped eyes narrowed on Onrack, then he nodded. 'Yes.'

As knowledge flowered before my mind's eye in the wake of the Ritual of Tellann's shattering. Very well, this I understand. 'Prepare for the telling of your tale, Trull Sengar. If instruction can be found within it, recognition is the responsibility of those to whom the tale is told. You are absolved of the necessity.'

Monok Ochem grunted, then said, 'These words are spurious. Every story instructs. The teller ignores this truth at peril. Excise yourself from the history you would convey if you must, Trull Sengar. The only lesson therein is one of humility.'

Trull Sengar grinned up at the bonecaster. 'Fear not, I was never pivotal among the players. As for excision, well, that has already occurred, and so I would tell the tale of the Tiste Edur who dwelt north of Lether as would they themselves tell it. With one exception – which has, I admit, proved most problematic in my mind – and that is, there will be no aggrandizement in my telling. No revelling in glory, no claims of destiny or inevitability. I shall endeavour, then, to be other than the Tiste Edur I appear to be, to tear away my cultural identity and so cleanse the tale—'

'Flesh does not lie,' Monok Ochem said. 'Thus, we are not deceived.'

'Flesh may not lie, but the spirit can, Bonecaster. Instruct yourself in blindness and indifference – I in turn intend to attempt the same.'

'When will you begin your tale?'

'At the First Throne, Monok Ochem. Whilst we await the coming of the renegades . . . and their Tiste Edur allies.'

Ibra Gholan reappeared with a broken-necked hare, which he skinned in a single gesture, then flung the blood-smeared body to the ground beside Trull Sengar. 'Eat,' the warrior instructed, tossing the skin aside.

Onrack moved off while the Tiste Edur made preparations for a fire. He was, he reflected, disturbed by Trull Sengar's words. The Shorning had made much of excising the physical traits that would identify Trull Sengar as Tiste Edur. The bald pate, the scarred brow. But these physical alterations were as nothing, it appeared, when compared to those forced upon the man's spirit. Onrack realized that he had grown comfortable in Trull Sengar's company, lulled, perhaps, by the Edur's steady manner, his ease with hardship and extremity. Such comfort was deceiving, it now seemed. Trull Sengar's calm was born of scars, of healing that left one insensate. His heart was incomplete. *He is as a T'lan Imass, yet clothed in mortal flesh. We ask that he resurrect his memories of life, then wonder at his struggle to satisfy our demands. The failure is ours, not his.*

We speak of those we have exiled, yet not to warn – as Monok Ochem claims. No, nothing so noble. We speak of them in reaffirmation of our judgement. But it is our intransigence that finds itself fighting the fiercest war – with time itself, with the changing world around us.

'I will preface my tale,' Trull Sengar was saying as he roasted the skinned hare, 'with an admittedly cautionary observation.'

'Tell me this observation,' Monok Ochem said.

'I shall, Bonecaster. It concerns nature . . . and the exigency of maintaining a balance.'

Had he possessed a soul, Onrack would have felt it grow cold as ice. As it was, the warrior slowly turned in the wake of Trull Sengar's words.

'Pressures and forces are ever in opposition,' the Edur was saying as he rotated the spitted hare over the flames. 'And the striving is ever towards a balance. This is beyond the gods, of course – it is the current of existence – but no, beyond even that, for existence itself is opposed by oblivion. It is a struggle that encompasses all, that defines every island in the Abyss. Or so I now believe. Life is answered by death. Dark by light. Overwhelming success by catastrophic failure. Horrific curse by breathtaking blessing. It seems the inclination of all people to lose sight of that truth, particularly when blinded by triumph upon triumph. See before me, if you will, this small fire. A modest victory . . . but if I feed it, my own eager delight is answered, until this entire plain is aflame, then the forest, then the world itself. Thus, an assertion of wisdom here . . . in the quenching of these flames once this meat is cooked. After all, igniting this entire world will also kill everything in it, if not in flames then in subsequent starvation. Do you see my point, Monok Ochem?'

'I do not, Trull Sengar. This prefaces nothing.'

Onrack spoke. 'You are wrong, Monok Ochem. It prefaces . . . *everything*.'

Trull Sengar glanced over, and answered with a smile.

Of sadness overwhelming. Of utter . . . despair.

And the undead warrior was shaken.

A succession of ridges ribboned the landscape, seeming to slowly melt as sand drifted down from the sky.

'Soon,' Pearl murmured, 'those beach ridges will vanish once more beneath dunes.'

Lostara shrugged. 'We're wasting time,' she pronounced,

then set off towards the first ridge. The air was thick with settling dust and sand, stinging the eyes and parching the throat. Yet the haze served to draw the horizons closer, to make their discovery increasingly unlikely. The sudden demise of the Whirlwind Wall suggested that the Adjunct and her army had reached Raraku, were even now marching upon the oasis. She suspected that there would be few, if any, scouts patrolling the northeast approaches.

Pearl had announced that it was safe now to travel during the day. The goddess had drawn inward, concentrating her power for, perhaps, one final, explosive release. For the clash with the Adjunct. A singularity of purpose locked in rage, a flaw that could be exploited.

She allowed herself a private smile at that. *Flaws. No shortage of those hereabouts, is there?* Their moment of wild passion had passed, as far as she was concerned. The loosening of long pent-up energies – now that it was done, they could concentrate on other things. More important things. It seemed, however, that Pearl saw it differently. He'd even tried to take her hand this morning, a gesture that she decisively rebuffed despite its pathos. The deadly assassin was on the verge of transforming into a squirming pup – disgust threatened to overwhelm her, so she shifted her thoughts onto another track.

They were running short on time, not to mention food and water. Raraku was a hostile land, resentful of whatever life dared exploit it. *Not holy at all, but cursed. Devourer of dreams, destroyer of ambitions. And why not? It's a damned desert.*

Clambering over the cobbles and stones, they reached the first ridge.

'We're close,' Pearl said, squinting ahead. 'Beyond that higher terrace, we should come within sight of the oasis.'

'And then what?' she asked, brushing dust from her tattered clothes.

'Well, it would be remiss of me not to take advantage of our position – I should be able to infiltrate the camp and stir up some trouble. Besides,' he added, 'one of the trails I am on leads into the heart of that rebel army.'

The Talons. The master of that revived cult. 'Are you so certain of that?'

He nodded, then half shrugged. 'Reasonably. I have come to believe that the rebellion was compromised long ago, perhaps from the very start. That the aim of winning independence for Seven Cities was not quite as central to some as it should have been, and indeed, that those hidden motives are about to be unveiled.'

'And it is inconceivable to you that such unveilings should occur without your hand in their midst.'

He glanced at her. 'My dear, you forget, I am an agent of the Malazan Empire. I have certain responsibilities . . .'

Her eyes lit on an object lying among the cobbles – a momentary recognition, then her gaze quickly shifted away. She studied the murky sky. 'Has it not occurred to you that your arrival might well jeopardize missions already under way in the rebel camp? The Empress does not know you're here. In fact, even the Adjunct likely believes we are far away from this place.'

'I am not uncomfortable with a supporting role—'

Lostara snorted.

'Well,' he amended, 'such a role is not entirely reprehensible. I can live with it.'

Liar. She settled down on one knee to adjust the greaves lashed to her leather-clad shins. 'We should be able to make that terrace before the sun sets.'

'Agreed.'

She straightened.

They made their way down the rock-studded slope. The ground was littered with the tiny, shrivelled bodies of countless desert creatures that had been swept up into the Whirlwind, dying within that interminable storm yet remaining suspended within it until, with the wind's sudden death, falling to earth once more. They had rained down for a full day, husks clattering and crunching on all sides, pattering on her helm and skidding from her shoulders. Rhizan, capemoths and other minuscule creatures, for the most part, although occasionally something larger had thumped to the ground. Lostara was thankful that the downpour had ended.

'The Whirlwind has not been friendly to Raraku,' Pearl commented, kicking aside the corpse of an infant bhok'aral.

'Assuming the desert cares one way or another, which it doesn't, I doubt it will make much difference in the long run. A land's lifetime is far vaster than anything with which we are familiar, vaster, by far, than the spans of these hapless creatures. Besides, Raraku is already mostly dead.'

'Appearances deceive. There are deep spirits in this Holy Desert, lass. Buried in the rock—'

'And the life upon that rock, like the sands,' Lostara asserted, 'means nothing to those spirits. You are a fool to think otherwise, Pearl.'

'I am a fool to think many things,' he muttered.

'Do not expect me to object to that observation.'

'It never crossed my mind that you might, Lostara Yil. In any case, I would none the less advise that you cultivate a healthy respect for the mysteries of Raraku. It is far too easy to be blindsided in this seemingly empty and lifeless desert.'

'As we've already discovered.'

He frowned, then sighed. 'I regret that you view ... things that way, and can only conclude that you derive a peculiar satisfaction from discord, and when it does not exist – or, rather, has no reason to exist – you seek to invent it.'

'You think too much, Pearl. It's your most irritating flaw, and, let us be honest, given the severity and sheer volume of your flaws, that is saying something. Since this seems to be a time for advice, I suggest you stop thinking entirely.'

'And how might I achieve that? Follow your lead, perhaps?'

'I think neither too much nor too little. I am perfectly

balanced – this is what you find so attractive. As a cape-moth is drawn to fire.'

'So I am in danger of being burned up?'

'To a blackened, shrivelled crust.'

'So, you're pushing me away for my own good. A gesture of compassion, then.'

'Fires neither push nor pull. They simply exist, compassionless, indifferent to the suicidal urges of flitting bugs. That is another one of your flaws, Pearl. Attributing emotion where none exists.'

'I could have sworn there *was* emotion, two nights past—'

'Oh, fire burns eagerly when there's fuel—'

'And in the morning there's naught but cold ashes.'

'Now you are beginning to understand. Of course, you will see that as encouragement, and so endeavour to take your understanding further. But that would be a waste of time, so I suggest you abandon the effort. Be content with the glimmer, Pearl.'

'I see ... murkily. Very well, I will accept your list of advisements.'

'You will? Gullibility is a most unattractive flaw, Pearl.'

She thought he would scream, was impressed by his sudden clamping of control, releasing his breath like steam beneath a cauldron's lid, until the pressure died away.

They approached the ascent to the last ridge, Lostara at her most contented thus far this day, Pearl likely to be feeling otherwise.

As they reached the crest the Claw spoke again. 'What was that you picked up on the last ridge, lass?'

Saw that, did you? 'A shiny rock. Caught my eye. I've since discarded it.'

'Oh? So it no longer hides in that pouch on your belt?'

Snarling, she plucked the leather bag from her belt and flung it to the ground, then drew out her chain-backed gauntlets. 'See for yourself, then.'

He gave her a startled glance, then bent down to collect the pouch.

As he straightened, Lostara stepped forward.

Her gauntlets cracked hard against Pearl's temple.

Groaning, he collapsed unconscious.

'Idiot,' she muttered, retrieving the pouch.

She donned the gauntlets, then, with a grunt, lifted the man and settled him over one shoulder.

Less than two thousand paces ahead lay the oasis, the air above it thick with dust and the smoke of countless fires. Herds of goats were visible along the fringes, in the shade of trees. The remnants of a surrounding wall curved roughly away in both directions.

Carrying Pearl, Lostara made her way down the slope.

She was nearing the base when she heard horses off to her right. Crouching down and thumping Pearl to the ground beside her, she watched as a dozen desert warriors rode into view, coming from the northwest. Their animals looked half starved, heads hanging low, and she saw, among them, two prisoners.

Despite the dust covering them, and the gloom of approaching dusk, Lostara recognized the remnants of uniforms on the two prisoners. *Malazans. Ashok Regiment. Thought they'd been wiped out.*

The warriors rode without outriders, and did not pause in their steady canter until they reached the oasis, whereupon they vanished beneath the leather-leaved branches of the trees.

Lostara looked around and decided that her present surroundings were ideal for staying put for the night. A shallow basin in the lee of the slope. By lying flat they would not be visible from anywhere but the ridge itself, and even that was unlikely with night fast falling. She checked on Pearl, frowning at the purple-ringed bump on his temple. But his breathing was steady, the beat of his heart unhurried and even. She laid out his cloak and rolled him onto it, then bound and gagged him.

As gloom gathered in the basin, Lostara settled down to wait.

Some time later a figure emerged from the shadows and stood motionless for a moment before striding silently to halt directly over Pearl.

Lostara heard a muted grunt. 'You came close to cracking open his skull.'

'It's harder than you think,' she replied.

'Was it entirely necessary?'

'I judged it so. If you've no faith in that, then why recruit me in the first place?'

Cotillion sighed. 'He's not a bad man, you know. Loyal to the empire. You have sorely abused his equanimity.'

'He was about to interfere. Unpredictably. I assumed you wished the path clear.'

'Initially, yes. But I foresee a certain usefulness to his presence, once matters fully . . . unfold. Be sure to awaken him some time tomorrow night, if he has not already done so on his own.'

'Very well, since you insist. Although I am already deeply fond of my newfound peace and solitude.'

Cotillion seemed to study her a moment, then the god said, 'I will leave you then, since I have other tasks to attend to this night.'

Lostara reached into the pouch and tossed a small object towards him.

He caught it in one hand and peered down to study it.

'I assumed that was yours,' she said.

'No, but I know to whom it belongs. And am pleased. May I keep it?'

She shrugged. 'It matters not to me.'

'Nor should it, Lostara Yil.'

She heard a dry amusement in those words, and concluded that she had made a mistake in letting him keep the object; that, indeed, it *did* matter to her, though for the present she knew not how. She shrugged again. *Too late now, I suppose.* 'You said you were leaving?'

She sensed him bridling, then in a swirl of shadows he vanished.

Lostara lay back on the stony ground and contentedly closed her eyes.

The night breeze was surprisingly warm. Apsalar stood before the small window overlooking the gully. Neither Mogora nor Iskaral Pust frequented these heights much, except when necessity forced them to undertake an excursion in search of food, and so her only company was a half-dozen elderly bhok'arala, grey-whiskered and grunting and snorting as they stiffly moved about on the chamber's littered floor. The scattering of bones suggested that this top level of the tower was where the small creatures came to die.

As the bhok'arala shuffled back and forth behind her, she stared out onto the wastes. The sand and outcrops of limestone were silver in the starlight. On the rough tower walls surrounding the window rhizan were landing with faint slaps, done with their feeding, and now, claws whispering, they began crawling into cracks to hide from the coming day.

Crokus slept somewhere below, whilst resident husband and wife stalked each other down the unlit corridors and in the musty chambers of the monastery. She had never felt so alone, nor, she realized, so comfortable with that solitude. Changes had come to her. Hardened layers sheathing her soul had softened, found new shape in response to unseen pressures from within.

Strangest of all, she had come, over time, to despise her competence, her deadly skills. They had been imposed upon her, forced into her bones and muscles. They had imprisoned her in blinding, gelid armour. And so, despite the god's absence, she still felt as if she was two women, not one.

Leading her to wonder with which woman Crokus had fallen in love.

But no, there was no mystery there. He had assumed the guise of a killer, hadn't he? The young wide-eyed thief from Darujhistan had fashioned of himself a dire reflection – not of Apsalar the fisher-girl, but of Apsalar the assassin, the cold murderer. In the belief that likeness would forge the deepest bond of all. Perhaps that would have succeeded, had she *liked* her profession, had she not found it sordid and reprehensible. Had it not felt like chains wrapped tight about her soul.

She was not comforted by company within her prison. His love was for the wrong woman, the wrong Apsalar. And hers was for Crokus, not Cutter. And so they were together, yet apart, intimate yet strangers, and it seemed there was nothing they could do about it.

The assassin within her preferred solitude, and the fisher-girl had, from an entirely different path, come into a similar comfort. The former could not afford to love. The latter knew she had never been loved. Like Crokus, she stood in a killer's shadow.

There was no point in railing against that. The fisher-girl had no life-skills of a breadth and stature to challenge the assassin's implacable will. Probably, Crokus had similarly succumbed to Cutter.

She sensed a presence close by her side, and murmured, 'Would that you had taken all with you when you departed.'

'You'd rather I left you bereft?'

'Bereft, Cotillion? No. Innocent.'

'Innocence is only a virtue, lass, when it is temporary. You must pass from it to look back and recognize its un-sullied purity. To remain innocent is to twist beneath invisible and unfathomable forces all your life, until one day you realize that you no longer recognize yourself, and it comes to you that innocence was a curse that had shackled you, stunted you, defeated your every expression of living.'

She smiled in the darkness. 'But, Cotillion, it is know-ledge that makes one aware of his or her own chains.'

'Knowledge only makes the eyes see what was there all along, Apsalar. You are in possession of formidable skills. They gift you with power, a truth there is little point in denying. You cannot unmake yourself.'

'But I can cease walking this singular path.'

'You can,' he acknowledged after a moment. 'You can choose others, but even the privilege of choice was won by virtue of what you were—'

'What *you* were.'

'Nor can that be changed. I walked in your bones, your flesh, Apsalar. The fisher-girl who became a woman – we stood in each other's shadow.'

'And did you enjoy that, Cotillion?'

'Not particularly. It was difficult to remain mindful of my purpose. We were in worthy company for most of that time – Whiskeyjack, Mallet, Fiddler, Kalam . . . a squad that, given the choice, would have welcomed you. But I prevented them from doing so. Necessary, but not fair to you or them.' He sighed, then continued, 'I could speak endlessly of regrets, lass, but I see dawn stealing the darkness, and I must have your decision.'

'My decision? Regarding what?'

'Cutter.'

She studied the desert, found herself blinking back tears. 'I would take him from you, Cotillion. I would prevent you doing to him what you did to me.'

'He is that important to you?'

'He is. Not to the assassin within me, but to the fisher-girl . . . whom he does not love.'

'Doesn't he?'

'He loves the assassin, and so chooses to be like her.'

'I understand now the struggle within you.'

'Indeed? Then you must understand why I will not let you have him.'

'But you are wrong, Apsalar. Cutter does not love the assassin within you. It attracts him, no doubt, because power does that . . . to us all. And you possess power, and

882

that implicitly includes the option of not using it. All very enticing, alluring. He is drawn to emulate what he sees as your hard-won freedom. But his love? Resurrect our shared memories, lass. Of Darujhistan, of our first brush with the thief, Crokus. He saw that we had committed murder, and knew that discovery made his life forfeit in our eyes. Did he love you then? No, that came later, in the hills east of the city – when I no longer possessed you.'

'Love changes with time—'

'Aye, it does, but not like a capemoth flitting from corpse to corpse on a battlefield.' He cleared his throat. 'Very well, a poor choice of analogy. Love changes, aye, in the manner of growing to encompass as much of its subject as possible. Virtues, flaws, limitations, everything – love will fondle them all, with child-like fascination.'

She had drawn her arms tight about herself with his words. 'There are two women within me—'

'Two? There are multitudes, lass, and Cutter loves them all.'

'I don't want him to die!'

'Is that your decision?'

She nodded, not trusting herself to speak. The sky was lightening, transforming into a vast, empty space above a dead, battered landscape. She saw birds climb the winds into its expanse.

Cotillion persisted, 'Do you know, then, what you must do?'

Once again, Apsalar nodded.

'I am . . . pleased.'

Her head snapped round, and she stared into his face, seeing it fully, she realized, for the first time. The lines bracketing the calm, soft eyes, the even features, the strange hatch pattern of scars beneath his right eye. 'Pleased,' she whispered, studying him. 'Why?'

'Because,' he answered with a faint smile, 'I like the lad, too.'

'How brave do you think I am?'

'As brave as is necessary.'

'Again.'

'Aye. Again.'

'You don't seem much like a god at all, Cotillion.'

'I'm not a god in the traditional fashion, I am a patron. Patrons have responsibilities. Granted, I rarely have the opportunity to exercise them.'

'Meaning they are not yet burdensome.'

His smile broadened, and it was a lovely smile. 'You are worth far more for your lack of innocence, Apsalar. I will see you again soon.' He stepped back into the shadows of the chamber.

'Cotillion.'

He paused, arms half raised. 'Yes.'

'Thank you. And take care of Cutter. Please.'

'I will, as if he were my own son, Apsalar. I will.'

She nodded, and then he was gone.

And, a short while later, so was she.

There were snakes in this forest of stone. Fortunately for Kalam Mekhar, they seemed to lack the natural belligerence of their kind. He was lying in shadows amidst the dusty, shattered fragments of a toppled tree, motionless as serpents slithered around him and over him. The stone was losing its chill from the night just past, a hot wind drifting in from the desert beyond.

He had seen no sign of patrols, and little in the way of well-trod trails. None the less, he sensed a presence in this petrified forest, hinting of power that did not belong on this world. Though he could not be certain, he sensed something demonic about that power.

Sufficient cause for unease. Sha'ik might well have placed guardians, and he would have to get past those.

The assassin lifted a flare-neck to one side then drew his two long-knives. He examined the grips, ensuring that the leather bindings were tight. He checked the fittings of the hilts and pommels. The edge of the otataral long-knife's blade was slightly rough – otataral was not an ideal metal for weapons. It cut ragged and needed constant sharpening, even when it had seen no use, and the iron had a tendency to grow brittle over time. Before the Malazan conquest, otataral had been employed by the highborn of Seven Cities in their armour for the most part. Its availability had been tightly regulated, although less so than when under imperial control.

Few knew the full extent of its properties. When absorbed through the skin or breathed into the lungs for long periods, its effects were varied and unpredictable. It often failed in the face of Elder magic, and there was another characteristic that Kalam suspected few were aware of – a discovery made entirely by accident during a battle outside Y'Ghatan. Only a handful of witnesses survived the incident, Kalam and Quick Ben among them, and all had agreed afterwards that their reports to their officers would be deliberately vague, questions answered by shrugs and shakes of the head.

Otataral, it seemed, did not go well with Moranth munitions, particularly burners and flamers. *Or, to put it another way, it doesn't like getting hot.* He knew that weapons were quenched in otataral dust at a late stage in their forging. When the iron had lost its glow, in fact. Likely, blacksmiths had arrived at that conclusion the hard way. But even that was not the whole secret. *It's what happens to hot otataral . . . when you throw magic at it.*

He slowly resheathed the weapon, then focused his attention on the other. Here, the edge was smooth, slightly wavy as often occurred with rolled, multi-layered blades. The water etching was barely visible on this gleaming, black surface, the silver inlay fine as thread. Between the two long-knives, he favoured this one, for its weight and balance.

Something struck the ground beside him, bouncing with a pinging sound off a fragment of tree trunk, then rattling to a stop down beside his right knee.

Kalam stared at the small object for a moment. He then looked up at the tree looming over him. He smiled. 'Ah, an oak,' he murmured. 'Let it not be said I don't appreciate the humour of the gesture.' He sat up and reached down to collect the acorn. Then leaned back once more. 'Just like old times . . . glad, as always, that we don't do this sort of thing any more . . .'

Plains to savanna, then, finally, jungle. They had arrived in the wet season, and the morning suffered beneath a torrential deluge before, just past noon, the sun burned through to lade the air with steam as the three T'lan Imass and one Tiste Edur trudged through the thick, verdant undergrowth.

Unseen animals fled their onward march, thrashing heavily through the brush on all sides. Eventually, they stumbled onto a game trail that led in the direction they sought, and their pace increased.

'This is not your natural territory, is it, Onrack?' Trull Sengar asked between gasps of the humid, rank air. 'Given all the furs your kind wear . . .'

'True,' the T'lan Imass replied. 'We are a cold weather people. But this region exists within our memories. Before the Imass, there was another people, older, wilder. They dwelt where it was warm, and they were tall, their dark skins covered in fine hair. These we knew as the Eres. Enclaves survived into our time – the time captured within this warren.'

'And they lived in jungles like this one?'

'Its verges, occasionally, but more often the surrounding savannas. They worked in stone, but with less skill than us.'

'Were there bonecasters among them?'

Monok Ochem answered from behind them. 'All Eres were bonecasters, Trull Sengar. For they were the first to carry the spark of awareness, the first so gifted by the spirits.'

'And are they now gone, Monok Ochem?'

'They are.'

Onrack added nothing to that. After all, if Monok Ochem found reasons to deceive, Onrack could find none to contradict the bonecaster. It did not matter in any case. No Eres had ever been discovered in the Warren of Tellann.

After a moment, Trull Sengar asked, 'Are we close, Onrack?'

'We are.'

'And will we then return to our own world?'

'We shall. The First Throne lies at the base of a crevasse, beneath a city—'

'The Tiste Edur,' Monok Ochem cut in, 'has no need for learning the name of that city, Onrack the Broken. He already knows too much of our people.'

'What I know of you T'lan Imass hardly qualifies as secrets,' Trull Sengar said. 'You prefer killing to negotiation. You do not hesitate to murder gods when the opportunity arises. And you prefer to clean up your own messes – laudable, this last one. Unfortunately, this particular mess is too big, though I suspect you are still too proud to admit to that. As for your First Throne, I am not interested in discovering its precise location. Besides, I'm not likely to survive the clash with your renegade kin.'

'That is true,' Monok Ochem agreed.

'You will likely make sure of it,' Trull Sengar added.

The bonecaster said nothing.

There was no need to, Onrack reflected. *But I shall defend him. Perhaps Monok and Ibra understand this, and so they will strike at me first. It is what I would do, were I in their place. Which, oddly enough, I am.*

The trail opened suddenly into a clearing filled with bones. Countless beasts of the jungle and savanna had been dragged here by, Onrack surmised, leopards or hyenas. The longbones he noted were all gnawed and split open by powerful jaws. The air reeked of rotted flesh and flies swarmed in the thousands.

'The Eres did not fashion holy sites of their own,' Monok Ochem said, 'but they understood that there were places where death gathered, where life was naught but memories, drifting lost and bemused. And, to such places, they would often bring their own dead. Power gathers in layers – this is the birthplace of the sacred.'

'And so you have transformed it into a gate,' Trull Sengar said.

'Yes,' the bonecaster replied.

'You are too eager to credit the Imass, Monok Ochem,' Onrack said. He faced the Tiste Edur. 'Eres holy sites burned through the barriers of Tellann. They are too old to be resisted.'

'You said their sanctity was born of death. Are they Hood's, then?'

'No. Hood did not exist when these were fashioned, Trull Sengar. Nor are they strictly death-aspected. Their power comes, as Monok Ochem said, from layers. Stone shaped into tools and weapons. Air shaped by throats. Minds that discovered, faint as flickering fires in the sky, the recognition of oblivion, of an *end* . . . to life, to love. Eyes that witnessed the struggle to survive, and saw with wonder its inevitable failure. To know and to understand that we must all die, Trull Sengar, is not to worship death. To know and to understand is itself magic, for it made us stand tall.'

'It seems, then,' Trull Sengar muttered, 'that you Imass have broken the oldest laws of all, with your Vow.'

'Neither Monok Ochem nor Ibra Gholan will speak in answer to that truth,' Onrack said. 'You are right, however. We are the first lawbreakers, and that we have survived this long is fit punishment. And so, it remains our hope that the Summoner will grant us absolution.'

'Faith is a dangerous thing,' Trull Sengar sighed. 'Well, shall we make use of this gate?'

Monok Ochem gestured, and the scene around them blurred, the light fading.

A moment before the darkness became absolute, a faint shout from the Tiste Edur drew Onrack's attention. The warrior turned, in time to see a figure standing a dozen paces away. Tall, lithely muscled, with a fine umber-hued pelt and long, shaggy hair reaching down past the shoulders. A woman. Her breasts were large and pendulous, her hips wide and full. Prominent, flaring cheekbones, a broad, full-lipped mouth. All this registered in an instant, even as the woman's dark brown eyes, shadowed beneath a solid brow, scanned across the three T'lan Imass before fixing on Trull Sengar.

She took a step towards the Tiste Edur, the movement graceful as a deer's—

Then the light vanished entirely.

Onrack heard another surprised shout from Trull Sengar. The T'lan Imass strode towards the sound, then halted, thoughts suddenly scattering, a flash of images cascading through the warrior's mind. Time folding in on itself, sinking away, then rising once more—

Sparks danced low to the ground, tinder caught, flames flickering.

They were in the crevasse, standing on its littered floor. Onrack looked for Trull Sengar, found the Tiste Edur lying prone on the damp rock a half-dozen paces away.

The T'lan Imass approached.

The mortal was unconscious. There was blood smearing his lap, pooling beneath his crotch, and Onrack could see it cooling, suggesting that it did not belong to Trull Sengar, but to the Eres woman who had . . . taken his seed.

His first seed. But there had been nothing to her appearance suggesting virginity. Her breasts had swollen with milk in the past; her nipples had known the pressure of a pup's hunger. The blood, then, made no sense.

Onrack crouched beside Trull Sengar.

And saw the fresh wound of scarification beneath his belly button. Three parallel cuts, drawn across diagonally, and the stained imprints of three more – likely those the

889

woman had cut across her own belly – running in the opposite direction.

'The Eres witch has stolen his seed,' Monok Ochem said from two paces away.

'Why?' Onrack asked.

'I do not know, Onrack the Broken. The Eres have the minds of beasts—'

'Not to the exclusion of all else,' Onrack replied, 'as you well know.'

'Perhaps.'

'Clearly, this one had intent.'

Monok Ochem nodded. 'So it would seem. Why does the Tiste Edur remain unconscious?'

'His mind is elsewhere—'

The bonecaster cocked its head. 'Yes, that is the definition of unconscious—'

'No, it is *elsewhere*. When I stepped close, I came into contact with sorcery. That which the Eres projected. For lack of any other term, it was a warren, barely formed, on the very edge of oblivion. It was,' Onrack paused, then continued, 'like the Eres themselves. A glimmer of light behind the eyes.'

Ibra Gholan suddenly drew his weapon.

Onrack straightened.

There were sounds, now, beyond the fire's light, and the T'lan Imass could see the glow of flesh and blood bodies, a dozen, then a score. Something else approached, the footfalls uneven and shambling.

A moment later, an aptorian demon loomed into the light, a shape unfolding like black silk. And riding its humped, singular shoulder, a youth. Its body was human, yet its face held the features of the aptorian – a massive, lone eye, glistening and patterned like honeycomb. A large mouth, now opening to reveal needle fangs that seemed capable of retracting, all but their tips vanishing from sight. The rider wore black leather armour, shaped like scales and overlapping. A chest harness bore at least a dozen weapons, ranging from long-knives to throwing darts. Affixed to the youth's belt were two single-hand crossbows, their grips fashioned from the base shafts of antlers.

The rider leaned forward over the spiny, humped shoulder. Then spoke in a low, rasping voice. 'Is this all that Logros can spare?'

'You,' Monok Ochem said, 'are not welcome.'

'Too bad, Bonecaster, for we are here. To guard the First Throne.'

Onrack asked, 'Who are you, and who has sent you here?'

'I am Panek, son of Apt. It is not for me to answer your other question, T'lan Imass. I but guard the outer ward. The chamber that is home to the First Throne possesses an inner warden – the one who commands us. Perhaps she can answer you. Perhaps, even, she will.'

Onrack picked up Trull Sengar. 'We would speak with her, then.'

Panek smiled, revealing the crowded row of fangs. 'As I said, the Throne Room. No doubt,' he added, smile broadening, 'you know the way.'

CHAPTER TWENTY-FOUR

In the oldest, most fragmentary of texts, will be found
obscure mention of the Eres'al, a name that seems to
refer to those most ancient of spirits that are the
essence of the physical world. There is, of course, no
empirical means of determining whether the
attribution of meaning – the power inherent in making
symbols of the inanimate – was causative, in essence
the creative force behind the Eres'al; or if some other
mysterious power was involved, inviting the accretion
of meaning and significance by intelligent forms of life
at some later date.

In either case, what cannot be refuted is the rarely
acknowledged but formidable power that exists like
subterranean layers in notable features of the land; nor
that such power is manifested with subtle yet profound
efficacy, even so much as to twist the stride of gods –
indeed, occasionally sufficient to bring them down
with finality . . .

Preface to the *Compendium of Maps*
Kellarstellis of Li Heng

The vast shelves and ridges of coral had been
worn into flat-topped islands by millennia of
drifting sand and wind. Their flanks were ragged
and rotted, pitted and undercut, the low ground in
between them narrow, twisting and filled with sharp-edged
rubble. To Gamet's eye, the gods could not have chosen

a less suitable place to encamp an army.

Yet there seemed little choice. Nowhere else offered an approach onto the field of battle, and, as quickly became evident, the position, once taken, was as defensible as the remotest mountain keep: a lone saving grace.

Tavore's headlong approach into the maw of the enemy, to the battleground of their choosing, was, the Fist suspected, the primary source of the unease and vague confusion afflicting the legions. He watched the soldiers proceeding, in units of a hundred, on their way to taking and holding various coral islands overlooking the basin. Once in place, they would then construct from the rubble defensive barriers and low walls, followed by ramps on the south sides.

Captain Keneb shifted nervously on his saddle beside the Fist as they watched the first squads of their own legion set out towards a large, bone-white island on the westernmost edge of the basin. 'They won't try to dislodge us from these islands,' he said. 'Why bother, since it's obvious the Adjunct intends to march us right into their laps?'

Gamet was not deaf to the criticisms and doubt hidden beneath Keneb's words, and he wished he could say something to encourage the man, to bolster faith in Tavore's ability to formulate and progress sound tactics. But even the Fist was unsure. There had been no sudden revelation of genius during the march from Aren. They had, in truth, walked straight as a lance northward. *Suggesting what, exactly? A singlemindedness worthy of imitation, or a failure of imagination? Are the two so different, or merely alternate approaches to the same thing?* And now they were being arrayed, as stolid as ever, to advance – probably at dawn the next day – towards the enemy and their entrenched fortifications. An enemy clever enough to create singular and difficult approaches to their positions.

'Those ramps will see the death of us all,' Keneb muttered. 'Korbolo Dom's prepared for this, as any competent, Malazan-trained commander would. He wants us crowded and struggling uphill, beneath an endless hail of arrows, quarrels and ballista, not to mention sorcery. Look at how smooth he's made those ramp surfaces, Fist. The cobbles, when slick with streaming blood, will be like grease underfoot. We'll find no purchase—'

'I am not blind,' Gamet growled. 'Nor, we must assume, is the Adjunct.'

Keneb shot the older man a look. 'It would help to have some reassurance of that, Fist.'

'There shall be a meeting of officers tonight,' Gamet replied. 'And again a bell before dawn.'

'She's already decided the disposition of our legion,' Keneb grated, leaning on his saddle and spitting in the local fashion.

'Aye, she has, Captain.' They were to guard avenues of retreat, not for their own forces, but those the enemy might employ. A premature assumption of victory that whispered of madness. They were outnumbered. Every advantage was with Sha'ik, yet almost one-third of the Adjunct's army would not participate in the battle. 'And the Adjunct expects us to comply with professional competence,' Gamet added.

'As she commands,' Keneb growled.

Dust was rising as the sappers and engineers worked on the fortifications and ramps. The day was blisteringly hot, the wind barely a desultory breath. The Khundryl, Seti and Wickan horse warriors remained south of the coral islands, awaiting the construction of a road that would give them egress to the basin. Even then, there would be scant room to manoeuvre. Gamet suspected that Tavore would hold most of them back – the basin was not large enough for massed cavalry charges, for either side. Sha'ik's own desert warriors would most likely be held in reserve, a fresh force to pursue the Malazans should they be broken. *And, in turn, the Khundryl can cover such a retreat . . . or rout.* A rather ignoble conclusion, the remnants of the Malazan army riding double on Khundryl horses – the Fist grimaced at the image and angrily swept it from his mind. 'The Adjunct knows what she is doing,' he asserted.

Keneb said nothing.

A messenger approached on foot. 'Fist Gamet,' the man called out, 'the Adjunct requests your presence.'

'I will keep an eye on the legion,' Keneb said.

Gamet nodded and wheeled his horse around. The motion made his head spin for a moment – he was still waking with headaches – then he steadied himself with a deep breath and nodded towards the messenger.

They made slow passage through the chaotic array of troops moving to and fro beneath the barked commands of the officers, towards a low hill closest to the basin. Gamet could see the Adjunct astride her horse on that hill, along with, on foot, Nil and Nether.

'I see them,' Gamet said to the messenger.

'Aye, sir, I'll leave you to it, then.'

Riding clear of the press, Gamet brought his horse into a canter and moments later reined in alongside the Adjunct.

The position afforded them a clear view of the enemy emplacements, and, just as they observed, so too in turn were they being watched by a small knot of figures atop the central ramp.

'How sharp are your eyes, Fist?' the Adjunct asked.

'Not sharp enough,' he replied.

'Korbolo Dom. Kamist Reloe. Six officers. Kamist has quested in our direction, seeking signs of mages. High Mages, specifically. Of course, given that Nil and Nether are with me, they cannot be found by Kamist Reloe's sorceries. Tell me, Fist Gamet, how confident do you imagine Korbolo Dom feels right now?'

He studied her a moment. She was in her armour, the visor of her helm lifted, her eyes half-lidded against the bright glare bouncing from the basin's hard-packed, crackled clay. 'I would think, Adjunct,' he replied slowly, 'that his measure of confidence is wilting.'

She glanced over. 'Wilting. Why?'

'Because it all looks too easy. Too overwhelmingly in his favour, Adjunct.'

She fell silent, returning her gaze to the distant enemy.

Is this what she wanted me for? To ask that one question?

Gamet switched his attention to the two Wickans. Nil had grown during the march, leading Gamet to suspect that he would be a tall man in a few years' time. He wore only a loincloth and looked feral with his wild, unbraided hair and green and black body-paint.

Nether, he realized with some surprise, had filled out beneath her deer-skin hides, a chubbiness that was common to girls before they came of age. The severity of her expression was very nearly fixed now, transforming what should have been a pretty face into a mien forbidding and burdened. Her black hair was shorn close, betokening a vow of grief.

'Kamist's questing is done,' the Adjunct suddenly pronounced. 'He will need to rest, now.' She turned in her saddle and by some prearranged signal two Wickan warriors jogged up the slope. Tavore unhitched her sword-belt and passed it to them. They quickly retreated with the otataral weapon.

Reluctantly, Nil and Nether settled cross-legged onto the stony ground.

'Fist Gamet,' the Adjunct said, 'if you would, draw your dagger and spill a few drops from your right palm.'

Without a word he tugged off his gauntlet, slid his dagger from its scabbard and scored the edge across the fleshy part of his hand. Blood welled from the cut. Gamet held it out, watched as the blood spilled down to the ground.

Dizziness struck him and he reeled in the saddle a moment before regaining his balance.

Nether voiced a hiss of surprise.

Gamet glanced down at her. Her eyes were closed, both hands pressed against the sandy ground. Nil had assumed the same posture and on his face flitted a wild sequence of emotions, fixing at last on fear.

The Fist was still feeling light-headed, a faint roaring sound filling his skull.

'There are spirits here,' Nil growled. 'Rising with anger—'

'A song,' Nether cut in. 'Of war, and warriors—'

'New and old,' her brother said. 'So very new . . . and so very old. Battle and death, again and again—'

'The land remembers every struggle played out on its surface, on all its surfaces, from the very beginning.' Nether grimaced, then shivered, her eyes squeezed shut. 'The goddess is as nothing to this power – yet she would . . . *steal*.'

The Adjunct's voice was sharp. 'Steal?'

'The warren,' Nil replied. 'She would claim this fragment, and settle it upon this land like a parasite. Roots of shadow, slipping down to draw sustenance, to feed on the land's memories.'

'And the spirits will not have it,' Nether whispered.

'They are resisting?' the Adjunct asked.

Both Wickans nodded, then Nil bared his teeth and said, 'Ghosts cast no shadows. You were right, Adjunct. Gods, you were right!'

Right? Gamet wondered. *Right about what?*

'And will they suffice?' Tavore demanded.

Nil shook his head. 'I don't know. Only if the Talon Master does what you think he will do, Adjunct.'

'Assuming,' Nether added, 'Sha'ik is unaware of the viper in her midst.'

'Had she known,' Tavore said, 'she would have separated his head from his shoulders long ago.'

'Perhaps,' Nether replied, and Gamet heard the scepticism in her tone. 'Unless she and her goddess decided to wait until all their enemies were gathered.'

The Adjunct returned her gaze to the distant officers. 'Let us see, shall we?'

Both Wickans rose, then shared a glance unwitnessed by Tavore.

Gamet rubbed his uncut hand along his brow beneath the helm's rim, and his fingers came away dripping with sweat. Something had used him, he realized shakily. Through the medium of his blood. He could hear distant music, a song of voices and unrecognizable instruments. A pressure was building in his skull. 'If you are done with me, Adjunct,' he said roughly.

She nodded without looking over. 'Return to your legion, Fist. Convey to your officers, please, the following. Units may appear during the battle on the morrow which you will not recognize. They may seek orders, and you are to give them as if they were under your command.'

'Understood, Adjunct.'

'Have a cutter attend to your hand, Fist Gamet, and thank you. Also, ask the guards to return to me my sword.'

'Aye.' He wheeled his horse and walked it down the slope.

The headache was not fading, and the song itself seemed to have poisoned his veins, a music of flesh and bone that hinted of madness. *Leave me in peace, damn you. I am naught but a soldier. A soldier . . .*

Strings sat on the boulder, his head in his hands. He had flung off the helm but had no memory of having done so, and it lay at his feet, blurry and wavering behind the waves of pain that rose and fell like a storm-tossed sea. Voices were speaking around him, seeking to reach him, but he could make no sense of what was being said. The song had burgeoned sudden and fierce in his skull, flowing through his limbs like fire.

A hand gripped his shoulder, and he felt a sorcerous questing seep into his veins, tentatively at first, then flinching away entirely, only to return with more force – and with it, a spreading silence. Blissful peace, cool and calm.

Finally, the sergeant was able to look up.

He found his squad gathered around him. The hand fixed onto his shoulder was Bottle's, and the lad's face was pale, beaded with sweat. Their eyes locked, then Bottle nodded and slowly withdrew his hand.

'Can you hear me, Sergeant?'

'Faint, as if you were thirty paces away.'

'Is the pain gone?'

'Aye – what did you do?'

Bottle glanced away.

Strings frowned, then said, 'Everyone else, back to work. Stay here, Bottle.'

Cuttle cuffed Tarr and the corporal straightened and mumbled, 'Let's go, soldiers. There's pits to dig.'

The sergeant and Bottle watched the others head off, retrieving their picks and shovels as they went. The squad was positioned on the southwesternmost island, over-looking dunes that reached out to the horizon. A single, sufficiently wide corridor lay directly to the north, through which the enemy – if broken and fleeing – would come as they left the basin. Just beyond it lay a modest, flat-topped tel, on which a company of mounted desert warriors were ensconced, the crest dotted with scouts keeping a careful eye on the Malazans.

'All right, Bottle,' Strings said, 'out with it.'

'Spirits, Sergeant. They're . . . awakening.'

'And what in Hood's name has that got to do with me?'

'Mortal blood, I think. It has its own song. They remember it. They came to you, Sergeant, eager to add their voices to it. To . . . uh . . . to you.'

'Why me?'

'I don't know.'

Strings studied the young mage for a moment, mulling on the taste of that lie, then grimaced and said, 'You think it's because I'm fated to die here – at this battle.'

Bottle looked away once more. 'I'm not sure, Sergeant. It's way beyond me . . . this land. And its spirits. And what it all has to do with you—'

'I'm a Bridgeburner, lad. The Bridgeburners were born here. In Raraku's crucible.'

Bottle's eyes thinned as he studied the desert to the west. 'But . . . they were wiped out.'

'Aye, they were.'

Neither spoke for a time. Koryk had broken his shovel on a rock and was stringing together an admirable list of Seti curses. The others had stopped to listen. On the northern edge of the island Gesler's squad was busy building a wall of rubble, which promptly toppled, the boulders tumbling down the far edge. Distant hoots and howls sounded from the tel across the way.

'It won't be your usual battle, will it?' Bottle asked.

Strings shrugged. 'There's no such thing, lad. There's nothing usual about killing and dying, about pain and terror.'

'That's not what I meant—'

'I know it ain't, Bottle. But wars these days are fraught with sorcery and munitions, so you come to expect surprises.'

Gesler's two dogs trotted past, the huge cattle dog trailing the Hengese Roach as if the hairy lapdog carried its own leash.

'This place is . . . complicated,' Bottle sighed. He reached down and picked up a large, disc-shaped rock. 'Eres'al,' he said. 'A hand-axe – the basin down there's littered with them. Smoothed by the lake that once filled it. Took days to make one of these, then they didn't even use them – they just flung them into the lake. Makes no sense, does it? Why make a tool then not use it?'

Strings stared at the mage. 'What are you talking about, Bottle? Who are the Eres'al?'

'Were, Sergeant. They're long gone.'

'The spirits?'

'No, those are from all times, from every age this land has known. My grandmother spoke of the Eres. The Dwellers who lived in the time before the Imass, the first makers of tools, the first shapers of their world.' He shook his head, fought down a shiver. 'I never expected to meet

900

one – it was there, *she* was there, in that song within you.'

'And she told you about these tools?'

'Not directly. More like I shared it – well, her mind. She was the one who gifted you the silence. It wasn't me – I don't have that power – but I asked, and she showed mercy. At least' – he glanced at Strings – 'I gather it was a mercy.'

'Aye, lad, it was. Can you still . . . speak with that Eres?'

'No. All I wanted to do was get out of there – out of that blood—'

'My blood.'

'Well, *most* of it's your blood, Sergeant.'

'And the rest?'

'Belongs to that song. The, uh, Bridgeburners' song.'

Strings closed his eyes, settled his head against the boulder behind him. *Kimloc, that damned Tanno Spiritwalker in Ehrlitan. I said no, but he did it anyway. He stole my story – not just mine, but the Bridgeburners' – and he made of it a song. The bastard's gone and given us back to Raraku . . .*

'Go help the others, Bottle.'

'Aye, Sergeant.'

'And . . . thanks.'

'I'll pass that along, when next I meet the Eres witch.'

Strings stared after the mage. *So there'll be a next time, will there? Just how much didn't you tell me, lad?* He wondered if the morrow would indeed be witness to his last battle. Hardly a welcome thought, but maybe it was necessary. Maybe he was being called to join the fallen Bridgeburners. *Not so bad, then. Couldn't ask for more miserable company. Damn, but I miss them. I miss them all. Even Hedge.*

The sergeant opened his eyes and climbed to his feet, collecting then donning his helm. He turned to stare out over the basin to the northeast, to the enemy emplacements and the dust and smoke of the city hidden within the oasis. *You too, Kalam Mekhar. I wonder if you know why you're here . . .*

* * *

The shaman was in a frenzy, twitching and hissing as he scuttled like a crab in dusty circles around the flat slab of bone that steadily blackened on the hearth. Corabb, his mouth filled with a half-dozen of the scarab shells strung round his neck to ward off evil, winced as his chattering teeth crunched down on one carapace, filling his mouth with a bitter taste. He plucked the necklace from his mouth and began spitting out pieces of shell.

Leoman strode up to the shaman and grabbed the scrawny man by his telaba, lifted him clear off the ground, then shook him. A flurry of cloth and hair and flying spittle, then Leoman set the shaman down once more and growled, 'What did you see?'

'Armies!' the old man shrieked, tugging at his nose as if it had just arrived on his face.

Leoman scowled. 'Aye, we can see those too, you damned fakir—'

'No! More armies!' He scrabbled past and ran to the southern crest of the tel, where he began hopping about and pointing at the Malazans entrenching on the island opposite the old drainage channel.

Leoman made no move to follow. He walked over to where Corabb and three other warriors crouched behind a low wall. 'Corabb, send another rider to Sha'ik – no, on second thought, you go yourself. Even if she will not bother acknowledging our arrival, I want to know how Mathok's tribes will be arrayed come the dawn. Find out, once you have spoken with Sha'ik – and Corabb, be certain you speak with her in person. Then return here.'

'I shall do as you command,' Corabb announced, straightening.

Twenty paces away the shaman wheeled round and screamed, 'They are here! The dogs, Leoman! The dogs! *The Wickan dogs!*'

Leoman scowled. 'The fool's gone mad . . .'

Corabb jogged over to his horse. He would waste no time saddling the beast, especially if it meant hearing more of the shaman's insane observations. He vaulted onto the animal, tightened the straps holding the lance crossways on his back, then collected the reins and spurred the animal into motion.

The route to the oasis was twisting and tortured, winding between deep sand and jagged outcrops, forcing him to slow his mount's pace and let it pick its own way along the trail.

The day was drawing to a close, shadows deepening where the path wound its way into high-walled gullies closer to the southwestern edge of the oasis. As his horse scrabbled over some rubble and walked round a sharp bend, the sudden stench of putrefaction reached both animal and man simultaneously.

The path was blocked. A dead horse and, just beyond it, a corpse.

Heart thudding, Corabb slipped down from his mount and moved cautiously forward.

Leoman's messenger, the one he had sent as soon as the troop had arrived. A crossbow quarrel had taken him on the temple, punching through bone then exploding out messily the other side.

Corabb scanned the jagged walls to either side. If there'd been assassins stationed there he would already be dead, he reasoned. Probably, then, they weren't expecting any more messengers.

He returned to his horse. It was a struggle coaxing the creature over the bodies, but eventually he led the beast clear of them and leapt onto its back once more. Eyes roving restlessly, he continued on.

Sixty paces later and the trail ahead opened out onto the sandy slope, beyond which could be seen the dusty mantles of guldindha trees.

Breathing a relieved sigh, Corabb urged his horse forward.

Two hammer blows against his back flung him forward. Without stirrups or saddlehorn to grab on to, Corabb threw his arms out around the horse's neck – even as the animal squealed in pain and bolted. The motion almost jolted loose his panicked grip, and the horse's right knee cracked hard, again and again, into his helm, until it fell away and the knobby joint repeatedly pounded against his head.

Corabb held on, even as he continued slipping down, then around, until his body was being pummelled by both front legs. The encumbrance proved sufficient to slow the animal as it reached the slope, and Corabb, one leg dangling, his heel bouncing over the hard ground, managed to pull himself up under his horse's head.

Another quarrel cracked into the ground and skittered away off to the left.

The horse halted halfway up the slope.

Corabb brought his other leg down, then pivoted around to the opposite side and vaulted onto the animal once more. He'd lost the reins, but closed both fingers in the horse's mane as he drove his heels into the beast's flanks.

Yet another quarrel caromed from the rocks, then hooves were thudding on sand, and sudden sunlight bathed them.

Directly ahead lay the oasis, and the cover of trees.

Corabb leaned onto the mount's neck and urged it ever faster.

They plunged onto a trail between the guldindhas. Glancing back, he saw a deep rip running down his horse's left flank, leaking blood. And then he caught sight of his lance, dangling loose now from his back. There were two quarrels embedded in the shaft. Each had struck at a different angle, and the impact must have been nearly simultaneous, since the splits had bound against each other, halting the momentum of both quarrels.

Corabb lifted the ruined weapon clear and flung it away.

He rode hard down the trail.

'A tiger's barbs,' she murmured, her eyes veiled behind

rust-leaf smoke, 'painted onto a toad. Somehow, it makes you look even more dangerous.'

'Aye, lass, I'm pure poison,' Heboric muttered as he studied her in the gloom. There was life in her gaze once more, a sharpness that went beyond the occasional cutting remark, hinting at a mind finally cleared of durhang's dulling fog. She still coughed as if her lungs were filled with fluid, although the sage mixed in with the rust-leaf had eased that somewhat.

She was returning his regard with an inquisitive – if slightly hard – expression, drawing steadily on the hookah's mouthpiece, smoke tumbling down from her nostrils.

'If I could see you,' Heboric muttered, 'I'd conclude you've improved some.'

'I have, Destriant of Treach, though I would have thought those feline eyes of yours could pierce every veil.'

He grunted. 'It's more that you no longer slur your words, Scillara.'

'What do we do now?' she asked after a moment.

'Dusk will soon arrive. I would go out to find L'oric, and I would that you accompany me.'

'And then?'

'Then, I would lead you to Felisin Younger.'

'Sha'ik's adopted daughter.'

'Aye.'

Scillara glanced away, meditative as she drew deep on the rust-leaf.

'How old are you, lass?'

She shrugged, 'As old as I have to be. If I am to take Felisin Younger's orders, so be it. Resentment is pointless.'

An awkward conversation, progressing in leaps that left Heboric scrambling. Sha'ik was much the same. Perhaps, he reflected with a grimace, this talent for intuitive thinking was a woman's alone – he admittedly had little experience upon which he could draw, despite his advanced years. Fener's temple was predominantly male, when it came to the holy order itself, and Heboric's life as a thief had, of necessity, included only a handful of close associations. He was, once more, out of his depth. 'Felisin Younger has, I believe, little interest in commanding anyone. This is not an exchange of one cult for another, Scillara – not in the way you seem to think it is, at any rate. No-one will seek to manipulate you here.'

'As you have explained, Destriant.' She sighed heavily and sat straighter, setting down the hookah's mouthpiece. 'Very well, lead me into the darkness.'

His eyes narrowed on her. 'I shall ... as soon as it arrives ...'

The shadows were drawing long, sufficient to swallow the entire basin below their position. Sha'ik stood at the crest of the northernmost ramp, studying the distant masses of Malazan soldiery on the far rises as they continued digging in. Ever methodical, was her sister.

She glanced to her left and scanned Korbolo Dom's positions. All was in readiness for the morrow's battle, and she could see the Napan commander, surrounded by aides and guards, standing at the edge of the centre ramp, doing as she herself was doing: watching Tavore's army.

We are all in place. Suddenly, the whole thing seemed so pointless. This game of murderous tyrants, pushing their armies forward into an inevitable clash. Coldly disregarding of the lives that would be lost in the appeasement of their brutal desires. *What value this mindless hunger to rule? What do you want with us, Empress Laseen? Seven Cities will never rest easy beneath your yoke. You shall have to enslave, and what is gained by that?* And what of her own goddess? Was she any different from Laseen? Every claw was outstretched, eager to grasp, to rend, to soak the sand red with gore.

But Raraku does not belong to you, dear Dryjhna, no matter how ferocious your claims. I see that now. This desert is holy unto itself. And now it rails – feel it, goddess! It rails! Against one and all.

Standing beside her, Mathok had been studying the

Malazan positions in silence. But now he spoke. 'The Adjunct has made an appearance, Chosen One.'

Sha'ik dragged her gaze from Korbolo Dom and looked to where the desert warchief pointed.

Astride a horse from the Paran stables. *Of course*. Two Wickans on foot nearby. Her sister was in full armour, her helm glinting crimson in the dying light.

Sha'ik's eyes snapped back to Korbolo's position. 'Kamist Reloe has arrived ... he's opened his warren and now quests towards the enemy. But Tavore's otataral sword defies him ... so he reaches around, into the army itself. Seeking High Mages ... unsuspected allies...' After a moment she sighed. 'And finds none but a few shamans and squad mages.'

Mathok rumbled, 'Those two Wickans with the Adjunct. They are the ones known as Nil and Nether.'

'Yes. Said to be broken of spirit – they have none of the power that their clans once gave them, for those clans have been annihilated.'

'Even so, Chosen One,' Mathok muttered, 'that she holds them within the fog of otataral suggests they are not as weak as we would believe.'

'Or that Tavore does not want their weakness revealed.'

'Why bother if such failure is already known to us?'

'To deepen our doubt, Mathok,' she replied.

He curtly gestured, adding a frustrated growl. 'This mire has no surface, Chosen One—'

'Wait!' Sha'ik stared once again at Tavore. 'She has sent her weapon away – Kamist Reloe has withdrawn his questing – and now ... ah!' The last word was a startled cry, as she felt the muted unveiling of power from both Nil and Nether – a power far greater than it had any right to be.

Sha'ik then gasped, as the goddess within her flinched back – as if stung – and loosed a shriek that filled her skull.

For Raraku was answering the summons, a multitude of voices, rising in song, rising with raw, implacable desire –

the sound, Sha'ik realized, of countless souls straining against the chains that bound them.

Chains of shadow. Chains like roots. From this torn, alien fragment of warren. This piece of shadow, that has risen to bind their souls and so feeds upon the life-force. 'Mathok, where is Leoman?' *We need Leoman.*

'I do not know, Chosen One.'

She turned once more and stared at Korbolo Dom. He stood foremost on the ramp, his stance squared, thumbs hitched into his sword-belt, studying the enemy with an air of supreme confidence that made Sha'ik want to scream.

Nothing – *nothing* was as it seemed.

To the west, the sun had turned the horizon into a crimson conflagration. The day was drowning in a sea of flame, and she watched shadows flowing across the land, her heart growing cold.

The alley outside Heboric's tent was empty in both directions. The sun's sudden descent seemed to bring a strange silence along with the gloom. Dust hung motionless in the air.

The Destriant of Treach paused in the aisle.

Behind him Scillara said, 'Where is everyone?'

He had been wondering the same thing. Then, slowly, the hairs rose on the back of his neck. 'Can you hear that, lass?'

'Only the wind . . .'

But there was no wind.

'No, not wind,' Scillara murmured. 'A song. From far away – the Malazan army, do you think?'

He shook his head, but said nothing.

After a moment Heboric gestured Scillara to follow and he set out down the alley. The song seemed suspended in the very air, raising a haze of dust that seemed to shiver before his eyes. Sweat ran down his limbs. *Fear. Fear has driven this entire city from the streets. Those voices are the sound of war.*

'There should be children,' Scillara said. 'Girls . . .'

'Why girls more than anyone else, lass?'

'Bidithal's spies. His chosen servants.'

He glanced back at her. 'Those he . . . scars?'

'Yes. They should be . . . everywhere. Without them—'

'Bidithal is blind. It may well be he has sent them elsewhere, or even withdrawn them entirely. There will be . . . events this night, Scillara. Blood will be spilled. The players are, no doubt, even now drawing into position.'

'He spoke of this night,' she said. 'The hours of darkness before the battle. He said the world will change this night.'

Heboric bared his teeth. 'The fool has sunk to the bottom of the Abyss, and now stirs the black mud.'

'He dreams of true Darkness unfolding, Destriant. Shadow is but an upstart, a realm born of compromise and filled with impostors. The fragments must be returned to the First Mother.'

'Not just a fool, then, but mad. To speak of the most ancient of battles, as if he himself is a force worthy of it – Bidithal has lost his mind.'

'He says something is coming,' Scillara said, shrugging. 'Suspected by no-one, and only Bidithal himself has any hope of controlling it, for he alone remembers the Dark.'

Heboric halted. 'Hood take his soul. I must go to him. Now.'

'We will find him—'

'In his damned temple, aye. Come on.'

They swung about.

Even as two figures emerged from the gloom of an alley mouth, blades flickering out.

With a snarl, Heboric closed on them. One taloned hand shot out, tore under and into an assassin's neck, then snapped upward, lifting the man's head clean from his shoulders.

The other killer lunged, knife-point darting for Heboric's left eye. The Destriant caught the man's wrist and crushed

909

both bones. A slash from his other hand spilled the assassin's entrails onto the dusty street.

Flinging the body away, Heboric glared about. Scillara stood a few paces back, her eyes wide. Ignoring her, the Destriant crouched down over the nearest corpse. 'Korbolo Dom's. Too impatient by far—'

Three quarrels struck him simultaneously. One deep into his right hip, shattering bone. Another plunging beneath his right shoulder blade to draw short a finger's breadth from his spine. The third, arriving from the opposite direction, took him high on his left shoulder with enough force to spin him round, so that he tumbled backward over the corpse.

Scillara scrabbled down beside him. 'Old man? Do you live?'

'Bastards,' he growled. 'That hurts.'

'They're coming—'

'To finish me off, aye. Flee, lass. To the stone forest. Go!'

He felt her leave his side, heard her light steps patter away.

Heboric sought to rise, but agony ripped up from his broken hip, left him gasping and blinded.

Approaching footsteps, three sets, moccasined, two from the right and one from the left. Knives whispered from sheaths. Closing . . . then silence.

Someone was standing over Heboric. Through his blurred vision, he could make out dust-smeared boots, and from them a stench, as of musty, dry death. Another set of boots scuffed the ground beyond the Destriant's feet.

'Begone, wraiths,' a voice hissed from a half-dozen paces away.

'Too late for that, assassin,' murmured the figure above Heboric. 'Besides, we've only just arrived.'

'In the name of Hood, Hoarder of Souls, I banish you from this realm.'

A soft laugh answered the killer's command. 'Kneel

before Hood, do you? Oh yes, I felt the power in your words. Alas, Hood's out of his depth on this one. Ain't that right, lass?'

A deep, grunting assent from the one standing near Heboric's feet.

'Last warning,' the assassin growled. 'Our blades are sanctioned – they will bleed your souls—'

'No doubt. Assuming they ever reach us.'

'There are but two of you . . . and three of us.'

'Two?'

Scuffing sounds, then, sharp and close, the spray of blood onto the ground. Bodies thumped, long breaths exhaled wetly.

'Should've left one alive,' said another woman's voice.

'Why?'

'So we could send him back to that fly-blown Napan bastard with a promise for the morrow.'

'Better this way, lass. No-one appreciates surprise any more – that's what's gone wrong with the world, if you ask me—'

'Well, we wasn't asking you. This old man going to make it, you think?'

A grunt. 'I doubt Treach will give up on his new Destriant with nary a meow. Besides, that sweet-lunged beauty is on her way back.'

'Time for us to leave, then.'

'Aye.'

'And from now on we don't surprise no-one, 'til come the dawn. Understood?'

'Temptation got the better of us. Won't happen again.'

Silence, then footsteps once more. A small hand settled on his brow.

'Scillara?'

'Yes, it's me. There were soldiers here, I think. They didn't look too good—'

'Never mind that. Pull the quarrels from me. Flesh wants to heal, bone to knit. Pull 'em out, lass.'

'And then?'

'Drag me back to my temple . . . if you can.'

'All right.'

He felt a hand close on the quarrel buried in his left shoulder. A flash of pain, then nothing.

Elder Sha'ik's armour was laid out on the table. One of Mathok's warriors had replaced the worn straps and fittings, then polished the bronze plates and the full, visored helm. The longsword was oiled, its edges finely honed. The iron-rimmed hide-covered shield leaned against one table leg.

She stood, alone in the chamber, staring down at the accoutrements left by her predecessor. The old woman reputedly had skill with the blade. The helm seemed strangely oversized, its vented cheek guards flared and full length, hinged to the heavy brow-band. Fine blackened chain hung web-like across the eye-slits. A long, wide lobster-tail neck guard sprawled out from the back rim.

She walked over to the quilted under-padding. It was heavy, sweat-stained, the laces beneath the arms and running the length of the sides. Boiled leather plates covered her upper thighs, shoulders, arms and wrists. Working methodically, she tightened every lace and strap, shifting about to settle the weight evenly before turning to the armour itself.

Most of the night remained, stretching before her like infinity's dark road, but she wanted to feel the armour encasing her; she wanted its massive weight, and so she affixed the leg greaves, footplates and wrist vambraces, then shrugged her way into the breastplate. Sorcery had lightened the bronze, and its sound as it rustled was like thin tin. The design allowed her to cinch the straps herself, and moments later she picked up the sword and slid it into its scabbard, then drew the heavy belt about her waist, setting the hooks that held it to the cuirass so that its weight did not drag at her hips.

All that remained was the pair of gauntlets, and the

under-helm and helm itself. She hesitated. *Have I any choice in all this?* The goddess remained a towering presence in her mind, rooted through every muscle and fibre, her voice whispering in the flow of blood in her veins and arteries. Ascendant power was in Sha'ik's grasp, and she knew she would use it when the time came. Or, rather, it would use her.

To kill my sister.

She sensed the approach of someone and turned to face the entrance. 'You may enter, L'oric.'

The High Mage stepped into view.

Sha'ik blinked. He was wearing armour. White, enamelled, scarred and stained with use. A long, narrow-bladed sword hung at his hip. After a moment, she sighed. 'And so we all make preparations . . .'

'As you have observed before, Mathok has over three hundred warriors guarding this palace, Chosen One. Guarding . . . you.'

'He exaggerates the risk. The Malazans are far too busy—'

'The danger he anticipates, Chosen One, lies not with the Malazans.'

She studied him. 'You look exhausted, L'oric. I suggest you return to your tent and get some rest. I shall have need for you on the morrow.'

'You will not heed my warning?'

'The goddess protects me. I have nothing to fear. Besides,' she smiled, 'Mathok has three hundred of his chosen warriors guarding this palace.'

'Sha'ik, there will be a convergence this night. You have readers of the Deck among your advisers. Command they field their cards, and all that I say will be confirmed. Ascendant powers are gathering. The stench of treachery is in the air.'

She waved a hand. 'None of it matters, L'oric. I cannot be touched. Nor will the goddess be denied.'

He stepped closer, his eyes wide. 'Chosen One! Raraku is *awakening*.'

'What are you talking about?'

'Can you not hear it?'

'The rage of the goddess consumes all, L'oric. If you can hear the voice of the Holy Desert, then it is Raraku's death-cry. The Whirlwind shall devour this night. And any ascendant power foolish enough to approach will be annihilated. The goddess, L'oric, *will not be denied.*'

He stared at her a moment longer, then seemed to sag beneath his armour. He drew a hand across his eyes, as if seeking to claw some nightmarish vision from his sight. Then, with a nod, he swung about and strode towards the doorway.

'Wait!' Sha'ik moved past him then halted.

Voices sounded from beyond the canvas walls.

'Let him pass!' she cried.

Two guards stumbled in, dragging a man between them. Smeared in dust and sweat, he was unable to even stand, so exhausted and battered was he. One of the guards barked, 'It is Corabb Bhilan Thenu'alas. One of Leoman's officers.'

'Chosen One!' the man gasped. 'I am the third rider Leoman has sent to you! I found the bodies of the others – assassins pursued me almost to your very palace!'

Sha'ik's face darkened with fury. 'Get Mathok,' she snapped to one of the guards. 'L'oric, gift this man some healing, to aid in his recovery.'

The High Mage stepped forward, settled a hand on Corabb's shoulder.

The desert warrior's breathing slowed, and he slowly straightened. 'Leoman sends his greetings, Chosen One. He wishes to know of Mathok's deployment—'

'Corabb,' Sha'ik cut in. 'You will return to Leoman – with an escort. My orders to him are as follows – are you listening?'

He nodded.

'Leoman is to ride immediately back to me. He is to take over command of my armies.'

Corabb blinked. 'Chosen One?'

914

'Leoman of the Flails is to assume command of my armies. Before the dawn. L'oric, go to Korbolo Dom and convey to him my summons. He is to attend me immediately.'

L'oric hesitated, then nodded. 'As you command, Chosen One. I will take my leave of you now.'

He exited the chamber, made his way through the intervening rooms and passageways, passing guard after guard, seeing weapons drawn and feeling hard eyes on him. Korbolo Dom would be a fool to attempt to reach her with his assassins. Even so, the night had begun, and in the oasis beyond starlight now played on drawn blades.

Emerging onto the concourse before the palace, L'oric paused. His warren was unveiled, and he made that fact visible through a spark-filled penumbra surrounding his person. He wanted no-one to make any fatal mistakes. Feeling strangely exposed none the less, he set out towards Korbolo Dom's command tent.

The Dogslayers were ready in their reserve trenches, a ceaseless rustling of weapons and armour and muted conversations that fell still further as he strode past, only to rise again in his wake. These soldiers, L'oric well knew, had by choice and by circumstance made of themselves a separate force. *Marked by the butchery of their deeds. By the focus of Malazan outrage. They know that no quarter will be given them.* Their bluster was betrayed by diffidence, their reputed savagery streaked now with glimmers of fear. And their lives were in Korbolo Dom's stained hands. Entirely. *They will not sleep this night.*

He wondered what would happen when Leoman wrested command from the Napan renegade. Would there be mutiny? It was very possible. Of course, Sha'ik possessed the sanction of the Whirlwind Goddess, and she would not hesitate to flex that power should Leoman's position be challenged. Still, this was not the way to ready an army on the night before battle.

She has waited too long. Then again, perhaps this was

intended. Designed to knock Korbolo off balance, to give him no time to prepare any counter-moves. If so, then it is the boldest of risks, on this, the most jagged-edged of nights.

He made his way up the steep pathway to the Napan's command tent. Two sentries emerged from near the entrance to block his progress.

'Inform Korbolo Dom that I bring word from Sha'ik.'

He watched the two soldiers exchange a glance, then one nodded and entered the tent.

A few moments later the sorceress, Henaras, strode out from the entrance. Her face knotted in a scowl. 'High Mage L'oric. You shall have to relinquish your warren to seek audience with the Supreme Commander of the Apocalypse.'

One brow rose at that lofty title, but he shrugged and lowered his magical defences. 'I am under your protection, then,' he said.

She cocked her head. 'Against whom do you protect yourself, High Mage? The Malazans are on the other side of the basin.'

L'oric smiled.

Gesturing, Henaras swung about and entered the command tent. L'oric followed.

The spacious chamber within was dominated by a raised dais at the end opposite the doorway, on which sat a massive wooden chair. The high headrest was carved in arcane symbols that L'oric recognized – with a shock – as Hengese, from the ancient city of Li Heng in the heart of the Malazan Empire. Dominating the carvings was a stylized rendition of a raptor's talons, outstretched, that hovered directly over the head of the seated Napan, who sat slouched, his hooded gaze fixed on the High Mage.

'L'oric,' he drawled. 'You foolish man. You are about to discover what happens to souls who are far too trusting. Granted,' he added with a smile, 'you might have assumed we were allies. After all, we have shared the same oasis for some time now, have we not?'

916

'Sha'ik demands that you attend her, Korbolo Dom. Immediately.'

'To relieve me of my command, yes. With the ill-informed belief that my Dogslayers will accept Leoman of the Flails – did you peruse them on your way here, L'oric? Were you witness to their readiness? My army, High Mage, is surrounded by enemies. Do you understand? Leoman is welcome to attempt an approach, with all the desert warriors he and Mathok care to muster—'

'You would betray the Apocalypse? Turn on your allies and win the battle for the Adjunct, Korbolo Dom? All to preserve your precious position?'

'If Sha'ik insists.'

'Alas, Sha'ik is not the issue,' L'oric said. 'The Whirlwind Goddess, however, is, and I believe her toleration of you, Korbolo Dom, is about to end.'

'Do you think so, L'oric? Will she also accept the destruction of the Dogslayers? For destroy them she must, if she is to wrest control from me. The decimation of her vaunted Army of the Apocalypse. Truly, will the goddess choose this?'

L'oric slowly cocked his head, then he slowly sighed. 'Ah, I see now the flaw. You have approached this tactically, as would any soldier. But what you clearly do not understand is that the Whirlwind Goddess is indifferent to tactics, to grand strategies. You rely upon her common sense, but Korbolo, she *has none*. The battle tomorrow? Victory or defeat? The goddess cares neither way. She desires *destruction*. The Malazans butchered on the field, the Dogslayers slaughtered in their trenches, an enfilade of sorcery to transform the sands of Raraku into a red ruin. This is what the Whirlwind Goddess desires.'

'What of it?' the Napan rasped, and L'oric saw sweat beading the man's scarred brow. 'Even the goddess cannot reach me, not here, in this sanctified place—'

'And you call me the fool? The goddess will see you slain this night, but you are too insignificant for her to act directly in crushing you under thumb.'

Korbolo Dom bolted forward on the chair. 'Then *who*?' he shrieked. 'You, L'oric?'

The High Mage spread his hands and shook his head. 'I am less than a messenger in this, Korbolo Dom. I am, if anything at all, merely the voice of . . . common sense. It is not who she will send against you, Supreme Commander. It is, I believe, who *she will allow* through her defences. Don't you think?'

Korbolo stared down at the High Mage, then he snarled and gestured.

The knife plunging into his back had no chance of delivering a fatal wound. L'oric's tightly bound defences, his innermost layers of Kurald Thyrllan, defied the thirst of iron. Despite this, the blow drove the High Mage to his knees. Then he pitched forward onto the thick carpets, almost at the Napan's boots.

And already, he was ignored as he lay there, bleeding into the weave, as Korbolo rose and began bellowing orders. And none were close enough to hear the High Mage murmur, '*Blood is the path, you foolish man. And you have opened it. You poor bastard . . .*'

'*Grim statement. Greyfrog must leave your delicious company.*'

Felisin glanced over at the demon. Its four eyes were suddenly glittering, avid with palpable hunger. 'What has happened?'

'*Ominous. An invitation from my brother.*'

'Is L'oric in trouble?'

'*There is darkness this night, yet the Mother's face is turned away. What comes cannot be chained. Warning. Caution. Remain here, lovely child. My brother can come to no further harm, but my path is made clear. Glee. I shall eat humans this night.*'

She drew her telaba closer about herself and fought off a shiver. 'I am, uh, pleased for you, Greyfrog.'

'*Uncertain admonition. The shadows are fraught – no path is*

918

*entirely clear, even that of blood. I must needs bob and weave,
hop this way and that, grow still under baleful glare, and hope
for the best.'*

'How long should I wait for you, Greyfrog?'

*'Leave not this glade until the sun rises, dearest she whom I
would marry, regardless of little chance for proper broods.
Besotted. Suddenly eager to depart.'*

'Go, then.'

'Someone approaches. Potential ally. Be kind.'

With that the demon scrambled into the shadows.

Potential ally? Who would that be?

She could hear the person on the trail now, bared feet
that seemed to drag with exhaustion, and a moment later a
woman stumbled into the glade, halting in the gloom to
peer about.

'Here,' Felisin murmured, emerging from the shelter.

'Felisin Younger?'

'Ah, there is but one who calls me that. Heboric has sent
you?'

'Yes.' The woman came closer, and Felisin saw that she
was stained with blood, and a heavy bruise marred her jaw.
'They tried to kill him. There were ghosts. Defending him
against the assassins—'

'Wait, wait. Catch your breath. You're safe here. Does
Heboric still live?'

She nodded. 'He heals – in his temple. He heals—'

'Slow your breathing, please. Here, I have wine.
Say nothing for now – when you are ready, tell me your
tale.'

Shadow-filled hollows rippled the hills that marked the
northwest approach to the oasis. A haze of dust dulled the
starlight overhead. The night had come swiftly to Raraku,
as it always did, and the day's warmth was fast dissipating.
On this night, there would be frost.

Four riders sat still on motionless horses in one such
hollow, steam rising from their lathered beasts. Their

armour gleamed pale as bone, the skin of their exposed faces a pallid, deathly grey.

They had seen the approaching horse warrior from a distance, sufficient to permit them this quiet withdrawal unseen, for the lone rider was not their quarry, and though none said it out loud, they were all glad for that.

He was huge, that stranger. Astride a horse to match. And a thousand ravaged souls trailed him, bound by ethereal chains that he dragged as if indifferent to their weight. A sword of stone hung from his back, and it was possessed by twin spirits raging with bloodthirst.

In all, a nightmarish apparition.

They listened to the heavy hoofs thump past, waited until the drumming sound dwindled within the stone forest on the edge of the oasis.

Then Jorrude cleared his throat. 'Our path is now clear, brothers. The trespassers are camped nearby, among the army that has marched to do battle with the dwellers of this oasis. We shall strike them with the dawn.'

'Brother Jorrude,' Enias rumbled, 'what conjuration just crossed our trail?'

'I know not, Brother Enias, but it was a promise of death.'

'Agreed,' Malachar growled.

'Our horses are rested enough,' Jorrude pronounced.

The four Tiste Liosan rode up the slope until they reached the ridge, then swung their mounts southward. Jorrude spared a last glance back over his shoulder, to make certain the stranger had not reversed his route – had not spied them hiding there in that hollow. *Hiding. Yes, that is the truth of it, ignoble as the truth often proves to be.* He fought off a shiver, squinting into the darkness at the edge of the stone forest.

But the apparition did not emerge.

'In the name of Osric, Lord of the Sky,' Jorrude intoned under his breath as he led his brothers along the ridge, 'thank you for that . . .'

At the edge of the glade, Karsa Orlong stared back at the distant riders. He had seen them long before they had seen him, and had smiled at their cautious retreat from his path.

Well enough, there were enemies aplenty awaiting him in the oasis, and no night lasted for ever.

Alas.

CHAPTER TWENTY-FIVE

> Hear them rattle
> These chains of living
> Bound to every moment passed
> Until the wreckage clamours
> In deafening wake
> And each stride trails
> A dirge of the lost.
>
> *House of Chains*
> Fisher kel Tath

He sat cross-legged in the darkness, perched in his usual place on the easternmost ridge, his eyes closed, a small smile on his withered face. He had unveiled his warren in the most subtle pattern, an unseen web stretched out across the entire oasis. It would be torn soon, he well knew, but for the moment he could sense every footpad, every tremble. The powers were indeed converging, and the promise of blood and destruction whispered through the night.

Febryl was well pleased. Sha'ik had been isolated, utterly. The Napan's army of killers were even now streaming from their places of hiding, as panic closed hands around Korbolo Dom's throat. Kamist Reloe was returning from his secret sojourn through the warrens. And, across the basin, the Malazan army was entrenching, the Adjunct whetting her otataral sword in anticipation of the morning's battle.

There was but one troubling detail. A strange song, faint

yet growing. The voice of Raraku itself. He wondered what it would bring to this fated night. Hood was close – *aye, the god himself* – and this did much to mask other . . . presences. But the sands were stirring, awakened perhaps by the Lord of Death's arrival. Spirits and ghosts, no doubt come to witness the many deaths promised in the hours to come. A curious thing, but he was not unduly concerned.

There will be slaughter. Yet another apocalypse on Raraku's restless sands. It is as it should be.

To all outward appearances, L'oric was dead. He had been roughly dragged to one wall in the command tent and left there. The knife had been yanked from his back, and he now lay with his face to the rough fabric of the wall, eyes open and seemingly sightless.

Behind him, the Supreme Commander of the Apocalypse was speaking.

'Unleash them all, Henaras, barring my bodyguards. I want every one of Bidithal's cute little spies hunted down and killed – and find Scillara. That bitch has played her last game.

'You, Duryl, take another and ride out to the Adjunct. Deliver my missive – and make certain you are not seen by anyone. Mathok has his warriors out. Fayelle will work sorcery to aid you. And impress upon Tavore the need to withdraw her killers, lest they do the Whirlwind Goddess's work for her.'

'Supreme Commander,' a voice spoke, 'what of Leoman of the Flails?'

'The 4th Company and Fayelle are to leave quietly with the next bell. Leoman will get nowhere near us, or the army. Corporal Ethume, I want you within crossbow range of Febryl – the bastard's hiding in the usual place. Now, have I missed anything?'

'My fear is deepening,' Henaras murmured. 'Something is happening . . . in the holy desert. Worse, I feel the approach of terrible powers—'

'Which is why we need the Adjunct and her damned sword. Are we safe enough in here, Henaras?'

'I think so – the wards Kamist, Fayelle and I have woven about this tent would confound a god.'

'That claim might well be challenged,' Korbolo Dom growled.

He added something more, but a strange gurgling sound, from just beyond the tent wall in front of L'oric, overrode the Napan's voice. A wetness, spattering the opposite side, then a sigh – audible to L'oric only because he was so close. Talons then raked along the base of the wall, reducing the fabric to ribbons. A four-eyed, immeasurably ugly face peered in through the gap.

'Brother, you look unwell.'

Appearances deceive, Greyfrog. For example, you have never looked prettier.

The demon reached in and grasped L'oric by one arm. He then began dragging him by increments through the tear. *'Confident. They are too preoccupied. Disappointed. I have eaten but two guards, the wards sleep and our path of retreat is clear. Things are coming. Suitably ominous. Frankly. I admit to fear, and advise we . . . hide.'*

For a time, yes, we do just that. Find us somewhere, Greyfrog.

'Assured. I shall.'

Then leave me there and return to Felisin. Assassins are out hunting . . .

'Delightful.'

Kasanal had been a Semk shaman once, but now he murdered at his new master's bidding. And he enjoyed it, although, admittedly, he preferred killing Malazans rather than natives. At least his victims this night would not be Semk – to slay those from his own tribe would be a difficult thing to accept. But that did not seem likely. Korbolo Dom had as much as adopted the last survivors of the clans that had fought for him and Kamist Reloe on the Chain of Dogs.

And these two were mere women, both servants of that butcher, Bidithal.

He was now lying motionless on the edge of the glade, watching the two. One was Scillara, and Kasanal knew his master would be pleased when he returned with her severed head. The other one was also familiar – he had seen her in Sha'ik's company, and Leoman's.

It was also clear that they were in hiding, and so likely to be principal agents in whatever Bidithal was planning.

He slowly raised his right hand, and two quick gestures sent his four followers out along the flanks, staying within the trees, to encircle the two women's position. Under his breath, he began murmuring an incantation, a weaving of ancient words that deadened sound, that squeezed lassitude into the victims, dulling their every sense. And he smiled as he saw their heads slowly settle in unison.

Kasanal rose from his place of concealment. The need for hiding had passed. He stepped into the glade. His four Semk kin followed suit.

They drew their knives, edged closer.

Kasanal never saw the enormous blade that cut him in half, from the left side of his neck and out just above his right hip. He had a momentary sense of falling in two directions, then oblivion swallowed him, so he did not hear the cries of his four cousins, as the wielder of the stone sword marched into their midst.

When Kasanal at last opened ethereal eyes to find himself striding towards Hood's Gate, he was pleased to find his four kinsmen with him.

Wiping the blood from his sword, Karsa Orlong swung to face the two women. 'Felisin,' he growled, 'your scars burn bright on your soul. Bidithal chose to ignore my warning. So be it. Where is he?'

Still feeling the remnants of the strange dullness that had stolen her senses, Felisin could only shake her head.

Karsa scowled at her, then his gaze shifted to the other woman. 'Has the night stolen your tongue as well?'

'No. Yes. No, clearly it hasn't. I believe we were under sorcerous attack. But we are now recovering, Toblakai. You have been gone long.'

'And I am now returned. Where is Leoman? Bidithal? Febryl? Korbolo Dom? Kamist Reloe? Heboric Ghost Hands?'

'An impressive list – you've a busy night ahead, I think. Find them where you will, Toblakai. The night awaits you.'

Felisin drew a shaky breath, wrapping her arms about herself as she stared up at the terrible warrior. He had just killed five assassins with five sweeping, almost poetic passes of that enormous sword. The very ease of it horrified her. True, the assassins had intended the same for her and Scillara.

Karsa loosened his shoulders with a shrug, then strode towards the path leading to the city. In moments he was gone.

Scillara moved closer to Felisin and laid a hand on her shoulder. 'Death is always a shock,' she said. 'The numbness will pass. I promise.'

But Felisin shook her head. 'Except for Leoman,' she whispered.

'What?'

'Those he named. He is going to kill them all. Except for Leoman.'

Scillara slowly turned to face the trail, a cool, speculative look stealing across her face.

The last two had taken down four warriors and come within thirty paces of his tent before finally falling. Scowling, Mathok stared down at the arrow-studded, sword-slashed corpses. Six attempted assassinations this night alone, and the first bell had yet to sound.

Enough.

'T'morol, gather my clan.'

926

The burly warrior grunted assent and strode off. Mathok drew his furs tighter about himself and returned to his tent.

Within its modest confines, he paused for a long moment, deep in thought. Then he shook himself and walked over to a hide-covered chest near his cot. He crouched, swept aside the covering, and lifted the ornate lid.

The Book of Dryjhna resided within.

Sha'ik had given it into his keeping.

To safeguard.

He closed the lid and locked it, then picked up the chest and made his way outside. He could hear his warriors breaking camp in the darkness beyond. 'T'morol.'

'Warchief.'

'We ride to join Leoman of the Flails. The remaining clans are to guard Sha'ik, though I am confident she is not at risk – she may have need for them in the morning.'

T'morol's dark eyes were fixed on Mathok, cold and impervious to surprise. 'We are to ride from this battle, Warchief?'

'To preserve the Holy Book, such flight may be a necessity, old friend. Come the dawn, we hover . . . on the very cusp.'

'To gauge the wind.'

'Yes, T'morol, to gauge the wind.'

The bearded warrior nodded. 'The horses are being saddled. I will hasten the preparations.'

Heboric listened to the silence. Only his bones could feel the tingling hum of a sorcerous web spanning the entire oasis and its ruined city, the taut vibrations rising and falling as disparate forces began to move across it, then, with savage disregard, tore through it.

He stirred from the cot, groaning with the stab of force-healed wounds, and climbed shakily to his feet. The coals had died in their braziers. The gloom felt solid, reluctant to yield as he made his way to the doorway. Heboric bared his teeth. His taloned hands twitched.

Ghosts stalked the dead city. Even the gods felt close, drawn to witness all that was to come. *Witness, or to seize the moment and act directly. A nudge here, a tug there, if only to appease their egos . . . if only to see what happens.* These were the games he despised, source of his fiercest defiance all those years ago. The shape of his crime, if crime it was.

And so they took my hands.

Until another god gave them back.

He was, he realized, indifferent to Treach. A reluctant Destriant to the new god of war, despite the gifts. Nor had his desires changed. *Otataral Island, and the giant of jade – that is what awaits me. The returning of power.* Even as those last words tracked across his mind, he knew that a deceit rode among them. A secret he knew but to which he would fashion no shape. Not yet, perhaps not until he found himself standing in the wasteland, beneath the shadow of that crooked spire.

But first, I must meet a more immediate challenge – getting out of this camp alive.

He hesitated another moment at the doorway, reaching out into the darkness beyond with all his senses. Finding the path clear – his next twenty strides at least – he darted forward.

Rolling the acorn in his fingers one last time, he tucked it into a fold in his sash and eased snake-like from the crack.

'Oh, Hood's heartless hands . . .'

The song was a distant thunder trembling along his bones, and he didn't like it. Worse yet, there were powers awakened in the oasis ahead that even he, a non-practitioner of sorcery, could feel like fire in his blood.

Kalam Mekhar checked his long-knives yet again, then resheathed them. The temptation was great to keep the otataral weapon out, and so deny any magic sent his way. *But that goes both ways, doesn't it?*

He studied the way ahead. The starlight seemed strangely muted. He drew from memory as best he could, from what he had seen from his hiding place during the day. Palms, their boles spectral as they rose above tumbled mudbricks and cut stone. The remnants of corrals, pens and shepherds' huts. Stretches of sandy ground littered with brittle fronds and husks. There were no new silhouettes awaiting him.

Kalam set forth.

He could see the angular lines of buildings ahead, all low to the ground, suggesting little more than stretches of mudbrick foundations from which canvas, wicker and rattan walls rose. Occupied residences, then.

Far off to Kalam's right was the grey smudge of that strange forest of stone trees. He had considered making his approach through it, but there was something uncanny and unwelcoming about that place, and he suspected it was not as empty as it appeared.

Approaching what seemed to be a well-trod avenue between huts, he caught a flash of movement, darting from left to right across the aisle. Kalam dropped lower and froze. A second figure followed, then a third, fourth and fifth.

A hand. Now, who in this camp would organize their assassins into hands? He waited another half-dozen heartbeats, then set off. He came opposite the route the killers had taken and slipped into their wake. The five were moving at seven paces apart, two paces more than would a Claw. *Damn, did Cotillion suspect? Is this what he wanted me to confirm?*

These are Talons.

Seven or five, it made little difference to Kalam.

He came within sight of the trailing assassin. The figure bore magically invested items, making his form blurry, wavering. He was wearing dark grey, tight-fitting clothes, moccasined, gloved and hooded. Blackened daggers gleamed in his hands.

Not just patrolling, then, but hunting.

Kalam padded to within five paces of the man, then darted forward.

His right hand reached around to clamp hard across the man's mouth and jaw, his left hand simultaneously closing on the head's opposite side. A savage twist snapped the killer's neck.

Vomit spurted against Kalam's leather-sheathed palm, but he held on to his grip, guiding the corpse to the ground. Straddling the body, he released his grip, wiped his hand dry against the grey shirt, then moved on.

Two hundred heartbeats later and there were but two left. Their route had taken them, via a twisting, roundabout path, towards a district marked by the ruins of what had once been grand temples. They were drawn up at the edge of a broad concourse, awaiting their comrades, no doubt.

Kalam approached them as would the third hunter in the line. Neither was paying attention, their gazes fixed on a building on the other side of the concourse. At the last moment Kalam drew both long-knives and thrust them into the backs of the two assassins.

Soft grunts, and both men sank to the dusty flagstones. The blow to the leader of the Talon's hand was instantly fatal, but Kalam had twisted the other thrust slightly to one side, and he now crouched down beside the dying man. 'If your masters are listening,' he murmured, 'and they should be. Compliments of the Claw. See you soon . . .'

He tugged the two knives free, cleaned the blades and sheathed them.

The hunters' target was, he assumed, within the ruined building that had been the sole focus of their attention. Well enough – Kalam had no friends in this damned camp.

He set out along the edge of the concourse.

At the mouth of another alley he found three corpses, all young girls. The blood and knife-wounds indicated they had put up a fierce fight, and two spattered trails led away, in the direction of the temple.

Kalam tracked them until he was certain that they led through the half-ruined structure's gaping doorway, then he halted.

The bitter reek of sorcery wafted from the broad entrance. *Damn, this place has been newly sanctified.*

There was no sound from within. He edged forward until he came to one side of the doorway.

A body lay just inside, grey-swathed, fixed in a contortion of limbs, evincing that he had died beneath a wave of magic. Shadows were flowing in the darkness beyond.

Kalam drew his otataral long-knife, crept in through the doorway.

The shadowy wraiths flinched back.

The floor had collapsed long ago, leaving a vast pit. Five paces ahead, at the base of a rubble-strewn ramp, a young girl sat amidst the blood and entrails of three more corpses. She was streaked with gore, her eyes darkly luminous as she looked up at Kalam. 'Do you remember the dark?' she asked.

Ignoring her question, he stepped past at a safe distance. 'Make no move, lass, and you'll survive my visit.'

A thin voice chuckled from the gloom at the far end of the pit. 'Her mind is gone, Claw. No time, alas, to fully harden my subjects to the horrors of modern life, try though I might. In any case, you should know that I am not your enemy. Indeed, the one who seeks to kill me this night is none other than the Malazan renegade, Korbolo Dom. And, of course, Kamist Reloe. Shall I give you directions to their abode?'

'I'll find it in due course,' Kalam murmured.

'Do you think your otataral blade sufficient, Claw? Here, in my temple? Do you understand the nature of this place? I imagine you believe you do, but I am afraid you are in error. Slavemaster, offer our guest some wine from that jug.'

A misshapen figure squirmed wetly across the rubble from Kalam's left. No hands or feet. A mass of suppurating sores and the mangled rot of leprosy. With horrible absurdity, a silver tray had been strapped to the creature's back, on which sat a squat, fired clay jug.

'He is rather slow, I'm afraid. But I assure you, the wine is so exquisite that you will agree it is worth the wait. Assassin, you are in the presence of Bidithal, archpriest of all that is sundered, broken, wounded and suffering. My own ... awakening proved both long and torturous, I admit. I had fashioned, in my own mind, every detail of the cult I would lead. All the while unaware that the shaping was being ... guided.

'Blindness, wilful and, indeed, spiteful. Even when the fated new House was laid out before me, I did not realize the truth. This shattered fragment of Kurald Emurlahn, Claw, shall not be the plaything of a desert goddess. Nor of the Empress. None of you shall have it, for it shall become the heart of the new House of Chains. Tell your empress to stand aside, assassin. We are indifferent to who would rule the land beyond the Holy Desert. She can have it.'

'And Sha'ik?'

'You can have her as well. Marched back to Unta in chains – and that is far more poetic than you will ever know.'

The shadow-wraiths – torn souls from Kurald Emurlahn – were drawing closer round Kalam, and he realized, with a chill, that his otataral long-knife might well prove insufficient. 'An interesting offer,' he rumbled. 'But something tells me there are more lies than truths within it, Bidithal.'

'I suppose you are right,' the archpriest sighed. 'I need Sha'ik, for this night and the morrow at least. Febryl and Korbolo Dom must be thwarted, but I assure you, you and I can work together towards such an end, since it benefits us both. Korbolo Dom calls himself Master of the Talon. Yes, he would return to Laseen's embrace, more or less, and use Sha'ik to bargain for his own position. As for Febryl, well, I assure you, what he awaits no-one but he is mad enough to desire.'

'Why do you bother with all this, Bidithal? You've no

intention of letting me leave here alive. And here's another thing. A pair of beasts are coming – hounds, not of Shadow, but something else. Did you summon them, Bidithal? Do you, or your Crippled God, truly believe you can control them? If so, then it is you two who are mad.'

Bidithal leaned forward. 'They seek a master!' he hissed.

Ah, so Cotillion was right about the Chained One. 'One who is worthy,' Kalam replied. 'In other words, one who is meaner and tougher than they are. And in this oasis, they will find no such individual. And so, I fear, they will kill everyone.'

'You know nothing of this, assassin,' Bidithal murmured, leaning back. 'Nor of the power I now possess. As for not permitting you to leave here alive ... true enough, I suppose. You've revealed too much knowledge, and you are proving far less enthusiastic to my proposals than I would have hoped. An unfortunate revelation, but it no longer matters. My servants were scattered about earlier, you see, defending every approach, requiring time to draw them in, to arrange them between us. Ah, Slavemaster has arrived. By all means, have some wine. I am prepared to linger here for that. Once you are done, however, I must take my leave. I made a promise to Sha'ik, after all, and I mean to keep it. Should you, by some strange miracle, escape here alive, know that I will not oppose your efforts against Korbolo Dom and his cadre. You will have earned that much, at least.'

'Best leave now, then, Bidithal. I have no interest in wine this night.'

'As you wish.'

Darkness swept in to engulf the archpriest, and Kalam shivered at the uncanny familiarity of the sorcerous departure.

The wraiths attacked.

Both knives slashed out, and inhuman screams filled the chamber. As it turned out, his otataral weapon proved sufficient after all. That, and the timely arrival of a god.

933

Korbolo Dom seemed to have unleashed an army upon his own allies this night. Again and again, Karsa Orlong found his path blocked by eager killers. Their corpses were strewn in his wake. He had taken a few minor wounds from knives invested with sorcery, but most of the blood dripping from the giant warrior belonged to his victims.

He strode with his sword in both hands now, tip lowered and to one side. There had been four assassins hiding outside Heboric Ghost Hands's dwelling. After killing them, Karsa slashed a new doorway in the tent wall and entered, only to find the abode empty. Frustrated, he set out for the temple round. Leoman's pit was unoccupied as well, and appeared to have been so for some time.

Approaching Bidithal's temple, Karsa slowed his steps as he heard fierce fighting within. Shrill screams echoed. Raising his weapon, the Toblakai edged forward.

A figure was crawling out from the doorway on its belly, gibbering to itself. A moment later Karsa recognized the man. He waited until Slavemaster's desperate efforts brought him up against the Toblakai's feet. A disease-ravaged face twisted into view.

'He fights like a demon!' Silgar rasped. 'Both blades cut through the wraiths and leave them writhing in pieces! A god stands at his shoulder. Kill them, Teblor! Kill them both!'

Karsa sneered. 'I take no commands from you, Slavemaster, or have you forgotten that?'

'Fool!' Silgar spat. 'We are brothers in the House now, you and I. You are the Knight of Chains, and I am the Leper. The Crippled God has chosen us! And Bidithal, he has become the Magi—'

'Yes, Bidithal. He hides within?'

'No – he wisely fled, as I am doing. The Claw and his patron god are even now slaying the last of his shadow servants. You are the Knight – you possess your own patron, Karsa Orlong of the Teblor. Kill the enemy – it is what you must do—'

Karsa smiled. 'And so I shall.' He reversed his grip on his sword and drove the point down between Silgar's shoulder blades, severing the spine then punching out through the sternum to bury itself a hand's width deep between two flagstones.

Vile fluids poured from the Slavemaster. His head cracked down on the stone, and his life was done. *Leoman was right, long ago – a quick death would have been the better choice.*

Karsa pulled the sword free. 'I follow no patron god,' he growled.

He turned from the temple entrance. Bidithal would have used sorcery to escape, drawing shadows about himself in an effort to remain unseen. Yet his passage would leave footprints in the dust.

The Toblakai stepped past the body of Silgar, the man who had once sought to enslave him, and began searching.

Twenty of Mathok's clan warriors accompanied Corabb Bhilan Thenu'alas on his return to Leoman's encampment. Their journey was unopposed, although Corabb was certain hidden eyes followed their progress.

They rode up the slope to the hill's summit and were challenged by sentinels. A more welcoming sound Corabb could not imagine. Familiar voices, warriors he had fought alongside against the Malazans.

'It is Corabb!' He had been given a hook-bladed sword drawn from the Chosen One's armoury, and he now raised it high in salute as the picket guards emerged from their places of hiding. 'I must speak with Leoman! Where is he?'

'Asleep,' one of the sentinels growled. 'If you're lucky, Bhilan, your arrival, loud as it was, has awakened him. Ride to the centre of the summit, but leave your escort here.'

That brought Corabb up short. 'They are Mathok's own—'

'Leoman's orders. No-one from the oasis is allowed to enter our camp.'

Scowling, Corabb nodded and waved back his fellow horse warriors. 'Take no offence, friends,' he called, 'I beg you.' Without waiting to gauge their reaction, he dismounted and hurried to Leoman's tent.

The warleader was standing outside the flap, drinking deep from a waterskin. He was out of his armour, wearing only a thin, sweat-stained linen shirt.

Corabb halted before him. 'There is much to tell you, Leoman of the Flails.'

'Out with it, then,' Leoman replied when he'd finished drinking.

'I was your only messenger to survive to reach Sha'ik. She has had a change of heart – she now commands that you lead the Army of the Apocalpyse come the morrow. She would have you, not Korbolo Dom, leading us to victory.'

'Would she now,' he drawled, then squinted and looked away. 'The Napan has his assassins between us and Sha'ik?'

'Aye, but they will not challenge our entire force – they would be mad to attempt such a thing.'

'True. And Korbolo Dom knows this—'

'He has not yet been informed of the change of command – at least he hadn't when I left. Although Sha'ik had issued a demand for his presence—'

'Which he will ignore. As for the rest, the Napan knows. Tell me, Corabb, do you think his Dogslayers will follow any other commander?'

'They shall have no choice! The Chosen One has so ordered!'

Leoman slowly nodded. Then he turned back to his tent. 'Break camp. We ride to Sha'ik.'

Exultation filled Corabb's chest. Tomorrow would belong to Leoman of the Flails. 'As it should be,' he whispered.

Kalam stepped outside. His clothes were in tatters, but he was whole. Though decidedly shaken. He had always considered himself one of the ablest of assassins, and he had drawn a blade against a veritable host of inimical, deadly foes over the years. But Cotillion had put him to shame.

No wonder the bastard's a god. Hood's breath, I've never before seen such skill. And that damned rope!

Kalam drew a deep breath. He had done as the Patron of Assassins had asked. He had found the source of the threat to the Realm of Shadow. *Or at least confirmed a host of suspicions. This fragment of Kurald Emurlahn will be the path to usurpation . . . by none other than the Crippled God.* The House of Chains had come into play, and the world had grown very fraught indeed.

He shook himself. Leave that to Cotillion and Ammanas. He had other, more immediate tasks to attend to this night. And the Patron of Assassins had been kind enough to deliver a pair of Kalam's favourite weapons . . .

His eyes lit upon the leprous corpse lying a half-dozen paces away, then narrowed. Kalam moved closer. *Gods below, that is some wound. If I didn't know better, I'd say from the sword of a T'lan Imass.* The blood was thickening, soaking up dust from the flagstones.

Kalam paused to think. Korbolo Dom would not establish his army's camp among the ruins of this city. Nor in the stone forest to the west. The Napan would want an area both clear and level, with sufficient room for banking and trenches, and open lines of sight.

East, then, what had once been irrigated fields for the city, long ago.

He swung in that direction and set out.

From one pool of darkness to the next, along strangely empty streets and alleys. Heavy layers of sorcery had settled upon this oasis, seeming to flow in streams – some of them so thick that Kalam found himself leaning forward in order to push his way through. A miasma of currents, mixed beyond recognition, and none of them palatable. His bones ached, his head hurt, and his eyes felt as if someone was stirring hot sand behind them.

He found a well-trod track heading due east and

followed it, staying to one side where the shadows were deep. Then saw, two hundred paces ahead, a fortified embankment.

Malazan layout. That, Napan, was a mistake.

He was about to draw closer when he saw the vanguard to a company emerge through the gate. Soldiers on foot followed, flanked by lancers.

Kalam ducked into an alley.

The troop marched past at half-pace, weapons muffled, the horses' hoofs leather-socked. Curious, but the fewer soldiers in the camp the better, as far as he was concerned. It was likely that all but the reserve companies would have been ensconced in their positions overlooking the field of battle. Of course, Korbolo Dom would not be careless when it came to protecting himself.

He calls himself master of the Talon, after all. Not that Cotillion, who was Dancer, knows a damned thing about them. Sparing the revelation only a sneer.

The last of the soldiers filed past. Kalam waited another fifty heartbeats, then he set out towards the Dogslayer encampment.

The embankment was preceded by a steep-sided trench. Sufficient encumbrance to a charging army, but only a minor inconvenience to a lone assassin. He clambered down, across, then up the far side, halting just beneath the crest-line.

There would be pickets. The gate was thirty paces on his left, lantern-lit. He moved to just beyond the light's range, then edged up onto the bank. A guard patrolled within sight on his right, not close enough to spot the assassin as he squirmed across the hard-packed, sun-baked earth to the far edge.

Another trench, this one shallower, and beyond lay the ordered ranks of tents, the very centre of the grid dominated by a larger command tent.

Kalam made his way into the camp.

As he had suspected, most of the tents were empty, and

before long he was crouched opposite the wide street encircling the command tent.

Guards lined every side, five paces apart, assault crossbows cocked and cradled in arms. Torches burned on poles every ten paces, bathing the street in flickering light. Three additional figures blocked the doorway, grey-clad and bearing no visible weapons.

Flesh and blood cordon . . . then sorcerous wards. Well, one thing at a time.

He drew out his pair of ribless crossbows. A Claw's weapons, screw-torqued, the metal blackened. He set the quarrels in their grooves and carefully cocked both weapons. Then settled back to give the situation some thought.

Even as he watched he saw the air swirl before the command tent's entrance, and a portal opened. Blinding white light, the flare of fire, then Kamist Reloe emerged. The portal contracted behind him, then winked out.

The mage looked exhausted but strangely triumphant. He gestured at the guards then strode into the tent. The three grey-clothed assassins followed the mage inside.

A hand light as a leaf settled on Kalam's shoulder, and a voice rasped, 'Eyes forward, soldier.'

He knew that voice, from more years back than he'd like to think. *But that bastard's dead. Dead before Surly took the throne.*

'Granted,' the voice continued, and Kalam knew that acid-spattered face was grinning, 'no love's lost between me and the company I'm sharing . . . again. Figured I'd seen the last of every damn one of them . . . and you. Well, never mind that. Need a way in there, right? Best we mount a diversion, then. Give us fifty heartbeats . . . at least *you* can count those, Corporal.'

The hand lifted away.

Kalam Mekhar drew a deep, shaky breath. *What in Hood's name is going on here? That damned captain went renegade. They found his body in Malaz City the morning after*

*the assassinations . . . or something closely approximating his
body . . .*

He focused his gaze once more upon the command tent.

From beyond it a scream broke the night, then the
unmistakable flash and earth-shaking thump of Moranth
munitions.

Suddenly the guards were running.

Tucking one of the crossbows into his belt, Kalam drew
out the otataral long-knife. He waited until only two
Dogslayers were visible, both to the right of the entrance,
facing the direction of the attack – where screams ripped
the air, as much born of horror as from the pain of wounds
– then surged forward.

Raising the crossbow in his left hand. The recoil
thrumming the bones of his arm. The quarrel burying itself
in the back of the further guard. Long-knife thrusting into
the nearer man, point punching through leather between
plates of bronze, piercing flesh then sliding between ribs to
stab the heart.

Blood sprayed as he tugged the weapon free and darted
into the tent's doorway.

Wards collapsed around him.

Within the threshold he reloaded the crossbow and
affixed it in the brace on his wrist – beneath the
voluminous sleeves. Then did the same with the other one
on his left wrist.

The main chamber before him held but a lone occupant,
a grey-robed assassin who spun at Kalam's arrival, a pair of
hooked Kethra knives flashing into guard position. The
face within the hood was expressionless, a narrow, sun-
darkened visage tattooed in the Pardu style, the swirling
artistry broken by a far heavier sigil branded into the man's
forehead – a talon.

The grey-clad assassin suddenly smiled. 'Kalam Mekhar.
I suppose you don't remember me.'

In answer Kalam drew out his second long-knife and
attacked.

Sparks bit the air as the blades clashed and whispered, the Pardu driven back two steps until, with a sweeping backslash, he leapt to the right and sidestepped round to give himself more space. Kalam maintained the pressure, weapons flashing as they darted out, keeping the Talon on the defensive.

He had skill with those heavy Kethra knives, and both quickness and strength. Kalam's blades took blocking blows that reverberated up the bones of his arms. Clearly, the Pardu was seeking to break the thinner weapons, and, well made as they were, nicks and notches were being driven into the edges.

Further, Kalam knew he was running out of time. The diversion continued, but now, along with the crack of sharpers ripping the air, waves of sorcery had begun rolling in deafening counterpoint. Whatever the nature of the squads attacking the Dogslayers, mages were giving answer.

Worse yet, this Talon didn't enter here alone.

Kalam suddenly shifted stance, extending the knife in his left hand and drawing his right hand back to take guard position. He led with the point, evading the parries, and, in increments, slowly retracted his left arm, beginning at the shoulder. The faintest pivoting of hips, drawing the lead leg back—

And the Pardu closed the distance with a single step.

Kalam's right hand shot across, beating aside both Kethra blades, simultaneously lunging high with his left hand.

The Pardu flung both weapons up to parry and trap the thrust.

And Kalam stepped in still closer, stabbing crossways with the long-knife in his right hand. Punching the tip into the man's lower belly.

A gush of fluids, the edge gouging along the spine, the point then plunging out the other side.

The parry and trap had torn the long-knife in his left hand from its grasp, flinging it to one side.

But the Talon was already sagging, folding over the belly wound and the weapon impaling him.

Kalam leaned closer. 'No,' he growled. 'I don't.'

He tugged his knife free and let the dying man fall to the layered rugs of the tent floor.

'A damned shame,' mused a voice near the back wall.

Kalam slowly turned. 'Kamist Reloe. I've been looking for you.'

The High Mage smiled. He was flanked by the other two Talons, one of whom held Kalam's second long-knife and was examining it curiously. 'We've been expecting a strike by the Claws,' Kamist Reloe said. 'Although an attack by long-dead ghosts was, I admit, not among our expectations. It is Raraku, you understand. This damned land is . . . awakening. Well, never mind that. Soon, there will be . . . silence.'

'He holds an otataral weapon,' the assassin on Kamist's right said.

Kalam glanced down at the blood-smeared long-knife in his right hand. 'Ah, well, that.'

'Then,' the High Mage sighed, 'you two shall have to take him in the, uh, mundane way. Will you suffice?'

The one holding the long-knife flung it behind him and nodded. 'We've watched. He has patterns . . . and skill. Against either one of us singly we'd be in trouble. But against both of us?'

Kalam had to agree with the man's assessment. He stepped back, and sheathed his weapon. 'He's probably right,' he rumbled. With his other hand he drew out the acorn and tossed it on the floor. All three men flinched back as it bounced then rolled towards them. The innocuous object came to a halt.

One of the Talons snorted. Kicked it to one side.

Then the two assassins stepped forward, knives flickering.

Kalam raised both arms, twisted his wrists outward, then flexed them hard.

Both Talons grunted, then staggered backward, each impaled by a quarrel.

'Careless of you,' Kalam muttered.

Kamist shrieked, unveiling his warren.

The wave of sorcery that struck the High Mage caught him entirely unawares, coming from one side. Death-magic closed around him in a sizzling, raging web of black fire.

His shriek escalated. Then Kamist Reloe sprawled, the sorcery still flickering over his twitching, burned body.

A figure slowly emerged from where the Talon had kicked the acorn moments earlier, and crouched down beside Kamist Reloe. 'It's disloyalty that bothers us the most,' he said to the dying High Mage. 'We always answer it. Always have. Always will.'

Kalam recovered his second long-knife, eyes on the closed flaps on the chamber's back wall. 'He's through there,' he said, then paused and grinned. 'Good to see you, Quick.'

Quick Ben glanced over and nodded.

The wizard was, Kalam saw, looking older. Worn down. *Scars not written on his skin, but on his heart. He will, I suspect, have nothing good to tell me when all this is done.* 'Did you,' he asked Quick Ben, 'have anything to do with the diversion?'

'No. Nor did Hood, although the hoary bastard's arrived. This is all Raraku.'

'So Kamist said, not that I understand either of you.'

'I'll explain later, friend,' Quick Ben said, rising. He faced the back flap. 'He has that witch Henaras with him, I think. She's behind some fierce wards that Kamist Reloe raised.'

Kalam approached the doorway. 'Leave those to me,' he growled, unsheathing his otataral long-knife.

The room immediately beyond was small, dominated by a map table, on which was sprawled the corpse of Henaras. Blood was still flowing in streams down the table's sides.

Kalam glanced back at Quick Ben and raised his brows.

The wizard shook his head.

The assassin gingerly approached, and his eyes caught something glimmering silver-white on the woman's chest.

A pearl.

'Seems the way is clear,' Kalam whispered.

Another flap slashed the wall opposite.

Using the points of his knives, Kalam prised it open.

A large high-backed chair filled the next chamber, on which was seated Korbolo Dom.

His blue skin was a ghastly grey, and his hands shook where they rested on the chair's ornate arms. When he spoke his voice was high and tight, jittery with fear. 'I sent an emissary to the Adjunct. An invitation. I am prepared to attack Sha'ik and her tribes – with my Dogslayers.'

Kalam grunted. 'If you think we've come with her answer, you'd be wrong, Korbolo.'

The Napan's eyes darted to Quick Ben. 'We assumed you were either dead with the rest of the Bridgeburners, or still on Genabackis.'

The wizard shrugged. 'Tayschrenn sent me ahead. Even so, he's brought the fleet across on mage-driven winds. Dujek Onearm and his legions reached Ehrlitan a week past—'

'What's left of those legions, you mean—'

'More than enough to complement the Adjunct's forces, I should think.'

Kalam stared between the two men. *The Bridgeburners . . . dead? Whiskeyjack? Onearm's Host – gods below, what happened over there?*

'We can salvage this,' Korbolo Dom said, leaning forward. 'All of Seven Cities, returned to the Empire. Sha'ik brought in chains before the Empress—'

'And for you and your soldiers a pardon?' Quick Ben asked. 'Korbolo Dom, you have truly lost your mind—'

'Then die!' the Napan shrieked, leaping forward, hands reaching for the wizard's throat.

Kalam stepped in and, knife reversed, struck Korbolo Dom hard against the side of the head.

The Napan staggered.

A second fist shattered his nose and sent him sprawling.

Quick Ben stared down at the man. 'Truss him up, Kalam. That diversion's over, from the silence outside – I'll find us a way out.'

Kalam began tying the unconscious man's hands. 'Where are we taking him?'

'I've a thought to that.'

The assassin glanced up at his friend. 'Quick? The Bridgeburners? Whiskeyjack?'

The hard, dark eyes softened. 'Dead. Barring Picker and a handful of others. There's a tale there, and I promise I will tell it in full . . . later.'

Kalam stared down at Korbolo Dom. 'I feel like cutting throats,' he rasped.

'Not him. Not now.'

Hold back on the feelings, Kalam Mekhar. Hold back on everything. Quick's right. In time. In time . . .

Oh, Whiskeyjack . . .

There was time for . . . everything. This night and for the day to come, Bidithal needed Sha'ik. And the Whirlwind Goddess. And perhaps, if all went well, there would be the opportunity for bargaining. *Once the goddess's rage has cooled, annealed into beauty by victory – we can still achieve this.*

But I know now what Febryl has done. I know what Korbolo Dom and Kamist Reloe plan for the dawn.

They could be stopped. The knives could be turned.

He hobbled as quickly as he could towards Sha'ik's palace. Ghosts flitted about on the edges of his vision, but his shadows protected him. In the distance he heard screams, detonations and sorcery – coming, he realized, from the Dogslayers' camp. *Ah, so that Claw's made it that far, has he? Both good and . . . troubling. Well, at the very least he'll keep Kamist occupied.*

945

Of course, the danger posed by the roving assassins still existed, though that was diminishing the closer he got to Sha'ik's abode.

Still, the streets and alleys were disturbingly deserted.

He came within sight of the sprawling palace, and saw with relief the pools of torchlight surrounding it.

Counter the Napan's gambit – awaken the goddess to the threat awaiting her. Then hunt down that gnarled bhok'aral Febryl and see his skin stripped from his writhing flesh. Even the goddess – yes, even the goddess will have to recognize me. My power. When flanked by my new pets—

A hand shot out of the darkness and closed about Bidithal's neck. He was lifted into the air – flailing – then thrown hard to the ground. Blinded. Choking.

His shadow-servants swarmed to defend him.

A growl, the hissing swing of something massive that cut a sweeping path – and suddenly the wraiths were gone.

Slowly, Bidithal's bulging eyes made out the figure crouched above him.

Toblakai—

'You should have left her alone,' Karsa Orlong said quietly, his voice devoid of inflection. Behind and around the giant were gathering ghosts, chained souls.

We are both servants of the same god! You fool! Let me speak! I would save Sha'ik!

'But you didn't. I know, Bidithal, where your sick desires come from. I know where your pleasure hides – the pleasure you would take from others. Witness.'

Karsa Orlong set down his stone sword, then reached between Bidithal's legs.

A hand closed indiscriminately around all that it found.

And tore.

Until, with a ripping of tendons and shreds of muscle, a flood of blood and other fluids, the hand came away with its mangled prize.

The pain was unbearable. The pain was a rending of his soul. It devoured him.

And blood was pouring out, hot as fire, even as deathly cold stole across his skin, seeped into his limbs.

The scene above him blackened, until only Toblakai's impassive, battered face remained, coolly watching Bidithal's death.

Death? Yes. You fool, Toblakai—

The hand around his neck relaxed, drew away.

Involuntarily, Bidithal drew in an agonizing breath and made to scream—

Something soft and bloody was pushed into his mouth.

'For you, Bidithal. For every nameless girl-child you destroyed. Here. Choke on your pleasure.'

And choke he did. Until Hood's Gate yawned—

And there, gathered by the Lord of Death, waited demons who were of like nature to Bidithal himself, gleefully closing about their new victim.

A lifetime of vicious pleasure. An eternity of pain in answer.

For even Hood understood the necessity for balance.

Lostara Yil edged up from the sinkhole and squinted in an effort to pierce the gloom. A glance behind her revealed a starlit desert, luminous and glittering. Yet, ahead, darkness swathed the oasis and the ruined city within it. A short while earlier she had heard distant thumps, faint screams, but now silence had returned.

The air had grown bitter cold. Scowling, Lostara checked her weapons, then made to leave.

'Make no move,' a voice murmured from a pace or two off to her right.

Her head snapped round, then her scowl deepened. 'If you're here to watch, Cotillion, there's little to see. I woke Pearl, and he hardly swore at all, despite the headache. He's in there, somewhere—'

'Aye, he is, lass. But already he's returning . . . because he can feel what's coming.'

947

'What's coming. Enough to make you hide here beside me?'

The shadow-shrouded god seemed to shrug. 'There are times when it is advisable to step back . . . and wait. The Holy Desert itself senses the approach of an ancient foe, and will rise in answer if need be. Even more precarious, the fragment of Kurald Emurlahn that the Whirlwind Goddess would claim is manifesting itself. The goddess is fashioning a portal, a gate – one massive enough to swallow this entire oasis. Thus, she too makes a play for Raraku's immortal heart. The irony is that she herself is being manipulated, by a far cleverer god, who would take this fragment for himself, and call it his House of Chains. So you see, Lostara Shadow Dancer, best we remain precisely where we are. For tonight, and in this place, worlds are at war.'

'It is nothing to Pearl and me,' she insisted, squinting hard into the gloom. 'We're here for Felisin—'

'And you have found her, but she remains beyond you. Beyond Pearl as well. For the moment . . .'

'Then we must needs but await the clearing of the path.'

'Aye. As I have advised, patience.'

Shadows swirled, hissed over sand, then the god was gone.

Lostara grunted. 'Goodbye to you as well,' she muttered, then drew her cloak tighter about herself and settled down to wait.

Assassins armed with crossbows had crept up behind him. Febryl had killed them, one after another, as soon as they arrived, with a host of most painful spells, and now his sorcerous web told him that there were no more. Indeed, Korbolo Dom and Kamist Reloe had been bearded in their den. By ghosts and worse – agents of the Malazan Empire.

Wide and bloody paths had carved messily across his web, leaving him blind here and there, but none stretched anywhere close to his position . . . so far. And soon, the oasis behind him would become as a nightmare wakened into horrid reality, and Febryl himself would vanish from the minds of his enemies in the face of more immediate threats.

Dawn was but two bells away. While, behind him, darkness had devoured the oasis, the sky overhead and to the east was comparatively bright with the glitter of stars. Indeed, everything was proceeding perfectly.

The starlight also proved sufficient for Febryl to detect the shadow that fell over him.

'I never liked you much,' rumbled a voice above him.

Squealing, Febryl sought to dive forward.

But was effortlessly plucked and lifted high from the ground.

Then broken.

The snap of his spine was like brittle wood in the cold night air.

Karsa Orlong flung Febryl's corpse away. He glared up at the stars for a moment, drew a deep breath into his lungs, and sought to clear his mind.

Urugal's withered voice was screaming in his skull. It had been that voice, and that will, that had driven him step by step from the oasis.

The false god of the Uryd tribe wanted Karsa Orlong . . . gone.

He was being pushed hard . . . away from what was coming, from what was about to happen in the oasis.

But Karsa did not like being pushed.

He lifted his sword clear of his harness rings and closed both hands about the grip, lowering the point to hover just above the ground, then forced himself to turn about and face the oasis.

A thousand ghostly chains stretched taut behind him, then began pulling.

The Teblor growled under his breath and leaned forward. *I am the master of these chains. I, Karsa Orlong, yield to none.*

Not gods, not the souls I have slain. I will walk forward now, and either resistance shall end, or the chains will be snapped.

Besides, I have left my horse tethered in the stone forest.

Twin howls tore the night air above the oasis, sudden and fierce as cracks of lightning.

Karsa Orlong smiled. *Ah, they have arrived.*

He lifted his sword's point slightly higher, then surged forward.

It would not do – it turned out – to have the chains sundered. The tension suddenly vanished, and, for this night at least, all resistance to Toblakai's will had ended.

He left the ridge and descended the slope, into the gloom once more.

Fist Gamet was lying on his cot, struggling to breathe as a tightness seized his throat. Thunder filled his head, in thrumming waves of pain radiating out from a spot just above and behind his right eye.

Pain such as he had never felt before, driving him onto his side, the cot creaking and pitching as nausea racked him, the vomit spraying onto the floor. But the emptying of his stomach offered no surcease from the agony in his skull.

His eyes were open but he was blind.

There had been headaches. Every day, since his fall from his horse. But nothing like this.

The barely healed knife-slash in his palm had reopened during his contortions, smearing sticky blood across his face and brow when he sought to claw the pain out from his head, and the wound now felt as if it was afire, scorching his veins.

Groaning, he clambered sideways from the cot and then halted, on his hands and knees, head hanging down, as waves of trembling shivered through him.

I need to move. I need to act. Something. Anything.

I need—

A time of blankness, then he found himself standing near the tent flap. Weighted in his armour, gauntlets

950

covering his hands, helm on his head. The pain was fading, a cool emptiness rising in its wake.

He needed to go outside. He needed his horse.

Gamet strode from the tent. A guard accosted him but he waved the woman away and hurried towards the corrals.

Ride. Ride out. It's time.

Then he was cinching the saddle of his horse, waiting for the beast to release its breath, then drawing it a notch tighter. A clever horse. Paran stables, of course. Fast and of almost legendary endurance. Impatient with incompetence, ever testing the rider's claim to being in charge, but that was to be expected from such a fine breed.

Gamet swung himself into the saddle. It felt good to be riding once more. On the move, the ground whispering past as he rode down the back ramp, then round the jagged island and towards the basin.

He saw three figures ahead, standing at the ridge, and thought nothing strange as to their presence. *They are what will come. These three.*

Nil. Nether. The lad, Grub.

The last turned as Gamet reined in beside them. And nodded. 'The Wickans and Malazans are on the flanks, Fist. But your assault will be straight up the Dogslayers' main ramp.' And he pointed.

Footsoldiers and cavalry were massing in the basin, moving through the thick gloom. Gamet could hear the whisper of armour, feel the thud of countless horse hoofs. He saw banners and standards, hanging limp and ragged.

'Ride to them, Fist,' Grub said.

And he saluted the child and set heels to his mount's flanks.

Black and rust-red armour, visored helms with ornate cheek-guards, short thrusting javelins and kite shields, the rumble of countless booted feet – he rode alongside one column, casting an appraising eye over the companies of infantry.

Then a wing of cavalry swept round to engulf him. One

rider rode close. A dragon-winged helm swivelled to face him. 'Ride with us, soldier?'

'I cannot,' Gamet replied. 'I am the Fist. I must command.'

'Not this night,' the warrior replied. 'Fight at our sides, as the soldier you are. Remember the old battles? When all that was required was the guarding of the companions flanking you. Such will be this night. Leave the commanding to the lords. Ride with us in freedom. And glory.'

A surge of exultation swept through Gamet. The pain in his head was gone. He could feel his blood racing like fire in his muscles. He wanted this. Yes, he wanted this very thing.

Gamet unsheathed his sword, the sound an echoing rasp in the chill air.

His helmed companion laughed. 'Are you with us, soldier?'

'I am, friend.'

They reached the base of the cobbled ramp, slowing to firm up their formation. A broad wedge that then began assailing the slope, hoofs striking sparks off the stones.

The Dogslayers had yet to sound an alarm.

Fools. They've slept through it all. Or perhaps sorcery has deadened the sounds of our preparation. Ah, yes. Nil and Nether. They are still there, on the ridge the other side of the basin.

The company's standard bearer was just a few horses to Gamet's left. He squinted up at the banner, wondered that he had never seen it before. There was something of the Khundryl in its design, torn and frayed though it was. A clan of the Burned Tears, then – which made sense given the archaic armour his comrades were wearing. Archaic and half rotting, in fact. *Too long stored in chests – moths and other vermin have assailed it, but the bronze looks sound enough, if tarnished and pitted. A word to the commanders later, I think . . .*

Cool, gauging thoughts, even as his proud horse

thundered alongside the others. Gamet glared upward, and saw the crest directly before them. He lifted high his longsword and loosed a savage scream.

The wedge poured over the crest, swept out into the unaware ranks of Dogslayers, still huddled down in their trenches.

Screams on all sides, strangely muted, almost faint. Sounds of battle, yet they seemed a league distant, as if carried on the wind. Gamet swung his sword, his eyes meeting those of Dogslayers, seeing the horror writ there. Watching mouths open to shriek, yet hardly any sound came forth, as if the sands were swallowing everything, absorbing sound as eagerly as they did blood and bile.

Masses surged over the trenches, blackened swords swinging and chopping down. The ramp to the east had been overrun by the Wickans. Gamet saw the waving standards and grinned. *Crow. Foolish Dog. Weasel.*

Out of the impenetrably black sky descended butterflies, in swarms, to flit above the carnage in the trenches.

On the ramp to the west there was the flash of Moranth munitions, sending grim reverberations through the earth, and Gamet could watch the slaughter over there, a scene panoramic and dulled, as if he was looking upon a mural – a painting where ancient armies warred in eternal battle.

They had come for the Dogslayers. For the butcherers of unarmed Malazans, soldier and civilian, the stubborn and the fleeing, the desperate and the helpless. The Dogslayers, who had given their souls to betrayal.

The fight raged on, but it was overwhelmingly one-sided. The enemy seemed strangely incapable of mustering any kind of defence. They simply died in their trenches, or seeking to retreat they were run down after but a few strides. Skewered by lances, javelins. Trampled beneath chopping hoofs.

Gamet understood their horror, saw with a certain satisfaction the terror in their faces as he and his comrades delivered death.

He could hear the battle song now, rising and falling like waves on a pebbled shore, yet building towards a climax yet to come – yet to come, but soon. *Soon. Yes, we've needed a song. We've waited a long time for such a song. To honour our deeds, our struggles. Our lives and our deaths. We've needed our own voice, so that our spirits could march, march ever onward.*

To battle.

To war.

Manning these walls of crumbled brick and sand. Defending the bone-dry harbours and the dead cities that once blazed with ancient dreams, that once flickered life's reflection on the warm, shallow sea.

Even memories need to be defended.

Even memories.

He fought on, side by side with his dark warrior companions – and so grew to love them, these stalwart comrades, and when at last the dragon-helmed horse warrior rode up and reined in before him, Gamet whirled his sword in greeting.

The rider laughed once again. Reached up a blood-spattered, gauntleted hand, and raised the visor – to reveal the face of a dark-skinned woman, her eyes a stunning blue within a web of desert lines.

'There are more!' Gamet shouted – though even to his own ears his voice sounded far away. 'More enemies! We must ride!'

Her teeth flashed white as she laughed again. 'Not the tribes, my friend! They are kin. This battle is done – others will shed blood come the morrow. We march to the shores, soldier – will you join us?'

He saw more than professional interest in her eyes.

'I shall.'

'You would leave your friends, Gamet Ul'Paran?'

'For you, yes.'

Her smile, and the laugh that followed, stole the old man's heart.

A final glance to the other ramps showed no movement. The Wickans to the east had ridden on, although a lone crow was wheeling overhead. The Malazans to the west had withdrawn. And the butterflies had vanished. In the trenches of the Dogslayers, an hour before dawn, only the dead remained.

Vengeance. She will be pleased. She will understand, and be pleased.

As am I.

Goodbye, Adjunct Tavore.

Koryk slowly settled down beside him, stared north-eastward as if seeking to discover what so held the man's attention. 'What is it?' he asked after a time. 'What are you looking at, Sergeant?'

Fiddler wiped at his eyes. 'Nothing . . . or nothing that makes sense.'

'We're not going to see battle in the morning, are we?'

He glanced over, studied the young Seti's hard-edged features, wanting to see something in them, though he was not quite certain what. After a moment, he sighed and shrugged. 'The glory of battle, Koryk, dwells only in the bard's voice, in the teller's woven words. Glory belongs to ghosts and poets. What you hear and dream isn't the same as what you live – blur the distinction at your own peril, lad.'

'You've been a soldier all your life, Sergeant. If it doesn't ease a thirst within you, why are you here?'

'I've no answer to that,' Fiddler admitted. 'I think, maybe, I was called here.'

'That song Bottle said you were hearing?'

'Aye.'

'What does it mean? That song?'

'Quick Ben will have a better answer to that, I think. But my gut is whispering one thing over and over again. The Bridgeburners, lad, have *ascended*.'

Koryk made a warding sign and edged away slightly.

'Or, at least, the *dead* ones have. The rest of us, we're just
. . . malingering. Here in the mortal realm.'

'Expecting to die soon, then?'

Fiddler grunted. 'Wasn't planning on it.'

'Good, because we like our sergeant just fine.'

The Seti moved away. Fiddler returned his gaze to the
distant oasis. *Appreciate that, lad.* He narrowed his eyes, but
the darkness defied him. Something was going on there.
*Feels as if . . . as if friends are fighting. I can almost hear sounds
of battle. Almost.*

Suddenly, two howls rose into the night.

Fiddler was on his feet. 'Hood's breath!'

From Smiles: 'Gods, what was *that?*'

No. Couldn't have been. But . . .

And then the darkness above the oasis began to *change*.

The row of horse warriors rode up before them amidst
swirling dust, the horses stamping and tossing heads in
jittery fear.

Beside him, Leoman of the Flails raised a hand to halt his
company, then gestured Corabb to follow as he trotted his
mount towards the newcomers.

Mathok nodded in greeting. 'We have missed you,
Leoman—'

'My shaman has fallen unconcious,' Leoman cut in. 'He
chose oblivion over terror. What is going on in the oasis,
Mathok?'

The warleader made a warding sign. 'Raraku has
awakened. Ghosts have risen, the Holy Desert's very own
memories.'

'And who is their enemy?'

Mathok shook his head. 'Betrayal upon betrayal,
Leoman. I have withdrawn my warriors from the oasis and
encamped them between Sha'ik and the Malazans. Chaos
has claimed all else—'

'So you do not have an answer for me.'

'I fear the battle is already lost—'

'Sha'ik?'

'I have the Book with me. I am sworn to protect it.'

Leoman frowned.

Shifting on his saddle, Corabb glared northeastward. Preternatural darkness engulfed the oasis, and it seemed to swarm as if filled with living creatures, winged shadows, spectral demons. And on the ground beneath, he thought he could see the movement of masses of soldiery. Corabb shivered.

'To Y'Ghatan?' Leoman asked.

Mathok nodded. 'With my own tribe as escort. Leaving almost nine thousand desert warriors at your disposal . . . for you to command.'

But Leoman shook his head. 'This battle will belong to the Dogslayers, Mathok. There is no choice left to me. I have not the time to greatly modify our tactics. The positions are set – she waited too long. You did not answer me, Mathok. What of Sha'ik?'

'The goddess holds her still,' the warleader replied. 'Even Korbolo Dom's assassins cannot get to her.'

'The Napan must have known that would happen,' Leoman muttered. 'And so he has planned . . . something else.'

Mathok shook his head. 'My heart has broken this night, my friend.'

Leoman studied the old warrior for a time, then he nodded. 'Until Y'Ghatan, then, Mathok.'

'You ride to Sha'ik?'

'I must.'

'Tell her—'

'I will.'

Mathok nodded, unmindful of the tears glistening down his lined cheeks. He straightened suddenly in his saddle. 'Dryjhna once belonged to us, Leoman. To the tribes of this desert. The Book's prophecies were sewn to a far older skin. The Book was in truth naught but a history, a telling of apocalyptic events survived – not of those to come—'

'I know, my friend. Guard well the Book, and go in peace.'

Mathok wheeled his horse to face the west trail. An angry gesture and his riders followed as he rode into the gloom.

Leoman stared after them for a long moment.

Howls shattered the night.

Corabb saw his commander suddenly bare his teeth as he glared into the darkness ahead. *Like two beasts about to come face to face. Spirits below, what awaits us?*

'Weapons!' Leoman snarled.

The company thundered forward, along the trail Corabb had now traversed what seemed countless times.

The closer they drew to the oasis, the more muted the sound of their passage, as if the darkness was devouring all sound. Those howls had not been repeated, and Corabb was beginning to wonder if they had been real at all. *Perhaps not a mortal throat at all. An illusion, a cry to freeze all in their tracks—*

The vanguard entered a defile and suddenly quarrels sprouted from riders and horses. Screams, toppling warriors, stumbling horses. From further back in the column, the clash of swords and shields.

Dogslayers!

Somehow, Corabb and his horse found themselves plunging clear. A figure darted close to his left and he shrieked, raising his weapon.

'It's me, damn you!'

'Leoman!'

His commander's horse had been killed beneath him. He reached up.

Corabb clasped Leoman's arm and vaulted him onto his horse's back.

'Ride, Bhilan! Ride!'

Black-armoured horse warriors plunged through the low wall, massive axes whirling in their gauntleted hands.

958

Quick Ben yelped and dived for cover.

Cursing, Kalam followed, Korbolo Dom's bound body bouncing on his shoulders. He flung himself down beside the wizard as hoofs flashed over them, raining sand and bits of mortar.

Then the heavy cavalry was past.

Kalam pushed the Napan off his back and twisted onto his side to glare at Quick Ben. 'Who in Hood's name were those bastards?'

'We'd best lie low for a time,' the wizard muttered with a grimace, rubbing grit from his eyes. 'Raraku's unleashed her ghosts—'

'And are they the ones singing? Those voices are right inside my head—'

'Mine, too, friend. Tell me, had any conversations with a Tanno Spiritwalker lately?'

'A what? No. Why?'

'Because that is what you're hearing. If it was a song woven around these ancient ghosts we're seeing, well, we'd not be hearing it. In fact, we'd not be hearing much of anything at all. And we'd have been chopped into tiny pieces by now. Kalam, that Tanno song belongs to the Bridgeburners.'

What?

'Makes you wonder about cause and effect, doesn't it? A Tanno stole our tale and fashioned a song – but for that song to have any effect, the Bridgeburners had to die. As a company. And now it has. Barring you and me—'

'And Fiddler. Wait! Fid mentioned something about a Spiritwalker in Ehrlitan.'

'It would have had to have been direct contact. A clasping of hands, an embrace, or a kiss—'

'That bastard sapper – I remember he was damned cagey about something. A kiss? Remind me to give Fiddler a kiss next time I see him, one he'll never forget—'

'Whoever it was and however it happened,' Quick Ben said, 'the Bridgeburners have now ascended—'

'Ascended? What in the Queen's name does *that* mean?'

'Damned if I know, Kalam. I've never heard of such a thing before. A *whole company* – there's no precedent for this, none at all.'

'Except maybe the T'lan Imass.'

The wizard's dark eyes narrowed on his friend. 'An interesting thought,' he murmured. Then sighed. 'In any case, Raraku's ghosts have risen on that song. Risen . . . to battle. But there's more – I swear I saw a Wickan standard back near the Dogslayer trenches just as we were hightailing it out of there.'

'Well, maybe Tavore's taken advantage of all this—'

'Tavore knows nothing of it, Kalam. She carries an otataral sword, after all. Maybe the mages she has with her sense something, but the darkness that's descended on this oasis is obscuring everything.'

Kalam grunted. 'Any other good news to tell me, Quick?'

'The darkness is sorcery. Remember whenever Anomander Rake arrived some place with his warren unveiled? That weight, the trembling ground, the over-whelming *pressure*?'

'Don't tell me the Son of Darkness is coming—'

'I hope not. I mean, I don't think so. He's busy – I'll explain later. No, this is more, uh, primal, I think.'

'Those howls,' Kalam grated. 'Two hounds, Quick Ben. I had a run in with them myself. They're like the Shadow Hounds, only somehow worse—'

The wizard was staring across at him.

'Stop it, Quick. I don't like that look. I got away because I loosed a handful of azalan demons at them. Didn't stop those hounds, but it was enough for me to make good my escape.'

Quick Ben's brows slowly arched. '"A handful of azalan demons," Kalam? And where have you been lately?'

'You ain't the only one with a few tales to tell.'

The wizard cautiously rose into a crouch, scanned the area on the other side of the crumbled wall. 'Two Hounds of Darkness, you said. The Deragoth, then. So, who broke *their* chains, I wonder?'

'That's just typical!' Kalam snapped. 'What *don't* you know?'

'A few things,' the wizard replied under his breath. 'For example, what are those hounds doing here?'

'So long as we stay out of their path, I couldn't care less—'

'No, you misunderstood.' Quick Ben nodded towards where his gaze was fixed on the clearing beyond. 'What are they doing *here*?'

Kalam groaned.

Their bristly hackles were raised above their strangely humped, massive shoulders. Thick, long necks and broad, flattened heads, the jaw muscles bulging. Scarred, black hides, and eyes that burned pure and empty of light.

As large as a steppe horse, but bulkier by far, padding with heads lowered into the flagstoned square. There was something about them that resembled a hyena, and a plains bear as well. A certain sly avidness merged with arrogant brutality.

They slowed, then halted, lifting glistening snouts into the air.

They had come to destroy. To tear life from all flesh, to mock all claims of mastery, to shatter all that stood in their path. This was a new world for them. New, yet once it had been old. Changes had come. A world of vast silences where once kin and foe alike had opened throats in fierce challenge.

Nothing was as it had been, and the Deragoth were made uneasy.

They had come to destroy.

But now hesitated.

With eyes fixed on the one who had arrived, who now stood before them, at the far end of the square.

Hesitate. Yes.

961

Karsa Orlong strode forward. He addressed them, his voice low and rumbling. 'Urugal's master had ... ambitions,' he said. 'A dream of mastery. But now he understands better, and wants nothing to do with you.' Then the Teblor smiled. 'So I do.'

Both hounds stepped back, then moved to open more space between them.

Karsa smiled. *You do not belong here.* 'You would let me pass?' He continued on. *And I have had my fill of strangers.* 'Do you remember the Toblakai, beasts? But they had been gentled. By civilization. By the soft trappings of foolish peace. So weakened that they could not stand before T'lan Imass, could not stand before Forkrul Assail and Jaghut. And now, they cannot stand before Nathii slavers.

'An awakening was needed, friends. Remember the Toblakai, if it comforts you.' He strode directly between the two hounds, as if he intended to accept their invitation to pass.

The hounds attacked.

As he knew they would.

Karsa dropped into a crouch that leaned far to his left, as he brought up the massive stone sword over his head, point sliding left – directly into the path of the hound charging from that side.

Striking it in the chest.

The heavy sternum cracked but did not shatter, and the rippled blade edge scored a bloody path down along the ribs.

Karsa's crouch then exploded after his weapon, his legs driving his shoulder forward and up to hammer the beast at the level of its collar bones.

Jaws snapped above the back of the Toblakai's neck, then the impact jolted through warrior and hound both.

And the latter's sword-gouged ribs splintered.

Jaws closed around Karsa's right leg just below the knee.

And he was lifted clear of the ground. Then thrown to

one side, though the jaws did not loosen. The wrench snapped the sword from his hands.

Molars ground against bone, incisors shredded muscle. The second hound closed on Karsa, savagely shaking the leg in its jaws.

The first hound staggered away a few paces, left foreleg dragging, blood spilling out beneath it.

Karsa made no effort to pull away from the beast seeking to chew off his lower leg. Instead, he pushed himself upright on his one free leg and lunged into the hound. Arms wrapping around the rippling body behind the shoulders.

With a bellow, the Teblor lifted the hound. Hind legs kicked in wild panic, but he was already wrenching the entire beast over.

The jaws were torn loose even as Karsa drove the creature down onto its back.

Flagstones cracked with explosions of dust.

The Teblor then sank to his knees, straddling the writhing hound, and closed both hands around its throat.

A snarling frenzy answered him.

Canines ripped into his forearms, the jaws gnawed frantically, chewing free chunks of skin and flesh.

Karsa released one hand and pushed it against the hound's lower jaw.

Muscles contracted as two unhuman strengths collided.

Legs scored Karsa's body, the claws tearing through leathers and into flesh, but the Teblor continued pushing. Harder and harder, his other hand edging up to join in the effort.

The kicks went wild. Panicked.

Karsa both felt and heard a grinding pop, then the flat head of the hound cracked against the flagstones.

A strange keening sound twisted out from the throat.

And the warrior pulled his right hand back, closed it into a fist, and drove it down into the animal's throat.

Crushing trachea.

The legs spasmed and went limp.

With a roar, Karsa reared upright, dragging the hound by its neck, then hammering it down once more. A loud snap, a spray of blood and saliva.

He straightened, shook himself, his mane raining blood and sweat, then swung his gaze to where the other hound had been.

Only a blood trail remained.

Karsa staggered over to his sword, retrieved it, then set off on that glistening path.

Kalam and Quick Ben slowly rose from behind the wall and stared in silence after the giant warrior.

Shadows had begun swarming in the darkness. They gathered like capemoths to the carcass of the Deragoth, then sped away again as if in terror.

Kalam rolled his shoulders, then, long-knives in his hands, he approached the hound.

Quick Ben followed.

They studied the mangled carcass.

'Wizard . . .'

'Aye?'

'Let's drop off the Napan and get out of here.'

'A brilliant plan.'

'I just thought it up.'

'I like it very much. Well done, Kalam.'

'Like I've always told you, Quick, I ain't just a pretty face.'

The two swung about and, ignoring the shadows pouring out of the burgeoning shattered warren of Kurald Emurlahn, returned to where they had left Korbolo Dom.

'*Friend?*'

Heboric stared at the four-eyed, squat demon that had leapt onto the path in front of him. 'If we'd met, demon, I'm sure I would have remembered it.'

'*Helpful explanation. Brother to L'oric. He lies in clearing twelve paces to your left. Hesitant revision. Fifteen paces. Your legs are nearly as short as mine.'*

'Take me to him.'

The demon did not move. *'Friend?'*

'More or less. We share certain flaws.'

The creature shrugged. *'With reservations. Follow.'*

Heboric set off into the petrified forest after the shambling demon, his smile broadening as it prattled on.

'A priest with the hands of a tiger. Sometimes. Other times, human hands glowing depthless green. Impressed. Those tattoos, very fine indeed. Musing. I would have trouble tearing out your throat, I think. Even driven by hunger, as I always am. Thoughtful. A fell night, this one. Ghosts, assassins, warrens, silent battles. Does no-one in this world ever sleep?'

They stumbled into a small clearing.

L'oric's armour was stained with drying blood, but he looked well enough, seated cross-legged, his eyes closed, his breathing steady. On the dusty ground before him lay a spread of the Deck of Dragons.

Grunting, Heboric settled down opposite the High Mage. 'Didn't know you played with those.'

'I never do,' L'oric replied in a murmur. 'Play, that is. A Master has come to the Deck, and that Master has just sanctioned the House of Chains.'

Heboric's eyes widened. Then narrowed, and he slowly nodded. 'Let the gods rail, he or she had to do just that.'

'I know. The Crippled God is now as bound as is every other god.'

'In the game, aye, after so long outside it. I wonder if he'll one day come to regret his gambit.'

'He seeks this fragment of Kurald Emurlahn, and is poised to strike, though his chances are less now than they were at sunset.'

'How so?'

'Bidithal is dead.'

'Good. Who?'

'Toblakai.'

'Oh. Not good.'

'Yet Toblakai has become, I believe, the Knight in the House of Chains.'

'That is damned unfortunate . . . for the Crippled God. Toblakai will kneel to no-one. He cannot afford to. He will defy all prediction—'

'He has already displayed that penchant this night, Ghost Hands, to the possible ruination of us all. Still, at the same time, I have come to suspect he is our only hope.' L'oric opened his eyes and stared across at Heboric. 'Two Hounds of Darkness arrived a short while ago – I could sense their presence, though fitfully, but could get no closer. Otataral, and the very darkness that shrouds them.'

'And why should Toblakai step into their path? Never mind, I can answer that myself. Because he's Toblakai.'

'Aye. And I believe he has already done so.'

'And?'

'And now, I believe, but one Deragoth remains alive.'

'Gods forbid,' Heboric breathed.

'Toblakai even now pursues it.'

'Tell me, what brought the hounds here? What or who has Toblakai just thwarted?'

'The cards are ambivalent on that, Destriant. Perhaps the answer is yet to be decided.'

'Relieved to hear some things remain so, truth be told.'

'Ghost Hands. Get Felisin away from this place. Greyfrog here will accompany you.'

'And you?'

'I must go to Sha'ik. No, say nothing until I finish. I know that you and she were once close – perhaps not in a pleasing manner, but close none the less. But that mortal child is soon to be no more. The goddess is about to devour her soul even as we speak – and once that is done, there shall be no return. The young Malazan girl you once knew will have ceased to exist. Thus, when I go to Sha'ik, I go not to the child, but to the goddess.'

'But why? Are you truly loyal to the notion of apocalypse? Of chaos and destruction?'

'No. I have something else in mind. I must speak with the goddess – before she takes Sha'ik's soul.'

Heboric stared at the High Mage for a long time, seeking to discern what L'oric sought from that vengeful, insane goddess.

'There are two Felisins,' L'oric then murmured, eyes half veiled. 'Save the one you can, Heboric Light Touch.'

'One day, L'oric,' Heboric growled, 'I will discover who you truly are.'

The High Mage smiled. 'You will find this simple truth – I am a son who lives without hope of ever matching my father's stride. That alone, in time, will explain all you need know of me. Go, Destriant. Guard her well.'

Ghosts pivoted, armour shedding red dust, and saluted as Karsa Orlong limped past. At least these ones, he reflected dully, weren't shackled in chains.

The blood trail had led him into a maze of ruins, an unused section of the city notorious for its cellars and pitfalls and precariously leaning walls. He could smell the beast. It was close and, he suspected, cornered.

Or, more likely, it had decided to make a stand, in a place perfectly suited for an ambush.

If only the slow, steady patter of dripping blood had not given away its hiding place.

Karsa kept his gaze averted from that alleyway of inky shadows five paces ahead and to his right. He made his steps uncertain, uneven with pain and hesitation, not all of it feigned. The blood between his hands and the sword's grip had grown sticky, but still threatened to betray his grasp on the weapon.

Shadows were shredding the darkness, as if the two elemental forces were at war, with the latter being driven back. Dawn, Karsa realized, was approaching.

He came opposite the alley.

And the hound charged.

Karsa leapt forward, twisting in mid-air to slash his sword two-handed, cleaving an arc into his wake.

The tip slashed hide, but the beast's attack had already carried it past. It landed on one foreleg, which skidded out from under it. The hound fell onto one shoulder, then rolled right over.

Karsa scrambled back to his feet to face it.

The beast crouched, preparing to charge once again.

The horse that burst out of a side alley caught both hound and Toblakai by surprise. That the panicked animal had been galloping blind was made obvious as it collided with the hound.

There had been two riders on the horse. And both were thrown from the saddle, straight over the hound.

The impact had driven the hound down beneath the wildly stamping hoofs. Somehow, the horse stayed upright, staggering clear with heavy snorts as if seeking to draw breath into stunned lungs. Behind it, the hound's claws gouged the cobbles as it struggled to right itself.

Snarling, Karsa lunged forward and plunged the sword's point into the beast's neck.

It shrieked, surged towards the Toblakai.

Karsa leapt away, dragging his sword after him.

Blood gushing from the puncture in its throat, the hound rose up on its three legs, weaving, head swaying as it coughed red spume onto the stones.

A figure darted out from the shadows. The spiked ball at the end of a flail hissed through the air, and thundered into the hound's head. A second followed, hammering down from above to audibly crack the beast's thick skull.

Karsa stepped forward. An overhead two-handed swing finally drove the hound from its wobbling legs.

Side by side, Leoman and Karsa closed in to finish it. A dozen blows later and the hound was dead.

Corabb Bhilan Thenu'alas then stumbled into view, a broken sword in his hand.

Karsa wiped the gore from his blade then glared at Leoman. 'I did not need your help,' he growled.

Leoman grinned. 'But I need yours.'

Pearl staggered from the trench, clambering over sprawled corpses. Since his rather elegant assassination of Henaras, things had gone decidedly downhill – *steeper than that trench behind me*. Countless guards, then the ghostly army whose weapons were anything but illusory. His head still ached from Lostara's kiss – *damned woman, just when I thought I'd figured her out . . .*

He'd been cut and slashed at all the way through that damned camp, and now stumbled half blind towards the ruins.

The darkness was being torn apart on all sides. Kurald Emurlahn was opening like death's own flower, with the oasis at its dark heart. Beneath the sorcerous pressure of that manifestation, it was all he could do to pitch headlong down the trail.

So long as Lostara stayed put, they might well salvage something out of all this.

He came to the edge and paused, studying the pit where he'd left her. No movement. She was either staying low or had left. He padded forward.

I despise nights like these. Nothing goes as planned—

Something hard struck him in the side of his head. Stunned, he fell and lay unmoving, his face pressed against the cold, gritty ground.

A voice rumbled above him. 'That was for Malaz City. Even so, you still owe me one.'

'After Henaras?' Pearl mumbled, his words puffing up tiny clouds of dust. 'You should be owing *me* one.'

'Her? Not worth counting.'

Something thumped heavily to the ground beside Pearl. That then groaned.

'All right,' the Claw sighed – *more dust, a miniature Whirlwind* – 'I owe you one, then.'

'Glad we're agreed. Now, make some more noises. Your lass over there's bound to take a look . . . eventually.'

Pearl listened to the footfalls pad away. Two sets. *The wizard was in no mood to talk, I suppose.*

To me, that is.

I believe I am sorely humbled.

Beside him, the trussed shape groaned again.

Despite himself, Pearl smiled.

To the east, the sky paled.

And this night was done.

CHAPTER TWENTY-SIX

On this day, Raraku rises.

xxxiv.II.l.81 'Words of the Prophecy'
The Book of Dryjhna the Apocalyptic

The whirlwind goddess had once been a raging storm of wind and sand. A wall surrounding the young woman who had once been Felisin of House Paran, and who had become Sha'ik, Chosen One and supreme ruler of the Army of the Apocalypse.

Felisin had been her mother's name. She had then made it her adopted daughter's name. Yet she herself had lost it. Occasionally, however, in the deepest hours of night, in the heart of an impenetrable silence of her own making, she caught a glimpse of that girl. As she once had been, the smeared reflection from a polished mirror. Round-cheeked and flushed, a wide smile and bright eyes. A child with a brother who adored her, who would toss her about on one knee as if it was a bucking horse, and her squeals of fear and delight would fill the chamber.

Her mother had been gifted with visions. This was well known. A respected truth. And that mother's youngest daughter had dreamed that one day she too would find that talent within her.

But that gift only came with the goddess, with this spiteful, horrific creature whose soul was far more parched and withered than any desert. And the visions that assailed Sha'ik were murky, fraught things. They were, she had

971

come to realize, not born of any talent or gift. They were the conjurings of fear.

A goddess's fear.

And now the Whirlwind Wall had closed, retracted, had drawn in from the outside world to rage beneath Sha'ik's sun-darkened skin, along her veins and arteries, careening wild and deafening in her mind.

Oh, there was power there. Bitter with age, bilious with malice. And whatever fuelled it bore the sour taste of betrayal. A heart-piercing, very personal betrayal. Something that should have healed, that should have numbed beneath thick, tough scar tissue. Spiteful pleasure had kept the wound open, had fed its festering heat, until hate was all that was left. Hate for . . . someone, a hate so ancient it no longer possessed a face.

In moments of cold reason, Sha'ik saw it for what it was. Insane, raised to such extremity that she understood that whatever had been the crime against the goddess, whatever the source of the betrayal, it had not earned such a brutal reaction. The proportions had *begun* wrong. From the very start. Leading her to suspect that the proclivity for madness had already existed, dark flaws marring the soul that would one day claw its way into ascendancy.

Step by step, we walk the most horrendous paths. Stride tottering along the edge of an unsuspected abyss. Companions see nothing amiss. The world seems a normal place. Step by step, no different from anyone else – not from the outside. Not even from the inside. Apart from that tautness, that whisper of panic. The vague confusion that threatens your balance.

Felisin, who was Sha'ik, had come to comprehend this. For she had walked that same path.

Hatred, sweet as nectar.

I have walked into the abyss.

I am as mad as that goddess. And this is why she chose me, for we are kindred souls . . .

Then what is this ledge to which I still cling so desperately? Why do I persist in my belief that I can save myself? That I can

972

return . . . find once more the place where madness cannot be found, where confusion does not exist.

The place . . . of childhood.

She stood in the main chamber, the chair that would be a throne behind her, its cushions cool, its armrests dry. She stood, imprisoned in a stranger's armour. She could almost feel the goddess reaching out to engulf her on all sides – not a mother's embrace, no, nothing like that at all. This one would suffocate her utterly, would drown out all light, every glimmer of self-awareness.

Her ego is armoured in hatred. She cannot look in, she can barely see out. Her walk is a shamble, cramped and stiff, a song of rusty fittings and creaking straps. Her teeth gleam in the shadows, but it is a rictus grin.

Felisin Paran, hold up this mirror at your peril.

Outside stole the first light of dawn.

And Sha'ik reached for her helm.

L'oric could just make out the Dogslayer positions at the tops of the cobbled ramps. There was no movement over there in the grey light of dawn. It was strange, but not surprising. The night just done would make even the hardest soldier hesitant to raise a gaze skyward, to straighten from a place of hiding to begin the mundane tasks that marked the start of a new day.

Even so, there was something strange about those trenches.

He strode along the ridge towards the hilltop where Sha'ik had established her forward post to observe the battle to come. The High Mage ached in every bone. His muscles shouted pain with every step he took.

He prayed she was there.

Prayed the goddess would deign to hear his words, his warning, and, finally, his offer.

All hovered on the cusp. Darkness had been defeated . . . somehow. He wondered at that, but not for long – there was no time for such idle musings. This tortured fragment of Kurald Emurlahn was awakening, and the goddess was about to arrive, to claim it for herself. To fashion a throne. *To devour Raraku.*

Ghosts still swirled in the shadows, warriors and soldiers from scores of long-dead civilizations. Wielding strange weapons, their bodies hidden beneath strange armour, their faces mercifully covered by ornate visors. They were singing, although that Tanno song had grown pensive, mournful, sighing soft as the wind. It had begun to rise and fall, a sussuration that chilled L'oric.

Who will they fight for? Why are they here at all? What do they want?

The song belonged to the Bridgeburners. Yet it seemed the Holy Desert itself had claimed it, had taken that multitude of ethereal voices for itself. And every soul that had fallen in battle in the desert's immense history was now gathered in this place.

The cusp.

He came to the base of the trail leading up to Sha'ik's hill. There were desert warriors huddled here and there, wrapped in their ochre telabas, spears thrust upright, iron points glistening with dew as the sun's fire broke on the east horizon. Companies of Mathok's light cavalry were forming up on the flats to L'oric's right. The horses were jittery, the rows shifting uneven and restless. The High Mage could not see Mathok anywhere among them – nor, he realized with a chill, could he see the standards of the warleader's own tribe.

He heard horses approach from behind and turned to see Leoman, one of his officers, and Toblakai riding up towards him.

The Toblakai's horse was a Jhag, L'oric saw, huge and magnificent in its primal savagery, loping collected and perfectly proportionate to the giant astride its shoulders.

And that giant was a mess. Preternatural healing had yet to fully repair the terrible wounds on him. His hands were a crimson ruin. One leg had been chewed by vicious, oversized jaws.

Toblakai and his horse were dragging a pair of objects that bounced and rolled on the ends of chains, and L'oric's eyes went wide upon seeing what they were.

He's killed the Deragoth. He's taken their heads.

'L'oric!' Leoman rasped as he drew rein before him. 'Is she above?'

'I don't know, Leoman of the Flails.'

All three dismounted, and L'oric saw Toblakai favouring his mangled leg. *A hound's jaws did that.* And then he saw the stone sword on the giant's back. *Ah, he is indeed the one, then. I think the Crippled God has made a terrible mistake . . .*

Gods, he killed the Deragoth.

'Where is Febryl hiding?' Leoman asked as the four of them began the ascent.

Toblakai answered. 'Dead. I forgot to tell you some things. I killed him. And I killed Bidithal. I would have killed Ghost Hands and Korbolo Dom, but I could not find them.'

L'oric rubbed a hand across his brow, and it came away wet and oily. Yet he could still see his breath.

Toblakai went on, inexorably. 'And when I went into Korbolo's tent, I found Kamist Reloe. He'd been assassinated. So had Henaras.'

L'oric shook himself and said to Leoman, 'Did you receive Sha'ik's last commands? Shouldn't you be with the Dogslayers?'

The warrior grunted. 'Probably. We've just come from there.'

'They're all dead,' Toblakai said. 'Slaughtered in the night. The ghosts of Raraku were busy – though none dared oppose me.' He barked a laugh. 'As Ghost Hands could tell you, I have ghosts of my own.'

L'oric stumbled on the trail. He reached up and gripped Leoman's arm. 'Slaughtered? *All of them?*'

'Yes, High Mage. I'm surprised you didn't know. We still have the desert warriors. We can still win this, just not here and not now. Thus, we need to convince Sha'ik to leave—'

'That won't be possible,' L'oric cut in. 'The goddess is coming, is almost here. It's too late for that, Leoman. Moments from being too late for everything—'

They clambered over the crest.

And there stood Sha'ik.

Helmed and armoured, her back to them as she stared southward.

L'oric wanted to cry out. For he saw what his companions could not see. *I'm not in time. Oh, gods below—* And then he leapt forward, his warren's portal flaring around him – and was gone.

The goddess had not lost her memories. Indeed, rage had carved their likenesses, every detail, as mockingly solid and real-seeming as those carved trees in the forest of stone. And she could caress them, crooning her hatred like a lover's song, lingering with a touch promising murder, though the one who had wronged her was, if not dead, then in a place that no longer mattered.

The hate was all that mattered now. Her fury at his weaknesses. Oh, others in the tribe played those games often enough. Bodies slipped through the furs from hut to hut when the stars fell into their summer alignment, and she herself had more than once spread her legs to another woman's husband, or an eager, clumsy youth.

But her heart had been given to the one man with whom she lived. That law was sacrosanct.

Oh, but he'd been *so* sensitive. His hands following his eyes in the fashioning of forbidden images of that other woman, there in the hidden places. He'd used those hands to close about his own heart, to give it to another – without a thought as to who had once held it for herself.

Another, who would not even give her heart in return – she had seen to that, with vicious words and challenging accusations. Enough to encourage the others to banish her for ever.

But not before the bitch killed all but one of her kin.

Foolish, stupid man, to have given his love to that woman.

Her rage had not died with the Ritual, had not died when she herself – too shattered to walk – had been severed from the Vow and left in a place of eternal darkness. And every curious spirit that had heard her weeping, that had drawn close in sympathy – well, they had fed her hungers, and she had taken their powers. Layer upon layer. For they too had been foolish and stupid, wayward and inclined to squander those powers on meaningless things. But she had a purpose.

The children swarmed the surface of the world. And who was their mother? None other than the bitch who had been banished.

And their father?

Oh yes, she went to him. On that last night. She did. He reeked of her when they dragged him into the light the following morning. Reeked of her. The truth was there in his eyes.

A look she would – could – never forget.

Vengeance was a beast long straining at its chains. Vengeance was all she had ever wanted.

Vengeance was about to be unleashed.

And even Raraku could not stop it. The children would die.

The children will die. I will cleanse the world of their beget, the proud-eyed vermin born, one and all, of that single mother. Of course she could not join the Ritual. A new world waited within her.

And now, at last, I shall rise again. Clothed in the flesh of one such child, I shall kill that world.

She could see the path opening, the way ahead clear and inviting. A tunnel walled in spinning, writhing shadows.

It would be good to walk again.

To feel warm flesh and the heat of blood.

To taste water. Food.

To breathe.

To kill.

Unmindful and unhearing, Sha'ik made her way down the slope. The basin awaited her, that field of battle. She saw Malazan scouts on the ridge opposite, one riding back to the encampment, the others simply watching.

It was understood, then. As she had known it would be.

Vague, distant shouts behind her. She smiled. *Of course, in the end, it is the two warriors who first found me. I was foolish to have doubted them. And I know, either one would stand in my stead.*

But they cannot.

This fight belongs to me. And the goddess.

'Enter.'

Captain Keneb paused for a moment, seeking to collect himself, then he strode into the command tent.

She was donning her armour. A mundane task that would have been easier with a servant at hand, but that, of course, was not Tavore's way.

Although, perhaps, that was not quite the truth. 'Adjunct.'

'What is it, Captain?'

'I have just come from the Fist's tent. A cutter and a healer were summoned at once, but it was far too late. Adjunct Tavore, Gamet died last night. A blood vessel burst in his brain – the cutter believes it was a clot, and that it was born the night he was thrown from his horse. I am . . . sorry.'

A pallor had come to her drawn, plain face. He saw her hand reach down to steady herself against the table edge. 'Dead?'

'In his sleep.'

She turned away, stared down at the accoutrements littering the table. 'Thank you, Captain. Leave me now, and have T'amber—'

There was a commotion outside, then a Wickan youth pushed in. 'Adjunct! Sha'ik has walked down into the basin! She challenges you!'

After a long moment, Tavore nodded. 'Very well. Belay that last order, Captain. You both may go.' She turned to resume strapping on her armour.

Keneb gestured the youth ahead and they strode from the tent.

Outside, the captain hesitated. *It's what Gamet would do . . . isn't it?*

'Will she fight her?' the Wickan asked.

He glanced over. 'She will. Return to Temul, lad. Either way, we have a battle ahead of us this day.' He watched the young warrior hurry off.

Then swung to face the modest tent situated twenty paces to his left. There were no guards stationed before its flap. Keneb halted before the entrance. 'Lady T'amber, are you within?'

A figure emerged. Dressed in hard leathers – light armour, Keneb realized with a start – and a longsword strapped to her hip. 'Does the Adjunct wish to begin her morning practice?'

Keneb met those calm eyes, the colour of which gave the woman her name. They seemed depthless. He mentally shook himself. 'Gamet died last night. I have just informed the Adjunct.'

The woman's gaze flicked towards the command tent. 'I see.'

'And in the basin between the two armies, Sha'ik now stands . . . waiting. It occurred to me, Lady, that the Adjunct might appreciate some help with her armour.'

To his surprise she turned back to her tent. 'Not this morning, Captain. I understand your motives . . . but no. Not this morning. Good day, sir.'

Then she was gone.

Keneb stood motionless in surprise. *All right, then, so I do not understand women.*

He faced the command tent once more, in time to see the Adjunct emerge, tightening the straps on her gauntlets. She was helmed, the cheek guards locked in place. There was no visor covering her eyes – many fighters found their vision too impaired by the slits – and he watched her pause, lifting her gaze to the morning sky for a moment, before she strode forward.

He gave her some distance, then followed.

L'oric clawed his way through the swirling shadows, scraped by skeletal branches and stumbling over gnarled roots. He had not expected this. There had to be a path, a way through this blackwood forest.

That damned goddess was *here*. Close. She had to be – if he could but find the trail.

The air was sodden and chill, the boles of the trees leaning this way and that, as if an earthquake had just shaken the ground. Wood creaked overhead to some high wind. And everywhere flitted wraiths, lost shadows, closing on the High Mage then darting away again. Rising from the humus like ghosts, hissing over his head as he staggered on.

And then, through the trees, the flicker of fire.

Gasping, L'oric ran towards it.

It was her. And the flames confirmed his suspicion. *An Imass, trailing the chains of Tellann, the Ritual shattered – oh, she has no place here, no place at all.*

Chthonic spirits swarmed her burning body, the accretions of power she had gathered unto herself over hundreds of thousands of years. Hatred and spite had twisted them all into malign, vicious creatures.

Marsh water and mould had blackened the limbs of the Imass. Moss covered the torso like dangling, knotted fur. Ropes of snarled, grey hair hung down, tangled with burrs. From her scorched eye sockets, living flames licked out. The bones of her cheeks were white, latticed in cracks from the heat.

Toothless, the heavy lower jaw hanging – barely held

in place by rotting strips of tendon and withered muscle.

The goddess was keening, a wavering, eerie cry that did not pause for breath, and it seemed to L'oric that she was struggling.

He drew closer.

She had stumbled into a web of vines, the twisted ropes entangling her arms and legs, wrapped like serpents about her torso and neck. He wondered that he had not seen them earlier, then realized that they were flickering, one moment there, the other gone – although no less an impediment for their rhythmic disappearance – and they were *changing* . . .

Into chains.

Suddenly, one snapped. And the goddess howled, redoubled her efforts.

Another broke, whipping to crack against a tree.

L'oric edged forward. 'Goddess! Hear me! Sha'ik – she is not strong enough for you!'

'*My – my – my child! Mine! I stole her from the bitch! Mine!*'

The High Mage frowned. *Who? What bitch?* 'Goddess, listen to me, please! I offer myself in her stead! Do you understand?'

Another chain broke.

And a voice spoke low behind L'oric. 'Interfering bastard.'

He spun, but too late, as a wide-bladed knife was driven deep between his ribs, tearing a savage path to his heart.

Or where his heart should have been, had L'oric been human.

The serrated tip missed, sliding in front of the deep-seated organ, then jammed into the side of the sternum.

L'oric groaned and sagged.

The killer dragged his knife free, crouched and pulled L'oric's head back by the jaw. Reached down with the blade.

'Never mind that, fool!' hissed another voice. 'She's breaking the chains!'

L'oric watched the man hesitate, then growl and move away.

The High Mage could feel blood filling his chest. He slowly turned onto his side, and could feel the warm flow seep down from the wound. The change in position gave him a mostly unobscured view of the goddess—

—and the assassins now closing in on her.

Sorcery streamed from their knives, a skein of death-magics.

The goddess shrieked as the first knife was driven into her back.

He watched them kill her. A prolonged, brutal butchering. Korbolo's Talons, his chosen assassins, who had been waiting in ambush, guided here by Febryl – no-one else could have managed that path – and abetted by the sorcerous powers of Kamist Reloe, Henaras and Fayelle. She fought back with a ferocity near to match, and soon three of the four assassins were dead – torn limb from limb. But more chains now ensnared the goddess, dragging her down, and L'oric could see the fires dying in her eye sockets, could see spirits writhe away, suddenly freed and eager to flee. And the last killer darted in, hammering down with his knife. Through the top of the skull. A midnight flash, the detonation flinging the killer back. Both skull and blade had shattered, lacerating the Talon's face and chest. Blinded and screaming, he reeled back, tripped over a root and thumped to the ground.

L'oric listened to the man moaning.

Chains snaked over the fallen body of the goddess, until nothing visible was left of her, the black iron links heaped and glistening.

Whatever high wind had lashed the treetops now fell away, leaving only silence.

They all wanted this shattered warren. This fraught prize. But Toblakai killed Febryl. He killed the two Deragoth.

He killed Bidithal.

And as for Korbolo Dom – something tells me the Empress

will soon speak to him in person. The poor bastard.

Beneath the High Mage, his lifeblood soaked the moss.

It came to him, then, that he was dying.

Twigs snapped nearby.

'I'm hardly surprised. You sent your familiar away, didn't you? Again.'

L'oric twisted his head around, stared upward, and managed a weak smile. 'Father.'

'I don't think much has changed in your room, son, since you left it.'

'Dusty, I would think.'

Osric grunted. 'The entire keep is that, I would hazard. Haven't been there in centuries.'

'No servants?'

'I dismissed them . . . about a thousand years ago.'

L'oric sighed. 'I'd be surprised if the place is still standing.'

Osric slowly crouched down beside his son, the sorcerous glow of Denul now surrounding him. 'Oh, it still stands, son. I always keep my options open. An ugly cut you have there. Best healed slowly.'

L'oric closed his eyes. 'My old bed?'

'Aye.'

'It's too short. It was when I left, anyway.'

'Too bad he didn't cut off your feet, then, L'oric.'

Strong arms reached under him and he was lifted effortlessly.

Absurdly – *for a man my age* – he felt at peace. In his father's arms.

'Now,' Osric said, 'how in Hood's name do we get out of here?'

The moment passed.

She stumbled, barely managing to right herself. Behind the iron mesh, she blinked against the hot, close air. All at once, the armour seemed immeasurably heavy. A surge of panic – the sun was roasting her alive beneath these plates of metal.

Sha'ik halted. Struggled to regain control of herself.

Myself. Gods below . . . she is gone.

She stood alone in the basin. From the ridge opposite a lone figure was descending the slope. Tall, unhurried, the gait achingly familiar.

The ridge behind Tavore, and those on every battered island of ancient coral, was now lined with soldiers.

The Army of the Apocalypse was watching as well, Sha'ik suspected, though she did not turn about.

She is gone. I have been . . . abandoned.

I was Sha'ik, once. Now, I am Felisin once more. And here, walking towards me, is the one who betrayed me. My sister.

She remembered watching Tavore and Ganoes playing with wooden swords. Beginning on that path to deadly familiarity, to unthinking ease wielding the weight of that weapon. Had the world beyond not changed – had all stood still, the way children believed it would – she would have had her turn. The clack of wood, Ganoes laughing and gently instructing her – there was joy and comfort to her brother, the way he made teaching subservient to the game's natural pleasures. But she'd never had the chance for that.

No chance, in fact, for much of anything that could now return to her, memories warm and trusting and reassuring.

Instead, Tavore had dismembered their family. And for Felisin, the horrors of slavery and the mines.

But blood is the chain that can never break.

Tavore was now twenty strides away. Drawing out her otataral sword.

And, though we leave the house of our birth, it never leaves us.

Sha'ik could feel the weight of her own weapon, dragging hard enough to make her wrist ache. She did not recall unsheathing it.

Beyond the mesh and through the slits of the visor,

Tavore strode ever closer, neither speeding up nor slowing.

No catching up. No falling back. How could there be? We are ever the same years apart. The chain never draws taut. Never slackens. Its length is prescribed. But its weight, oh, its weight ever varies.

She was lithe, light on her feet, achingly economical. She was, for this moment, perfect.

But, for me, the blood is heavy. So heavy.

And Felisin struggled against it – that sudden, overwhelming weight. Struggled to raise her arms – unthinking of how that motion would be received.

Tavore, it's all right—

A thunderous clang, a reverberation jolting up her right arm, and the sword's enervating weight was suddenly gone from her hand.

Then something punched into her chest, a stunning blossom of cold fire piercing through flesh, bone – and then she felt a tug from behind, as if something had reached up, clasped her hauberk and yanked on it – but it was just the point, she realized. The point of Tavore's sword, as it drove against the underside of the armour shielding her back.

Felisin looked down to see that rust-hued blade impaling her.

Her legs gave way and the sword suddenly bowed to her weight.

But she did not slide off that length of stained iron.

Her body held on to it, releasing only in shuddering increments as Felisin fell back, onto the ground.

Through the visor's slit, she stared up at her sister, a figure standing behind a web of black, twisted iron wire that now rested cool over her eyes, tickling her lashes.

A figure who now stepped closer. To set one boot down hard on her chest – a weight that, now that it had arrived, seemed eternal – and dragged the sword free.

Blood.

Of course. This is how you break an unbreakable chain. By dying.

I just wanted to know, Tavore, why you did it. And why you did not love me, when I loved you. I – I think that's what I wanted to know.

The boot lifted from her chest. But she could still feel its weight.

Heavy. So very heavy . . .

Oh, Mother, look at us now.

Karsa Orlong's hand snapped out, caught Leoman before the man fell, then dragged him close. 'Hear me, friend. She is dead. Take your tribes and get out of here.'

Leoman lifted a hand and passed it across his eyes. Then he straightened. 'Dead, yes. I'm sorry, Toblakai. It wasn't that. She' – his face twisted – 'she *did not know how to fight!*'

'True, she did not. And now she's dead, and the Whirlwind Goddess with her. It is done, friend. We have lost.'

'More than you know,' Leoman groaned, pulling away.

In the basin below, the Adjunct was staring down at Sha'ik's corpse. From both armies lining the ridges, silence. Karsa frowned. 'The Malazans do not cheer.'

'No,' Leoman snarled, turning to where Corabb waited with the horses. 'They probably hate the bitch. We ride to Y'Ghatan, Toblakai—'

'Not me,' Karsa growled.

His friend paused and then nodded without turning around, and vaulted onto his horse. He took the reins from Corabb then glanced over at Toblakai. 'Fare well, my friend.'

'And you, Leoman of the Flails.'

'If L'oric returns from wherever he went, tell him . . .' His voice trailed away, then he shrugged. 'Take care of him if he needs help.'

'I shall, but I do not think we will see him again.'

Leoman nodded. Then he said to Corabb, 'Tell the warchiefs to scatter with their tribes. Out of Raraku as fast as they can manage it—'

'Out of the Holy Desert, Leoman?' Corabb asked.

'Can't you hear it? Never mind. Yes. Out. Rejoin me on the western road – the ancient one that runs straight.'

Corabb saluted, then pulled his horse round and rode off.

'You too, Toblakai. Out of Raraku—'

'I will,' Karsa replied, 'when I am done here, Leoman. Now, go – officers are riding to the Adjunct. They will follow with an attack—'

'Then they're fools,' Leoman spat.

Karsa watched his friend ride off. Then strode to his own mount. He was tired. His wounds hurt. But some issues remained unsettled, and he needed to take care of that.

The Teblor swung himself onto Havok's back.

Lostara walked down the slope, the cracked ground crunching underfoot. At her side marched Pearl, breathing hard beneath the weight of Korbolo Dom's bound, limp form.

Tavore still stood alone on the flats, a few paces from Sha'ik's body. The Adjunct's attention had been fixed on the Dogslayer trenches, and on the lone, ragged standard rising from the highest ground at the central ramp's summit.

A standard that had no right being here. No right existing at all.

Coltaine's standard, the wings of the Crow Clan.

Lostara wondered who had raised it, where it had come from, then decided she didn't want to know. One truth could not be ignored, however. *They're all dead. The Dogslayers. All. And the Adjunct did not need to even raise a hand to achieve that.*

She sensed her own cowardice and scowled. Skittering away, again and again, from thoughts too bitter with irony to contemplate. Their journey to the basin had been nightmarish, as Kurald Emurlahn swarmed the entire oasis, as shadows warred with ghosts, and the incessant rise and fall of that song grew audible enough for Lostara to sense, if not hear. A song still climbing in crescendo.

But, at the feet of . . . *of everything*. A simple, brutal fact. They had come too late.

Within sight, only to see Tavore batter Sha'ik's weapon out of her hands, then thrust that sword right through her . . . *name it, Lostara Yil, you damned coward. Name it! Her sister. Through her sister. There. It's done, dragged out before us.*

She would not look at Pearl, could say nothing. Nor did he speak.

We are bound, this man and I. I didn't ask for this. I don't want it. I'll never be without it. Oh, Queen forgive me . . .

Close enough now to see Tavore's face beneath the helm, an expression stern – almost angry – as she turned to watch their approach.

Officers were riding down, though slowly.

There would be time, Lostara realized, for a private conversation.

She and Pearl halted six paces from the Adjunct.

The Claw dumped Korbolo Dom onto the ground between them. 'He won't wake up any time soon,' he said, taking a deep breath, then sighing and looking away.

'What are you two doing here?' the Adjunct asked. 'Did you lose the trail?'

Pearl did not glance at Lostara, but simply shook his head in answer to Tavore's question. A pause, then, 'We found her, Adjunct. With deep regret . . . Felisin is dead.'

'Are you certain?'

'Yes, Adjunct.' He hesitated, then added, 'I can say one thing for certain, Tavore. She died quickly.'

Lostara's heart felt ready to explode at Pearl's quiet words. Jaws clenching, she met the Adjunct's eyes, and slowly nodded.

Tavore stared at them both for a long moment, then lowered her head. 'Well, there is mercy in that, I suppose.'

And then sheathed her sword, turned away and began walking towards her approaching officers.

Under her breath, so low that only Pearl could hear

her, Lostara said, 'Yes, I suppose there is . . .'

Pearl swung to her suddenly. 'Here comes Tene Baralta. Stall him, lass.' He walked over to Sha'ik's body. 'The warrens are clear enough . . . I hope.' He bent down and tenderly picked her up, then faced Lostara once more. 'Yes, she's a heavier burden than you might think.'

'No, Pearl, I don't think that. Where?'

The Claw's smile lanced into her heart. 'A hilltop . . . you know the one.'

Lostara nodded. 'Very well. And then?'

'Convince them to get out of Raraku, lass. As fast as they can. When I'm done . . .' he hesitated.

'Come and find me, Pearl,' she growled. 'Or else I'll come looking for you.'

A flicker of life in his weary eyes. 'I will. I promise.'

She watched his gaze flit past her shoulder and she turned. Tavore was still twenty paces from the riders, who had all but Baralta halted their horses. 'What is it, Pearl?'

'Just watching her . . . walking away,' he replied. 'She looks so . . .'

'Alone?'

'Yes. That is the word, isn't it. See you later, lass.'

She felt the breath of the warren gust against her back, then the day's heat returned. Lostara hitched her thumbs in her belt, and waited for Tene Baralta.

Her once-commander would have wanted Sha'ik's body. A trophy for this day. He would be furious. 'Well,' she muttered, 'that's just too damned bad.'

Keneb watched her approach. There was none of the triumph there he thought he would see. Indeed, she looked worn down, as if the falling of spirit that followed every battle had already come to her, the deathly stillness of the mind that invited dire contemplation, that lifted up the host of questions that could never be answered.

She had sheathed her sword without cleansing it, and

Sha'ik's blood had run crooked tracks down the plain scabbard.

Tene Baralta rode past her, on his way, Keneb suspected, to Sha'ik's body. If he said anything to the Adjunct in passing, she made no reply.

'Fist Blistig,' she announced upon arriving. 'Send scouts to the Dogslayer ramps. Also, a detachment of guards – the Claw have delivered to us Korbolo Dom.'

Ah, so that was what that man was carrying. Keneb glanced back to where the duel had taken place. Only the woman stood there now, over the prone shape that was the Napan renegade, her face turned up to Tene Baralta, who remained on his horse and seemed to be berating her. Even at this distance, something told Keneb that Baralta's harangue would yield little result.

'Adjunct,' Nil said, 'there is no need to scout the Dogslayer positions. They are all dead.'

Tavore frowned. 'Explain.'

'Raraku's ghosts, Adjunct.'

Nether spoke up. 'And the spirits of our own slain. Nil and I – we were blind to it. We'd forgotten the ways of . . . of seeing. The cattle dog, Adjunct. Bent. It should have died at Coltaine's feet. At the Fall. But some soldiers saved it, saw to the healing of its wounds.'

'A cattle dog? What are you talking about?' Tavore demanded, revealing, for the very first time, an edge of exasperation.

'Bent and Roach,' Nil said. 'The only creatures still living to have walked the Chain the entire way. Two dogs.'

'Not true,' Temul said from behind the two Wickan shamans. 'This mare. It belonged to Duiker.'

Nil half turned to acknowledge the correction, then faced Tavore once more. 'They came back with us, Adjunct—'

'The dogs.'

He nodded. 'And the spirits of the slain. Our own ghosts, Adjunct, have marched with us. Those that fell around

990

Coltaine at the very end. Those that died on the trees of Aren Way. And, step by step, more came from the places where they were cut down. Step by step, Adjunct, our army of vengeance *grew*.'

'And yet you sensed *nothing*?'

'Our grief blinded us,' Nether replied.

'Last night,' Nil said, 'the child Grub woke us. Led us to the ridge, so that we could witness the awakening. There were *legions*, Adjunct, that had marched this land a hundred thousand years ago. And Pormqual's crucified army and the legions of the Seventh on one flank. The three slaughtered clans of the Wickans on the other. And still others. Many others. Within the darkness last night, Tavore, there was war.'

'Thus,' Nether said, smiling, 'you were right, Adjunct. In the dreams that haunted you from the very first night of this march, you saw what we could not see.'

'It was never the burden you believed it to be,' Nil added. 'You did not *drag* the Chain of Dogs with you, Adjunct Tavore.'

'Didn't I, Nil?' A chilling half-smile twisted her thin-lipped mouth, then she looked away. 'All those ghosts . . . simply to slay the Dogslayers?'

'No, Adjunct,' Nether answered. 'There were other . . . enemies.'

'Fist Gamet's ghost joined them,' Nil said.

Tavore's eyes narrowed sharply. 'You saw him?'

Both Wickans nodded, and Nether added, 'Grub spoke with him.'

The Adjunct shot Keneb a querying look.

'He can be damned hard to find,' the captain muttered, shrugging. 'As for talking with ghosts . . . well, the lad is, uh, strange enough for that.'

The Adjunct's sigh was heavy.

Keneb's gaze caught movement and he swung his head round, to see Tene Baralta riding back in the company of two soldiers wearing little more than rags. Both were unshaven, their hair long and matted. Their horses bore no saddles.

The Fist reined in with his charges. His face was dark with anger. 'Adjunct. That Claw has stolen Sha'ik's body!'

Keneb saw the woman approaching on foot, still twenty paces distant. She looked . . . smug.

Tavore ignored Tene Baralta's statement and was eyeing the two newcomers. 'And you are?' she asked.

The elder of the two saluted. 'Captain Kindly, Adjunct, of the Ashok Regiment. We were prisoners in the Dogslayer camp. Lieutenant Pores and myself, that is.'

Keneb started, then leaned forward on his saddle. Yes, he realized, through all that filth . . . 'Captain,' he said in rough greeting.

Kindly squinted, then grimaced. 'Keneb.'

Tavore cleared her throat, then asked, 'Are you two all that's left of your regiment, Captain?'

'No, Adjunct. At least, we don't think so—'

'Tell me later. Go get cleaned up.'

'Aye, Adjunct.'

'One more question first,' she said. 'The Dogslayer camp . . .'

Kindly made an involuntary warding gesture. 'It was not a pleasant night, Adjunct.'

'You bear shackle scars.'

Kindly nodded. 'Just before dawn, a couple of Bridgeburners showed up and burned out the locks.'

'What?'

The captain waved for his lieutenant to follow, said over one shoulder, 'Don't worry, they were already dead.'

The two rode into the camp.

Tavore seemed to shake herself, then faced Keneb. 'You two know each other? Will that prove problematic, Captain?'

'No.'

'Good. Then he won't resent your promotion to Fist. Now ride to your new legion. We will follow the fleeing tribes. If we have to cross this entire continent, I will see them cornered, and then I will destroy them. This rebellion will be ashes on the wind when we are done. Go, Fist Keneb.'

'Aye, Adjunct.' And he gathered his reins.

'*Weapons out!*' Temul suddenly shouted.

And all spun to see a rider cantering down from the hill where Sha'ik had first appeared.

Keneb's eyes thinned, even as he drew his sword. There was something wrong . . . a skewing of scale . . .

A small squad from Blistig's legion had been detailed as guard to the Adjunct, and they now moved forward. Leading them was one of Blistig's officers – none other, Keneb realized, than Squint. The slayer of Coltaine, who was now standing stock still, studying the approaching horse warrior.

'That,' he growled, 'is a Thelomen Toblakai! Riding a damned Jhag horse!'

Crossbows were levelled.

'What's that horse dragging?' asked the woman who had just arrived on foot – whom Keneb now recognized, belatedly, as one of Tene Baralta's officers.

Nether suddenly hissed, and she and her brother flinched back as one.

Heads. From some demonic beasts—

Weapons were readied.

The Adjunct lifted a hand. 'Wait. He's not drawn his weapon—'

'It's a stone sword,' Squint rasped. 'T'lan Imass.'

'Only bigger,' one of the soldiers spat.

No-one spoke as the huge, blood-spattered figure rode closer.

To halt ten paces away.

Tene Baralta leaned forward and spat onto the ground. 'I know you,' he rumbled. 'Bodyguard to Sha'ik—'

'Be quiet,' the Toblakai cut in. 'I have words for the Adjunct.'

'Speak, then,' Tavore said.

The giant bared his teeth. 'Once, long ago, I claimed the Malazans as my enemies. I was young. I took pleasure in voicing vows. The more enemies the better. So it was, once. But no longer. Malazan, you are no longer my enemy. Thus, I will not kill you.'

'We are relieved,' Tavore said drily.

He studied her for a long moment.

During which Keneb's heart began to pound hard and fast in his chest.

Then the Toblakai smiled. 'You should be.'

With that he wheeled his Jhag horse round and rode a westerly path down the length of the basin. The huge hound heads bounced and thumped in their wake.

Keneb's sigh was shaky.

'Excuse my speaking,' Squint rasped, 'but something tells me the bastard was right.'

Tavore turned and studied the old veteran. 'An observation,' she said, 'I'll not argue, soldier.'

Once more, Keneb collected his reins.

Surmounting the ridge, Lieutenant Ranal sawed hard on the reins, and the horse reared against the skyline.

'Gods take me, somebody shoot him.'

Fiddler did not bother to turn round to find out who had spoken. He was too busy fighting his own horse to care much either way. It had Wickan blood, and it wanted his. The mutual hatred was coming along just fine.

'What is that bastard up to?' Cuttle demanded as he rode alongside the sergeant. 'We're leaving even Gesler's squad behind – and Hood knows where Borduke's gone to.'

The squad joined their lieutenant atop the ancient raised road. To the north stretched the vast dunes of Raraku, shimmering in the heat.

Ranal wheeled his mount to face his soldiers. Then pointed west. 'See them? Have any of you eyes worth a damn?'

Fiddler leaned to one side and spat grit. Then squinted to where Ranal was pointing. A score of riders. Desert warriors, likely a rearguard. They were at a loping canter. 'Lieutenant,' he said, 'there's a spider lives in these sands. Moves along under the surface, but drags a strange snake-like tail that every hungry predator can't help but see. Squirming away along the surface. It's a big spider. Hawk comes down to snatch up that snake, and ends up dissolving in a stream down that spider's throat—'

'Enough with the damned horse-dung, Sergeant,' snapped Ranal. 'They're there because they were late getting out of the oasis. Likely too busy looting the palace to notice that Sha'ik had been skewered, the Dogslayers were dead and everyone else was bugging out as fast as their scrawny horses could take 'em.' He glared at Fiddler. 'I want their heads, you grey-whiskered fossil.'

'We'll catch them sooner or later, sir,' Fiddler said. 'Better with the whole company—'

'Then get off that saddle and sit your backside down here on this road, Sergeant! Leave the fighting to the rest of us! The rest of you, follow me!'

Ranal kicked his lathered horse into a gallop.

With a weary gesture, Fiddler waved the marines on, then followed on his own bucking mare.

'Got a pinched nerve,' Koryk called out as he cantered past.

'Who, my horse or the lieutenant?'

The Seti grinned back. 'Your horse . . . naturally. Doesn't like all that weight, Fid.'

Fiddler reached back and readjusted the heavy pack and the assembled lobber crossbow. 'I'll pinch her damned nerve,' he muttered. 'Just you wait.'

It was past midday. Almost seven bells since the Adjunct cut down Sha'ik. Fiddler found himself glancing again and again to the north – to Raraku, where the song still rushed out to embrace him, only to fall away, then roll forward once more. The far horizon beyond that vast basin of sand, he now saw, now held up a bank of white clouds.

Now that don't look right . . .

Sand-filled wind gusted suddenly into his face.

'They've left the road!' Ranal shouted.

Fiddler squinted westward. The riders had indeed plunged down the south bank, were cutting out diagonally – straight for a fast-approaching sandstorm. *Gods, not another sandstorm . . .* This one, he knew, was natural. The kind that plagued this desert, springing up like a capricious demon to rage a wild, cavorting path for a bell or two, before vanishing as swiftly as it had first appeared.

He rose up on his saddle. 'Lieutenant! They're going to ride into it! Use it as cover! We'd better not—'

'Flap that tongue at me one more time, Sergeant, and I'll tear it out! You hear me?'

Fiddler subsided. 'Aye, sir.'

'Full pursuit, soldiers!' Ranal barked. 'That storm'll slow them!'

Oh, it will slow them, all right . . .

Gesler glared into the blinding desert. 'Now who,' he wondered under his breath, 'are they?'

They had drawn to halt when it became obvious that the four strange riders were closing fast on an intercept course. Long-bladed white swords flashing over their heads. Bizarre, gleaming white armour. White horses. White everything.

'They're none too pleased with us,' Stormy rumbled, running his fingers through his beard.

'That's fine,' Gesler growled, 'but they ain't renegades, are they?'

'Sha'ik's? Who knows? Probably not, but even so . . .'

The sergeant nodded. 'Sands, get up here.'

'I am,' the sapper snapped.

'What's your range, lad, with that damned thing?'

'Ain't sure. No chance to try it yet. Fid's is anywhere

from thirty to forty paces with a cusser – which is ugly close—'

'All right. Rest of you, dismount and drive your horses down the other side. Truth, hold on good to their reins down there – if they bolt we're done for.'

'Saw Borduke and his squad south of here,' Pella ventured.

'Aye, as lost as we are – and you can't see 'em now, can you?'

'No, Sergeant.'

'Damn that Ranal. Remind me to kill him when we next meet.'

'Aye, Sergeant.'

The four attackers were tall bastards. Voicing eerie warcries now as they charged towards the base of the hill.

'Load up, lad,' Gesler muttered, 'and don't mess up.'

The lobber had been copied from Fiddler's own. It looked decent, at least as far as lobbers went – *which ain't far enough. Thirty paces with a cusser. Hood roast us all . . .*

And here they came. Base of the slope, horses surging to take them up the hill.

A heavy thud, and something awkward and grey sailed out and down.

A cusser – holy f— 'Down! Down! Down!'

The hill seemed to lift beneath them. Gesler thumped in the dust, coughing in the spiralling white clouds, then, swearing, he buried his head beneath his arms as stones rained down.

Some time later, the sergeant clambered to his feet.

On the hill's opposite side, Truth was trying to run in every direction at once, the horses trailing loose reins as they pelted in wild panic.

'Hood's balls on a skillet!' Gesler planted his hands on his hips and glared about. The other soldiers were picking themselves up, shaken and smeared in dust. Stormy closed on Sands and grabbed him by the throat.

'Not too hard, Corporal,' Gesler said as Stormy began

shaking the sapper about. 'I want him alive for my turn. And dammit, make sure he ain't got any sharpers on his body.'

That stopped Stormy flat.

Gesler walked to the now pitted edge of the hill and looked down. 'Well,' he said, 'they won't be chasing us any more, I'd say.'

'Wonder who they were?' Pella asked.

'Armour seems to have weathered the blast – you could go down and scrape out whatever's left inside 'em . . . on second thought, never mind. We need to round up our horses.' He faced the others. 'Enough pissing about, lads. Let's get moving.'

Lying on the smoking edge of the crater, sprayed in horse-flesh and deafened by the blast, Jorrude groaned. He was a mass of bruises, his head ached, and he wanted to throw up – but not until he pried the helm from his head.

Nearby in the rubble, Brother Enias coughed. Then said, 'Brother Jorrude?'

'Yes?'

'I want to go home.'

Jorrude said nothing. It would not do, after all, to utter a hasty, heartfelt agreement, despite their present circumstance. 'Check on the others, Brother Enias.'

'Were those truly the ones who rode that ship through our realm?'

'They were,' Jorrude answered as he fumbled with the helm's straps. 'And I have been thinking. I suspect they were ignorant of Liosan laws when they travelled through our realm. True, ignorance is an insufficient defence. But one must consider the notion of innocent momentum.'

From off to one side, Malachar grunted. 'Innocent momentum?'

'Indeed. Were not these trespassers but pulled along – beyond their will – in the wake of the draconian T'lan

Imass bonecaster? If an enemy we must hunt, then should it not be that dragon?'

'Wise words,' Malachar observed.

'A brief stay in our realm,' Jorrude continued, 'to re-supply and requisition new horses, along with repairs and such, seems to reasonably obtain in this instance.'

'Truly judged, brother.'

From the other side of the crater sounded another cough. At least, Jorrude dourly reflected, they were all still alive.

It's all the dragon's fault, in fact. Who would refute that?

They rode into the sandstorm, less than fifty strides behind the fleeing horse warriors, and found themselves flounder-ing blind in a maelstrom of shrieking winds and whipping gravel.

Fiddler heard a horse scream.

He drew hard on his own reins, the wind hammering at him from all sides. Already he'd lost sight of his com-panions. *This is wide-eyed stupid.*

Now, if I was the commander of those bastards, I'd—

And suddenly figures flashed into view, scimitars and round shields, swathed faces and ululating warcries. Fiddler threw himself down against his horse's withers as a heavy blade slashed, slicing through sand-filled air where his head had been a moment earlier.

The Wickan mare lunged forward and to one side, choosing this precise moment to buck its hated rider from the saddle.

With profound success.

Fiddler found himself flying forward, his bag of munitions rolling up his back, then up over his head.

Still in mid-air, but angling down to the ground, he curled himself into a tight ball – though he well knew, in that instant, that there was no hope of surviving. No hope at all. Then he pounded into the sand, and rolled – to see, upside-down, a huge hook-bladed sword spinning end over end across his own wake. And a stumbling horse. And its rider, a warrior thrown far back on his saddle – with the munition bag wrapped in his arms.

A surprised look beneath the ornate helm – then rider, horse and munitions vanished into the whirling sands.

Fiddler clambered to his feet and began running. Sprinting, in what he hoped – what he prayed – was the opposite direction.

A hand snagged his harness from behind. 'Not that way, you fool!' And he was yanked to one side, flung to the ground, and a body landed on top of him.

The sergeant's face was pushed into the sand and held there.

Corabb bellowed. The bulky, heavy sack was hissing in his arms. As if filled with snakes. It had clunked hard against his chest, arriving like a flung boulder out of the storm, and he'd time only to toss his sword away and raise both arms.

The impact threw him onto the horse's rump, but his feet stayed in the stirrups.

The bag's momentum carried it over his face, and the hissing filled his ears.

Snakes!

He slid on his back down one side of the mount's heaving hindquarters, letting the bag's weight pull his arms with it. Don't panic! He screamed.

Snakes!

The bag tugged in his hands as it brushed the ground.

He held his breath, then let go.

Tumbling clunks, a burst of frenzied hissing – then the horse's forward charge carried him blissfully away.

He struggled to right himself, his leg and stomach muscles fiercely straining, and finally was able to grasp the horn and pull himself straight.

One pass, Leoman had said. Then wheel and into the storm's heart.

He'd done that much. One pass. Enough.

Time to flee.

Corabb Bhilan Thun'alas leaned forward, and bared muddy teeth.

Spirits below, it is good to be alive!

The detonation should have killed Fiddler. There was fire. Towering walls of sand. The air concussed, and his breath was torn from his lungs even as blood spurted from his nose and both ears.

And the body lying atop him seemed to wither in shreds.

He'd recognized the voice. It was impossible. It was . . . infuriating.

Hot smoke rolled over them.

And that damned voice whispered, 'Can't leave you on your own for a Hood-damned minute, can I? Say hello to Kalam for me, will ya? I'll see you again, sooner or later. And you'll see me, too. You'll see us all.' A laugh. 'Just not today. Damned shame 'bout your fiddle, though.'

The weight vanished.

Fiddler rolled over. The storm was tumbling away, leaving a white haze in its wake. He groped with his hands.

A terrible, ragged moan ripped from his throat, and he lifted himself onto his knees. 'Hedge!' he screamed. 'Damn you! *Hedge!*'

Someone jogged into view, settled down beside him. 'Slamming gates, Fid – you're Hood-damned alive!'

He stared at the man's battered face, then recognized it. 'Cuttle? He was here. He – you're covered in blood—'

'Aye. I wasn't as close as you. Luckily. 'Fraid I can't say the same for Ranal. Someone had taken down his horse. He was stumbling around.'

'That blood—'

'Aye,' Cuttle said again, then flashed a hard grin. 'I'm wearing Ranal.'

Shouts, and other figures were closing in. Every one of them on foot.

'—killed the horses. Bastards went and—'

'Sergeant! You all right? Bottle, get over here—'

1001

'Killed the—'

'Be quiet, Smiles, you're making me sick. Did you hear that blast? Gods below—'

Cuttle clapped Fiddler on one shoulder, then dragged him to his feet.

'Where's the lieutenant?' Koryk asked.

'Right here,' Cuttle answered, but did not elaborate.

He's wearing Ranal.

'What just happened?' Koryk asked.

Fiddler studied his squad. *All here. That's a wonder.*

Cuttle spat. 'What happened, lad? We got slapped down. That's what happened. Slapped down hard.'

Fiddler stared at the retreating storm. *Aw, shit. Hedge.*

'Here comes Borduke's squad!'

'Find your horses, everyone,' Corporal Tarr said. 'Sergeant's been knocked about. Collect whatever you can salvage – we gotta wait for the rest of the company, I reckon.'

Good lad.

'Look at that crater,' Smiles said. 'Gods, Sergeant, you couldn't have been much closer to Hood's Gate and lived, could you?'

He stared at her. 'You've no idea how right you are, lass.'

And the song rose and fell, and he could feel his heart matching that cadence. Ebb and flow. *Raraku has swallowed more tears than can be imagined. Now comes the time for the Holy Desert to weep.* Ebb and flow, his blood's song, and it lived on.

It lives on.

They had fled in the wrong direction. Fatal, but unsurprising. The night had been a shambles. The last survivor of Korbolo Dom's cadre of mages, Fayelle rode a lathered horse in the company of thirteen other Dogslayers down the channel of a long-dead river, boulders and banks high on either side.

Herself and thirteen battered, bloodied soldiers. All that was left.

The clash with Leoman had begun well enough, a perfectly sprung ambush. And would have ended perfectly, as well.

If not for the damned ghosts.

Ambush turned over, onto its back like an upended tortoise. They'd been lucky to get out with their lives, these few. These last.

Fayelle well knew what had happened to the rest of Korbolo's army. She had felt Henaras's death. And Kamist Reloe's.

And Raraku was not finished with them. Oh no. Not at all finished.

They reached a slope leading out of the defile.

She had few regrets—

Crossbow quarrels whizzed down. Horses and soldiers screamed. Bodies thumped onto the ground. Her horse staggered, then rolled onto its side. She'd no time to kick free of the stirrups, and as the dying beast pinned her leg its weight tore the joint from her hip, sending pain thundering through her. Her left arm was trapped awkwardly beneath her as her own considerable weight struck the ground – and bones snapped.

Then the side of her head hammered against rock.

Fayelle struggled to focus. The pain subsided, became a distant thing. She heard faint pleas for mercy, the cries of wounded soldiers being finished off.

Then a shadow settled over her.

'I've been looking for you.'

Fayelle frowned. The face hovering above her belonged to the past. The desert had aged it, but it nevertheless remained a child's face. *Oh, spirits below. The child. Sinn. My old . . . student . . .*

She watched the girl raise a knife between them, angle the point down, then set it against her neck.

Fayelle laughed. 'Go ahead, you little horror. I'll wait for you at Hood's Gate . . . and the wait won't be long—'

The knife punched through skin and cartilage.

Fayelle died.

Straightening, Sinn swung to her companions. They were, one and all, busy gathering the surviving horses.

Sixteen left. The Ashok Regiment had fallen on hard times. Thirst and starvation. Raiders. This damned desert.

She watched them for a moment, then something else drew her gaze.

Northward.

She slowly straightened. 'Cord.'

The sergeant turned. 'What – oh, Beru fend!'

The horizon to the west had undergone a transformation. It was now limned in white, and it was *rising*.

'Double up!' Cord bellowed. '*Now!*'

A hand closed on her shoulder. Shard leaned close. 'You ride with me.'

'Ebron!'

'I hear you,' the mage replied to Cord's bellow. 'And I'll do what I can with these blown mounts, but I ain't guaranteeing—'

'Get on with it! Bell, help Limp onto that horse – he's busted up that knee again!'

Sinn cast one last glance at Fayelle's corpse. She'd known, then. What was coming.

I should be dancing. The bloodied knife fell from her hands.

Then she was roughly grasped and pulled up onto the saddle behind Shard.

The beast's head tossed, and it shook beneath them.

'Queen take us,' Shard hissed, 'Ebron's filled these beasts with *fire*.'

We'll need it . . .

And now they could hear the sound, a roar that belittled even the Whirlwind Wall in its fullest rage.

Raraku had risen.

To claim a shattered warren.

The Wickan warlocks had known what was coming. Flight

1004

was impossible, but the islands of coral stood high – higher than any other feature this side of the escarpment – and it was on these that the armies gathered.

To await what could be their annihilation.

The north sky was a massive wall of white, billowing clouds. A cool, burgeoning wind thrashed through the palms around the oasis.

Then the sound reached them.

A roar unceasing, building, of water, cascading, foaming, tumbling across the vast desert.

The Holy Desert, it seemed, held far more than bones and memories. More than ghosts and dead cities. Lostara Yil stood near the Adjunct, ignoring the baleful glares Tene Baralta continued casting her way. Wondering . . . if Pearl was on that high ground, standing over Sha'ik's grave . . . if that ground was in fact high enough.

She wondered, too, at what she had seen these past months. Visions burned into her soul, fraught and mysterious, visions that could still chill her blood if she allowed them to rise before her mind's eye once more. Crucified dragons. Murdered gods. Warrens of fire and warrens of ashes.

It was odd, she reflected, to be thinking these things, even as a raging sea was born from seeming nothing and was sweeping towards them, drowning all in its path.

Odder, still, to be thinking of Pearl. She was hard on him, viciously so at times. Not because she cared, but because it was fun. No, that was too facile, wasn't it? She cared indeed.

What a stupid thing to have let happen.

A weary sigh close beside her. Lostara scowled without turning. 'You're back.'

'As requested,' Pearl murmured.

Oh, she wanted to hit him for that.

'The task is . . . done?'

'Aye. Consigned to the deep and all that. If Tene Baralta still wants her, he'll have to hold his breath.'

She looked then. 'Really? The sea is already that deep?' *Then we're—*

'No. High and dry, actually. The other way sounded more . . . poetic.'

'I really hate you.'

He nodded. 'And you'll have plenty of time in which to luxuriate in it.'

'You think we'll survive this?'

'Yes. Oh, we'll get our feet wet, but these were islands even back then. This sea will flood the oasis. It will pound up against the raised road west of here – since it was the coastal road back then. And wash up close to the escarpment, maybe even reach it.'

'That's all very well,' she snapped. 'And what will we be doing, stuck here on these islands in the middle of a land-locked sea?'

Infuriatingly, Pearl simply shrugged. 'A guess? We build a flotilla of rafts and bind them together to form a bridge, straight to the west road. The sea will be shallow enough there anyway, even if that doesn't work as well as it should – but I have every confidence in the Adjunct.'

The wall of water then struck the far side of the oasis, with the sound of thunder. Palms waved wildly, then began toppling.

'Well, now we know what turned that other forest to stone,' Pearl said loudly over the thrashing roar of water—

That now flowed across the ruins, filling the Dogslayer trenches, tumbling down into the basin.

And Lostara could see that Pearl was right. Its fury was already spent, and the basin seemed to swallow the water with a most prodigious thirst.

She glanced over to study the Adjunct.

Impassive, watching the seas rise, one hand on the hilt of her sword.

Oh, why does looking at you break my heart?

The sands were settling on the carcasses of the horses. The

three squads sat or stood, waiting for the rest of the legion. Bottle had walked up to the road to see the source of the roar, had come staggering back with the news.

A sea.

A damned sea.

And its song was in Fiddler's soul, now. Strangely warm, almost comforting.

One and all, they then turned to watch the giant rider and his giant horse thunder along that road, heading westward. Dragging something that kicked up a lot of dust.

The image of that stayed with Fiddler long after the clouds of dust had drifted off the road, down the near side of the slope.

Could have been a ghost.

But he knew it wasn't.

Could have been their worst enemy.

But if he was, it didn't matter. Not right now.

A short while later there was a startled shout from Smiles, and Fiddler turned, in time to see two figures stride out from a warren.

Despite everything, he found himself grinning.

Old friends, he realized, were getting harder to find.

Still, he knew them, and they were his brothers.

Mortal souls of Raraku. Raraku, the land that had bound them together. Bound them all, as was now clear, beyond even death.

Fiddler was unmindful of how it looked, of what the others thought, upon seeing the three men close to a single embrace.

The horses clambered up the slope to the ridge. Where their riders reined them in, and one and all turned to stare at the yellow, foaming seas churning below. A moment later a squat four-eyed demon scrabbled onto the summit to join them.

The Lord of Summer had lent wings to their horses – Heboric could admit no other possibility, so quickly had they covered the leagues since the night past. And the beasts seemed fresh even now. As fresh as Greyfrog.

Though he himself was anything but.

'What has happened?' Scillara wondered aloud.

Heboric could only shake his head.

'More importantly,' Felisin said, 'where do we go now? I don't think I can sit in the saddle much longer—'

'I know how you feel, lass. We should find somewhere to make camp—'

The squeal of a mule brought all three around.

A scrawny, black-skinned old man was riding up towards them, seated cross-legged atop the mule. 'Welcome!' he shrieked – a shriek because, even as he spoke, he toppled to one side and thumped hard onto the stony trail. 'Help me, you idiots!'

Heboric glanced at the two women, but it was Greyfrog who moved first.

'Food!'

The old man shrieked again. 'Get away from me! I have news to tell! All of you! Is L'oric dead? No! My shadows saw everything! You are my guests! Now, come prise my legs loose! You, lass. No, you, the other lass! Both of you! Beautiful women with their hands on my legs, my thighs! I can't wait! Do they see the avid lust in my eyes? Of course not, I'm but a helpless wizened creature, potential father figure—'

Cutter stood in the tower's uppermost chamber, staring out of the lone window. Bhok'arala chittered behind him, pausing every now and then to make crooning, mournful sounds.

He'd woken alone.

And had known, instantly, that she was gone. And there would be no trail for him to follow.

Iskaral Pust had conjured up a mule and ridden off earlier. Of Mogora there was, mercifully, no sign.

Thoroughly alone, then, for most of this day.

Until now.

'There are countless paths awaiting you.'

Cutter sighed. 'Hello, Cotillion. I was wondering if you'd show up . . . again.'

'Again?'

'You spoke with Apsalar. Here in this very chamber. You helped her decide.'

'She told you?'

He shook his head. 'Not entirely.'

'Her decision was hers to make, Cutter. Hers alone.'

'It doesn't matter. Never mind. Odd, though. You see countless paths. Whilst I see . . . none worth walking.'

'Do you seek, then, something worthy?'

Cutter slowly closed his eyes, then sighed. 'What would you have me do?'

'There was a man, once, whose task was to guard the life of a young girl. He did the best he could – with such honour as to draw, upon his sad death, the attention of Hood himself. Oh, the Lord of Death will look into a mortal's soul, given the right circumstances. The, uh, the proper incentive. Thus, that man is now the Knight of Death—'

'I don't want to be Knight of anything, nor for anyone, Cotillion—'

'The wrong track, lad. Let me finish my tale. This man did the best he could, but he failed. And now the girl is dead. She was named Felisin. Of House Paran.'

Cutter's head turned. He studied the shadowed visage of the god. 'Captain Paran? His—'

'His sister. Look down upon the path, here, out the window, lad. In a short time Iskaral Pust will return. With guests. Among them, a child named Felisin—'

'But you said—'

'Before Paran's sister . . . died, she adopted a waif. A sorely abused foundling. She sought, I think – we will never know for certain, of course – to achieve something . . . something she herself had no chance, no opportunity, to achieve. Thus, she named the waif after herself.'

'And what is she to me, Cotillion?'

'You are being obstinate, I think. The wrong question.'

'Oh, then tell me what is the right question.'

'What are you to her?'

Cutter grimaced.

'The child approaches in the company of another woman, a very remarkable one, as you – and she – will come to see. And with a priest, sworn now to Treach. From him, you will learn . . . much of worth. Finally, a demon travels with these three humans. For the time being . . .'

'Where are they going? Why stop here, as Iskaral's guests?'

'Why, to collect you, Cutter.'

'I don't understand.'

'Symmetry, lad, is a power unto itself. It is the expression, if you will, of nature's striving for balance. I charge you with protecting Felisin's life. To accompany them on their long, and dangerous, journey.'

'How epic of you.'

'I think not,' Cotillion snapped.

Silence, for a time, during which Cutter regretted his comment.

Finally, the Daru sighed. 'I hear horses. And Pust . . . in one of his nauseating diatribes.'

Cotillion said nothing.

'Very well,' Cutter said. 'This Felisin . . . abused, you said. Those ones are hard to get to. To befriend, I mean. Their scars stay fresh and fierce with pain—'

'Her adopted mother did well, given her own scars. Be glad, lad, that she is the daughter, not the mother. And, in your worst moments, think of how Baudin felt.'

'Baudin. The elder Felisin's guardian?'

'Yes.'

'All right,' Cutter said. 'It will do.'

'What will?'

'This path. It will do.' He hesitated, then said, 'Cotillion.

1010

This notion of . . . balance. Something has occurred to me—'

Cotillion's eyes silenced him, shocked him with their unveiling of sorrow . . . of remorse. The patron of assassins nodded. 'From her . . . to you. Aye.'

'Did she see that, do you think?'

'All too clearly, I'm afraid.'

Cutter stared out the window. 'I loved her, you know. I still do.'

'So you do not wonder why she has left.'

He shook his head, unable to fight back the tears any more. 'No, Cotillion,' he whispered. 'I don't.'

The ancient coast road long behind him, Karsa Orlong guided Havok northward along the shore of the new inland sea. Rain clouds hung over the murky water to the east, but the wind was pushing them away.

He studied the sky for a moment, then reined in on a slight rise studded with boulders and slipped down from the horse's back. Walking over to a large, flat-topped rock, the Teblor unslung his sword and set it point downward against a nearby boulder, then sat. He drew off his pack and rummaged in an outside pocket for some salted bhederin, dried fruit, and goat cheese.

Staring out over the water, he ate. When he was done, he loosened the pack's straps and dragged out the broken remains of the T'lan Imass. He held it up so that 'Siballe's withered face looked out upon the rippling waves.

'Tell me,' Karsa said, 'what do you see?'

'My past.' A moment of silence, then, 'All that I have lost . . .'

The Teblor released his grip and the partial corpse collapsed into a cloud of dust. Karsa found his waterskin and drank deep. Then he stared down at 'Siballe. 'You once said that if you were thrown into the sea, your soul would be freed. That oblivion would come to you. Is this true?'

'Yes.'

With one hand he lifted her from the ground, rose and walked to the sea's edge.

'Wait! Teblor, wait! I do not understand!'

Karsa's expression soured. 'When I began this journey, I was young. I believed in one thing. I believed in glory. I know now, 'Siballe, that glory is nothing. Nothing. This is what I now understand.'

'What else do you now understand, Karsa Orlong?'

'Not much. Just one other thing. The same cannot be said for mercy.' He raised her higher, then swung her body outward.

It struck the water in the shallows. And dissolved into a muddy bloom, which the waves then swept away.

Karsa swung about. Faced his sword of stone. He then smiled. 'Yes. I am Karsa Orlong of the Uryd, a Teblor. Witness, my brothers. One day I will be worthy to lead such as you. Witness.'

Sword once more slung on his back, Havok once more solid beneath him, the Toblakai rode from the shoreline. West, into the wastes.

EPILOGUE

And now here I sit,
on my brow a circlet of fire,
and this kingdom
I rule
is naught but the host
of my life's recollections,
unruly subjects,
so eager for insurrection,
to usurp the aged man
from his charred throne
and raise up
younger versions
one by one.

The Crown of Years
Fisher kel Tath

By any standards, she was a grim woman.

Onrack the Broken watched her stand in the centre of the chamber and cast a harsh, appraising eye upon the disposition of her young killers. The grimace that twisted her handsome features suggested that she found nothing awry. Her gaze fell at last upon the Tiste Edur, Trull Sengar, and the grimace shifted into a scowl.

'Must we watch our backs as well, with you here?'

Seated on the hewn floor, his back to an equally rough wall, Trull Sengar shrugged. 'I see no easy way of convincing you that I am worthy of your trust, Minala. Apart from weaving for you my lengthy and rather unpleasant story.'

'Spare me,' she growled, then strode from the room.

Trull Sengar glanced over at Onrack and grinned. 'No-one wants to hear it. Well, I am not surprised. Nor am I even stung. It is a rather squalid tale—'

'I will hear your story,' Onrack replied.

Near the entrance, Ibra Gholan's neck creaked as the T'lan Imass looked back over one shoulder to regard Onrack for a moment, before returning to his position guarding the approach.

Trull Sengar barked a laugh. 'This is ideal for an unskilled weaver of tales. My audience comprises a score of children who do not understand my native tongue, and three expressionless and indifferent undead. By tale's end, only I will be weeping . . . likely for all the wrong reasons.'

Monok Ochem, who was standing three paces back from Ibra Gholan, slowly pivoted until the bonecaster faced Onrack. 'You have felt it, then, Broken One. And so you seek distraction.'

Onrack said nothing.

'Felt what?' Trull Sengar asked.

'She is destroyed. The woman who gave Onrack her heart in the time before the Ritual. The woman to whom he avowed his own heart . . . only to steal it back. In many ways, she was destroyed then, already begun on her long journey to oblivion. Do you deny that, Onrack?'

'Bonecaster, I do not.'

'Madness, of such ferocity as to defeat the Vow itself. Like a camp dog that awakens one day with fever in its brain. That snarls and kills in a frenzy. Of course, we had no choice but to track her down, corner her. And so shatter her, imprison her within eternal darkness. Or so we thought. Madness, then, to defy even us. But now, oblivion has claimed her soul at last. A violent, painful demise, but none the less . . .' Monok Ochem paused, then cocked its head. 'Trull Sengar, you have not begun your tale, yet already you weep.'

The Tiste Edur studied the bonecaster for a long moment, as the tears ran down his gaunt cheeks. 'I weep, Monok Ochem, because he cannot.'

The bonecaster faced Onrack once more. 'Broken One, there are many things you deserve . . . but this man is not among them.' He then turned away.

Onrack spoke. 'Monok Ochem, you have travelled far from the mortal you once were, so far as to forget a host of truths, both pleasant and unpleasant. The heart is neither given nor stolen. The heart *surrenders*.'

The bonecaster did not turn round. 'That is a word without power to the T'lan Imass, Onrack the Broken.'

'You are wrong, Monok Ochem. We simply changed the word to make it not only more palatable, but also to empower it. With such eminence that it devoured our souls.'

'We did no such thing,' the bonecaster replied.

'Onrack's right,' Trull Sengar sighed. 'You did. You called it the Ritual of Tellann.'

Neither Monok Ochem nor Ibra Gholan spoke.

The Tiste Edur snorted. 'And you've the nerve to call Onrack *broken*.'

There was silence in the chamber then, for some time.

But Onrack's gaze remained fixed on Trull Sengar. And he was, if he was anything, a creature capable of supreme patience. *To grieve is a gift best shared. As a song is shared.*

Deep in the caves, the drums beat. Glorious echo to the herds whose thundering hoofs celebrate what it is to be alive, to run as one, to roll in life's rhythm. This is how, in the cadence of our voice, we serve nature's greatest need.

Facing nature, we are the balance.

Ever the balance to chaos.

Eventually, his patience was rewarded.

As he knew it would be.

This ends the fourth tale of the
Malazan Book of the Fallen

GLOSSARY

Ascendants

Anomander Rake: Son of Darkness
Apsalar: Lady of Thieves
Beru: Lord of Storms
Bridgeburners
Burn: The Sleeping Goddess
Cotillion: The Rope, Patron of Assassins, High House Shadow
Dessembrae: Lord of Tears
Draconus: an Elder God and forger of the sword Dragnipur
D'rek: The Worm of Autumn
Fener: the Bereft
Gedderone: Lady of Spring and Rebirth
Hood: King of High House Death
Jhess: Queen of Weaving
K'rul: an Elder God of the Warrens
Mael: an Elder God of the Seas
Mowri: Lady of Beggars, Slaves and Serfs
Nerruse: Lady of Calm Seas and Fair Winds
Oponn: Twin Jesters of Chance
Osserc/Osseric/Osric: Lord of the Sky
Poliel: Mistress of Pestilence and Disease
Queen of Dreams: Queen of High House Life
Shadowthrone: Ammanas, King of High House Shadow
Sister of Cold Nights: an Elder Goddess
Soliel: Lady of Health

The Azath: the Houses
The Crippled God: The Chained One, Lord of High
House of Chains
The Deragoth: of the First Empire of Dessimbelackis
The Seven Hounds of Darkness
The Whirlwind Goddess
Togg and Fanderay: The Wolves of Winter
Treach/Trake: The Tiger of Summer and Lord of War

The Gods of the Teblor (The Seven Faces in the Rock)

Urugal the Woven
'Siballe the Unfound
Beroke Soft Voice
Kahlb the Silent Hunter
Thenik the Shattered
Halad the Giant
Imroth the Cruel

Elder Peoples

Tiste Andii: Children of Darkness
Tiste Edur: Children of Shadow
Tiste Liosan: Children of Light
T'lan Imass
Eres/Eres'al
Trell
Jaghut
Forkrul Assail
K'Chain Che'Malle
The Eleint
The Barghast
The Thelomen Toblakai
The Teblor

The Warrens

Kurald Galain: The Elder Warren of Darkness
Kurald Emurlahn: The Elder Warren of Shadow, the Shattered Warren
Kurald Thyrllan: The Elder Warren of Light
Omtose Phellack: The Elder Jaghut Warren of Ice
Tellann: The Elder Imass Warren of Fire
Starvald Demelain: The Eleint Warren
Thyr: The Path of Light
Denul: The Path of Healing
Hood's Path: The Path of Death
Serc: The Path of the Sky
Meanas: The Path of Shadow and Illusion
D'riss: The Path of the Earth
Ruse: The Path of the Sea
Rashan: The Path of Darkness
Mockra: The Path of the Mind
Telas: The Path of Fire

The Deck of Dragons

High House Life
King
Queen (Queen of Dreams)
Champion
Priest
Herald
Soldier
Weaver

High House Death
King (Hood)
Queen
Knight (once Dassem Ultor, now Baudin)
Magi
Herald

Soldier
Spinner
Mason
Virgin

High House Light
King
Queen
Champion (Osseric)
Priest
Captain
Soldier
Seamstress
Builder
Maiden

High House Dark
King
Queen
Knight (Anomander Rake)
Magi
Captain
Soldier
Weaver
Mason
Wife

High House Shadow
King (Shadowthrone/Ammanas)
Queen
Assassin (The Rope/Cotillion)
Magi
Hound

High House of Chains
The King in Chains
The Consort (Poliel?)

Reaver (Kallor?)
Knight (Toblakai)
The Seven of the Dead Fires (The Unbound)
Cripple
Leper
Fool

Unaligned
Oponn
Obelisk (Burn)
Crown
Sceptre
Orb
Throne
Chain
Master of the Deck (Ganoes Paran)

Places in House of Chains

Seven Cities

Aren: a Holy City
Balahn: a small village north of Aren
Ehrlitan: a Holy City north of Raraku
Erougimon: a tel north of Aren
G'danisban: a city east of Raraku
Jhag Odhan: the wastes west of Seven Cities
Lato Revae: a city west of Raraku
Sarpachiya: a city west of Raraku
Thalas River: west of Raraku
The Oasis: Holy Desert Raraku
The Whirlwind Warren
Vathar Crossing: site of battle on Chain of Dogs
Y'Ghatan: self-styled First Holy City

Genabackis

Culvern: a town
Genabaris: a city
Laederon Plateau
Malybridge: a town
Malyn Sea
Malyntaeas: a city
Ninsano Moat: a town
Silver Lake
Tanys: a town

Drift Avalii: an island southwest of the continent of Quon Tali
The Nascent: a flooded world

Steven Erikson's
epic fantasy sequence continues in

MidNight
Tides

Available now from Tor Books

The First Days of the Sundering of Emurlahn
The Edur Invasion, the Age of Scabandari Bloodeye
The Time of the Elder Gods

From the twisting, smoke-filled clouds, blood rained down. The last of the sky keeps, flame-wreathed and pouring black smoke, had surrendered the sky. Their ragged descent had torn furrows through the ground as they struck and broke apart with thunderous reverberations, scattering red-stained rocks among the heaps of corpses that covered the land from horizon to horizon.

The great hive cities had been reduced to ash-layered rubble, and the vast towering clouds above each of them that had shot skyward with their destruction – clouds filled with debris and shredded flesh and blood – now swirled in storms of dissipating heat, spreading to fill the sky.

Amidst the annihilated armies the legions of the conquerors were reassembling on the centre plain, most of which was covered in exquisitely fitted flagstones – where the impact of the sky keeps had not carved deep gouges – although the reassertion of formations was hampered by the countless carcasses of the defeated. And by exhaustion. The legions belonged to two distinct armies, allies in this war, and it was clear that one had fared far better than the other.

The blood mist sheathed Scabandari's vast, iron-hued wings, as he swept down through the churning clouds, blinking nicitating membranes to clear his ice blue draconian eyes. Banking in his descent, the dragon tilted his head to survey his victorious children. The grey banners of the Tiste Edur legions wavered fitfully above the gathering warriors, and Scabandari judged that at least eighteen thousand of his shadow-kin remained. For all that, there would be mourning in the tents of the First Landing this night. The day had begun with over two hundred thousand Tiste Edur marching onto the plain. Still . . . it was enough.

The Edur had clashed with the east flank of the K'Chain Ch'Malle army, prefacing their charge with waves of devastating sorcery. The enemy's formations had been assembled to face a frontal assault, and they had proved fatally slow to turn to the threat on their flank. Like a dagger, the Edur legions had driven to the heart of the K'Chain Che'Malle army.

Below, as he drew closer, Scabandari could see, scattered here and there, the midnight banners of the Tiste Andii. A thousand warriors left, perhaps less. Victory was a more dubious claim for these battered allies. They had engaged the K'ell Hunters, the elite blood kin armies of the three Matrons. Four hundred thousand Tiste Andii, against sixty thousand K'ell Hunters. Additional companies of both Andii and Edur had assailed the sky keeps, but these had known they were going to their own deaths, and their sacrifices had been pivotal in this day's victory, for the sky keeps had been prevented in coming to the aid of the armies on the plain below. By themselves, the assaults on the four sky keeps had yielded only marginal efficacy, despite the short-tails being few in number – their ferocity had proved devastating – but sufficient time had been purchased in Tiste blood for Scabandari and his Soletaken draconian brother to close on the floating fortresses, unleashing upon them the warrens of Starvald Demelain, and Kuralds Emurlahn and Galain.

The dragon swept downwards to where a jumbled mountain of K'Chain Che'Malle carcasses marked the last stand of one of the Matrons. Kurald Emurlahn had slaughtered the defenders, and wild shadows still flitted about like wraiths on the slopes. Scabandari spread his wings, buffeting the steamy air, then settled stop the reptilian bodies.

A moment later he sembled into his Tiste Edur form. Skin the shade of hammered iron, long grey hair unbound, a gaunt, aquiline face with hard, close-set eyes. A down-turned, broad mouth that bore no lines of laughter. High, unlined brow, diagonally scarred livid white against the dusky skin. He wore a leather harness bearing his two-handed sword, a brace of long-knives at his hip, and from his shoulders hung a scaled cape – the hide of a Matron, fresh enough to still glisten with natural oils.

He stood, a tall figure sheathed in droplets of blood, watching the legions assemble. Edur officers glanced his way, then began directing their troops.

Scabandari faced northwest then, eyes narrowing on the billowing clouds. A moment later a vast bone-white dragon broke through. If anything larger than Scabandari himself when veered into draconian form. Also sheathed in blood – and much of it his own, for Silchas Ruin had come to the aid of his Andii kin against the K'ell Hunters.

Scabandari watched his ally approach, stepping back only when the huge dragon settled onto the hilltop to then quickly semble. A head or more taller than the Tiste Edur Soletaken, yet terribly gaunt, muscles bound like rope beneath smooth, almost translucent skin. Talons from some raptor gleamed from the warrior's thick, long white hair. The red of his eyes seemed feverish, so brightly did they glow. Silchas Ruin bore wound, sword-slashes across his body. Most of his upper armour had fallen away, revealing his chest where the blue-green of his veins and arteries tracked branching paths beneath the thin, hairless skin. His legs were slick with blood, as were his arms. The twin scabbards at his hips were empty – he had broken both weapons, despite the weavings of sorcery invested in them. His had been a desperate battle.

Scabandari bowed his head in greeting. 'Silchas Ruin, brother of mine. Most stalwart of allies. Behold the plain – we are victorious.'

The albino Tiste Andii's pallid face twisted in a silent snarl.

'My legions were late in coming to your aid,' Scabandari said. 'And for that, my heart breaks at your losses. Even so, we now hold the gate, do we not? The path to this world belongs to us, and the world itself lies before us ... to plunder, to carve for our people worthy empires.'

Ruin's long-fingered, stained hands twitched, and he faced the plain below. The Edur legions had reformed into a rough ring around the last surviving Andii. 'Death fouls the air,' Silchas Ruin growled. 'I can barely draw it to speak.'

'There will be time enough for making new plans later,' Scabandari said.

'My people are slaughtered. You now surround us, but your protection is far too late.'

'Symbolic, then, my brother. There are other Tiste Andii on this world – you said so yourself. You must needs only find that first wave, and your strength will return. More, others will come. My kind and yours both, fleeing our defeats.'

Silchas Ruin's scowl deepened. 'This day's victory is a bitter alternative.'

'The K'Chain Che'Malle are all but gone – we know this. We have seen the many other dead cities. Now, only Morn remains, and that on a distant continent – where the short-tails even now break their chains in bloody rebellion. A divided enemy is an enemy quick to fall, my friend. Who else in this world has the power to oppose us? Jaghut? They are scattered and few. Imass? What can weapons of stone achieve against our iron?' He was silent a moment, then continued, 'The Forkrul Assail seem unwilling to pass judgement on us. And each year there seem to be fewer and fewer of them in any case. No, my friend, with this day's victory, this world lies before our feet. Here, you shall not suffer from the civil wars that plague Kurald Galain. And I and my followers shall escape the rivening that now besets Kurald Emurlahn—'

Silchas Ruin snorted. 'A rivening by your own hand, Scabandari.'

He was still studying the Tiste forces below, and so did not see the flash of rage that answered his offhand remark, a flash that vanished a heartbeat later, Scabandari's expression returning once more to equanimity. 'A new world for us, brother.'

'A Jaghut stands atop a ridge to the north,' Silchas Ruin said. 'Witness to the war. I did not approach, for I sensed the beginning of a ritual. Omtose Phellack.'

'Do you fear that Jaghut, Silchas Ruin?'

'I fear what I do not know, Scabandari . . . Bloodeye. And there is much to learn of this realm and its ways.'

'Bloodeye.'

'You cannot see yourself,' Ruin said, 'but I give you this name, for the blood that now stains your . . . vision.'

'Rich, Silchas Ruin, coming from you.' Then Scabandari shrugged and walked to the north edge of the heap, stepping carefully on the shifting carcasses. 'A Jaghut, you said . . .' He swung about, but Silchas Ruin's back was to him, as the Tiste Andii stared down upon his few surviving followers on the plain below.

'Omtose Phellack, the Warren of Ice.' Ruin said without turning. 'What does he conjure, Scabandari Bloodeye? I wonder . . .'

The Edur Soletaken walked back towards Silchas Ruin.

He reached down to the outside of his left boot and drew out a shadow-etched dagger. Sorcery played on the iron.

A final step, then the dagger was driven into Ruin's back.

The Tiste Andii spasmed, then roared—

Even as the Edur legions turned suddenly on the Andii, rushing inward from all sides to deliver the day's final slaughter.

Magic wove writhing chains about Silchas Ruin, and the albino Tiste Andii toppled.

Scabandari Bloodeye crouched down over him. 'It is the way of brothers, alas,' he murmured. 'One must rule. Two cannot. You know the truth of that. Big as this world is, Silchas Ruin, sooner or later there would be war between the Edur and the Andii. The truth of our blood will tell. Thus, only one shall command the gate. Only the Edur shall pass. We will hunt down the Andii who are already here – what champion can they throw up to challenge me? They are as good as dead. And so it must be. One people. One ruler.' He straightened, as the last cries of the dying Andii warriors echoed from the plain below. 'Aye, I cannot kill you outright – you are too powerful for that. Thus, I will take you to a suitable place, and leave you to the roots, earth and stone of its mangled grounds . . .'

He then veered into his draconean form. An enormous taloned foot closed about the motionless form of Silchas Ruin, and Scabandari Bloodeye rose into the sky, wings thundering.

The tower was less than a hundred leagues to the south, only its low battered wall enclosing the yard revealing that it was not of Jaghut construction, that it had arisen beside the three Jaghut towers of its own accord, in answer to a law unfathomable to god and mortal alike. Arisen . . . to await the coming of those whom it would imprison for eternity. Creatures of deadly power.

Such as the Soletaken Tiste Andii, Silchas Ruin, third and last of Mother Dark's three children.

Removing from his path Scabandari Bloodeye's last worthy opponent among the Tiste.

Mother Dark's three children.

Three names . . .

Andarist, who long ago surrendered his power in answer to a grief that could never heal. All unknowing that the hand that delivered that grief was mine.

Anomandaris Dragnipurake, who broke with his Mother and with his kind. Who then vanished before I could deal with him. Vanished, likely never to be seen again.

And now, Silchas Ruin, who in a very short time will know the eternal prison of the Azath.

Scabandari Bloodeye was pleased. For his people. For himself. This world he would conquer. Only the first Andii settlers could pose any challenge to his claim.

A champion of the Tiste Andii in this realm? I can think of no-one . . . no-one with the power to stand before me . . .

It did not occur to Scabandari Bloodeye to wonder where, of the three sons of Mother Dark, the one who had vanished might have gone.

But even that was not his greatest mistake . . .

On a glacial berm to the north, the lone Jaghut began weaving the sorcery of Omtose Phellack. He had witnessed the devastation wrought by the two Soletaken Eleint and their attendant armies. Little sympathy was spared for the K'Chain Che'Malle. They were dying out anyway, for a myriad host of reasons, none of which concerned the Jaghut overmuch. Nor did the intruders worry him. He had long since lost his capacity for worry. Along with fear. And, it must be admitted, wonder.

He felt the betrayal when it came, the distant bloom of magic and the spilling of ascendant blood. And the two dragons were now one.

Typical.

And then, a short while later, in the time when he rested between weavings of his ritual, he sensed someone approaching him from behind. An Elder god, come in answer to the violent rift torn between the realms. As expected. Still . . . which god? K'rul? Draconus? The Sister of Cold Nights? Osseric? Kilmandaros? Sechul Lath? Despite his studied indifference, curiosity finally forced him to turn to look upon the newcomer.

Ah, unexpected . . . but interesting.

Mael, Elder Lord of the Seas, was wide and squat, skin a deep blue, fading to pale gold at throat and bared belly. Lank blonde hair hung unbound from his broad, almost flat pate. And in Mael's amber eyes, sizzling rage.

'Gothos,' Mael rasped, 'what ritual do you invoke in answer to this?'

The Jaghut scowled. 'They've made a mess. I mean to cleanse it.'

'Ice,' the Elder god snorted. 'The Jaghut answer to everything.'

'And what would yours be, Mael? Flood, or . . . flood?'

The Elder god faced south, the muscles of his jaw bunching. 'I am to have an ally. Kilmandaros. She comes from the other side of the rent.'

'Only one Tiste Soletaken is left,' Gothos said. 'Seems he struck down his companion, and even now delivers him into the keeping of the Azath Tower's crowded yard.'

'Premature. Does he think the K'Chain Che'Malle his only opposition in this realm?'

The Jaghut shrugged. 'Probably.'

Mael was silent for a time, then he sighed and said, 'With your ice, Gothos, do not destroy all of this. Instead, I ask that you . . . *preserve*.'

'Why?'

'I have my reasons.'

'I am pleased for you. What are they?'

The Elder god shot him a dark look. 'Impudent bastard.'

'Why change?'

'In the seas, Jaghut, time is unveiled. In the depths ride currents of vast antiquity. In the shallows whisper the future. The tides flow between them in ceaseless exchange. Such is my realm. Such is my knowledge. Seal this devastation in your damned ice, Gothos. In this place, freeze time itself. Do this, and I will accept an indebtedness to you . . . which one day you might find useful.'

Gothos considered the Elder god's words, then nodded. 'I might at that. Very well, Mael. Go to Kilmandaros. Swat down this Tiste Eleint and scatter his people. But do it quickly.'

Mael's eyes narrowed. 'Why?'

'Because I sense a distant awakening – but not, alas, as distant as you would like.'

'Anomander Rake.'

Gothos nodded.

Mael shrugged. 'Anticipated. Osseric moves to stand in his path.'

The Jaghut's smile revealed his massive tusks. 'Again?'

The Elder god could not help but grin in answer.

And though they smiled, there was little humour on that glacial berm.

* * *

1133rd Year of Burn's Sleep
Year of the White Veins in the Ebony
Three years before the Letherii Seventh Closure

He awoke with a bellyful of salt, naked and half-buried in white sand amidst the storm's detritus. Seagulls cried overhead, their shadows wheeling across the rippled beach. Cramps spasming his gut, he groaned and slowly rolled over.

There were more bodies on the beach, he saw. And wreckage. Chunks and rafts of fast-melting ice rustled in the shallows. Crabs scuttled in their thousands.

The huge man lifted himself to his hands and knees. And then vomited bitter fluids onto the sands. Pounding throbs wracked his head, fierce enough to leave him half-blind, and it was some time before he finally rocked back to sit up and glared once more at the scene around him.

A shore where no shore belonged.

And the night before, mountains of ice rising up from the depths, one – the largest of them all – reaching the surface directly beneath the vast floating Meckros city. Breaking it apart as if it were a raft of sticks. He had seen nothing like it. Meckros histories recounted nothing remotely like the devastation he had seen wrought. Sudden and virtually absolute annihilation of a city that was home to twenty thousand. Disbelief still tormented him, as if his own memories held impossible images, the conjuring of a fevered brain.

But he knew he had imagined nothing. He had but witnessed.

And, somehow, survived.

The sun was warm, but not hot. The sky overhead was milky white rather than blue. And the seagulls, he now saw, were something else entirely. Reptilian, pale-winged.

He staggered to his feet. The headache was fading, but shivers now swept through him, and his thirst was a raging demon trying to claw up his throat.

The cries of the flying lizards changed pitch and he swung to face inland.

Three creatures had appeared, clambering through the pallid tufts of grass above the tide-line. No higher than his hip, black-skinned, hairless, perfectly round heads and pointed ears. Bhoka'ral – he recalled them from his youth, when a Meckros trading ship had returned from Nemil – but these seemed to be muscle-bound versions, at least twice as heavy as those pets the merchants had brought back to the floating city. They made directly for him.

He looked round for something to use as a weapon, finding a piece of driftwood that would serve as a club. Hefting it, he waited as the bhoka'ral drew closer.

They halted, yellow-shot eyes staring up at him.

Then the middle one gestured.

Come. There was no doubting the meaning of that all-too-human beckoning.

The man scanned once more the strand – none of the bodies he could see were moving, and the crabs were feeding unopposed. He stared up once more at the strange sky, then stepped towards the three creatures.

They backed away and led him up to the grassy verge.

Those grasses were as nothing he had ever seen before,

long tubular triangles, razor-edged – as he discovered once he passed through them to find his low legs crisscrossed in cuts. Beyond, a level plain stretched inland, bearing only the occasional tuft of the same grass. The ground in between was salt-crusted and barren. A few chunks of stone dotted the plain, no two alike and all oddly angular, unweathered.

In the distance stood a lone tent.

The bhoka'ral guided him towards it.

As they drew near, he saw threads of smoke drifting out from the peak and slitted flap that marked the doorway.

His escort halted and another wave directed him to the entrance. Shrugging, he crouched and crawled inside.

In the dim light sat a shrouded figure, hood disguising its features. A brazier was before it, from which heady fumes drifted. Beside the entrance stood a crystal bottle, some dried fruit and a loaf of dark bread.

'The bottle holds spring water,' the figure rasped in the Meckros tongue. 'Please, take time to recover from your ordeal.'

He grunted his thanks and quickly took the bottle.

Thirst blissfully slackened, he reached for the bread. 'I thank you, stranger,' he rumbled, then shook his head. 'That smoke makes you swim before my eyes.'

A hacking cough that might have been laughter, then something resembling a shrug. 'Better than drowning. Alas, it eases my pain. I shall not keep you long. You are Withal, the Swordmaker.'

The man started, then his broad brow knotted. 'Aye, I am Withal, of the Third Meckros city – which is now no more.'

'A tragic event. You are the lone survivor . . . through my own efforts, though it much strained my powers to intervene.'

'What place is this?'

'Nowhere, in the heart of nowhere. A fragment, prone to wander. I give it what life I can imagine, conjured from memories of my home. My strength returns, although the agony of my broken body does not abate. Yet listen, I have talked and not coughed. That is something.' A mangled hand appeared from a ragged sleeve and scattered seeds onto the brazier's coals. They spat and popped and the smoke thickened.

'Who are you?' Withal demanded.

'A fallen god ... who has need of your skills. I have prepared for your coming, Withal. A place of dwelling, a forge, all the raw materials you will need. Clothes, food, water. And three devoted servants, whom you had already met—'

'The bhoka'ral?' Withal snorted. 'What can—'

'Not bhoka'ral, mortal. Although perhaps they once were. These are Nacht. I have named them Rind, Mape and Pule. They are of Jaghut fashioning, capable of learning all that you require of them.'

Withal made to rise. 'I thank you for the salvation, Fallen One, but I shall take my leave of you. I would return to my own world—'

'You do not understand, Withal,' the figure hissed. 'You will do as I say here, or you will find yourself begging for death. I now own you, Swordmaker. You are my slave and I am your master. The Meckros own slaves, yes? Hapless souls stolen from island villages and such on your raids. The notion is therefore familiar to you. Do not despair, however, for once you have completed what I ask of you, you shall be free to leave.'

Withal still held the club, the heavy wood cradled on his lap. He considered.

A cough, then laughter, then more coughing, during which the god raised a staying hand. When the hacking was done, he said, 'I advise you to attempt nothing untoward, Withal. I have plucked you from the seas for this purpose. Have you lost all honour? Oblige me in this, for you would deeply regret my wrath.'

'What would you have me do?'

'Better. What would I have you do, Withal? Why, only what you do best. Make me a sword.'

Withal grunted. 'That is all?'

The figure leaned forward. 'Ah well, what I have in mind is a very particular sword . . .'

TOR

Award-winning authors
Compelling stories

Please join us at the website
below for more information
about this author and other great
Tor selections, and to sign up for
our monthly newsletter!

Oblat can be ... taken care of, as a show of our appreciation.'

Stormy scowled and glanced back at Gesler.

The sergeant slowly rose from the couch. 'Well, lass, the corporal here's better with the scary ones ... since he tells them so bad they ain't so scary any more. Since you're being so kind with ... uh, our recent push of the Lord at knuckles, me and the corporal will both weave you a tale, if that's what you're here for. We ain't shy, after all. Where should we start? I was born—'

'Not that early,' Lostara cut in. 'I will leave the rest to Pearl – though perhaps someone could get him something to drink to assist in his recovery. He can advise you on where to start. In the meantime, where is Pella?'

'He's out back,' Gesler said.

'Thank you.'

As she was making her way to the narrow, low door at the back of the stables, another sergeant emerged to move up alongside her. 'I'll escort you,' he said.

Another damned Falari veteran. And what's with the finger bones? 'Am I likely to get lost, Sergeant?' she asked as she swung open the door. Six paces beyond was the estate's back wall. Heaps of sun-dried horse manure were banked against it. Seated on one of them was a young soldier. At the foot of a nearby pile lay two dogs, both asleep, one huge and terribly scarred, the other tiny – a snarl of hair and a pug nose.

'Possibly,' the sergeant replied. He touched her arm as she made to approach Pella, and she faced him with an enquiring look. 'Are you with one of the other legions?' he asked.

'No.'

'Ah.' He glanced back at the stables. 'Newly assigned to handmaid the Claw.'

'Handmaid?'

'Aye. The man needs ... learning. Seems he chose well in you, at least.'

'What is it you want, Sergeant?'

'Never mind. I'll leave you now.'

She watched him re-enter the stables. Then, with a shrug, she swung about and walked up to Pella.

Neither dog awoke at her approach.

Two large burlap sacks framed the soldier, the one on the soldier's right filled near to bursting, the other perhaps a third full. The lad himself was hunched over, holding a small copper awl which he was using to drill a hole into a finger bone.

The sacks, Lostara realized, contained hundreds of such bones.

'Pella.'

The young man looked up, blinked. 'Do I know you?'

'No. But we perhaps share an acquaintance.'

'Oh.' He resumed his work.

'You were a guard in the mines—'

'Not quite,' he replied without looking up. 'I was garrisoned at one of the settlements. Skullcup. But then the rebellion started. Fifteen of us survived the first night – no officers. We stayed off the road and eventually made our way to Dosin Pali. Took four nights, and we could see the city burning for the first three. Wasn't much left when we arrived. A Malazan trader ship showed up at about the same time as us, and took us, eventually, here to Aren.'

'Skullcup,' Lostara said. 'There was a prisoner there. A young girl—'

'Tavore's sister, you mean. Felisin.'

Her breath caught.

'I was wondering when somebody would find me about that. Am I under arrest, then?' He looked up.

'No. Why? Do you think you should be?'

He returned to his work. 'Probably. I helped them escape, after all. The night of the Uprising. Don't know if they ever made it, though. I left them supplies, such as I could find. They were planning on heading north then west ... across the desert. I'm pretty sure I wasn't the only one aiding them, but I never found out who the others were.'

Lostara slowly crouched down until she was at his eye-level. 'Not just Felisin, then. Who was with her?'

'Baudin – a damned frightening man, that one, but strangely loyal to Felisin, though . . .' He lifted his head and met her gaze. 'Well, she wasn't one to reward loyalty, if you know what I mean. Anyway. Baudin, and Heboric.'

'Heboric? Who is that?'

'Was once a priest of Fener – all tattooed with the fur of the Boar. Had no hands – they'd been cut off. Anyway, them three.'

'Across the desert,' Lostara murmured. 'But the west coast of the island has . . . nothing.'

'Well, they were expecting a boat, then, weren't they? It was planned, right? Anyway, that's as far as I can take the tale. For the rest, ask my sergeant. Or Stormy. Or Truth.'

'Truth? Who is he?'

'He's the one who's just showed up in the doorway behind you . . . come to deliver more bones.' He raised his voice. 'No need to hesitate, Truth. In fact, this pretty woman here has some questions for you.'

Another one with the strange skin. She studied the tall, gangly youth who cautiously approached, carrying another bulging burlap sack from which sand drifted down in a dusty cloud. *Hood take me, a comely lad . . . though that air of vulnerability would get on my nerves eventually.* She straightened. 'I would know of Felisin,' she said, slipping some iron into her tone.

Sufficient to catch Pella's notice, and he threw her a sharp look.

Both dogs had awakened at Truth's arrival, but neither rose from where they lay – they simply fixed eyes on the lad.

Truth set down the bag and snapped to sudden attentiveness. Colour rose in his face.

My charms. It's not Pella who'll remember this day. Not Pella who'll find someone to worship. 'Tell me about what happened on the western shore of Otataral Island. Did the rendezvous occur as planned?'

'I believe so,' Truth replied after a moment. 'But we weren't part of that plan – we just happened to find ourselves in the same boat with Kulp, and it was Kulp who was looking to collect them.'

'Kulp? The cadre mage from the Seventh?'

'Aye, him. He'd been sent by Duiker—'

'The imperial historian?' *Gods, what twisted trail is this?* 'And why would he have any interest in saving Felisin?'

'Kulp said it was the injustice,' Truth answered. 'But you got it wrong – it wasn't Felisin that Duiker wanted to help. It was Heboric.'

Pella spoke in a low voice quite unlike what she had heard from him moments earlier. 'If Duiker is going to be made out as some kind of traitor . . . well, lass, better think twice. This is Aren, after all. The city that watched. That saw Duiker delivering the refugees to safety. He was the last one through the gate, they say.' The emotion riding his words was now raw. 'And Pormqual had him *arrested*!'

A chill rippled through Lostara. 'I know,' she said. 'Blistig loosed us Red Blades from the gaols. We were on the wall by the time Pormqual had his army out there on the plain. If Duiker was seeking to free Heboric, a fellow scholar, well, I have no complaint with that. The trail we are on is Felisin's.'

Truth nodded at that. 'Tavore has sent you, hasn't she? You and that Claw inside, listening to Gesler and Stormy.'

Lostara briefly closed her eyes. 'I am afraid I lack Pearl's subtlety. This mission was meant to be . . . secret.'

'Fine with me,' Pella said. 'And you, Truth?'

The tall lad nodded. 'It doesn't really matter anyway. Felisin is dead. They all are. Heboric. Kulp. They all died. Gesler was just telling that part.'

'I see. None the less, please say nothing to anyone else. We will be pursuing our task, if only to gather her bones. Their bones, that is.'